OUT
OF THE
ASHES

OUT
OF THE
ASHES

A NOVEL

A.E. KAYSER

Out of the Ashes

Printed in the United States of America.

Kayser, Ann Elizabeth
Out of the ashes / by A.E. Kayser
Tarentum, Pennsylvania : Word Association Publishers, 2024. |

ISBN: 978-1-63385-525-0
Library of Congress Control Number: 2024908664

BISAC: FICTION / Coming of Age | FICTION / Romance / Military
| FICTION / Native American & Indigenous

Published by
Word Association Publishers
205 Fifth Avenue
Tarentum, Pennsylvania 15084

www.wordassociation.com
1.800.827.7903

ACKNOWLEDGEMENTS

Special thanks to all the wonderful people at Georgetown Medical School, especially those who worked in the Med School Library as I researched old curriculums and other bits of interest.

To the Jicarilla Apaches of New Mexico, I have the utmost respect for your Nation and hope I was able to portray your strength and determination in my main character.

There are so many people that without whom this book would never have been written.

To my original Editor-in-Chief, my mother, Virginia Tamburro. I'm so sorry that you never saw this finally in print. You always said that if I didn't get this book published you would come back to haunt me—well here it is. I made sure to get those apostrophes where they belonged!

To the editing group of Straub, Shapiro, and McNeil. Aunt Ellen, thank you for your insight and nursing expertise. Unfortunately, you never saw this published, either. The punch, however, because I made you cry, I could have done without! Jody, you have been there through it all. During our many brainstorming sessions at various eateries, I always worried we were going to get thrown out because of how long we lingered! Glad you saw the gang as friends and loved them like I did. And dearest Emily, who grew up as I was living in two worlds, you filled the important shoes that Gma left. You also had to put up with me stressing and was the best helper a person could ask for.

To Janet Rozycki—the catalyst. I swear you put these people in my head. I know you are smiling from above. The coincidences are scary, especially Jesse William.

To Captain Ken Rozycki, DMD (retired) without whom the Vietnam section of the book would never have been written. Janet was looking down as, day after day at lunch and between patients, I picked your brains as you recounted numerous tales of Vietnam and gave explanations and details of a time that is now considered almost ancient history. I think our discussions helped to fill the void that Janet left. At least for me, anyway.

To Dr. Charles Graff, MD for responding to all my crazy emails and to Paula Holmes, RN for all your help.

To Sue Goodwin, my first non-family reader. It was like leaving my baby with a sitter for the first time. I'm so glad I did! Thank you for all your wonderful critiques and advice. We are always on the same wavelength.

To Alejandra Bernal, one of my Beta readers, who was also my Spanish editor and to Dr. Stan, MD who also added his medical input, I am forever grateful to you both.

To the rest of my Beta readers especially cousin Leigh Hanchar and Jasmine Karnavas who were so helpful and took time out to read the manuscript and give their feedback.

To Mr. Robitusin in humble gratitude. Although you came late to the party, your comments, criticisms, and insights were a wonderful addition to this book. Danke, mein Freund.

To all Vietnam Veterans—especially Lenny Roolf (US Marine Corps), Rich Miller (US Army) and Rick Ciesielski (US Army) for their service, information and inspiration. Thank you so much.

Most importantly, to Dr. Tom, Francine, Jason and Emily my wonderful team at Word Association Publishers. I couldn't have done it without you. Special thanks to Dr. Tom Costello, who is one of the best editors a writer could ask for. You read those first pages years ago, filled it full of red ink, then said, "Great idea and outline, now tell me a story." Jason, thank you! You took my manuscript and worked miracles with the layout and also designed the greatest cover and put it all together beautifully. Thank you for being so patient and putting up with all my crap and first time jitters.

Finally, to Greg who put up with me all these years and gave me support, encouragement, and great advice. This book would not have been written without you.

In loving memory of
Janet, Gabe, and Virginia

PART ONE

> *"The art of living is more like wrestling*
> *than dancing*
> *in as much as it, too*
> *demands a firm and watchful stance*
> *against any unexpected onset."*
>
> ~
>
> *"Consider where each thing originates,*
> *what goes into its composition,*
> *what it is changing into,*
> *what it is going to be after the change,*
> *and that it will be no whit the worse for it."*

Marcus Aurelius

BILLY

Spring, 1960

The air above the asphalt shimmered. The runners crouched low, their hands burning on the hot pavement. Billy's focus narrowed as he stared down the track, sweat stinging his eyes. When the gun went off, he sprang from the blocks, his muscles uncoiling like springs. Billy attacked the hurdles with a mixture of defiance and pleasure. He could already taste the sweetness of victory as he left the rest of the field far behind.

The hurdles flew under him like white lines, blurring completely as he neared the finish. His legs were burning as he hit the tape well ahead of the rest. Slowing to a jog, he caught his breath as he waited for his times to be posted.

"Fuckin'…Injun!" a tall, muscular blond yelled, as he pounded up behind his friend. "You…beat me…every…time."

"If you'd moved…your lazy…white ass, Lewis," Billy coughed, bending at the waist, "you might…have caught me."

Cal Lewis slapped the slight, agile Billy Running Fox on the back. "Just you wait," Cal said, spitting into the dust. "Someday…when you least expect it…I'll whip ya good."

"When pigs fly," Billy retorted, as they made their way from the track to the locker room.

Billy Fox took his running seriously, as he did with everything else. It was a necessity. From the reservation in New Mexico to Arizona State University, Billy had come too far to let anything—or anyone—get in his path. His prowess on both the track and cross-country high school teams had awarded him an athletic scholarship toward a pre-med degree. But between now and the completion of his education, there were still many hurdles to face and overcome.

In the steam of the shower room, Cal's voice boomed, "Did you change your mind about the party? It's gonna be a good time."

"No!" Billy spat, as he rinsed the soap from his dark brown, waist-length hair. "I got a huge genetics test tomorrow. I gotta hit the books."

"You're such a drag. Two girls off campus are throwin' it. We're all goin'. Study later."

"Oh sure, and if I don't keep up an 'A' average, it's 'so long, redskin.' Count me out."

Cal shook his head. "You're like a goddamned monk! What's one hour of your time to go and have a little fun? There'll be lots of chicks there. Hell, ya might even get lucky."

"I said no!"

"Come on, Fox. Don't be such a fuckin' pussy."

"All right, I'll go," Billy growled, "one hour, that's it. Now lay off."

Billy took his time dressing and braiding his hair. But eventually, Cal hustled him out to his car. The ride across town was short since Cal kept his foot pressed to the accelerator. Billy held tightly to the door handle, already regretting saying yes.

Cal skidded the tires against the curb in front of a dilapidated, three story, apartment building. He jumped from the car and headed for the door. Billy continued to sit, staring at the building with trepidation.

"Let's go, Fox," Cal called. "The party's already started. We don't want to miss anything."

"We're going in there?" Billy asked weakly.

"Sure, come on," Cal said.

Billy scowled and extracted himself from the car. He trailed Cal up a flight of sagging, wooden stairs. At the door, a cockroach, bigger than his thumb, scuttled away.

Cal didn't bother to knock. He entered the smoke-filled room as if he'd been there before, greeting the many members of the track team as he did so. Cal immediately headed for a keg of beer in the corner with Billy following at his heels.

"Holy shit! Look who's here!" yelled a teammate, who was seated on the floor with a young woman draped across his legs. "Hey Lewis, how did you get the nerd to come to the party?"

Cal grinned. "I got lots of talents, boys. In fact, one of them is just bustin' to come out and show off."

The other young men hooted with laughter while Cal poured two plastic cups of beer. He handed one to Billy, who protested, "You know I don't drink."

"Well, it's about time you started. A little fire water's good for you," Cal commented absently, surveying the crowd. His blue eyes lit on a pert brunette seated across the room. She stared back, licking her parted lips.

Billy reached into his shirt pocket for his cigarettes. "A little fire water is what fucked up my people in the first place."

One teammate murmured to his friends, "That son of a bitch always burns us on the track. Let's see if we can return the favor." He handed Billy an odd looking, hand-rolled cigarette. "Here Foxy, put your smokes away and take a hit of one of these."

Billy eyed the cigarette suspiciously. He shrugged and took a deep drag, filling his lungs with bitter smoke. He took another drag and sipped at his beer.

"Hey, you gonna smoke the whole thing yourself?" the teammate laughed. "Come on, pass it around."

Billy handed back the cigarette. "Here, it tastes like shit, anyway." He finished his beer, then put the empty cup down by the keg. Another teammate refilled it and handed it back. "Geez Fox, drink up. It's free."

Billy took the proffered cup. "Nothing in life is free," he mumbled, then took another swallow. The beer didn't taste too bad and went down easily. He gulped it down, then drank another. His teammates laughed and encouraged him to drink more.

Billy lit a Marlboro, and looked around for Cal. His roommate had disappeared. Shit, he thought, and panicked. Now what? He chugged another beer, then began to search for his friend. The heat of the packed room made him dizzy, and all the noise and confusion made his head throb. He didn't want to be here, nor did he belong.

After a while, he gave up looking and lurched toward the door. Billy had dodged through the crowd, looking for a place to set his empty cup, when he bumped into a young woman.

Billy's mouth went dry, and he flushed. It was Jessie Tsosie. Jessie worked at the same printing company where Billy was employed. She was a stunning Navajo with a waterfall of silky, blue-black hair. Her body was curvaceous, her peat brown eyes like a doe's.

Jessie made Billy squirm, and he avoided her. She didn't go to ASU, even though she and her friend hung out on the campus. It was said they were fast, easy, and ready for anything.

"Fox! I didn't expect to see *you* here at our party," said Jessie, as she walked toward him. "I thought all you did was work and study."

"Hi Jessie," Billy mumbled, and backed away. So, this was *her* place. The rough stubble of the plaster wall bit into his back as Jessie pressed closer.

The smell of her perfume and touch of her breast grazing his arm excited yet terrified him.

"Have some beer," she said, refilling his empty cup from a pitcher.

Billy wondered how many beers he had already drunk.

"Hey! What gives?" Jessie asked, grabbing his arm as his beer spilled to the floor.

Billy stared at the spreading puddle and shook his head. "Man, I'm sorry… need some air."

Jessie dragged him down the hall passed an occupied room. The guy's trousers were bunched around his ankles. Billy blinked. It was Cal humping a young woman from behind, her skirt tossed casually over her ass.

Billy took a deep breath, trying to erase what he had just seen. He felt trapped in a nightmare. The other party guests were laughing and jostling him. They wove in and out of his field of vision in slow motion. Some spoke, but he couldn't comprehend what they were saying.

I've got to get out of here, he thought. But something terrible had happened. His arms and legs were no longer his own and his head and stomach seemed to be spinning in opposite directions.

"Come on," said Jessie. "Why are you just standing there?"

"Feel sick," he complained. "Think I'm gonna puke."

"Out here," Jessie said, hauling him by the arm. She pushed him up against the metal rail of the fire escape and unzipped his jeans.

"S'matter with me?"

"You're drunk, you dumb ass," Jessie sneered. "Here, I'll make you forget all about that." She pushed him up against the metal rail of the fire escape, her fingers unzipping his jeans.

The warm breeze hit his bare skin and sobered Billy slightly. "What are you doing?" he asked, and pushed feebly at Jessie's hands. "Don't."

"Oh, for God's sake, shut up and relax. You'll love this." She knelt in front of him, and Billy's olive green eyes widened first in alarm, then in surprise, when Jessie began to do things to him unlike any he had ever known.

Billy again tried to push Jessie away but eventually quit fighting. A low moan escaped his lips. He closed his eyes in an effort to savor what Jessie was doing. But when he did, his head snapped back with a clunk against the railing. If only the world would stop its crazy spinning.

Meanwhile, Jessie's mouth and tongue continued their erotic dance, coaxing Billy's body to respond. Billy exploded then leaned over the fire escape and began to vomit. He fell to his knees and rested his head against the hot iron of the railing. Dazed, Billy barely heard Jessie's wicked laughter as she got up and returned to the party.

The whirling of the world went on forever. With his head down, Billy could see his pants pushed to his knees. He thought of Cal and was sick again.

He had stumbled to his feet and managed to get his jeans zipped up when Jessie returned with a beer in her hand. "A little hair of the dog?" she smirked, offering him the beer.

"No!" said Billy. He turned to run but, abruptly stopped in his tracks when faced with the rickety, narrow metal rungs of the fire escape. "I've got to get out of here!"

"Wait a minute, brainy boy," she said, her fingers biting into his upper arm. "You owe me."

Billy panicked and eyed the stairs again. At twenty years of age, he knew more about chemical formulae than sex. Now, here was a beautiful girl wanting him, but all he wanted to do was to get out of that apartment fast.

Jessie pulled him back inside and into her room. She pushed him down onto the bed, shoving a well-worn teddy bear out of the way. She yanked off his boots and was in the process of unfastening his pants, when her roommate called her to the phone.

"Don't you dare move," she commanded. "I'll be right back."

Once she had gone, Billy jumped to his feet. The room spun and closed in on him. He grabbed onto the dresser to keep from falling. When his vision cleared, he hurriedly searched for his boots. Having no luck, he stumbled barefooted past the partying people and out into the late afternoon sunshine.

The hammering went on and on. After several minutes, Billy realized the hammering was inside of his head. He groaned, rolled over and looked at the clock on the nightstand.

"Shit!" he swore, when his eyes finally focused. His genetics class began at 9:30 a.m., and he was already half an hour late.

Dr. Joe Benson was a stickler for being on time and usually locked the door the moment a test began. If you were late, you were screwed. Damn! Why had he let Cal talk him into going to that crazy party? If he blew this exam, he was dead.

He tumbled out of bed and hastily pulled on jeans and a t-shirt. His brain was fuzzy and seemed disconnected from his body. His knees buckled, and he flopped down heavily on the bed. He looked at his dirty, bruised feet in perplexity, then around the room. Where the hell were his boots? Then he remembered.

He dragged himself down the hall to the bathroom, splashed cold water onto his face, then staggered out. Gingerly, he ran to the lecture hall in his bare, bruised feet. With each excruciating step, Billy kicked himself mentally. His one and only pair of boots, gone—so fucking stupid! Thank God his dormitory was close to the lecture hall.

He hesitated at the door, then knocked. Billy prayed that Benson would be lenient. He stared at the window of the door until he saw his professor's face framed in the glass. Benson's eyes widened when he saw who stood there. The door immediately opened a crack. "Where have you been?" he hissed. "The test has already begun."

"Please Dr. Benson, I know I'm late. But could you please at least let me start the test? I've never been late or missed an exam before."

Benson stepped into the hall, closing the door behind him. At six feet four inches, he towered over Billy.

"Please!" Billy begged. "I have to take this test."

Benson blinked at Billy's tone of desperation and appraised his best and favorite student. The usually neat braid of hair was now snarled. His normally clean clothing was rumpled and dirty—his feet bare. Something was very wrong with this picture. "My God, Billy! Are you all right? You look terrible. What happened?"

"It's a long story, sir. Please, will you let me take the exam?"

Benson considered Billy for a long moment, then glanced at his watch. "All right. I'll let you in, but you get graded on whatever you can finish in the time left. Understand?" he replied.

"Yes, sir."

"And Fox, you're lucky. I could have said no."

"Thank you, sir." Billy went in and sat down. Some of his classmates snickered, but he didn't care. He perused the test quickly, then attacked it as yet another hurdle. When Benson called time, Billy had completed a large portion of the test, giving him a chance at a B. He still had to ace his other classes, if he wanted to return to ASU for his final year. Then, if he made it through, and the Army helped him, he'd be on his way to medical school.

Yesterday's stupidity could have hurt him badly. He could not afford to make any more mistakes. One wrong move could dump his red butt back on the Rez. From now on, he cautioned himself, no more screwing around.

Later that afternoon, Billy sat on the floor; textbooks and notes cluttering the carpet.

"I'm goin' to dinner," Cal announced, nudging his roommate with his foot. "You comin'?"

Billy looked up in surprise. "When did you come in?"

Cal threw up his hands. "Shit Fox, I've been here all afternoon. If you hadn't been in a study trance, you'd have known that."

"Oh."

With a pained expression, Cal sighed and repeated. "Are you comin' with me to dinner?"

"No," Billy murmured, "maybe later." He pushed his silver, wire-rimmed glasses up off the end of his nose and went back to his book.

Cal shook his head and walked out, "What a goof ball," he said.

A few minutes later, repeated knocking interrupted Billy's train of thought. Getting up, he automatically walked to the door, his eyes still glued to his book.

"That was fast. Did you forget your key again?" he asked without bothering to look up.

"Key? What are you talking about?"

The voice snapped Billy's head from the page and his jaw dropped. Jessie stood in the doorway, his missing boots dangling from her hand. He stood dumbstruck as Jessie pushed past him into the room.

"You owe me, remember?" Without any preamble, Jessie quickly stripped. There was nothing sensual about the act. She peeled off her clothes like a sweaty, shower starved athlete, then carelessly dropped them in a heap on the floor. Very slowly, she walked toward Billy allowing him to take in her nicely rounded curves.

Billy fought to keep sane, but the urge of all young men was coursing through his veins. Trying to look Jessie in the eye, he wanted to say, 'get out' but he couldn't drag his eyes from her nakedness.

Jessie was sleek and beautiful with dusky, rose-colored skin and a body that was willowy and firm. Full breasts made her waist appear even smaller, and her long hair flowed loosely down her back. Billy couldn't make his eyes, or his body behave. They were responding to a call as old as mankind and one that knew no bounds.

She plucked the textbook from his hand, tossing it onto the floor with her clothes.

Billy swallowed hard as Jessie gyrated in front of him in a little dance. Beckoning to him with her finger, she ordered, "Come here."

Billy felt light-headed and realized he was holding his breath. "Oh fuck," he muttered, his resistance and reasoning caving in rapidly.

"Yeah, that's what we're gonna do," Jessie laughed as she reached for Billy's belt.

CAL

Cal sauntered back to their room from dinner and realized he had forgotten his key, yet again. He was about to knock when he noticed that the door was slightly ajar.

He peered through the crack and witnessed Billy's and Jessie's naked bodies entwined. He quietly closed the door and headed back down the hall. He was stunned. Of all the girls he had imagined with his friend, Jessie Tsosie was not one of them.

Jessie was a well-known whore who hung out on the campus. She solicited undergraduates and teachers for both money and drugs. Jessie was a man's fantasy who did things that no decent young woman would ever think of doing.

Whether it was in the back seat of a car or up against the wall, it didn't matter to Jessie. Her skills left men breathless and begging for more. In fact, it was joked about in quiet corners that one had to take a number and wait in line.

Cal had been one of many. With Jessie there was no pretense of romance—only pure ecstasy. Sex with no strings attached. But after a while, it became disconcerting. Cal prided himself on his own sexual expertise and liked to impress the women he took to his bed.

Yet Jessie was never fazed by his skills. She performed mechanically with an air of boredom that Cal eventually found annoying. Most of the women Cal took to his bed were not in the same league as Jessie, but they found him exciting and didn't come with a price.

Jessie's fee also posed a problem for Cal. The last time he had experienced her clever wares it had cost him a bag of marijuana. It had been difficult to purchase, and clandestine arrangements had to be made.

Money was never an issue, but with drugs, he had to be careful. He could toke on joints at a party, provided someone else brought the grass. Getting it himself was another story. Cal's father had bailed him out of a few scrapes already. He told Cal that the next time he got into trouble, he was on his own.

Mr. Lewis was a wealthy, well-respected attorney who demanded that his two sons keep their noses' clean. Cal's older brother had followed in their father's footsteps. Currently in his third year of law school, Curt had always been the perfect son. He had never been in trouble and had always received the highest grades and honors.

Cal was the total antithesis of Billy. He was lazy and never felt the need to study or do well. Women and fun came first.

The two men were brought together by a campus housing lottery. In the beginning, Cal and the poor, scholarship Indian boy had not known what to say to each other. But, as days passed, they found some common ground. For one, both ran track. They were also pre-med. Cal planned on specializing in cardiology, and Billy had hopes of becoming a surgeon. But that's where the likeness ended.

Upon graduation, Cal would be attending Cornell Medical School—his father had seen to that. Billy, on the other hand, had interviewed at a few schools and was waiting to hear whether he had been accepted. Cal often wondered what Billy was going to do with a BS in Biology, a BA in English Lit, and a minor in Chemistry if he wasn't accepted to a medical school.

For three years, they had been roommates and friends. Billy was easy to live with. He kept his side of their tiny, spartan room neat—his few possessions tucked away.

However, knowing Billy completely was almost impossible. His friend never talked about himself or his family. Cal knew that he had grown up on an Apache reservation in New Mexico, but Billy never offered more information, and Cal didn't push for answers.

Cal once invited Billy to his home in Flagstaff during a holiday break. Cal's parents had been very taken with his roommate. The serious and studious young man would be a good influence on their wayward son.

It seemed evident to Cal, however, that being in their palatial home, made Billy uncomfortable. Though Billy never said a word, Cal noticed that he always had an excuse for remaining on campus thereafter.

Now, his shy, backward friend was 'going a round' with the queen of sex. Cal scratched his head. It just didn't fit—not Billy. Hell, Billy was so naive that Cal doubted he had even dated a girl let alone screwed one.

Did Billy realize that Jessie's favors came with a price? Although a magician with the way she used her body, Jessie was a viper that sucked you dry. Where would Cal's penniless roommate get the cash for such a romp? And what would someone like Jessie want with Billy?

Maybe Cal didn't know Billy as well as he thought he did. Perhaps while Cal was away on a break, his buddy had entertained many a girl. This may have just been the first time he had caught Billy in the act. His mother always said that 'still waters run deep'. Whatever that meant, Cal thought and shrugged. Continuing down the hall, he considered his options for where to crash for the night.

Billy stared at the brush burn on his knee and couldn't believe what had just happened. Is this how it's supposed to be, he wondered? It wasn't exactly how his grandfather had explained it so many years ago. Instead of making love to Jessie, he felt as though he had been a participant in a weird wrestling match…and had lost.

With Jessie, sex was a game in which she made up the rules as she went along. Billy had to learn quickly to give her what she wanted. It had begun in a whirlwind and was over just as swiftly.

Afterward, Billy had tried to pull her close and kiss her, but she had shoved him away. "What do you think you're doing? I'm not into *that* kind of stuff," she chastised. Crawling to her clothes, she searched through her things and brought back a hand-rolled cigarette and matches.

"What is that?" Billy questioned, as she lit it and took a deep puff. "People were passing them around at the party."

"God, for someone who's supposed to be so smart, you sure are dumb!" Jessie said, handing Billy the cigarette. "Haven't you ever smoked grass?"

Billy's eyes widened. "I smoked one at the party but didn't feel anything," he said and quickly handed the cigarette back to her as if it had burned him.

"You have to smoke a couple the first time before you get high," Jessie advised with as much sincerity as a naked woman can give. "Don't worry, I have a few joints with me. Baby, we're gonna get high tonight."

"Look Jessie, I don't really want to get high. Hell, I have another test tomorrow. I can't afford to be doing this."

"You really *are* a nerd, aren't you?" Jessie snorted. "Listen to you whining 'cause you can't study. What the hell's wrong with you?"

"Nothing's wrong with me," Billy retorted. "But if I don't keep up my grades, the school will cancel my scholarship. That's something I can't afford to lose."

"What kind of test?"

"Anatomy."

"Well, hot damn, anatomy. Even *I* know all the important parts." She pushed him down onto his back and took hold of his genitals. Then straddling his body, she writhed like a wild animal on top of him.

Billy surrendered and moved with her feverishly, wanting her warm softness. The feel of her skin against his was addictive and he couldn't get enough of her. The remainder of the evening was a shock to his senses, a blur of skin and sweat mingled with the acrid aroma of marijuana.

Afterward, he reached out, wanting to hold her. But Jessie squirmed away and abandoned him, leaving him alone with his scrambled thoughts.

"What the hell happened to you yesterday?" Cal asked, the next morning in the cafeteria.

"What are you talking about?" Billy asked defensively.

"You know. You were studyin' your ass off when I went to dinner and screwin' your head off when I came back."

"What's it to you?"

"Just wondered that's all. I ended up bunkin' with Dave last night. I don't know how his roommate can stand it. He's the slob of the year."

"Yes, I know," Billy said. "I've experienced his floor on the numerous occasions when I have found myself on the other side of our door."

"He also snored and snorted in his sleep like a hog in heat."

"That's too damned bad."

"I never slept a wink," Cal whined.

"It's funny, you never cared where or how *I* slept when *you* were the one with the chick."

Cal blinked and stared at Billy. He had never heard such anger in his roommate's voice. "Hey, if it bothered you, why didn't you say somethin'?"

Billy shrugged, "It wouldn't have made any difference, would it?"

Cal grinned. "Hell no, why quit when you're on top of things…so to speak?"

"Right," Billy agreed, a slow grin creasing his cheeks.

"But…Fox," Cal continued, "about your choice of women…"

Billy clenched his jaw. "My choice of women isn't any of your business."

"But, that Tsosie broad, she's not the best choice of dating material."

"Really? Well, unlike you, I don't have many options. If you've noticed, there aren't many Indian girls on campus to choose from."

"What about an Anglo? There are lots of them here."

"Oh yeah, there's a whole slew of them. But what respectable Anglo chick would want to spend time with a redskin?"

Cal shrugged and had nothing to say.

"Besides," Billy continued, "I don't rag you about who you screw around with, do I?"

Cal stared at Billy for another long moment. "No, you don't. But Fox…this chick, she comes with a price, man."

"What do you mean?"

"You know, she wants money or something for it."

"Really, that's news to me! She never said anything about wanting to be paid. She came looking for me not the other way around."

"Trust me, Billy. Next time she'll have her hand out."

Billy's eyes narrowed. "And how would you know that?"

Cal studied Billy's face and squirmed. "I've heard things about her."

"You sure you haven't been in her pants, too?"

"I'm just sayin' she comes with a price," Cal said, running his finger under his collar.

"Lay off, Lewis, everything comes with a price."

"You're right, sorry. Forget I said anything."

"I will. Now shut up and eat your breakfast."

"Fine. Don't mind if I do," Cal said, his face once again split into a grin.

"Not bad, Fox. It's taken you a couple days, but you're learning," Jessie said, passing a joint to Billy as they lay on her ancient, stained mattress.

Billy inhaled the drug and closed his eyes. The taste was still bitter, but he liked how it made him feel. With grass, he felt split in two. The quiet, shy Billy sat back and watched while another Billy danced to whatever tune Jessie was playing at the moment. It was like sex. Once he got a taste of both, he couldn't get enough of either. The marijuana made being with Jessie bearable. When he was high, it didn't matter that she didn't want him to touch her.

But sometimes he forgot. Now, still feeling good from the after-effects of sex and the grass, he put his arms around her.

She roughly pushed him away. "Do you always have to paw me?"

"No, but I don't get it. One minute we're all over one another and the next, you act like I'm a stranger. What gives?"

"I told you before, I'm not *into* that shit."

"What the hell *are* you into, then?"

"Will you leave it alone! You always want to talk. Where're you from? Who's your clan? What do you want to do with your life?" she mimicked. "Can't we just fuck?"

She got up and grabbed a fashion magazine that was lying on her scarred, rummage sale dresser. Turning her back on him, she flipped through the pages as she finished the joint. Jessie flaunted her nakedness, knowing the power she held over him. Billy, on the other hand, hurriedly collected his clothes from where they had fallen and dressed. Unless she wanted something more, she'd pretend that he didn't exist. When they weren't screwing, and even sometimes when they were, Jessie acted as if she hated him and couldn't stand the sight of him.

I don't think I like you much either, Billy thought, and jammed his feet roughly into his boots. The ragged teddy bear lay discarded next to him—its jaunty grin mocking. The good feelings from the pot and sex had quickly dissipated, leaving Billy confused and lonely. He looked at Jessie one last time. Her back was a solid wall of silent disdain. Billy started to say something but changed his mind. He shook his head and without a word, left the apartment.

JESSIE

He walked toward her—his arms outstretched; his step unsteady. She quickly put the rough, splintered kitchen table between them. But even when drunk, he was too fast and too strong for her to elude for long.

He wrestled her to the floor, his long greasy hair swinging in her face. His wet lips closed over hers, suffocating her with the putrid smell of rotting teeth and whiskey. As he fumbled with his trousers, the weight of his body pressed her into the hard-packed earth floor of the hogan. Twisting her head away, she could smell decay in the dirt.

It was a silent, exhausting battle and over quickly. As her father forced himself into her small, slight body, the five year old girl let out a scream of pain and fury.

Jessie's screams mingled with the shrill shriek of the alarm. Throwing out an arm, she knocked the clock off the bedside table with a ringing clatter. Jessie's heart thumped wildly; her insides quivered with nausea.

She grabbed her teddy bear, a gift from one of the mission ladies, and silently rocked back and forth. Pressing her face against the bear's warm security, her tears anointed the soft matted fur and muffled her sobs.

No matter how many miles or years Jessie had put between herself and her father, the recurring nightmare was still as vivid as the day it occurred.

There had never been a mother in the picture. Whether she was dead or had taken off, Jessie didn't know. She had never asked her drunken, abusive father, and he had never volunteered the information.

For the first twelve years of her life, the bleak Navajo reservation on the outskirts of Tuba City had been Jessie's home. Then, she had run—still running, she thought morosely.

After a few moments, Jessie took a deep breath, gave the bear a final squeeze, and laid it aside. Untangling herself from the sweat dampened sheets, she rose and looked at herself in the cracked, wavy mirror on the wall. Two puffy, blood-shot eyes peered back at her.

The apartment was silent, as if embarrassed by the noise she had made. Jessie staggered over some of Billy's books piled on the floor. She caught herself on the doorjamb and gave the books a malicious kick. "Fuckin' men," she swore loudly.

"You okay?" Anita Lopez, her roommate, called from the kitchen.

"Yeah," Jessie called. "Just tripped over Fox's stupid books."

"I guess that means he'll be back later."

"Oh yeah, he'll be back," Jessie muttered, and stomped into the kitchen. "He's fuckin' his goddamned ass off and lovin' every minute of it. Why wouldn't he be back?"

"Speaking of which, it's a wonder you can walk this morning," Anita commented. "You two were really rockin' and rollin' last night. You had me twitching for a man of my own."

Jessie snorted. "Why? They're all pigs. All they care about is getting off. It makes me sick."

"Geez, the way you talk, you'd think you hated men."

"I do. They're all the same. They use you over and over till they're empty, then out comes the booze and more fun begins."

"If you hate men so much, why are you foolin' around with Fox?"

"I have plans for him."

"Why's he so special?"

"He's my way outta this dump," Jessie replied, pouring herself a cup of coffee from the battered percolator. She dragged a metal stool next to Anita. Plunking herself down heavily, Jessie grabbed up a pack of cigarettes and a lighter lying on the table. "I hear he's in med school," she said, as she savored her first lungful of smoke for the day.

"So?"

"So. When he becomes a doctor, he'll be rolling in bucks. I want to be rolling with him."

"How're you gonna do that?"

"He's a nerd, right? A real goody two shoes. I figured if I pulled his awkward ass into the sack, I could do anything with him I want. Guys like Fox are almost too easy. They're so hungry and eager for their first taste of pussy that their dick takes over. I taught him a few tricks, and now I got him eatin' out of my hands. It won't take much to finish him off."

Jessie stabbed out her cigarette viciously and rose. She had said too much, but Anita had caught her off guard with all her nosy questions. "I gotta go to work."

A short time later, she arrived at the print shop and found Billy already there. He was in the process of painstakingly changing the blade to the cutter.

'The Guillotine,' as the finishers called it, had a blade about thirty inches long and six inches wide. It was a hazard that everyone respected.

Jessie stared at Billy's back and was filled with revulsion and loathing. The morning's dream returned to her, and she shuddered, fighting the urge to vomit. Quietly, she walked up behind Billy and ran her hand over his butt. "Hi handsome," she whispered, running her tongue around the outer edge of his ear.

Billy jerked back in surprise and impaled his index finger on the blade. "Jesus!" he exclaimed. He grabbed his finger and held it tightly to slow the bleeding. His white t-shirt was speckled red, and someone hurriedly handed him some paper towels.

Jessie's face paled. "Shit, Fox!"

Worried co-workers rushed over and pushed Jessie away. Billy's boss instructed someone to take him to the hospital. Jessie stood alone. She glanced down at her hands, noticing the blood on the floor and a couple of splotches on her own shirt.

"Why the hell did that stupid fool go and cut himself," she grumbled to no one in particular. "It was just a pat on the ass," she shrugged. "Who'd have figured he'd be so jumpy."

A woman, stapling a booklet together, looked at Jessie with disgust. She muttered 'trash' under her breath and went back to what she was doing.

Later, Jessie snuck up to Billy's dormitory room. "You alone?" she asked, when he answered the door.

"For the moment," Billy replied.

"I see you're still alive."

"Yeah, I'm still here, no thanks to you."

Jessie grabbed Billy's hand. His finger was thickly wrapped in gauze. "Don't complain. It looks okay to me."

Billy winced and jerked his hand away. "Okay? I had to have a half dozen stitches. Plus, a fuckin' tetanus shot."

"Sorry. Does it hurt?"

"Like hell."

"Poor baby. Bet it's throbbin'?" she asked, her eyes locked on his.

"It's throbbing all right."

Her eyes were molten chocolate. "What? Your dick or your finger?" Jessie moved closer, her eyes penetrating deep within Billy's gaze like a cobra. "I could take your mind off it," she said.

Billy was spellbound and couldn't seem to put two thoughts together. "Uh," he swallowed, "how do I know you won't hurt me again?"

"You'll just have to take your chances," Jessie said, her body now rubbing against him. She smiled and pushed Billy into the room, firmly closing the door behind her.

Before Billy could say another word, Jessie had his shirt and pants half removed. Billy wondered fleetingly if she'd find his brain when she got to his undershorts.

A few weeks later when the term came to an end, Jessie persuaded Billy into staying in Tempe for the summer break. "Why're you going home?" she asked. "You've got a job here."

"Where am I going to stay? I can't live in the dorm, and I can't afford to rent an apartment."

"Stay with me. Anita won't care. You're here most of the time, anyway."

"I don't know, Jessie. It's not right, me living with the two of you."

"You're such a square. What's the diff? We *are* sleeping together. You afraid people are gonna talk?" she sneered.

"No, you're right. It would be silly for me to go home. Are you sure Anita won't mind?"

"She won't. 'Sides, it's none of her business what I do."

"Well, in that case, I guess I'll stay."

"It'll be a real blast, I promise," Jessie said, a smile curving her lips.

BILLY

Billy awoke on the living room floor, his face resting on a shoe. He groaned, rolled over, and sat up slowly. With bleary eyes, he looked around the apartment and was shocked. Empty bottles and glasses were everywhere. Ashtrays overflowed onto the mangy carpet, adding to the accumulated debris.

Billy's thoughts turned to that first party he had attended in this apartment. Since then, his life had dramatically changed. There had been more parties than he could count—a lifetime of bacchanalian orgies compressed into a few short weeks.

On his way to the bathroom, he stumbled over several people who were crashed on the floor. He didn't know them. In the bathroom, his bare feet slipped on vomit and urine that covered the linoleum. The smell made him gag, and he threw up as well.

He scuffed his feet on the carpet as he inched his way to Jessie's bedroom. She slept—sprawled across the bed. Billy stared at her a long time. The sight of her nakedness no longer stirred feelings of arousal and lust, only a grim ache of emptiness. Billy's fascination and excitement with sex had faded. Jessie's mood swings and cold dismissals had him frustrated, hurt, and extremely angry with his lack of self-control.

He went over to the dresser and searched for Jessie's bag of grass. Finding it, he deftly rolled and lit a joint, desperate for the drug to take over. To hurry things along, he shuffled into the kitchen and reached for an open bottle of cheap whiskey. Swiping the rim of the bottle with his palm, he drank a long swallow, consuming breakfast.

He tried not to drink too much, since he had to go to work later. The few times he had gone to work stoned or drunk, he had made several costly mistakes and was now on probation. He couldn't afford to lose this job. It paid for the means to forget. For Billy, life had become one endless muddle of noise and confusion. Every once in a while, the inner Billy would try to surface, but was squelched by Jessie and her bag of goodies. How much worse could his life get?

"You're pregnant? That can't be possible. I've been using protection. You know that," Billy shouted.

"Yeah, well sometimes when you're drunk or high, you forget," Jessie answered coolly. "Who else could the father be? We've been screwing all summer. It's gotta be you."

Billy had let this woman get under his skin, and now, he was trapped. He had secretly condemned Cal's behavior, yet he was acting just like him, only worse.

"Hey! I'm talking to you."

"Huh," Billy mumbled, shaking himself.

"You didn't hear a shittin' thing I said, did you?"

"You said you're pregnant."

"I said we gotta get married."

"What!"

"It's the only thing to do. You gotta take care of me."

"What! Why?"

"It's your fault."

"How can this be my fault?"

"You're the one with the dick, remember?"

Billy put his head into his hands. "That's just great, I'll never be a doctor now," Billy muttered.

Jessie felt a stab of fear. "Of course you will."

"And how will I do that? The school already owns my red-skinned ass. I can't afford you, let alone a kid."

"You'll think of something."

"It really doesn't matter anyway," he shrugged.

The hopelessness Billy felt was something he had lived with much of his young life. As a small child, Billy always knew he wasn't wanted. His mother made that clear to him from the beginning, by either completely ignoring him or hurting him physically. "I don't want you, you brat," she'd say over and over as she struck or kicked him. "You wrecked my life."

In turn, Billy watched helplessly as his father beat his mother in drunken rages. When he was older, he became a victim as well—to black eyes, bruises, and welts.

When Billy was eight, he stole his father's hunting knife vowing never to take any more abuse. When his father came at him to beat him, Billy took out the knife. Instead of attacking him, he held the knife out to his father. "Either you do it or I do it. The knife is quicker than you and her beating me to death," Billy said quietly. In that instant, Billy's intent was clear.

Daniel Running Fox looked into his son's eyes—really looked. He saw the same despair that was mirrored in his own. In that instant, Billy earned his father's pride and respect. He was truly an Apache and worthy of his name. Billy's father decided right then and there that Billy would have a better life—a life like he once had before his wife Sarah had turned him into a monster.

Since the time before time, there were always horses. They were part of Billy's blood—his legacy. From his grandfather to his father, their lives focused around raising, training, and riding the four-legged gifts from the gods.

While others on the Jicarilla Apache reservation were herding sheep or growing crops, Billy's grandfather, Ben, was continuing the tradition of raising and selling the finest mustangs and quarter horses in all of Arizona, Colorado, and New Mexico. He was a master at his craft, and people from all over the country came to him for strong, dependable, and beautiful mounts.

Billy's father, Daniel, had followed in his father's footsteps. No one could break and gentle a horse like Daniel, not even Ben. To the Apaches, Daniel had a horse's spirit. Ranching, however, was too tame. Stirred by the testosterone coursing through his veins, he hit the rodeo circuit at the age of fifteen, much to his parents' dismay.

Daniel was in a class by himself. When he was riding, the arena fence was filled with the curious, the awestruck, and the young 'catbirds' who waited for a glimpse of their hero.

Daniel always gave his fans what they wanted; a thrilling, chilling ride of great magnitude—outriding, outperforming, outlasting all the rest.

Sarah was one of those 'catbirds'. At fourteen, she followed Daniel's successes like a star-struck fan. She was determined that Daniel Running Fox would be hers. She got exactly what she wanted.

When Sarah was eighteen, she and Daniel ran off and got married. Daniel's parents were shocked. In their minds, she was too young, too silly, and much too Navajo. But their concerns fell on deaf ears. Daniel and Sarah were in love and things were good. Daniel was winning—winning a lot. He won the usual trophies, saddles and belt buckles at Native events. Once he started riding in Anglo rodeos, he also won large amounts of prize money.

Nothing pleased Daniel more than to better an Anglo horseman. He looked on those 'cowboys' with scorn. Perhaps it was his pride that proved to be his undoing.

At one particular rodeo on the Rez that was open to Anglos, Daniel took a bet. The bet was that he couldn't ride a nasty brute of an animal, that no one could get near, for at least ten seconds. Not only did the Anglos participate in this bet, but it seemed that everyone on the reservation also put in money. Most people bet that Daniel would win, although besides the Anglos, it seemed that a few Apaches had also bet against young Running Fox.

If Daniel won the bet, he wouldn't have to worry about finances for at least a year or more. Daniel actually lasted eight of those ten seconds before the horse threw himself over backwards, falling on top of his rider and crushing his legs.

To Daniel's horror, he survived the fall. In his mind, he would have been better off dead. Oh yes, he still had the use of his legs, but they were now twisted and stiff and pained constantly. He had lost his money and his status as a rider.

The rumor on the Rez was that the Anglo cowboys had 'got one over on Daniel Running Fox'. He never knew that a sharp piece of metal barbed wire had been placed under his saddle blanket, making the horse 'out of his mind' with pain the minute Daniel mounted him.

But the worst thing that happened to Daniel, however, was that there now was fear—a consuming fear so deep and painful that it was worse than any excruciating, physical injury. There was no way in his mind that he would ever ride a horse again. In fact, he wasn't even sure that he could stand being around the animals that he had felt akin to and loved. But there was nothing else that he could do.

Despite Sarah's pleadings to ride again, he began to work with his father on the ranch. The couple moved in with Daniel's parents; and while Daniel worked long hours with his father, Sarah had no choice but to spend her day with Daniel's mother.

When Sarah became pregnant, she sulked and fumed, blaming Daniel for doing this terrible thing. If she could have rid herself of this moving being within her, she would have. But Daniel's mother kept a close, watchful eye on her every move. When Billy was born, Sarah made no effort to conceal her feelings. She wanted no part of this child.

By the time Billy was a year old, Sarah had had enough. She was tired of her mother-in-law telling her what to do and how to care for her unwanted son. She forced Daniel to relocate to her home village of Rough Rock, Arizona. The move crushed Daniel's parents. They had become very attached to the silent baby with the sweet smile. The move also ruined Daniel.

Rough Rock was an obscure, desolate little smudge of a town within the confines of the Navajo reservation. There were no horses to work, no farming, no employment of any kind. Poverty was rampant.

With their manhood stripped away, some of the men on the reservation drank or turned to peyote. They became abusive, taking their anger and despair out on their women and children.

Daniel also turned to alcohol, hating his woman and young son more each day. Because of them, he was in this alien place among strangers with no livelihood, no future…no hope.

When Billy rebelled, Daniel took him back to New Mexico to live with his parents where he would be loved. Sarah didn't even protest. She was glad to be rid of her son.

For Billy, it was like rising from the depths of hell into heaven. He loved his new home, *Abuelo* and *Abuela*, all the horses and dogs, and the cats that multiplied so frequently.

When Billy was on a horse, one could never tell where he ended and where the horse began. People who came to the ranch used to call him 'One with Horses'. They felt he was even more gifted with the animals than his father.

His grandparents were very proud of this young boy who brought such joy to their lives. He had a rare mix of common sense and intelligence. With that combination, his grandparents knew that he could go far and be much more than a cowboy or rancher.

Billy's grandmother, Isabella, was a *curandera*, or healer. Not only did she perform the tasks of midwife, but she was also an herbalist who used plants to create medicines for all types of ailments and injuries. Isabella would sometimes travel for days in order to aid and treat people living in their sparsely populated and far-reaching section of the reservation.

Billy was fascinated and learned as much as he could. He would squat in the dirt alongside his *abuela*, helping her grow, gather, and prepare her herbs and plants. Many times, he traveled with her, helping in any way he could. He decided that he, too, would be a *curandero*.

When he got older, however, his grandmother decided that instead of a traditional healer, Billy should become a doctor. An Anglo Medicine Man could treat his people in both the old way and the new.

The Jesuits at the mission school that Billy attended agreed this was a good idea and encouraged Billy. With his brain and determination, the priests believed Billy could achieve his goals, thereby rising above the desperation and depression that were prevalent on the reservation.

Fortunately, Billy also excelled in sports. Once his academic path was laid, the high school track coach took over, providing guidance. Under his tutelage and a physically demanding training schedule, Billy earned a full athletic scholarship to Arizona State University. He was on his way.

Billy and Jessie filled out and signed the official paperwork in front of the local Justice of the Peace. Peace, Billy thought, there would be no peace for him now. He was ashamed and heartsick. Now there could never be any hope of fulfilling the dream he and his grandparents had planned with such care.

When his senior year started in the fall, he began skipping classes in order to work. If he did show up, he was late. He had failed to show for cross country practice and had missed several important meets. He was haggard and seemed to have the weight of the world on his shoulders. Drinking became as much a part of his life as breathing.

One day, he came home early to find Jessie having sex with a stranger. He stood for a moment in the doorway of the bedroom, numb and confused. Jessie and the man on the bed stared back, surprised to see him.

Without missing a beat, the man grunted, "Cool your heels, red boy. You're next. I'll be through in a minute. After that, she's all yours."

Billy reddened in embarrassment and hastily left the apartment, his mind a jumble of thoughts. He headed to the bar down the street and swallowed mouthfuls of fiery whiskey, hoping to dull his senses and ease the hurt.

Later, when he stumbled into the apartment, Jessie was lighting a joint. "Look what I got. Real good shit. Not bad for only a half hours' worth of fucking, huh?" she said proudly.

"S'not bad 'nough you're fuckin' some guy behind my back," Billy slurred. "But you're takin' shit for it. Whore! Fucking whore!" Billy staggered against Jessie, grabbing her shirt collar and tearing it as they fell against the wall of the kitchen. He tried to slap the joint from her hands, but missed, slapping at her face instead.

"You bitch!" he yelled.

"Gonna hit me?" Jessie sneered, "you can't even do *that* right. Loser!"

The anger and rage that had been slowly building, seethed inside of him. "Fucking slut!" he shouted, as again, he tried to slap at Jessie.

"Loser," she yelled again. "Like this asshole," she said, punching him in the gut. They grappled together then Jessie's fist connected with Billy's jaw, knocking him off balance.

The back of Jessie's head hit first as together they awkwardly tumbled to the floor. Out of breath, Billy lay on top of her, staring into her eyes as though seeing her for the first time. Shocked by what had just happened, he rolled to the side of her. "God, Jessie, you okay? I'm…so…sorry."

Jessie pushed herself into a seated position and rubbed at the back of her head, Billy tried to put his arms around her, but she shoved him away.

"Don't touch me, you bastard," she growled and spit into his face. "I…hate…you!"

In a daze, Billy wiped at his face, stumbled to their room, and passed out on the bed. When he awoke in the morning, he wasn't sure if the events of the day before were an alcohol induced dream or had really happened. It wasn't until he saw Jessie's torn shirt he knew. He walked past her and got out the whiskey. His nightmare had become reality.

For Billy, the next few days blended together into one continuous drunk. He finally sobered up when he ran out of alcohol that Sunday afternoon. Sitting at the kitchen table, he cradled his head on his arms.

"Good doctor you'll make," Jessie jeered.

"Doctor?" he snorted and raised his head. "That's a laugh! Shit, at this rate, I'll never even graduate let alone get into a med school."

"What do you mean? You're already there."

"I wish," he shook his head. "I haven't even been accepted to a school yet."

"What're you talking about? I thought, I mean…ASU's got a med school. I just thought, you know, you were already there. You said you had one year to go."

"Well, Jess. You thought wrong. I still have one year of pre-med left. Hell, I'll be lucky if I don't get thrown out. I haven't been to classes in over a week, and I haven't been to a cross country practice or meet all season. Don't think I'm gonna go, either. Not now. What's the use? It's over. I'll never be anything." Under his breath, he muttered angrily, "Just like my old man. Don't know why I thought I could be any different."

He got up, went to the cupboard, and pushed the contents around viciously. "No damn whiskey, no drugs, nothing. Why don't you go out and fuck somebody, Jessie?" he spat. "Maybe you could get us some grass."

Jessie stared at Billy's back, stunned. "Not in med school?" she kept repeating. "Not a doctor?"

"Have you fucked your brains out? You sound like an idiot. Man, this kid's really gonna be screwed up."

"What kid?" Jessie asked absently.

"Our kid."

"Huh?"

"You're pregnant, remember?"

"Oh that," she replied. "I didn't mean it."

"What!" he said, turning away from the cupboard to stare at her.

"I'm not pregnant."

"You mean you lied to me?" he asked, advancing on her.

"Kinda," she laughed nervously, backing away from him.

"The kid, this marriage…it was all a lie?" He could see the defiance in her eyes.

"Yeah, doesn't matter now," she shrugged. "You aren't in med school."

"What the hell does that have to do with anything?"

"Money," she said, turning away from him. "Don't doctors make lots of money?"

"You made all this up because you thought I'd have money?" He yanked her around to face him. "You fucked up my life!" he shouted, shaking her. "Do you hear me?"

Jessie glared back. "Gonna hit me?" she taunted. "Go ahead, hit me."

Billy looked at the table. An empty whiskey bottle stood in the midst of the trash. He picked it up and with a growl of frustration hurled it against the wall, spraying the room with shards of glass. "Fucking bitch!" he growled.

"You're the one who's fucked up," Jessie shouted and pushed him backward. "I should have known. You're nothing but a loser. Just like the rest of the Indian men I've known."

Billy lunged at Jessie and knocked her to the floor. He wanted to wipe the smirk from her face and aimed a kick at her head. But before his foot connected, something inside of him snapped.

He looked down at Jessie, but saw instead, his mother, cringing at his father's feet. He blinked at the image, then saw himself on the floor, waiting for his mother's punishing blows. Blinking again, he thought, my God, what are you doing? What's happening to you?

Billy started to shake. He stared at Jessie for a long moment, then abruptly ran past her and out the door. Jessie lay on the glass littered floor; her defiance gone. She had gambled and lost. Her dreams had ruined them both.

Billy slouched in his chair as he faced Dr. Benson and his counselor, Dr. Elena Sanchez. "You're failing not one but three subjects, Billy. I don't understand," Dr. Sanchez commented. "You're cutting classes, missing exams. The cross country coach is so angry that he is pushing for you to be expelled. When school started this fall, you seemed like a different person."

Boy, you got that right, thought Billy. How different can a person get. Now they are going to ask you to leave, cancel your scholarship. He could feel the failure deep inside and knew he had no one to blame but himself.

"What's wrong, Billy? You haven't been yourself since last spring," Dr. Benson observed. "Is it Jessie Tsosie? I've seen you with her. That girl is trouble. She could corrupt the Easter Bunny."

"I had no choice, sir. I married Jessie before the term began."

The room was silent—too silent. Billy felt like he was suffocating as he waited for the explosion.

"What! Why would you do a thing like that?" Benson yelled, slamming his hands down on the desk.

"I said I had no choice."

"No choice? I thought you were going on to medical school. You were going to do something with your life."

Billy stared down at his hands and mumbled something.

Dr. Benson paced angrily in front of his desk. His face was red and the veins in his temples were throbbing. "I can't believe this! You just threw it all away. All of it!"

Dr. Sanchez stood up and laid a calming hand on Benson's shoulder. She said quietly, "Billy, we knew how you felt. We were all pulling for you. You were an excellent, straight A student and worked so very hard. What about the ROTC program, medical school, everything? Don't you care that it's slipping away?" she questioned.

"Of course, I care," Billy whispered. He stared down at his hands—the hands he had so often fantasized performing surgery. He would have cried if he could, but crying was something Billy Fox had never done. It was not the Apache way.

"Jessie said she was pregnant. I believed her even though I was careful and thought I took every precaution. I wanted to do the right thing. Yesterday, she told me she lied about being pregnant so that I would marry her. It seems she was under the impression I was already in med school. I'm going to try to move back to my old dorm room today. It'll be safer."

"Safer?" asked Dr. Sanchez. "For you?"

"No," Billy said, "for Jessie." He hung his head, refusing to look at the teachers who had encouraged him, the ones who had advised and helped him. He had let them down.

Dr. Benson glanced at Dr. Sanchez. "You say you're moving back on campus. Does this mean you're still interested in pursuing your dream?"

"I'd like to try, sir. If the school will let me. I'm willing to work extra hard."

Cal didn't recognize him. He was emaciated and his eyes were dull and sunken. "Billy? What the hell happened to you? Where've you been? I haven't seen you since school ended last term. I kinda thought you dropped out. I felt really bad."

"Is my bunk still available?" Billy asked, hoping Cal would let him stay.

"Sure, come on in. I was just headin' to the cafeteria for dinner. You look like you could use some chow."

"I'm not very hungry, just tired." Billy trembled and wrapped his arms around himself.

Cal noticed the flash of silver on his finger and sucked in his breath. "What the hell? Is that a wedding ring on your finger?"

Billy studied the plain band. He remembered buying those rings, trying to make a wrong situation right. They had been all he could afford. Hell, they probably weren't even solid sterling. Now, the band mocked him, reminding him of his stupidity. "Yeah, I married Jessie over the summer."

"Jessie! Holy shit, Fox! I can't believe it!" Cal slapped him on the back and Billy lurched forward, stumbling into the room.

"I've got to lie down," Billy mumbled, rubbing his forehead.

Cal glanced into the hallway. "But…where's Jessie?" he asked, stunned and bewildered.

"I left her."

"What? When?"

"Yesterday."

"Why? What the hell happened?"

"I'm scared, Cal," Billy shivered. "I don't want to hurt her."

"Billy, you aren't makin' any sense. Are you high? What are you talkin' about?"

Billy looked at Cal, then down at his shaking hands. The hands that had wanted so much to heal, were now hands that could cause pain. "I was so stupid. You were right," he whispered. "She did want something. It's just with me, she wanted so much more."

He collapsed onto the bunk where he had once made love to Jessie. This time, a different kind of pain welled inside of him. Love, he thought, pulling the quilt over himself. I don't know what the hell that means.

Cal felt helpless. He had never seen Billy like this. Billy was steady and dependable, a friend you could bring your problems to who would really listen. He was smart and helped Cal out many times in class. He was going to make a great doctor. He couldn't blow it now.

Billy had paid the fees and sat for the MSATs, then spent last year's Christmas break interviewing at several schools. Borrowing a suit from one of his classmates, he had taken the bus across the country to do so. It had been a long haul. Was he going to let all that work and the application fees go down the drain?

If he had already left Jessie, maybe there was still hope. Since Cal didn't have any classes this term with him, he didn't know how he was doing academically. He'd find out later.

Meanwhile, he'd get some dinner and bring something back for Billy, who looked like a scarecrow. Wonder if he's doing drugs? Cal thought. It made sense, knowing Jessie and her reputation.

When Billy woke up, the two of them were going to have a long talk. Cal would then get some answers. After that, they'd make plans on how to redeem his buddy.

JESSIE

Billy rounded the back of Jessie's apartment building, hoping he wouldn't have to face her. Unfortunately, she was sitting on the fire escape, her head down and her arms wrapped around her knees. He hesitated, then taking a deep breath, climbed the rickety metal rungs and sat beside her.

"Hi Jess," he said.

"What do you want? Sex? A joint? How 'bout some whiskey?" she spat out from under her arms.

"Please, Jessie. I just came to talk."

"Talk, huh?"

"Yes, it's something we've never done. You never wanted to talk, never listened, either."

"Why?" she asked, her voice muffled. "What do we have to talk about?"

"Us."

When Jessie lifted her head, Billy was shocked. There was a cut above Jessie's eye and black and blue bruising around her mouth. "Oh my God," he said gently touching the cut over her eye. "Did I do that?"

She had meant to pull back, meant not to let him touch her. His touch was a caress, as though he was touching something fragile. Jessie realized she was holding her breath. "No."

"What do you mean, no? I threw that bottle. It must have cut you when I knocked you down." Billy looked sick.

"I…uh…fell yesterday," she muttered, turning away from him.

Billy stared at her a long moment then shook his head. "I'm sorry, Jess. I never wanted to hurt you. It'll never happen again. I promise."

"Sure," she laughed. "Over and over again you all apologize as you knock us around. You men are all the same, no matter how old—no matter what color."

"No, we're not, Jess. You never let me get close enough to be a different kind of man. It's as if you wanted me to hurt you all along."

"I'm used to pain. It's all I know. Ever since my old man put his fuckin' paws on me as a kid, it's never stopped. Do you know how much I hate you—hate all of you?" Jessie laid her head back down onto her knees as tears streamed down her face.

Billy watched her rock silently back and forth to a lullaby only she could hear. He longed to hold her and comfort her—to erase the abuse she had suffered from her father, from other men, and mostly, from himself. Unfortunately, it was too late.

He got up wearily and walked past her into the apartment. Anita was sitting at the kitchen table reading a magazine. For a brief instant, Billy did a double take. He never realized before just how closely the girls resembled one another. God, where have I been the last couple of months, he thought? I didn't even notice that the two women could have passed for twins.

Then Anita looked up, and Billy changed his mind. It was the long, dark hair and stature that gave one the illusion that they were similar. Anita's face and body, however, were much more fleshy and less appealing.

She stared at him quizzically with mature, calculating, street-hardened eyes. It was a look that Jessie was either too young to have developed or was still able to hide.

Ignoring her, he went into the room that he and Jessie had shared. There wasn't much to pack, just a few shirts, some jeans, and a couple of books.

"What are you doing?" Jessie asked from the hallway, as Billy crammed his clothes and books into his backpack.

"I'm taking my things," he said, straightening. Slinging the pack over his shoulder, he walked from the room.

"Where are you going?"

"Back to the dorms. I can't live like this any longer, and I refuse to hurt you. The best thing for the both of us is for me to get out."

"But we're married. Who's going to take care of me?"

"I don't get you," Billy said, facing her in the hall. "You tell me you hate me and yet you want me to stay. You were fine before I came along. What's the difference now?"

Jessie was shaking and her arms were wrapped around herself. "I need you."

"No, Jess, you don't need anyone, especially me." Billy squinted and took a long look at Jessie. He grabbed her wrist, exposing the length of her arm and two long, red marks.

"Christ, Jessie!" he yelled, shaking her arm. "Isn't grass enough? Where are you getting the money for heroin? Are you whoring for it? Is that how you really got this?" he asked, again touching her cut face.

"Don't touch me!" Jessie screamed, pulling her arm away. "What I do is none of your business."

"You're wrong. It *is* my business. I made a promise to care for you when we got married. But I refuse to support your drug habit. Right now, I'll pay the rent. But for everything else, you're on your own."

"You can't do that."

"I have nothing, Jessie. I'm trying to somehow resurrect my ruined GPA, and I'm working my ass off to pay for books and food and to continue to save for medical school."

"So, you're still gonna go to med school?"

"I don't know. I haven't been accepted anywhere yet."

"What if you don't?"

Billy shrugged. "I haven't thought that far ahead. I'm just trying to take care of you, go to school, and make money. I can only do so much. Hell, you're working. You probably make more than I do, and you don't have the expenses I have. In all fairness, *you* should be helping *me*."

"Will you always take care of me?"

"Is that all that matters to you?"

"I need to know."

"I'll do whatever I can. It might not be much."

Finally, she said, "I guess that's fair. Um…will you still come by?"

"You mean, will I still screw you?"

"Well, we are married."

"I doubt it. I've already made a mess of things because of that. I'm trying to straighten out my life. Besides, I don't think you really want me, anyway. You made that pretty clear from the beginning. If you need me for anything, I'll be around. At least for the rest of the school year," he said and walked out.

Jessie watched him go.

Anita put down her magazine. "Do you really think he'll keep paying our rent?"

"Who knows?" Jessie shrugged.

Anita shook her head, what a fool, she thought.

JOE

When Billy was summoned to the department office, his face was pale and drawn.

Joe Benson looked stern. "You'd better sit down," he cautioned, pointing to a chair.

Billy however, remained standing, expecting the worst. "What's wrong?"

Benson leaned against his desk with his arms crossed on his chest and glowered at Billy. "You know Billy, since your mail is now being forwarded to the department, we have been sent some information that probably never reached you when you weren't in the dorms."

"I'm being expelled?"

"Joe, stop it! You're being cruel," said Dr. Sanchez. "Relax, Billy," she said with a smile, you've been accepted to Temple, Georgetown, and the University of Pennsylvania for medical school. You made it! Between you and the scores from your MSATs, you really impressed them."

"Yes!" he yelled, raising his fists into the air. He grabbed Dr. Benson's hand and pumped it up and down, then grabbed Dr. Sanchez's as well. "I can't believe it! I made it!"

He had done the impossible. He had been accepted to three prestigious schools in the country—schools that had what he wanted. "I feel light-headed. Maybe I'd better sit down after all. Wow! I thought you were going to tell me I was being thrown out. You sure had me scared for a minute."

"Sorry kid," Benson chuckled. "Just wanted to pull your chain a bit. We're very proud of the way you turned things around. Do you have a preference? I think that no matter which school you select, the Army will foot some of the bill. You'll have to set up an appointment with the recruiting office. But first, you should choose a school so that we can get the paperwork rolling."

"I don't know. I never expected to be accepted by any of them. Do you have any suggestions?"

"All of these schools are good," said Dr. Sanchez. "Was there any reason why you applied to these three?"

"I knew they had good surgical programs, especially Georgetown. The Jesuits at my high school encouraged me to go there and helped to set up my interview."

Dr. Benson said, "My sister Marian and her family live in Georgetown. They could be a big help."

"Georgetown is a good school," Dr. Sanchez commented. "It's near DC but not in the middle of the city. Why don't you think it over for a few days and let us know at the end of the week?"

"In the meantime, I'll give Marian a call," Dr. Benson added. "We'll see you on Friday."

It had been an unusually chilly autumn day in Georgetown. After dinner, Marian and Rusty Wilson sat companionably in front of a crackling fire, the Washington Post scattered at their feet. When the phone rang, Marian groaned. There went their cozy evening together. Surely it was the hospital calling for Rusty.

Marian was pleasantly surprised to hear her brother's voice on the line. "Hello, Joe," Marian said. "I'm so glad it's you. How are you and Dorothy?"

They made small talk for several minutes, then Joe moved on to the purpose of his call. "I have a problem, Marian, and I wondered if you and Rusty could help me out?"

"Sure. Rusty's at home right now. Why don't I put him on and you two can talk?"

"That would be great. Give the girls a kiss for us."

"Hey, Joe, what's up?" Rusty's voice boomed over the line.

"Rusty, I have a favor to ask." Joe Benson then proceeded to tell Rusty about Billy, his academic background and his tentative plans for the future. "He really wants this badly, but…" he concluded, his voice drifting off.

"So, what's the favor?" Rusty asked brusquely.

"I was hoping maybe you'd have some ideas about where Billy can get either low or no cost housing."

"In Georgetown? Are you kidding? If he can't afford it, why can't he go to some state school?"

"Billy is interested in surgery. From experience, you know what an excellent surgical program Georgetown has to offer. Of all the schools that accepted him, Georgetown was probably the best."

"Isn't he working?"

"Yes, very hard but he also has a wife to support."

"Can't his folks help him?"

"I don't know much about his family, but I don't think so."

"You really like this kid, don't you?"

"Yes, Rusty, I do. I think with a little help and guidance he could go far. He's not afraid of hard work. With the exception of one bad term, he's been an A student. He had a little problem with this woman he married, but he seems to have straightened himself out. If I offered him the money, he wouldn't take it."

"Ahhh, I think I know where this is going. I know how your mind works. What you're really calling for is to ask if he can stay with us. Right?"

Joe gave a nervous little laugh. "Well, now that you mentioned it, it would be a great idea."

"What!"

"The way I see it, Rusty, I'm the only one willing to stand up for this kid and help him. He has this dream that, at this point, I don't think he'll be able to achieve. I remember what it was like to have dreams, don't you? Your dream of being a surgeon was realized. You remember who helped you?"

"Are you blackmailing me?" Rusty questioned.

"No, Rusty," Joe said tiredly, "I'm not blackmailing you. I'm just appealing to you since I can't do anything for him here. Billy has worked very hard to get to where he is today. It would be a terrible shame to let it all go to waste. Or to put off med school for a year or two until he has the additional funds."

"All right! We'll give it some thought. But I'm not making any promises, you understand?"

"I understand. I'll call you back in a couple of days, okay?"

"Okay."

"And Rusty?"

"Yeah?"

"Thanks."

Rusty grunted into the phone and hung up.

Marian looked at him. "What was that all about?"

"I'm not quite sure." Crossing the room, he poured himself a liberal amount of bourbon from the decanter on the gleaming mahogany sideboard. This was his domain of peace and sanity away from the hospital. He looked at his lovely wife. In the soft glow of lamp light, her eyes were full of love and trust. It was because of her and her family that he had been able to become a doctor. Joe was right. If it hadn't been for his father-in-law, he wouldn't have anything.

Rusty's own father had died when he was young, and he hardly remembered him. After serving in the Army during World War I, his father returned home and invested all that the small family possessed in stocks and bonds. When the market crashed several years later, he lost everything—their money, the house, his life.

Rusty's mother had never gone into detail about what happened. All she told him was that his father had accidentally fallen from the third story window of their home.

Afterward, his mother took several jobs and Rusty began selling newspapers and running errands. Between the two of them, they managed to eke out a life for themselves.

Rusty aspired to one day becoming a doctor. He worked hard, saving every penny for college. After high school, he entered Georgetown University and studied in earnest. But money was scarce. He applied for every scholarship, loan, and grant available. Although he received good grades, until he met Marian, there was never any chance he could fulfill his dreams.

Marian was secretary to the dean of the School of Arts and Sciences at Georgetown University. They had met at several school functions, becoming friends. Rusty had been very taken with her. She was bright and extremely pretty. But when he found out she came from one of the wealthy old families of Georgetown, Rusty ended their friendship. Not only could he not afford to take her out, but he was also afraid Marian would think he was after her money. The separation, however, didn't last.

When he met her widowed father, Rusty was terrified and man enough to admit it. He swallowed his pride and told the old man everything—his dreams and his growing attraction to Marian. The old man took him at face value. He liked Rusty's determination and ambition, seeing in him a little of himself. He loaned Rusty the money to go to medical school, interest free.

After interning and completing his residency at District of Columbia General Hospital, he and Marian were married and moved in with Marian's father. When the old man passed away several years later, the house and a clearing of the debt was their inheritance.

Joe Benson had also used his inheritance to pursue an education. After graduating from ASU, he moved to Arizona permanently and was extremely happy. Joe disliked the stress and bustle of the Nation's capital and thoughts of ever moving back east never occurred to him.

Rusty looked around at all that Marian's father had bequeathed to them. The home was a graceful, elderly, brick Georgian with character and charm. The crystal, china, and furniture were just a few gentle reminders—possessions Rusty would never have had without his father-in-law's help.

But Marian's father had provided so much more than material wealth, a home, and the means in which to live. He had provided guidance, friendship, and something Rusty never really had—a father.

Billy and Cal sat on the floor surrounded by brochures, maps, and filled ash trays. "Where should I go?" Billy asked.

"None of them are close to me. I was hopin' we'd be at the same school, or at least nearby."

"You're just saying that because I won't be around to bail you out anymore," Billy said, blowing a stream of smoke at Cal. "It'll be interesting to see how you do when you're on your own. I'm sure it won't take you long to find someone to cheat from. If you pay them enough, that is," he laughed.

"Cheat! I never cheat," said Cal, shoving Billy over onto his side. "Well, almost never anyway."

Billy laughed again, his white teeth flashing in contrast to his bronze skin. The drawn, haggard look was gone, and he had filled out a bit. Righting himself, he picked up a brochure and leafed through the pages.

Cal was suddenly hit by a feeling of melancholy. He was going to miss all this—sitting around, smoking, shooting the bull. He'd miss his running buddy. Many nights, when they were up late studying, Billy would say, "Come on, Hound, let's hit the pavement, blow the fog from our brains." Billy had nick-named him that when they'd first started running track. "You can't catch the Fox!" he'd say and take off with Cal at his heels. And no, Cal never did catch him.

"Somehow I doubt whether there'll be many Indians at either Temple or U of PA," Billy commented, shaking Cal from his reverie. He picked up the brochure from Georgetown and looked at its formal lettering. "Of course, I don't think this place will be any different. Just look at this fancy thing. How the hell could I fit in here?"

"Don't know, Foxy. You'll never know until you get there. DC should be full of all kinds of people. Maybe you'll be surprised."

"Yeah, and maybe they'll all drink tea and hold their pinkies in the air."

"Better switch beverages then, Fox. When in Rome…"

"I don't know, Cal. I'll be like a fish out of water or an 'Indin' off the Rez."

"Look, you said you'll be seein' Benson and Sanchez at the end of the week. They'll help you out. They aren't gonna steer you wrong. That's what they're here for, right?"

"I guess," Billy replied.

The next few days passed slowly—each worse than the day before. By the time Billy entered the department office later that week, his mind was addled, and he was exhausted from lack of sleep. Dropping his books at his feet, Billy slumped into a chair.

"Good heavens. What's the matter?" Dr. Sanchez asked.

"I can't do this," Billy answered. "I just can't."

"Can't what?" Benson asked.

"You know. All this crap. I just can't do it. It was stupid for me to even try. I've looked at all the stuff from those schools. None of it makes any sense."

"Come on, Billy. It's not as bad as you're making it out to be. Let's talk about this. Together we can make some sense of it all."

"No, Dr. Sanchez, it was a crazy idea. What was I thinking? Why didn't I apply to some state schools? I'll never fit in at any of these places. Look at me," he said, pulling at his t-shirt. "What's a goddamned Indian gonna do at George-town or Temple? They'll crucify me there."

"They will if you let them," Benson spat out. "Of course, I thought you were tougher than this. I thought you were an Apache," he said with squinty eyes as he stood over Billy. He pointed a finger accusingly at him, "They aren't beaten by anything, are they? Geronimo sure as hell didn't go running away from his problems. He faced them like a man."

Billy squirmed in his chair, refusing to look at Benson.

"Now Joe, calm down," Dr. Sanchez said. "Yelling isn't going to solve anything."

"But he's come this far, damn it!" Benson said, frowning. He plunked down on the edge of his desk and crossed his arms. "Are we just going to let him give up?"

"I never said that. I'm sure that we'll come to a solution. I think right now, Billy is just a little overwhelmed. Aren't you?"

Billy looked dazedly at his two teachers. "It's too much. Not just deciding where to go but how to pay for everything. If I don't get the scholarship, then what? Where will I live? I can't think anymore."

"Perhaps that's part of your problem," Dr. Sanchez commented. "I think you've been thinking too much. Why don't we address your concerns one at a time? For instance, you talk about finances. Okay, let's talk about them. If you don't mind us asking, do you have money put aside?"

"Yes, I do. I've always had a job. I've been sticking almost everything I make into a savings account. But with paying Jessie's rent and this last batch of books, there's not as much as I'd hoped."

"Can't she pay her own rent?" Benson asked.

Billy shrugged. "I told her I would take care of her. I can't go back on my word."

Benson growled in exasperation and looked as though he was going to explode again. Dr. Sanchez stepped in saying, "You're working at a print shop right now, aren't you? What kind of money are you making there?"

"Minimum wage," Billy said, his head low on his chest.

"Is that all?" Benson muttered.

Dr. Sanchez gave him a dark look, then continued. "This morning, I happened to glance at the bulletin board. There's an opening in the Biology Lab for a research assistant. I think that what they're offering would probably double that. I could call them and set up an interview if you'd like."

"That would be great," Billy said, lifting his head. "Last month, I looked into teaching CPR as an extra job. But I need to have transportation for that."

"Eventually, you are going to have to address that problem," Dr. Benson stated. "You can't walk or take the bus everywhere."

"I know. But how can I possibly buy a car, even a cheap used one? I can't afford to drain my savings."

"Hmm," Benson said, rubbing his chin. "A friend of mine is selling his '52 Harley Panhead. It's in decent shape. I could find out what he's asking for it.

Something like that may be within your reach. They're cheaper to run than a car and wouldn't deplete your finances, either."

"If I had the bike, I could take both jobs. The CPR classes are only on weekends. That shouldn't screw up my schedule."

"Hold on, Billy. We don't want you to run yourself ragged," warned Dr. Sanchez, holding up her hand. "Remember how you started this last term."

"I won't forget. But even with the added salaries, I'm afraid I'll still come up short."

"There are always grants and loans available," Dr. Sanchez said reasonably.

"I know, but I hated to do that unless it was absolutely necessary. I wanted to do this all on my own."

"What's wrong with borrowing money? Everybody does it," Benson asked.

"I'd be ashamed."

"There's nothing to be ashamed of. There are times when you have to," Benson added.

"But I hate the thought of owing somebody something, especially money."

"Well, get those thoughts out of your head."

"What if they won't give me a loan?"

"If you're worried about not qualifying or needing someone to countersign, I'll go with you to the bank."

"And in the meantime, I'll check into some government grants for you," Dr. Sanchez said. "I'm sure we'll be able to find a few that don't have to be paid back."

Billy was at a loss for words.

"Now that money is no longer an issue, we need to address where you will go to school," Sanchez remarked.

"Maybe I can help there, too," Dr. Benson said. "I mentioned before that my sister lives in Georgetown. Her husband is a surgeon and works out of Georgetown University Hospital. He teaches a course at the med school every semester and is also in the Army Reserves. I spoke to them the other day and told them about you."

"About me?"

"Yes, Billy, if you decide on Georgetown, it would be a plus to know that my family's nearby. They can help you if you run into trouble. Also, you wouldn't feel so alone and out of your element."

"But they don't know me. Why would they want to help me?"

"Because I asked them to," Benson smiled. "My brother-in-law is coming out here next month for a seminar at the University of Arizona in Phoenix. He's going to be staying with me while he's here. I think it would be a good idea if the two of you were to meet. Maybe he can give you some advice."

Billy's thoughts were whirling—this time, not in confusion but hope. He stared at his teachers. "Why're you guys doing this for me?" Billy asked, incredulous.

Benson paused a moment and smiled again. "Uh…free medical treatment when you graduate," he replied. "We're not always going to be young and in the best of health. We're just thinking ahead," he said, grinning at Dr. Sanchez.

"Thank you both. I don't know what else to say. I just wonder if you would have helped me as much if I had wanted to be a proctologist?"

"Billy, you're already a pain in the ass!"

"Oh, you two are terrible," Dr. Sanchez said, laughing. "But seriously Billy, just make us proud of you. That's all the thanks we need."

BILLY

Billy took the job in the biology department, working four nights a week. It was tedious but doubled his income. On Saturdays, he began taking classes for his certification to teach cardiopulmonary resuscitation and first aid. Once certified, he would be able to conduct classes at the local Red Cross and also at the University. He would be paid a fee for every class he gave. If he wanted to work every weekend, that could be arranged if he had the transportation.

With Cal's help and encouragement, Billy got a motorcycle license and purchased the Harley, Dr. Benson had told him about. The motorcycle was great. It was fuel efficient and didn't cost an arm and a leg to operate. The only downside was that it sounded like a herd of thundering horses.

Billy finished the written portion of the test, then turned in his papers.

"If you'll wait a few minutes, I'll check this. That way, if you passed, we can finish the paperwork for your certification," said the instructor.

"Okay," said Billy. "I'll just hang out in the hall."

At this time of day, the Red Cross building was almost empty. Except for his class, there wasn't anything else going on at the moment. Billy lit a cigarette and walked around, looking at the other classrooms. If he got his certification, he would probably be teaching a class in one of these rooms in a few weeks.

"Hey Fox," the instructor called. "You want to come in here?"

"Sure," Billy said.

"You did fine. Fill out this form, and we'll get things moving. Someone here at the office will be calling you to give you a list of class times that are available. Good luck."

"Thanks," said Billy, shaking his hand.

Billy had to ride past Jessie's apartment and felt obligated to stop. He parked in front of her building, hesitated, then finally walked up the stairs and knocked.

Anita answered. Crossing her arms against her chest, she leaned into the doorframe. "Look what the cat dragged in. What do we owe this honor? Let me guess? You're horny?"

Billy shifted uncomfortably. "Is Jessie here?"

Anita stared at him a long moment, then replied, "Come on in." Turning, she yelled into the apartment, "Hey Jess, your *hubby's* here."

Jessie walked out of her room and froze when she saw Billy. "What do *you* want?"

"I had a few bucks on me, so I stopped to see if you needed anything. But I guess you don't," he shrugged and turned to go.

"Wait. We could use some stuff. What do we need, Anita?" The two girls disappeared. A few minutes later, Jessie returned with a list saying, "Okay big spender, let's go." Seeing the bike parked at the curb, she said, "Cool. Is it yours?"

Billy handed Jessie his helmet. "Yes, put this on."

He scanned Jessie's list, scratched off many items, and bought instead necessary staples that could be carried on the bike in his saddlebags.

Jessie trailed Billy as he hauled the groceries up the steps. Her eyes lingered on his jeans. The age softened material molded to his backside, and Jessie fought to keep her hands from reaching out and stroking the fabric.

"Wanna stay for dinner?" she asked impulsively.

"Sure," said Billy. "I'm starving. But are you really going to cook? I don't have any money left for anything else."

"Well, we did get stuff today. What'd we buy?"

Billy walked into the kitchen. "May I?" he asked, as he deposited the bags on the counter and began to remove items.

"Go ahead. You know *I* can't cook."

"I knew there was a catch to the invite," he said, shaking his head.

Jessie twisted her lips into a smug smile. "Of course."

"Well, don't just stand there and watch. Put a pot of water on to boil."

"That's what doctors always say. Boil water," she said wryly.

Anita wandered into the kitchen as Billy cut tomatoes, onions, and garlic, tossing them into a skillet. After throwing some pasta into the boiling water, he started making a salad. He moved around the kitchen efficiently and neatly, cleaning up as he went. When the food was ready, the three of them sat down.

"Pretty nice, Jess. He buys us food and cooks it, too," said Anita, taking a bite, "Not bad, either. You can cook for me anytime."

Billy ate quickly. "Thanks for dinner. I hate to eat and run but I got a paper to write."

"He's such a nerd, isn't he Anita?"

"Yeah, see ya 'round Billy."

Jessie walked Billy to the door. "Do you really have to go? I mean, you could stay awhile," she said. Sidling up to him, she ran her fingers down the buttons of his shirt.

Billy backed away and said, "Sorry, Jess. I gotta run. See ya."

"You sure?" she asked, grabbing his belt.

"Positive," he said, gently loosening her fingers, and taking the stairs at a run.

"Hey, Fox?"

Pausing halfway down the steps, Billy turned to look up at her.

"Um…thanks," she mumbled.

"You're welcome."

Jessie watched until he was swallowed up into the darkness of the stairway. She shut the door and went to the window, watching him mount the bike and ride away. She then wandered back into the kitchen where Anita had cleared away most of the dirty dishes.

"Did he leave?"

"Uh huh."

"Geez, I thought sure you'd have had him in the sack by now. You're losing your touch. What happened?"

"He left."

"That's it?"

"Yeah," Jessie said puzzled. "He didn't ask for any money for the food or anything. I don't get it. He didn't even try to kiss me."

"Weird," said Anita, putting the last dish into the cupboard.

"Yeah, really weird."

"Where the hell have you been all day?" Cal greeted Billy.

"I spent most of the day getting certified at the Red Cross. The rest of the day, I spent with Jessie."

"What? Are you crazy?"

"Calm down. I didn't do anything stupid. You'd have been proud of me."

"I'd have been more proud if you hadn't stopped at all, you dumb shit. You're askin' for trouble. Just watch your ass, buddy."

"I know, I know," Billy sighed. "Don't worry. Hell, if you worried as much about your own ass as you did about mine, you'd win some kind of award."

"Yeah, well don't go givin' me any gray hairs, Fox. If I'm not a good doctor, I'm gonna have to rely on my good looks to make money."

"Asshole," Billy said, shoving Cal out of his way. "You have neither brains nor looks in my opinion, you pale faced, blue-eyed devil."

"Go to hell, redskin," said Cal, as he wrestled Billy to the floor.

RUSTY

When Frank "Rusty" Wilson walked into the ASU classroom, desks were pushed back, and bodies were strewn on the floor. A mantra of one and two and three and four and five, breathe could be heard. Students, in teams of two and three, practiced chest compressions and ventilations on mannequins. A young man in jeans and a Red Cross t-shirt walked around the room. He lingered at each group and watched for a while. Sometimes, he stopped the students and repositioned their hands or offered advice.

Finally, the instructor had the students take their seats. "In a few minutes, I'm going to test each one of you individually on what you've been practicing. You'll be asked to complete a whole cycle of CPR for the practical part of your test. If you pass both this and the written exam you completed earlier, the Red Cross will mail your cards and certificates to you within two weeks. If you fail, you'll have another chance to take the tests next week. Does anyone have any questions?"

While the young man was speaking, Rusty quietly sat down at the back of the room. He watched and listened very carefully. Joe Benson hadn't told him everything and now he knew why. Joe never said Billy was an Indian, that he wore earrings, or that his hair hung in a plait down his back. Rusty mentally shook his head. He would have to get to know this kid a lot better before he could make any kind of decision.

At forty years of age, Rusty thought he was a good judge of character. Aside from college and medical school, he also spent some time in the Army and knew what made a good officer. He would scrutinize Billy with the same detachment that served him so well both in the service and in the hospital. Now, however, if Rusty made a poor decision, his family would be affected.

Upon further inspection, Rusty put all his prejudices aside. Billy's jeans were well worn but free of stains. He was clean and his hair was wrapped in a tight braid. His skin was a little darker than most of the other students' but not a very noticeable difference. He had a patient manner about him that, if he became a doctor, would be beneficial. He spoke quietly and was very attentive to what his students had to say.

When the testing was over, Billy held back a few students and went over the procedure again with them. He seemed to be apologizing. Must have failed them, Rusty thought. At least he's not a pushover. After the students left, Rusty walked over to Billy who was kneeling on the floor cleaning the mannequins. The smell of rubbing alcohol permeated the room.

"Are you Billy Fox?" Rusty asked.

Billy looked up startled. He didn't remember seeing the tall, thin, red-haired man earlier and his appearance threw him momentarily. Concern showing in his eyes, Billy replied, "Yes, I am. Can I help you?"

"I'm Frank Wilson, Joe Benson's brother-in-law. He told me I could find you here today. I thought when you were finished, we might go somewhere and talk."

"Oh, that's right, he said you were coming out here," Billy said, putting down the bottle of alcohol and wiping his hands on a rag. "Glad to meet you," he said, sticking out his right hand. "I'll be done here in just a few minutes. Do you mind waiting?"

"Take your time," said Rusty.

Billy packed the dummies into their cases and, with Rusty's help, stored them in a closet. It was late in the afternoon and Rusty could hear Billy's stomach growling.

"Hungry?" he laughed.

"Just a little bit," Billy smiled. "We went straight through since nine this morning. The kids had a break, but I ended up working with someone who was having trouble, instead."

"What do you say we get something now?"

"Sure, you have anything in mind? The food in the cafeteria is passable."

"How about some authentic Mexican food? I've been really hungry for something hot and spicy, but Joe has an ulcer."

"I know of a place. The food's great, but it's not very fancy. You interested?"

"Sounds good to me," said Rusty. "Except I walked here from Joe's house."

"That's okay if you don't mind sitting on the back of a motorcycle."

"I won't get saddle sore, will I?"

"The place I have in mind is close. I can drop you off at Dr. Benson's afterward."

Rusty thought there was a mistake when Billy pulled up in front of a dive at the edge of town. There were several Mexicans and Indians sitting on the veranda, a few dogs of uncertain ancestry lay at their feet, panting in the dust.

"Are you sure about this place?" Rusty asked a little nervously, as the occupants on the veranda stared at them with unsmiling intensity.

"I told you it wasn't fancy," Billy replied, nodding to the occupants of the veranda. "Those dogs better move their asses though if they don't want to become someone's dinner," he said as he opened the wooden screen door.

Again, Rusty had to put his prejudices aside. The façade was deceiving. Inside, the restaurant was very clean—the scents of garlic and onions made Rusty's mouth water. A young Hispanic boy escorted them to a booth; its cracked vinyl seats were patched neatly with industrial tape. The fading sunlight created dancing shadows across the red-checked piece of oil cloth covering the table.

The boy brought a basket of warm tortilla chips, a bowl of salsa and two glasses of water.

"Be careful of the salsa," Billy warned. "It's usually pretty lethal."

"Okay. You want a beer?" Rusty asked, as he loaded up a chip and popped the whole thing into his mouth.

"No thanks. The water will be fine." Billy stared at Rusty, whose face turned the color of his hair, making his green eyes and freckles stand out.

"Oh my God!" Rusty coughed. He hastily grabbed his water glass, tears streamed down his face.

"I told you it was lethal."

"Yes, but that's…wicked!" he said, gulping his water. "You ate a hell of a lot more than that, and it didn't even phase you."

Billy laughed. "I was raised on hot stuff. I don't think there's anything I can't handle. Besides, these are only jalapeños. For a gringo like you though, I guess they're pretty hot."

Rusty wiped at his eyes with his napkin. "Hot! I can't feel my lips anymore! We could use this as an anesthetic at the hospital. Do I dare order for myself?"

"Just don't order the Chihuahua," Billy grinned.

By the time they got their orders, Rusty had gotten to know Billy pretty well. Hot food can do that to a person.

"So, why do you want to be a doctor?" Rusty questioned abruptly, cutting into his tamale.

"Actually, I originally wanted to be a *curandero*."

"What's that?"

"A *curandero,* or healer, is someone who uses herbs and other medicinal plants, as well as alternative remedies, to help people who are injured or sick. They usually grow their own plants and make poultices or infusions with them, among other things. My people depend on them since there aren't many doctors on the reservation. And the ones we have are only part time and found in small clinics in more populated areas."

"Why is that?"

"You want to work out in the middle of nowhere for nothing?" Billy smiled.

"I guess not," Rusty said, with a rueful grin. "How did you become interested in medicine in the first place?"

"Well, to understand that you have to understand my grandmother. *Abuela* is a very uh…interesting woman. She's the *curandera* and midwife on our part of the Rez. I spent a lot of time helping her when I was growing up. It's incredible the amount of knowledge she possesses for never having gone to school and being basically illiterate."

"She sounds fascinating."

"She is. I know many Anglos wouldn't understand, but she and others like her are essential to the reservation. I was lucky to learn everything she could teach me." Billy took a sip of water. In a hushed voice, he continued, "Some of the people on the Rez think she's pretty radical and a bit *loca*. They think she's a *bruja*."

"A what?"

"*Bruja*—you know, a witch."

"Why?"

"Because she always seems to see and think beyond what others do. That scares a lot of people."

"Well, is she a witch?"

"Probably," Billy laughed. "She always seems to know what I'm thinking and doing, especially if it's something wrong."

"Sounds just like my mother," Rusty chuckled. "I wonder what she'd say if I told her *she* was a witch?"

Billy wiped his eyeglasses with his shirt tail. "I don't know, man. But if she's anything like my *abuela,* you'd be in for a real tongue lashing."

"Probably, so why didn't you become a healer?"

"*Abuela* felt my people needed more than just traditional healers. She knew from experience that they weren't always enough. Sometimes Anglo medicine was needed. And since I had the interest…," Billy shrugged.

"I see. Um, you talk about your grandmother but how do your parents feel about this? Joe says you're married. What about your wife? Are they all giving you their support?"

Billy sobered. He forked up the remains of his rice and beans and chewed thoughtfully. "I don't live with my wife," he stated, pushing his empty plate aside. "It doesn't matter what she thinks. My parents…," he paused, "my old man's dead, and I haven't seen my mother since I was about eight. I've lived with my grandparents since then."

Rusty put down his fork and picked at a cigarette burn in the oil cloth. "I'm sorry," he said. "My own father died when I was five. It was hard. I know how you must have felt."

Sitting quietly, Billy looked down to see that he had twisted his paper napkin into a rope. "My father was a very unhappy man, and he drank—a lot. He was not...you know...the greatest of fathers," he said with an air of resignation.

Staring out the window into the growing darkness, Billy said, "He killed himself. In front of me. I couldn't stop him."

Reaching into his pocket, he pulled out his cigarettes. Shaking one out of the pack, he tapped it down and took his time striking the match. Inhaling the smoke, Billy went back to looking out the window.

Rusty closed his eyes, rubbing them with a thumb and index finger. He was suddenly very tired. He remembered his own father's broken and bleeding body on the pavement in front of their house. It was funny, he couldn't remember his father's face, but the image of his body never went away.

How similar we are, Rusty thought. Two different people from two different walks of life, yet here we are, basically the same. When he opened his eyes, Billy was staring at him. Their eyes held and something seemed to pass between them. After that, a long silence fell until the waiter interrupted their thoughts by presenting the check. Billy quickly reached for the bill, then stood and pulled out a worn leather wallet.

"Hold it," Rusty said. "Let me take care of that."

"No," Billy replied. "You're my guest."

"Come on, Billy. This is crazy. Give me that check."

"Sorry, Dr. Wilson, they don't take Anglo money here," Billy said, as he handed money to the waiter.

"Well, they sure as hell will take it at Georgetown. Any and all the money they can get. Do you have those kinds of finances?"

Slowly shaking his head, Billy said, "No, I don't."

"Well, if you don't have it, where are you going to get it? Loans, grants, what?"

Billy sank back down into his seat and sighed. "I'm working on getting a scholarship through the Army."

"That's great. But knowing the Army, they surely aren't going to pay for everything."

"You're right. The funds will only cover tuition and provide me with a small stipend. I'll need that to cover the costs of books and some of the required instruments."

"If you do get the scholarship, how will you pay for the rest?"

"I'll have to apply for some government grants and maybe take out a loan."

"When will you know if you get the scholarship?" Rusty questioned.

"I won't know until the end of my first year."

"What? You mean you have to wait that long before you know?"

"Yes. Look, they want to be sure that the recipient can handle the course and will be in it for the long haul."

"God, a whole year," Rusty shook his head in disbelief. "That's a long time to be uncertain, isn't it?"

"I know. Even if I get straight A's, I'll still have to pass several other tests to qualify. I'm hoping that being ROTC will give me an edge."

"What about housing?"

"I'm not sure there'll be enough left for that."

"If there were, where would you stay?"

"I don't know. I already checked into on and off campus housing. So far, things don't look too good."

"Why not?"

"Well, the places off campus that are nearby cost a small fortune. Even the ones further away are pretty expensive."

"What about on-campus housing?"

"Getting a place on campus is done through a lottery. Undergrads get first dibs. If there are any rooms left over, the rest of the pack fight for them."

"Have you put in an order for a dormitory room?"

"Yes, but I doubt I'll get one. There are already too many ahead of me. Maybe next year, if I'm lucky."

"That's leaving a lot of things up in the air, isn't it?"

"Yes, but I can't do it any other way. I'm basically flying by the seat of my pants."

"But what if things don't work out? Then what are you going to do?"

"I guess I'll have to go home."

"And throw all that money and time away?"

Billy shrugged. "What else can I do? It's either take a chance or sit on my ass on the Rez and drink myself to death. There's really no other way."

Rusty steepled his index fingers together, pursing his lips against them. Billy had painted himself into an impossible corner. Silently, he cursed his brother-in-law. Joe was right, damn it. This kid *was* different. How could Rusty in good conscience take away Billy's opportunity to do something with his life? He thought again about his father-in-law and the chance that he himself had been given.

Rusty hated to make a snap decision, especially without first talking to his wife, but felt that in this case, it was necessary. After a moment, he took a deep breath, "How would you like to stay with my family, at least for your first year of school?"

"What? Are you serious?"

"Yes. I am."

"But I can't stay with you, Dr. Wilson. You don't even know me."

"I don't know about that. I think I know you pretty well. Look, a few years ago someone helped me when I wanted to go to medical school. Now I want to do the same thing for you."

"I don't want anyone's charity."

"Come on, Billy, it's not charity. I want to help. And please, call me Rusty."

"I don't know, uh...Rusty. I mean, that's a lot to do for someone you don't know. It would be great, but...what about your wife and the rest of your family?" Billy asked, flustered.

"Let me worry about that."

"This is too much," Billy said, shaking his head. "I can't take it all in."

"You don't have to make any decision right now. I'm not leaving until next Wednesday. You'll have a few days to think things over. Is that fair?"

"That's more than fair."

Rusty glanced around the restaurant. He and Billy were the only patrons left. The young boy was quietly mopping the floor on the other side of the room.

Rusty stood. "I think we'd better hit the road before we're asked to leave."

Billy also stood. He looked at Rusty for an awkward moment, then stuck out his hand. "I can't thank you enough for offering to help me."

"You're welcome. I'll even forgive you for the heartburn I have now," Rusty grinned.

"Hey, I told you not to order the Chihuahua!" They both burst out laughing and headed out the door into the night.

BILLY

Billy rose early the morning of graduation. He was too keyed up to sleep. It was only seven a.m., but it was already stiflingly hot in their tiny dorm. Billy glanced around the empty room. Most of Cal's things were gone with the exception of a few necessities.

This was the day they had talked about for months. Today, Cal would leave this room for the last time. Tomorrow, it would be Billy's turn.

"Turn off that light," Cal groaned. "It's killin' me."

"It wouldn't be bothering you if you hadn't gotten plastered last night."

"Hell, I had to celebrate. It would've been more fun if you'd have joined us."

"For whom?" Billy retorted. "I thought you were dead when I found you lying in front of the door last night."

"I was restin'."

"No, you weren't. You were getting ready to puke. You make tossing your cookies an Olympic event. I hope that's the last time I have to clean up after you."

"Make fun, go ahead. You'll miss me, ya know."

"I know," Billy said. "I'm gonna miss you a lot, you big, dumb asshole."

"Thanks. Now turn off that fuckin' light before I hurt ya."

Later that morning, Billy and Cal readied themselves for the graduation exercises. "I look stupid," said Billy, scrutinizing himself in the mirror. "The damn dress is bad enough without this goofy hat to go with it." He placed the white stole around his neck. It would have been gold for Suma Cum Laude, if he hadn't screwed up last term. Still, Magna wasn't too bad.

"Think you're smart, don't ya?" said Cal, eyeing the stole.

"You could have had one too, if you had studied more."

"There are more important things in life than studyin'."

"Uh huh, women, beer, and puking on your shoes," Billy ticked off on his fingers. "What time will your parents be here?"

"Any minute, I reckon. They're always early. Is Jessie comin' to Commencement?"

"Are you kidding? What the hell for? She'd be the last person I'd expect to see. She's already pissed I'm going to be staying with her until I have to leave for

San Antonio. I just wish my grandparents could have made it. It's because of them I'm here in the first place."

"Why didn't they come?"

"How would they have gotten here? *Abuelo* has an old, beat-up truck that could hardly get them to Albuquerque, let alone Tempe. Besides, they would feel out of place. They probably wouldn't have come even if they lived in Phoenix," Billy shrugged. "Come on, let's go. It's getting late."

As Billy and Cal went to meet Mr. and Mrs. Lewis after Commencement, however, Billy spied another couple. The gentleman was in his late fifties and wore a plaid shirt tucked into a pair of dungarees. A belt with a large turquoise buckle adorned his waist. His black hair was shot with gray and twisted into a braid. At his side stood a woman, slightly younger, wearing a long, colorful dress. Her high cheekbones were deeply tanned, and her bright eyes were creased with lines of laughter. A tight bun was drawn at the nape of her neck, and she held herself very erect. Both man and woman appeared tired, yet their eyes were filled with a quiet pride.

Billy's heart skipped a beat when he saw them. "*Abuela! Abuelo!*" He ran to greet the couple, his Commencement gown billowing out behind him. "I can't believe it!" he said. "How did you get here?"

"This young man and his parents helped us," Ben Running Fox nodded in Cal's direction. "He thought we'd want to be here with you today. He was right. We are very proud of you."

Billy didn't know what to say and didn't quite trust his voice. The back slapping and vomiting forgotten, he looked at Cal in amazement.

Cal grinned stupidly and slapped Billy on the back. "Sly as a fox, eh Billy? I almost bust a gut tryin' to keep from laughing when we were talkin' about your grandparents earlier."

Billy grinned back. "Didn't think you had it in you to keep your big mouth shut."

"I'm just full of surprises, aren't I? Now come on, Dad's takin' all of us out for lunch before we have to leave. Let's go get out of these dresses before someone takes us to a convent," Cal said, hauling Billy away.

The afternoon passed quickly in a flurry of small talk. Unfortunately, Billy only had a few moments alone with his grandparents while Cal and his family packed his remaining belongings.

"I hope you don't mind that I'm going so far away," Billy said. "But it worked out for the best. I'm just sorry that I won't be seeing you for a while."

"Whatever happens, William, you will be in our hearts. We'll think of you every day and pray you are well," his grandmother said, holding his hand. She noticed the ring on his finger but didn't say anything.

He bowed his head. "I made some very big mistakes this past year. You would have been ashamed of me," he said quietly. "I almost failed you."

"You will never fail us, William," his grandmother said firmly. "Even if you fail yourself. No matter what, we will always love you. Never forget that. You made us very proud today."

"I'm so happy you were here with me," Billy replied. "We planned this day for so long."

"Now the hard part begins," Ben advised. "Remember William, one needs wisdom to know they are ignorant. Remember also," he cautioned, "that finding wisdom does not mean forgetting who and what you are."

"I'll remember."

Soon afterward, everyone gathered by the car. On their way back to Flagstaff, the Lewis family would drop Ben and Isabella off at the bus station for their long ride home.

"Here's my address in New York City," Cal said, shoving a scrap of paper into Billy's hand. "I don't know if you'll want to write or have the time, but… well, here it is. So long, Billy. Good luck at Georgetown. Stay out'a trouble."

"You too, and Cal, thanks…for everything. This meant a lot to me," he nodded at his grandparents.

"I know." Cal slapped Billy on the shoulder, then the two hugged awkwardly. "See ya," Cal said, getting into his vehicle along with his brother.

Billy saw the pride in his grandparents' eyes and knew he had completed the first step. Could he possibly finish? Their eyes told him yes. He took both of their hands in his and squeezed them gently. "I promise, I won't let you down," he said, swallowing hard. "*Te amo.*"

His grandfather blinked and nodded. Releasing Billy, he got into the waiting car. "*Te amo,*" said his grandmother quietly, placing her hand against his chest. "I love you." Then lightly touching his cheek, she followed her husband into the Lewis sedan.

Billy waved as the cars pulled away. What a day! He still couldn't believe his grandparents had come all this way. He was amazed that Cal and his parents had secretly arranged such a wonderful surprise.

He continued to stand on the sidewalk even though the cars were gone from sight. Billy finally came back to earth as he realized that he was now on his own and very much alone. He already missed Cal's laughter and easy friendship. Facing a new challenge, with no one except strangers, was going to be a very scary proposition.

His thoughts traveled to Jessie. He wondered how the next few weeks would pan out. She hadn't been happy that he was going to stay with her. He wasn't too thrilled about the situation himself. Billy never knew what to expect from her and didn't think he'd ever be comfortable in her presence.

He lit a cigarette and wandered back to his room. Someone was throwing a party, and the sounds of laughter and music filtered down the hall. He sat in the middle of the deserted room, lit another cigarette and grabbing a book, began to read. After a while his doubts and fears faded. All noises ceased, as he became immersed in the complex workings of the human body.

JESSIE

Although Billy was back in the apartment, if it weren't for a small pile of clothes and a stack of books in the corner, Jessie wouldn't have known he existed.

She had assumed that since he was again living with her, he would expect to share her bed and all that it entailed. Instead, he wrapped himself in a blanket and fell asleep on the couch. This confused Jessie. She would lay awake at night listening for any sounds from Billy in the other room. If he got up to go to the bathroom, she'd think that surely, he was coming for her, wanting her. But he would go straight back to the couch.

Billy also resumed working at Printer's Ink. He'd take Jessie with him, disappearing into the press room for the day. Afterward, he'd drop her off at the apartment, then head to the Bio lab for the evening. On Saturdays, he continued working for the Red Cross and was gone all day. With that kind of schedule, he didn't have much free time. Most days, Billy packed a lunch and dinner, eating at work. Only on weekends would he eat at the apartment, usually doing the cooking.

When Billy wasn't working, he would often leave and go for a run, sometimes being gone for hours. He would come back soaked, take a shower, then hit the couch.

The few times that she and Anita had a party, Billy took off. It seemed he wasn't taking any chances. He never drank, never touched any of the drugs they had available, never raised his voice to her, never noticed her. When she'd smoke grass, he'd shake his head and walk away.

It was a strange arrangement and one that made Jessie uncomfortable.

"What're you reading?" Jessie asked, sitting on the arm of Billy's chair.

"It's *Meditations* by Marcus Aurelius."

"Who?"

"Marcus Aurelius was a Roman emperor and a philosopher."

"Is there any sex in it?"

"No."

"I probably wouldn't like it then," she said, tossing her hair back.

"Hell Jessie, you wouldn't even understand it."

"Wanna go out?" she said, flicking her tongue in his ear and pressing her breasts against his shoulder.

"No," he pushed up his glasses and turned the page.

"How come?"

"Not interested and can't afford it. You're in my light. Go sit somewhere else."

Jessie could see she was getting to him. He was very uncomfortable when she got too close and would start to fidget. Instead of moving, Jessie slid down the side of the chair so that she was sitting in Billy's lap.

"Get off, Jessie," he said, a flush creeping up his neck.

"Okay. Let's get off," she giggled. "I want it bad." Putting her hand to his crotch, she fondled the denim fabric.

"Wow! Feels to me like you do, too."

Pushing her off his lap, he got up. "I'm going for a run. Go find someone else to play with." He laced up his shoes and slammed out of the apartment.

Another night, she sat curled up on the couch, her battered teddy bear hugged to her chest. She noticed his look of disapproval as she lit up a joint. "You know, you really piss me off," she said, tossing the spent match into an ashtray. "You act so goddamned prim and proper like you never did drugs."

"I hate to see you messing up your mind and your life."

"It didn't bother you when *you* did it."

"Maybe I wised up. It's never too late to change."

"Go to hell. I don't need any motherly advice," she snapped.

"I just wish someone had given my old man some advice. Maybe if they had, he'd be alive today. Not that he was much of a father, but…" Billy shrugged.

"What happened to him?"

"He and his friends used a lot of peyote. On my thirteenth birthday, he took me up to the mountains. You know, an Apache manhood thing. He started chewing some buttons and wanted me to do it, too. That was his idea of a vision quest, and I didn't like it. But it didn't last long because he started tripping, and thought he was some kind of fucking bird. He dove off a cliff before I could stop him. What a waste," he said in disgust.

"Nice birthday present," Jessie snorted.

"Yeah, real nice, that's why I especially hate it when you get stoned. It makes me think of him and it scares me. I'd hate to have to pick up the pieces."

"Like you care."

"Hell, I'm surprised you're still alive. You're self-destructive and it shows."

Jessie shrugged and tightened her grip on the bear. "Why bother living, no one gives a shit about me anyway. All my old man wanted to do was fuck me. You, too."

"I don't know, Jess," he said sadly. "I think you've done your own share of screwing. Sometimes I wonder who's screwing whom."

"Just fuck me, beat me, leave me. Go ahead run," she murmured to herself, ignoring him. "Run, run, run," she repeated, then began to laugh hysterically. Her laughter turned into tears, as she rocked back and forth on the couch. Abruptly she stopped, rose, and threw her stuffed animal at Billy. "I hate you!" she screamed, then ran to her room, slamming the door behind her. Billy looked down at the bear in his hands, exhaled, and slowly shook his head.

The next day was Sunday. Jessie watched Billy dust and vacuum the living room. Feeling a little guilty, she went into the bathroom to clean up the mess in there. On her way out the door, she ran into him, losing her balance. As she went to fall, Billy held her arm to steady her. She could feel the heat of his body as she leaned against him.

"Sorry," he said, quickly releasing her. "Are you done in there?"

"As done as I'll ever be."

"Good, I'm going to take a shower. Dr. Benson and his wife asked me to come over this afternoon. I most likely won't see him again before I leave. They invited me for dinner, so I'll probably be gone the rest of the day."

"Want some company in there? I wouldn't want you to be lonely," she said, stroking his arm.

"No thanks," he replied, shaking off her hand.

"You sure?"

"I'm sure."

"I guess I'll go and clean up the kitchen and wash the dishes. That way I can use up all the hot water."

"That's okay, I'm used to cold water," he shrugged.

"If you need someone to warm you up, give me a call."

"I'll keep it in mind," he said, firmly shutting and locking the door behind him.

With such a hectic schedule, Billy's time with Jessie passed quickly. Before she realized it, it was time for him to leave.

The night before he left, Jessie crept into the living room and stood by the couch. "Fox?" she whispered.

"Um?" he mumbled. "What is it?"

She slid next to him, her hand roaming over his body. She heard his heart beating, felt it racing as she caressed his bare, muscular chest. She lingered on his flat, hard abdomen before sliding her fingers down and under the waistband of his boxer shorts. His breath caught, becoming ragged, as her hand closed around his erection, rubbing and fondling him.

He groaned deep in his throat and rolled on top of her. "If we do this, we do it my way," he said into her ear. His lips were soft and warm against her eyelids, against her neck, against her mouth. They were nothing like her father's sloppy, drunken kisses. Billy's kisses were fire—his probing tongue, searing and insistent. She forgot to breathe as his hands slowly and gently caressed her breasts and stroked her hair. This wasn't what she expected at all. She sighed and closed her eyes. For the first time in her life, Jessie let go.

BILLY

When Billy felt Jessie beside him, he was alert and awake. Damn it! He was tired of fighting, tired of running from her. The past three weeks had been hell. She had been relentless—always touching him, getting too close, making him ache.

"If we do this, we do it my way," Billy said. Patiently he loved her, kissing and caressing her face and body—doing all the things he had longed to do but had always been denied. This time however, Jessie didn't fight him.

Billy could feel her responding to him—at first tentatively, then with a hunger and passion that matched his own. Scooping Jessie up, Billy carried her to her room—to the room they once shared. The bed was soft compared to the lumpy old couch he had slept on all those lonely nights. He held back for as long as he could, wanting to make the moment last. Her body enthralled him, and he reveled in touching her. When he finally took her, it was almost more than he could bear.

Afterward, Jessie lay quietly, her hair in damp tangles against his chest. She breathed softly, holding him close.

"I'm sorry, Jess."

"Hmm," Jessie mumbled. "About what?"

"Everything. I never meant to hurt you. But I was so angry."

"Guess I made a mess of things for you?"

"You're not kidding," he said, lightly stroking her face. "Of course, it was my own fault for letting you."

"Can you ever make it right?"

"I don't know. I can only do one thing at a time. Right now, I'm just trying to get my future squared away. There's no time to worry about anything else."

"What about us?"

"Us? Hell, I don't know. Tomorrow, I'll be gone, and I won't be back until Christmas, if I'm lucky. It's a long way and a long time."

"But what's gonna happen to me?"

"What do you mean?"

"You said you'd always take care of me."

"Look Jessie, I'll help you as much as I can. But it won't be a lot. Like the rent. Anita's going to have to pay every other month like she used to. I can't afford to keep both of you. She's going to have to kick in. Besides, you're both working. It's not like you don't have any money. Before I was in the picture, you both managed to live, eat, pay rent."

"I know," Jessie sighed with a pout. "But still…"

"Don't worry," he said, his fingers caressing her back, feeling the warmth of her skin. "You'll be fine."

"I guess," she said, then cuddled closer to him. "Maybe if I'd let you kiss me sooner, things would've been different. But I couldn't get my old man out of my mind. He'd hold me down and slobber all over me until I couldn't breathe. Then he'd fuck me. So now, any time a man tries to kiss me, I freak."

Billy held Jessie's face in his hands. He looked into her eyes and read the story of pain and fear that for the first time she allowed him to see. He kissed her gently. "I'm sorry, Jessie, about your dad, about hurting you myself. I never meant for any of that to happen. I promise, I'll never hurt you again." He ran his hand over her breast, feeling the nipple tighten under his fingers. "All I ever wanted was to love you. Like I did just now." He rubbed his nose against hers, then brushed her lips with his own. "Was it really all that bad?"

Jessie sighed. "It was okay, I guess. Different, you know. Kinda nice." Her face turned up towards his expectantly. "Kiss me some more," she demanded.

As he drifted off to sleep, Billy looked at Jessie's face, innocent and vulnerable in sleep and wished things had started out differently.

In the morning, he rushed to finish packing. "Do you have to leave?" Jessie asked, as Billy stowed the last of his gear into the saddle bags.

"You know I do. I should have left hours ago. I wanted to reach El Paso before dark. But that's not going to happen now. I'm not going to be able to stop very often. My ass will be awfully sore when I finally get there."

"And I won't be there to kiss it."

"I know. And tomorrow will be another killer." With his hands in the back pockets of her jeans, he pulled her tightly against his body and kissed her.

"Please Jessie," he pleaded. "Behave yourself. At least try and stay away from the drugs."

"Come on, get off my back. I'm too hooked and you know it."

"Don't say that. It's never too late."

She looked away. "Be careful. Do good at school."

"I'll try."

"When are you coming back?"

"I don't know for sure. I'll try to get back here for Christmas. We'll see what happens then. See if we can save this mess. Don't think one night will change things…or us. It won't." He held her tightly for a moment, then kissed her one last time. "See ya, Jess." He mounted the bike and started the engine. Then fastening his helmet, he waved and roared away.

Basic training was interesting. All the protocol was like a very complex game. For a month, he marched, drilled, saluted, and was tested on what a member of the United States Army should and shouldn't do and how to act in every possible situation. It was amazing.

San Antonio was sweltering. At night on his metal framed cot, he would lay awake sweating, listening to the sounds and snores of the other occupants of the barracks. All this togetherness was not his bag.

There were some guys who had never been away from home before. At lights out, he could hear their muffled crying and couldn't believe his ears. These were grown men! How his people would laugh. Billy had no sympathy for them. Hell, the women of his tribe were tougher than these guys. These men were like infants.

During the day, many men got ill in the heat when they drilled around the base. Billy was lucky. His grandfather had taught him early on how to handle the heat and to conserve his strength. Thanks to *Abuelo*, Billy could go for days at a steady trot and never show a sign of discomfort. His camp mates, however, had a hard time running a mile without having to stop to vomit or pass out. Basic had been enlightening, and he was glad it was over.

Now, he faced a new hurdle. The long trip to DC loomed and the uncertainty of what was to come made him slightly queasy. He left San Antonio in the middle of the night with aspirations of making it to Little Rock by the end of the day. But his plans fell short. He had made it as far as Texarkana, when common sense made him quit for the day. His butt was sore, and he was incredibly tired.

He set out before dawn the next day hoping to make it at least to Tennessee by nightfall. Unfortunately, things again didn't go as he had planned. It was becoming clear to Billy that he stood out far too well in this part of the country.

When he stopped for lunch, he found himself in the middle of hostile territory. Billy entered a dingy eatery and proceeded with caution. The white customers gave him unfriendly sidelong looks, making him uncomfortable.

He edged onto a stool at the counter and scanned the menu in haste. He ordered a sandwich to take with him and tried to make himself invisible while he waited. On his way out, he could feel the weight of dozens of eyes boring into his back and was happy to get back on the bike.

The sun was merciless, and the dust and dirt choked him. Bikes were great for short distances but not for the long haul. Billy's shoulders, back, and butt ached. His cheeks and chin were wind burned. He would have loved to stop for a long period of time, but it was too dangerous.

By rights, he should have stopped in Memphis, but he decided to keep moving for as long as he could. After that, things went from bad to worse. When he stopped at a filling station for gasoline, a couple of locals kept him from using the rest room. They stood in front of the door to the facility, their arms crossed against their chests. Grinning wickedly at Billy, they made their intentions clear.

He hurriedly got back on his bike and kept going. But it wasn't long before his bladder and stomach were urging him to stop. The first place he found was another diner on the outskirts of a forgettable, nameless town. He nervously entered and ordered a burger to carry out. Before he left the diner, he tried to use the men's room. But a bearded giant stopped him.

"Where ya goin' in such a hurry, red man?"

Billy ignored him and kept walking toward the rest room, hoping the big bruiser was all piss and wind.

"I said, where ya goin'? The crapper's for white boys only."

Billy ignored him. But the guy stuck out his foot and sent Billy stumbling. The men at the bar laughed, making rude remarks about drunken Indians.

Billy was stopped from falling when the guy who tripped him, grabbed his braid and hauled him upright. "We like reds here, don't we boys? We like to chew scum like you up and spit ya out." He yanked Billy's head back hard, breathing foul breath into his face. "What d'ya say we scalp this boy fellas? Nice bit of hair here." The giant's mean, little eyes glared into Billy's.

Be passive Billy thought. Don't end up in jail, don't give them anything to fight about, and most of all, don't piss yourself.

"Leave him be," said the woman behind the bar. "Don't you dare break this place up again. Remember what y'all did to me last week," she said, nodding to a hole in the wall.

The giant shoved Billy toward the entrance saying, "Ya runt, ya ain't worth my time. Don't y'all be coming back. This here bar's for white folks only. Next time, ya won't be so lucky. Ya hear?"

Billy exited into the dark parking lot, clutching his bag of food. He tried not to run, but his insides felt like jelly. Please don't follow me out here, he prayed. He got on the bike and hit the throttle.

He went about ten miles before pulling over and relieving himself along the side of the road. He wasn't hungry anymore, but he didn't want to waste the food. The cold, soggy burger stuck in his throat. A strong cup of coffee would have helped wash it down, but Billy was afraid to stop again. He got back on the bike and kept moving.

By the time the gas tank was almost empty, he was approaching Nashville. He couldn't hold out much longer. His eyes were gritty and kept threatening to close.

He spied the orange roof of a Howard Johnson's. It would be expensive but much safer. Plus, there was a service station next door. He went in and registered without any problems, showered, then fell into bed minutes later.

The room was spinning. He had pushed too hard and gone too far. Tomorrow, he'd have to take his time. It would be a little safer, he hoped. He missed Jessie's warm body and was lonely. It was going to be a long time until the holidays. He couldn't wait for this trip to be over.

PART TWO

"Remember the country mouse's encounter
with the town mouse,
and the flurry and agitation
into which it threw him."

~

"Adapt yourself to the environment
in which your lot has been cast,
and show true love to the fellow-mortals
with whom destiny has surrounded you."

Marcus Aurelius

MARIAN

August, 1961

Marian Wilson paced through the house, peering anxiously from windows. On their quiet, tree lined street, cars infrequently came and went, with none showing any interest in their home.

The day dragged as rain pelted down, at times obscuring her view. Jagged streaks of lightning pierced the dismal sky followed by booming thunder. The heat and humidity were oppressive and made Marian even more anxious. She was alone with one of her little girls, waiting for a stranger—a stranger who was going to be living with them for about nine months.

That morning, she had begged Rusty, yet again, to take the day off or to shift his schedule so that he would be at home with her.

"I'm sorry, Marian," he had replied. "You know I'll be in surgery all day. Besides, you've entertained company before without me. I know you'll be the perfect hostess as always. Don't worry, everything will be fine. He may not even arrive until after I get home."

"But Rusty, that's not the point," Marian said. "I know nothing about this young man. All you've said was that he's nice, intelligent, and needs our help."

"There isn't anything more to tell. I want you to form your own opinions. I have no qualms about Billy or the fact that he will be staying with us, neither does Joe. Trust us."

Trust us, Marian thought as she waited and sighed. She entered the formal living room and restlessly repositioned a cut crystal vase full of fresh flowers on the cherry coffee table.

Unlike her older brother Joe, Marian was petite. She was the picture of refined gentility in a sleeveless, linen floral dress, a strand of pearls gracing her neckline. Nylon stockings and black leather pumps completed her ensemble.

The humidity had made Marian's shoulder length, dark brown hair curl up slightly at the ends. She looked at her reflection in a mirror. A pair of striking hazel eyes flecked with gold gazed back. At the moment, the almost feline orbs were full of concern.

Just then, a loud noise from the street startled her. A low rumble of an idling motorcycle sent Marian scurrying to the window. Rain was coming down as the rider glanced at a paper in his hands, looked at the house, then back at his paper. He shook his head and cut the engine. He stared at the house a moment longer, then dismounted. Rubbing his lower back, he walked to the front door.

No, it couldn't be, Marian panicked. This person had to be lost. This isn't someone Rusty would allow in their home.

When the doorbell rang, Jennifer ran into the room. "Is he here?"

"I don't think so, dear. But I'd better go and see. No, no, you stay here."

Marian's breath caught as she peered out the sidelight. On the doorstep stood an extremely wet young man. He was of medium height with high cheekbones and swarthy skin. Removing his helmet, he shook out a very long, braid of hair. His old, worn, denim jacket and torn dungarees were drenched. Water trickled down his slender nose, running over full lips to his chin. From pierced ears, silver crosses dangled. In comparison, his wire-framed glasses were mundane.

Oh my God, Rusty, what have you done, Marian thought. She felt rooted to the spot and couldn't bring herself to answer the door.

"Well, is he here?" Jennifer asked, tugging at her sleeve.

Marian blinked and looked down at Jennifer. "What? Oh, I'm not sure." She glanced back out the sidelight. The man had turned and was walking away from the house. Taking a deep breath, she opened the door slightly. "Yes?" she questioned.

The young man stopped and returned to the doorstep. "Hi, can you help me? I'm trying to locate Q Street; however, there seems to be two parts of it. I'm looking for the Wilson home. Is this it?" he asked in a soft baritone, as he swiped the back of his hand under his dripping nose.

"Are you Billy Fox?"

"Yes, ma'am, you must be Marian Wilson?"

"Yes, please come in."

Billy glanced into the house and through a second set of french doors that opened into a massive entrance hall and hesitated. A beautiful light blue and cream Oriental rug adorned the polished hardwood floor. "I'm pretty wet," he said.

Marian saw the direction of his look. "Don't worry. You can stand on that carpet. That's what it's there for."

"Okay," he said still hesitating. Then kicking off his boots, he entered the house in his bare feet, leaving his boots just inside the front doors.

Marian noticed his footwear. There were holes in both soles; the heels worn smooth.

"Is he here, Mommy?" Jennifer asked again, peeking into the entrance way.

"Yes, sweetheart. Billy, this is our youngest daughter, Jennifer. She just turned seven."

"Hi, Jennifer, your daddy told me a lot about you," Billy said, solemnly shaking her hand.

"Are you going to be a doctor?" Jennifer asked.

"I hope so."

"Me too! That's what *I* want to be when *I* grow up." She handed him a doll with its leg out of the socket. "Can you fix this? This leg came off, and I can't push it back in. Daddy usually operates on her, but he's not here right now."

"Jenny, Billy is wet. Don't bother him with that. Daddy can fix it later." To Billy, she said, "Let me go and get you a towel. I'll be right back," and hurrying off, disappeared down the hall.

Billy stood frozen; the doll still held awkwardly in his hands. He looked at the leg, then back at the little girl. He had never held a doll before—any toy for that matter. He was even less familiar with seven-year-old girls.

"Uh, let's see." Billy exhaled and studied the leg and socket for a few seconds. After several unsuccessful attempts, he finally heard a loud snap confirming that the leg was back in the socket, at least for the time being. He handed the doll back to Jennifer.

"Oh, thank you. You fixed her. Come on, I'll show you to your room."

Before Billy had a chance to reply, Jennifer had taken his hand and pulled him further into the house and up a large flight of stairs. At the first landing, the stairs split then proceeded up to the second floor from either side.

"Here's where Barbara and I usually race to see who beats. Your room is at the top of the stairs across the hall from Mommy and Daddy," she said.

She skipped down the hall. "This is their bedroom. It's huge! They even have their very own bathroom. Next to that, is Daddy's office," she whispered. "We're not allowed in there. And this is Barbara's room. There's a bathroom in the middle that we share, and my bedroom is on the other side. It's just like Barbara's. See? Come on in."

Jennifer ran and jumped onto the double bed that was complete with canopy and filmy curtains cascading from the top. "I'm like a fairy princess in a castle. Everything is pink and green," she announced, bouncing up and down on the mattress. "Like it? Over there are all my books," she waved as she bounced. "Want to read one?"

Billy was dumbstruck. He felt caught up in a whirlwind and couldn't quite comprehend what was happening. Jennifer talked so fast and flitted from one subject to another that Billy had a hard time keeping up.

Taking a final bounce, Jennifer rejoined Billy and continued her tour. "Next to me is the room that used to be the nanny's when mommy was little. Mommy uses it now for extra company and she also has closets for her sewing stuff. Next to that is the old nursery. It's been redone. My Grandma Jean stays there when she comes to visit. She's Daddy's mommy. Here's another bathroom that connects to both her bedroom and yours. Barbara and I like to play in there when we are playing hide and seek. And now, here we are. Ta da!" Jennifer spread her arms wide. "This one's yours," she crowed, and pulled him into the room at the head of the stairs. "Do you like it?"

The room was spacious and bright. Two large, lace covered windows faced the street on either side of a chest of drawers. Opposite those windows, against the inner wall stood a very tall queen-sized sleigh bed, and a nightstand. On the other side of the bed was the door that led to the bathroom. A working fireplace flanked by a closet on one side and another window on the other graced the outer wall. On the opposing inner wall was a desk with shelves mounted above it and a small dresser and mirror.

"Well?" Jennifer asked, nudging Billy in the side.

"Uh…it's very nice," he said, swallowing hard.

"Where are all your clothes and stuff?"

"They're still outside."

"Jennifer!" Marian called a little frantically. "Where are you?"

"Up here, Mommy. I'm showing Billy his room," Jennifer called.

Marian hurried into the room a little breathlessly. "Jennifer, you should have waited downstairs. I was worried when I came back, and you weren't there."

"I was giving Billy a tour of the upstairs," Jennifer replied. "Why would you be worried?"

"Uh…I didn't know where you were," she said, lamely. She handed Billy a towel. "Here, you can use this. I hope the room will be all right," she said.

Billy appeared to be in a daze. He absently took the towel. "Holy shit," he muttered.

"Excuse me!" Marian gasped.

"Oh fuck! I said shit!"

Marian gasped again, her face a bright red.

"Oh shit! I said fuck!" Billy spit out, looking like he wanted to fall through the floor. "Jesus! I'm…sorry," he said flustered. "The room is…uh…great. But I can't stay in here."

"What do you mean? Is there something wrong?" Marian asked, and walked over to the bed and straightened the spread. "What could possibly be wrong?"

"Wrong? No, no! It's just, I mean, this is…too nice. God! Rusty never said he lived in a friggin' mansion. Look, don't you have servants' quarters or maybe a room in the attic or over the garage or even a tent out back?"

"I'm sorry, Billy. We don't use the third-floor servant's quarters anymore except for storage. It was too expensive to heat. This is all we have."

Billy looked around the room again and shook his head. Marian studied the young man and was at a loss. He was out of his element—so was she. Marian mentally cursed her husband for putting them all into such a predicament.

Marian took a deep breath and tried to calm the panic rising within her chest. Fortunately, her motherly instincts kicked in. "You really should get out of those wet clothes. Why don't you get the rest of your things, then you can take a hot shower and get cleaned up for dinner? Rusty should be home in about an hour after he picks up our older daughter from a friend's house."

"Okay." Retracing his steps, Billy headed outside. He was stunned. He had never expected this. Once outside, he lit a cigarette, smoking it in the rain, then immediately lit another. While smoking a third, he went down to the bike, returning with two small saddlebags and his backpack.

"Is this everything?" Marian asked in amazement, when he dropped the bags on the towel he had placed on the floor of the bedroom. "Where are all of your clothes?"

"This is it except for a couple of uniforms and a jacket that'll be sent to me later. Should I have more?" he asked a little defensively, eyeing the dresser, the chest of drawers and closet.

Marian didn't know what to say. "Well, I guess not." She looked again at the clothes Billy was wearing, taking in their poor condition and glanced, as well, at the dresser, chest and closet. She held her tongue, not wanting to hurt his feelings. But she made a mental note to consult Rusty about how to deal with the matter.

"Has Jenny pointed out your bathroom? You can get to it from the hall or here in your room. It's also connected to the bedroom next to you from the other side," she said as she walked toward the bathroom. "When you are in there, just remember to close and lock the door from all sides or you may get unwanted company. Especially if Grandma Jean is visiting, since her room is on the other side. There's also a bathroom between the girls' bedrooms and another full bath on the first floor under the staircase."

Marian went into the bathroom and opened one of two huge closets. She pulled out several large, plush bath towels and a washcloth. "Here," she said, laying everything on the counter. "You can use these. There is shampoo and soap in the shower. Please make yourself at home. If you don't see something you need, just ask."

Billy gaped. The room was almost the size of an ASU dormitory bathroom. On one wall, a marble vanity with double lavatory basins faced a mirrored wall, as well as a toilet and closet. On the opposite wall was another closet and an extra-large, walk-in shower. All the faucets and handles were of polished brass that gleamed with a rich luster.

"If you leave your wet clothes outside the door on the floor in the hall, I'll put them into the dryer for you."

"Please don't fuss," Billy murmured. "They'll dry eventually."

"Leave the clothes in the hall. I'm not fussing."

When he emerged in dryer versions of his original jeans and t-shirt, Jenny was in the hall waiting for him.

"Daddy will be home soon. Till then, do you want to see the rest of the house? After that, you could read me a story." She showed him a well-thumbed copy of *The Pokey Little Puppy*. "This is my favorite book in the whole world."

Billy stared down at the little elf of a girl and didn't know what to think. She was unlike anything he had ever come across. He looked at the book and gulped.

"Come on," she said, taking his hand. They descended the stairs and peeked into the room on the right. This room was filled with elegant, antique furniture, and a marble fireplace. "This room is for special company. Barbara and I aren't really allowed in here. Too many things to break," Jennifer smiled impishly.

They crossed the entrance hall and entered an immense, formal dining room. There was a banquet sized dining table that could seat at least a dozen and a half comfortably, if not more.

"This is where we eat when we have lots of company." Jennifer moved so quickly, that Billy's impression was only one of fancy cut glass, china, glossy wood, and another fireplace. "And here's the kitchen," she said, passing through a door into a butler's pantry that opened into a huge farmhouse kitchen, complete with a trestle table and another fireplace. Copper pots and pans hung from the ceiling. To the side of the kitchen, in an alcove, was a modern utility room with a washer, dryer, and a powder room. A back door led to a patio and detached garage.

"Hi Mommy, I'm giving Billy a tour of the rest of the house."

Marian looked at them and smiled faintly. "I see you got the dry clothes I brought up."

"Yes, thank you," Billy replied.

"Is there anything else you need?"

"No, thanks. The dry clothes are great."

"Dinner will be ready in about an hour. If you're hungry, I could get you a snack."

"No, thank you. I'm fine."

"What about me?" Jennifer asked. "I'm hungry."

"You can wait like the rest of us, Jennifer."

"But it smells so good."

"Then it will be worth the wait. Now run along and finish showing Billy around."

"Okay. Come on," she said, and once again taking Billy by the hand, pulled him from the kitchen. Crossing the hall, they passed the other full-sized bathroom then walked into a large, light-filled room.

"Here's all the books," Jennifer said, throwing her arms wide.

Billy was aghast. The room held a baby grand piano, leather furniture, a mahogany sideboard that held several decanters and crystal glasses, a television set, and thousands of books. He itched to peruse the shelves, but Jennifer took him through large, open French doors instead. "In here is the sunroom. It has all these plants, and you can get to the back yard and the patio from here, too."

She pointed, "That's the garage and the back yard. See our swing set and tree house? Maybe after dinner if it stops raining, we can go out and play. Or maybe Barbara will play the piano for you. She takes lessons, you know."

From the library, they peered through another set of French doors that led to the side of the house. "This is the pool room. Not the kind you swim in, but the one with sticks. We aren't allowed in here, either. Daddy usually comes in here with his friends. There's also a huge bar and chairs and even a little baby refrigerator. Then, from the library that doorway leads back to the living room. And that's it, we're back to the beginning again. It's like a big square, kind of. Barbara and I like it 'cause we can run the whole way around the house without stopping. But don't tell Mommy," she said conspiratorially. "She doesn't know we do that."

Jennifer pulled Billy over to the overstuffed leather couch and flopped down, her book hugged to her chest. "Now we can read."

Billy gingerly sat on the edge of the seat. Easing back, he was enfolded in soft, buttery leather. He thought back to the decrepit couch he had slept on in Jessie's apartment. There were two broken springs in the middle that jabbed him every time he sat down.

Jenny snuggled against him and handed over the book. Billy let out an inward sigh and began to read.

Once in a while, Marian would nervously glance in, then return to the kitchen. She heard Rusty's old Volvo sedan before he rounded the drive to the garage. When he and Barbara entered the back door, Marian was lying in wait.

"Hello sweetheart," Rusty said, hugging his wife. "I see the bike. Has Billy been here long?"

"About two hours," she said aloud. Into his ear, however, she whispered, "You and I need to have a little talk, dear."

Rusty smiled and kissed her cheek. "Of course, dear. We'll talk later. But now, I'd better go and greet our guest."

By the time Rusty entered the library, Billy was on his fifth story and craving a smoke.

"Daddy!" Jennifer yelled, running to him.

Rusty picked her up and gave her a big hug. "Hi ya, Tiger." Putting her down, he greeted Billy while Barbara hid behind her father. "Barbara, come out and meet Billy. He doesn't bite." Barbara shyly glanced around her father, said, "hi" and retreated behind his back again.

"Billy fixed my doll, Daddy," said Jennifer. "He's going to be a good doctor. He put her leg back on just like you always do. He has been reading me all my favorite books." Smiling a big gap-toothed grin, with her red hair and freckles, she was a miniature version of her father.

"Well Billy, I see you did your first successful re-attachment. Jenny, you and Barbara run along and let Billy and I talk." He went to the sideboard and picked up a decanter. "How about a drink? I'm going to have a bourbon and water. What would you like?"

Billy thought longingly of a glass of whiskey before replying, "Nothing, thanks."

"You sure? This is really good bourbon."

Of course, it's good, Billy thought. Bet he never drank the cheap shit I used to quaff down by the fifth. "No, thanks," he said slowly. "I uh…don't drink."

"We have soda and water, too, if you prefer it. You must be thirsty after reading all those stories," he grinned.

"Okay, thanks. A glass of water does sound pretty good right now."

Rusty went into the pool room and poured Billy a glass of water from the mini fridge. "So how was the trip?" Rusty asked, handing Billy the glass and sitting down opposite him.

"Long. My ass is killing me."

Rusty laughed. "Saddle sore, eh? I don't think I could have done it."

"You would have if you had to."

"I hope Jenny hasn't been driving you crazy. She can be a real pest."

"She loves to be read to."

"The understatement of the year," Rusty said dryly, looking at the pile of books at Billy's feet. "She knows a sucker when she sees one and takes full advantage."

A few minutes later, Marian called them to dinner. The polished mahogany table was now set at one end with fine china and crystal which sparkled in the glow from the twin chandeliers. On the table sat a platter of roast beef with mashed potatoes, vegetables and gravy.

Rusty glanced at Billy who looked as if someone had just kicked him in the privates.

"Something wrong, Billy?" he asked.

"Yeah, Rusty," Billy muttered. "Why didn't you warn me? You never said you lived in a damn museum."

"Museum? Nonsense, it's just a house."

"Bullshit, I've been in houses before. None of them were like this. Hell, I'm afraid to touch anything. Just look at this room. All done up like Buckingham Palace. I've never in my life sat down to a table fixed up like this. You know the kind of places I'm used to."

"If I'd have told you what the house was like, would you have come?"

"Hell no, right then and there, I would have become a gas station attendant or something and thrown in the towel."

"Then I'm glad I didn't tell you. Eventually, you'll get used to us. And we'll get used to you."

"I don't know," Billy said, frowning.

"Don't worry. We usually eat in the kitchen without all this fuss. But tonight, you're a guest. Now come on, I'm hungry. Let's eat."

When plates had been filled, the Wilson family began eating. Billy, however, bowed his head and sat there.

"What are you doing?" asked Jenny.

"I'm thanking the Creator for this food."

"We never say grace, do we Mommy? Why don't we?"

Marian blushed, "I don't know, honey. We just never did. But we probably should."

"Maybe Billy would say it?" Jenny asked.

Marian said, "Please Billy, that would be nice."

Billy flushed, then cleared his throat nervously. "*Gracias a Dios.* Thank you, God, for this food, the woman who prepared it, and the family who has taken me into their home to share it with them, amen."

"Thank you, Billy," said Marian. "From now on, we'll say grace at dinner. I suppose we've been acting like a bunch of heathens."

At her choice of words, there was silence at the table. Billy stared at his plate, Marian reddened, shifting in her seat, and Rusty looked askance at his wife. The girls glanced at each of the adults, not understanding the silence.

"Speak for yourself," Rusty finally commented with a snort. "Now can we all eat?"

Just then, Barbara piped up, "Are you really a wild Indian?"

"Barbara!" Marian snapped.

Billy looked up from his plate. "I don't know about the wild part, but yes, I am an American Indian."

"Do you live in a tipi and ride horses in your underwear and scalp people like the Indians on TV?" asked Jennifer.

"Jennifer!" Marian scolded, her face scarlet with embarrassment. "Of course, Billy isn't like that. He's civilized just like we are. Oh Billy, I…I'm so sorry."

"It's okay, Marian. They're just curious. I don't suppose they see too many of my kind around here. Actually Jenny, I live with my grandparents on a reservation in New Mexico. I do ride horses but uh…I usually wear jeans," he said, trying hard not to smile. "And no, I've never scalped anyone, nor do I plan on doing that in the future. However, I have built and stayed in a tipi when we have gone hunting. And we also have a wikiup, which is kind of like a tipi but longer, near our horses where we camp out sometimes. *Abuelo* wanted me to learn the old ways and traditions of our people."

"What's Aaab…welo?" asked Jennifer, wrinkling her nose.

"*Abuelo* is the Spanish word for grandfather."

"But you said you're an Indian, not Spanish."

Billy smiled tolerantly. "I am. But besides English and the language of my people, I also speak Spanish."

"How come?"

"Many, many years ago, first Spaniards then Mexicans came onto my people's land. Initially, we learned their language in order to trade with them," Billy said, as he cut into a piece of beef and began to eat.

"Well," Marian prompted, when he appeared to have finished his narrative. "What happened after that," she asked, her chin resting on her fist.

Billy looked up at her in surprise. "Uh, all hell broke loose after that. First the armies came—the missionaries followed. My people were forced to learn the language and to practice the religion of the white man instead of our own."

"Why?" Jennifer asked.

"Um…well, because they said we were uh…heathens."

Marian reddened again, remaining silent.

"That wasn't very nice," Jennifer pouted.

"No, it wasn't. But eventually, the armies left to go conquer someone else."

"But you still speak Spanish," Marian commented.

"Yes, unfortunately, the missionaries returned and stayed. That's why I can speak Spanish and am a Christian."

"That still wasn't nice," Barbara commented.

"I guess. But we at least got one good thing out of the whole mess. The Spaniards brought horses with them."

"Oh, I love horses," Barbara said. "Do you have a horse?"

"Yes, I do. In fact, we have several. My grandfather raises horses to sell. Although my motorcycle is the closest thing to a horse that I ride these days."

"Will you take us for a ride?" Jennifer questioned.

"Well, motorcycles are kind of dangerous and you're both pretty little. Maybe someday, but not right now. And only if your mom and dad say it's all right."

"Okay everybody," Rusty interrupted with a quick look at his wife, "that's enough questions for now. Let Billy eat. He's probably starving, and his food is getting cold. We'll have lots of time to get to know our guest. He isn't going anywhere. Are you?"

Billy thought of all that had transpired so far that afternoon. He swallowed hard. "At least not today," he smiled rather weakly.

BILLY

I t was difficult for Billy to get used to his new family and their different way of life. Rusty was great, but he wasn't home very much. He worked out of Georgetown University Hospital and had an office in an adjacent building. One night a week, Rusty taught a class at the University and neither his family nor Billy saw him for long periods of time.

The girls had started back to school after Labor Day. Since Billy's classes didn't begin until the middle of September, he found himself at loose ends. During the day, he felt drawn to the library. There were more books in that one room than there had been at the mission school.

One day, as he stood before the shelves, Marian came up behind him. "You know, Billy, you can borrow any book you want from those shelves. Help yourself."

"Thanks. There are so many I wouldn't know where to start."

"My father tried to keep some order to all of them. Most of the books on the top shelves are either very old or are history books of the area. Father was greatly interested in the pre-colonial and colonial periods of Georgetown and the surrounding parts of Virginia and Maryland."

"Then this house belonged to your family," Billy stated.

"Yes, this house has been in the Benson family since it was built over 200 years ago. My grandfather was the one to bring us out of the dark ages though, by updating the plumbing and electrical work. But he was very particular when it came to changing the original structure."

"It's quite a home."

"Yes, it is. I guess it can be overwhelming," Marian smiled.

Billy grinned. "A little."

Marian walked around the room, touching and straightening things as she did. "This has always been my favorite room. When I was growing up, the whole family used to congregate here most evenings. We were all avid readers, and the girls are following in our footsteps. If you thought Jenny liked to read, Barbara is ten times the reader. And it looks as though we've added another reader to the family," she said, looking at Billy. "Are your grandparents readers?"

Billy turned back to the bookshelf. "Neither of my grandparents can read," he said. "Besides, books cost money. At the mission school, my favorite padre was the librarian. He would lend me books, not just from the library but his own reading material as well. Every day, I would bring books and magazines home, and at night, after our work was done, I'd read aloud to my grandparents. I think that by the time I graduated, I had read almost every book in the library."

"That's wonderful."

"For me, it was everything."

"Everything?"

"Sure, not only did I learn things, but it was also my way out—my…escape."

Marian looked at him sharply, but he had his back to her, his eyes focused on the books.

"Well, don't be afraid to borrow any book that you care to read."

"Thanks."

After a moment, Marian cleared her throat. "Uh, there's something else that I think you and I need to discuss."

"Yes?" he said, turning to her, concern filling his eyes.

"It's about your clothing."

Billy looked down at his t-shirt and jeans. "My clothing?"

"You really need to get some dress clothes."

"Why?"

"You can't go to school like that. If I'm not mistaken, the medical school at Georgetown has a dress code. At least it did when Rusty was a student."

"What do you mean?"

"In medical school you are expected to *look* professional," Marian pointed out. "Dungarees and t-shirts are fine for when you're at home but not for going to classes. If you want me to, I'll take you to the men's shop where Rusty buys his clothes. The salespeople are very nice there and will be able to help you. Just let me know when you want to go," she finished in a rush, then quickly exited the room.

Billy thought back to the other day when he had gone with Marian and the girls to run some errands. They had stopped at a men's wear shop in Leesburg to pick something up for Rusty, and Billy had been shocked at the prices. While Marian had conducted her business, Billy had wandered around the store. A clerk had tailed him as he looked at different displays.

"May I help you?" the gentleman finally asked haughtily.

"No thanks. I'm just looking."

"There's really nothing for your kind of people here. I suggest you *look* somewhere else," the clerk said, taking Billy by the elbow and escorting him to the door.

"What's going on?" Marian asked, as she and the girls came up behind the clerk.

"Nothing to worry about ma'am," the clerk replied. "This young man was just leaving. He won't be bothering you."

"Why would he?" Marian asked, taking Billy firmly by the other arm. "He's with us. And by the way," she said, putting down the socks that she had in her hand. "You just lost a sale and a future customer." With that she propelled Billy and the girls from the store.

The incident had haunted him. It seemed that everywhere he went, he was stared at with suspicion. He hated to leave the house, but at the same time, he knew that Marian wasn't quite comfortable with him being in the house alone, either. Did people think he was some kind of thief?

He walked out the French doors to the patio and lit a cigarette. At this point, he couldn't wait for his classes to begin so that he could get out during the day.

Now, Marian was on his back about his clothes. Didn't she understand that he had no money? Hell, that was the main reason he was here. In Leesburg, he couldn't even afford a handkerchief let alone pants and shirts. Why would the prices be different at another store? He'd seen the kind of clothing Rusty wore. Even to Billy's uneducated eye, they were expensive.

He ground out his cigarette and lit another. All this superficial shit was starting to eat at him, and he didn't know how to handle the stress. He felt like a time bomb waiting to go off.

The explosion occurred a few days before his classes were to start. After picking up some groceries, Marian and Billy were headed back to the car when they passed a barbershop.

"Oh Billy," Marian announced, "this is where Rusty gets his hair cut. Why don't we stop in, and you can make an appointment?"

"For what?"

"Why to get all that hair cut off. Maybe they can take you right now. Let's go and see."

"Hold on," Billy said, puzzled. "What are you talking about? I'm not getting a haircut."

"You aren't?"

"Hell no," he said, his voice rising. "Why should I get it cut? It was fine for ASU."

"I know it was all right for ASU," Marian placated, her hand on his arm. "But Billy, this is *Georgetown*. Things are different here. You are going to have to conform to some extent."

In frustration, Billy finally lost his temper. He shook her hand from his arm and began to expostulate loudly. "What the hell does the length of my hair have to do with anything? It's my culture, goddamn it! Those white bastards can't take that away from me. If someone doesn't like the length of my hair, they can go to fucking hell!"

Marian flinched at his words and hastily backed away from him. Her face showed a mixture of emotions—hurt, embarrassment, and fear. Passersby made a large arc around the two and hurried on their way. Billy spit on the sidewalk in front of the barbershop, then turning from Marian, walked alone to the car.

The ride home was uncomfortably silent. Marian drove with both hands clenched tightly to the wheel, her face pinched and white. Billy stared straight ahead, his countenance rigid with anger. This wealthy Anglo woman was getting to him. First, she nagged at him to get fancy new clothing he couldn't afford. That, he could take, to a certain extent. But now, she had gone too far. She had personally attacked him. Didn't Marian realize that his hair was the only thing of his culture he still possessed. To cut his hair was to strip himself of his identity. Without his hair, he was lost. Who was he? *What* was he?

After that, Billy stuck to his room and steered clear of Marian. Although worried, Rusty refused to interfere and instructed the girls to do the same.

Billy got his schedule and found that much of his first semester would be devoted to the study of anatomy. He'd have lectures and labs every day and a conference every other Saturday. There wouldn't be much time for anything else.

On the first day of class, Billy wore a clean pair of jeans and his one and only dress shirt. Marian frowned when she saw him but made no comment. Fuck it, Billy thought until he walked into the lecture hall and found he was the only student not wearing dress pants, shirt, and tie.

Several young men laughed when they saw him while others seemed embarrassed for him.

At the end of the class, his professor stopped him. "What's your name?"

"It's William Fox, sir."

The prof studied his roster. "Oh yes, you're in the army. Didn't you know we have a strict dress code here? You are required to wear a shirt, tie, and dress slacks for class every day. Don't worry, we provide lab jackets for our students to wear over their clothing for protection when in the laboratory," he said sarcastically. "I hope tomorrow you will be better attired. Also, I'm surprised that the Army hasn't made you cut your hair."

"Sir, I am an American Indian. No one told me I had to have it cut."

"You're in a white school in a white world. You want to play with us, then act like us."

Billy clenched his hands into fists and ground his teeth. Fucking bigot, he thought to himself. He was still fuming when he returned to the Wilson home later that afternoon. He had been read the riot act by not one but all of his professors. His classmates had laughed and ridiculed him. He should have listened to Marian instead of being such a hard head. Now, he was going to have to go and get some clothes before tomorrow.

"What's the matter?" Marian questioned as he stomped in the back door.

"Fucking bastards didn't like the way I was dressed. I made a jackass of myself and was the laughingstock of the medical school. I should've listened and got some dress clothes. I don't suppose there's a Goodwill or a St. Vincent DePaul store in this highfalutin town, is there?"

Marian closed her eyes and bit her lip. Oh God, she thought, I wish I knew how to handle this strange, young man. "We don't have either one of those stores here; however, the women's auxiliary at the hospital has a resale shop on M Street. You could probably get some things there. Most of the men's clothes were donated by doctors at the hospital and are very nice. The prices are reasonable, too. Do you want me to take you there?"

Billy stood with his arms folded across his chest and stared at the floor. "I don't have much choice," he mumbled, his face flushed with embarrassment. "I should have done this before I got here, but I never realized that medical school would be so different. On top of that, there is only so much room on the bike. I feel so stupid."

"No, you're not stupid. They should have told you when you were being interviewed."

"They might have. But I could have missed a few details. It was a lot of information at one time, and I was here by myself."

"Would you rather wait for Rusty and go with him?"

Billy shrugged. "It doesn't matter. Besides, he'll be tired when he comes home. The last thing he needs to do is to take me shopping. Let's just get it over with."

For Billy, the trip proved to be a humiliating and nerve-wracking experience. The girls ran around the store and played hide and seek in the clothes racks, while he tried to find some decent dress clothes in his size. Marian led him around like a little kid, selecting things then sending him off to a dressing room.

Billy had never given much thought to his clothes in the past. A few pairs of jeans, some t-shirts, a sweatshirt and a flannel shirt or two were good enough for him. Now, he had to rethink everything from his underwear and socks to neckties and shoes.

He and Marian got into a heated discussion before heading to the checkout when Marian tried to give him some money. Billy shook his head angrily. "I don't want your money. It's bad enough I'm living on your charity. I'm already in your debt. I'll never be able to repay you."

"Listen to me," Marian retorted, her hands on her hips. "We don't expect any payment. Besides, you're already doing chores I never asked you to do. You live here now. You are a member of the family. Consider it an allowance for doing chores around the house. The kids get one, why not you?"

When they arrived home, Billy retreated tired and frustrated to his room, tossing his purchases on the bed. The clothes reeked of mothballs, and he envisioned more taunting in the morning on top of a huge dry-cleaning bill.

He lit a cigarette and went to the open window. His head was pounding, and he felt like vomiting. This new life was sweeping him along, out of control. There was no way to stop or slow down its frantic pace or the constant changes that had assaulted him since his arrival.

Billy looked at his reflection in the window glass, smoothing back some wispy strands of hair. He pulled the braid over his shoulder, studying it a long time. He shook his head—his mouth grim.

It was a painful decision but, once made, had to be acted upon immediately. He went into the sewing room then found Marian in the kitchen preparing the evening meal. "Marian?"

"Yes?" she asked, then reared back in fright when she saw the sharp pair of sewing shears, glinting in his hands like a knife.

In his preoccupation, he didn't notice her look of alarm. "Please, will you do this for me. I have a rubber band where I want you to cut. I hope a foot is enough for them. I still want *some* hair. I haven't had a haircut in over ten years."

Marian slowly breathed a sigh of relief. "Wouldn't you rather go to a barber?"

"No!" he said, handing her the scissors. "Just do it quickly, before I chicken out."

"Let's go outside," she said and pushed open the back door to the patio. Once outside, Marian stood behind Billy. "I'm going to slide the rubber band down a little in case I need to straighten things out. That way, I won't have to cut off any more than you want," she suggested.

He tensed as she took his hair in her hands. For a second, he panicked and almost stopped her. Then with one quick cut, it was too late to change his mind.

Shaking out the remaining hair, Marian evened the ends. It was beautiful and glinted with copper highlights in the sun. As she re-braided his hair, it slipped through her fingers like silk.

"It's still long," she said, handing him the piece she had cut off. "But it looks much better now. I can't see them complaining about this, especially if you keep it braided or tied back, which you do anyway."

Billy held the braid in his hands and bent his neck from side to side. "Wow! My head feels…funny. You know, lighter. I guess I should have done this sooner. It really was too long. It's a wonder I didn't choke on it in my sleep." He paused for a moment, then said quietly, "Thank you, Marian for everything. The clothes, this," he said, holding out the braid.

"You're welcome."

"Marian, uh…about the other day, I'm really sorry. I shouldn't have yelled at you."

"I'm sorry, too. I didn't understand how you felt. I was a bit patronizing."

"That's okay, you were only telling it like it is. I just overreacted. I'm sorry."

"Peace?" Marian smiled, putting out her hand.

"Peace," Billy grinned, taking the hand. "Oh, Marian. There's just one more thing."

"What's that?"

He pulled a necktie out of his pocket. "How the heck do you tie one of these things?" he asked.

Marian laughed lightly, her nervousness and fear of him completely evaporating. "Rusty can show you when he gets home."

The next morning, Billy came down to breakfast dressed in his new clothing. "I feel trapped," he complained, tugging at his collar.

Rusty glanced up from his breakfast. "You'll get used to it." He scrutinized Billy. "I see you managed the tie. It doesn't look bad."

"It shouldn't, it's still the knot you tied last night. I just loosened it a little to take it off."

"Cheater!"

"There was no way I was going to fight with it this morning. It's bad enough I had to stuff my feet into these stupid shoes. Now I know why you white people are always in a bad mood. You have sore feet."

"Bad mood, huh? Look here Cochise, I'll have you know, I'm always in a good mood."

"Sure, you wear sneakers at work. What do you care?"

"So, I do," Rusty laughed. Draining his coffee cup, he stood. "Want a ride to school?"

"No thanks, I'll walk," Billy said, then considering his feet, looked at Rusty. "On second thought, I think I'll take you up on that ride."

The professors who had scolded him the day before, now nodded with approval. It was amazing what a difference clothing made. Some of his classmates still snickered and made war whoop sounds behind his back. But several students seemed friendly and exchanged hellos.

One afternoon, several weeks into classes, Billy was sitting on the steps outside of the Medical School building. He was smoking a cigarette and reading. The top buttons of his shirt were undone, and his tie was jammed into his shirt pocket. A couple of his classmates walked by.

"Look. It's Geronimo," said a short, stocky guy with a buttoned-down collar and a white bread last name. "Why don't you go back to the reservation, redskin? You don't belong here."

Billy ignored him and continued to smoke.

"I think he's deaf, too. Or maybe he doesn't understand English. How about this? Getum your assum back to the…"

"Get off his back!" No one had seen the tall, young man come from inside the building.

"Hey, Simple Simmonds is standing up for Geronimo."

"God, you're such a jackass, Dwight. Why don't you grow up? The only reason you're here is because your Daddy's a rich podiatrist. Leave the guy alone."

"And what if I don't?"

The man named Simmonds towered over Dwight. Swinging his heavily laden backpack, he said, "Well, I could make you a little shorter. If that's possible?"

Dwight looked a bit uncomfortable. He glanced at his cronies who were watching the interplay carefully. "Why would I want to dirty my hands on poor scum like you? It's amazing the riff raff they are allowing into this school these days. Money must really be tight for those poor 'mick' priests. Come on," he said to his friends. "These two aren't worth our time."

Simmonds watched them walk away, a look of disgust on his face. "Assholes," he muttered under his breath.

Billy checked his watch, stood up, and began walking in the other direction. Simmonds caught up with him. He was gangly with wavy dark hair and glasses.

"Hey! Why do you let them pick on you every day like that?" he asked. As he spoke, his rather large Adams apple bobbed up and down.

"I have better things to do than get involved with a bunch of pansy-assed rich boys who think their shit doesn't stink. If I'd say anything, it would start a fight. And I sure as hell know it would be me not pansy ass that would get into trouble. I could be suspended or expelled. Hell, I'm having enough trouble just dressing to suit these rich snobs."

"I hear you. By the way, I'm John Simmonds," he stuck out his hand.

"Billy Fox."

"You're in the Army, aren't you?"

"Uh huh."

"So am I. Do you live here in Georgetown?"

"On Q Street."

"In one of the townhouses?"

"No on the other end."

John whistled. "Up with all the muckety mucks?"

Billy shrugged. "I guess. I'm staying with a family until I can find a place I can afford."

"Here?" John laughed. "Good luck, buddy."

"Is it that hard to find?"

"In Georgetown, if you weren't born with it, you aren't ever gonna have it. Where you are living, those digs are really something. People up there are from old bread."

"What about you? Where do you live?"

"Me? I live across the river in Rosslyn, Virginia with my poor, debt-ridden, middle-class parents. I made it through Georgetown for my pre-med by the grace of God and loans coming out my wazoo. That's how I know the illustrious Dwight Carrington-Brown that you so fortunately had the pleasure of meeting a few days ago."

"Oh, I see."

They reached a bus stop shelter and John stopped. "So where are you from, really?"

"New Mexico, though I did my pre-med at ASU."

"Cool beans. Well, here's where I catch my bus. Unfortunately, the limo is in the shop today."

Billy grinned. "Lucky you, at least you get to ride. I have to hoof it up the hill."

"How very bourgeois," John laughed. "I didn't know those people up there knew how to do that. I'll see you tomorrow."

"See ya. And John, thanks for earlier."

"It was no big deal."

Billy continued to the neighborhood bus stop to meet Jennifer and Barbara. Initially, it had just been for their first day of school, then it became a regular occurrence on the afternoons he was finished early, and Marian was volunteering.

He didn't mind. It gave him a chance to get in a good nicotine fix before he went home, since Marian had recently requested that he not smoke in the house.

"You really should quit. It's such a dirty habit. I hate to say this, but you're smelling up the house. I also don't think it's setting a very good example for the girls."

"I know it's a bad habit, but I've been smoking since I was a kid. I'm too hooked to stop now. I promise though, I won't smoke in the house or in front of the girls, okay?"

"That will have to do. Thank you."

She also chastised him for the language that came out of his mouth. "Billy, you have to remember that two, young, impressionable girls live in this home. You can't talk like that in front of them and frankly, I don't like it either. You speak like you came from the gutter."

"But that's where I came from," he argued.

"I don't believe that for one minute. Do you speak crudely in front of your grandmother?"

"No," he answered sheepishly.

"I didn't think so. But even if you did, that's no excuse. You are going to be a doctor. How many times must I remind you to act professionally, like the intelligent human being you are?"

"Yes, mother," Billy said, good-naturedly. "I'll try to be a good boy from now on."

"Thank you."

Billy smiled to himself. Marian sometimes acted just like his *abuela*. They were both small, fierce women who pushed their men around shamelessly. As he pondered the women in his life, Billy saw the school bus approaching and crushed out his cigarette.

When the bus pulled up, Jenny and Barbara were last off. Both were crying.

"Hey, what's wrong?" Billy asked.

"Oh Billy," Jenny said, throwing herself into his arms. "They were saying such terrible things about you. I don't believe it for one minute. Tell Bubba it's not true."

"What's not true?"

"They said you're gonna cut our throats and burn the house down."

"Is that all?" Billy asked. "Geez, I was afraid they'd said something awful."

"It *was* awful," Jenny sobbed.

"Who said this? Surely not all the kids were saying things about me."

"Jeffrey Little started it, and the rest joined him," Jenny explained.

Billy noticed that several of the parents and children were watching them curiously. "Come on. People are staring."

When they got home, Marian had just returned and was putting away some groceries. "What's the matter?" she asked, as both girls burst into fresh tears.

"The kids on the bus were picking on us today. And it's all *his* fault," Barbara said, pointing at Billy. "I hate you!" she yelled, glaring at him. "I wish you had never come to live with us!" she cried and ran from the kitchen.

"Barbara Jean Wilson, come back here this instant and apologize! Oh dear, I'm so sorry, Billy. I don't know what to say," she said, as she went to follow Barbara out of the room. "I'll go and talk with her."

"Wait, Marian. Why don't you stay here, and Jenny can tell you what happened. Let me talk to Barbara. If she has a problem with me, maybe I should be the one to handle it."

"Are you sure?" Marian asked.

Billy nodded, then went upstairs and stood outside of Barbara's room. He could hear her crying as he knocked on the door.

"Barbara, may I come in?"

"Go away!"

He turned the knob, and slowly opened the door. Barbara was face down across her bed sobbing uncontrollably. Sitting on the edge of the bed, he waited for her to calm down.

"Go away," she said again, but not as vehemently as the first time.

"Barbara, what happened? Please sit up and tell me. I want to know. Who's Jeffrey Little?"

After many long moments, Barbara sat up on the bed and wiped at her eyes with her hand. She sniffed. "He lives down the street. He's mean."

"What did he say to you?"

"Jeffrey says…you're…a savage and can't be trusted. And…that you'll kill us and scalp us like in those John Wayne movies. He says that the only good Indian…is a dead Indian and that Mommy and Daddy are crazy…for letting you live with us."

"Do you believe that?"

"I don't know," Barbara muttered, looking at the floor.

"Look at me," Billy said. "Do I look like a savage to you?"

Barbara looked up quickly, then back at the floor. She shrugged.

"Do you really think I'd kill you or hurt you in any way?"

Again, she shrugged. Billy picked up her hand and held it gently in his. "I'm just like you and your parents. The only difference I see between us is that my skin color is just a little bit darker than yours. It hurts me when people don't like me just because of that. How would you feel if people didn't like you just because you had, say, brown hair and hazel eyes? Wouldn't that make you feel bad?"

Barbara nodded; her head still bowed.

"Each and every one of us is different in some way. That doesn't make us uncivilized or not real. There are, however, a lot of people, who for one reason or another, are savage no matter what their skin color. These people are cruel and mean like Jeffrey. They refuse to accept people who are different. Are you going to let someone like Jeffrey tell you what to believe and who to like and dislike?"

Barbara shook her head, then looked up at him with hazel eyes so much like her mother's. Right now, they were huge and very, very red.

Billy met her stare head on. "I would never do anything to hurt you or your family in any way. Do you believe me?"

In a voice he could hardly hear, she said, "Yes."

"Do you really hate me and want me to leave?"

"No," she answered.

"Are you sure?"

"Yes."

"Are we still friends?"

"Uh huh," she nodded solemnly. "Can I have a hug?" she whispered, putting her arms up. After a moment's hesitation, he put his arms around her and held her tightly. She was too little to be hurt so badly. And he felt responsible.

"Let's go downstairs," he smiled, wiping a stray tear from her cheek with his thumb. She smiled back weakly and let him help her off the bed.

When they returned to the kitchen, Marian looked like she was ready to scold Barbara, but seeing Billy shake his head, she asked instead, "Is everything all right between you two?"

"Yes," said Billy. "Barbara why don't you go and play with Jenny. I want to talk to your mommy alone, okay?"

"Okay, Billy."

When she was gone, Billy patted his shirt pocket and pulled out a crumpled pack of cigarettes and matches. At Marian's look, he said, "Can we go outside?"

Marian nodded and followed him out onto the patio. Billy immediately lit a cigarette and stood facing away from Marian. After a moment, he turned and asked, "did Jenny tell you what happened on the bus?"

"All she would say was that the kids on the bus were picking on them. She wouldn't elaborate."

As they stood there, Rusty drove up and parked by the garage. He emerged and walked over to them, a worn briefcase hanging from his hand. He looked from one to the other and his face filled with concern.

"What's going on? Did someone die?"

"No, no one died," Marian answered. "But something very disturbing happened, nonetheless. Billy, why don't you tell Rusty what Barbara told you."

"When the girls got off the bus today, they were crying. A kid named Jeffrey Little was picking on them because of me. Saying stuff like your mom and dad are crazy for letting that savage stay with you. He's going to kill you some night, burn your house down, you know, that kind of garbage. And I guess a few of the other kids chimed in as well. Barbara was very upset and told me she hated me and wished I had never come here. I followed her to her room and we talked a little bit about racial discrimination. I also said that what he was saying was not true."

"Oh geez, Billy, I'm so sorry," Rusty said, putting his arm around Marian. "I forget that this can be a very prejudiced neighborhood. Heck, why only a couple hundred years ago, many of these people would have owned slaves. Since we don't think that way, we are probably a minority."

Billy lit another cigarette. "I don't care what people say about me. I mean, I'm used to this crap. But God, it makes me ill that someone is saying this behind your backs, or to the kids."

He turned and faced Rusty and Marian. "Rusty, I know you're not home very much and many nights I'm here alone with your wife and children. Do you trust me?"

Rusty tightened his hold on his wife and kissed her hair. "If I didn't trust you, you wouldn't *be* here. I'm actually glad you're here because I know someone is with them when I can't be. Jeffrey's father, Paul, is a real asshole."

Marian made a noise of disapproval and Rusty smiled. "Sorry, Marian, but he is. I'd like to have a long, violent discussion with that jerk."

"If he's saying these things, others are too. I don't want anyone cutting you down on my account. Maybe I'd better leave. You've been really great, but it's not worth having your children harassed and your name damaged because of me."

"You're not going anywhere. These people can't push me or my family around. And Billy, when I say family, I include you. You are one of us now. Perhaps this will all blow over if we don't say or do anything. If not, I may have to damage my precious hands on that bastard's face."

Billy continued to meet the bus on the days his lectures were over in the middle of the afternoon. Some of the kids taunted him, some stared. He completely ignored them and told the girls to do the same.

One day, a woman turned to Billy and said quietly, "I want you to know that many of us are opposed to what is happening here. Unfortunately, this is a very prejudiced neighborhood. We try and teach our children that race doesn't matter, but many of our neighbors don't agree—especially Paul Little. We're sorry. We know what he's saying isn't true. Marian's family has always lived in this neighborhood. She and Frank do so much in the community. For the most part, we all think very highly of both of them. We're ashamed of how people are reacting. I just wanted you to know that."

"Thank you," Billy said. "I appreciate your honesty. I'll tell the Wilsons what you said. I just hope this all blows over soon because the girls are really suffering."

Just then, the bus came, and the children flowed out. Except for Jeffrey, none of the other children had much to say, and Barbara was talking with another little girl. Things did seem to be settling down.

CAL

Cal was lonely. Cornell Medical School was very different from ASU and New York City was a far cry from Tempe. The people, their accent and the area were very strange. The massive skyscrapers towering over him made him feel claustrophobic. He had no one to talk to which made him miss Billy even more.

Cal wondered how his old roommate was getting along. Hell, Georgetown was probably as unlike ASU as Cornell. Neither were very big schools. At ASU, there were so many students that you were bound to fit in somewhere. One could get lost in the crowd and be comfortable. In a smaller school, someone who was different would stick out like a sore thumb. Right now, Cal was feeling like that thumb.

To get to know the neighborhood, Cal found himself running—a lot. He had rented an apartment on 75th Street that was simple, but had everything he needed, and was only two blocks away from the school. It had a high student population, accommodating students either going to the medical school or to nearby Rockefeller University.

His classmates were decent, but none of them seemed to be interested in cultivating new friendships. Now, instead of fooling around, he actually found himself studying and learning something. There would be no more wild nights for him, at least for the moment.

He could have kicked himself for not getting Billy's address. But there had been such confusion as they were leaving. Besides, if Billy was the type to write letters, he was probably too busy with his own life to take the time.

One day after class, however, Cal came home to find a letter in his mailbox. He assumed it was his mother's weekly missive, until he noticed the Washington, DC postmark. He quickly ripped open the envelope and began to read.

10/10/61

Dear Hound,

¿Que pasa? I'm having a <u>great</u> time here in DC. Major culture shock. But I'm surviving. Fortunately, the family I'm living with is pretty cool.

Living here isn't bad, except the house is like a goddamned museum. On top of that, I'm not allowed to smoke or swear. That's sort of like asking me not to breathe.

I have inherited two sisters ages seven and nine. The seven-year-old is something else. In fact, she's a lot like you without the sex and the vomit. The nine-year-old is kind of quiet except when she told me she hated me!

We had a little problem when I first arrived. The school kids were picking on the girls because they were living with a 'Savage.' You know, that kind of shit. But things have calmed down since then.

Med School is okay, I guess. I fit in about as well as a round peg in a square hole. Most days, I want to kill one of my classmates. He runs around calling me Geronimo. If he knew he was paying me a compliment, it would piss him off! He's lucky I'm not Geronimo. I'd have had his throat cut a month ago. He's a stupid jerk by the name of Carrington-Brown. All he needs is an ascot. I'm sure you get the picture.

Got a haircut. It was very traumatic, although necessary. No, I didn't get an Army buzz. Are you kidding! Me with a burr, no way! There's still enough for a tail but at least a foot is gone. On top of that, Georgetown has a strict dress code and I have to wear a tie to school. Can you dig it? I look like some fucked up white boy. I've enclosed my address, write if you can.

Adios, Fox

Cal went inside and got a beer. He pushed a stack of papers out of the way and sat down at the kitchen table. Lighting a cigarette, he re-read the letter. Poor Billy. Sounds like he's having it rough. The next four years are going to be hell, Cal thought. At least I'm white, all of his classmates were except for one Negro student who kept to himself. It wasn't that the other guys made fun of him, they just acted as if he didn't exist. Cal was the only one to acknowledge him and say hello. He seemed nice but wary of everyone.

A week later, Cal attended a reception for all first-year medical students. Usually the life of the party, Cal felt uncomfortable in such a formal gathering. He got a drink then found himself standing next to the Negro student. From out of the corner of his eye, he checked out his neighbor. He was well built in a muscular, athletic way. However, at the moment, he seemed ill at ease and was staring at his shoes.

Cal said, "How's it goin'?"

"About as good as it'll ever get," the guy shrugged.

"I'm Cal Lewis," Cal said, sticking out his hand.

"Terrence Johnson," he replied, returning the shake.

"This is just not my speed. I'm not used to this sort of thing," said Cal.

"You and me both," Terrence said with a smile. "You're not from around here, are you? The accent is wrong."

"Got that right," said Cal. "I'm from Flagstaff, Arizona."

"You're about as far as I am close. I come from Harlem. You know, you're the only person here who has spoken to me since classes started. Most of these boys are afraid the color is going to rub off or something. You aren't afraid. Why?"

"My best buddy is an American Indian. He always says that everyone is the same inside. We all got the same parts; the covering just happens to be a little different. Unfortunately, to some, that outer covering is too important."

"Amen, brother. Your friend sounds cool."

"He is. He's going to be a doctor, too. Right now, he's at Georgetown, fightin' his own version of the Indian Wars. You run?"

"Yeah, I can run. These days, it's usually from things."

For the first time in over a month, Cal Lewis laughed.

BILLY

It was Friday and Billy was home early. Since the girls were staying at a friend's house for a slumber party, he was off-the-hook for school bus duty. Opening the back door to the kitchen, he was greeted by the fragrance of chocolate. Marian stood at the oven decked out in a frilly apron.

"Good timing," she said, waving a metal spatula. "Tollhouse cookies, hot out of the oven."

"I wondered what smelled so great."

"You want some coffee? I just made a pot."

"Sure. Coffee sounds good. Want me to pour us some?"

"That would be nice. How were your classes today?"

"Okay," he said, removing his tie and unbuttoning the top buttons of his shirt.

"Is Dwight still making your life miserable?"

"He's a pain in the aa…butt," he finished lamely, swallowing his words at Marian's look. "Thank God he's kind of let up. It was getting old."

"Well, that's good."

Billy got out cream and sugar, then poured mugs of steaming coffee, giving one to Marian.

"Thanks. Here, have a cookie."

"Mmm," he said, taking a bite. "It's sure quiet without the kids. I don't know if I'll be able to study in the silence."

"Are you focusing on anything in particular?"

"Right now, we're working on the muscles of the hand."

"Sounds interesting. How is everything else going?"

"Most of my classes are pretty straight forward."

"That's not exactly what I meant. I mean, have you gotten settled?" she asked, putting another tray of cookies into the oven.

"I guess," he shrugged.

"That doesn't sound very encouraging."

He leaned back against the kitchen counter and sipped his coffee. "I'm sorry. It's just that I'm so overwhelmed right now, my head is spinning. It's hard enough going to school to learn something as difficult as medicine without all the other stuff. I mean, I feel like I'm constantly walking on eggs both here and at school."

"Is it that bad?"

Billy drank another swallow of coffee. Going to the sink, he ran some hot water and gathered dirty utensils off of the counter.

"What are you doing?"

"The dishes."

"Leave those. I'll do them."

"Come on, I can't just stand around and watch you work. I need to do something. Let me do this, please." He wiped off the counters and started washing the dirty mixing bowls.

"Is there anything we can do to make things easier for you?"

"No, you've all been great. The problem is within me, and I'll have to solve it myself." Changing the subject he asked, "So, do you two have any plans for this evening since the kids are away? A movie, dinner? You should go out and do something."

"We can't do that. You'd be all alone."

"Don't worry about me. I'll be at the library all evening, at least until they kick me out at ten. I have a paper to write. That should keep me out of trouble for a little while."

"We'll see if Rusty's up to it. Now that you mentioned it, it would be rather nice."

The medical school library was quiet. Billy was amazed at how much information there was on tendinitis. He was so absorbed in his work, that when he felt a tap on his shoulder, he jumped, tossing his pen into the air and onto another table, startling the student seated there.

"Sorry," John Simmonds chuckled, retrieving the pen. "Hope you're better with a scalpel than you are with this."

"Thanks for the infarct, you bastard." Billy leaned back against his chair, staring at the long, red line he had drawn across his notes.

John looked over his shoulder at the line, as well. "Speaking of infarcts," he laughed, "I think you're a goner. What're you up to? Writing the paper for Gregson's class?"

"Yeah, what're you doing yours on?"

"Bursitis."

"Thrilling! Mine's on tendinitis."

"Equally thrilling! I hear Dwight's doing his on sprains. I wonder who's gonna write it?"

"Can't he even write a paper by himself?" Billy asked.

"You kidding? Hell, C-B's mom still wipes his ass! Or perhaps it's the maid. So, what are you doing on your day off tomorrow?"

"I was thinking about going for a little run and finishing this paper. The girls have been hounding me to take them to the park while the weather's still nice. I might do that, too. Why?"

"The run sounds interesting. Mind if I tag along? I like to run but hate going alone."

"I was actually thinking of coming over your way. I was going to run to the cemetery, then jog past the White House and see what Kennedy was up to before going home."

"What? You call that a little run?"

"It's not like a marathon or anything."

"Maybe I'll just go with you to the cemetery. That way, if I burn myself out, I can get a bus back home."

"What a wuss, I thought you were in the Army?"

"Army yeah, not the Marines!"

"A poor example of the defenders of this fine country," Billy snorted. "I don't know, Simmonds. You may slow me down if I have to carry you home to your mommy."

"Hell's bells, Fox! I guess I can hold my own with a puny guy like you. I'll meet you across the Key Bridge tomorrow morning at seven. First one around the cemetery gets to flip the bird at the president."

"You're on."

It was a beautiful fall morning. There was a crispness in the air that was exhilarating. Billy had hardly broken a sweat when he crossed the bridge and found John jogging in place.

"Took you long enough," Simmonds whined. "I was waiting for hours."

"What? Did you sleep here last night to conserve your strength? I have a feeling you're nothing but hot air, Simmonds. You're puffing already, and we haven't even run a block."

"Just gettin' in gear. Takes me a while to find my rhythm."

"At the rate you're going, the band will have gone home before you find it."

"You run track at ASU?"

"Yeah, the 120 and 440 yard hurdles, the 50 and 100 yard dashes and ran on the cross country team. You run for Georgetown?"

"Uh huh, I did the 220 and the 440," he said, wiping at the sweat on his forehead and looked at his watch. "What was your best time?"

"The 100 in 00:09.40."

"Holy shit! You were flying."

"Yeah, crazy, huh? My regular times were at least 00:09.50. What about you?"

"I once did the 220 in 00:25.00 and thought I was King Shit from Turd Island. Then I realized I still came in second. Burned my ass."

Before they knew it, Arlington Cemetery loomed up ahead of them. They decided not to go all the way around but to head across the Potomac instead.

"What do you think of our fair city?"

"Don't know. Today's the first I've seen it."

"You're kidding?"

"Nope, never had the time. That's why I did this today."

They jogged past the back of the Lincoln monument then up Constitution Avenue to 17th Street, passing the White House on their way to Pennsylvania Avenue.

"Walking or running here's…much easier than driving," John said, spitting into the street. "Never know which street's one way…and you never can get there from where you are."

They cruised up Pennsylvania to M Street then back to the Key Bridge. "Thanks," John said, puffing. "See? You didn't have to carry me home. Though I never did hit my stride."

"We'll have to go further next time. How 'bout all the way 'round the cemetery before going into town? You should be singin' by then," Billy laughed. "See ya Monday."

"With bells on."

Marian had coffee perking when Billy let himself in the back door. "You're soaked," she stated, then poured him some orange juice. "Did you have a good run?"

"Uh huh, it's a beautiful morning. Is Rusty awake? I don't want to make any noise."

"Barely," Rusty said, shuffling into the kitchen in his pajamas. "Thanks to your advice, I was out until the wee hours last night with my wife, Audrey Hepburn and George Peppard. The movie was good but, I'm not used to doing that anymore. See what kids can do to a relationship?"

"You don't look too bad for all that. A little coffee does wonders. You should have gone running with us this morning. Get your blood all stirred up."

"I don't need to leave the house to do that," Rusty said, grabbing Marian from behind and planting a kiss on her cheek. "Do I honey?"

"Oh Rusty," she said, blushing. "Stop it."

"I'll leave you two alone," Billy remarked, finishing his juice. Then running up the stairs two at a time, he headed for the bathroom.

MAGGIE

The streetlights were on, and the city was waking up for its second wind when Maggie Sullivan ran into her building. She had been living in New York City for over four years and still wasn't used to all the noise and confusion. After the quiet of Watkins Glen, the city could be jarring to the senses and very frightening.

Upon graduation from the Cornell School of Nursing, she had taken a job on the Medical/Surgical Ward of New York Hospital. Maggie was on daylight this week and hated being out after dark. She picked up some groceries at the corner market, then hurried home.

The hallway light in front of Maggie's apartment was still burned out. She had complained to her landlord to no avail. He had met her at his door wearing a dirty, sleeveless undershirt, pants that threatened to fall and a leer. Picking his teeth with a toothpick, he said that he'd take care of things. What year? Maggie thought grimly.

The whole building was dimly lit to begin with, creating dark shadows. As Maggie nervously looked around, she ran into something solid in front of her door. Letting out a scream, she dropped her sack.

"Hey! Are you all right?" the big blond guy asked with a look of surprise. "Here, let me help you." He bent down and began picking up her spilled groceries.

"No really, that's all right. You don't have to help me. I'm sorry, I wasn't looking where I was going. My fault. Thanks." She quickly unlocked her door, grabbed her sack and slammed the door in the man's face.

Her heart was pounding as she leaned against the wall in the entryway. She had to get a grip. He was probably harmless. But she had heard too many stories about how men raped young women without a moment's hesitation. Maybe I should go back home, she thought. If I'm going to be constantly jumping at shadows, I don't belong here.

For the first time in over a month, Maggie had a Saturday free. She gathered her dirty laundry and headed to the laundromat down the street. If she got there early enough, she wouldn't have to wait for a machine.

When she arrived, there was only one other person in the place—the blond guy she had run into the night before. He was sitting in front of a dryer reading a textbook.

Turning her head and averting her eyes, she quickly went to the opposite side of the room and began loading her clothes into a washing machine. Out of the corner of her eye, she noticed him get up and walk her way. Her heart started thumping. Oh dear God, please don't let him hurt me. She couldn't decide whether to run or wait to see whether he attacked her. If he attacked her, she'd kick him as hard as she could, then run.

"I see you're out bright and early, too. This place can get pretty crowded. Sorry for scarin' you last night. This city has a way of keepin' people on edge." His voice had a slight drawl to it. Definitely not from around here, Maggie thought.

"My name's Cal, I live in apartment four."

"Uh…hi, my name's Maggie," she said. "You're not from this area, are you?"

"You know, I must stick out like a cactus in a flower garden. Everyone I meet says the same thing. Is it that noticeable?"

"Yes," she smiled. "It is. You sound kinda like John Wayne in a cowboy movie."

"That bad?" he laughed. "And here I thought I was fittin' in so well. I guess all I need is a horse to complete the picture."

"I know, Texas," she guessed.

"Yup, born there. But my parents relocated to Arizona when I was in high school."

"What in the heck are you doing in the middle of New York City?"

"I'm a first-year med student at Cornell."

"Really? I graduated from Cornell Nursing School last spring. Nice, isn't it?"

"I guess the school's okay. But everything moves so quickly in this city, I always get the feelin' that if I slow down for anything, I'll be in the middle of a damn stampede. It was never as hectic in Arizona. Where's everyone rushin' to?"

"I'm rushing home or to work, hoping I don't get mugged in the process. I'm not originally from the city and I know what you mean about the pace. I'm from a little town in the southeastern end of the state. It's so quiet there that you can hear yourself breathing."

Maggie was amazed at the perfectly normal conversation they were having. It had been a long time since she had a conversation, of any kind, with anyone that didn't revolve around a medical issue. It struck her at that moment, how very lonely she was. She snuck a look at Cal from under lowered lashes and noticed he was ruggedly handsome. If you liked tall, blond, football player types.

"You ever play football?" It was out of her mouth before she could give it some thought.

"No, but I did run track. I know, people look at me and say, 'You should have played ball.' But I was never interested."

"You don't look like a runner," she said, smiling.

"Don't let looks deceive you," he smiled back. "I'm not goin' to attack you, either. Not unless you want me to, that is," he laughed and winked at her.

Maggie grinned back.

"Where are you headed after your clothes are done?"

"Back home. Cleaning comes next."

"Hell, I got to draw the line somewhere. Even though my apartment's such a mess, it looks like I was robbed."

"That bad?"

"Yeah," he laughed.

Nice laugh, Maggie thought. "Are you planning on becoming a GP or do you have a specialty in mind?"

"My granddaddy was a cardiologist. I thought I'd try keepin' it in the family."

"Well, Cornell is a good place for it. I know a few cardiology residents here. The program's tough, but you'll be glad in the long run."

"Oh, I wish you wouldn't have said tough. That's one word I try to avoid. I'm basically lazy, if you know what I mean."

"Somehow I'm not surprised after what you told me about your apartment."

"I'll bet you're gonna be all in when you're done with that cleanin'. How about lettin' me take you out to dinner tonight, somewhere nice. I promise I won't make any lewd suggestions or passes. And you won't have to go slammin' your door in my face."

Maggie blushed. "Was I that bad?"

"Darlin,' you were pretty crazy. I thought I was living next to a psycho. Still not sure, either."

She tried to swat him with a wet towel, but he dodged away in time. "Okay. But remember, no lewd suggestions."

Putting his hand over his heart, he replied, "I promise. How does six o'clock sound?"

"Fine. Thank you."

"See you then," he said, sauntering back to retrieve his clothes.

Maggie finished doing her laundry, then whipped through her apartment in a frenzy. She was nervous and excited about the upcoming evening. She couldn't remember the last time she had a date. It would be nice to get out of her apartment and do something fun for a change.

Her only worry was that Cal was more than she could handle. There was something about his drawl and saunter that gave Maggie the impression he had done it all before and with many a girl. She had a feeling that if she let her guard down for an instant, she'd find herself flat on her back. But as the evening approached, she pushed her fears aside and reasoned that dinner couldn't be that dangerous.

BILLY

With the holidays approaching, Billy had a major decision to make. Should he go home for Christmas? He hadn't given it much thought until the fundraiser dinner dance the women's auxiliary had put together for the hospital. Marian was on the committee and of course she and Rusty were attending.

When Billy came home, he found Rusty sporting an elegant black tuxedo and Marian in a stunning, amber satin gown. They looked great together and Billy promised to babysit.

He finally put his notes aside and was readying for bed when the Wilsons returned around 1:00 in the morning. Rusty was a little unsteady on the stairs, and the two of them did a lot of giggling on their way to their bedroom. The giggling subsided and was soon replaced by the distinct sounds of lovemaking.

At that moment, Billy had never felt so lonely. Until then, he had successfully blocked those kinds of feelings from his mind as he studied and went about his new life. Now they all came racing back—the feel of Jessie's skin, the way her body clung to his. It was more than he could stand. He quietly closed his door. But how could he possibly fall asleep now?

After a long night of mental tossing and turning, Billy decided to go home for Christmas. He knew the drive was a killer, but for his own sanity, he was going to have to make the trip.

Later in the day, Rusty took him to the country club where he was a member. Since Billy had no interest in golf, Rusty was teaching him how to play tennis. After a couple of sets, they went in and had a sauna.

Billy loved the sauna. "It is a cleansing, Rusty. You sweat out all the bad stuff. When I lived on the Rez, we would have a sweat as often as we could. I mean, it wasn't like a ceremonial sweat, but it did the same thing."

"How did you do that?"

"There's a wooden shelter *Abuelo* and I built behind the house. *Abuelo* would place rocks that he'd heated on the stove inside this shelter on the ground. He'd throw water on them to make them steam, then we'd sit in the heat and sweat. When we had enough, we'd jump into the icy stream flowing behind the house and scrub ourselves raw with sand. It was great."

"You people have a strange way of feeling great," Rusty commented, wiping his face with a towel. "You know, you always speak of your grandparents, but I never hear you mention your wife. I'm not sure whether I should ask about her or not."

"You can ask," Billy shrugged. "But there isn't much to tell."

"Don't you miss her?"

"Actually, I hadn't thought about Jessie or missed her until about 1:00 this morning."

"This morning, why then? Oh…I see," Rusty coughed and reddened. "Were we that loud?"

"Well, you were pretty tanked when you came home, and you didn't close the door completely. Plus, my door was open because I was listening for the kids. I think you thought you were being quiet, but…"

"Geez, I must have really been loaded. We never forget to close and lock the door. I'm really sorry. I hope that doesn't happen again."

"Don't worry about it. I didn't hear a thing once I closed my door."

"It must be difficult being away from home. I keep forgetting you have a family and life outside of ours."

"That's okay, sometimes I forget, too."

"So, what's she like?"

"Who? Jessie?"

Rusty nodded.

"Jessie, hmm, she's knock down, drop dead, gorgeous. She's got long, thick, black hair, big brown eyes, and is stacked just right."

"Sounds great. How can you stand being away from her?"

Billy's eyes filled with sadness. "Sounds great until you find out she'll have sex with anybody to get what she wants. And she'll take any drug she can get her hands on. Real great, huh? Looks aren't everything," he shook his head.

"Is that why you weren't living with her when we first met?"

Billy let out a deep breath. "One reason."

"Was she like that when you married her?"

"At the time, I had only heard rumors about her that I didn't want to believe. Then, I figured once we were married, she wouldn't screw around."

"Why'd you marry her in the first place?"

"She told me I knocked her up."

"Shit, you never told me you had a kid. Why didn't you say something?"

"It was all a lie. She was never pregnant. Hell, I was always careful and used condoms."

"Then why did you believe her?"

Billy hung his head and was silent. Then quietly he answered, "She said that when I was drunk or…high, I'd forget to put one on."

"What? God, Billy! Joe said you had some problems, but he never mentioned drugs."

"I don't think he knew, and I was too ashamed to tell him."

"Are you still using them?"

"No, and as I said before, I don't drink either. But it really doesn't matter now, anyway."

"What do you mean?"

"I mean, you trusted me, and I blew it. I should have been up front with you when we first met. But I was so afraid I'd lose my chance of getting here, I didn't tell you. I'm really sorry, Rusty. I'll pack and get out as soon as we get home."

"Who said anything about you leaving?"

"Come on. You couldn't possibly want me to stay, especially now. Think about your wife and kids. I'm really nothing but trash."

"Is that what you think?"

"Of course. I don't belong here in this beautiful club with all these wealthy men. I see the way they look at me when I come in here with you. They barely tolerate me. This whole thing has been nothing but a stupid farce."

"A farce?" Rusty asked.

"Sure, I should have known that I'd never fit in here. *Abuelo* warned me this might happen. I keep forgetting who and what I am. Hell, I start thinking I'm white. Then I'm reminded, not too gently, that I *am* different. That I belong back on the reservation."

Rusty crossed his arms against his chest and stared at Billy for a long moment. "So, you're going to throw it all away. This whole semester, wasted?"

"What's the use? I'm just fooling myself into thinking I can be a doctor."

"I'm really surprised at you. I thought you were tougher than that. But I can see I was wrong. Things get hot and you run. Are you going to keep running all your life?"

Billy got off the bench and slammed out of the sauna. By the time Rusty had showered and dressed, Billy was gone. In fact, he was halfway home by the time Rusty pulled alongside of him.

"Come on, get in," Rusty said, through the open passenger seat window.

After a moment's hesitation, Billy opened the door and got in, silently staring straight ahead as Rusty drove down the street.

Rusty sighed. "I'm ashamed. Everything's so easy for me now, that I've become too quick to judge. I forget my own humble beginnings. I just wonder what *I* would have done if I were in your shoes."

Billy lit a cigarette and looking out the window said, "My people say, 'Great Spirit grant that I may not criticize my neighbor until I have walked two moons in his moccasins.'"

"We whites have a similar saying. Although I don't think we ever do that, do we?"

"I think we all assume far too much."

"How's that?"

"We assume we know another person because of who and what they are. We try to fit them into a category, just to make things neat and easy. But things are never neat and easy. They're messy as hell."

Billy flicked ash out the window and stared off into space. "I'm trying to make myself fit, in a place I don't belong," he said, shaking his head. "All my life I've been doing that. Trying to be what everyone else wants me to be. After a while, you go crazy trying," he said, and took a drag on his cigarette.

"That sounds like a lot of pressure to put on a person," Rusty commented.

Billy snorted. "Here I am, living in luxury. Going to a white man's school to be a white man's doctor. I was told the clothes I wear, the way I talk, and my way of life are all wrong. Now I'm trying to change myself just like Eliza *Fucking* Doolittle."

"I'm sorry, Billy. I'm afraid we've been part of that pressure."

"Do you know what I really am?" he said, facing Rusty. "I'm nothing but a poor Indian," he said. "My drunken father beat my mother and me because he was away from all the things *he* loved, living a life *he* hated. I went to college to better myself—to break that chain of helplessness. Instead, I got trapped by another abused Indian who was haunted by her own past, trying to survive the only way *she* knew how. In the long run, I ended up doing things that I am ashamed of." Billy disgustedly flicked his cigarette butt out the window.

Rusty didn't know what to say. Billy meanwhile shivered and reached into his pocket for another cigarette. He tapped it against the pack but didn't light it, toying instead with the matches in his hands.

"It's a vicious cycle," he pointed out. "I should never have come here. And saying that isn't running," he said, glancing at Rusty. "No matter what my old man did to me, I never ran from him, never ran from the problem."

He finally lit his cigarette, then looked back out the window. "Aren't you glad you invited me to live with your family? Jeffrey Little was right. Don't ever trust me. I *am* a savage," he said, his voice cracking in misery.

Rusty pulled the car to the side of the road and parked, turning off the engine. For several minutes, neither man spoke. Finally, Rusty took a deep breath and let it out gustily. "Is there anything else you haven't told me?" he asked.

"No," Billy said, tossing his cigarette out the window, "that's about it."

After a long pause, Rusty finally spoke. "What do you really want, Billy? If you were a white kid from the right side of the tracks, what would you do with your life?"

Billy stared at his hands clenched in his lap. Finally, he said, "I guess I would still want to be a surgeon."

"Why can't that be possible for you?"

"Because I'm not white, goddamn it!" he spit out, pounding his fist against his leg.

"What does color have to do with anything?"

"Everything," Billy said, defeated.

"You just think that. It doesn't, really. You're being too sensitive. If you would just give yourself a break, maybe everyone else would."

"That's easy for you to say. You're white."

"Billy, you're so full of shit." Rusty paused, then said, "You know what you need?"

"What?"

"You need to get laid. That's your whole problem right there in a nutshell," he said, nodding his head sagely.

Billy stared at Rusty. All of a sudden, he grinned and shook his head, then started to laugh. Rusty joined him, and they laughed so hard that Rusty had tears coming from his eyes.

"Let's go home," Rusty said at last and turned the key in the ignition.

"Yeah, home," said Billy, smiling weakly.

Thanksgiving was an interesting experience for Billy. Jennifer banged on his door early in the morning and burst in on him. "Hey! How come you're still in bed? You said you were taking us to the parade. Remember?"

After being up half the night studying, the last thing Billy wanted to do on his day off was go to the neighborhood parade with the girls. He pulled the pillow over his head and rolled over.

"Come *on,* Papa Fox. Get up!" she said, planting her small fists on her tiny hips.

"Go 'way," Billy mumbled. "Lemme sleep."

"You promised." Jennifer grabbed the pillow and pulled it away. Then, she started working on the blankets.

Billy's eyes snapped open, and he grabbed at the covers. Christ, he thought, panicking. He couldn't remember if he had thrown on a pair of shorts before he went to bed. "All right," he muttered. "I'm up. Get out of here and let me get dressed or I won't take you."

"Promise?"

"Yeah, now beat it."

She was gone as quickly as she had come. Billy stretched, craving a cigarette and some caffeine. It took about five minutes under a cold shower before he started to feel alive again. He could smell pancakes cooking on his way downstairs. Bypassing the table, he headed for the coffee.

"What? Aren't you eating breakfast?" Marian asked. "I made these for you."

"Marian, please," Billy groaned. "I can't keep eating like this. My pants are getting tight. Can't I just have a bowl of cereal or a piece of toast?"

"Won't you be hungry later?"

Billy looked around the kitchen at Marian's dinner preparations. He nodded at the huge turkey sitting on the counter. "If that's for dinner, I don't think you need to worry."

Marian smiled. "Well, if you're sure, the cereal's in the pantry."

After the parade, Billy and the girls got into the family station wagon Billy had nicknamed 'The Tank,' and went to pick up Rusty's mother who lived in Rockville, Maryland. She was coming to spend the weekend with the family, and the girls couldn't wait to see her.

Jean Wilson was a tall, large-boned woman who resembled her son, although her once red hair was now more silver. Jenny and Barbara made a fuss over her, and there were many hugs and kisses going around. Billy hung back, not wanting to intrude.

"Grandma, this is Billy," Jenny said, grabbing Billy by the hand and drawing him in. "He lives with us now. Billy, this is Grandma."

Jean's eyes flickered over Billy. "Marian has told me quite a lot about you, young man. I hear you are going to my son's alma mater to study medicine."

"Yes, ma'am."

"Good luck. It won't be easy, you know."

"Yes, ma'am, I know. Most important things never usually are," Billy replied.

"Spoken like someone who knows firsthand," Jean nodded. Then smiling broadly, she offered her hand. "Welcome to the family, Billy."

Billy smiled shyly. "Thanks, Mrs. Wilson. Now, what can I take out to the car?"

She handed him a small suitcase. "Here's my overnight bag, and there are two pies in a box on the counter in the kitchen. That's it. And please, call me Jean or Grandma."

Jenny said matter-of-factly. "You're lucky, Grandma. Billy just got his regular license last week. We'd never have been able to fit the pies on the back of his motorcycle."

"Good gracious! I highly doubt you'd have gotten *me* on the back, either!" She laughed and winked at Billy as he opened the front door for her and helped her inside.

When they returned home, Marian was in the middle of a cooking frenzy. The smell of turkey filled the house and potatoes bubbled on the stove. Rusty had done his rounds at the hospital and was home early.

Marian shooed a protesting Grandma from the kitchen and into the library. Rusty joined her and the girls took turns entertaining their grandmother and father by playing the piano and telling stories about their new school year.

Billy found himself at loose ends. "What can I do?" he asked, wandering back into the kitchen.

"Not a thing, go and visit with Grandma. I can handle this," Marian answered.

"Do I have to? I'm really not good at that. Let me help. Please."

"Well, you could start by opening this can for me then draining the potatoes. I guess I really could use the help. Thanks."

Billy never saw so much food at one time. This would feed my grandparents for a week, maybe longer, he thought. After dinner, he helped Marian clear the plates, then started to wash the dishes. It felt good to be on his feet.

"Do you celebrate every holiday like this?" he asked, putting away a platter.

"What do you mean?" Marian questioned, wrapping up leftovers.

"I'm not used to all this food."

"Don't your people celebrate Thanksgiving?"

"Ah, not really. It's not exactly our holiday."

"But I thought, you know, the Indians and the pilgrims."

Billy looked very uncomfortable. "Um…well…for my family, every day was a day to be thankful."

"Oh. Well, if this surprised you, Christmas will overwhelm you."

Billy turned to Marian. "Didn't Rusty tell you? I'm going home for the holidays. I'll be leaving on the 21st and won't be back until the first of January."

"What! Rusty never told me. The girls will be disappointed. We were looking forward to having you here."

"Gee Marian, I'm really sorry. But I haven't been home in over six months. I haven't seen my wife or grandparents since May," he said, sitting down at the kitchen table.

"We didn't think, Billy. I'm sorry. We keep forgetting you have a family somewhere else. I'm going to hate telling the girls. Maybe next year you could spend the holidays with us."

"We'll see. It'll depend on how things go this year. I'm not too sure Jessie will be happy to see me. She hasn't answered any of my letters. It may be a wasted trip."

"If you change your mind, you know you're always welcome to stay here for the holidays."

"Are you talking about Christmas?" Jenny asked, skipping into the kitchen.

"Yes, Miss Nosy," said Billy, flicking his dish towel at her.

"When you were a boy, what did Santa bring you?"

Billy looked at her oddly. "Um, you know, it's been…uh so long ago I don't remember."

"You can't remember? Gee, Mommy and Daddy remember and they're old."

"Thanks a lot, Jenny," her mother said dryly.

"Do Indians celebrate like we do?"

"It depends," he said. "My grandparents are Roman Catholic, so we celebrate the holiday. Usually, the only thing different about Christmas is going to midnight mass at the mission church."

Jenny crawled up into Billy's lap. "How come you never talk about your mommy and daddy?"

"Jenny, how many times do I have to tell you? It's not polite to ask people personal questions," Marian admonished.

"Billy doesn't mind, do you?"

"I never talk about them because my father is dead and my mom…well," his voice trailed off.

"Is she dead too?" Jenny asked.

"I uh…really don't know. I haven't seen her in a long, long time. If she is alive, I don't think she would want to see me. She isn't like your mommy."

"I'm sorry about your daddy, Billy, and your mommy. But you know what? You have a mommy and daddy right here. Right, Mommy?" she said, grabbing Billy's arms and wrapping them around her slight body.

"That's right," Marian said, clearing her throat and quickly turning away.

"I'm a very lucky person, Jenny Wren," Billy said, and after a moment's hesitation, tightened his arms around her.

Jenny leaned back against Billy's chest and looked up at him. "Now that Thanksgiving's over, Christmas will be here soon. I can't wait. It's gonna be so much fun with you here. Bubba and I are going to get you a special present."

"Honey, Billy isn't going to be here for Christmas. He's going home to spend the holidays with his family."

Jennifer turned in Billy's lap slightly so that she was facing him. Her eyes immediately filled with tears. "But Billy, I thought *we* were your family now? Don't you want to be with us?"

"Of course, I want to be here, Jenny. But I also need to go home for a little while. And the only time I can do that is during my break. I'd be here if I could."

"But it was going to be so special. You spoiled it!" She pushed his arms away and jumping off his lap, ran from the room.

Billy rubbed his forehead. "I didn't think she would take it so hard."

"Don't worry," Marian said, patting his shoulder. "You know Jenny, stormy one minute, sunshine the next."

Billy looked at her glumly.

"Come on, cheer up. My mother had a saying, 'Things always come out in the wash.' She was right. They always do. Now let's go join the rest of the family. You deserve a break. Thanks for all your help. I could never have done this without you."

CAL

What Cal hated most about doing the laundry was the folding and putting away. It was just easier to take the clothes out of the basket as needed. But maybe I'll have some company tonight, he thought as he jammed his underwear into a drawer. I don't want her to think I'm a total slob.

He made dinner reservations at the Tavern on the Green. He and his parents had eaten there when they were scouting out the school. It was elegant and expensive—the perfect place to impress a date. He straightened a few things in the apartment then cleaned up the bathroom. It'll do, he thought. He dressed carefully then went to get Maggie.

She answered the door right away. "Standing by the peep hole, eh?" he said.

"Of course. I had to be sure it was you."

"You look very nice in something other than white."

"Gee, thanks for the compliment, I think."

She really did look good, thought Cal. She was pretty in a gamine way with short, softly curling, reddish blond hair that framed a pixie face. She reminded Cal of a sprightly, curvaceous Peter Pan. Her forest green sweater contrasted with her hair and made her emerald eyes stand out.

She tilted her head from side to side. "You don't look too bad yourself."

He laughed, his white teeth flashing. "Now that we got that out of the way, shall we go?"

They caught a cab to the restaurant and, just as Cal had hoped, Maggie was very impressed.

"Wow, I've heard about this place. Other girls on the floor have mentioned it. But I've never been able to go here—too expensive. It looks like something out of a fairy tale, doesn't it?"

Nestled among the trees of Central Park, the restaurant and the surrounding shrubbery twinkled with hundreds of white lights. The inside was ornate and filled with antiques and mirrors.

"I've never seen anything like this," said Maggie, once they were seated and their orders taken. "It's unbelievable."

After the waiter brought their drinks, Cal said, "There's something I've been meanin' to ask you."

"What's that?"

"If you're so scared of everything, why did you come to New York City, of all places?"

"I know. It seems really stupid, doesn't it?" Maggie replied. "But my best friend and I decided to go to Cornell. At the time, New York sounded exciting. We were two country bumpkins and the girls from the city made fun of us. But I liked the school a lot. Unfortunately, after a semester, my friend chickened out and left me to fend for myself," she shrugged. "Now, after four years, I guess I'm getting used to it. Still, every day I read in the papers about young women getting mugged, and it scares me."

"Why do you stay?"

"I guess I feel I have something to prove. All my life I was sheltered. I was the only girl sandwiched between two older brothers and one younger brother. They fought my battles for me. When I dated in high school, it was someone my parents and brothers both knew and approved of. I never did an exciting thing in all my life."

"So, you decided to break out."

"Something like that. And I don't want to go crawling back to hear, 'I told you so.'"

Cal leaned back in his chair and reached for his cigarettes.

"Do you have to smoke?"

"I guess not. Does it bother you?"

"Yes, actually it does. If you don't mind."

He put the pack and his lighter back in his shirt pocket, then took a long swallow of beer. "So would your parents approve of me?"

Maggie laughed. "I'm not sure. But you do remind me a bit of the guy I dated throughout high school."

"Let me guess, tall, blond, blue eyed, incredibly handsome and the kind of man young women swoon over."

"Well, sort of. But the hair color is wrong. Mike had thick, black, wavy hair. God, he was full of the devil. I think you are too."

"Me? Full of the devil?" Cal asked in mock surprise, his hand over his heart. "Darlin' I don't know where you get such ideas."

"Really, I thought I was a pretty good judge of character."

"So, what happened to this guy. How could you let someone like that slip through your fingers?"

Maggie's face saddened for a few seconds. "I guess you could say that our dreams took us on different paths. Mike was accepted to the prestigious Air Force Academy in Colorado. I think he proposed so that I could stand at his side and applaud all his accomplishments. Not to mention, mass producing children, in keeping with the Irish Catholic tradition of trying to populate the world single handedly."

"Ah, the old barefoot and pregnant routine."

"You guessed it."

"And I take it, that's not what you wanted?"

"Not exactly, and not right away, either. I wanted to be here, doing what I'm doing."

"So, Mr. Wonderful went to Colorado alone?"

"Yes, he's probably a pilot by now. We wrote for a while, but you know how that is. The distance was too much. Eventually the letters dwindled to nothing."

"That's too bad, but hey, his loss is my gain."

Their orders came shortly afterward. The meal was excellent, and Cal enjoyed Maggie's company. As they were leaving the restaurant, Cal spotted a horse and buggy sitting out in front. "Want to go for a ride?"

"Sure, that would be neat."

They got in the carriage and the driver wrapped a blanket snugly around them. Pulling out into traffic, they headed down Fifth Avenue enjoying the sights along the way. The steady clip clop of the horse's feet on the pavement seemed unreal in the middle of the large noisy city. Cal managed to put his arm around Maggie without her objecting. It was a perfect evening and Maggie appeared to be enjoying herself.

Feeling his gaze, she smiled. "Do you treat all your women to elegant dinners followed by romantic carriage rides?"

"Well, darlin,' I usually don't work that hard. Most of my dates are beer and bed. But I don't think you're that kind of gal, are ya?"

"No, I'm not."

"I guess that means that you don't want to take the mattresses at the Plaza for a test drive!" He laughed when he saw the look on her face. Throwing his hands up in surrender, he said, "not to worry, just kiddin.' I don't have a hankerin' to take a bite out of you yet. I kinda think you might be worth the wait," he said, winking.

After their buggy ride, they caught a cab in front of the Plaza. Cal cocked his head toward the luxurious, New York icon. "You sure?" he questioned, his eyes laughing.

Maggie grinned. "I'm sure."

At their apartment building, Cal escorted Maggie to her door. "No screamin' tonight?" he laughed.

"No," she smiled. "Thank you for a wonderful evening. I had a lovely time."

"Thanks for comin' with me, Maggie. I enjoyed being with you. Is a good night kiss permissible or is that considered lewd behavior and unacceptable?"

"I think I can handle a kiss good night without kicking you or calling a policeman."

Cal leaned down and very lightly kissed Maggie on the lips. It was sweet and he didn't linger. Another night, he thought. It will give her something to look forward to.

He watched her go into her apartment, then smiled to himself as he heard her throw the bolt on the door. Once she was safely inside, he headed toward his own apartment, whistling a tuneless song through his teeth. Things were definitely looking up, he thought.

He went inside the apartment and threw his tie and jacket on the arm of a chair. Going to the refrigerator, he got out a bottle of beer and sat down at the kitchen table. Lighting a cigarette, he thought about Billy. He felt bad, he had never written back. Billy probably thought he had forgotten all about him.

Pulling out some notebook paper, he took another puff on his cigarette. Writing was never easy for him. It took several beers, a couple of cigarettes and a lot of mulling to find the right words. Finally, he grabbed up his pen and began to write.

November, 1961

Hey Billy,

How are ya? Thanks for writing. It was great to hear from you. Sorry it took so long to write back, but you know me, I couldn't find a pencil or paper! And when I did, it was too much of an effort.

Things here were pretty bad at first. But I guess they're beginning to settle down. New York City is a hell of a sight different from Tempe.

I never heard so many car horns beeping in all my life. They never stop, even in the middle of the night. Add to that all the sirens and I can see why they call this the 'city that never sleeps.' They mean it!

My classes aren't too bad. You'd be proud of me, I'm actually studying. I even wrote several papers. <u>All by myself</u>. Had you been here, I probably would have begged you to do it, but since you weren't...

Anyway, the guys here are very competitive and not very friendly. There's one guy who's pretty cool. He reminds me of you. He likes to run, and we've gone for a jog a couple of times. But it's not very easy to run here. Too many cars.

Most of the time, we go to Central Park. That's a problem, too. There, you have to fight the dogs, their shit and their crazy owners.

Are you going home for Christmas? I think I'm going to fly home for the break. There's not too much here to keep me occupied except this chick I met recently in my building. She's pretty nice but very refined. Not the kind of girl I'm used to.

If you come home, let me know. I'll be there till the end of December.

Cal

He scribbled the letter hurriedly as the words came to him. It was sloppy, but hell, Billy was used to his writing. Cal got out another beer and wondered what Billy would think of Maggie. It was funny, Maggie was the kind of girl he would have picked for Billy. She was intelligent, demure and not a party person.

He laughed when he thought about it. Maybe it's like they say, opposites attract. There was quiet, backward Billy married to Jessie—the girl most likely to…anything. Then there was genteel Maggie, who was hanging around with Mr. always-at-the-ready Lewis.

Maggie was so different that he didn't know where to go next with the relationship. In the past, his tactics were simple. Take a girl out, get her drunk and into bed. If she didn't want him, it was no big deal. There were always other girls.

Billy said if Cal would have been an Indian, his name would have been 'Rutting Bull' or 'Hound in Heat'. He remembered a story that Billy used to tell about a young Indian boy who wanted to know how he came to be named. The father in the story told how each of his son's sisters and brothers had been named by an animal that happened to be outside the tipi when they were born. People would hang onto every word as he described little bear, running deer and soaring eagle. When Billy was almost through, Cal would ruin it by saying, "Why do you ask, Two Dogs Fucking?" and the two of them would howl at the punch line.

Yeah, he sure as hell hoped he'd get to see Billy over the holidays. He could use a good laugh.

BILLY

By taking a different route and heading to Colorado first, Billy was able to spend Christmas Eve, Christmas Day and the 26th with his grandparents. It was about the same distance but in much safer territory. After the lavishness of Georgetown, the ranch seemed small, cramped, and very primitive. Until now, Billy had never noticed how rank the outhouse really smelled. When he offered to dig out a new one, his *abuela* had turned and looked at him sharply.

The realization that he was changing took him by surprise. Being with the Wilsons had opened his eyes to another way of life. Now, he looked differently at all that had once been familiar. It struck him that he had always taken his *abuela* for granted. In all the years he had lived with her, he had never once heard her utter a complaint. She hauled in wood for the wood burning stove and pumped water from a well or carted it from the stream. She used an outhouse, washed their clothes in a galvanized tub on the stove, and had no privacy whatsoever. Her quiet acceptance of her lot in life humbled him, and he wanted to do something to show how much he appreciated and loved her.

After he had dug out and moved the outhouse, Billy helped his grandmother dig up some roots that were planted in the winter-hardened earth near the house. As they worked, *Abuela* questioned him about what he was learning. She listened raptly, nodding in understanding as Billy told her about his classes and labs. Billy, in turn, questioned her about what she was doing and how many babies she had brought into the world since he had seen her last.

Afterward, Billy went with his grandmother to get water from the ice-cold stream. Not thinking, he took the buckets from her and proceeded to fill and carry them back to the house.

"Do you think I am too old and feeble to carry water, William?" his grandmother asked, her eyes filled with hurt.

"Of course not. But I'm here. Why can't I carry the water for you? I used to when I was young."

"You are a man now. You should not do my work. I am quite capable of doing it myself."

"I know you are. But I want to do this for you," he said firmly and continued walking.

His *abuela* shook her head sadly and followed him back to the house. Again, Billy felt as though he was walking on eggs. But this time, it was with his own family.

Midnight Mass at the Mission, however, hadn't changed. It was still magical with flickering candlelight and hymns sung in Spanish. It always felt so peaceful and holy. Billy sat on the worn, wooden pew of the chapel and tried to clear his mind. He felt so small in the big picture of things. It was too much to consider who he was and where he was going in this life.

In the chapel behind the altar was a stained-glass window depicting San Francisco, the mission's patron. Francisco's arms were open wide to encompass the animals that surrounded him. Both saint and animals alike radiated a quiet peace.

It was to this window that Billy was drawn, when as a young boy, he was filled with uncertainty, confusion, and anger. The window always seemed to calm Billy and the quiet of the chapel offered solace to the troubled youngster.

Now, looking at that window, Billy again felt peace and serenity. He felt ready to face whatever the creator had in store for him, to give thanks for each new day, and to enjoy life's journey to the fullest without leaving tracks.

After the holiday, Billy met with a friend of his grandfather's to discuss some summer employment, then headed to Flagstaff. When he pulled in front of the Lewis home at lunchtime, Cal was leaning against the gate of the stucco wall waiting for him, a cigarette dangling from his lips. "It's great to see ya, Fox," he grinned, slapping Billy on the back, as he climbed off the bike.

"Some things never change," Billy winced as he rubbed his shoulder. "Someday you're gonna break my fuckin' back, ya know that?"

"Can't help it. Don't know my own strength. Besides, you're such a runt, a fart could blow you over. Anyway, how's it goin'?" he asked as they made their way onto the back patio where Mrs. Lewis had sandwiches and a cold pitcher of iced tea waiting.

While they ate, Cal questioned Billy about his first semester. "Tell me about Georgetown. You fittin' in any better than when you first got there?"

"I guess. I really like what I'm learning. It's just taking a lot longer to get used to the snotty rich geezers who go there. What's sad is they only want to be doctors because they think they'll make lots of money. Not because they want to help people."

"I find that, too. Of course, I *am* one of those geezers," Cal laughed.

"So, this chick you mentioned—she sounds like more than an average notch on your headboard," Billy commented, taking a long swig of tea.

"She is. She's not my type at all. Not only is she very pretty, but she also knows her shit when it comes to medicine. In fact, she's helped me out on a number of occasions. She scares the hell out of me, Fox. I don't know what to do with her. In the past, if I didn't screw 'em, I had no use for 'em."

"If that's the case, what *are* you doing with her?"

Cal spread out his hands. "I'm not really sure. But at any rate, I'm makin' lotsa brownie points. You know, takin' her to fancy places for dinner and movies when our schedules allow. For some crazy reason, I can't seem to stay away from her."

"God, that *is* scary. I've never known you to be with one girl for more than a night. Hell, who can stand your company for more than a few hours? Especially if she has a brain." He laughed and ducked as Cal reached over and tried to wallop him for the second time.

Unfortunately, time was short. It was hard to get in everything they wanted to talk about. They compared the two curriculums, discussing the differences in teaching methods by their respective professors. But most of all, they talked about old times.

"Where're ya headin' now?" Cal asked as Billy prepared to leave.

"Tempe."

"You stayin' with Jessie?"

"Don't know yet. She never answered my letters. I don't know what the hell I'm gonna find when I get there. If she throws me out, you'll see me with my tail hangin' between my legs. If that should truly happen, can I swing back and crash for the night?"

"You know you can stay anytime. You don't have to ask."

"Thanks. I guess I'd better take off. I'm not really looking forward to this."

"Good luck," said Cal, and went to clap his hand on Billy's shoulder yet again.

"Goddamn it! Quit putting your ham hock paws on me, you asshole! My arm will be good for shit. And who knows, if I get lucky with Jessie, I just might need that arm," Billy said as he mounted his bike and fastened his helmet.

"Pussy," Cal said, shaking his head.

"God, I hope so," Billy grinned and started the bike as Cal smartly saluted with his thumb to his nose. Billy returned the gesture, then pulled away from the curb and headed south.

It was early in the evening by the time Billy got to Tempe. He felt many emotions as he drove past the ASU campus. Though most of his time spent in Tempe had been good, there were also grim reminders of past mistakes and the consequences he now had to face.

His stomach churned as he entered the dark entranceway of Jessie's building. The stairs creaked with age and neglect as he made his way slowly to the second floor apartment. He took a deep breath, and rapped against the faded, chipped paint.

"Hey Jessie, Doctor Kildaire's here," Anita smirked.

Billy felt self-conscious standing in the doorway with the girls staring at him. Anita finally said, "I guess I'll disappear for a while. I'm sure you two have *lots* of catching up to do," she winked. "See ya later."

Jessie stood with her arms crossed against her chest, eyeing Billy with a mix of uncertainty, hostility, and suspicion. "You gonna just stand there lookin' at me or are you gonna get your ass in here so I can shut the door?"

Billy flinched and entered the apartment.

"You hungry?"

"Yeah, I could eat," Billy replied after a moment's thought.

"There's stuff in the fridge. You can make a sandwich if you want," she said. Walking ahead of him down the dingy, gray hallway, Billy noticed a definite sashay to Jessie's backside.

When she got to the kitchen, Jessie placed half a loaf of stale bread on the counter along with some bologna and cheese. "Help yourself. Want a beer?" she asked, as she opened a bottle and took a small sip, running her tongue along the rim of the bottle suggestively.

"No, thanks."

"Still dry, huh?" As she leaned back against the counter, the move drew the thin fabric of her sweater tight across her heavy breasts. Billy tried not to stare. He focused instead on the bread, concentrating on trying to find two slices that weren't speckled with mold. He quickly made a sandwich, then went outside and gingerly sat down on the top step of the fire escape. Jessie joined him. When he finished his sandwich, he pulled out his cigarettes and lit one.

Jessie held out her hand and he passed the pack and matches to her. "How's school?" she asked, exhaling a stream of smoke.

"It's tough but okay."

She flicked at his ponytail with her index finger. "What the hell happened to your hair? Those white people you live with scalp you?"

"Got it cut," he said. "Did you get my letters? I never heard from you."

"I got them. But shit," she snorted, "I'm not *into* that. What would I have written? Did you want me to tell you I *missed* you?"

"The thought crossed my mind." He paused, then asked, "Did you?"

She was silent for a little while, smoking. "I don't know. Maybe," she finally answered, her hand shielding her eyes from the setting sun. "How long're you staying?"

"I just got here. You want to get rid of me already?"

"Just wondered."

"Only two days, I have to be back at school by the 2nd."

He took a sidelong look at his wife. Jessie was just as beautiful as he remembered. He wanted to take her in his arms and kiss her but was afraid. He lit another cigarette instead and watched the smoke curl up and away from him. There were so many things he wanted to say but didn't know how to say them.

After a while, Billy had had enough of the hard wooden stair. He stood up, flicked his cigarette butt over the railing, and stretched. "Mind if I take a shower?"

"Go ahead. You know where the bathroom is."

She followed him in and watched him retreat down the hall. She wandered over to the kitchen counter. After sitting out so long, the bologna was beginning to curl, and the cheese was sweaty. Jessie carelessly tossed both back into the refrigerator.

Billy got his backpack and went into the bathroom. The hot water felt good on his tired, aching muscles. With his eyes closed and his head being pelted by the water, he never heard her until she was beside him under the spray.

Reaching out blindly, he pulled her against his wet, soapy body. His mouth found hers and he kissed her hard. At first, she fought his kisses, turning her head to the side. He backed away, holding her at arm's length. "I'm not going to hurt you, Jessie," he said. "You have to trust me."

He waited for her to make the next move. She stared at him a long time through water-clogged lashes. At last, she moved back against him. He touched her face, caressing her lips with his thumb. He pulled her close and kissed her lightly. He didn't want to scare her. Soon however, she was asking for more. Closing his eyes, he gave her what she wanted.

For Billy, it was like a dam breaking. They made love in the bathroom, on the floor in the hall and finally in bed. All the desires and feelings he had kept tightly under wraps the past seven months came flooding back full force.

"What're you gonna do while you're here?" Jessie asked, leaning back against his chest.

"I want to go and see Dr. Benson tomorrow. And I need to get presents for the Wilson girls. I promised we'd celebrate Christmas when I got back. I wish I could afford gifts for all of them. Maybe I'll be able to pick up something small for Rusty and Marian at the craft center in Phoenix. But other than that, I have no plans."

"What about me? You bring me anything?"

"You want more than what I just gave you?"

"Of course," she said, elbowing him in the ribs. "Don't I always?"

He pushed her aside and hurriedly retrieved his overturned backpack and clothes from the bathroom floor, hoping Anita wouldn't return and catch him naked in the hall. Handing her a wrapped package, he crawled back into bed. Jessie tore off the paper and pulled out a powder blue Georgetown Medicine sweatshirt.

"I figured if you wouldn't see me or I didn't make it back, I could keep it," he grinned. "Good thing we're the same size," he said. "With one big exception of course," he smiled as he fondled her breast.

"Thanks," she said, starting to pull it over her head.

"Wait," he whispered into her ear. "Don't put it on yet." He ran his finger down the inside of her arm, causing her to shiver. "You look too good the way you are now," he said, kissing her shoulder.

"What was that other thing you said you brought me?" she asked innocently, while groping under the covers.

"Never satisfied, are you," he smiled wryly. Rolling her onto her back, he slowly ran his tongue across her breasts and down her belly.

"Never," she replied, twisting her fingers tightly into his hair and arching up against his roving mouth.

Much later, as the shadows deepened on the bedroom wall, Jessie said, "I didn't get you anything."

"I didn't think you would."

"Why?"

"Because you're not *into* that sort of thing. Are you?" he mocked her, smiling.

"What d'ya want?"

"Do you need to ask?"

She got up and went to her dresser, pulling out a small plastic bag and some papers. She rolled a joint, lit it and slowly inhaled, returning with it to the bed.

"You know what you *could* do for me?" he asked, taking the joint she handed him.

"What?"

He held the marijuana a long time, considering it, watching the smoke drift up into the air around him. The acrid smell jarred memories and for a very brief moment he recalled how good it felt to be high and was tempted. He gave himself a mental shake and the moment passed. "Don't do drugs while I'm here," he said, putting the cigarette out in the ash tray on the nightstand.

"What the hell!"

"Come on, Jess, just one day. Please," he begged.

"What if I say no," she pouted.

Billy got up and started shoving things into his backpack. He found his underwear and pants and began to get dressed.

"What are you doing?"

"Leaving."

"You're walking out because of a joint?"

"Yes."

"Why?"

"Because I can't deal with you on drugs."

"You did them too, remember?"

"I know." It seemed as though time stood still as he stared at her. "So, what'll it be Jess, me or the grass?"

She appraised him slowly from head to toe, then sighed. "You, I guess. Don't leave." Reaching out her hand, she pulled him back to the bed. "When did you say you were leaving?"

The luminescent hands on his wristwatch read 3:00 a.m. Time to hit the road. Jessie lay curled away from him, innocent in sleep. Wondering if he should waken her, he quietly slipped out of bed and dressed in the dark.

He slung his backpack over his shoulder and glanced at her one last time. He couldn't tell whether she was really asleep. He thought about kissing her but changed his mind and walked out of the apartment without saying goodbye.

Like a trusty steed, the Harley ate up the long, tedious miles without a complaint. The rumble of the engine as well as the hypnotic passing of white dotted lines, lulled Billy. His mind wandered and he replayed his stay in Tempe.

He thought about his visit with his old professor. At first glance, he would never have thought Dr. Benson and Marian Wilson were related, let alone brother and sister. But after a while, he realized how similar their personalities were.

Benson pumped him for information about school and how everything was going. He seemed to know just how to draw Billy into conversation. Joe understood Billy's frustration in dealing with a different culture and a different way of life. Even for himself, Georgetown would have taken some getting used to again. Although he had grown up there, it was the complete opposite of what was familiar. Benson had uprooted himself and moved out west because there was a lot less pressure. And with his personality, extra pressure was something he tried to avoid.

Except for the time he was with Benson, the remainder of Billy's short stay was spent with Jessie. But it was very unsettling. He felt like he was trying to make something from nothing. The only thing they had in common was sex. Hell, Billy thought, that's not enough.

He had seen couples together, from his grandparents and Cal's parents to the Bensons and Wilsons. There had to be something more. Rusty and Marian talked and had discussions about important things. Content in each other's company, they were also good friends.

Unfortunately, he and Jessie couldn't carry on a decent conversation. She had nothing important to say and didn't think about anything except fooling around and drugs. It was sad and depressing. Desperately trying to make their pretense of a marriage work, Billy kept coming up empty. What did that leave him? Nothing.

Thinking of Jessie got him down, and he turned his thoughts to what lay ahead. At least this time, he knew what he would find at the end of the trail. Before he left for Arizona, he promised the Wilson girls that when he returned, they would celebrate Christmas.

The postponed holiday was a success. At the craft center in Phoenix, Billy managed to purchase two inexpensive sterling silver pins for the girls—a horse for Barbara and a road runner for Jenny. Unfortunately, he couldn't find anything for Rusty and Marian. The appropriate or nice items were too expensive. He didn't want to give them just anything, so he bagged the whole idea. He was sure they'd understand.

The girls were delighted with the pins. Using their pocket money, they bought Billy a pen with a light on the end. For when he studied late at night, they explained.

Billy's second semester was filled with more conferences and studies of case histories, which didn't leave much time to dwell on Jessie. Instead, he had one lecture after another and spent a lot of time in the library.

When John was overheard complaining about their schedule, a third-year student laughed and said, "Just wait. This is nothing. Next year will be a real drag. Have fun while you can."

"Fun? This is fun?" John asked.

"Yeah," replied the older student. "Next fall, the crap will hit the fan for you guys, if you can last that long."

John turned to Billy. "Maybe we should just move into this library. What do you think?"

"We're already here too long. As crazy as home can get, I think I prefer it to this place." Billy checked his watch and began to gather his papers. "And right now, we're about to be tossed out. Let's get going."

With such a hectic schedule, time sped along. Billy was past the midway point in his second semester and final examinations were fast approaching.

RUSTY

usty was tired. It had been a long night at the hospital. A three-car collision had kept him, and the other doctors who were on duty, occupied for the next eight hours. Then, after only a few hours of sleep, he had gone into the office for a little while.

When Rusty returned home, he talked Billy into going with him to the club for some tennis. He thought a few games would revive him.

"I've been meaning to ask if your plans for the summer are definite?" Rusty questioned as they changed into gym clothes.

"Yes, I promised a friend of *Abuelo's* that I'd work some horses for him. Why?"

"We were hoping you might change your mind and stay for the summer. I had a job myself to offer you."

"What? Head babysitter?"

"Not exactly," Rusty smiled, closing his locker door and picking up his racquet. "Though I'm sure the girls would approve. My nurse is taking a leave of absence and I was going to ask if you would fill in for her. It would be good experience, you'd be helping me out, *and* making money."

"Gee Rusty, thanks for asking," Billy said as they walked onto the court. "But I already told Jake I'd work for him. Besides, I can't pass up making that kind of money. If I don't get the scholarship, I'll need every last penny."

The two men warmed up, then Billy served. His game had improved so much that he could put a nasty top spin on the ball that was almost impossible to return.

"Son of a bitch!" Rusty swore. "How was I supposed to return that?"

"Move it. You act like you got lead in your legs."

"My ass."

"Okay, your ass too!" Billy grunted, as he served again then ran into position.

Rusty missed that shot, and a few easy lobs later, Billy won the first game.

"Why the hell couldn't you learn to play golf like all the rest of the doctors in the world?" Rusty asked, wiping sweat from his face.

"Golf," Billy retorted, "is the most boring game in the world."

"Boring!" Rusty shook his head. "Your hopeless."

"Do you want to play another, or have you had enough humiliation?" Billy asked.

"I'm done!"

As Billy walked around the net, picking up balls on his way, Rusty asked, "When will you hear if you get the scholarship?"

"Probably not until the term ends and my grades are forwarded to the Army. Between now and then, I'll have my finals."

"You've worked very hard and you're doing very well. I'm sure you'll ace your tests."

"I hope so."

"Has the Army said anything about taking those qualifying tests?"

"Actually, I've already taken a few, and next week, I have a complete physical scheduled. After that, I'll only have to do the vision test and another written test," he said, as he held the door to the locker room open for Rusty.

"By the way," Rusty commented, "I noticed the other day, you had circled several apartments for rent in the real estate section of the Post. Have you checked into any of them?"

"Not yet."

"Good. Marian and I were talking and agreed that we don't want you to leave."

"No way, Rusty, I can't do that."

"Why? Don't you like living with us?"

"Of course, I do, but I've already stayed here long enough. If I get the scholarship, with that and the money I'll make over the summer, I should be okay."

"And what if you don't get the scholarship?"

"Then," he shrugged, "I don't know what I'll do."

"Come on, kid. If you stay here, your problems are solved. You already got that grant money and if you get the scholarship, you can devote all your thoughts to school and not have to worry about every last penny."

"I refuse to keep sponging off of you and your family."

"Get it through your thick head, you're not sponging. You're giving us money, helping around the house, and babysitting whenever we need you. Hell, we should be paying you."

Billy looked at Rusty a long time. "I might consider it only if you take more money from me as rent, and I contribute toward groceries."

"I don't want or need your money."

"Then I won't stay," Billy said stubbornly, his arms crossed tightly against his chest.

Rusty glared at him. "All right, you win. God you're a pain in the ass."

Billy grinned. "I am, aren't I?"

Billy couldn't believe his first year was over.

"Do you have to leave?" asked Jennifer as he packed. "I'm going to miss you."

"Don't worry, I'll be back. Wow, I can't believe all the stuff I've accumulated this year," he said, stuffing some socks into a saddlebag. "Thank God I don't have to worry about taking everything with me."

Marian walked into the room with a laundry basket. "Besides the clothes in here, I just finished ironing some of your dress shirts. Do you need any of them? They're still downstairs."

"Marian, if I needed any of those, it would be a real miracle. I think I got everything I'll need," he said, smiling at her.

"How many days will it take you to get there?"

"Probably three and a half to four, depending on how fast and far I drive each day. I made it in less than four at Christmas. I'm hoping I can do it again. It saves me a night's stay."

"I hate to see you making such a long trip on that motorcycle. It's so dangerous."

"I'll be okay."

"I wish there was a way you could phone us when you get home to let us know you arrived in one piece."

"I could call you from the Colorado border, but I'll still have an hour or so to go from there."

"I guess I'll just have to wait to get a letter."

"If that is a hint, I got it."

"Smart boy."

"Don't worry Marian. I'll stay in one piece. I promise."

CAL

Billy lay on his back in the dust and coughed. "I'm getting too old for this shit."

"Are you sure you can break him without killin' yourself?" Cal looked at his friend and shifted his butt on the split rail fence. "That's the umpteenth time today you've been thrown."

Billy rose slowly and smacked at the dirt and dried manure on his backside. He spit in disgust. "He's one hell of a horse, but he's tougher than any I've ever worked. He'll be worth bucks if I can break him, and Jake's counting on me."

"In the meantime, you're gonna break your neck."

The stallion circled the enclosure on stiff legs, tossing his head and flaring large, red nostrils. Bucephalus in the flesh, his muscles rippled under a shiny black coat now flecked with sweat.

The two-year-old quickly stopped in front of Billy, then screamed and reared, pawing the air with deadly legs. Cal felt the small hairs on the back of his neck rise. If it would have been him, he would have gone running and never got near that brute again.

But not Billy—he stood his ground and eyed the horse thoughtfully, his hands resting on his hips. When Roughneck laid his ears back, he was as ugly as a mule and just as stubborn. "He's too keyed up to do anything more today," Billy said as he slowly climbed the fence and sat next to Cal. "But I'll break that son-of-a-bitch eventually, even if it *does* kill me."

"You're crazy," Cal said, offering Billy a cigarette. "You couldn't pay me enough to get near that devil, let alone ride him."

Billy pulled the bandana from around his head and wiped the sweat from his eyes. He lit the cigarette. As he exhaled, he laughed. "Hell, you won't get anywhere near anything that doesn't have breasts, hips and a nice ass."

"Now *that* kind of filly I don't mind ridin'," Cal said, lighting a cigarette for himself.

Billy shook his head and laughed. "Bareback of course."

"Damn right. It's the only way to ride."

"In this crew's case, Jake is expecting me to not only get saddles on them, but to train them for trail riding as well."

"Are the rest as bad as the stallion?"

"The mares, so far, have actually been pretty easy. I spent a couple of days talking to them and walking around. They're so damn funny. Got to the point where they were following me around like dogs. Couldn't get away from them."

"Is that what you wanted?"

"Sure, they were practically begging me to ride them. Shit, once I got on one, the others wouldn't leave me alone until I had ridden them all."

"Do you think if I brought Maggie out here, you could train her, too?" Cal laughed.

"What do you mean?"

"Set a fire under her ass and get her into my bed. I'll pay you big bucks to do it."

"Sounds like you got it bad, buddy."

"Christ Almighty, bad isn't the word. This has been the longest self-imposed drought I've ever had. Maggie's really draggin' her feet. I'm as horny as a toad and Mary Palm and her five sisters are seein' way too much action."

Billy laughed and shook his head. "I have a feeling Mary and her sibs are going to be busy for quite some time. From what you tell me, I think your chick would be tougher than this stud. And he's bein' a real bastard."

"Dang it, I was afraid you were goin' to say that."

"Of course," Billy said, "on the other side of the coin, there's Jessie. Now how the hell do I get *her* to stop?"

"Stop?"

"Yeah, when I was home at Christmas which, mind you, was only for two days, she acted like she couldn't wait for me to get the hell out. Kept asking when I was going to leave. Every time we were in bed together, I felt like the meter was running. At any minute my time would be up, and I'd be replaced by someone else."

"Have you seen her at all this summer?"

"No, I haven't had the time and don't feel like driving all that way to be disappointed. Christmas was bad enough." He wiped again at the sweat in his eyes, leaving his face streaked with dirt. "What's so depressing is that when we aren't screwing, we have nothing to say to one another."

"I find that to be true with most of the women I've laid."

"But you aren't married to any of those sluts."

"Also true."

"Do you talk to Maggie?"

"Oh yeah, we've had some very *meaningful* conversations. Which, unfortunately, is all we ever do."

Billy leaned forward on the fence rail and looked over at Cal. "But talking… that's normal, isn't it? I mean, I'm not much of a talker, but hell, Jessie doesn't say anything at all. I ask her a question and she shrugs. I start a conversation; she yawns or says she's not into something and walks away. Is there something wrong with me, or is it Jessie?"

"There isn't a thing wrong with you, Fox. You just happened to hook up with one cold bitch who's missing a shit load of brain cells. Why don't you ditch her? You know, get a divorce."

"That takes money—money I don't have. Besides, I feel bad for her. She's had it rough and needs my help."

"Help? You still think you're gonna save her?"

Billy hung his head. "Yes," he said quietly.

"Fat chance. You can't save someone like Jessie. She's a lost cause."

"But I gave her my word. I said I'd be there for her."

"Your word. Shit. Take it back."

"Just like that?"

"Sure, I would."

"You do a lot of things that I wouldn't do."

"Well, I can tell you one thing. I sure as hell wouldn't let my spunk go dormant because of a whore like her."

"Is sex all you ever think about?"

"What else is there?" Cal said with a wolfish grin.

Billy gave him a disgusted look. "You know, you really *are* a dickhead." He threw his leg over the rail and jumped off the fence. "Come on, let's get something to drink. I've been out in the sun too long," he said, grinding out his cigarette with his boot. "I'm as ornery as Roughneck."

After being home for only one week, Billy felt as though he had never left. The many constraints of Georgetown were gone, leaving him relaxed and at ease with his family. Secretly, Billy had been worried that he would again feel like a stranger in his home.

It seemed as though he wasn't the only one who was worried. When he first arrived, his grandparents appeared to be holding their breath as if they were afraid he would be greatly changed.

All their fears were groundless. His new job had him up and out of the house before dawn. He was gone all day and came home mentally and physically exhausted. Many evenings, all he could manage to do was eat his dinner, nod his thanks to his grandmother, and fall into bed.

When he did have some free time, however, his help was appreciated out in the garden digging and cultivating the earth where his grandmother grew her herbs and plants. Just as when Billy was a child, he enjoyed the time spent at his grandmother's side. But this time, he found himself listening more attentively.

Abuela was a constant source of information. Her words of wisdom and her gently given advice made Billy feel as though he were back in the classroom in the presence of a truly gifted professor.

Billy had his grandmother re-explain what she was doing, the herbs and plants she used, and the many treatments and remedies that, in the past, Billy had taken for granted. His admiration and respect for her grew steadily, especially now that he had some medical schooling behind him.

At Georgetown, he was learning new methods and a scientific approach toward medicine. He shared these ideas with his grandmother and was slightly surprised that she didn't laugh or shrug off some of the more novel theories.

"William," she would say patiently, "ideas are like shoots on a tree. They are constantly sprouting. Just because something is new, doesn't mean it's bad. What you are learning right now may be something that *I* might find useful. Just like what I know may be useful to *you* despite what you have learned. The old and the new need to work together."

Abuela's advice had always been so on the mark that Billy made a mental note to never disregard the old ways and the holistic methods of healing just because of some new technological advance. He had to keep reminding himself of who he was and where his path was leading. This road he had chosen to take was proving to be very long and very arduous. He just hoped that he had the determination and stamina to continue his journey.

ANITA

J essie snapped her suitcase shut with a click.

"How long'll you be gone?" Anita asked, leaning against the doorjamb.

"He didn't say."

"You going to Vegas again?"

"Uh huh, he wants to hit it big this time. He says I bring him luck."

"How can you stand him touching you? He's old, fat, and ugly. I wouldn't want him touching me."

"Shit. I'll screw him blind as long as he pays me. I don't care what the hell he's like."

"I don't know, Jessie. This guy looks scary to me. I know he has money and all the drugs you could want, but still…"

"Don't be a sap. As long as I'm putting' out and stayin' outa his way, he won't hurt me. I'm not stupid. I take what he gives me and don't ask questions."

"It's your life," Anita shrugged and returned to her room. She had tried to warn her friend, but Jessie's mind was set. Since before Christmas, Jessie had been selling it to this so-called businessman. Anita didn't like when he showed up at the apartment. He appraised her as if she was for sale. She might turn a trick or two with some college kid for drugs, but this guy was in a different league. She was afraid Jessie was going to get hurt or worse.

The knock on the door took her by surprise. Leaving the chain in place, Anita peered out into the hall. It was Billy. What in the hell was *he* doing here? And what was she going to tell him? She removed the chain and opened the door slightly. "Fox."

"Hi, Anita, how's it going?"

Anita stood like a statue at the door. "What do you want?"

"I'm here to see Jessie."

"She's not here."

"That's okay, I'll wait," he said and made a move to enter the apartment.

Anita squirmed and barred the door with her body. "Why should I let you in?"

Billy frowned. "I have nowhere else to go. I just arrived from New Mexico, my ass is sore, and I'm tired."

"So go find a hotel."

"What the hell for?" Billy replied heatedly. "I'm paying for this apartment, and I plan on staying here while I'm in town. Now let me in. What the hell's wrong with you? You got some guy in there?"

Anita stared at him for a long moment before finally stepping aside.

"Where's Jessie?" Billy asked, as he walked past her into the apartment. "Is she at work?"

"She's…away."

"Away? Where?"

"I don't know."

"I take it she's not alone."

"You can take it any way you want."

"Who's she with now?"

"I don't know, and I don't care. If you want to know, ask her when she comes back."

"I will. When's she coming back?"

"I don't know. She didn't say."

"You don't know too much, do you Anita?"

"What Jessie does is up to her and none of my business. I'm not her mother. If she wants to go to Vegas with some sleaze ball that's her business."

"Vegas? With some sleaze ball?"

"Yeah, that's all I know. Now why don't you beat it. She could be gone for weeks. She was gone for almost a month last time."

"Last time?" Billy asked.

"Yeah, last time," she said, crossing her arms. "You know, you kill me. Did you really think she was pining away for you all this time? You're away doing your own thing in DC. You don't give a shit about her, why should she give a shit about you?"

"Is that what you think?"

"Yeah."

"How long's she been with this guy?"

"Since before Christmas, if you really care," Anita smirked. She leaned toward him. "You know what you remind me of Fox, a big ole tom cat. Always sniffing around when you're hot and bothered and in the neighborhood. Tell you what, for twenty bucks, I'll jerk you off, so you don't have to do it yourself. I could use the money."

Billy walked around Anita to the door. "The next time you see Jessie, tell her I was here. You can also tell her that, from now on, she's completely on her own. She isn't getting another fucking penny from me. That means you, too. Do you understand?" He slammed the door and was gone.

Oh shit, thought Anita, Jessie was going to be pissed now. She depended on the rent money Billy sent directly to the landlord every other month. Actually, Billy was right. Anita depended on that money, too. What was she going to tell Jessie when she came home? Maybe she should've lied to Billy—thought up some crazy song and dance. But what would she have told him?

Jessie had never seemed too worried about the rent. In fact, she had quit her job several months ago. She always took it for granted that Billy would come through with the money even when she was off gallivanting. Anita knew that she herself couldn't produce the rent every month on her own. If Jessie or her new friend couldn't come up with the cash, she would have to start looking for another apartment or a new roommate.

BILLY

Billy walked down the street in a daze. He couldn't believe Jessie was gone, yet it didn't surprise him. Hell, she screwed around when he lived with her for God's sake. Why would she stop when he wasn't there? Now he also understood why she had been eager to get rid of him during the holidays.

It infuriated him that he had been paying her rent, and she hadn't even been there. Instead, she was using her ass to latch onto another sucker.

His aimless wandering took him past one of his old haunts. The familiar lights and sounds of the Tempe Tavern beckoned to him. He stood on the sidewalk for a long time. Finally, he went in and sat down at the bar. He ordered a shot of whiskey, then another.

The alcohol went down easily, searing his throat with its heat. All this way, he thought. He should have called first, should have known better. He ordered another drink and chugged it, getting madder with every minute. He was not a tom cat, damn it, he thought, slamming the shot glass down onto the bar. She was his wife for Christ's sake! Why shouldn't he see her? He ordered another drink, letting the alcohol take over.

By the time the bar closed, he was completely numb and couldn't remember where he had left his motorcycle. He thought it was back at the apartment but wasn't sure.

Somehow, he got to Joe Benson's house, stumbled up to the front door, and leaned against the bell. After a moment, lights winked on in the house. Billy looked with half-closed eyes as the door partially opened.

"Billy!" Benson exclaimed. "What are you doing here?"

Billy mumbled and slid slowly down the adobe wall of the house. He violently threw up in the bushes near the door, then passed out.

"What the hell?" Benson said. He grabbed Billy under the arms and pulled him into the house. God, he smells like a distillery, Joe thought. I wonder what's happened now. He rolled Billy onto the couch, yanked off his boots and went to find a blanket.

"What is it?" his wife asked groggily.

"It's nothing, honey, go back to sleep. I'll tell you in the morning." Joe threw a light cotton blanket over Billy and got another for himself. He didn't want to leave Billy alone and wanted to be around when he awoke. Joe hoped he wouldn't be sick again. Settling into his recliner, he wrapped himself in the blanket and put up his feet. It was going to be a long night.

When Billy finally woke up the next day, he had no idea how he had gotten to Benson's. All he remembered was that Jessie was gone, and he had tried to drown himself in alcohol.

"What do you mean, gone?" Joe asked, pouring both himself and Billy another cup of coffee.

"Gone to Vegas with some guy."

Billy blinked in the morning sunlight and groaned. His head felt as though it would split. He closed his eyes and laid his head down on his crossed arms.

Joe got up and rooted through a cupboard for some aspirin. He returned to the table and handed Billy two pills. "Take these."

Benson looked at Billy thoughtfully. He resembled a ghost. At Christmas, he had been so excited about med school and his new life. Joe couldn't believe the same kid was sitting in front of him. He thought, oh God, please not again.

"How did you get here?"

"Here?"

"Arizona."

"Oh, I drove."

"Where's your motorcycle?"

"I think it's parked in front of Jessie's apartment."

"Are you okay to drive?"

"I guess. Why?"

"Come on. We're going to go and get it. Hopefully, it'll still be there."

They got into Benson's car and drove across town. Joe had no idea how Billy had gotten to his home in the condition he had been in the night before. It was a miracle he hadn't gotten himself killed.

The bike was still in front of the rooming house. Billy slowly climbed on, then glanced up at Jessie's window. It was dark and empty.

When they got back to Benson's, Billy couldn't decide whether to hang around Tempe for a couple of days and wait for Jessie or go back home.

"What good will seeing her do?" Joe asked.

"I don't know. The thing is, if I do see her, what am I going to say to her. Frankly, I'm afraid of what I might do. I don't know if I can trust myself anymore. After what I did last night, God knows."

"Just because you tied one on, doesn't mean you're going to go on the warpath with her if you see her. You figured she was running around anyway."

"But damn it! She's a whore. Why the hell did I get messed up with her in the first place? I was so fuckin' stupid."

"Come on, Billy. Don't be so hard on yourself. Everyone makes mistakes."

"What am I going to do?"

"You'll figure something out. Maybe the best thing is to do nothing. Stay married but don't give her any money."

"I already told Anita I wasn't going to pay the rent anymore."

"Good, see how she likes that."

"Cal says I should get a divorce."

"Spoken like a true attorney's son. Look Billy, hiring a lawyer takes money and time. Two things you don't have. Maybe when you're out of school and making money, you can give it more thought. But for now…let it go."

"And in the meantime, live like a damn priest."

"I never said that. Jessie isn't living like a nun, is she?"

"No, but just because she whores around, doesn't make it right."

Benson sighed and shook his head. "We could go around and around on this. There are no easy answers. You're going to have to do what your gut tells you. And if that's to live like a priest until you can afford a divorce, then that's what you're going to have to do."

Billy rubbed his forehead with the palm of his hand. "It's all a bunch of shit, isn't it?"

"Yes, it is. But life *can* be shit sometimes. Jessie aside, how is everything else going?"

"I found out last week I got the scholarship," Billy said. "That's one of the reasons I came to Arizona. I couldn't wait to tell you."

"Hey! That's great! I had no doubt you'd get it. And see, not everything is shit!"

"I was so excited. Now, my head throbs so bad I just want to puke again."

"Don't worry. Those aspirin should kick in soon," Benson commented. "So how will the scholarship work?"

"They're going to pay the next three year's tuition and give me a stipend for books and stuff."

"That's terrific. I hear you also got that grant we applied for."

"Yes, that's going to be a big plus. It's one that doesn't have to be paid back. You and Dr. Sanchez were so great to help me with all those applications. I would never have known what to do on my own. Thanks again. I owe you both so much."

"You're welcome. I also heard through the Georgetown grapevine that Rusty and Marian put the pressure on you to move in with them indefinitely."

"Yeah, that was even better than the money. Again, I can't thank you enough for that. I'd never have been able to go to school if they wouldn't have offered me a place to stay."

"I'm glad it worked out for you."

"Since I'm not going to pay Jessie's rent anymore, maybe I'll be able to save some money again. I'll also be able to give the Wilsons more for my room and board. I give them so little right now."

"Listen, they don't expect that or need it."

"I know. But I don't want to be a freeloader. This job I have now is going to be a big bonus, too."

"How's that coming along?"

"Okay, except for the stallion. He's giving me a hard time."

"I always wanted a horse. I'd give anything to do what you're doing or at least watch."

"It's not very glamorous or exciting. I spend most of my day spitting horse shit out of my mouth."

Benson laughed. "Now that, I'd really like to see."

"Cal Lewis is coming up for another visit after the fourth of July. Why don't you come with him? He'd probably like the company. If you don't mind sleeping in the barn, you're welcome to watch as much as you want."

"Boy, that sounds really tempting. I'd love it."

"Think about it. I'll give you Cal's number before I leave, and I'll also tell him you might be joining him."

Billy left the next day. As he passed the apartment, he didn't see anything to indicate that Jessie had returned. If she wanted to play games, he could play games, too. *Just try to find me when you need money for the rent or anything else. I can disappear as well,* he thought.

RUSTY

For the past several weeks Marian had been on Rusty's back. She and the girls had been clamoring for a family vacation.

"You work too hard. You have a practice, you work at the hospital, and you teach a class. What are you trying to do? We haven't gone on a vacation together for years. It's about time you took a break. Let's go somewhere quiet where we can relax."

"Where do you have in mind?"

"What do you think about Arizona?" asked Marian. "Joe's off for the summer, and he's been asking us to come out for a long time. We could go for the holiday and stay for a couple of weeks."

"I don't know, Marian. I'm not sure I could get away for that amount of time."

"How about two weeks? I'll call Joe. You know Ken will fill in for you at the office. All you need to do is talk to the people at the hospital. Everyone else goes on vacation. Why can't you?"

Joe was waiting at the airport. As they walked to his car, Barbara asked, "Who turned on the oven?"

"Kiddo, you ain't seen nothing yet! It's only ninety degrees right now. It'll get hotter today. Maybe one hundred or so!"

"One hundred! We'll melt!"

"I don't think so," Joe laughed, as he and Rusty loaded the suitcases into the trunk of his car. "Don't worry, it'll be cooler at home."

Joe had a stucco ranch house that his wife Dorothy had surrounded with heather, poppies, palm trees and cacti. The family room at the back of the house opened up into a large flagstone patio that surrounded an in-ground swimming pool. A large round dining table with an umbrella and several lounge chairs were scattered around the deck.

The Wilsons were sunning themselves by the pool when Cal called. With all the recent events that had transpired, Joe had completely forgotten about his earlier conversation with Billy.

"Hey Doc, Billy told me to give you a call. I hear you want to go and watch him break his neck. I'll be leavin' in a couple of days and thought I'd see if you still wanted to come with me."

"Darn. I forgot all about it. My family from DC is here visiting. I don't think I'll be able to get away now. I'm really sorry. I would have loved to come with you. When did you say you were going again?"

"I was thinkin' of leavin' after the holiday. I wanted to get up there for Fox's birthday on the 7th."

"I didn't know it was Billy's birthday."

"He doesn't talk about it much so I'm not sure that he even celebrates it. But anyway, if you change your mind about goin', call me."

"Thanks, I will."

Jenny had run in to get a glass of water and was now standing by the sink. "Did I hear you talking about Billy, Uncle Joe?"

"Yes, you did, Nosy," he said, ruffling her hair. "I was talking to a friend of his."

"I thought we'd see Billy while we were here. Doesn't he live in the same town as you?"

"When he went to school, he did. He was just here visiting a week or so ago but had to get back to his grandparents' home and his job. I was supposed to go and see him next week. Since you all are here now, I had to change my plans."

"Couldn't we all go?"

"I don't know," he hesitated.

"Oh please, let's ask Daddy. Daddy!" she called and ran back out to the pool. "Can we go and see Billy? Uncle Joe was going to visit him but can't because we're here."

"What's all this?" Rusty said, as Jennifer dashed over to him and onto his lap.

"Say we can visit Billy. Please! I'd love to see his horses. Uncle Joe, didn't you say something about it being Billy's birthday? We could go for his birthday."

Barbara looked up from her book. "Did you say we were going to see Billy? Goody! I'll get to see some horses. When are we going?"

"Hold on!" Rusty yelled. "What is going on? What are you all talking about?"

"Jenny overheard me talking to a friend of Billy's," Joe explained as he took a seat on a chaise lounge next to Rusty. "The two of us were supposed to visit

Billy next week. But when you made plans to visit, I completely forgot about going and told Cal I couldn't make it. End of story."

"We could all go," Jenny pleaded.

"Now hold on, Jenny. You can't go arranging people's lives. It's bad enough we're putting your Uncle Joe and Aunt Dorothy through the wringer. We can't just pile into the car and drive to God knows where to see Billy."

"Why not?"

"For one thing, we weren't invited. For another, we don't know anything about his family and his home. We can't just burst in on him."

"We'd get to see a reservation and some real Indians."

"Billy *is* a real Indian, Jennifer," said Marian, putting down her magazine. "Do you think Billy would mind, Joe, if we all went?"

"I don't think so. He invited me. I'm sure you'd be welcome. But it's a long drive. It's up to you."

"What do you think, Rusty? It would be an experience for all of us. Plus, it might help us better understand Billy if we knew where he came from."

"I guess you're right."

"Hooray! We can go. Oh, thank you!" Jenny ran from adult to adult hugging each one of them. "I can't wait!"

They made arrangements with Cal, deciding what day they would leave. "We'll just have to show up," said Cal, when Rusty asked him how he was going to let Billy know they were coming en masse. "He doesn't have a phone out there, and we'll arrive before he could get another letter. When I last wrote to him, I told him I'd be there on the 7th—that's Billy's birthday. But I didn't mention that in the letter."

"Why not?" asked Rusty.

"Billy never talks about it. I only found out by accident. He once said his birthday was just another day and no reason to celebrate. Maybe it's an Indian thing."

Leaving Dorothy at home, Joe and the Wilsons piled into the Benson's station wagon before dawn and headed to Flagstaff. There, they picked up Cal and continued on their way.

"Unfortunately," said Joe, "the biggest tourist attraction our state has to offer isn't anywhere near where we are going."

"What's that?" asked Jenny.

"The Grand Canyon."

"What's that?"

Cal laughed. "It's kind of a fancy hole in the ground."

"Well, I'd rather see Billy than a hole in the ground."

"Me too," Barbara chimed in.

"Talk about a gross misrepresentation," Marian remarked. "Girls, the Grand Canyon is a very beautiful, magnificent place."

"We don't care."

"I thought that we could stop for lunch and see some of the Painted Desert and part of the Petrified National Park instead," said Joe. "In fact, I actually prefer those to the canyon. They're not as touristy and are quite incredible and a beautiful sight to see as well. Then, we'll head to Gallup for the night."

"As in a horse moving fast?" asked Barbara.

"Always got horses on the brain, don't you?" her uncle commented.

Aside from wanting to know whether there was a gift shop at the Painted Desert, the girls were more interested in the part of the Navajo reservation that their route took them through. It was a sobering experience for all when they saw the poverty in which the Indians were living.

"Does Billy live in a house like this?" Barbara asked frowning, as they passed a run-down cabin.

"No, it's not that bad," said Cal, who was now driving. "Though it's not like anything you're used to. To you, I guess it'll probably be terrible."

"You mean, it's not like Georgetown or Uncle Joe's house?" Jenny asked.

"No, Jenny, but it's also not a cabin or trailer like we've seen or a traditional round hogan like others we've passed on the Navajo reservation. It's a small, one-story house. Inside, there's just one huge room with a wooden floor. A combined living area and kitchen are on one side and a partitioned sleeping area is on the other. In the center of the room is a wood stove for cookin' that also supplies them with heat. A large trestle table functions as both a place to eat and workspace for preparing food. Then around back is the outhouse."

"What's an outhouse?"

"It's a shack outside where you go to the bathroom."

"Outside?"

"That's right, honey," said Marian. "Some people don't have indoor plumbing. They have to go outside to go to the potty."

"That's terrible! Do you mean when we're visiting Billy, we have to go to the bathroom outside?"

"I'm afraid so," Marian replied.

"Yuck! I don't think I'm going to like that."

"Just remember, you were the one who wanted to come."

"Let's see," said Cal. "Behind the house is a tiny stream and a small area of piñon trees." Seeing the girls' puzzled faces, he added, "Piñon trees are a kind of pine tree."

"Oh, I thought he lived in the desert?" Jenny remarked.

"Where the Foxes live is in the lower part of the reservation and is kind of near the Santa Fe National Forest. So, there are still a few trees and lots of rocks."

"Where are the horses?" asked Barbara.

"The barn is to one side of the house next to the chicken coop. This is where they keep a couple of dairy cows and also have a few horses. Above the stalls, a hayloft runs the length of the barn. When I visited last month, this was where Billy and I slept."

"You slept in the barn? With the horses?" asked Barbara.

"Sure, it sounds worse than it was," Cal replied.

"I don't know if I'll like that either," said Jennifer, wrinkling her nose.

"Whether you do or not, don't say anything to Billy," Marian said. "You don't want to hurt his feelings, do you?"

"No, Mommy."

They stopped at a motel on the outskirts of Gallup for the night, then started out early the next morning. Before leaving, they purchased some gifts for Billy's grandparents and bought a cake and some candles. It was in the middle of the afternoon when they pulled into the Fox's yard. Everyone was quiet. Cal was right. It wasn't as bad as some of the homes they had passed earlier. But it was nothing like Georgetown. The look of shock was evident on the girls' faces.

"I can't believe Billy lives here," Jenny whispered and started to get out of the car. Cal stopped her.

"We have to wait here," he said, blowing the horn.

"Why?"

"It's a form of courtesy. I let Mrs. Running Fox know we're here by blowing the horn. It gives her a chance to be able to show us hospitality. If we just barged right up to the door, that would be considered bad manners. Our hostess might not be prepared for us and would be embarrassed. At least that's how Billy explained it to me."

"I wonder where he is?" Barbara asked.

"You'll find out soon enough," said Rusty. "Although I do hope we don't have to wait too long, I really need to stretch my legs."

Just then, the door of the house opened, and a small woman came outside and approached the car. She wore an old-fashioned blouse and a long, tiered, brightly colored skirt. Her dark hair was shot with silver and pulled back into a bun. An old pair of tennis shoes completed her outfit.

"*Hola, Tia,*" Cal called, emerging from the automobile. "I've brought you some company. This is the family Billy lives with in Washington. They've come to visit."

"Welcome," the woman said. "I'm sorry my grandson is not here to welcome you. But I am making tea for myself and my husband. Please come in and join us. You must be tired."

Cal gave Isabella a kiss on the cheek then, taking her hand in his, walked toward the house. The Wilsons and Joe trailed behind. The rough exterior of the hand-hewn logs gave the house a rustic look. As they got closer, they could see green gingham curtains in the windows and a rock garden in front of a wrap-around porch, that boasted several handmade rocking chairs. No, it wasn't Georgetown, but it was very homey.

About an hour later, they were all seated around the kitchen table when they heard the sounds of a motorcycle approaching.

"Here he comes!" yelled Jennifer, jumping up and down.

"Quiet, Jenny. Let's surprise him," said Barbara.

The engine was cut, and they heard yips and murmurings followed by the sounds of footsteps on the wooden stairs. When the door opened, everyone yelled, "Surprise! Happy Birthday!"

Billy stood in the doorway, stunned and confused. Jenny ran to him but stopped at the last moment. At his side was an animal that resembled a wolf. The animal stepped between Billy and Jenny, growling deep within its throat.

Jenny let out a small scream and the dog began to bark. Billy put his hand on the dog's head, saying something to it in another language, then led it outside.

When he returned, Jenny asked, "Was that a wolf?"

"That's Dog Too, she's only half wolf. She won't hurt you. She just wasn't expecting all of you. Of course," Billy smiled wanly, "neither was I."

Jenny stared at the man before her. There was nothing familiar about him. His skin was deeply tanned, and his clothes were dusty, old, and torn. He had a red bandana wrapped around his head Apache style and silver earrings in his ears. She stared at him for a moment, then ran to him, jumping into his arms. "Surprise!" she yelled at the top of her lungs.

Billy staggered under her weight. "I can't believe you're all here." He looked at each smiling face and shook his head in disbelief.

"You kind of scared me for a minute, Papa Fox. You're different from at home."

"Sorry kid, but this is the real me, and this is my home." He looked around and felt he was taking a step back in time. His eyes took in the unpolished wooden floor, his grandmother's colorful, hand-woven rag rugs, and the simply furnished dwelling. The oil burning lamps were primitive. The bench and old chrome kitchen chairs around the battered pine dining table and the wood burning stove were nothing like what they're used to, he thought, and was embarrassed. Embarrassed for his grandparents, who had worked so hard to provide what little they had. Embarrassed for himself that his new family should see the way in which they lived.

"I hope you don't mind the company," said Joe Benson. "When my house guests heard I planned on visiting you, they drove me crazy until I told them we could all come. Luckily, my wife opted to stay at home. As it is, we have a small army on your doorstep."

"No, this is great. It's uh…really good to see all of you. What a surprise."

"I've had a wonderful time getting to know your grandmother," Marian said. "You're very lucky, she's a special lady."

Billy still hadn't moved from the doorway. "I'm glad you and *Abuela* are getting along. You're right. She's very special." He looked solemnly at his grandmother who glanced at him shyly, then lowered her eyes.

"Cal told us it's your birthday," Marian added. "We brought you a cake to celebrate. So, how old are you today?"

Abruptly, Billy changed the subject. "If you guys don't mind, I'm going to get cleaned up. I smell like horseshii…a horse."

Putting Jenny down, he turned and walked out the door. The Wilsons, Joe and Cal exchanged looks. Billy's grandparents, however, sat calmly, not noticing anything odd about their grandson's behavior.

Rusty excused himself and followed Billy outside. He heard sounds of splashing coming from behind the house. Billy was kneeling by a small pump with his head and back under a stream of water, a ragged towel by his side.

"How's everything going?" Rusty asked, sitting down on a large rock by the pump. "Joe told us you got the scholarship. That's terrific! We're all very happy for you."

"Thanks," said Billy, drying his face and chest. "I didn't hear right away and got worried. But I guess that's the way the Army works."

"I'm sorry we barged in on you like this. I think we put you on the spot. Marian thought we all needed a vacation. Which is why we're here in the first place. Joe's been asking us to visit, and the girls really put on the pressure."

"It's okay. I can't hide where I live. I just wish I'd known you were coming. I would have tried to make things look…better."

"Billy, there's nothing wrong with your home."

"It's not Georgetown."

"No, it's not. Who wants it to be? It's a perfectly good home. Your grandfather told me how the two of you re-built this house and barn and made some of the furniture."

"Well…"

"Really, Billy, it's amazing and beautiful. I didn't realize you were so talented. A lot of hard work and love went into this house and barn. You should be very proud of your accomplishments."

"I guess." He ran a comb through his wet hair, trying to get out the tangles.

"The girls have been so excited the last couple of days that I thought we were going to have to sedate them. When they found out it was your birthday, they couldn't be contained."

Billy turned and faced Rusty, tucking the comb into his back pocket. "Please don't make a big deal out of my birthday. I haven't celebrated it in years and don't intend to start now."

"How come? Surely, you're too young to worry about your age," Rusty laughed.

There was no sparkle in Billy's eyes today. "I told you; I don't celebrate it. Let's not make an issue of it, all right?"

"Okay. But the girls are going to be upset. They're expecting a party."

Billy rolled his shirt into a ball and sat down on the rock next to Rusty. With the heel of his boot, he scraped at the dirt at his feet. "There was never any reason to celebrate when I was little," he muttered. "Hell, all I ever heard was 'I don't want you.' Why would they celebrate my birthday? My mother acted like it was the worst day of her life."

Rusty was at a loss for words. Out of the corner of his eye, he glanced at Billy who was staring at the marks his boots had made. After a moment, Billy stood. "You up for a short walk? There's something I'd like to show you."

"Sure, it'll be good to get the kinks out of my legs."

They walked together into the area behind the house. It was quiet and smelled of pine.

"When I was eight, my father brought me here. Just dumped me off and left. I was filthy and full of lice from sleeping under the rusted-out trailer where we lived," he said. "My grandparents had to corner me to give me a bath. I remember how I kicked and screamed and bit them. I thought for sure they were going to hurt me.

"Eventually, I began to trust them. That was hard. I was so used to being abused; I didn't understand anything else." He shook his head. "I had never been to school and was truly an ignorant savage. But my grandparents took me to the mission that fall and talked to the priests. They put me into a class with first graders and other kids who were slow."

"Did they have to do that?"

"What else could they do," Billy shrugged. "The other kids made fun of me and bullied me. But after a month or two, they moved me to second grade. Once I started to learn, they couldn't slow me down. I went from first to third grade in a year."

The level ground began to climb and became more rocky. They walked single file the rest of the way. At the crest of the slope, they came to an out-cropping of rocks that pitched into a deep canyon. Billy went no further. Rusty however, walked toward the edge and stared down into the depths. Rocks and scrub trees stuck out at odd angles on the sides of the canyon.

"That's quite a drop," Rusty commented.

"Yes," Billy said shortly. "The day before my thirteenth birthday, my father showed up. I was scared. I thought he was going to take me back to Arizona. Instead, he told me to get some things together because we were going hunting. He took me up here to this spot."

"It's quite a climb."

"Are you all right?"

"I'm fine."

"When we got here, he said it was time I became a man. He gave me a cross-bow and some arrows and told me to get our dinner. It took a while, but I finally tracked and killed a jackrabbit. While my father chewed some peyote, I skinned and gutted the animal. Then I cooked the meat over a fire I started manually."

"How old did you say you were?"

"Basically thirteen."

"Didn't he help you?"

"It was a test. After we ate, he pointed to those rocks over there," Billy said, pointing to a rock formation in the distance. "He told me I was to hike to that spot. When I got there, I was to gather some rocks, then find my way back here by morning, bringing the rocks with me. I wasn't allowed to take any food or bedding—only a knife for protection." Billy shook his head. "That formation is about five miles away over some pretty rugged territory."

"How did you do it?" Rusty asked incredulous.

"It wasn't easy. But *Abuelo* had taken me out there a couple of times, so I was familiar with the area. In any case, I would have done it even if it killed me."

"Why?"

"I wanted to show him I could do something difficult. That I was worth something."

"Was he happy?"

"When I returned before dawn on my birthday, he was ecstatic. In his eyes, I was truly an Apache. He handed me some peyote and told me to chew it to help me have a vision. He had already been chewing some. I didn't want that stuff. I didn't like the way it made me feel. But he got pretty forceful about the whole thing. I took some and pretended to chew and swallow then spit it out into the grass. By then he was pretty high and didn't notice."

Billy turned to Rusty and extended his arm, pointing. "This is where he threw himself off. Said he could fly. I tried to grab him, but he was too fast." Billy kicked hard at some loose stones. They rattled on their way over the side and down to the ground far below. "He never made a sound until he hit the ground. I was afraid to look down, but I forced myself to the edge."

Billy paused, crossing his arms against his bare chest. Even though the day was warm, gooseflesh covered his skin. "*Abuelo* found me a couple of hours later. By then, the buzzards had already circled and even though I yelled and waved my arms, they moved in and began to fight over him. I said, 'I couldn't stop him or…them.' *Abuelo* looked at me sadly, touched my head and said, 'Let's leave this place.'"

Neither Billy nor Rusty moved or spoke. Even the sounds of nature had stilled—the silence complete. When Billy continued speaking, Rusty started at the sound of his voice. "We returned to the ranch. He and *Abuela* went outside and talked a long time. She was alone when she came back. There were tears in her eyes, but she never broke down in front of me, never said a word. Just went back to what she was doing. *Abuelo* returned later, looking like an old man. Like his spirit had been sucked out of him. Neither one of them laughed as much as before, and from then on, we never celebrated my birthday."

Billy eyes blazed with anger. "I'll never forgive him for what he did! That bastard cheated me," he spit out. "Cheated all three of us. He came back and got my hopes up. Made me feel as though he cared. That maybe he was sorry. That maybe…he loved me." Billy's chest heaved as though he had run a mile. His hands were clenched into fists as he struggled to maintain his composure.

Several minutes later, he spit in the dust, turned abruptly, and strode away from the cliff, starting down the slope toward home.

Rusty had to move quickly to catch up with him. "Wait, Billy."

Billy stopped and turned.

"So, because of that, you've written yourself off," Rusty continued, slightly out of breath. "Have never acknowledged that you're alive?"

Billy crossed his bare arms, rubbing them. "Why bother? The memories hurt all of us too much."

"My father never cried out either. I was looking out my bedroom window when I saw him fall, saw him hit the pavement. My mother said it was an accident. But even then, I think I always knew that he jumped. He was also trying to escape in the only way he knew how."

Billy was startled. "I'm sorry."

"So am I."

"What I can't understand is, even after all these years, why does it still hurt so much?"

"I don't know," Rusty shook his head. "But we can't let their pain, and what they did, continue to interfere with our lives. If we did, we'd go crazy."

After several moments, Rusty finally said, "We'd better get moving. Everyone's probably wondering where we went. Besides, we have a birthday cake to eat."

"With candles?" Billy asked, looking sheepishly at Rusty. "I mean, I just thought I'd ask."

"Now tell me, would it be a birthday cake without candles?" Rusty smiled, putting his arm around Billy's shoulder and giving him a one-armed hug.

An odd, mismatched assortment of chairs, dishes and cutlery were placed around the table for dinner. But everyone had a place to sit and a plate of food before them.

"May I say grace?" Barbara asked Billy timidly.

"Sure," Billy answered.

She bowed her head and in a quiet voice said, *"Gracias a Dios* thank you God for this food, the women who prepared it and the family who welcomed us into their home to share it with them, amen."

Billy smiled and winked at her, *"Gracias,* Bubba."

Dinner was a silent affair. Billy and his grandparents made no attempt at conversation. Ben Running Fox ate quickly, then stomped out the door. Billy likewise ate quickly. He left his dirty plate on the table, nodded to his grandmother, and followed his grandfather outside.

After everyone else finished eating, Marian and the girls helped clean up despite Isabella's protests, then joined the men out on the porch. Ben recruited Rusty, Joe and Cal for a poker game and Isabella promised the girls a trip to the barn to see some newborn kittens.

Billy was sitting on the wooden steps, a lit cigarette in his hands when Marian came from the house. She brushed at the step then gingerly settled down next to him, smoothing her skirt over her legs.

Billy took a long drag on his cigarette, then averting his head away from where Marian sat, exhaled the smoke. Marian glanced at him and cleared her throat. When he continued to smoke, she cleared her throat again and looking pointedly at his cigarette said, "Are you going to put that out?"

Billy stared at her. "Why? I just lit it. I'm outside and the girls are in the barn. Is it bothering you?"

"Well, no, not really."

"So why do you want me to put it out?"

"I'm just surprised. You never did this at home."

"But Marian, the girls are in the barn."

"I know. You're right. But Billy…"

"Yes?"

"I have to tell you, I'm very disappointed in your behavior."

"My behavior?"

"Yes, what happened to your manners?"

"What do you mean?"

"When you stayed with us you had such nice manners. You were so different. So…"

Billy exhaled smoke through his nostrils. "So white, you mean?" he finished, with bitterness in his voice.

"No! That's not what I meant," she replied vehemently. "It's just that you were such a…a gentleman."

"You mean, I conformed." Billy smiled without humor, staring off into the distance. After a moment, he waved his hand out in front of him.

"Marian, this is my home, for what it's worth. It isn't Georgetown."

Marian glanced down at her sandal-clad feet. The expensive, white, Italian leather was covered in dust and sand, her exposed toes, filthy. "No, it isn't. But that has nothing to do with being a gentleman. Nor does it give you the right to be rude."

"Rude? By whose standards? You can't expect your rules to apply here."

"Why not?"

"Look Marian, I can understand having to adapt to your rules and lifestyle when I'm living with you. But don't you think you're being a little unfair to expect that kind of behavior from me here in my own home? That's sort of what the missionaries did. Don't you remember how you all thought it was terrible that outsiders came and ordered my people to live differently?" He cocked his head, raising his eyebrows at her.

Marian looked slightly abashed and didn't answer. Billy noted the look then continued, more gently, "You have to understand something, Marian. The mores of my people are different than yours. Our men and women have certain accepted behaviors. For example, you probably offended my grandmother."

"Offended her?" Marian asked, startled.

"Yes, by helping her to prepare the meal then cleaning up afterward. *Abuela* prides herself on the running of this home. She is almost arrogant in the meticulous way she performs her chores and shows hospitality to guests. But since you're an Anglo, she'll forgive you your ignorance. On the other hand, if I offered to help or cleared my dirty plate, she would be hurt that I didn't think she could do her job."

"Oh dear, I'm sorry. I hope I didn't hurt her feelings. Should I apologize to her?"

"No, I think she understood that you were being helpful out of kindness."

"I hope so."

"You're lucky these are modern times, Marian," Billy said with a smile. "A couple hundred years ago, Rusty may have been expected to sleep with *Abuela* tonight and you might have been given to *Abuelo*…or me."

"What!"

"Sharing one's woman was considered hospitable in some tribes," he grinned, as he ground out his cigarette with his boot. He then snorted. "Hell, my wife's been spreading her hospitality all over town for years."

As they watched the sun sink below the horizon, Billy's dog came and put her head on his knee. He absently scratched her behind the ears. After a while, Marian said, "I'm sorry. I wish I understood you and your people better. This is very difficult."

"The day I pulled in front of your home, I had never seen a house like that let alone been inside of one. Since then, it hasn't been easy. Every day, I have to merge two worlds, trying to be something I'm not, yet trying to hold onto my identity and sanity at the same time. Everyone is constantly telling me that who and what I am is wrong. My clothes're wrong, my hair's wrong. Don't wear jewelry. Don't wear those boots. Don't cuss, don't smoke. God Marian, it's a wonder I haven't lost my mind."

"Was it really that bad?"

"Yes. And sometimes, it still is. Every day, I have to tell myself why I am in Georgetown and why I need to remain. If you all hadn't been so nice, I'd never have stayed."

"You know, Billy. This was one reason why I agreed to come here in the first place. I was hoping this would help us to better understand the problems you face."

"Don't get me wrong, it wasn't all bad. After a few months, I got used to things. I had to adapt or go crazy. Some people will do anything to get what they want."

"And what is it you want?" Marian asked, laying her hand on his arm.

Billy looked down at her hand and thought a long time. "Indoor plumbing," he said finally, patting Marian's hand.

"You came all the way across the country for a flushing toilet? Amazing," she laughed.

"Yeah, amazing," he said, standing up. "Now, I should literally hit the hay. I've got to be up by 4:30. Long day tomorrow. I'm glad you're all here. Thanks for the cake and everything. It's been quite a day."

"I'm glad we came. Though, I feel bad about taking your bed tonight."

"Don't worry about it, I don't mind. But I'm going to give you a little advice. Make sure you stuff your socks into any closed shoes, put Barbara's sleeping bag on the couch, and check between the sheets before you get into bed. I wouldn't want you to be surprised by a scorpion or two. Also, *Abuelo* snores like crazy so try to fall asleep quickly."

"Scorpions?" Marian asked faintly.

Billy grinned. "The bane of desert living."

BARBARA

It was still dark outside when Barbara heard Billy enter the house. She was snuggled in a sleeping bag on the couch near the sleeping area. Crawling out of her bag, she went to him as he pumped water into a coffee pot.

"What are you doing up?" He poked at the ashes in the wood stove, then laid in some kindling. "You should be sleeping."

"I couldn't sleep. What are you doing?"

"Making coffee."

"What time is it?"

Billy checked his watch. "it's almost five."

"Wow. Why so early?"

"I have to work some horses."

"Can I come?"

Billy hesitated then said, "I guess. But let's get something to eat first."

Billy's grandmother appeared and quietly made some oatmeal. Billy's grandfather joined them, and they sat down to breakfast. The smell of fresh coffee was fragrant in the air, but Marian and Jennifer slept on in Billy's bed behind the partition.

After eating, Billy and Barbara silently made their way to the barn. The horses nickered and stomped their feet. Billy murmured to them, then bridled and saddled two of the horses and brought them outside.

"Do you want the black or the gray?" Billy asked.

"You mean I can ride one of them?"

"Yes, they both need exercise. This will save me time. Besides, I know you're just dying to ride. So, which will it be, the black or the gray?"

"The gray. Are you sure I can ride one of them?"

"Sure, these two are mine. The black one is Conchita and the gray, that you chose, is Sombrita."

"They're very beautiful."

"They were payment for some work I did. I couldn't have afforded horses like these any other way. They're both very special," he said, rubbing the nose of the black horse. She bumped his chest with her head and snuffled at his shirt until he gave her some of the carrot pieces he had in his pocket.

"Here," he said, handing Barbara a few. "Keep your palm flat and your fingers out of the way. Sombrita won't bite you. But having eyes on either side of her head like that, she can't always see if there's a thumb in the way or not." After Barbara fed Sombrita some carrots, Billy lifted her onto the animal's back.

For Barbara, it seemed a long way down. "Billy, I'm scared. I've never been on a horse before. What if I fall off?"

"If you're scared, she'll feel it. I could walk you around a few times first. Would that be better? Or we could ride together. What would you rather do?"

"Could we go together just this once?"

"I guess," he sighed, tying Conchita to the rail. He held on to Sombrita's saddle horn and before Barbara knew it, was behind her, holding her with one hand and the reins with the other.

As they walked Sombrita into the corral, Billy explained to Barbara how to rein the horse and move with her gait. When Barbara was comfortable with walking, he touched his heels to Sombrita's side, and she broke into a trot. Barbara started to giggle when her rear end smacked the saddle.

"I'm sorry," she said. "I can't help it. It sounds funny."

"Move with her, Bubba, and keep your legs tucked close to her side. You don't hear my butt banging, do you?"

"No," she giggled.

"Here, we'll go faster." As they started to canter, Barbara got the hang of moving with the horse. Her butt didn't slap the saddle, and she was able to think about what she was doing.

"No fair," Jenny cried, running over to the fence. "How come you get to ride?"

"Because I'm older," Barbara retorted. "I also got up before you."

"Don't worry, you'll get a chance to ride, too," said Billy, reining in Sombrita. "Just remember, if you ride, you get to shovel out stalls when you're done."

"Shovel what?" asked Jennifer.

"Poop!" Barbara laughed. Billy dismounted, then plucked Barbara from the saddle. He walked Sombrita out of the corral, tied her and brought in Conchita.

"Next," he said, motioning to Jennifer. He went through the same routine with Jenny. After the workout, they all went back to the barn and cleaned stalls and horses.

"What's all this racket?" asked Cal, climbing down the ladder from the loft. He rubbed his eyes and stretched. "You guys woke me up."

"It's about time, Sleeping Beauty. Did you think you were getting breakfast in bed?" Billy asked.

"I'm forever hopeful, Fox. Unfortunately, you treat those big dumb animals better than you treat your human guests."

"They're worth a lot more than you are. Besides, you aren't paying me to feed you."

"Anything going in the house?"

"There's always oatmeal and coffee. But hell," he said, looking at his watch, "it's almost lunchtime. Why bother with breakfast now?"

The rest of the company were on the porch sipping coffee. Billy deposited the girls with their mother. "If you don't mind, I need a lot of quiet when I work Roughneck. You two will have to amuse yourselves for a while."

He worked the stallion for about an hour and a half. The horse was finally responding to all his efforts and although still skittish, was coming along nicely. Out of the corner of his eye, he saw that Joe, Rusty and Cal were watching from a distance. Later, as Billy walked Roughneck back to the barn, he passed the other men.

Joe let out a low whistle. "That is one beautiful animal. What I wouldn't do to have a horse like that."

"He's doin' great, Fox. What did you do to him since I last saw you gettin' dumped on your ass?" asked Cal.

"Lots of hard work. Something you would never understand."

"I'd rather watch than do, you know that. Except when it comes to chicks," he laughed.

"Don't I."

"You done for the day? We were talkin' about how long it would take to get these folks back to Phoenix."

"Anglo time or 'Indin' time?"

"They need to catch their flight home at the end of the week. So, I think 'Indin' time is out. In fact, we were thinkin' that if we left after lunch, we could spend the night in Albuquerque and see some sites. Or we could go home by way of Farmington and see the Canyon. Either way, we would have them back in Tempe before they have to leave and still have a couple of days to relax."

"That's a good idea, except that means that you'll all be leaving soon."

"I know. But that's the best plan we could come up with. Plus, we don't want to put you all out any more than we have."

"You're right, I guess. It's probably best. I have some things that I need to order for *Abuelo* in La Jara. I can follow along until then, if you're heading to Albuquerque."

Lunch was followed by a flurry of activity. The car was packed and last-minute trips to the outhouse were made.

"Thank you for everything," Marian said, taking Isabella Running Fox's hand in hers. "It was wonderful to meet you."

"You're very welcome. We also enjoyed meeting you and having you here with us. Thank you for all that you are doing for William. He is all that we have. It's good to know that he's with such fine people. Please come again."

Marian then turned to Billy. "You'll be back the first week of August, right?"

"Yes, I'll write you with the exact date, okay?"

"That will be fine. Be careful and take your time."

"Yes, ma'am," Billy replied.

"I'm sorry we put you all out."

"You didn't put us out. In fact, I'm very glad you came. It was good that my grandparents got to meet you."

"Are you sure about that?"

"Yes, I'm sure. What about you? By the way," he said, looking down. "I think those poor sandals are shot."

"I don't care," Marian said. "It was worth it. Although, I think I behaved a bit like those missionaries before you set me straight. I'm sorry."

Billy smiled. "It's okay. *Abuela* always says that anytime something is learned it's a good thing. Even if what you learned is unpleasant or not exactly what you expected."

"She is a very wise woman."

"Yes. She kind of reminds me of you," he said and smiled.

Marian laughed and gave Billy a quick hug. "We'll see you at home."

"Yes," Billy said, returning the hug. "Home."

PART THREE

*"See what things consist of:
resolve them into their matter,
form, and purpose."*

~

*"Give your heart to the trade
you have learnt,
and draw refreshment
from it."*

Marcus Aurelius

JESSIE

November, 1962

The suitcase and overnight bag sat forlornly in the hall outside of the hotel room. The scruffy bear lay on its side several feet away. It took a few minutes for their significance to slowly sink into Jessie's brain. Shock and confusion were replaced by a flood of anger. How could he just throw her out like that?

Although, if she really thought about it, the signs had been there. Her companion had no longer been winning and had begun to get restless—his eyes constantly straying to other women. And now, her possessions lay in the hall.

The bus ride back to Tempe was long. Jessie had ample time to mentally kick herself. After buying her ticket, Jessie found herself almost penniless. With no money for a taxi, she hauled herself and her bags the many blocks back to her apartment—only to find another problem.

The key to the door no longer worked in the latch. Anita must have changed the lock. Nice, she thought and began to bang angrily on the door.

"Quit that poundin'," a voice shouted from within. "I'm comin'."

Jessie was surprised when a strange woman answered the door. But then again, there were always people coming and going from their apartment.

"Where's Anita?" Jessie asked, dragging her bags into the apartment.

"Who?" the woman asked.

"You know, Anita? She lives here."

The woman pushed against Jessie, sending her back out into the hall and kicked her bags as well. "This is my apartment, sister. I don't know anyone named Anita. If you were a smart Injun, you'd get your ass and your things out of my hallway and take off before I call the police."

"Wait!" Jessie said, bewildered. "I live here. Where's Anita?"

"Honey, I don't know anything about you or your roommate. Now take a hike."

"How long have you been living here?"

"I moved in about a month ago. I don't know anything about the former tenant. I got the place from an agent. As far as I know, nobody was living here. Now vamoose," she said, slamming the door in Jessie's face.

Jessie stared at the door a long moment, then slowly hauled her bags back down the stairs and outside. Looking at the mailboxes, she saw that only two other apartments were occupied. The names were unfamiliar. She knew nothing about Anita or her family, if she had one. There weren't many options left.

In a daze, Jessie sat down on the curb. She pulled out her wallet and slowly began to count what was left of her money.

With Thanksgiving almost upon them, the topic of Christmas break had been discussed. This year the Wilsons had talked Billy into staying with them for the holidays. It hadn't taken much coaxing. Billy didn't seem to care and was very quiet as of late. Since his return in August, Billy had tried to call Jessie on several occasions, but she hadn't been home.

"When I talked to Anita in August, she said Jessie had never come back from Vegas. I tried to call several times since then, but first there was no answer and now, the line's been disconnected. I don't know whether to be angry or worried," Billy said.

"Have you stopped sending money?" Marian asked.

"I haven't sent money since June. But now I feel guilty. I told her I would take care of her, but..." he shrugged.

"If she hasn't been home, she doesn't even know you're not paying the rent."

"I know. I just hope she isn't into something she can't handle."

"The only thing I can tell you, Billy, is that from how you describe Jessie, I think she's the kind of girl who can take care of herself. I'm sure she'll be fine."

"I hope so."

Two days after Thanksgiving, Marian and the girls were doing some pre-holiday cookie baking when the doorbell rang. Marian wiped her hands and went to the front door. Peering out the window, she saw a young woman standing on the doorstep. She was very pretty, with high cheekbones and a face the color of a cinnamon stick. Her long black hair blew loose in the wind. Her coloring and facial structure reminded Marian a little of Billy. "Yes?" she asked, opening the door.

"You Marian Wilson?"

"Yes, I am."

"Is Fox here?"

"Billy? He's at class right now. Can I help you?"

"I'm Jessie, his wife."

"Oh!" Marian said, startled. "Please…come in." She checked her watch. "Billy should be home in about an hour."

Jessie entered the house carrying a small suitcase and an overnight bag. She closed the door behind her and looked around. "Kee-rist! Billy never told me that he lived in a fuckin' mansion. There's enough room here for a small tribe of Navajos."

"Uh, here," Marian said, her face bright red. "Let me take your jacket. Why don't you put your things down and come out to the kitchen? My daughters and I are baking."

"What? No servants or slaves? Or is that Fox's job when he's here?" Jessie said, partially to herself, as she followed Marian down the hall.

Upon entering the kitchen, Marian turned and asked, "Are you hungry? Can I get you something to eat or drink?"

"No, thanks," Jessie replied.

Barbara and Jennifer stopped what they were doing and looked up in surprise.

"Jessie, these are my daughters, Barbara and Jennifer. Girls, this is Jessie," Marian explained.

"Hi," Jessie said.

The girls smiled shyly and continued to get out spoons and measuring cups.

"Are you sure I can't get you something to eat?"

"No," Jessie replied, settling herself on a chair and taking stock of the kitchen.

"Did you drive here or take a bus?" Marian asked, trying to make conversation.

"Hitched."

"What?"

"Hitchhiked. Got rides from truckers, you know?"

"Isn't that dangerous?"

Jessie shrugged. "It's amazing the protection a piece of ass can buy."

"What!" Marian blurted out. Oh, dear Lord, she thought, what am I going to do with this young woman until Billy comes home. Not only was talking to her like pulling teeth, but when she did reply, it was definitely not suitable conversation fit for her children's ears. She finally decided to start baking and left Jessie to her own thoughts. Every so often, she'd glance at the clock, hoping Billy wouldn't be late.

After a while, Jessie stood and wandered around the kitchen, noting the pictures on the wall and the knickknacks in the hutch.

"Nice stuff," Jessie commented.

"Thank you," Marian replied nervously, questioning her lack of judgment. She shouldn't have allowed this strange woman into her home without asking more questions.

Just as her uneasiness had built to a fever pitch, Jennifer saw Billy from the window. "Billy's coming! I'm going to meet him."

"Put on a coat," Marian admonished, as Jenny ran out the door without one.

"Billy! Guess what?" Jennifer said, tugging on his sleeve. "Jessie's here to see you."

"What?" Billy was stunned. It couldn't be. How had she found him? How would she even know where to look? He turned to Jenny. "How long has she been here?"

"About an hour, Mommy has been trying to talk to her, but she doesn't say very much. And when she does, she says funny things that make Mommy's face turn colors."

"Oh my God!" Billy mumbled. "Sounds like Jessie." They walked up the driveway and entered the back door. From the laundry room, Billy could see Marian talking with someone as he took off his outer jacket.

"Here he is now. Billy, you have a visitor," Marian said brightly, her smile forced.

He walked into the kitchen with a feeling of dread. Jessie turned and faced him. "Fox."

"Jessie," he nodded.

They stared at one another without saying a word. The tension between them made Marian uncomfortable.

"Come on, girls," she said. "Let's give Billy and Jessie some privacy. They haven't seen one another for a long time."

"Surprised to see me?" Jessie asked, when they were alone.

"Shocked is more the word. What are you doing here?"

"Thought I'd come and see how the other half lives," she said, running her fingers along the kitchen table. "Pretty fucking nicely, it seems. And look at you," she said, as he loosened his tie. "Fancy duds—a tie even. Wow, Fox, very sexy."

"How did you find me?"

"You wrote me letters, remember?"

"I don't get it. You fall off the face of the earth, then suddenly reappear on the doorstep months later. What are you up to?"

"I haven't seen you for a long time."

"I came to see you over the summer, but you weren't around."

"I was away."

Billy leaned back against the kitchen counter; his arms folded across his chest. "For how long? I've been trying to call you since the end of June."

"A while."

"A while? What's going on, Jessie? The last time I called, your phone was disconnected."

"That bitch Anita took off, and the apartment got rented to someone else."

"So where have you been living?"

"Nowhere, till now."

Billy narrowed his eyes. "What do you mean?"

"I guess I'll be living here with you."

"Here? Are you crazy? You can't stay here."

"Why not?"

"For one thing, you haven't been invited."

"Then invite me."

"It's not my house."

"You live here, don't you?"

"Yes but…"

"I'm your wife. I belong with you, don't I?"

"Oh sure, if you truly belonged with me, where were you this summer?"

"With friends."

"Friends," Billy snorted. "You don't have any friends. You were selling your ass in Vegas. Anita told me. Don't lie."

"Ok, I was in Vegas. If you knew, why'd ya ask? What's it to you?"

"Did you have a good time?"

She stared at the floor. "It was okay."

"You got tossed out, didn't you?"

"I wouldn't say that."

"And what *would* you say?"

"Uh…replaced?"

"I was right. You got tossed. And now Anita's gone, and you decided to find your sucker of a husband."

"What's wrong with me coming to visit?"

"If you were any other woman, I'd hope that you missed me and wanted to be with me. But unfortunately, I know you too well. There has to be a motive here. It's not because you've been pining away for me."

"I told you. I want to see how the other half lives," she smiled.

"Well, take a good look 'cause you're not staying."

"You mean you'd throw me out?"

"Damn right."

"But where would I go? You don't want me to whore for money now, would you? How would your new family feel about you if they knew you treated me so poorly that I had to sell my ass to make a buck? Besides, this house is so fuckin' huge, no one will even know I'm here."

Billy looked at Jessie and her sly grin and wanted to strike her. He ground his teeth and counted to ten, trying to remain calm. But his mind was reeling. What was he going to do? She couldn't stay here. But damn it, he had made her a promise. He said he'd take care of her. He also knew that the chances of her changing were slim. The only thing he could do would be to remove Jessie from the Wilson's home until he could find a place for them both to live.

Later that evening, he and the Wilsons heatedly discussed the latest turn of events. "I'll get a hotel room until I can find us a place to stay."

"That won't be necessary," Marian replied.

"Yes, it is. It's bad enough that I'm here. The last thing you both need is another person in your home, especially Jessie."

"That is the most ridiculous thing I've ever heard. Neither of you are going anywhere," Marian said.

"You don't understand," Billy pleaded. "This won't work. She's not a normal woman. I am going to have to take her somewhere."

"And where are you going to take her?" Rusty asked. "Not only will most of the hotel and motel rooms be booked through the holidays, they're also very expensive. You don't have that kind of money."

"She can't stay here," Billy argued, stubbornly.

"I know she's not the kind of woman we're used to," Marian replied, "but she's your wife."

"I don't care if she were my mother, she can't stay here," he said again.

"I'm surprised at you, Billy," Marian said. "You're being very selfish."

"Selfish?"

"Yes, you say she's had a rough life, why not let us help to make it better for her?"

"You have no idea what you are letting yourself in for."

"Oh, come now," Marian laughed. "You're being so dramatic. She's a young woman. How much trouble could she possibly cause?"

"You'd be surprised," Billy grunted. "Just don't say I didn't warn you."

The Wilson family tried to pretend that Jessie was a welcome addition to the family, but her presence was definitely a strain. During the day, Jessie flipped through magazines or wandered around the house admiring the Wilson's possessions. She did nothing to help Marian and didn't have much to say.

As Christmas approached, Jessie's existence in the house threw a gloom over the happy holiday season. No one knew what to say to her, and when she did speak, it was something crude or sexually charged.

One night, several days after Christmas, the family was gathered in the kitchen. Billy was trying to study, the girls were doing homework, and Marian was cleaning up from the evening meal. Rusty was at the hospital.

Jessie, instead of helping Marian clear the table, was hanging all over Billy. Marian tried to ignore what was going on, but it was difficult. Billy's face was flushed in embarrassment, and he tried to push her away.

"Come on, Fox," she said, starting to unbutton his shirt. "I want it."

"Want what?" asked Jennifer. "Can I have it, too?"

"Jenny, please!" Marian exclaimed, looking close to tears.

Billy pushed Jessie's hands away. "Knock it off, Jessie. How many times have I told you not to talk like that in front of the family."

"Shit, Fox, Mama Marian's no virgin. She's got two brats. That means she's been fucked at least twice. Of course, she's probably one of those women who just lays there waiting for her man to get it over with. She's not like me, huh? I can really throw down the moves."

"Shut up!" Billy yelled, standing so quickly that his chair fell over backward.

"What're you gonna do? Hit me?"

Marian gasped, her eyes filling with tears.

"You've got to stop this, Jessie," Billy pleaded.

"Gonna hit me?"

"No! For God's sake! But for the last *fucking* time, you can't talk like that. Can't you try to act civilized for just a little while?"

"Civilized? Is that what you call kissing these rich Anglos' asses?"

"I don't kiss their ass."

"Yes, you do. They say jump and you say how high. What are you afraid of?"

"I wasn't afraid of anything until you showed up. Look, you have Marian in tears, again. The kids are confused, and Rusty is finding excuses to stay at work. I'm so embarrassed."

"What are you embarrassed about?"

"You."

"Me?"

"Yeah, I don't want everyone to think that I'm like you."

"But you *are* like me," Jessie said, stabbing Billy in the chest with her finger.

"I was never like you."

"I don't know about that, Mr. Goody-Two-Shoes. You were plenty like me before. Does your family know about all the drugs you used to do—all the wild sex. What about the crazy parties where you'd heave your guts out after you downed a fifth then down another and pass out. God!" she said, looking at Marian, "Did they cut off your balls as well as your hair when you moved in? I thought you were a man, not a fuckin' pussy." She again poked his chest.

Marian gasped and a sob escaped her lips. She urged the girls to their feet and out of the room. "Jenny, Barbara, let's go!"

"I am *not* a pussy!" Billy ground out. "And no matter *what* I did before, I am *not* like you!" he said, grabbing her finger.

"The truth hurts, doesn't it?" Jessie asked, yanking her finger from his hand. "Once a drunken Injun, always a drunken Injun. You think you're so damn smart. You think you're white now, don't you? Well, guess what? You'll never be white. You'll always be treated like scum because you're still nothing but a fuckin' Indian!"

"God...damn...you!" Billy yelled. The slap rang out as Billy's hand caught the side of Jessie's face. For a moment, all that was between them was an angry, shocked silence.

"See?" Jessie said finally, rubbing her cheek. "You'll never change." Then turning, she walked from the room.

Billy let out a groan of anguish and ran for the door. He headed down the driveway and out into the street, running as if demons were after him.

It was Rusty, coming home from work an hour later, who spied him in the beam of his headlights. Billy was blocks from home and soaking wet with sweat. His chest rose and fell heavily with exertion.

Rusty slowed the car and rolled down the window. "Kind of late to be out for a stroll, isn't it?" Billy checked his pace to a jog but didn't answer. "Want a lift home?" Rusty asked, stopping the car.

After a moment's hesitation, Billy stopped running and got into the car. They drove the rest of the way home in silence. The back door light was on as Billy walked over to the girls' swing set and sat down on a swing. He pulled out a very crumpled pack of cigarettes and lit one. For a long time, he sat—a shadow in the dark. Only the glow from his cigarette gave him life.

Sitting down next to him, Rusty asked, "Shall I assume that there is something wrong?"

"Yes."

"Want to elaborate?"

"No."

"When I get in the house, will Marian be crying again?"

"Probably."

"That bad?"

"Yes."

"Shit," Rusty said, sighing. "I know, I know. You warned us."

The back door suddenly opened and the lights by the patio came on as well, illuminating the two men on the swings. Marian appeared in the doorway. After a moment, she came outside, a jacket clutched around her shoulders. She stood in front of Billy and tears welled and fell. "I met Jessie on the stairs. I saw her face. I don't care what she said about me or to me," Marian hiccuped. "You didn't have to…to slap her."

Rusty looked from his wife to Billy. "You struck her?" he asked.

Billy's bowed head nodded in the dark. Rusty shook his head slowly, "Oh God." For many minutes, no one moved or spoke. Finally, Rusty said, "This is all our fault, Marian. We should have listened to Billy. We should have let him take her away. Instead, we let things get out of control and forced him to do something he didn't want to do."

After a moment, Billy said, "That's not true. This had nothing to do with Marian. I mean, that was only part of it. Jessie threw the truth in my face, and I couldn't take it."

"The truth?" Marian asked.

"Yeah, that I'll never be anything but a drunken, worthless Indian, and I'm pretending to be white by being here. She's right," he said, putting his head in his hands. "And because of it, I put you all through hell. You've been so good to me, and this is what I do in return." He slowly stood and looked Marian in the eye. "I'm just sorry you had to find out that I'm nothing but an animal."

As Marian went to speak, Billy interrupted, saying, "We'll be gone in the morning."

He waved off their protests and hurried to the house. He remembered the first day he had come here. This crazy, huge Anglo house had become home to him, and now, he was going to have to leave.

He trudged up the stairs and into the room that had been his. Jessie was seated on the bed, her bags packed. He walked to the closet and pulled out his backpack. Methodically, he began to pack things he would need right away.

"What're you doing?" Jessie asked him.

"What does it look like? I'm packing."

"Why?"

"Come on, Jessie. Neither one of us can stay here now."

"They threw you out?"

"No, I'm leaving." He glanced at her things. The bedraggled teddy bear peeked out from the overnight bag. There was something so sad and sorry about that damned bear that Billy just wanted to sit on the bed and cry. He wanted to take the bear and hold it, because he knew he could never hold Jessie.

"But…I thought you lived here. That they wanted you."

"What difference does it make now? They know what I really am. You made sure of that, didn't you?"

"But I thought you paid to be here. You know. Like rent."

"Yes, Jessie, I give them money. But it isn't exactly like rent. You can't pay someone for the privilege of being treated as one of the family. I really blew it."

"What are we gonna do now?"

"I don't know about you, but I'm going back home."

"Home?"

"Yeah, home, maybe there, I can redeem myself."

"Home? As in the Rez?"

"That's where I belong. In fact, if I ever became a doctor, that was where I was going to practice eventually."

"You can't be serious?"

"I'm very serious. If you'd asked a few questions and maybe talked to me once in a while, you'd have known that."

"Why would you waste your life in some piss hole?"

"Because 'The People' need me."

"You'd throw your life away and rot on the Rez because of 'The People?'" Jessie sneered. "I can't believe that."

"Believe what you want," he said, continuing to pack.

Jessie looked at Billy a long time. Finally, she said, "You would really do that?"

"Yeah."

"Then you shouldn't leave."

"It's too late for that now."

"No, it's not. If I go, they'll let you stay."

"I can't stay."

"Sure, you can. If I get out of the way, you can be what you want."

"They'd never let me stay now. Not after all the shit that happened tonight."

"Maybe I could get them to change their minds."

"Yeah sure, Jessie and how would you do that?"

"I could offer to blow Rusty a few times."

"Are you crazy?"

Jessie's lips turned up in a small smile. "Relax, Fox. I'm kidding."

"Could have fooled me."

"How about if I just hit the road?" With her guard down, he saw the sadness in her face.

"No, we'll go together."

"You mean like a couple?"

"Well, we are, aren't we?"

"Oh yeah, a real Ozzie and Harriet," Jessie jeered, standing. "I can see it now. Living happily ever after in a one room, dirt floor hogan with no running water, how romantic!" she spat at him. With her arms out as if presenting him, she continued, "Add to the fairy tale a drunken, slap happy Prince, with no job and a death wish, who'll fill my gut with a baby every fucking year? No thank you!" She pointed her thumb at her chest. "You won't get *my* ass back on the

Rez, not for anything. I'd rather hook, if you don't mind. At least then, I can pee inside." Then pointing a finger at Billy, she said, "You want to go back to the Rez? Baby, you're on your own."

"If you won't come with me, what are you going to do?"

"Maybe I'll head back to Vegas," Jessie shrugged. "Who knows? Don't worry. I'll be fine." She picked up her bags and headed for the door.

"You can't leave tonight. You have nowhere to go. We'll leave together in the morning."

"No, it's better if I go now, alone. I've caused enough trouble."

Billy looked at Jessie a long time. He would rather have fought with her. Seeing her defeated made him feel horrible. He wanted to touch her, to love her, to change things. But that was impossible. The distance between them was a chasm that could not be bridged.

"God Jess, why does it always have to be like this with us? Why can't we ever seem to get it together?"

The corner of Jessie's lips lifted in a wry smile. "Don't know, Fox. I guess I'm just not *into* what you're into."

"Do you have any money?"

"Some," she lied.

Billy pulled out his wallet. It contained the withdrawal he had made the previous day. The money was earmarked to purchase books for his next term and to pay Rusty for his room and board for January. He thumbed through it, then took out some of the bills. He shook his head, then hesitantly he asked, "Will you promise me you'll not use this to buy drugs?"

Jessie stared at the money, refusing to look Billy in the eye, then went to take it.

"Promise me, Jessie," Billy said, withholding the money from her.

She sighed, then mumbled, "I promise," so quietly that Billy could hardly hear her.

When he handed her the cash, she finally looked at him. They stared at one another for a long moment. Then, she turned and walked from the room, down the stairs, and out the door.

Billy went to the window and watched her head down the sidewalk. After she had melted into the night, he went back to the bed and continued to pack. He was almost finished, when there was a knock on his door. Rusty and Marian stood in the doorway.

"Can we come in?" Rusty asked.

"Sure, it's your house."

"Where's Jessie?" Marian questioned.

"She left."

"Left? Now? But it's so late. Will she be all right? Where will she go?"

"I don't know, Marian. I didn't want her to leave now. She could have waited until tomorrow and left with me. But after what I did, I guess she doesn't want to be around me."

"You know, kid," Rusty said, sitting down on the bed. "You put up with quite a bit. Most men would have had a hard time keeping their cool in the same situation."

"You wouldn't have hit her, no matter what."

"I don't know about that. A couple of times at dinner, I wanted to smack her myself."

"But you didn't. Thinking about it and doing it are two different things."

"Again, I'm not so sure. Why do you think I was at work so much? Look, all of that aside, Marian and I have been talking. We don't want you to leave. You've come so far; you can't quit now."

Billy looked at Rusty then turned to Marian. He was so ashamed that he had a hard time looking into her eyes, especially when he saw the pain in their hazel depths.

"Please stay," Marian said, her look unwavering. She held out her hand to him.

"How can I stay now? How can you even look at me?"

"You are part of the family," Marian said, her hand still outstretched. "You can't turn love off just because someone you care about does something you disagree with. No matter how wrong."

"Besides, what would happen to your scholarship?" Rusty questioned. "You can't back out of that now."

Billy sank down on the bed beside Rusty. "I never even gave that a thought." With his eyes still steadily on hers, he asked Marian, "Are you really sure you want me?"

"I said we did, didn't I?"

"Yes, but I want this to be your decision, not Rusty's."

"It's *our* decision," she said. "We…I want you to stay. A lot of what happened here tonight was, as Rusty said, our fault. I know I didn't make things any easier.

I just didn't know what to do. I tried to talk to Jessie, but she wouldn't respond. And when she did, it wasn't the kind of response that I expected. In fact, I hate to admit this, but Jessie kind of scared me."

Billy smiled wanly. "At first, she scared me, too. Now, she just confuses and depresses me."

"I'm still afraid that you hit Jessie in my defense, didn't you?"

"Look Marian, I told you before, that was only part of it. Jessie knows how to push people's buttons and make them do things they regret. I can usually ignore her but, when she verbally abused you, then taunted me as well, she went too far. Don't blame yourself for any of this. I should have insisted on taking her away from here."

Billy stood and went to the window. He stared out at the shadows of the night and thought about Jessie's lone figure somewhere out there in the dark. He shook his head sadly.

"Here I am, being given yet another chance, and out there somewhere, Jessie's alone again." He let out a gust of breath. "All that time, I was so worried about her, then she showed up and I got mad. God! She makes me so crazy! And now, where do I go from here?"

"You go back to school and finish one of the most important things that you have ever started," Rusty replied. "Don't forget, when you finish, it will benefit *both* of you. But remember, you have to finish first. Come on Marian, let's leave Billy to unpack, I'm starving. I hope the kitchen is still open."

"I think I can scare something up for you," Marian smiled at both men. "When you're finished, come down and get something to eat, too," she said to Billy. "Food always calms the soul."

"How about the savage beast?" Billy muttered.

When they left, Billy began to put his clothing back. He thought again of Jessie, and the misery crept back. How could she survive? And for how long?

Several days later, Billy's break ended, and he finished out his term and finals. Although he was relieved that Jessie was gone, her visit had affected him deeply. He became withdrawn, spending his free time at the library or in his room studying or brooding. He couldn't shake his melancholy mood. It was almost worse than his initial loneliness and homesickness.

Marian hated to see him so down and hoped that something would happen to bring his laughter back into the house. In the small amount of time he had lived with them, Billy had become so much more than a house guest. He was now a member of the family and treated the girls like young sisters. Whether it was taking the training wheels off Jennifer's bicycle and encouraging her riding or aiding Barbara with troublesome math homework, he was there for them like an older brother.

Now, he had distanced himself from the family and Marian was at a loss as to how to rectify the situation. There had to be some catalyst to bring about the change. But what?

When the second semester began, however, Marian got her wish. Billy met Harry. It was Harry who returned Billy to the family, adding an extra element of excitement to Billy's usually serious demeanor. Harry brought laughter back into the house, proving that there are different ways of looking at things. In fact, it was Harry who taught Billy what life and death were truly all about.

JOHN

His name was Harry. He was tall, bald, hung like a horse, and very, very dead. John and Billy examined this fine specimen of a human being. He was all theirs, and they couldn't wait to cut into him.

Dissection lab was not for the faint of heart. Learning anatomy through textbooks and lectures was one thing, but cutting into dead human beings was another story. It separated the men from the boys. Most of the students found the sights and smells hard to take except for Billy. John had never seen anyone so matter of fact about anything in his life.

"How did you make out on your Pathology report?" Billy asked, as he made a thoracic-abdominal or 'Y' incision on Harry. He cut from shoulder to shoulder, then made an incision down the entire length of the abdomen as calmly as if he were gutting a deer.

"Okay, I guess." John couldn't keep his eyes from the blade in Billy's hand and the seemingly expert way he was wielding it. "Uh, how about you?" he swallowed nervously, knowing the next procedure was his.

"I didn't get it back yet. Here," he said, "your turn."

"I was afraid you were going to say that," John gulped.

"Don't be such a sissy."

"Give me that scalpel."

Every day, they removed organs as directed by their instructor; examining, weighing, and measuring each one. Cross sections were then cut, and tissue samples were studied under microscopes. It wasn't the actual tasks but the pervading odor of formaldehyde that finally got to John. "I just can't take it anymore," he said to Billy. "The smell is getting to me."

Billy stared at Harry. By now, he had ceased to resemble a human being. His scalp had been pulled down over his face and his skull had been sawed open to expose and remove his brain. His internal organs lay neatly in bags and John had tied a blue ribbon around his exceptional member. "I doubt that a shower or deodorant will help him now," Billy replied.

"Man, you're a nut! Why do I talk to you?"

Each student was also given a box containing the bones of a disarticulated skeleton. "Gentlemen, these bones are for you to study for the remainder of this term," Dr. Gravis, their professor, stated. "You will be expected to return them in perfect condition. Please take advantage of this fine tool in order to learn the entire skeletal system. You will need to know each and every bone for your exams."

Gravis, who John referred to as Graves, was one of their most difficult instructors so far. In fact, since the second semester began, everything was much more serious. Now, except for an occasional run, the rest of their time was spent in the library studying, writing papers, doing research, or going to conferences.

One Sunday a month, however, John's mother invited Billy for dinner. He enjoyed being with the Simmonds family and always felt comfortable with them. They were down to earth, middle-class people. John likewise enjoyed spending time at the Wilson home. He and Billy would pick Rusty's brain and pump him for information about his career, his time in Korea and any number of things.

At the dinner table, they would sit and discuss Harry's dissection and all the fascinating things they were learning. Marian finally objected after John and Billy began to go into a detailed description of the contents of Harry's stomach.

"Oh Mommy, make them stop. That's disgusting," said Barbara. "I'm going to be sick."

"Yes, please," said Marian. "I think we've heard quite enough about Harry. This is a dinner table not an operating theater. The next one of you to discuss a body part at this table unnecessarily will be banned from the dining room for a month." She looked directly at Rusty, shaking her finger. "That includes you!"

"Me? I never talk shop at home, do I girls?"

"Yes, you do," said Jennifer. "We always have to hear about how you took out somebody's golf bladder. I don't know what golfing has to do with peeing. I wish someone would tell me!"

John snorted his water and coughed into his napkin. "I think our little Jenny Wren is about to be banned from the dining room," John said. "She just mentioned a body part, sort of."

"Did not. I just want to know what golfing has to do with peeing and nobody will tell me," she retorted, crossing her arms against her chest. "I'm not a doctor! At least not yet!"

John and Billy exchanged a look, then glanced at Marian who was trying hard not to laugh. "Well, should we correct her now or wait until after dinner?" John asked.

"It's gall bladder, dear, and it doesn't have anything to do with golfing or…
um well peeing," Marian said, putting her hand over her mouth laughing. "And
now, that is truly enough," she said smiling.

"Boy, she sure is pretty," John mentioned to Billy one night in the medical
school library. He was referring to the young woman who was working at the
information desk. The woman's long, honey colored hair hung straight down
her back. Her face, that was devoid of makeup, was clear and rosy cheeked.

Billy grunted; his face buried in a textbook.

"Should I ask her out?" John questioned wistfully, pretending to read a peri-
odical as he surreptitiously eyed the young woman working at the desk.

"Sure, why not?" Billy replied.

"What if she says no?"

"Ask someone else, I guess."

"How did you go about asking your wife out?"

"Didn't," Billy mumbled, scribbling into a notebook.

"What?"

"Never had a date. Hell, I wouldn't know the first thing about it. I'm not the
best role model, Simmonds."

"If you never had a date, how the hell did you end up marrying her?"

"She said I got her pregnant," Billy muttered under his breath.

"What did you say?"

"She said I got her pregnant!" Billy said a little louder than he had intended.
The occupants of the library, including the young woman, looked their way in
disapproval.

"Oh," John said, looking a little confused. "Oh!"

"Shit, John. That's just how it happened. I'd much rather have done it the
right way."

"Oh…so, what do you have?"

"What?"

"You know, your kid. What do you have? A boy or a girl?"

Billy shook his head. "Neither, she hauled my ass to the JP, then the kid
disappeared."

"Oh man, you've got to be kidding."

"No, I wish I was."

"They're not all like that, are they?"

"You mean women?"

"Yeah."

"I hope not," Billy said, smiling ruefully. "Look, if you like this chick, ask her out. She might say yes. Who knows?" He returned to his book. "After that, you're on your own."

She did say yes. The only problem was trying to find a day and time. They wanted to go to a movie, but on the nights that Mary Agnes was free, John had a class. It seemed hopeless.

"Why don't you take her out for breakfast? If you go early enough, neither one of you will be at work or class," Billy suggested.

"That's a great idea!"

Her name was Mary Agnes Kuchta. She had just transferred to Georgetown from Duquesne University in Pittsburgh at the beginning of the semester. She was a third year, second semester Library Science major.

"So that's why I've never seen you before," John said as he sat across from her in the school cafeteria, his fried eggs congealing on his plate, his toast forgotten.

"My family moved back to Arlington from Pittsburgh at the beginning of the year. When I found out that my credits would transfer without a problem, and when Georgetown accepted me, I figured it was a good idea to move with them."

"Back?"

"My dad got transferred to Pittsburgh when I was a toddler. But both sets of grandparents still live here and are getting up in years and not in the best of health. When dad was offered a position in DC, he jumped at it. It's not that we didn't like PA, we did. We especially loved the ethnicity of the area and, with a name like Kuchta, well, we fit right in. Pittsburgh was kind of like a mini DC without all the traffic. But, as much as I loved Duquesne, it just seemed easier to move here with the family."

"Hopefully to stay," John said, giving her a meaningful look.

Mary Agnes blushed and said, "I hope so."

Breakfast was such a huge success that it became a Tuesday morning ritual. The only problem was finding a location other than the campus or hospital cafeterias. But after a few weeks, they were too engrossed in getting to know one another to worry about the quality of the food.

At the beginning of the term, John and his classmates had been split into several groups and sent to various hospitals in the area. During these sessions, they were taught methods of physical examination and diagnostic interpretation.

Billy also began working at Rusty's office on a part time basis. It was a great experience. He answered the telephone and scheduled patients. By the end of the semester, he was weighing patients, taking blood pressures and temperatures. It didn't seem like much, but it got Billy familiar with the workings of a medical office. While other students were practicing these things on one another, Billy was actually doing the tasks.

"I wish I could be doing that. You're so lucky," John said one night in the library.

"Umm," Billy riffled through a sheaf of papers and checked some notes he had made.

"Do you think Rusty would give me a job this summer?"

"I don't know. You'll have to ask him."

"Mary Agnes is getting tired of me practicing on her."

"You mean you're only practicing?" Billy raised his eyebrows.

"Oh man, you know what I mean," John said, turning several shades of red. The flush contrasted sharply with the beard and mustache he was in the process of growing. "Practice does make perfect, though. I guess."

"Be glad you have someone to practice on. By the time I actually have sex again, I'll probably have forgotten how."

"Do you really think so? I mean, isn't it sort of like riding a bicycle?"

"A bicycle? God! If you ride a woman like a bicycle, Simmonds, your ass is gonna get awfully sore," Billy replied with a grin.

"Aw, you know what I mean. Anyway, have you heard from your wife since she split?"

"No, I haven't heard from her, and I have no clue where she is."

"Oh."

"Is there any reason why you're suddenly worried about my marital situation?"

"Well, kinda out of morbid fascination and truthfully, I've been thinking about marriage myself lately."

"You have?"

"Yeah, it's just that knowing your situation has slowed me down some."

"At least I'm good for something. I'm the learning experience of the year. I don't know why you even compare us. Do you love Mary Agnes? Or is it some other young woman that has sent you into the throes of passion?"

"It's Mary Agnes. And yes, I think I love her."

"You haven't known her very long."

"Three months."

"Is that all?"

"Isn't that enough?"

"What the hell do I know? In less than three months, I was…well…you know what I was. Anyway, do you like her?"

"I said I loved her, didn't I?"

"Yes, but that isn't the same thing."

"It's not?"

"No."

"What do you mean?"

"I mean, I have sex with Jessie, yet we're strangers. I don't like how she acts, what she says, what she does. I never thought about what life with her would be like without sex. Sad isn't it," he said, shaking his head. "We were never friends. We have nothing in common. I have never laughed with her or held her hand."

"Well, Mary Agnes and I talk about all kinds of stuff. Besides you, she's my best friend."

"Is that it, two friends? Man, you need to get out more. Now, will you quit buggin' me? This paper is due at the end of the week."

JESSIE

Las Vegas was a town of illusions. At night, the lights of the city were so bright that they gave a false sense of daylight. Patrons would step out into the streets, blinking in the glare, like animals emerging from deep beneath the recesses of the ground.

Inside the lavish, elegant, and sometimes gaudy casinos sat row upon row of gamblers, feeding endless supplies of coins into slot machines. The craps and card tables were a never-ending kaleidoscope of color as men and women revolved from table to table, like hummingbirds, flitting from flower to flower.

In this glittering splendor, the illusion was that everyone was beautiful, rich and a winner. But it was all a sham. Jessie walked the strip in a slinky, low-cut dress in the midst of this ersatz gaiety and knew the city for what it was.

Chartered buses disgorged hundreds daily, all emerging hopeful and excited. Jessie saw the same people re-boarding the buses after hours or days at the casinos. She could always tell the gambler apart from the tourist who went for the sights or shows. With the exception of those bragging about a big win or wearing pleased, sly looks, most appeared shell shocked, their faces slack and gray. She saw the disappointment and disillusionment in so many gamblers' faces and felt the same.

Most of the men Jessie serviced were either high on the thrill of a big win or needing comfort after watching their money slip from their fingers in a quick twist of fate. All the girls wished for the rich ones—the ones who paid extra due to extravagance and luck. They were the men who were less likely to leave you with no money and a black eye for your trouble.

But one never knew the kind of man 'Lady Luck' would send. Life on the street was a bigger gamble than most of the action taking place in the casinos. But instead of a small fortune at stake, it was a young woman's life.

After she left Georgetown, Jessie had hitched rides until she landed back in Vegas. The lure of the city coursed in her veins. But this time, she didn't arrive on the arm of a prosperous companion. She was now alone and almost penniless. By the end of her first week back, she had been picked up by the police several times for soliciting.

The other girls that worked the streets told Jessie that she needed a pimp. A pimp was a good manager and could command higher fees. He would also keep the police off her back to a certain extent. The girls didn't tell Jessie, however, that once you signed on with a pimp, there was no getting out of the deal unless he dumped you or you ended up dead.

Most of the girls recommended a pimp named Cliff. Cliff was decent with the money and didn't beat his women too often—except when he felt they weren't pulling their weight. He had no problem adding Jessie to his already large stable of call girls. Women with foreign or striking looks, like Jessie's, were highly prized. With them, he could demand a higher fee. In a world of plentiful, plain women, men sought and paid dearly for the exotic and colorful. They wanted beautiful women on their arm in the casinos who would later do their bidding between the sheets with no questions asked.

For Jessie, time no longer had any meaning. Weeks drifted into months. Whoring paid for a rat-infested room above a low-life bar on a back street to hell. The drugs she used kept her from caring. It was a dead-end job in a dead-end existence. The pieces of her life scattered like dry leaves in the wind, and her battered teddy bear mocked her in silent reproach. She should have stuck with Billy, the bear's look said. But just when things seemed the bleakest, Jessie's life took a different turn.

One night, as Jessie walked the streets, she looked for a place to lean to give her feet a rest. Her legs ached from her stiletto heels, but they were "advertising" Cliff always said. 'Fuck me shoes,' she thought. That's what brings in the bucks.

As Jessie surreptitiously rubbed her calves, a black Lincoln Continental pulled up alongside of her. The passenger window rolled down and a very handsome man leaned over and appraised her from head to toe.

"Hey Babe, ya busy?" he asked in an accent that said New York City.

"Got time for you, if you're asking."

"Get in," the face commanded, as the car door opened up for Jessie.

Jessie hesitated, then looked over her shoulder and saw Cliff approaching. Although his face showed no emotion, Jessie knew that he was quickly calculating what this could mean for him in terms of money. He went to the door and leaned inside.

"You interested in one of my girls?"

"Yes."

"Jessie doesn't come cheap."

"I have money."

"Good, half now, half when you bring her back."

"Fine."

The two men haggled over Jessie while she stood waiting impatiently. She just wanted to get in the car so that she could sit on her ass. Hopefully, this guy would keep her off her feet for a few hours.

"Well, sweetheart, get in," the man said, as Cliff backed away from the car, a wad of bills in his hand. "I feel like dancing tonight."

"Jessie loves to dance, don't you babe?" Cliff winked as Jessie slid into the car.

Jessie thought about her leg cramps. Sighing to herself, she said, "Dancing's great," as the car pulled away from the curb and into traffic.

"Good," the man responded. "I want to dance the night away."

Jessie mentally winced. But, like an actress making an entrance onto the stage, she smiled and drew close to the man. Rubbing his thigh, she purred, "With legs like these, I bet you're good at it."

"Dancing?"

"Oh, I'm sure at anything," Jessie giggled.

"You better believe it," the man answered, taking Jessie's hand and moving it upward.

His name was Nick Vitone, and he made Jessie feel like a woman. Nick was handsome and charming. Jessie enjoyed the time she spent with him, even though it was only a buyer/seller relationship. After all, she *was* a hooker. What else could she expect? At least he treated her well, paid lavishly and gave her all the drugs she wanted.

When Jessie was with Nick, the glamor of Vegas returned. At his shoulder in the casinos, she again felt the excitement that had always drawn her to this crazy place. Nick was a businessman from New York City, who spent several weeks at a time in Vegas, wining and dining prospective and influential clients.

One evening, Nick approached Jessie. "Hey babe, my latest client is looking for a little action. Do you think you could help me out?"

"Sure, Nick, what do you want me to do?"

"Mr. Martarelli is interested in having a good time. Why don't you show him around, take him to the nicer casinos? Show him where the best, most elaborate buffets are. Whatever he wants. Kind of like a tour guide with benefits," he winked. "I'll make it worth your while."

Jessie hesitated thinking about Cliff. As if reading her mind, Nick said. "Don't worry, I'll pay your boss. He doesn't need to know that I'm giving you something on the side. I just don't want my client to know that I'm buying you for his pleasure."

"Okay, Nick. I can do that."

"Remember, Jessie. Mr. Martarelli is very important. Show him a lot of respect and don't ask any questions."

"Oh, for cryin' out loud! This isn't my first time around the block, you know."

"I know. I'm just making sure. I need to stay on very good terms with this guy."

After Martarelli, Jessie found herself entertaining quite a few of Nick's special clients. Most of the men were well dressed and professional looking, not the scruffy lowlifes she found back in Tempe. These men had class.

Nick paid Cliff the fees that he required but always made sure that Jessie got a little extra and had a safe place to squirrel it away.

Jessie still wasn't quite sure what kind of business Nick was in, but she had an idea. If she played her cards right and kept her mouth shut, she could be very happy. Nick was better than a pimp. He gave her generous, secret tips, the clients were decent, and she was treated to some top-notch drugs as well.

The only problem was that when Nick went back to New York, Jessie was left where he had found her—on the streets, working hard for every dollar that Cliff squeezed from her.

"Do you have to go?" Jessie asked, as Nick packed to go back to New York.

"It's business, babe. But don't worry, I'll be back. Maybe in the meantime, you could do me a favor."

"What's that?"

"I have a client who's gonna be in town for about a month. He's interested in someone to keep his bed warm at night. If you get my drift?"

"Of course, Nick. I'll be very happy to help you out."

"Good, it's settled. I'll get in touch with my client then I'll get in touch with your boss," Nick smirked. "Show him a good time, Jessie. Do what he wants and make him very happy."

"Of course. That's what I do best," Jessie said with a trace of sadness in her voice. "Make people very happy."

JOHN

It was a bright September day, perfect for being outdoors. John and Billy sat in the courtyard behind the medical school alongside the University Hospital. Students and medical personnel alike found this the perfect place to enjoy lunch or spend a few quiet moments.

John looked at his watch. "Nuts, only ten minutes of peace left before we have to go back inside. I know. Let's play hooky for the rest of the day. It's too nice to be cooped up in the hospital. What d'ya think?"

Billy was sitting with his arms wrapped around his knees. He exhaled a stream of cigarette smoke and squinted up at the cloudless, cerulean blue sky. "Great day for a run!"

"Sure is," John agreed.

There were quite a few people taking the opportunity to enjoy the sunshine and seating was at a premium. John, who was staring intently at all those entering the courtyard, abruptly stood up.

"Mary Agnes!" he called, waving. "Lots of room over here."

"Thanks," she smiled, as she made her way to their bench. "What a gorgeous day! It seems like everyone is taking advantage of it." She opened a brown paper bag and took out a sandwich.

"Ah, the heady aroma of peanut butter," John said. "Makes my mouth water every time."

"If that's a line, you really need to do better than that," she said.

"Sweetheart, after smelling all the things we've been around today, I meant the comment wholeheartedly."

"Uh oh, I don't think I want to know where your noses have been."

"All I will say, without going into detail and being extremely gross, is that Billy and I give new meaning to the term stool pigeon!" John said. "We were studying someone's fecal matter in order to figure out what was giving patient X the, shall we say, shits."

"Ahhh. I see. Bet whoever it was ate in the hospital cafeteria. And no, I'm not making fun of our little dates!"

"Light of my life, it's not just you, I'm afraid. Hell, even with my cast iron gut, I get the runs every time I eat there. We really need to have an official date that doesn't purge our innards," John commented, then checked his watch.

"Come on, Igor, we must get back to the lab and leave this young lady to her peanut butter."

John grabbed Mary Agnes' hand and kissed it. "Parting can be such sweet sorrow, my love. Until we meet again, which will probably be while standing on the local public transportation of choice." He performed a curtly bow, then he and Billy went back into the hospital.

Mary Agnes chuckled, shook her head, and finished her sandwich.

John was enjoying the clerkship portion of his education. Each day was a new experience. Since third year began in early August, most of his time was spent at the hospital. Along with attending over 250 hours of conferences, each student now rotated through all the major departments of the hospital, working a regular shift.

Besides Georgetown Hospital, students were scattered at other clinical facilities in the area. After their shift, they would race back to the University for a follow-up lecture. They discussed what they had seen and done and procedures they'd witnessed or actually performed.

Many students couldn't handle the grueling schedule and dropped out. Sleep and free time were things of the past. But despite the drawbacks, John and Billy agreed that what they were doing was interesting and exciting.

"Man, I'm whipped," said John, biting into a sandwich the next day in the courtyard.

"Long night at DC General?" Billy asked.

"You're not kidding. Must've been a full moon. The ER was packed. The resident, intern, and I were running around like one-armed paperhangers. We never had a chance to hit the bunks in the call room. The damn paging system kept us on our feet all night. And the attending was that scary, son-of-a-bitch Jenssen. Fortunately, he wasn't around much, but when he was, I thought the resident was going to shit his pants and run."

"Did he?"

"Close."

"Sounds like a fun night!"

"That depends on your idea of fun," John retorted.

"Uh, speaking of fun, are you doing anything tonight?" Billy asked.

"Isn't this our first Friday off in over a month?"

"Yep."

"My God, the options are limitless."

"Sitting home alone abusing yourself doesn't count."

"Spoil sport. You have something better in mind?"

"I don't know if it's better, but it's somewhat less messy. Rusty has tickets for tonight's football game but has to work. Marian flat out refuses to go and watch a bunch of young men rolling around in the mud for a ball. So, I'm taking the girls, who are not as refined as their mother. That leaves two tickets. Do you and Mary Agnes want to come with us?"

"Hum…if the combatants were female that could lend itself to my original option."

"Wishful thinking will get you nowhere," Billy said, shaking his head.

"I know. But it would be entertaining."

"On a very basic level."

"Face it Fox, women rolling around are entertaining on any level."

"Yeah, well I don't have any tickets for that. Beggars can't be choosers. You want to go or not? The tickets are free, if that's any consolation."

"Wow! Something that is free and not messy. I suppose I could handle that. Uh…no pun intended—or maybe it was."

"Why don't you check with Mare, and let me know later? I think they're playing Duquesne University if that makes any difference. Didn't you say that's where Mare transferred from?"

"Yes, she may want to go," John commented. "I'll call you when I get home and let you know if we're going to tag along."

"Sounds good," Billy said, throwing away his sandwich wrapper. "I guess we have to go back in," and with that, the two men returned to the hospital.

Billy wasn't home long when John phoned. "Those tickets still up for grabs?"

"You both want to go?"

"Yes, thanks. I'm excited! A free date without the heartburn!"

"Your lucky night. Just don't buy a hotdog."

"Ha! Shall I pick you guys up?"

"You have room in that clunker of yours for the three of us?"

"Sure, the more the merrier, we'll pick you up in half an hour."

"Okay. Thanks. I guess a nap is definitely out now," Billy sighed as he hung up.

Marian fussed, making sure the girls were dressed warmly since it had gotten chilly after the sun went down. "Are you sure you want to go to the game?" she asked. "It'll be past your bedtime when it's over. I don't want you two whining for Billy to take you home if you're tired."

"We won't. We promise," said Barbara.

"All right, then. Here, take this blanket to wrap around you. And listen to Billy."

"Yes, Mommy," they nodded. "We'll be good."

Billy looked out the window. "All right everybody, let's go. John's here."

They climbed into John's very old, dilapidated Chrysler. No one was sure what the original color had been, since it had faded to some nondescript hue. But as John said, it was easy to spot, and no one would think of stealing it. The little girls got in back with Mary Agnes, and they headed to the stadium.

"Thanks again for the invite," Mary Agnes called up to Billy. "It's nice to have someone to go with."

"A whole gang, actually," Billy smiled back.

"And see, we made it," John announced, easing the car into a lone parking spot on the street. "Who said this car wouldn't make it around the block?"

"That's only about as far as it went," Billy retorted.

Both teams' defense were playing well and neither was allowing the other to score. By the end of the first half, the game was tied at 7. The wind had picked up and everyone reached for jackets and blankets. Although Mary Agnes had brought a sweater, John noticed she was still shivering with cold.

"Here," he said, draping his field jacket over her shoulders. "Your lips are turning blue."

"Don't you need this?"

"Not really, I brought it just in case."

"Thanks," she said, pulling the olive drab material around her. "It's nice and warm."

The game ended in a 10 to 7 Georgetown victory. Mary Agnes tried to be non-biased but ended up cheering louder for Georgetown. "I didn't want to yell too loudly for the Dukes," she said, as they followed the herd from the stadium. "For fear I'd be attacked by a bunch of Hoyas. Whatever a Hoya is."

"What kind of history buff are you?" John jokingly chided. "You need to know this for your finals, so pay attention! I don't know how a bulldog became affiliated with this," John said, "but…being an inquiring, Georgetown student,

I found that back in the dark ages of our Alma Mater, when all Georgetown students, poor sods, were forced to study not only Greek but Latin, the University's teams were nicknamed 'The Stonewalls.' It is suggested that a crazy student, probably from the medical school, mashing Greek and Latin terms, started the cheer 'Hoya Saxa!', which translates into 'What Rocks!' No, wait, it couldn't have been a med student. It was probably an Anthro student into Archeology. A med student would have said Quid Cacat or 'What shits!'

"Also," John said, continuing his dissertation, "the first mascot was not a bulldog, but a terrier named Stubby."

"I don't know if I would have wanted to be affiliated with that," Billy commented.

"Gee guys, thanks for all the useless info," Mary Agnes said.

"You are so welcome. We aim to please. We are a wealth of useless shit, aren't we Billy?"

"Of course, *faex* of all kinds."

The girls were worn out. In fact, Jennifer fell asleep the minute she hit the seat. A few minutes later, John pulled up in front of the Wilson home.

"Thanks guys. I really enjoyed going with all of you. It was fun, despite the shitty lecture," Mary Agnes giggled, the dimple working in her cheek.

"Yes, thanks for the tickets. We'll have to do this again sometime," said John. "School and work permitting. See you Monday, Billy."

"Good night, thanks for the ride," he said, guiding the two sleepy girls in front of him and waving as John drove off.

About a month later, the courtyard was strangely deserted when John entered the medical school building. Mary Agnes was waiting for him at the door to the library. She immediately rushed to him and began to sob.

"What's wrong?" John asked, folding her into his arms.

"Didn't you hear?"

"Hear what?" he asked, worriedly. "What is it, sweetie?"

"President Kennedy was killed this afternoon. It was on the news."

"What!

"It's true," she said, nodding her head.

"Oh my God! That's horrible! Where?"

"Texas. He was shot while driving through Dallas. Why would anyone want to kill him? He was such a good president. Everyone loved him."

"I wondered why it was so quiet. Everyone must be gathered around radios and TVs," John said, rubbing her back.

"I'm sorry. I got your shirt messed up," Mary Agnes said, looking at John's chest.

He glanced down and smiled. "It's only water."

"And snot," Mary Agnes said, wiping her nose.

"What's a little snot? Come on. Let's go."

As they made their way to the bus stop, people they passed were talking about the assassination. The mood was somber, and more than a few people were openly weeping.

When he arrived home, his mother was in front of the television set. "John, did you hear? The president was killed a little while ago," Mrs. Simmonds remarked as he entered the room.

"I heard at school."

"That poor woman," his mother said.

"Do they know who killed him?" John asked, sitting down.

"They're not quite certain. Walter Cronkite says they've arrested a man named Lee Harvey Oswald. They're holding him for questioning. But it appears as though he did it."

"Will Johnson take over now?"

"That's what the news people are saying."

Every channel on the television told the story of the assassination over and over, making many speculations. It would be interesting to see what Johnson would do and how he would continue to lead the country.

John had always found politics boring and had never kept abreast of political matters. Maybe he should pay more attention to these things. But in the long run, did it really matter? How could politics have an effect on his life?

CAL

Cal's head dropped onto his desk with a loud clunk. Dr. Harris, in the middle of a lecture on congestive heart failure, mentally shook her head. When she dismissed class, she stopped him. "Mr. Lewis, do you find congestive heart failure boring?"

"Uh…no, Doctor, I'm sorry. I was working last night and didn't get any sleep."

"That's no excuse. Other students were also working or taking call. You aren't the only one who is sleep deprived. Twice this week you've used my class as nap time. If you're thinking of becoming a cardiologist, this class is extremely important. Of course, at the rate you're going, you'll never make it."

"What do you mean?" Cal asked.

"You're failing my course and will have to repeat it next rotation. If you don't bring up your grades, you'll have to repeat the entire year."

"Repeat the whole year?"

"Yes."

Failing the course! Part of him was angry, another part didn't care. He hated going to classes by day, then doing drudge work under smart-assed residents by night. It was around-the-clock torture. He should have followed his brother into Law, but Cal wanted something different. Curt had always been the perfect child, and Cal hated the competition that his parents had elicited between them. Had he gone into Law, the competition would have been too fierce.

Unfortunately, Cal hated everything about medicine—especially the patients. Most of the patients that he and the other students observed were, in Cal's opinion, merely hypochondriacs or people wanting attention. He listened with half an ear as patients whined about their problems. Instead, he checked out cute nurses, making sure that they noticed him.

The residents told him he was spoiled. "Poor little rich boy," they crooned. "Are you afraid to get shit on your nice clean hands?" Or they would say, "Here, pretty boy. Take this down to the pharmacy and have it filled, STAT." They gave him the worst tasks and laughed.

Now Harris was giving him a hard time. Cal couldn't make her out. She was very attractive. But as the only female professor at the school, she took no flak from anyone. The other students felt her methods were very good. All except

Cal, who thought she was too demanding. And now, he was failing her course. Usually full of answers, Cal was clueless as to how to save his butt now.

"Hello? Billy?" Cal questioned into the phone.

"Cal! It's been a long time. How the hell are you?"

"Not bad, I missed ya this summer. How are things in DC?"

"Okay, I guess. You know, SOS."

"I hear ya."

"How's everything at Cornell?"

"Third year stinks. Man, I wish you were here."

"Tsk, tsk, can't find a sucker to help you out, huh?"

"Not just that. I'm havin' second thoughts about bein' a doctor."

"What's the problem?"

Cal let out a gust of breath. "I'm failin'."

"Failing? Failing what?"

"I have to redo a rotation in cardiology."

"You're kidding?"

"I wouldn't lie."

"How are you doing in everything else?" Billy asked.

"I'm floundering. I don't know if I can handle all this stuff."

"Come on. It can't be that bad, can it?"

"When Maggie was here, it was okay. But her mother had a stroke, and she went back home to help her. I heard later that her mother died."

"Geez, I'm sorry to hear that."

"Thanks, but it gets worse. I was talkin' to a friend of hers the other day. Seems she got married this past summer to an old boyfriend. Some guy in the Air Force that she talked about once in a while. Now, I'm so freakin' down, I can't stand it," he said, his voice trailing off.

"So…what else is going on?" Billy asked, uncomfortable with the silence on the other end.

"I don't know what I want. I hate workin' in the hospital. The residents pick on me."

"They pick on everybody. The attending physicians are making their lives miserable, and the residents have to take it out on someone, us…interns, nurses…janitors, you name it."

"I don't like it."

"Who does? But, you have to put up and shut up. The more you bitch, the worse it is."

"I bet they don't pick on you."

"Ha! You really believe that? Hell, they're still trying to send *me* back to the reservation."

"But you seem to like what you're doing."

"Yes, I do. I'm so fascinated with everything I'm learning that I tune out the crap."

"Fascinated?" Cal said. "I don't know, Fox. You really dig the long hours of hard work, the crazy shifts, and the crap from above?"

"It's not that I dig it, I tolerate it. Look, I've lived in this house for three years. I see the long hours Rusty puts in, and the calls in the middle of the night. It's all part of it. No one ever said that being a doctor was a nine to five job, five days a week."

"I think that's part of my problem. It scares me when I think about giving so much of my time. Will I have anything left?"

"Sure, you will. Rusty has time to go to the country club and play some golf or tennis. We do things as a family. He goes places with Marian. They have two children…and me. What else could he possibly want?" Billy said.

"But what we're doin' now, will we always be doin' it?"

"What do you mean?"

"Eatin' shit and having endless responsibilities?"

"To a certain extent," Billy said, patiently. "No matter what field or profession you choose, you're always going to have someone telling you what to do."

"But I don't like that."

"Of course, you don't. What *you* want is no responsibility, no job, and plenty of money." Billy stated. "What *you* want is to be a rich kid forever. Don't you think it's time you grew up?"

"So, you think I'm a spoiled, rich kid, too?"

"No, Cal, I don't think it, I know it."

"What?"

"Compare us," Billy said. "I work; you don't. I pay for everything I have; your parents pay your way. I'm living on the Wilson's charity; you're living on your own. You're kidding yourself if you think we're on the same level."

"I thought you were my friend."

"Only a *true* friend would tell you something you didn't want to hear in order to help."

"You think pickin' on me is gonna help?"

"Is that what you think I'm doing?"

"Aren't you?"

"I'm merely pointing out facts."

"You think you're so damned smart, don't you?"

"No, I don't," Billy said, tiredly. "But I know one thing, no matter what you do, no one is going to hand you anything. What you are and what you make of yourself can't be bought. So, if you don't want to work hard, go home. Maybe your parents will pay you to watch the grass grow."

"You bastard. I call you for help and you turn on me."

"I am *not* turning on you. Look, why do you want to be a doctor anyway?"

"I don't know, family pressure, money—you know, that kinda stuff. Tell me, Fox. Why do *you* want to be a doctor?"

"None of those reasons. Mostly I want to help people, especially my people. I'm fascinated with what makes the human body work and what fixes it when it breaks."

"Man, there has to be something wrong with me. Except for Maggie, nothin's ever motivated me like that. But I've come so far, I can't quit now. Four years pre-med, three years med school. Hell, that's seven years of my life down the drain if I throw in the towel. But I keep thinkin' I still have forever to go."

"It does seem like forever sometimes, doesn't it? I keep telling myself it's worth it."

"Is it?"

"I hope so. Everything I've ever done has led me to this point—all the planning and hard work to get scholarships and grants. I try not to think about the price I've had to pay to be here. If you don't like med school or being a doctor, get out now. You'll be a lousy doctor if you don't really want to be one. About Maggie, I don't know what to say. I'm not the best expert on women."

"Have you seen Jessie lately?" Cal questioned.

"Not since she showed up on the Wilson's doorstep last Thanksgiving."

"You're kiddin'?"

"I wish I was. She was a shock to everyone. You know Jess. She was as outrageous and crazy as ever. Yet she also seemed lost and lonely. I don't know. I probably screwed up big time. She actually showed up and instead of trying to do something to help her, I pretty much threw her out. I still feel like a rat about the whole thing."

"Maybe we should both give up women forever."

"I have. I don't expect to see Jessie again for a good long time. Now I'm trapped. Got a wife I don't love. Can't get interested in any other women because I'm married. Not that I'd have time for any kind of relationship anyway."

"Oh well, I just hope Maggie's happy."

"And maybe someday, Jessie and I will get it together. Stranger things have happened."

"Yeah, I might even become a doctor," Cal laughed.

"I don't know which thought is scarier."

"Me, either. Well, take it easy and thanks for listenin'."

"Anytime."

MARY AGNES

Mary Agnes always felt left out. All through grade and high school, she had been quiet, shy, and on the fringe of things. She liked sports and was good at them but didn't enjoy competing. A good student, Mary Agnes received high marks, but never stood out among the rest of her classmates. In fact, nothing about her was memorable. She was thin, of medium height, and wore her straight, honey colored hair, long.

She loved Duquesne University, however, and its' Library Science program. It was English, history and books! Everything that Mary Agnes loved.

But when her dad had the chance to move back to the DC area, Mary Agnes had the choice of either staying in Pittsburgh and finishing her degree or trying to transfer to a school closer to Arlington.

She applied and was accepted to Georgetown. With only a few extra credits to make up, she was able to transfer to Duquesne's southern relation. A commuter, she made some wonderful friends and finally felt a sense of belonging.

It was Sunday and Mary Agnes stopped to see John. When she arrived, he was in the driveway bent under the open hood of his car.

"I don't think you have any idea what's under there," she said, standing at his shoulder.

"I'd have better luck if it were a human being," John grinned. He wiped his hands on a rag and pulled Mary Agnes against him for a kiss. "What're you up to?"

"I'm going to help my cousin make decorations and favors for a baby shower."

"Hey, knock your socks off."

Mary Agnes heard the Harley before she saw it. Glancing up the street, she saw a shiny black motorcycle coming their way. Pulling behind John in the driveway, the rider cut the engine, dismounted, and took off his helmet.

John stuck his head out from under the hood. "I thought you were going to be here sooner."

"Sorry, I was working on a paper and lost track of time," Billy said. "I hustled over as quickly as I could. Hope your mom doesn't mind. I'm a little ratty."

Billy wandered over to the car. He leaned against the side and stuck his head under the hood. "You have no idea what's under there, do you?"

"Aw, come on, you too?"

Mary Agnes laughed. "I said the same thing. He just pokes and prods things under there but doesn't do anything except mutter curses."

"Ever hear the word mechanic?" Billy asked, leaning on the fender. "Is there something in particular you're looking for, or are you just browsing?" He and Mary Agnes laughed again.

"Go ahead. Make fun of me. Sticks and stones," John retorted.

Billy straightened and looked at Mary Agnes. "Are you here for dinner, too?"

"No, I'll be leaving shortly," she said.

"That's too bad, Mrs. Simmonds makes a mean pot roast."

"I know. She makes the best, doesn't she?"

"Yes, but please don't tell Marian I said that. I'll deny it."

"Speaking of pot roast, Mom said everything's about ready," John replied. "We were just waiting for you."

"I've got to run, too," Mary Agnes said, kissing John goodbye. "See you tomorrow."

"Same time, same channel," John said, pointing his index finger at her like a gun.

The holiday season came rapidly for John. During Christmas break, he promised to take Mary Agnes to the city for a day of exploration. Mary Agnes was in her element. Although John had been to the Smithsonian Museums many times, Mary Agnes showed him those places in a new light. She gave him a history lesson in every building. But, instead of being bored, John was fascinated. More like storytelling than lecture, Mary Agnes brought history to life.

The rest of the afternoon was spent admiring monuments and other places of interest. After a long discussion, they decided on Chinatown for dinner. Although the walk proved longer than anticipated, the meal was memorable. Eating with chopsticks, they tried many different items, enjoying the exotic seasonings and textures.

John was amazed by Mary Agnes. She wasn't like other girls he had dated. She was adventurous and never made fun of anything or anybody. As they sat companionably, savoring each course, John was finding more and more things to discuss with Mary Agnes. He knew, without a doubt, that this lovely woman was his soul mate and if he was smart, he would do everything he could to make her his.

The bus ride back was quiet. "My brain feels numb," John said.

"Sensory overload," Mary Agnes smiled. "I think it hit us pretty hard. Still, it was a very nice day. I enjoyed myself. What about you?"

"It sure beats listening to a bunch of patients giving a group of us vague symptoms or telling us how they haven't had a bowel movement in over three months. Geez, when I think about it, it all narrows down to shit, doesn't it? I mean, that's what makes the human being tick."

Mary Agnes laughed. "Here we go again! Are you going to give me another lecture about shit?"

"Not exactly. But, three years of med school, all the exams, rotations and papers. Couldn't they have just told us this up front?" John laughed as well.

"And they say doctors don't have a sense of humor."

"Don't forget, I'm not one yet. Maybe when I finally graduate, I'll have lost it. Although, many doctors I know still have one. But it's kind of scatological and a bit on the raunchy side."

"You mean like yours?"

"I guess," he smiled and wrapped an arm around her, giving her a gentle squeeze.

John couldn't believe how quickly the four years of medical school had flown. Graduation was just around the corner. This last year had been a killer. With such a hectic schedule, he had no free time. Occasionally he met Billy for lunch in the courtyard. But, other than that, there were no more runs, no Sunday dinners. Work and study were the only items on both men's agendas.

A week before graduation, John and Billy were hurriedly taking a break for lunch when Mary Agnes stopped by. "Hi guys," Mary Agnes said. "I picked up your uniform at the cleaners, John. You're all set for the army banquet." She turned toward Billy. "Are you going?"

"No."

"Billy won't go because he doesn't have a date," John replied. "Since it's a dinner followed by a dance, mostly couples attend. But I told him there was no reason why he couldn't go. Especially since he is getting the same award as me."

"You are? That's wonderful! Why don't you come with us?"

"You know how I hate those kinds of things. Besides, I refuse to be a third wheel. You guys go and have a great time."

The formalities of the banquet didn't take long. John was presented with an award for academic excellence. Although, he wasn't at the dinner, Billy's name was mentioned as well. It also came as no surprise that both men were awarded Walter Reed hospital for both their internships and residencies.

Mary Agnes was very proud and much relieved that John wouldn't be sent far away. During the last year and a half, their relationship had evolved from a tentative, getting to know you—to I think this is forever.

When they first found out about Walter Reed, John and Billy had kicked around the idea of renting an apartment in Takoma Park.

"Why would you do that?" Mary Agnes asked, when the subject had been brought up.

"It's much closer to the hospital. From home during rush hour, the drive can sometimes take up to forty-five minutes," John replied. "But the cost of an apartment, plus the hue and cry that the Wilsons put up with Billy, made us change our minds. It's a shame that the metro system isn't finished, since one of the proposed stops is in Rosslyn. It would have made life a whole hell of a lot easier for both of us."

When dinner was cleared away, the lights were dimmed. As the opening strains of *Can't Help Falling in Love* were heard, John took Mary Agnes' hand and led her out onto the small dance floor. "Now, how do I do this without crippling you for life," he said, putting his arm around her waist.

Mary Agnes moved against him and took his hand, wrapping her other around his neck. "I guess we just stand close and sway to the music," she said, glancing at the other couples on the dance floor. "It looks like that's all they are doing," she said smiling.

It was a beautiful song and John wished it would have gone on forever. When it was over, he took Mary Agnes' hand and led her out to the veranda. The night was filled with the heady aroma of flowers.

John took both of her hands in his. Taking a deep breath, he looked into her eyes and said, "I love you, Mare. Have since the moment I first saw you. I know right now, I'll only be a lowly intern, then an over-worked resident, but eventually, I'll be able to offer you something. I know I have nothing at the moment, and you are still finishing your own degree, but would you ever consider joining me in an adventure that would last a lifetime?"

Mary Agnes said softly, "There is no one on earth that I would rather share an adventure with than you."

John smiled and pulling her against him, kissed her softly on the lips. Then throwing caution to the wind, crushed her against him and let his lips tell her how he really felt.

BILLY

The day of graduation was finally upon them. Marian sat with pride in the crowded auditorium at the Medical School. As the graduates stood and recited the Hippocratic oath, she took Rusty's hand. It was very stirring to hear those passages. It brought her back to Rusty's graduation and the pride she felt for the man beside her.

When the ceremony ended, they went out for dinner. While they waited to be served, the family made Billy open his gifts. During med school, Billy had used instruments that were either purchased second-hand or ones that Rusty had passed on to him. They were functional but a little out-dated. Wrapped individually were a new otoscope with five different specula, a Taylor percussion hammer, a stethoscope and a sphygmomanometer. Billy was overwhelmed.

The most overwhelming gift of all, however, was a plain white envelope containing account information for a Certificate of Deposit.

"What's this?" he asked fearfully.

"It's all of the money that you have given us the past four years," Rusty replied. "I told you we didn't need or want it, but you refused to take no for an answer. Marian and I decided to bank it for you and when we had enough, we rolled it over into a CD in your name. When it comes due, it will help you with whatever you may need. Just a little nest egg."

Billy bowed his head and looked like he was ready to cry.

"What's wrong?" Jenny asked him.

He swallowed hard. "There's nothing wrong, Jenny Wren. It's difficult for me to say what I feel inside." He stood and turned to Marian and Rusty. "You took me in, a stranger. Gave me so much—a roof over my head, a bed to sleep in," he paused, "a place to call home. I never thought when I came here, you would become my family." He cleared his throat. "A family like I never had. These gifts are wonderful, and I appreciate them more than you'll ever know. But what I treasure most are the things that couldn't be bought. A mother, a father, two sisters," he said softly. "A family who has stood behind me with unconditional love despite everything." He swallowed again, trying to keep his composure. Marian reached out and took his hand.

"I love you all so very much," he said, squeezing her fingers. "Thank you."

The girls jumped up from their chairs and ran to hug him.

"We're so glad you're here with us," Marian said with tears in her eyes. "You're the son we wanted but couldn't have. And we love you, too." She stood and clasped Billy into her arms.

"You made us very proud today," Rusty added, standing as well. "I think I am safe in my masculinity to join this hug. Congratulations, Doctor Fox," he said, and the whole family hugged as one.

Walter Reed was an amazing place. During his internship, Billy rotated through all the departments of the hospital and spent time at other hospitals in the area as well. There was so much to do and still so much to learn.

Occasionally, he ran into John. They would stop briefly and say hello. But there never was longer than a moment to talk. It wasn't until their internships were over and they were sent to San Antonio for Officer Candidate School that they had the chance to finally catch up.

Endless drilling and exercise left them exhausted. At first, they collapsed onto their adjacent bunks at night and fell asleep quickly. Eventually, as they got acclimated to all the physical and mental demands OCS put on them, they would quietly recap their day at lights out, smiling at the snorts and farts of the other occupants of the room.

While they were in Texas, the talk in the barracks kept returning to Asia and the troops President Johnson was sending by the thousands into Vietnam. Instead of things being settled quickly, the United States' involvement continued to escalate.

As the civil war became more intense, the American troops found themselves embroiled in something that couldn't be contained. Like fighting an out-of-control forest fire, the firemen sent in to stop the blaze were unable to back out and escape.

For Billy and John, being sent to Vietnam was a very real possibility. They were already in the army. The question now wasn't *if* they were sent but when. With the army, nothing was certain. Pulling active duty in Asia hung over their heads like a threat.

In the meantime, John and Mary Agnes set a date for their nuptials. They would be married in the chapel at the medical school building in May of 1968. Even though John would still have two more years of residency, he was earning a salary, albeit a meager one. Mary Agnes now worked full-time as a librarian at the medical school library. They didn't need much money to live. They were young and had each other.

The week of the wedding, John and Billy attended a seminar in California. The day of the rehearsal, Mary Agnes was to pick them up at the airport. The men were already outside and waiting with their bags, when Mary Agnes pulled up in front of the terminal half an hour late.

"I'm sorry. I just had my final fitting and picked up your uniforms at the cleaners for tomorrow," Mary Agnes explained as she got out of the car. "I thought I'd never get here." Handing John the keys, she continued, "You're driving home. I've had it. I hate driving in this crazy city. Everything's so congested and torn up due to the new metro that it's a wonder I got here at all."

As the men got in the car, she asked, "how was California?"

"Very informative," John replied.

"What was the seminar about?"

"Amputations."

"Oh? I thought you already knew how to cut things off."

Billy smiled. "We do. God! Remember how Dwight shit himself when Dr. Gravis brought out that hack saw?"

"He puked," John laughed. "Just like he did when we first began dissection lab. He was always such a wuss."

"Well, if they didn't teach you how to cut things off, what *did* they teach you?" Mary Agnes persisted.

"A few prosthetic companies came and discussed new procedures and techniques of amputation." John smiled at her through the rear-view mirror. "Get the picture?"

"I see. But why would the army send you guys to something like that?"

"Vietnam," Billy answered shortly. "With these new procedures, we should be able to send amputees home to be more easily fitted for prosthetics. It used to be that some army surgeons would just basically hack the limb off and leave the rest to nature. So that by the time the wounded would get back to the States, the damage wasn't always able to be repaired. In fact, some of those procedures hadn't changed since the Civil War. Since prosthetics have changed for the better, there are now updated methods of padding the skin around the bone so that a prosthetic will fit more snugly and won't cause as many sores."

"Well, thank God for that!" Mary Agnes said.

"It's sad to think," John commented, "doctors are being sent to Asia to repair the damage to human lives that politics is dictating. What a bunch of shit! At least in our civil war, it was mainly our own people fighting. And, in World War 1 & 2, we were fighting for our country. Korea was questionable. But now, this makes no sense."

The next day was clear and sunny, promising to be hot later in the day. The two men waited in the sacristy with the priest until the wedding began. John stalked around the room, rubbing nervously on his now smooth chin. He had shaved off his facial hair, much to Mary Agnes' delight. She had been nagging him for months, complaining that kissing him was like kissing a porcupine.

"Will you calm down! You're making me nuts," Billy said, exasperated.

"Can't help it. I just wish it was over. I hate being the center of all this attention."

"Hell, no one's even going to notice you. All eyes will be on Mare. You could be a fence post as far as the rest of the people are concerned."

"Fence post? Thanks, I feel much better now. Seriously though, Billy, I appreciate you being my best man. I'm very glad you agreed to do this. I'm lucky to have you as a friend. Thanks too for covering for me this weekend."

"Don't thank me until you get my bill. I just hope the emergencies hold off until after dinner. I'd hate to leave in the middle of the ceremony." The music then began, and the men walked out into the church.

It was a beautiful service. The reception that followed, with only the closest of family and friends, was simple and elegant.

Before dinner was served, champagne was poured. John turned to Billy and said, "Well buddy, your moment has arrived. You *do* have a toast planned, don't you?"

"I thought I'd do a twenty-minute presentation about cirrhosis of the liver, complete with a slide show. What do you think?"

"I think I should have had Dwight for a best man."

At that, Billy stood and cleared his throat. "John and I have been friends for a long time. When he met Mary Agnes, I thought I was going to lose my running buddy. But instead of losing John, I gained Mare." He bent down and kissed Mary Agnes on the cheek then shook John's hand. "Here's to John and

Mary Agnes, may they have a long and happy life together. Friends always," he said, raising his glass.

"Not bad, Fox," John said, wiping moisture from his eye. "Thanks."

"After dinner, I'll do the cirrhosis thing."

"You're such a jerk," John said.

During dinner, Billy was called to the phone. When he returned to his seat, John asked, "What was that all about?"

"It was Curtis. He said he'd stay until eight o'clock." Billy checked the time. "I have about an hour before I turn into a pumpkin."

Once dinner was cleared, John and Mary Agnes were introduced and made their way to the center of the dance floor.

John smiled. "Now, how do I do this without crippling you for life?"

"Just hold me close and step back and forth," Mary Agnes replied. And together they swayed to the music, lost in the light of each other's eyes.

Billy, in the meantime, was gathering his things together. "I'll probably see you late tomorrow night," he told the Wilsons. "I got called in for John. After that, I'll work my own shift. It'll be a long night at the funny farm."

"We haven't seen you since you went to California," Jenny complained, pouting.

"And you promised that you'd dance with me," Barbara said sadly.

"I'm sorry. It's been crazy at the hospital. With all this crap going on in Asia, we're working tons of overtime. We've been getting a lot of convalescent wounded as well as patients that need more extensive surgery. I should be home all day Monday, I hope. See you then."

He took one last look at his friends. As he watched the couple, John stepped several times on Mary Agnes, but the look in their eyes proved that nothing would ruin the moment. He smiled and shook his head. Billy was happy for his friends, yet a little sad knowing he would never have a moment like that.

JESSIE

When Rusty walked in the back door, Billy was seated at the kitchen table, his head cradled on his arms. As the door banged shut, Billy awoke with a start and jumped to his feet.

"Holy shit! What time is it?"

"Eight," Rusty replied.

"Christ, I'm late! Oh my God! How could I fall asleep like that?"

Rusty looked at Billy closely, then asked, "Are you sure you were on your way out?"

Billy stared at Rusty, a look of puzzlement on his face. "I don't know. I don't remember."

Rusty chuckled. "I remember when I was a resident. I used to show up for work on days I wasn't scheduled, simply because I was working so much, I couldn't remember what was happening from one day to the next. With you, it's even worse. You guys at Reed are really putting in the overtime."

"Yeah," Billy mumbled. "But now I don't know whether I was coming or going."

"By the look of your uniform, I'd say you just came in."

"How can you tell?"

"Your tie's askew and your uniform is rumpled."

"Really?" Billy said, looking down at his clothes. "What day is it?"

"Tuesday," Rusty said, checking the two schedules hanging on the refrigerator door. "Yep, you're coming in. It appears as though you did a double starting on Sunday."

"Whew," Billy said. "Thank God. My ass would have been in a sling if I'd been late."

"It looks as though you have the whole day off," Rusty said. "How exciting! This will give you a chance to play a round or two of golf."

Billy yawned as he got up and shuffled down the hallway. "Pfft, not very likely, I'm getting my mean ass to bed. Don't call me unless the house is on fire."

"Sweet dreams," Rusty called. "I'll be right on your heels."

It wasn't the house on fire but the phone ringing in his ear that jolted Billy awake. He squinted at his watch as he picked up the receiver. "Um," he mumbled into the phone.

"Fox?" a male voice asked.

"Who's this?"

"It's Cal. You sound pretty groggy. Did I wake you?"

"Kind of, I just came off a double plus OT."

"Sorry buddy, but this is important."

"It's been a while. What is it now?"

"Actually, this concerns you."

"Me?"

"I have something that belongs to you. I need to know what you want me to do with it."

"What's that?"

"Jessie."

Billy's eyes snapped open, and he sat up in bed. "What the hell are you doing with her?"

"I found her walkin' the streets, sellin' her wares. She's in some kind of trouble. But you know Jessie. Her mouth is shut tighter than a seventy-year-old virgin's twat."

"Shit! Let me talk to her."

"Before you start yelling," Jessie began, "it wasn't my fault. So, spare me a lecture."

"Your fault? I don't even know what you're talking about and you're already pointing fingers at someone else. I want you to get your ass on a bus to Washington. I'm in no shape to deal with you now. We'll sort this out when you get here."

"What if I don't want to come?"

"Then you go back to the streets. I won't let Cal become responsible for you."

"What if he likes my ass and all its tricks."

"Then he'll have to answer to me."

"What? Are you my pimp now?"

"You know what I mean. Don't get smart."

"But I like it here. He's got more to offer than you, in more ways than one."

"I'm sure he does, but that isn't the purpose of this call. I'm assuming that since he was the one to do the phoning, he's trying to get rid of you. Am I right?"

Jessie was silent.

"The first bus, Jessie. Have Cal call me when he knows what time you'll be due in. I'll meet you at the station."

"All right," she sighed and hung up.

"Where'd ya get the heap?" Jessie asked the next day, as she slipped into the front seat of the station wagon. Her black mini skirt almost covered her butt, showing off her shapely legs. And the tight, off-the-shoulder top she was wearing accentuated all her other curves. She smirked as she noticed Billy glancing surreptitiously at her exposed skin. "It's really cool."

"Don't start, Jessie," Billy said, throwing her bags into the back seat then getting behind the wheel. "I borrowed the Wilson's car since I didn't know how much stuff you'd have with you. There's only so much room on the bike. Besides, with all that bare skin, you'd probably cause an accident. Now, what's going on?" he asked, as he pulled out into traffic from Union Station.

"For a minute there, you had me worried, doctor. It is doctor now, isn't it? Or do you prefer your royal highness?"

"Don't change the subject. How did you end up in New York City? I'm assuming that's not where you went after you left the last time."

Jessie stared sullenly ahead, refusing to answer.

"Look Jess, I'm in no mood for playing games. I want some answers and I want them now. Where did you go when you left here? Vegas?"

Jessie nodded. Her eyes straight ahead.

"And what did you do there? I'm also assuming that you didn't check into a convent."

Jessie shot him a dirty look. "What do you think I was doing?"

"Great! A question with a question. You're gonna make me work for this, aren't you? Okay. Let me tell you what I think happened, then you can tell me if I'm wrong."

Jessie shrugged and watched the other drivers jockey for position in the snarl of downtown DC traffic. Billy swore under his breath as he tried to maintain a safe distance from the other cars without getting killed or smashed into. "This is what I think. You went to Vegas and sold your ass to make money. Eventually, you pissed someone off. How you got to New York is a mystery, although, you have been known to hitchhike, that's one possibility. Am I right so far?"

Jessie bit at her lower lip. "Close enough, I guess," she finally said.

"Now, you can fill in the blanks."

"What if I don't want to?"

"Do you want my help or not?"

"I don't need your help."

"Really? Then why are you here?"

"I didn't call you. It was your buddy who got me into this mess. I was doing fine until he picked me up. I don't need you or anyone else."

"That's not what Cal said when I spoke to him earlier."

"What does he know?"

"Plenty from the sound of it," Billy replied, grinding his teeth and trying to maintain his composure. He looked at her from out of the corner of his eye. Even though she was arguing with him, her bravado seemed half-hearted, and she looked very tired. Billy let her be. He concentrated instead on maneuvering through traffic, thinking again how much easier running was than driving.

He finally relaxed as he reached the familiar streets of Georgetown. Jessie, in the meantime, stared silently out the window, her hands worrying the strap of her handbag.

A few blocks from home, Billy pulled over and stopped the car. "All right, Jessie. Your time's up. I want to know everything—no lies, no arguments, just the truth for once. Please."

"You won't understand," she said, her eyes full of unshed tears.

"Try me."

Jessie took a deep breath, then said, "I think someone got killed because of me."

Billy stared at her for a long moment, his face a blank. "What happened?"

"He was gonna take me away from Vegas," she said, as tears ran down her cheeks, "to New York City. He lived there and he needed me for his business. I didn't mind. He was good to me. All I had to do was keep his clients happy. But first, he had to get me away from my pimp."

"You had a pimp?"

"Look, Fox. I needed to live. And there was no way I was getting any help from you."

Billy looked out the window then finally back at Jessie. "I'm sorry. Please…," he gestured with his hand.

"He said he had it all figured out. He gave me my ticket and some money and told me to meet him on the plane, but he never came. I'm so afraid he got killed because of me."

"Do you know for a fact that he's dead?"

"No, but what else can I think. He was supposed to be on that plane. When I got to New York, I waited at the airport for a week, thinking he got another flight. But he never showed. He has to be dead. He wouldn't have just left me like that after he had given me a ticket and money." Jessie turned to the window and wiped her eyes with the back of her hand. "I took a bus into the city and wandered the streets. I had some cash, plus what he had given me, but not enough to live on. I was trying to make money the only way I know how when Blondie found me."

"When was that?"

"A week ago."

"A week? What were you doing all that time?"

"Trying to talk the big, rich boy into letting me stay."

"You wore out your welcome rather fast."

"There was another chick with him. She didn't want me on her turf," Jessie shrugged.

"And now, you're here again." Billy sat silently. After a while, he seemed to come to some sort of decision. He turned to her and put his hands on both sides of her face.

Jessie tried to break free. "What're you doing?"

"I want you to look at me and listen to me very carefully," he said, his hands still firmly on her face. "You are my wife. You are going to stay with me."

"You mean with those uppity Anglos?"

"I'll find an apartment for us, but in the meantime, we'll have to stay with the Wilsons. *If* they'll have you. But this time, things will be different. I won't tolerate any rude or crude language or actions from you. You will be polite and helpful. You won't smoke in the house or sit around on your butt all day, making smart remarks like you did before. You'll either be looking for a job, working or helping Marian."

"A job?"

"Yes, a job. When we move out, you'll be gainfully employed in a reputable place, not hooking. You'll pull your weight and help out by doing things that normal wives do."

"And you, Mr. Doctor? What will *you* be doing?"

"Me? I'll be eating shit and hauling ass at the hospital. I won't be home very much; but when I am, I'll probably be sleeping. I'll support you as best as I can, but I'm warning you, I make next to nothing as a resident. Don't expect a grand apartment in a fancy neighborhood."

"Great! From one slum to another."

"Yeah, well, at least you can pee inside."

"Joy."

"And lastly and most importantly, there will be no drugs to speak of in your possession at any time. Do you understand?"

Jessie nodded her head, her eyes burning hatred into his face.

"I want you to promise me that you'll toe the line."

"And if I don't?"

"Then you're on your own."

"What you're really saying is that I don't have a choice."

"Smart girl."

"You're a fucking tyrant."

"With you I have to be."

"I hate you."

"I know," he said quietly, taking his hands from her face.

"This isn't gonna work."

"You're right. But I have to try."

"How about sex?"

"Sex? With me? Somehow, I don't think you'd want that."

"How come?"

"After all the men you've had, I'm sure I'd fall short of your expectations."

Jessie snorted. "You'd be surprised. Compared to most of the animals I've had to screw, you weren't all that bad."

"Gee, thanks. I'll put it on my resume." He started the motor of the station wagon and let out the brake. "Now, we are going home. You will be on your very best behavior. I promise, I won't hit you no matter how hard you provoke me. But I will, however, throw your ass as far out into the street as I can if you fail to act accordingly."

"God, did they give you a new tongue in medical school? I'm not sure what you just said was in English."

"All you need to understand is that I expect you to behave."

Again, Billy was shot down by the Wilsons. "Suppose you actually find a suitable apartment?" Rusty questioned. "Then what?"

"What do you mean?" Billy replied a little defensively.

"The kind of apartment you can afford will never be furnished. If it is, it won't be the kind of furniture you'd want."

"Then I'll have to buy some."

"Listen Billy, *when*, not if, Jessie takes off again, you'll be stuck with an expensive lease and useless furniture you'll either have to sell or store. You don't need that hanging around your neck like a millstone, too."

"Come on guys, you saw what happened the last time. I won't have that happen again."

"Neither do we," Marian admitted. "But this time, we're prepared. We…*I*… know what to expect. You've already laid down the law to her. I'll do everything I can to help her get a job. In fact, I think they're looking for a paid salesclerk at the auxiliary resale shop."

"Otherwise known as Fox's fashions," Billy said wryly.

"Tomorrow, I'll bring her with me and introduce her to the manager. I'm already working there three days a week as a volunteer. I'll be able to keep an eye on her and make sure she stays out of trouble. Unfortunately, as Rusty said, I have a feeling she won't be here long."

"And what if she stays. What if she moves in permanently?"

"That's when you go looking for an apartment," Rusty replied.

A few days later, Jessie sat on Billy's bed, frowning. "Where are we going again?"

"John and Mary Agnes are good friends and invited us for dinner."

"You mean I have to be nice to these people all evening?"

"They're very easy going. It shouldn't be hard."

"I don't know about this, Fox. Why don't you go alone? I'll be a good prisoner and stay in my cell all night."

"The reason we're going is because of you. I already explained that."

"But they don't know me. And they probably won't like me."

"Whether they like you is up to you. They'll be nice to you, but you have to be nice back."

"Stupid white shits."

"Uh, by the way, that outfit isn't gonna cut it. You're not working the streets tonight. How about a pair of jeans and a t-shirt?"

"Hiding my light under a bushel, aren't you."

"I don't want you to look like a whore. That top you're wearing is just a bit too snug for mixed company. Not to mention the tiny fact that you aren't wearing a bra."

"Do you like it?" she asked, sidling up to him.

Billy flushed. "Whether I like it or not isn't the point. You can't go wearing something so revealing to someone's home for dinner," he answered, as he hurriedly buttoned up his shirt and tucked it into his jeans.

"You're no fun anymore," she said, stripping off her top and digging through the drawers of Billy's dresser. She grabbed one of his t-shirts and pulled it over her head.

"Uh, aren't you forgetting something?"

Jessie looked down and sighed. "Bras're so damn uncomfortable," she grumbled.

"Come on, Jess. You can't go like that."

"You're such a grandma," she said. Pulling off the shirt, she rummaged around in her suitcase on the floor looking for a bra. She took her time, knowing that she was making Billy uncomfortable. Finally, she put everything back on then said, "Am I presentable now?"

"Yes, that's much better."

Jessie snorted. Brushing her hair she continued, "By the way, do they know about me?"

"You mean do they know what you did to earn a living?"

"Yeah."

"Uh huh, but don't worry, they aren't going to ask how many men you've had or how to choose a pimp. I don't think those questions will come up this evening."

"Speaking of things coming up, I think you need to change your mind about having sex with me. I don't think you were meant to be a priest as well as a doctor."

"Look, I don't feel like explaining to my attending physician at the hospital why I have a case of Clap. Thanks, but no thanks. Now come on, let's go. Try to have a good time. It's very kind of them to have us. Don't spoil it. Just remember to think before you say anything."

The evening was not a success. In fact, in Billy's mind, it was a total failure. John and Mary Agnes tried to include Jessie—working hard to pry small talk from her. But it was almost impossible to get her to join in the conversation. After a while, John and Billy talked shop while Mary Agnes worked in the kitchen preparing the meal. Jessie was left to her own devices, drinking bottle after bottle of beer. When the evening ended several hours later, all four persons breathed sighs of relief.

The job at the resale shop was a yawn, as far as Jessie was concerned. Run by a gaggle of self-important doctors' wives, the shop was filled with over-priced, musty old clothing that, in Jessie's mind, no one would want to wear.

Marian was the only woman who didn't act like a snob. She treated Jessie like an equal, not a paid employee. However, the other women weren't impressed that she also was the wife of a doctor. First of all, Billy was only a lowly resident. Secondly, no matter what Billy was, it didn't matter. He and Jessie were both redskins and would never be included in their circle.

The women treated Jessie civilly, provided Marian was also in the shop. But on days that Marian didn't volunteer, Jessie was treated like dirt. The other women whispered cattily behind her back and sometimes even to her face, their biting remarks sarcastic and snide. Jessie did her best to tune them out, but some days it was difficult. On those days, she came home tired and depressed.

Life on the street had been bad, but she had never had to deal with mean, rich women before. The saying about sticks and stones wasn't true. Jessie would rather have been beaten by a john than have to deal with these women. Their words wounded far more than a fist ever did.

Billy, when he was around, noticed her depression and Jessie knew that he went out of his way to be nice to her. He would try to talk to her, but as always, Jessie never knew what to say. Hurtful words and a raised fist were things that she knew and understood. But it was the kindness shown to her by Billy and the Wilsons that Jessie couldn't accept.

Marian was always ready to help her in any way either at work or at home. No matter what Jessie said or did, Marian was patient and never took offense. That was something that Jessie couldn't seem to handle.

One night, Marian said to Jessie, "The girls are away at a friend's slumber party this evening. Since the guys are actually coming home at a normal time tonight, why don't we make a special dinner for them. Something nice," Marian suggested.

Jessie shrugged. "Okay."

"I know, let's make a roast. We can eat in the dining room and make it special."

"Fine," Jessie answered, sighing. "What do you want me to do?"

"You could set the table. Let's get out the good china, silver and cloth napkins, and we can light candles. How about that?"

"Why?"

"Because it's a special occasion. How many evenings do we get to see both Rusty and Billy at the same time. My goodness, Billy hasn't been home for three days, you should be happy to see him." Jessie shrugged again. "Come now, Jessie, Billy's your husband. He works so very hard. You have no idea what residents go through. I remember when Rusty was doing his residency, he would come home so tired that he could hardly talk. As a resident, Billy is responsible for so many things, yet has no control over any matter. He takes all the flak when something goes wrong and puts in all the overtime."

"Okay, okay. I get the picture," Jessie replied.

Marian smiled and bustled ahead of Jessie into the dining room. She showed Jessie where to find all the things that she had previously mentioned. "While you're doing this, I'll be in the kitchen. If you need me, call."

Jessie looked at all the fine objects in front of her. She fingered the linen napkins and touched the delicate crystal. She had never seen anything like them before. For a brief moment, she found herself almost enjoying the task.

By the time Rusty got home, dinner had been put into the oven, and the table was set, complete with candles and flowers.

Marian greeted him at the door with a kiss. "It's so nice to have you home. How was your day?"

"Tolerable," Rusty answered, giving her a hug and returning the kiss. "You sure are a sight for sore eyes. I'm glad to be home."

"I should hope so. Not only are we good to look at, but Jessie and I have been slaving away all day over a hot stove. We have a wonderful meal prepared for you which we'll finish when Billy gets home. In fact, I think I hear the bike coming up the drive right now."

When Billy walked in, Marian greeted him warmly. She then looked over at Jessie and motioned to her with a slight cock of her head and a smile.

Jessie hesitated, then walked over to him and took his backpack, shyly kissing him on the cheek. "Hi," she said.

Billy was startled and stared at Jessie for a fraction of an instant. "Hi."

"Tough couple of days?" Jessie asked. Again, Billy stared at her for a second before answering.

"Uh, not bad, could have been worse."

"Why don't you two go change and wash up?" Marian suggested. "Dinner will be ready in about an hour. I'll finish up in here, Jessie. Why don't you go and spend some time with Billy?"

Jessie slowly followed Billy up the stairs to their room. As Billy took off his shirt, he bent his neck from side to side and rolled his shoulders.

"Sore?" Jessie asked, coming up behind him.

"Yeah, I spent the better part of the past three days bent over the insides of a bunch of faceless, nameless kids."

"Here," Jessie said, rubbing his shoulders and massaging his back and neck. "How's that?"

Billy groaned. "Mmm, I'll give you an hour to quit it." Jessie continued to rub his shoulders, getting into the spirit of the moment. If she thought about it, it was almost like when she was working. Make the guy feel good, give him what he wanted, and pretend to have fun at the same time. She ran her hands down his arms and over his chest. Nuzzling up against him, she began kissing his neck and shoulders.

Her hands worked their way down his chest, stopping at his belt. She was starting to undo the buckle when Billy turned toward her, taking her hands. "Stop, Jessie," Billy said.

"No, I *want* to do this," she said and leaning forward, she kissed him on the lips. Rearing back in surprise, Billy looked into her eyes. She smiled at him slightly, then pulling his head down toward hers, she kissed him again.

Dinner was a quiet, peaceful event, with Jessie making an effort to join the conversation at the table. Afterward, the men fussed and complimented the women on the excellence of the meal, until Marian pleaded with them to stop.

"Why don't you two go and read the newspaper or watch television. We'll clean up here."

"You sure you don't want help?" Billy questioned.

"Go," Jessie surprised everyone by answering. "You worked hard today, remember?"

"I won't be asked twice," Rusty commented, heading to the library. He gave the paper a cursory glance, then walked through the French doors and out onto the patio.

Night had fallen and the crickets and cicadas were serenading the neighborhood. Rusty settled himself in a rocker while Billy took a seat on the glider. "That was nice," Rusty remarked.

"Sure was," Billy replied, as he lit a cigarette.

"By the way, you looked like the cat that swallowed the canary during dinner," Rusty commented.

"Really?" Billy retorted. "Are you fishing or were we so loud that the neighbors could hear us?" Billy laughed.

"Neither. You just seemed so relaxed, and Jessie was on her very best behavior. I just wondered."

"She was, wasn't she?"

"Do you think she's finally getting used to being here?"

"No," he said, shaking his head. "In fact, even though she seemed to be fitting in this evening, I could feel bad vibes."

"What do you mean?"

"Well, did you notice how quiet she got when we started talking about Vietnam?"

"Not really," Rusty shrugged apologetically. "She's always pretty quiet to begin with."

"No, there was a definite change in her. Even earlier, when we were…uh… upstairs, something was going on in her head. Since she won't talk to me, I wouldn't know if something was bothering her or not." He sighed. "She just seems so lost, so out of her element. And there doesn't seem to be a damn thing I can do about it. Hell, I don't even know what her element is."

"I'm sorry. I wish we could do something to help."

"You already are. You're being nice to her, letting her live here, accepting her. What more could anyone do?"

A few minutes later, Marian and Jessie joined the men. Jessie settled next to Billy on the glider, her hand extended for his cigarettes.

"Why don't we leave the kids alone, Rusty? Come on inside and see if you can help me with the crossword puzzle I'm doing. This one is really challenging."

"Can't do anything without me, can you?" Rusty laughed and followed his wife into the house.

"Puzzle my ass," Jessie said under her breath. "She hates the smoke."

"I know. It's her right."

"I guess."

"That was a good dinner, Jess. I was really proud of you tonight."

"Why?"

"You went beyond trying. I'm sure it wasn't easy."

"I don't know. I guess I'm getting pretty good at acting."

"Acting? What about before dinner? Was all that acting, too?" he asked quietly, trying to mask the hurt that he felt.

Jessie was silent for a moment. "I…I'm not sure. I think I was at first, but then I…oh…I don't know."

Billy looked down at his smoldering cigarette. "I guess to do what you used to do, you had to act."

"Yeah."

"It must have been terrible."

"Not always, some guys treated me nice."

"Like the guy you think died?"

Jessie turned her head away. Finally, she said, "Yeah, like him."

"I'm sorry."

"Doesn't matter now. Nothing does."

"Look Jessie, I know you don't love me, and I don't love you. But we are married. I mean, you got what you wanted. I'm on my way. No, I'm not making a fortune, but I'm not starving, either. I know you don't want to live on the Rez, but at least while I'm here, we could work things out. Couldn't we?"

"Oh sure, and what about that place in Asia? I heard you guys talking at dinner. What if they send you there? What if you have to leave tomorrow? Then what? I can't stay here without you."

"Sure, you can. You have a good job. You'd just keep doing what you're doing until I came back."

"A good job, huh? I'd rather hook."

"How can you say that?"

"You've never had to work with a bunch of mean, stuck-up bitches who treat you like last week's garbage."

"Is it really that bad?"

Jessie snorted. "You'd be surprised."

"Why don't you say something to Marian? Maybe she could help you find another job. One that you'd like."

"She's already helped me enough. I don't want to be a pain."

"What about a job at the hospital as an aide or something?"

"No way, no blood or guts for me."

Billy sighed. "Then I don't know what to tell you."

"I don't know how much longer I can take this gig, Fox."

"I know."

"It's just that…I just don't…I can't handle…"

"Can't handle what?" Billy prodded.

Jessie sighed. "Oh fuck it, never mind." She got up from the glider and went into the house. Billy remained—alone once again. He lit another cigarette and tried to understand the nonsense of Jessie's and his life.

Later that evening when he crawled into bed, he tried to snuggle against her. But she pulled away from him, huddling into a tight ball of misery.

Despite her unhappiness, Jessie remained with them over three months. Some days she was able to get into the act of being the good wife and all that it entailed. Other days, it was a constant struggle not to tell each and every person in the house and at work to go fuck themselves.

What she needed was some drugs. That was what she missed the most. Jessie felt that if she only had some pot to smoke, living with the Wilsons could have been more tolerable.

In the end, the struggling just got to be too much for Jessie. She finally slipped away early one morning, as the days of autumn were fast approaching.

When Billy came home from work and entered his room, he knew something was wrong. There was no sign of Jessie anywhere. When Billy saw that the bedraggled teddy bear was no longer on Jessie's pillow, he knew for sure that she was gone. A note was on his pillow instead. It was short and to the point.

> *Sorry Fox couldn't take it anymore.*
> *I took all the money I could find.*
> *Don't worry about me, I'll manage.*
> *P.S. I was right. The sex <u>was</u> good.*

Even though they had been expecting it, her disappearance was a slight shock. They had tried to make Jessie fit, but unfortunately it was all in vain. However, with all the work that Billy was doing, it wasn't hard to push thoughts and worries of her from his mind. Each week, he saw new faces at Walter Reed while many old faces were missing. Letters came daily, summoning all areas of medical personnel to Southeast Asia. Billy and John knew that now it was only a matter of time.

PART FOUR

"To nature, whence all things
come and wither
all return,
the cry of the humble
and well-given heart is,
'Give as thou wilt,
take back as thou wilt;'
yet uttered with no heroics,
but in pure obedience and good will."

~

"Loss is nothing more than change,
and change is Nature's delight."

Marcus Aurelius

JOHN

November, 1969

They arrived at Bien Hoa in the middle of the night. The flight up to that point had been uneventful. But as the plane circled preparatory to landing, streaks of light flashed into the sky.

"Holy heck!" John exclaimed; his face pressed to the window. "They're shooting at us!"

"What are you talking about?" Billy asked, leaning across John to look out the window. "Why would they be shooting at us? We're a commercial flight." As he spoke, another round reached the sky. There was an air of uneasiness as well as faint murmurings among the men.

The plane however, continued its path of descent and proceeded to land. When it came to a complete stop, John looked at Billy relieved. "I don't know what that was all about, but I hope we have no more surprises," he commented.

They grabbed their gear and joined the rest of the men shuffling toward the exit. They were disoriented, and the dark of the Vietnam night didn't help. "I can't see a thing," John complained, as he walked across the tarmac.

"Maybe it's better that way. I'm not so sure I want to see where I'm going," Billy said, as they were herded onto buses.

A jeep with a machine gun mounted to its hood led the way. Each time the road curved, all lights on the vehicles were turned off until the road straightened.

"Do you know where we're going?" John asked the man across the aisle.

He shrugged. "Someone said a processing center, whatever the hell that is."

It was mid-morning by the time the bus pulled in front of three quonset huts. Inside, lines of men snaked throughout the buildings. John and Billy joined the queue. As usual, it was hurry up and wait.

For John, the night had been endless and the day before, even longer. When he left Dulles Airport four days ago, the goodbyes had been traumatic and gut wrenching. Only a week before, he and Mary Agnes had been so happy when they discovered that she was expecting. Then, he received the letter that turned their world upside down.

At the airport, Mary Agnes tried to smile, but her lips kept quivering and tears kept falling. All John could do was hold her. Placing his hand against her

"

abdomen, he said, "I'll be back before you know it. Take good care of our little one. I love you, sweetheart." He kissed her, then ran to the waiting plane.

Billy's letter had come the same day. Even though it was no surprise, it was still upsetting. Unlike John, Billy requested that the Wilsons not see him off at Dulles. Instead, they opted for a quiet dinner together the night before he left. "You know how I hate all that drama at airports," Billy said. "I'd rather say goodbye this way."

"I can't believe you're going to miss my high school graduation," Barbara exclaimed. The graceful and very tall young woman had been sulking ever since they had been given the news.

"I'm sorry, Bubba," Billy said, hugging her. "I'm going to hate missing that, too. But I can't say no to the army."

The next day, Billy stowed his gear into the car and Rusty drove him to Dulles, dropped him at the curb, and with a final wave, left.

From Dulles, John and Billy flew to San Francisco. Buses then took them to Travis Air Force Base where they changed from their dress khakis to fatigues. It had seemed silly to wear uniforms, but that was the only way they could get a reduced military rate on a commercial flight.

At Travis, they were no longer civilians. They joined a sea of olive drab and had something to eat before boarding a plane chartered by the army. They landed briefly in Hawaii to refuel and pick up men returning from R & R.

John had no idea what time it was or what day. He had forgotten to wind his watch and figured he'd wait and reset it when he got to Vietnam. After one last stop at Wake Island, John tried to doze but kept jerking awake. He stared out the window, wishing he knew where they were going. Their letters simply said to go to Vietnam. There were no orders, no location. Hopefully, they would soon find out.

When John finally reached the desk at the processing center, he was given form after form to sign. After his orders were cut, he found that he was assigned to a place called Chu Lai. He would be at a Battalion Aid Station or BAS on the outskirts of town. Billy was to go to an aid station at Tam Quan.

John swallowed his disappointment at being separated from Billy, then went to find out how to get to Chu Lai. Everyone gave him the run around. First, he needed to fly to Da Nang, then to Chu Lai. Once there, he'd have to either find a jeep or maybe hitch a ride on a deuce and a half to get to the BAS.

John looked at Billy. "I hear what they're saying, but I'm not sure it's English."

"I'm having the same problem. By the way, did you get a map of the country?"

"Yes, what's it for? To see where we're going?"

"Yes and no. You see how it's separated into little blocks?" Billy pointed.

"Uh huh."

"We're supposed to fill in a block every day. When the map's filled in, we've been here 365 days and can go home."

"I'm supposed to rely on a stinkin' map to tell me when I can go home?"

"No, but it's better than making slashes on the wall."

"Thanks. I'll remember that. Are you going to Da Nang, too?"

"Yes, the sergeant told me there's a C-130 going there early tomorrow morning. We need to find a spot and plant it until then," Billy advised. "Unfortunately, the only food going is in those machines. Oh, and remember when we landed and thought we were being shot at?"

"I almost wet myself."

"I'm glad you didn't. They were only illumination flares the army uses to look for the enemy. If there were any bad guys out there, our guys would hopefully see them first and shoot them before they could shoot down our plane. Just thought you'd want to know."

"Thanks. I can't tell you how relieved I am," John replied. "I wonder if there's a men's room around here anywhere."

"I'll stay here and hold our piece of floor if you want to find one. Then we can trade places."

"Sounds good," John said and pushed his way through the noisy throng until he finally snagged a corporal hurrying past. "Can you tell me where I can find a men's room?"

"If you need to take a leak, there's a piss tube outside and around the corner. If you have to shit, there's a six-holer behind the next building." He imparted those words of wisdom without breaking stride.

"Thanks," John said.

Outside, he found a line of men in front of a crude stall against the side of the quonset hut. What appeared to be a large funnel was attached to rubber tubing that ended in a bed of gravel on the ground. Guess this is it, he thought. Maybe if I'm lucky, I won't have to shit for the next 12 months. I really don't want to know what a six-holer is.

He returned to Billy. "There's a piss tube around the side of this building and a six-holer behind the next," he said with authority.

"All the comforts of home," Billy said standing. He shook his head and was swallowed into the crowd.

John settled against his duffel and tried to sleep. He was exhausted and wasn't sure what the morning would bring.

The following day was frustrating. He and Billy got a flight to Da Nang. But once there, they were stonewalled. A steady torrential rain had canceled all remaining flights for the day. A jeep took them to an army depot where they got a bunk for the night and a hot meal.

The next day, they returned to the airport. But again, rain grounded all planes. After several attempts by shortwave radio, both men finally got through to their superior officers to tell of the delay. A few days later, the rain finally let up and they were able to continue their journeys. Now, they were on their own.

Chu Lai was boring. After twelve to sixteen-hour shifts at Walter Reed, the BAS was a vacation. John became part of an artillery unit that was out on maneuvers most of the day or night. He spent his days reading, sweating and missing his wife. Meals were C-rations which mostly consisted of canned chili, spaghetti or hot dogs and beans.

"Gas in a can," one GI remarked.

He saw no casualties. The wounded were taken directly from the field to a hospital by helicopter. The only doctoring he did was trivial. He removed some splinters, did 'short-arm inspections,' treated a few snake bites and aided some soldiers with dysentery.

After two months, he was transferred to Dong Ha. At first, he couldn't find his new unit. Not only did the Army have a hospital and supply station there, but the Marines and Air Force as well. Located only a few miles from the DMZ, Dong Ha was central to fighting in the North and was also near the important point of Hue to the South.

Casualties were brought in and stabilized, then sent further south to hospitals or to hospital ships for treatment. Less severe casualties were treated, then sent back to the field. Surgeons only operated on the most serious cases.

Dong Ha was a bit more permanent than a BAS. The hospital was scattered among submerged bunkers and tents and serviced casualties as well as the personnel of the 99th artillery unit. There was a sick bay, a pre-op with x-ray equipment and a post-op tent that functioned as a small ward. These areas were clustered around the main hospital bunker where surgery, when necessary, was performed. John shared a 'hooch' with two other doctors. A roofed platform on stilts, the hooch had roll up screens for walls to let in any available breeze. They were sandbagged for protection since Dong Ha got shelled on a regular basis.

John couldn't sleep. He never knew when he'd hear the piercing whistle of 'incoming' and have to throw himself out of his bunk and onto the floor. If the shelling was heavy, he and his hooch mates would run and take cover in one of the many bunkers placed around the encampment. He felt like he was back in Basic, crawling around on the ground with shells flying overhead. But this time, the ammo was live. It scared the hell out of him.

After three months 'in country,' John was starting to get the hang of the lingo and the feel of the war. He tried to become hardened to the fact that these young men, who seemed so brave and so willing to fight for their country, were going to die and there was a possibility he could die as well.

He once patched up and sent back to the field the same kid three times. A week later, he pronounced him and wrote his last ticket home. Death was everywhere and like it or not, he was there for the ride.

He got letters from Mary Agnes at least once a week. Sometimes he hated getting those letters; they brought him another reality. Mary Agnes told of visits to the obstetrician and how she was now feeling life. He would never get the chance to lay his hand on her and feel the baby move. It made him bitter to think that another doctor would be taking care of her—that another man would be beside her when the baby was born. By the time his tour ended, the baby would be almost three months old. But just as soon as the depression settled in, another batch of wounded would arrive to take his mind off home and family.

The CO of the medical corps was a 'full-bird' colonel who was picky as hell about everything. He was a huge man named Patrick McDonald who ran an organized, well stocked camp. An excellent surgeon, with over ten years of experience, he was great to have on your side but a bastard if you ticked him off.

There was one GP who liked to sleep until the very last minute. McDonald would be waiting for him at the entrance to the hospital, a pocket watch in hand. The GP, who was a 'short timer' with only one month left 'in country,' would salute, then look at his own watch. "8:30," he would say. "Is that what you got Colonel?"

McDonald's face would redden, and he'd snarl. "I'd hate to be one of your patients, doctor. By the time you showed up for work, I'd be well or dead."

The other doctors were decent, but John didn't have much in common with them. All they talked about was sex, their practices, or their golf scores. Lonely, scared, and homesick, John filled in his map and longed for home.

When Billy got out of the C-130, he looked around in surprise. Dong Ha was a bustling little complex of tents and bunkers. He walked into the largest tent and found himself face to face with John.

"Billy! What are *you* doing here?"

"Hey, John! It's great to see you. I just got assigned here."

"That's the best thing I've heard in a long time. How was Tam Quan?"

"About as exciting as an ingrown toenail. I was getting desperate for a snake bite or a case of dysentery. The only excitement I had was getting shot at every once in a while."

"Man, I can't believe it." John threw his arm across Billy's shoulder. "Everything will be fine now that you're here. It's like the army read my mind and sent you to keep me company."

"How long have you been here?"

"About four weeks."

"If that's what a month will do, I don't think I want to stay."

John waved him off saying, "I got a letter from Mare yesterday, and I'm still feeling the effects. I get so lonely when I read her letters. You know, all that talk about the baby." Bending down, he picked up Billy's backpack. "Come on, we have an empty bunk in our hooch. You can stay with us."

John introduced Billy to the other occupants, then went with him to the colonel's quarters. "Mac's an excellent doctor and a fair man. Just don't screw with him," John cautioned.

Mac reminded Billy of a deuce and a half—approximately six foot four, about 240 in the buff, all muscle and no nonsense. His sandy brown hair was streaked with grey and always appeared tousled because of Mac's tendency to run his hands through his hair in agitation.

He studied Billy's paperwork and said, "I see everything's in order. Welcome to Dong Ha," he said, extending a beefy hand across his desk and swallowing Billy's fingers in a crushing shake. "I run a smooth operation with everything in its place. In a camp this size, with so much below ground, organization is the key," he commented. "John, why don't you show your friend around while it's quiet."

"Yes, sir."

"I look forward to working here, sir," Billy said.

"Good, you'll see plenty of action. There's never a dull moment."

Later, John and Billy were knee deep in wounded. Choppers landed long enough for their cargo to be evacuated, then rising like giant, awkward birds, went back for more. Corpsmen brought the wounded into the triage area where GPs evaluated conditions and started treatments.

As the surgeons in the camp, John and Billy checked to see if there were any extreme casualties. Presently, there were three. John showed Billy where to scrub, and they began working in earnest. There was only one anesthesiologist. And he, as well as John, Billy and Mac, when necessary, were on call twenty-four hours a day.

There were no female nurses in Dong Ha. Since male nurses were few and far between, GPs, internists, or corpsman would scrub for the surgeons. The corpsmen, like the 'grunts' on the field of battle, were indispensable. They not only risked their lives bringing back wounded soldiers, but in the field hospital, ran the radiology department, the blood bank and charted patients. They also performed bedside nursing and alerted doctors to changes in patients' conditions. Without the corpsmen, the running of the hospital would falter.

Mac's hospital ran like a well-oiled machine, and he prided himself on the excellence of his corpsmen. If a kid came in green, he would train him himself. His motto was simple—get the patients in, treat them and move them out so that more could replace them.

Joey was one of Mac's hand trained corpsmen and was excellent. He had just started his first semester of pre-med, when he decided to enlist. Joey gave at least a hundred percent every day and was McDonald's favorite. Friendly, smart, and sincere, Joey was short and wiry with a spattering of freckles and short chestnut hair that stuck up at odd angles. He had been in Dong Ha for close to two months and Mac was worried he'd be moved out to the field soon.

Unfortunately, corpsmen did not have a long life expectancy and were moved frequently. The longer they stayed in the field, the more their chances of getting wounded or killed. Mac didn't want Joey to be a statistic and tried his best to see that Joey stayed out of the action.

Joey handed an x-ray to Billy, "Hey Doc, here's the neg for Baker. Got a bad gut. We already started an IV and typed him. He's all yours now. You need anything, shout. We'll come running. The gas passer will be in any sec. He's finishing up next door."

"Thanks," Billy said, studying the x-ray.

"Hey, no problem! See ya later, Doc." Joey turned and dashed back to triage.

"That's Dong Ha for you," John said later in the mess. "All hustle and hurry, then nothing."

"Man, I've never seen so much action in less than twelve hours. It makes Walter Reed look like a nursing home. And we were plenty busy there."

Just then, Joey stopped at their table. "You're the new doc, aren't you? I'm Joey Mahoning, one of the corpsmen here."

"One of the best, too," John commented, putting down his coffee cup. "Joey, I'd like you to meet Captain Fox. He's a buddy of mine."

"You did a good job today," Billy said. "Thanks for all your help."

"No problem! Well, see ya later. I hear we got grape Kool-Aid today. It's my favorite." He walked quickly to the chow line, waving and calling to men as he went.

"What a great kid," John said. "I've never seen him mad or upset. No matter what happens, he's always smiling. His cheeks must be sore by the end of the day."

"I don't know about his facial cheeks, but he sure works his ass off," Billy pointed out.

"He sure does, and Mac knows it. He trained Joey himself, and he's the Big Guy's pet. Speaking of the devil, here comes Mac now," John said, under his breath.

"Heard good things about you today, Captain." He laid a hand on Billy's shoulder. "Keep up the good work." Without another word, he was gone.

"Uh oh, Joey better watch his step, McDonald may have a new fave."

"Get lost," Billy said. "So, can you still do a lap without passing out, Simmonds?"

"I think I can go the distance against a puny bastard like you. Come on. There are a few safe places where we can run and not worry about getting our feet blown off by a mine."

"You're on."

"Damn, it's good to have you here," John smiled and followed Billy from the tent.

Life in Dong Ha had a pattern; breakfast, choppers, shelling, choppers, dinner, bed, breakfast. John and Billy worked harder than ever before, seeing and treating more patients in one month than the average doctor would sometimes have in three back home.

They got used to the chronic athlete's foot resulting from blood seeping into their boots. They learned when to stay put, when to run, and when to hit the ground. The casualties they saw were enlisted men, ranking officers, civilians, children. Their favorite equipment was the ever-present flak gear that sat at the end of their cots. It was an ugly, raw waste of humanity, and they were there to pick up the pieces.

"Hey Billy, listen to this." John lay on his bunk reading his latest letter from home. "The baby rolled completely around today. Mare thought she was going to throw up, it felt so weird. Isn't that cool?"

"What? The baby moving or Mare tossing her cookies?"

"The baby, you jerk. Did you get anything in the mail?"

"A letter from Marian and Rusty, three mysteries from Bubba and shampoo from Jenny."

"Wow! You had a field day."

"One of the best! The mail works much better here than at a BAS, doesn't it?"

"It sure does. Oh boy, our moose of a dog chased the paperboy and peed on the neighbor's flowers again. Mare had to practically get down on her knees to apologize. That's the third time this month."

"Rusty's going to quit teaching at the University. It's become too much for him. I'm glad. He didn't need that hassle."

John looked at Billy. "This is weird."

"What?" Billy asked, rolling over to face John.

"We're talking about them, but I can't picture it. It feels as if when we left, everybody back home stopped. Yet here they are, continuing with their lives while we're gone."

Billy stared at John. "It does seem strange, doesn't it? Like we're the only ones living, and they're frozen in time."

"It kind of ticks me off, you know. They're carrying on without us."

"Hell, John. Maybe they feel the same way about us. We're carrying on without them, too."

"Maybe. But *we* don't want to be here. I guess *that's* the difference."

"I guess."

Suddenly, they heard a faint whistling sound. Without a word, they threw themselves to the floor, their arms crossed over their heads. Kabooom! The earth shook with the impact.

"Should we hit the bunkers?" John asked, reaching for his flak gear and helmet as a second blast filled the air.

Billy squirmed into his gear. "Shit!" he said, hearing another piercing whistle, as the sound of another incoming was heard. "Let's get out of here!"

"Right behind ya," John yelled, as the ground shook again. They raced to the closest bunker about fifty feet away from their hooch. Several men were already there.

"Sounds like the fuckin' fourth of July," one guy grumbled, "I will forever hate that fuckin' holiday!"

They slid down inside the bunker and wondered how long the shelling would last. In the midst of the shelling, a truck pulled into the camp, spraying gravel in its wake. One of the corpsmen yelled for a surgeon.

John popped his head up, then quickly ran to the hospital bunker with Billy on his tail. Joey was already there. "We just put a kid with a ripped-up spleen in the next tent. He's bleeding like crazy and we're afraid to move him."

The men listened. The shelling and the return fire seemed to have stopped for the moment. They looked in on the kid. Joey was right, he was losing blood fast. If they didn't remove his spleen quickly, he'd bleed to death.

"Let's do it," John said. "Finish prepping him Joey, and make sure to get a cross match on his blood. He'll probably need a pint or two at the rate he's going. We'll also need the gas passer in here on the double. While you're seeing to that, we'll go scrub."

"Yes, sir," Joey saluted and hurried off. Without taking off their flak gear and helmets, they scrubbed and with Joey's help got partially gowned. Once gloved, they got down to work. While John removed the spleen, Billy fished out shrapnel from the surrounding area. John glanced at the kid's bare arm and the tattoo he sported.

"Special Forces Unit," he grunted. "Kid's either extremely brave or crazy as hell."

"Both," Joey commented as he reentered the tent. "Heard he was riding the skids of a chopper, picking off VC when he was hit. You have to be pretty damn crazy…"

"Hey! What the hell was that?" John asked.

Billy heard a strange popping, whining sound and felt a slight stinging sensation in his arm. "I don't know, but I think I was just stung by a bee," he said.

"That was no bee!" John said horrified, as a bloodstain appeared on Billy's sleeve. Another popping sound followed. "You've been hit!" he yelled. The gas passer turned white and fled.

"Holy shit!" Billy stared in amazement at the rapidly spreading stain of blood on his arm.

"Let's get this kid down! Fast!" John instructed. Joey had remained and the three men got the litter to the ground. They laid on their stomachs and continued to suture the wound. One side of the tent was being ripped with holes. A moment later, they heard the whistle of more incoming.

"Get out of here!" Billy yelled to John and Joey. "Go back to the bunkers."

Joey didn't hesitate. He crawled to the flap and crossing himself, made a run for it.

"Go on John, beat it," Billy said through clenched teeth, his arm beginning to throb.

"I can't leave you here alone. You need help. You're hurt."

A mortar round shook the earth. John pulled his helmet low over his head. "Jesus! Don't they care that this is a hospital?"

Another shell crashed to the ground, it's whistle made Billy's stomach contract, and he wanted to vomit. "John, go! Get the hell out of here. I don't need you."

"You're going to get killed!"

"No use both of us getting killed. Go on, before it's too late."

"I can't leave you!"

"Don't fuckin' argue. By the time I finish this kid, it'll be over. Go!"

John's face was full of indecision and fear.

"Go, damn it!"

Running from the tent, John headed for the nearest bunker. It was only a few yards away. Hell, he'd run races longer than that. His heart was pounding so loudly in his head that he never heard the shell until it was too late.

Billy, who had just put in the last suture, heard it and threw himself over the wounded boy. The shell hit with a sickening crunch, rocking the ground around Billy. Christ, he thought, that was close! In fact, it sounded like it was right outside!

He crawled over and raised the flap. Through the dissipating smoke and dust, Billy saw a huge hole between the tent and the nearest bunker. Oh my God, Billy thought. John! He had to have gotten to the bunker in time. He just had to.

Billy lay in the opening, listening to the eerie sound of silence. He counted seconds—no whistles, no whines, no sound at all. Men began to emerge from the bunkers like corpses rising from the grave.

Billy ran to the hole and saw a boot several feet away. "Oh God! No!" A sob came from his throat. John lay face down in the dirt, his body soaked in blood. Billy ran to him and gently turned him over. "John! Oh God! John! Somebody help me!" he yelled, as he felt for the carotid. There was only a faint whisper of a pulse. John looked at Billy and coughed up blood.

"Never…could…hit…stride…tell…Mare…love…"

"NO!" Billy cried as John's head fell slack onto his arms, his eyes staring sightlessly. The blood from Billy's wound had soaked his shirt and ran over his hand, mingling with the blood of his friend.

Patrick McDonald ran and squatted next to Billy. He felt for a pulse for a long time, then closed John's eyes. "He's gone, son," he said softly, touching Billy's shoulder.

"NO!"

"Come on, let's go see to your arm. You can't do anything for him now. Joey!" he called. "Get another corpsman and a litter, please. We also need to see to that wounded soldier."

Billy knelt on the ground, his arms around John. He wouldn't let go. Mac had to pry Billy's fingers away from his friend.

"Come on, Billy. We need to get you fixed up." He gently helped Billy to stand.

Billy looked down at John in horror. "I…killed…him," Billy whispered. "I made him go."

"No, Billy, you didn't kill him, the NVA killed him. It was a freak thing."

"I sent him to his death," Billy said, his eyes glazed.

Putting his arm around Billy, Mac walked him toward the hospital. A small cluster of men stood by, as Joey and another young boy placed John on a litter and started toward the morgue.

MARIAN

John was dead. It just didn't seem possible. Marian saw his face, heard his voice telling one of his corny doctor jokes. He had been like a son. And now, he was being buried from the St. Ignatious Loyola Chapel at the medical school; the same chapel where he and Mary Agnes had said their vows and where their baby was going to be baptized in a few short months.

Marian had been to funerals before but never one like this. Most of the time, people who died were old or sick. This was different. What words of comfort could be offered to Mary Agnes, her body swelling to show the baby nestled within? How do you comfort a grieving mother and father? Parents should never outlive their children. It wasn't natural. It cut Marian deeply.

Later they stood by the freshly dug grave in the cemetery where John and Billy had often run. The casket was draped with the flag of the United States. Marian would never be able to see another flag without thinking of it as a shroud or later in its perfect triangle being placed in Mary Agnes' unsteady hands.

He was a doctor, for God's sake. Doctors weren't supposed to get killed. The Vietnamese had been shelling a hospital? Marian thought of Billy and was ill. It could have been him.

Rusty would find her sitting in Billy's room, reading his letters—the letters that had stopped after John's death. Finally, he said, "Marian, you're making yourself sick sitting up here day after day. It won't bring John back or keep Billy safe."

Walking to the window, he glanced out at the street. "Police action," he snorted, "what a bunch of bureaucratic bullshit. It's a goddamned war. How many of our boys have come home wrapped in the flag of the country that sent them to slaughter? And how many more will die? And for what?" He let the curtain fall back into place and went to Marian. He put his arms around her. There was no substance to her at all. She had to start eating again, had to come back to them. If she didn't, they would lose her, too.

It was midnight when the phone rang. Rusty quickly answered, thinking it was the hospital.

"Rusty?" Billy's voice sounded strange, disjointed.

"Billy? Are you all right?" At the sound of Billy's name, Marian was awake and at Rusty's side.

"You have to keep talking, Rusty. I'm using the MARS shortwave since there's no phone here," Billy explained. "They're trying to get the best channel so you can hear me better. Over?"

"Where are you?"

"Can't ask questions. Just talk. Tell me what's going on. How is everyone? Over?"

They talked for several minutes about general things. In the meantime, the radio operator at the mobile army radio station, or MARS, scanned for the best frequency to transmit to the West coast, then patch through to Washington. It was a strange conversation. They couldn't both talk at the same time.

"I got R & R to Hawaii. Can you guys meet me there? I know it's short notice, but I just found out myself. I'll be leaving for Oahu in a week. Over?"

Marian, who had her ear pressed to the phone said, "tell him yes. We'll be there."

"The boss has spoken. Over," Rusty laughed and grabbing a pencil and a piece of paper on the nightstand, scribbled down the particulars.

When he hung up, Marian was at his shoulder. "What did he say? How did he sound? Did he say anything about John?"

Rusty put up a hand. "Hold on, Marian, not so fast. First of all, he didn't say much of anything. He was using the radio system, and the reception wasn't the best. Anyone in the world with a shortwave radio could listen in to our conversation, including the enemy. And no, he didn't say anything about John. We'll see him soon. Now, let's go back to sleep, I have to get up early tomorrow. We can talk about it then. We have a lot to discuss."

Billy looked ill with dull, sunken eyes. His uniform hung loosely. The Wilsons waved and went to meet him. Marian said quietly, "Don't talk about John unless Billy says something first."

She put out her arms and went to him, her smile frozen in place. "Billy! It's so good to see you." She hugged him, gasping at his thinness and his haggard appearance. The girls' faces registered shock as they fought for hugs. Rusty stood back; his face unreadable.

"It's good to see you all. I'm glad you could make it." Billy's words were stilted, as if he had rehearsed them on the plane. He reached into his pocket and pulled out a pack of cigarettes, his hands shaking as he lit one. Marian was about to say something, but his look silenced her.

They got his duffel from baggage claim and flagged a taxi to the hotel. In the cab, Barbara couldn't wait to tell Billy all about her interview at Georgetown and her upcoming graduation. Jenny, in the meantime, chattered about her classes at school.

Billy remained silent. Lighting one cigarette after another, he stared out the open car window oblivious to the family and their surroundings.

The Wilsons had booked a beautiful, three-bedroom suite in a luxurious, ocean front hotel. "Come and check out the view," Jenny called from the balcony.

"No thanks," Billy mumbled.

"Let's go to the beach then, the water's great." She went to him and grabbed his arm. "Come on. Last one in is a rotten egg."

"Let go!" He flinched and held his arm against his side.

Jenny released him as if she had been burned, her eyes filling with tears.

Billy exhaled. "I'm sorry, Jenny Wren. I'm just very tired. It was a long way, and I haven't slept for a long time. I'll go to the beach with you later. I promise." He took his duffle, walked into his room and closed the door.

Rusty motioned for everyone to go out into the hall. "I tried to explain to you that Billy might be different. He needs us right now and we have to help him. But the thing is, none of us, including Billy, knows how we can do that. We're going to have to play these first few days by ear. But for now, let him rest. He needs that more than anything."

Billy spent the first day in bed, getting up only to pick at the food they brought him and to smoke one cigarette after another. He hardly spoke. On the second day, however, Barbara marched into Billy's room and opened the curtains on the windows. With hands on her hips, she faced Billy, who was blinking groggily.

"I can't stand this," she said. "We've toured the island, gone swimming and shopping, eaten dinner at fancy places, and you just sit or lay in this room. You drag us all the way here, then ignore us. What the hell kind of vacation is that!"

"Barbara Jean Wilson!" Marian exclaimed. "How dare you talk that way! Billy needs to rest. Leave him alone."

"No, mother, I am *not* going to leave him alone. He needs us and we need him. We're a family, aren't we? Are we just going to pretend that everything's fine? That John didn't die? That we're all here to lay in the sun and get a tan?" She put her hands out to Billy. "Do you remember how you sat on my bed the day Jeffrey tormented us on the bus? Do you remember how you wiped away my tears and asked me if we were still friends? Except for a few years of my young life, you have been a part of this family. I love you, Billy Fox. We all do. We need to know how we can help you. Talk to us. Please!" Tears streaked her face as she again held out her hands.

Billy looked at her, then at the family he loved so much. He grasped her hands and pulled her to him. She fell across the bed and Marian and Jenny joined her. Rusty stood against the wall for a moment then said, "Oh, what the hell," and joined the crowd.

The five of them hugged and laughed and cried until the bed began to groan under the weight. "Everybody off!" Rusty cried. "We're going to collapse!"

"That's much better," Jenny nodded. "Now, the last one into the ocean is a rotten egg!" she yelled, then pointed a stern finger at Billy. "That includes you. Do I have to tear your clothes off or are you going to come willingly?"

Billy put both hands up into the air. "All right. You win. I'll get my bathing suit on if you guys remembered to bring it." Jenny disappeared then came back and threw something at Billy.

"Thank you. I needed that," Billy said. "I'm not sure what else I need, but we'll figure that out as we go, okay? And you," he said to Jennifer, "are going to be a rotten egg."

They went to the beach and played in the water. Billy attempted to join in, but Marian could see what an effort it was for him. They noticed the bandage on his upper arm, but Billy never offered an explanation, and no one asked.

"Anyone care to go for a walk?" Marian proposed a little while later. The girls looked up sleepily from their towels and shook their heads. Rusty was engrossed in an article and didn't even acknowledge her question.

Billy stood. "I'll go," he said.

They wandered down the beach, walking close to the water's edge. After a while, Marian glanced at Billy and said, "So, how are you, really?"

"Some days are worse than others," Billy shrugged. "Most days, I just do my job, pretending it was all a bad dream. But then, I'll walk past the spot where it happened or someone will say something he would say, and I end up in the CO's office shaking. If it hadn't been for him, I don't know how I'd have gotten through the last couple of weeks."

"Do you want to talk about it?" Marian asked.

"I'm not sure I can." He turned to Marian. "It hurts too much," he said, with anguish in his eyes. Marian hugged him. Although it was warm, Billy was shivering. "Can we go back to the room?" he asked.

"Sure, I'll let Rusty and the girls know that we're going back to the hotel."

When they returned, Billy sat on the couch, hugging his knees up to his chest.

"What happened to your arm?" Marian asked, sitting down beside him.

"I got hit."

"When?"

"The day…uh he died. And every time I bump or hit it, everything comes back to me."

"I thought you were in a hospital."

"It is a hospital, sort of. It's a field unit. But the thing is, it's also a supply station and it's located only a few miles away from the DMZ or the Demilitarized Zone, which means it's a free for all. The NVA shoot at us and shell us at odd hours to keep us off balance."

"However do you live like that?"

"When…he was there, it was all right. But now, every time I hear a whistle or a whine, I throw myself to the ground and lay there trembling. I can't move. I can't sleep. When I close my eyes, I see the scene over and over. Him coughing up blood, his sightless eyes. Hell, it's not like I'd never seen that happen before to someone else. But this time, it was…him.

"When I do fall asleep, I dream about it. I hear the shelling, see the blood on my arm. I hear myself telling…him to get to a bunker. I'm pushing him, forcing him to go. Then I see…him getting hit and I wake up in a cold sweat, screaming. I think I'm losing my mind."

Marian put her arms around him, and he curled in to her, laying his head on her chest like a small boy. He started to cry silently, his body shaking. Marian held him and rocked him like a baby, her heart aching for him and for herself.

After a while, Billy stopped shaking and was quiet. His deep, even breathing led Marian to believe he had dozed off. How fragile we are, she thought. Unconsciously, her arms tightened around him. She wished she could protect him—keep him safe. But like John, he too could be hurt or worse. She must have accidentally touched his wound for he jerked awake.

He sat up and wiped at his eyes. "I'm sorry, Marian," he mumbled.

"For what? Being human? Needing to be comforted? You have always kept your emotions tucked away from everyone, including yourself. Sometimes you have to let them out. If you don't, you *will* lose your mind. I visit Mary Agnes and she always seems so in control. So stoic and brave. But I keep waiting for the other shoe to drop and I'm afraid."

"I've wanted to talk to her, but I don't know what to say," Billy said. "I felt so guilty about…John's death. I should have called her to see how she was. To ask her to…forgive me," he looked away.

"Look at me," Marian said sternly. "You have nothing to feel guilty about. You did not kill John. You didn't know he was going to get hit. You cannot live the rest of your life thinking you sent him to his death. I will not allow you to! Do you hear me?" With her eyes flashing in her face, Billy had never seen her so angry.

"That's what Mac says."

"You see? I know everyone thinks I'm just a pretty face, but I'm not stupid." As she said this, Rusty and the girls walked into the room.

"Now sweetheart," Rusty said, "I never called you stupid…to your face."

"Oh, get out of here. And you, if you were so smart, Mr. Doctor, you'd have known to get your freckled, lily-white skin out of the sun. Just look at you, you're glowing."

Marian smiled and squeezed Billy's hand. He returned the squeeze and the smile. They'd all get through this, Marian thought. It wasn't going to be easy. But somehow, their love would get them through.

CAL

After was posted on the bulletin board outside the call room asking young doctors to volunteer for the US Armed Forces. With openings in all four major areas of service, many of Cal's compatriots signed up. Cal perused the lists and figured that by the time he was done with his residency, the war would be over. He'd be damned if he'd give Uncle Sam two plus years of his life. Why sign up?

However, as months passed and Cal got closer to completing his residency, the war was still going strong. If he didn't sign up now, he could be drafted, and his practice would be shot before it began. Maybe his fellow doctors were right. If he joined now, he would also be able to choose which branch of service he preferred. Everyone said the Navy was the way to go. They always seemed to get the best of everything: food, locations, even uniforms. But by the time Cal enlisted, the Army was the only branch with openings left.

Basic training was a nightmare. Cal was so out of shape that he could barely run a mile, let alone five, with a loaded pack on his back. He couldn't understand why a doctor had to be trained like some grunt. He found crawling under barbed wire with ammo being fired over his head distasteful and ridiculous. He wasn't going to Vietnam to fight.

A portion of every day was spent on the firing range practicing the loading and firing of both his forty-five service revolver and M-16 rifle. With an air of boredom, he halfheartedly cleaned both. Surely, he grumbled, he wouldn't need these in a hospital. This was a useless exercise.

He trained with a group of men consisting of physicians and dentists. During the wire drill, one dentist crawling under the wire would always panic, stand up and run. He was 'killed' every time they did that particular exercise. The same man cried himself to sleep each night. Instead of being trained, then going to an army facility in the states to await his summons to 'Nam, he was to go directly there after Basic. He was young and scared and had no wish to go to Southeast Asia.

After training, Cal was sent to Fort Dix in New Jersey to wait and to work. A couple of months later, he was sent to an Evacuation Hospital twenty miles northeast of Saigon. The Evacuation hospital was a break from New York and all the craziness that working in an inner-city hospital brought. For the first time in his life, Cal began to feel useful and needed. Seeing those kids everyday made him realize how lucky he was to be a doctor.

Now he had a sense of purpose. Maybe that was what was missing all those years. He never felt needed. But when a young private thanked him for just patching him up, he felt something tug at him.

Located in an air conditioned, metal quonset hut, the Evac was just like a regular hospital. Cal thought again about basic training and considered it a waste of time. He couldn't see himself using any of the skills he had been taught. His revolver lay unused in his nightstand; a helmet and flak gear gathered dust at the foot of his bed.

There were plenty of nurses at the Evac. Many were young and in awe of the doctors. Cal could have a different girl every night. If he wanted a native, he could go into any one of the local bars and get a prostitute for a few hours. All the comforts of home and more, he thought. This wasn't so bad.

He wondered about the war stories he heard from time to time. Must have been a different war, he thought. Those guys were exaggerating. He didn't find this horrifying at all.

He had been in Vietnam over six months, when he was reassigned to a field hospital outside of Pleiku. Suddenly Cal lost his smugness. Here, there were casualties by the hundreds: dirty, bloody and many times screaming in pain. There were no pretty young nurses or whores readily available. If he wanted action of that kind, he had to go into Pleiku.

Once a week, a group of doctors commandeered a jeep and went into town. One Sunday, Cal joined them. He was out of cigarettes, and someone recommended a local tobacco shop. A tiny hole in the wall, the shop was owned by an old man with chipped, tobacco-stained teeth and a ready smile. He managed to communicate through hand motions and very elementary French. They had a lively, but limited, conversation about the merits of American versus Vietnamese tobaccos. The man's wife brought in tea and Cal spent a pleasant hour.

Cal got into the habit of going into town and visiting the tobacco shop. He enjoyed the time spent with the Le family, and the tea and conversation became a ritual. In order to better communicate, Cal even learned some basic Vietnamese.

The Le's three young grandsons, ranging in age from eight to thirteen, lived with them. Cal had no idea where the parents of these children were. His grasp of the language was too limited to ask those kinds of questions.

When he found out how much the family enjoyed hot, spicy food, he brought them some canned jalapeño peppers his parents had sent him. The Le's likewise gave Cal some of the Vietnamese spicy fish sauce called *nu'oc m'am pha.* Like the tobacco, the topic of hot food brought about quite a debate.

Cal's hooch mates couldn't understand him spending time with a family of peasants.

"Don't trust them, Cal," one of the doctors warned. "You never know who's side they're on. One minute they're your friend, the next, they're handing you an early ticket home."

Cal paid the warnings no heed. They were two old people and three small children. They were harmless. Besides, his visits with them made being in Vietnam bearable.

With three months left 'in country,' Cal was moved to a BAS on the other side of Pleiku. Even though he was in an out of the way spot, he could still visit his friends. Compared to the field hospital, the BAS was boring. Going into town became something to look forward to during the long days spent at the aid station.

One night, while the company was out on maneuvers, Cal was left at the BAS with only two wounded men for company. The men had been badly injured when their jeep overturned—one man had a broken arm; the other had head and eye injuries. They were awaiting a chopper to take them to the hospital in Da Nang.

Earlier in the evening, Cal heard faint harassment and interdiction, or H & I, fire coming from beyond the trees around the camp. He hurried the men into a bunker to await their transport just to be on the safe side.

Once night had fallen, Cal realized it was too late for a chopper. Making the men as comfortable as possible, he settled down for a long night. Around midnight, Cal was wakened from a doze by a rustling sound. He and the man with the broken arm looked out into the night, straining to hear any more sounds, searching for the cause, and hoping against hope the noise had been made by an animal.

As they searched the shadows, they saw five black shapes moving stealthily out from the trees, creeping into the camp like wraiths. The other man handed Cal his M-16. "Here, sir, you'll need this."

Cal stared at the corporal. "What do you mean?"

"They're VC, Captain and they're gunning for us. Look," he pointed. In the hands of all five silhouettes were rifles with fixed bayonets. "Don't let them get close enough to kill us."

The VC heard the whispers and changed their course, heading toward the bunker. "Jesus, get them now, sir. Don't wait!"

Cal shouldered the rifle and fixed one of the VC in his sights. He had scoffed at Basic Training, yet here he was with a loaded rifle in his hands. One of the VC stopped and took aim at the bunker. Without waiting for anything more, Cal squeezed the trigger and fired several rounds of ammunition. He shot blindly, hoping to hit something in the process.

Waiting for the report of return fire, he looked out through a cloud of smoke, his heart pounding wildly. He was so terrified that his hands were wet with sweat and shaking. When the smoke cleared, the VC lay motionless and crumpled on the ground.

Cal left them where they lay, too afraid to see if they were dead or only wounded. For the rest of the night, the men huddled in the bunker, vigilant for more movement. Listening in the dark, their fear was like icy fingers at the base of their necks.

At dawn, Cal slowly climbed from the bunker, his rifle at the ready. Five, motionless, mounds lay in the dirt—pools of blood spread out around them. The buzzing from hundreds of insects gorging on flesh and blood assaulted Cal's ears.

He went to the closest bundle of dusty black cloth and nudged it over with his foot. Old Mr. Le faced him, eyes wide and staring, ragged chunks of flesh ripped from his body.

Cal turned to the next bundle and was horrified to see Mrs. Le, her rifle frozen in her grip. About him, the three children lay scattered.

The man who had given him the rifle came up behind him. "Fuckin' VC! They're like shit," he said, spitting into Mrs. Le's blood encrusted face, then gave Mr. Le a kick.

In his mind, Cal heard the old man calling for tea. Looking again at the wide-open eyes, he fell to his knees and began to vomit.

"You all right, sir?"

Cal heard the echo of his hooch mate's voice, "Don't trust them. You don't know who's side they're on." He couldn't stop the tears making their way silently down his cheeks and dripping into the dust next to the old man. In the distance, sounds of a chopper were heard as well as the sounds of the returning artillery group. Cal's vision swam as the chopper landed and another day began.

MAC

Patrick McDonald knew about loss. Ten years ago, he lost his wife in childbirth. The baby died several days later. He had never gotten over it and had never looked at another woman. He understood Billy's feelings of guilt and pain and was there for him. Consequently, they spent many late nights sitting in Mac's quarters commiserating.

When Billy returned from Hawaii, Mac called him into his office. "How are you?" he asked, his eyes searching Billy's face.

"I'm all right."

"Are you sure? In Phu Bai, they still have a psychiatrist if you need to talk to someone."

"I don't need a shrink, thank you," Billy said curtly.

"Okay. Anyway, I have some news for you. I've recommended you for a promotion."

"Promotion?"

"Yes, you're being promoted to Major."

"What? Why?"

"I've seen the way you work. And last month, you demonstrated what kind of doctor you are by putting yourself on the line to save the kid with the ruptured spleen."

"But that was nothing," Billy disagreed.

Mac put up his hand. "You don't think you did anything out of the ordinary. But it was. First, you were in a tent, because the kid couldn't be moved. Two, you were injured. Three, you were being shot at. Look, the gas passer didn't even think twice. He took off. Plus, you're a good doctor and a good surgeon. That's often hard to find."

"But there are lots of docs and surgeons over here," Billy argued. "As you know, most of them have a hell of a lot more experience than I do."

Mac stood in the doorway, overseeing the camp. "Just because someone's an attending doesn't necessarily mean they know their shit. I've seen doctors come and go. Unfortunately, some just don't give a damn. That's one of the reasons I'm in charge of the medical units in this quadrant—I care." He shook his head, "Sometimes, too much."

He turned away from the door and faced Billy. "I can see myself in you. You're someone who can get the job done and care at the same time. *That* is a rare commodity." Mac strode to his desk and pushed some papers around. "The head of medical personnel in Phu Bai is a short timer. He'll be rotated back to the states soon, and there doesn't seem to be a lot to choose from waiting in the wings. They need someone to replace him. Once a lot of these guys are approaching their drop date, they no longer give a shit—if they ever did. I hear that the hospital there is a mess. With my guidance, I can have you ready to fill his shoes when he leaves."

"But sir, I don't know anything about running a hospital."

"Look, we have a few weeks. There's not much to it. The hardest part is all the paperwork. But if you have a good clerk, it'll be smooth sailing."

"I don't know," Billy shook his head doubtfully.

"Don't worry. I have faith in you." He pulled a small envelope out of his desk drawer and handed the bronze oak leaves to Billy. "Congratulations, you deserve this. Sorry we couldn't do this with more pomp and circumstance."

Billy held the new insignia in his palm and was overwhelmed. All he had ever wanted was to be a doctor. He wasn't sure he could handle the new rank and title. He had never held a position of management or authority before and was content to be an underling. He still felt uncomfortable when the enlisted men saluted him. Now, it would be worse.

Mac was staring at him expectantly. "Uh…thanks, Colonel. I don't know what else to say. This is a surprise. I hope you aren't making a mistake. I don't know if I can do this."

"Don't worry," Mac said again. "I'm never wrong. I thought I was once, but I was mistaken." He smiled at Billy. "Just don't take yourself too seriously and you'll be all right. I'm sure you'll be at least one hundred percent better than the last guy."

From then on, Billy spent most of his time with McDonald. He learned about ordering drugs, supplies and all the necessities that it took to running a hospital. Dong Ha's requirements were meager compared to what a field hospital like I-Corps needed. Billy tried to absorb everything. It was a lot of information in a small amount of time.

Mac also helped Billy out in the OR. "Over here, we don't always have the luxury of time to do things according to textbooks and lectures," he said. "I've noticed you already take some short cuts. They are either instinctive or someone has been schooling you on battle surgery."

"Back home, I live with a surgeon who served in the Korean War. He told me a few things to help save time."

"Really? I was in Korea. What's his name?"

"Frank Wilson."

"Wilson? Hmm…I knew a Rusty Wilson."

"That's him, Rusty's his nickname."

"I'll be damned. Rusty was a great guy. Haven't heard from him in years. What's he doing these days?"

"He's a surgeon at Georgetown University Hospital. He and his family invited me to stay with them while I went to medical school then while I was at Walter Reed. That's who I spent my R & R with when I went to Hawaii."

"No kidding? Small world, isn't it?"

"It sure is."

The morning Billy left, he stopped at Mac's office to pick up his papers. "Joey will be going with you," Mac stated. "That should keep him out of trouble for at least another month or two. He's such a good kid, I'd hate to see him get wounded…or worse. He's been so damned eager to get out into the field and is going to be disappointed with his new assignment. I hope you don't mind, but I told him you needed his help at your new post."

"Sure. That's fine with me, and not too far off the mark, either."

"I did hear that the Army CO is also fairly new to Phu Bai. The grapevine says that he's a decent guy who's an old timer and knows the ropes. I'm sure if you have any problems, he'll help you out. Although from past experience," Mac warned, "the army guys don't like to get involved in medical concerns. They aren't around to solve petty doctor disputes. Remember that."

"Are you sure I can do this, Mac?"

"Of course, I'm sure. And remember, if you get stuck, I'm only a radio call away. At least until they send me home at the end of the month. Then, you'll be on your own. You have good instincts. Just remember, order and discipline. Without them, you have chaos." Mac walked around his desk and put his hand out. As Billy went to shake hands, McDonald said, "And Billy, don't take any shit from anyone…open your mouth!"

Billy laughed. "Thanks for the advice, I think." Sobering, he said, "Seriously Mac, thank you for everything. Without you, I probably would've needed that shrink. Thanks." His throat tightened and he couldn't continue.

Mac walked back to his chair and shuffled papers around his desk, refusing to look at Billy. Finally, he cleared his throat and said, "Good luck, son. Take care of yourself. And take care of Joey. I'll…uh…miss you both. Say hello to Rusty for me when you get back home."

"I will. Goodbye, Mac."

When they landed in Phu Bai, Billy and Joey were amazed. I Corps was a small, horseshoe shaped village, two times the size of Dong Ha. A tall, gray-haired man waited for them impatiently.

"Are you Fox?" he asked. "I'm Colonel Barnes, the CO here." He gave Billy the once over, noting the braided hair with a trace of disgust. He shook his head. "I hope you're not like the last chief of medical personnel, Major. I won't take that in my company. I always try to let you medical boys go your own way. However, I want you to know that the situation we have here now won't do. I run my company strictly by the books. Do you understand?"

"Yes, sir," Billy said.

"Good, because if you don't, your ass will be history," Barnes said. "I don't care who I have to petition for your immediate removal, even if it's the president, himself. Have I made myself clear, Major?"

"Yes, sir," Billy replied.

"Good. Now, let me show you around. This is our hospital," he said, walking into the quonset hut nearest to the air strip. "I hope you like hard work," Barnes continued. "You're in for quite a bit. This place is filthy. Don't know how the docs can work in these conditions." He walked quickly, giving Billy and Joey no time to take more than a cursory glance.

Apart from the camp sat another, larger quonset hut. A steady hum emanated from the building. "What's that building, sir?" Joey pointed.

"Oh that," he said, with a dismissive flap of his hand, "that's the morgue. It's the only fully air-conditioned building we have. Alongside the hospital is my office, Major. You'll have the small office next to me. It's not much, but it'll do. It also houses the pharmacy. I hear we were having some problems with drug theft as well," he said, giving Billy a pointed look.

A long, low building formed the U of the shoe. "This is the mess hall. Don't forget," he said, addressing Joey, "officers eat on one side and enlisted men on the other. Behind the mess, Major, you'll find the Officer's Club."

Across from the hospital squatted a cluster of raised shacks. Barnes waved his arm in the direction of the buildings. "The officer's hooches are over there. You can bunk in which ever one has the room. The Vietnamese and enlisted men have quarters behind them. If you have any questions, Corporal Higgins, the company clerk, will be able to help you. Good luck." With that, he strode back to his office, leaving Billy and Joey with their mouths gaping.

"I feel like I just got sucked up into a tornado," said Billy.

"Well, we sure as hell ain't in Kansas, Toto," Joey laughed. "But hey, that hospital gave me the willies. The mayo trays were kind of just lying around. I wonder if they were even clean. And did you see all those bloodstains on the floor? I think they must have been there for months."

"I saw them. Mac would have heart failure if he saw this. That chief must have been a real pig. God Joey, we have our work cut out for us. I don't know where to begin."

As he spoke, they heard the whomp of an approaching chopper.

"I guess we start with that," Joey said, as a cluster of people began hurrying to the hospital.

"I guess so," Billy said, as they went out to meet the landing helicopter.

MAGGIE

"This is ridiculous!" Mike yelled.

"What is ridiculous?" Maggie replied calmly.

"You know very well what I mean. You went and joined the army, that's what."

"The army needs nurses. Why shouldn't I enlist?"

"Because you're a married woman," he replied. "You know, I'm sick of this discussion. When we got married, I cut you some slack. You wanted to work, you wanted a career, you wanted everything that I was against. And now, you've really gone in for the kill, haven't you?"

"Michael Reynolds you are taking this all the wrong way."

"Am I? You should be at home raising fat, Irish babies. We could have at least six by now."

"A half dozen? Geez Michael, you don't want a family, you want a herd."

"As a Reynolds, it's expected. All my brothers and sisters have at least four kids. Do you realize I'm the laughingstock of my family. My one brother actually took me aside the other day and wanted to know if I was shooting blanks."

"That's not my fault."

"Oh yes, it is. They all think you run me around by the nose, and I have no balls."

"Oh, for goodness sake! Just because I want to work?"

"Yes, in this family, the women don't work. They stay home and have babies. That's what they're for. And the more babies the men produce, the better men they are."

"That is such crap!"

"No, it's not crap. It's the way it is."

"Well, I don't like it."

"I know. You'd rather spend time in that damn hospital than here where you belong. You care more about your patients than me. Night after night, I come home to an empty house and a cold stove. I'm tired of having to make my own dinner."

"You're exaggerating. One night a week is not night after night. And since when do you cook for yourself? You don't cook and you know it. How many of those nights do you eat at the bar on base? And what about the nights you spend cuddling up to other women, even when I *am* at home? At least *I'm* faithful."

"If you were home more often, perhaps I wouldn't have to look to strangers for comfort. A man has needs, Maggie, and you are doing nothing to fulfill mine."

"I do plenty, Michael and you know it. I work at the hospital, cook, clean, do the laundry, shop for food and yes, I even satisfy your needs."

"Hmph, is that what you call laying there staring at the ceiling?"

"Maybe if you took the time to treat me as something more than a sperm receptacle or baby factory, I might get more involved in what you were doing. I sure hope you treat your "girlfriends" better than you treat me. All you give me is a perfunctory kiss, then a slam, bam, and off to sleep you go."

"Just because you're frigid, don't blame me. Your problem is you want to wear the pants in this family at all times. Well, when it comes to sex, you can't have it your way."

"Ugh! That's it! I've had enough of this childish conversation. I've enlisted and that's that. If they send me overseas, I'll have to go. I'm sorry you're upset, but I did what I felt was right."

"What was right?" Mike said, shaking his head. "Wasn't it enough for one of us to be headed to Vietnam? I'm the man, I'm supposed to go to war, not you."

"I never said I was going to Vietnam to fight. I'm going there to help people."

"You don't know what you're getting yourself into. I was already there for six months, remember? You want to go into a godforsaken jungle full of snakes and bugs? How about the monsoons?"

"I can't think about those things. Our boys and those poor people need help."

"You have no clue. You can't trust those people, Maggie. You think you're on some mission to save the world? Those people don't want us in their country. Even little old helpless ladies and cute-as-a-button kids have killed our soldiers. Anyone can turn into the enemy. And you'll never know until it's too late."

"Surely I'll be safe in a hospital."

"You won't be safe anywhere except here, where you belong."

"Here we go again."

"Look Maggie," Mike said, going to her and putting his arms around her. "I know you think I'm a chauvinistic bastard. And maybe I am. But I love you.

I really do. I don't want to see you get hurt. It's my job to take care of you, no matter what you think. Can't you let me be a man?"

"Of course, I can. But why can't you let me be me? You continually expect me to be the cardboard cutout of a woman that your mother is. I can't do that. I refuse to rear ten children single-handedly while *you* be a man like your father. I don't want to wear the pants. I just want to be the one to decide what I'm wearing, not you. I love being a nurse and helping people. But I also love you. Why can't I be able to love both? You love flying, and me. You do both."

Mike stared at her a long time, then gustily exhaled. "If you feel that strongly about this Maggie, I won't stop you, but I want you to know, I'm not happy. I'd feel much better knowing that you were safe and sound here rather than in some hospital over there."

"I'll only be a letter away."

"That's not a very comforting thought."

"That's the best I can offer."

In the end, Mike accepted her decision grudgingly. He didn't have much time to fuss, however. Several weeks later, he was sent overseas, and Maggie followed soon after. It was going to be a strange year for both of them.

Maggie hated Saigon. The hospital personnel worked regular shifts just like in the states. The sick and wounded were brought to them fairly cleaned up and prepped for surgery or other treatments. In fact, life in Saigon was very similar to being home with one major exception. Some of Maggie's co-workers felt that, because they were away from their homes and families, they could get away with anything.

Maggie was constantly on her guard after one particularly annoying doctor decided to grab her butt in the presence of another doctor. The two men thought the situation was hilarious and something that was either condoned or overlooked on a day-to-day basis.

Billeted in a run-down hotel the army had taken over, Maggie had many of the comforts of home and felt guilty. She knew that Mike wasn't enjoying air conditioning and a nice bunk to sleep on at night. Although they had their problems, Maggie still missed Mike terribly and was counting the days until she could go home to him. She vowed to herself that when they were together again, she would try harder to be the kind of wife that he wanted. After this experience, having Mike's baby would be welcome.

His letters came like clockwork every Wednesday. Even if he just scribbled 'I Love You' on an envelope, she got something from him every week without fail, and did her best to reciprocate. It seemed as though Mike was also trying to make up for past sins.

Besides Mike's letters, the only other bright spot in Saigon was a young nurse named Deena Cramer. Deena was tall and shapely, got along with everyone, and always knew the dirtiest jokes. She was one quarter Japanese on her mom's side, and was endowed with thick, black hair that she usually wore in two long ponytails. Her dark brown eyes were always crinkled in laughter.

Deena made Saigon tolerable for Maggie. They shared a room and although she was single and several years Maggie's junior, the girls hit it off right away. They had many interests in common and shared many late-night confidences.

After the first week however, it became apparent that beneath Deena's happy manner there was a very troubled young woman. At first, Maggie thought Deena was nervous. She would find her doing something incorrectly and would gently remind her how to do it properly. "Don't do it like that, you Dodo. Do it this way."

Somehow the name 'Dodo' stuck, and Deena accepted it good-naturedly. On the surface, she seemed intelligent, then she'd do something very stupid and out of character, causing Maggie to worry about her friend.

One night, Maggie heard muffled crying from the other bed. "Deena? Are you all right?"

Deena sniffled. "I…guess."

Maggie got out of bed and went to her. "What's wrong?"

"Nothing."

"I don't believe you. Come on. What is it?"

"Oh Maggie, I did something terrible, and I don't know how to fix it."

"Tell me. Maybe I can help."

"I don't see how."

"You don't know unless you tell me."

"I'm not really a nurse," she cried.

"What do you mean? Of course you're a nurse."

"I'm not. I never finished school. I had a year left."

"How did you get into the army? You had to have some credentials."

"I did my training at a small community hospital in the little town where I live. It was easy to fudge them."

"But Do, why?"

Deena turned on the bedside light, grabbed a tissue, and blew her nose. "My brother was in the army and came over here almost two years ago. He's been MIA for the past ten months. I thought if I was here, I could check out hospitals. See if anyone remembered him. It was a stupid idea. I'll never find him. He has to be dead," she said, miserably.

Maggie hugged her. "I'm so sorry, Deena. Why didn't you tell me?"

"I couldn't. I didn't want to involve you in this mess."

"But that's what friends are for."

"Thanks Maggie. I'm glad you're still my friend."

"Of course, I am. But Deena, what if you're caught?"

"I'll have to figure that out if, or when, the time comes."

"Did you really think that by putting yourself into this predicament, you'd find out about your brother?"

"I don't know. But it was so awful at home. My parents couldn't function anymore. Everyday they'd wait for the mail, hoping to hear some word. I couldn't stand to see their pain. When I suggested coming here to search for him, they were appalled. They didn't want me to disappear as well. But then, the more we thought about it, the more sense it seemed to make."

She blew her nose again. "When people are desperate, the most outrageous schemes seem to make sense. And now I'm here. I'll never find him, and I'll soon be caught. I can't fake everything. You can only save my butt for so long." She started crying again. "Oh Maggie, what am I going to do?"

"We'll figure something out. In the meantime, I'll try to stick close and help you. There are a lot of things you *do* know. It's the surgical stuff that's giving you problems."

"I know. I never had any med/surg training. See what I mean? Dumb, dumb, dumb. What did I think I was going to do here? Empty bedpans and hold soldier's hands?"

At dinner the next day, Maggie overheard a conversation between two nurses that gave her an idea. The nurses were dissatisfied in Saigon. They came to Vietnam, not to work in a sterile hospital, but to get into the country where they could be of better help. They wanted to go to one of the field hospitals in the North where they felt they would be more useful.

"When I heard them talking about field hospitals," Maggie said, "the wheels in my head started turning. If you were in a field hospital, you could maybe find out about your brother and do less technical work. Many of those units merely stabilize casualties. You could do that."

With Maggie as their spokesperson, the four nurses petitioned the CO of their medical unit for permission to go to one of those hospitals. Maggie argued that they'd be of better use there. In the meantime, Deena could nose around, and Maggie could help her out when she ran into trouble. It was a great plan. It was fool proof.

The motion of the lumbering C-130 Hercules was making Maggie sick. She and her companions were holding on for dear life to the webbed sling seats that ran against either side of the cavernous plane. How Mike would laugh at her discomfort. He, who fought the G-forces of jets on a daily basis, would have found this flight comparable to the loft of a gently thrown softball.

The C-130 was definitely *not* a jet. Not even close. It was the biggest, strongest aircraft the US had in their possession. It was a workhorse that transported troops, artillery, tanks—whatever was needed, wherever it was needed. It was like the corpsman of the sky.

After some pitching and rolling, the engine's roar changed as the plane began its descent. Deena was ashen and Maggie had a grip on the straps with white knuckled hands. The servicemen, that the plane was also transporting, smiled at the girls either in encouragement or fun. Maggie couldn't be sure. Then, all at once, they were down.

"Thank God," said Deena. "I thought we'd never make it. If we'd have been in the air much longer, I'd have thrown up."

"Me too," Maggie replied. "Let's get out of this monster and find out where we need to go," she said, as the girls stuck their heads out of the plane and prepared to disembark.

"What the heck! Where are we?" Deena asked. There was nothing to indicate that they were at a hospital. A short distance away from where the plane had landed sat a small cluster of buildings; some crude huts on stilts, a few wooden structures, and two metal quonset huts. Sandbagged bunkers dotted the perimeter at regular intervals.

"I don't know. But I'm going to find out quickly, so that we can get back on that plane before it takes off again." Maggie walked over to the young pilot. "We were supposed to be going to Phu Bai. This can't be it. Where's the hospital?"

The pilot grinned at her and pointed to the cluster of buildings. "This *is* Phu Bai, and *that* is the Army hospital. What were you expecting, Walter Reed or Bethesda?"

"Who's in charge here?"

"The commander's office is over there," he pointed.

The women trooped to the office, Maggie in the lead. A corporal sat at a desk typing. "We need to see the commander right away," Maggie announced.

The corporal looked up, then went back to his typing. "Colonel Barnes is out."

"I think we're in the wrong place."

"Are you the four Army nurses from Saigon to I-Corps Field Hospital, Phu Bai, Vietnam?"

"Yes."

"No mistake, this is it. Next door," he motioned with his head, mumbled something and kept on typing.

The next room Maggie entered was neatly stocked with medical supplies. Padlocked glass doored cupboards contained large bottles of drugs. Facing away from her, a person with a long dark braid of hair sat, writing at a desk, a cigarette smoldering in an overflowing kidney bowl.

"Pardon me, ma'am. I was sent in here." The person turned and Maggie flushed. The braid belonged to a man. Maggie muttered under her breath, "Oh for the love of God…"

"Excuse me?" he said, his eyebrows pulled together into a frown. "You must be one of the nurses we're expecting. Paperwork?" he said, holding out his hand.

"I'm Lieutenant Reynolds." She handed over a sheaf of papers. "The rest of the girls are outside. Can you show us to our quarters, Corporal?"

He raised his eyebrows and stared at her through silver wire-framed glasses, making Maggie squirm uncomfortably under his scrutiny. Finally, he looked heavenward and shook his head, sighing. "I suppose I can," he said, rising. "Come on."

He walked past Maggie and went outside, surprising the rest of the girls. In the light, Maggie was able to get a better look at him. Outside, she would never have mistaken his gender. Although he was slim, the bare legs sticking out of his cut-off fatigues were tan and very muscular. There was a Mexican look about him, from the high cheekbones and thin nose to the full lips and cinnamon colored skin.

He crossed the open ground to the raised shacks, stopping in front of one. "This is your hooch. You should be happy to know you displaced five doctors."

"A hooch?"

"Yes, where you are bunking. The mess is that large wooden building over there. Remember, officers and noncoms are segregated. By the way, you'll have to share a latrine with the Vietnamese women who work here. It's that rectangular structure," he pointed. "You'll share the shower with them also. There's only a fifty-gallon holding tank for the water, so remember: get wet, soap up and rinse, no lingering. This isn't Saigon. Oh, and there's usually a movie every night at ten behind the officer's club, which is that building over there. Any questions?"

"Where's the hospital?"

"The larger of the two quonset huts."

"And the smaller one?"

"That's the morgue."

"Oh."

"Report to the hospital tomorrow morning at oh seven hundred unless someone gets you sooner. The corpsmen will tell you what to do and where you're needed."

"We're to take orders from a corpsman?"

"They know more than anyone here about the hospital, how it works and what needs to be done." He turned to go. "Oh, and make sure to use your mosquito netting and take your quinine tablets. Unless, of course, you want a good case of malaria," he said over his shoulder, as he headed back to the supply room.

Around five p.m., the girls joined the parade of men making their way toward the mecca of the mess hall.

"What is that?" Deena asked a young man, who stood behind the battered buffet chafing pans, making motions to place something brown on Deena's plate.

"Meat," he smiled.

"What kind of meat?"

"For you princess, spam a l'orange."

"I think I'll pass." She took her tray and went to get something to drink.

"Coffee or Kool-Aid. That's all they have." Anna Marie said when Deena caught up to her.

"Man, if anything, maybe I'll lose some weight while we're here. This makes the stuff we had in Saigon look like gourmet delicacies."

"Pretty bad, huh?" said Trisha. "But remember, we asked for this. It was all our idea."

"That's right, girls," said Maggie. "We wanted this experience. Well, here it is in its full glory. I don't think we're going to be welcomed with open arms either. You saw how that medical supply clerk treated us. And he said we took the hooch of a bunch of doctors. You know what they're like when they're in a good mood. Now, they're really gonna be ticked at us. Oh well, it's only for a month or so, right?"

"Right," said Deena. "So, let's make the best of it," she said, taking a seat at a long wooden table. "Careful of the bench," she advised. "I think I just got a splinter in my butt."

As they ate, they were aware of the looks they were receiving. Some of the men acted as though they had never seen a woman before. Others seemed disgusted and some, like the man who was approaching, clearly had sex on the brain.

"Here comes a live one," said Trisha, under her breath.

"Ladies, ladies, ladies! Let me be the first to welcome you to our humble abode. I'm Captain Galbreath, otherwise known as Lucky. I'm one of the GIs here."

"General Infantry?" Trisha asked innocently.

"Aren't you funny," he laughed, "GI, General Internist. I'm one of the staff doctors."

"Oh, I see. How silly of me. Tell me, Doctor, do you get very busy here?"

"Pretty busy. Most days we see well over fifty casualties of some sort or another. We have two general surgeons, an orthopedic guy, me, two GPs and a couple of gas passers. But who wants to talk shop. If you like Bogie, they're showing the *African Queen* tonight."

"Moving in on the chicks already, Lucky?" A skinny blond man approached followed by several others. They all sat down with the nurses. "Don't trust him," said the blond. "I'm Ray Krause, one of the surgeons here. After dinner, we'd like to buy you all a drink at the 'O' Club."

"Thank you, Doctor," said Maggie. "That's very nice of you, maybe some other time. We still have a lot of unpacking to do and our hooch, or whatever it's called, is filthy and we plan on giving it a good cleaning."

"Lucky, did you leave a mess again?"

"How was I supposed to know that a bunch of women were throwing us out? I think they owe us a little something since they're taking our beds. Actually, we could have just shared the hooch. Two fit quite comfortably on my cot. Especially when they're one on top of the other. Don't you agree?" He leered at the women collectively. "No one has turned me down yet."

"There's a first time for everything," Maggie said. "Sorry, Captain. No, thanks." As a group they stood and walked out of the mess hall with as much dignity as they could muster. What have I done, Maggie thought?

Loud whomping vibrations shattered the stillness of dawn at oh six hundred the next morning. Maggie, as well as the rest of the camp, was immediately awake and moving. Corpsmen pounded to the arriving helicopters; their yells muffled by the thumping rotor blades as they rushed to unload the wounded. A little disoriented, Maggie frantically dressed and hurried to the hospital. She was fast on the heels of Lucky Galbreath, who was in the process of pulling a t-shirt over his sleep tousled hair. His untied boot laces flapped against the ground as he walked.

"Eight, fifteen and six, sir," a corpsman greeted him, as he entered the building. Lucky acknowledged the corpsman, then saw Maggie behind him, a puzzled expression on her face.

"Eight on stretchers, fifteen walking and six that need to be pronounced," Galbreath explained. "Which is my first order of the morning, counting stiffs. Since you chicks weren't very obliging, the dead are the only stiff things we have in this camp at the moment," he said gruffly.

Just then, a ginger haired kid with freckles rushed up to Maggie. "Lieutenant, we need someone to scrub for OR, quick," he said. "Bad gut in OR 1. That's the first partitioned area you come to. Doc's getting started. I'd go, but it's crazy right now. Got to type and cross match some blood, then pick up some films."

"Where do I scrub?"

Freckles pointed to the far door of the hospital and kept walking.

Maggie scrubbed and went to the OR as directed. The OR was nothing more than a partitioned stall in the capacious metal building. A large light hung overhead, and equipment was tightly packed around a gurney located in the center of the stall. At the moment, a young man of about twenty occupied the gurney. His abdomen was a ragged, bloody mess. A gowned and gloved man sat at his head giving anesthesia while a surgeon was already trying to tie off vessels, his Bovie humming; the smell of burnt flesh permeating the air.

"Hand me a Kelly," the surgeon said without looking up. "This kid's never gonna make it if we can't slow this flow down. He's bleeding like a stuck pig and has so many holes in him I don't know which one to fix first. He's also full of buckshot. If it's not a hole, it's pieces of metal. I'm going to need some sponge sticks and suction. I can't see a thing down here."

Maggie stood at his shoulder doing as she was told. The surgeon grunted, his voice muffled by his mask, "Stand across from me, will you. I'm left-handed and it works better that way."

Moving into position, Maggie did her best to anticipate the surgeon's every move. He wore glasses with an added nose piece that had magnifying lenses attached. Maggie was fascinated by his hands. The slender fingers seemed to dance inside the patient.

As he cauterized and sutured, Maggie watched, mesmerized. Though he grunted and cursed under his breath, and every once in a while, even hummed bits of Beatles' tunes, he quickly assessed the wounds and systematically took care of each one. He didn't rush or panic when something went wrong but kept going.

Maggie always felt she had a strong stomach, but some of the injuries were hard to take. One after another in a gory parade came boys who would never be the same again. She had thought things were bad in Saigon. But back there, the wounded were already prepped and cleaned up to a certain extent. Here however, the wounded came straight from the field where they had fallen. She assisted the surgeon as he performed several bowel resections, cleaned up a few missing fingers and toes and patched up a myriad of wounds.

Later in the day, the young, freckled corpsman stuck his head in, holding a mask over his nose. "Need anything, Doc?"

"What's it like out there, Joey?"

"Kids really took a pounding last night. But rush hour is over. Most of the wounded still arriving are in pretty good shape. The GPs are taking care of them. Then they'll be shipped out."

"Got many left?"

"Naw, just one and Doc Krause is gonna take him."

"Thank God."

"How's my replacement doin'?"

"Not bad. She'll do."

"Good," Joey said, winking at Maggie.

When the surgeon finished suturing their last patient, he shook his head. "I don't know about this one," he said, peeling off his gloves. "I have a bad feeling I'm going to see him again." Without removing his mask, he rubbed the back of his neck and flexed his shoulders. "Good job today, thanks," he said, as he walked from the room.

Maggie helped Joey clean and disinfect the OR, then both went to the overflowing mess for dinner. Maggie filled a tray and searched the throng for her comrades. They were scattered. She noticed a seat next to the clerk with the braid from the medical supply office. He was reading a book, smoking, and drinking some coffee; an empty plate of food was pushed to the side.

"Wow, what a day," she said, plunking down next to him.

"I guess," he replied. "I've seen worse."

"Really?"

"Mmm," he mumbled then went back to his book.

"I don't know who the doctor was that I worked with today and I never saw his face, but he was something else. I've never seen hands like his before in my life. Even though he was wearing gloves, I'd know those hands anywhere. The anesthesiologist called him Billy. Do you know who I'm talking about?"

The man grunted and kept reading.

"You don't talk much, do you?"

"I'm very tired. I didn't ask you to sit here. I was minding my own business, when you bounced down beside me like some freakin' schoolgirl."

"Ha! You couldn't have worked nearly as hard as the guy I worked with today. He really busted his butt."

"That so?"

"Yeah," glancing down to see the title of the book he was reading, Maggie took notice of his hands. They were rather small, and the fingers were slender and familiar. She began to feel confused and uncomfortable.

"So, what did *you* do today that has you so whipped?" she asked, still looking at his hands.

"Oh, a little of this and that," he replied nonchalantly, taking a long pull on his cigarette.

"By the way, didn't you tell me that noncoms were supposed to be sitting on the other side of the room. Or is it a free for all when it's this crowded?" Maggie asked.

He exhaled a stream of smoke, studying her over the top of his wire-rimmed glasses. His olive-green eyes were piercing, and she felt herself drowning in his gaze.

"Hey Doc," Joey called, running up to their table. "That last kid you did, he's spiking and his pressure's dropping fast."

The man's eyes shifted, and the spell was broken. "Son of a bitch," he said, viciously stabbing out his cigarette. "I knew I'd see him again." Then rising, he followed Joey from the room, leaving Maggie and her burning face behind.

The next morning, Maggie went early to the hospital. "Hey, Lieutenant," Joey stopped her. "Doc Krause could use some help in OR 3."

"Sure, Joey, by the way, where's the doctor from yesterday?"

"You mean Doc Fox? He's sleeping. He was with that kid half the night and had to open him up again. I hear he lost him about oh four hundred. Damn shame. When I came on this morning, he was just heading to his hooch. I told him I'd wake him only if he was needed. But so far, it's been pretty slow. We have less than 10 casualties right now and half of them are ambulatory. Anytime we have more than ten on litters though, that's considered mass casualties. Everyone runs when they hear that."

"Gotcha! Well, I'd better go and scrub for Dr. Krause. See you later."

"Okay."

Ray Krause was not a bad surgeon, but he wasn't quite Billy Fox. Billy worked quickly, efficiently, and meticulously. Krause rushed the work in a slightly sloppy manner. He seemed more interested in impressing her and talking sports with the gas passer, as they all called the anesthesiologists, than in his patient.

"So, Maggie, what do you think of our little set up here?"

"When we arrived yesterday, we were all shocked. We were expecting a real hospital. This seemed so primitive. Yet, on the other hand, it's run better than the hospital in Saigon. It's cleaner, more organized and efficient. I find it amazing."

"Well, Billy does his best. When he came here about two months ago, things were pretty shoddy. He reorganized and cleaned this place up like you wouldn't believe."

"Billy?"

"Major Fox. I hear you got to work with him yesterday."

"Major?" Maggie said faintly.

"What's your opinion of our boss?"

"He's…very good."

"Yeah, he is. Nice guy too, when you get to know him. Or rather, *if* he lets you get to know him. For the record, his bark is a lot worse than his bite."

"Thanks. I'll remember that."

"Are you girls all unpacked and disinfected now?"

"I think so," Maggie replied, absently.

"Good, how about that drink later?"

Maggie hesitated.

"Look Lieutenant, we're not all like Lucky. Most of us are very happily married men. We just want to buy you girls a drink, not get into your pants. Having you here and being able to buy you a drink makes this place more civilized, that's all."

"In that case, we'll be happy to accept. Thank you."

Later at dinner, Ray and a few other men, including Billy, were seated at a table.

"Girls, over here," Ray called. "There's lots of space. Come on guys, shift your butts and give the ladies some room."

The four nurses took places at the table. Maggie, unfortunately, found herself next to Lucky. "Wanna play doctor later?" he asked Maggie, leering.

"That's the story of your life, Lucky. All you ever do is *play* doctor," Billy said, lighting a cigarette. "And by the way, I want you to tear down the partition you so cleverly built around your bunk. I refuse to live in a whorehouse."

"Yeah, you and the waitress from the 'O' Club had us awake half the night with your fun and games," Ray added. "Her kids were standing outside watching while the two of you copulated your fannies off. Aren't you ashamed?"

"Ashamed? Hell no, I perform better for an audience," Galbreath laughed. "Besides, she wasn't a bad piece, for a gook. Although she could have been a little tighter, but…"

"I want that partition down tonight," Billy interrupted.

"Gonna scalp me if I don't?"

"In your case, I'd rather nail your nuts to the wall."

"You know what your problem is *Major*? You need to get laid."

Billy's look was withering. "Get it down, *Captain*," he said, standing, "that's an order."

"Yes, sir," Galbreath said, saluting with his middle finger extended as Billy left the mess.

Maggie ate quickly, wanting to get away from Lucky. She had received a letter from Mike in the day's mail, that she was anxious to read. Leaving the mess, she headed for a bench she had spied earlier. She was almost upon it, when she realized someone was already there. Sitting with his knees up, smoking and reading a letter was Billy.

"May I sit here, Major?" she asked.

"Not my bench, do what you like," he said, sliding over.

"I'm sorry you lost your patient," she said, taking a seat.

He snorted. "Which one?"

"The boy we had yesterday."

He glanced at her for a long moment, then said, "Can't save them all." But the look on his face suggested that he felt differently. He then went back to his letter.

Maggie shifted uncomfortably on the bench in mental debate with herself. Finally, she cleared her throat and spoke. "I also want to apologize for the other day. I burst into your office, assumed the wrong thing, and was rude and insulting on more than one occasion. I'm very sorry, sir," she said.

Billy looked up from his letter and stared at her. "You can knock off the sir crap, Lieutenant. I don't care about titles or rank. It doesn't do a thing for me. The only time I use it is with an asshole like Galbreath. About the other day, forget it." He went back to his mail, dismissing her.

After that, she hastily tore open her envelope. She was thrilled Mike had found her so quickly. When she finished reading, she noticed Billy was tucking his letter into an envelope emblazoned with a Washington, DC postmark. He slipped it into his shirt pocket, then reached for another cigarette.

"You sure smoke a lot, Doctor," she commented.

"Tell me something, Lieutenant, do you always just blurt out whatever you're thinking?"

Maggie flushed. "I'm just surprised you're not more conscious of being healthy since you're a doctor. Why don't you quit?"

"Why don't you mind your own business?" He snapped his lighter shut with a loud clink and exhaled a stream of smoke through his nostrils.

"Sorry," she glanced down, then back at him. "So why don't you?"

"You know, Reynolds, you remind me of a mosquito, constantly buzzing around, making a nuisance of itself," he said, shaking his head. "For your information, I don't quit because I don't want to. Okay?"

"But it's so unhealthy."

"Look," he growled, "the damn surgeon general wasn't pushing his warnings when I was six and my old man gave me my first cigarette. Besides, between cigarettes and alcohol, I think the government would like to see us annihilate ourselves. It would save them the trouble of doing it themselves. In fact, it's a wonder they don't provide them for us."

"Who's us?"

"My people."

"So, you *are* a Mexican?"

"Mexican? Where the hell did you get that idea?"

"You look Mexican."

"Well, I'm not."

"Oh?" She looked at him questioningly.

"For God's sake! Don't you ever stop?" He shook his head again, sighing. "I'm an American Indian."

"That's interesting, what kind?"

"Kind?" he asked, rising. "We're not pickles, Reynolds. We don't come in varieties," he said. "If you must know, I'm from the Apache and Navajo Nations."

She was quiet for a minute, mulling over what he told her.

"Satisfied?" he asked, with a look that said the conversation and questioning were over.

"Yes," she paused. "I'm sorry. I think I put my foot in it again, didn't I?"

He looked down at her shoes. "Just one foot? It's a damned good thing you have small feet, Lieutenant," he commented, disgustedly. "*Mañana*," he said and stalked off into the dusk.

"*Mañana*," she mumbled to herself.

BILLY

Billy found his new job interesting. Phu Bai was a busy field unit and between the administrative and surgical aspects of his job, he didn't have much time to dwell on John.

Initially, he was overwhelmed. Records were missing, supplies were scattered, the hospital was filthy and poorly arranged. Since the radiology department was not adjacent to the hospital, getting an x-ray sometimes took too long.

The first thing Billy did was sit down with the other doctors to discuss a reorganization of the hospital. They decided to flip the morgue with the hospital so that the scrub room, ORs, radiology, and recovery were all under the same roof. Between all medical personnel, it took about a month of hard work to have the hospital cleaned up and running more efficiently.

Colonel Barnes proved to be a fair and decent CO. He was pleased there were no problems with the medical company, and the hospital was no longer a disgrace. Billy, however, was so busy that he didn't see Barnes much. But when he did, the colonel usually had a compliment to give.

Having four females foisted on him put a wrench into the works. Maggie, especially, seemed to have been sent to test his patience. For Billy, who usually went out of his way to avoid confrontations, Maggie was constantly putting him on guard. In one week, he was on the offensive and defensive more than he had ever been with Jessie or anyone else for that matter. It was as though she went out of her way to antagonize him.

"I don't see why women haven't been here before now," Maggie said, as she helped him inventory the pharmacy one day.

"You don't, huh?" Billy replied.

"No, I think you're all just a bunch of male chauvinists."

"There you go spouting off again. You have no idea what you're talking about. The reason women haven't been here before is simple. It's dangerous. We're too close to the fighting. It's bad enough *we* have to be here."

"You sound just like my husband."

"Well, he sounds like a sensible person."

"Sensible? All he ever does is rag on me about being a nurse. I shouldn't have a career or work. I'm supposed to stay home—where it's *safe*, and mass produce children. All that other stuff is for men, including the fooling around on the side."

"I don't know about the fooling around part, but in the past, that's how it was."

"And how you all still want it to be."

"I never said that."

"You implied it," Maggie argued.

"The hell I did!"

"You're all the same. Admit it."

"Why would I admit to something that isn't true? You can have any career you want. You could even be a doctor for all I care. What does a career have to do with safety?"

"Are you serious?"

"About what?"

"About the doctor thing?"

"You mean, about a woman being a doctor?"

"Yes."

"Sure, if that's what she wants."

"I find that hard to believe."

"What? That I don't fit into *your* definition of what a man should be. Or what an Indian should be, for that matter? Hell Reynolds, you're the one who's being sexist *and* racist."

Maggie blushed and studied the label on the bottle she was holding. "I guess," she muttered.

"If you'd get off your soap box for one minute and listen to me. All I said is that this place is dangerous. I never said that women shouldn't be here in Vietnam. There's nothing wrong with having women working in an Evac or hospital or hospital ship where things are relatively safe. I don't think that's being sexist. Is it?"

"I guess not."

"Before you girls got here, this camp was geared for men. Urinals were against the buildings; the showers were big semi-open spaces with faucet heads. Men ran around here half naked. I had one hell of a time changing things around. The only women that came into the camp were the Vietnamese women who work here."

"What do they do here anyway?" Maggie asked, trying to change the subject.

"They're our 'hoochie coochies,'" Billy replied with a small smile.

"What?"

"If you want, they'll clean your hooch and wash your clothes. They also tend bar and wait on tables in the 'O' Club."

"Boy, that's nice they do that for the army."

"You don't think they do this out of the goodness of their hearts, do you? Each hooch costs several thousand piasters a week to clean. Each shirt or pair of pants is another couple hundred piasters to wash. You want them ironed? Guess what?"

"More piasters?"

"You got it. That's how they make a living."

"Oh," she said, then paused. "Uh, Doctor?" Billy sighed and stared at her, waiting for more. "I'm sorry about the sexist stuff."

"You're a real thorn in my side, Reynolds. Do you know that?"

Maggie looked down at her feet. "I'm sorry," she said quietly.

Billy shook his head and grinned. "So, how many of those quinine tabs do we have?"

Maggie looked at him and smiled shyly, "Uh, ten bottles of five hundred."

"Thanks," he said, making a note on his clipboard.

The next day, Maggie came running into the hospital. "Dr. Fox!" she yelled. "The camp is on fire!"

Billy ran to the door and looked out. Thick, oily, black clouds of smoke hung in the air. He rolled his eyes. "Maggie, it's Monday," he said impatiently. "The Vietnamese men are burning shit."

"What?" Maggie asked, confused.

"You share a six-holer with the Vietnamese women, right?"

"Yes."

"Under each of those plywood holes sits an oil drum filled with diesel fuel."

"Is that what that odd smell is?"

"Yes, and every Monday, those drums are removed and replaced. The waste is then taken out to the perimeter of the camp and burned. *We* are not on fire, our *shit* is."

Maggie turned bright red. "Oh, I see, Doctor. Thanks for the explanation."

"Hey, no problem!"

"You sound just like Joey."

"I know. I've been hanging around him too long."

"You could sound worse, I guess."

"Yeah, I could start sounding like Lucky."

"Oh please, no," Maggie said, her hands to her face in mock horror. Billy smiled and went back to what he was doing.

For the next few days, a steady stream of casualties kept the medical personnel busy. But toward the end of the week, things had again slowed down. During the lull, Billy took the opportunity to catch up on some reading. He had just finished his dinner and was in the middle of the latest novel that Barbara had sent him, when Maggie plopped down beside him. He nodded hello and kept reading.

"You sure read a lot."

"Mmm."

"What do you have this time," she asked, tilting the cover so that she could see the title. "The Phantom of the Opera?"

"Do you mind? He's about to kill Joseph Buquet."

"What do you do with the books you've already read?"

Billy put down his book and glared at Maggie in exasperation. "Would you like to read one of them?"

"Sure, I'm getting a little bored. Would you really loan me one?"

"I'd do anything to get you to shut up for a while so that I could read in peace."

"Oh, I'm sorry."

Billy got up. "Come on, let's get you something to keep you out of my hair." Maggie had to almost run to keep up with Billy's long, even strides as he walked to his hooch. As he was stepping inside, Maggie hesitated, "Shall I wait out here?"

"Why? I'm not dragging this heavy box outside."

"I just wasn't sure if I was allowed in your hooch."

"If you think I'm going to rape you, think again. I'm not Lucky. Your integrity is safe with me."

Maggie blushed, then followed him inside. She looked around at the vacated interior. "Where is everyone?"

"Probably at the 'O' Club getting sloshed."

"How can they do that every night?"

Billy shrugged. "Who knows or cares," he said, peering under his bunk. "I know I have a box of finished books here somewhere," he muttered under his breath.

As he said this, Maggie glanced at a small double picture frame sitting on the table by his cot. On one side was a snapshot of an attractive white couple and two young women in their teens. In the other was an older Indian couple.

"Is this your family?" Maggie asked, picking up the frame.

Billy dumped a cardboard carton of books on his bed, then took the frame out of her hands. "Help yourself," he said, as he opened the drawer of the bedside table, placed the picture frame in it, then closed it with a bang. Going over to Ray's bunk, he sat down and thumbed through his book to find his place.

"Who sends you all the reading material?" Maggie asked, as she sifted through the paperbacks.

"I have two semi-adopted sisters. One sends me books and one sends me other stuff."

"Other stuff?"

"Things like shampoo, soap, and herbal teas," he said absently, once more engrossed in his novel.

"What do you mean semi-adopted?" Maggie persisted.

Billy blew out an exasperated breath and threw his book down with a thud. "You won't shut up, will you?" He crossed his arms against his chest and said in annoyance. "I've lived with this family for about nine years. We kind of adopted one another."

"Is that the family in the picture?"

"God! I thought you wanted something to read?"

"If you weren't so secretive, I wouldn't have to ask."

"I'm not being secretive. I just feel that the finer details of my life are neither you nor anyone else's business."

"I don't see how asking you about your family is so intrusive."

"You really bust my ass; you know that?"

"So, you've said."

"You're not going to quit, are you?" He stared at Maggie who calmly returned the look. Finally, he shook his head, sighed and going over to the nightstand, pulled the picture frame out of the drawer, handing it to Maggie. "This is the Wilson family. That's Rusty and Marian and this is Barbara and Jennifer. Barbara is the book-a-holic. Jenny is more eclectic with what she sends."

"Who is the other couple?"

"My grandparents."

"I see the resemblance," she said, scrutinizing the photo. "You look a lot like your grandfather."

"I guess," he shrugged.

"I don't see a picture of your wife anywhere," Maggie commented, looking around.

"No, you don't."

"Why not?" she persisted.

"Because I don't possess a picture of her," he said, clenching his teeth.

"Did it really hurt for you to tell me all this?"

"No," he said, looking down at himself. "I don't see any visible wounds. Are you satisfied you know all this now?"

"Yes, I'll be able to sleep much better tonight."

"Good. Now beat it," he said, ushering her out the door. "Sweet dreams."

"Same to you, Doctor," she smiled. "Thanks for the books."

A few days later, Billy took the information that he and Maggie had gathered and sat down to fill in a drug requisition order. He was just about finished, when there was a knock on the door.

"Major, can I have a few minutes," Colonel Barnes said, sticking his head into the office.

"Sure, Colonel," Billy got up and walked to the door. Barnes cocked his head toward the Officer's Club.

"Come on, it's happy hour."

Billy hesitated, then followed Barnes to the wooden shack across the camp.

"I have some information for you," Barnes said, as they entered the dimly lit building. At this time of day, the club was doing a booming business. The small room was full of patrons, cigarette smoke, and raucous laughter.

Barnes walked up to the bar and ordered a whiskey and soda. "What do you want, Fox?" Barnes asked, his money out.

"Uh…how about an orange juice?" Billy said.

Barnes gave him a strange look, then put in the order.

The Vietnamese girl behind the counter said, "Vodka?"

"No, just orange juice," Billy replied.

"Silly Joe, you get juice for free in mess," the Vietnamese girl muttered, as she took Barnes' money.

The two men found seats in the corner and the colonel pulled out some papers. "I got these in the mail today. I think they concern you more than me. A wild strain of virus is running rampant up here. There's going to be a meeting in Saigon in a couple of weeks to discuss it."

"Oh?" Billy said, and reached his hand out for the papers that Barnes presented. "Do I have to go?"

"As chief of medical personnel in this camp, you'd be expected to be there."

"What if we have casualties?" Billy questioned.

"It doesn't matter. You'll have to go. You know how the army is."

"I hope there aren't any problems."

"You know what they say, wish in one hand and shit in the other, Fox. See which one fills up first. Crap happens whether you want it to or not."

Billy was originally scheduled to fly to Saigon on an early morning fixed wing, then return the next morning. The morning of the meeting however, I-Corps received mass casualties at oh five hundred from a bad night out in the field. Half an hour later, Billy found himself up to his elbows in a perforated bowel instead of preparing to leave. It was a difficult procedure and he hated to rush for fear of missing shrapnel or additional holes in the bowel.

With his eyes focused on the light box, he studied the negative. "Hand me those Babcocks," he said to Maggie, his hand out. With them, he explored a section of bowel. "I don't see anything on the neg, but I feel something small and hard down here," he mumbled.

"If you'd get your hands out of your pants and back into the patient where they belong, you wouldn't have that problem," the gas passer snorted.

"Good things come in small packages," Billy muttered. "There you are, you little bastard," he said, as he fished out a tiny piece of metal and dropped it into a kidney bowl with a clink.

"Uh huh, they *come* all right."

"You two have the filthiest minds," Maggie complained.

"Hands too," Billy commented, holding up a brown and bloody glove. "I think that's it."

"Now, what are you doing?" Maggie asked, as he stuck his nose down close to the open abdomen.

"I'm smelling for shit."

"Oh? Is this something you do for kicks or is there a good reason why you would want to smell that?"

"This is not a perverse pleasure, Reynolds. I'm hoping not to smell shit. If I smell it, there may be another hole somewhere, perhaps on the underside of the bowel."

"I see. And what do you smell?"

"Shit," he muttered.

"I hate to tell you doctor, but you have some smeared on your forehead. Do you think that's what you're smelling?"

"At this point, I don't have the faintest idea. This kid is just going to have to take his chances."

The clock on the wall showed oh nine hundred when he finally tied the last knot. Another fixed wing was due at any moment.

"I guess I don't have time to shower, set my hair, or do my nails," Billy said to Maggie as he pulled off his gloves with a snap and examined his fingers.

"You also have a little souvenir from our last patient on your immaculate trousers," she said, pointing to his pants as she helped untie and remove his gown.

"Oh shit."

"Yep, that's what it looks like, I'm afraid."

As she said this, Billy's ride approached for a landing, bouncing down on the small runway of the air strip.

"No time to change. Maybe I'll have a chance when I get there." He grabbed up his backpack and ran to the plane.

"Have fun," Maggie called. "Don't do anything we wouldn't do."

Held in a downtown Saigon hotel, the meeting was already in progress when Billy finally arrived. He hurriedly found the conference room and entered. Dressed in crumpled fatigues, Billy's hair was dirty and coming loose from its braid in little wisps. There was dried blood and other foreign matter spattered on his boots and a smear of feces on his pants.

Attired in their dress khakis, the doctors quit talking and stared. One rose from his seat and approached him. "Can we help you? The uh...psychiatric unit is across the street."

"Is this the meeting of chiefs of medical personnel?"

"Yes, it is. And as I said before, the psychiatric unit is across the street." He went to grab Billy's arm to move him toward the door but got a good whiff and cut a hasty retreat.

"So you say, but I'm here for the meeting. I'm *Major* Fox from the field hospital in Phu Bai," he said, reaching into his shirt pocket for the information he had been sent.

"*You* are Major Fox?" the doctor said in disbelief.

"Yes, sorry about the clothes, but we got mass casualties this morning. I didn't have time to change before I left."

"What is that on your pants?"

"It sure looks like fecal matter from the bowel resection I did this morning."

"Hope you don't mind sitting in the back," the doctor stated. "You smell like a barn." When the others laughed, he continued. "I didn't know they *had* real doctors up there. I thought they were just a bunch of butchers. From the looks of you, I guess I was right."

"Who said he's even a doctor," another man commented. "Look at him. He's either a stoned hippie or maybe he's a medicine man pretending to be a doctor."

Billy took a seat at the very back of the room and lit a cigarette, trying to ignore the rude comments being spoken. A young man walked over with a pot of coffee and a mug. "Care for some coffee, Major?"

"Yes, please."

Under his breath, the corporal said, "Don't mind them, sir. Half of these guys have never even seen a casualty. And if they did, they wouldn't know what to do with it. Cream and sugar?"

Billy smiled and took the coffee. "Real cream?"

The corporal smiled, "For them? Of course."

"Then cream, thanks."

"How about something to go with it? These guys already had a full breakfast. You're probably starving."

"I am. Anything you got would be great. Thanks."

Most of the meeting was a waste of time. Billy nodded off, while the other men talked about which bars to hit later in the afternoon as well as which prostitutes were the cleanest and the least expensive. There was also a heated debate about whether taking antibiotics after sex actually kept one from getting VD.

The reason Billy came to the meeting took about twenty-five minutes to discuss then dismiss. There was a presentation addressing a virulent strain of virus that was causing bronchitis and, in some instances, pneumonia. The virus was spreading up north into Billy's area and, because of the climate and approaching wet weather, measures were being taken to halt its progress. So far, the different antibiotics being used were obtaining good results.

Unfortunately, since most of the doctors attending were from actual hospitals and hospital ships, those in attendance who were from the areas where the virus really mattered weren't given the chance to ask questions. And, even though Billy tried to ask, he was ignored.

The discussion immediately went back to a certain hooker, who sounded to Billy like a contortionist in a circus. He should have stayed in Phu Bai. He felt guilty that he had left his comrades with mass casualties while he sat there and listened to a bunch of crap. Now it was too late to get another plane back.

The meeting adjourned late in the afternoon, and the same corporal came to Billy's aid once again. "There are a few rooms set aside for doctors who need to stay the night. Not all of them are taken." He led Billy to a room and told him about some of the nicer restaurants in town. "If you want room service, it's available. If you want a clean whore, Mama San's Bar on the corner is the best. If you need anything, give me a call, here's my extension. Call any time. If I don't answer, someone else will."

"Thanks for everything today," Billy said, shaking the young man's hand. "You were a lifesaver." The corporal smiled, saluted, and left.

The first thing Billy did was take a shower. It was wonderful to stand under hot, scalding water without worrying about depleting the water tank. It was a shame he couldn't have gotten there earlier. He felt like such a jerk. The other doctors steered clear of him with the exception of making some nasty remarks about his race and odor. It was a hell of a long way to come for a shower and clean sheets.

As he was leaving early the next morning, several of the remaining doctors, milling about in the lobby, noted his clean dress khakis. One man smirked and said, "I see you cleaned up your act. Too bad you're going back to the bush." The other doctors laughed, one adding that the only bush they had in Saigon was one hundred piasters for ten minutes.

Billy was happy to return to Phu Bai and hoped he never had to go back to Saigon. From what he saw and heard, the doctors he came in contact with may as well have been back in the states for all the war they saw. All they seemed to care about was drinking and whoring around. It was a recess from responsibility. To them, Billy was a freak.

He knew that there had to have been good doctors attending the meeting that were either decent or needed more information, but as usual, the good men always seemed to disappear into the woodwork when the jerks took over. It was amazing how stupid men in large groups could stifle intelligence.

At dinner later that night, the other doctors questioned him about his trip. "What did you think of Saigon?" Ray asked.

"It was like being in any other large city."

"Was the hotel nice?"

"The sheets were clean, and this morning I got to take a shit all by myself without anyone else there to hold my hand."

"Did you get any good sex?" Lucky asked.

"You wouldn't know good sex if it came up to you and bit you on the dick," Ray retorted. "In your case, quantity over quality is generally the rule." Ray then turned to Billy. "So. Did you?"

"Not that it's any of your business," Billy said with a smile. "But the closest thing I had to an orgasmic experience was the twenty-minute hot shower I had last night and again this morning."

"Soap and everything?"

"Of course."

"Geez Fox, are you turning queer or something?" Lucky sneered. "Soap and everything? Bet they were those little perfumed jobs. You must smell like a queen."

"You would know, wouldn't you," Billy replied.

"Is sex all you guys ever think about?" Maggie asked.

"Yes," Lucky replied. "What else is there?"

"Plenty," Maggie countered.

"Like what?" Lucky pushed.

Maggie, for once, was speechless. "Well, you know, life…in general."

"And what creates life, Nurse Smarty?" Lucky continued.

"Sex," Deena answered, gleefully. "Besides, twenty minutes in the shower with Dr. Fox sounds pretty orgasmic. With or without soap! I would pay money to see his butt wet and naked. Come on Maggie, you would too. Admit it."

The doctors all hooted with laughter with the exception of Billy, who was trying to ignore the direction the conversation was taking. Maggie turned a deep shade of red. "I will not admit anything of the kind," she replied hotly. "There is *no* man in this camp that I would want to see wet and/or naked. *Even* Doctor Fox. As far as I'm concerned, most men are animals with very little brains. I don't know why you encourage them, Dodo. They're all bad enough on their own." Maggie stood, grabbed her tray, and returned it to the counter with a bang before exiting the mess. Deena giggled again, then blew a kiss in Billy's direction.

"So Doc, how about a twenty second one later on? Wouldn't want to deplete the tank!"

Billy flushed and also rose. "This conversation has gotten way out of hand; and, as far as I'm concerned, is over." He followed Maggie from the building, the sounds of laughter echoing in his wake.

He stomped off to his office and sorted through all the mail that had come in during his short absence. In the pile was an official document that usually meant reassignments. He opened the envelope and scanned the list. What Mac had dreaded finally came to pass. Assigned to an artillery group, Joey was to leave immediately. Billy felt sick. The two had been together for so long, that Joey was like family. Billy hated to see him go.

Joey, on the other hand, was excited when Billy broke the news to him. "Cool beans! I'm finally going to see some action. Not that I want to leave you, Doc," he said, as he began to pack his duffel. "But I'll be a big help to those guys. I can't wait."

"Don't be a hero, Joey. Stay down. Don't go getting yourself shot to hell and back. I don't want to see you being brought in on a litter."

"Hey, no problem! I'll keep low. Don't worry about me. I know how to take care of myself."

"Who the hell's gonna help me run this place now?"

"Aw, you got Lieutenant Reynolds. She can take my place. You two already work well together."

"Work well together? You mean we fight well together," Billy said dryly. "I think I'd rather have a case of malaria."

"Oh, come on, sir. I've seen the two of you together. You're not *always* fighting."

"What would you call it, then?"

"Well, back home in Galveston, my daddy would probably call it foreplay," Joey laughed.

Billy's face turned an odd shade of red. "What!"

"You know what I mean."

"No. I do not."

"Beggin' your pardon, sir, but I think you know what foreplay is, don't you?"

"Yes, smart ass I do. But that has nothing to do with me and Lieutenant Reynolds."

"I won't argue with you, especially since you outrank me. But I know what I see."

"You're so full of shit Joey, you stink."

"Well, I haven't taken a dump today, so maybe I do. But that has nothing to do with the fact that Lieutenant Reynolds is good. You can't argue with me on that one."

"You're right. She is good. In fact, she's the best damned nurse I've ever worked with. If I could just get her to shut up, she'd be about as close to perfect as a woman could get. But God, she's always asking questions, always talking."

"That's funny, I never heard her talking to anyone else like that. In fact, she's a little mouse when it comes to the other doctors. It must be you, sir."

"Me?"

Joey laughed. "Yeah, never heard a peep out of her any other time."

"Well, 'Mighty Mouse' sure makes up for it when she's with me. Some days she gives me such a headache, I can't think straight."

"Take two aspirin and call me in the morning."

"Thanks for the swell advice, *Doctor* Mahoning."

"Hey, no problem! I'll send you my bill," he said, picking up his bag.

Billy ruffled Joey's hair. "Remember Joey, stay down."

"Like a snake, man. See ya, Doc. Keep cool." He threw his duffel over his shoulder and sauntered toward the airstrip to wait for his ride out. Billy shook his head and watched him go.

DEENA

The casualties had been very light. Both sides seemed to be taking a much needed respite. This left the medical personnel of I-Corps with some free time on their hands. Deena and Maggie lay on their cots and watched life go by through the screened walls of their hooch. Their attention was drawn to Billy and Ray who were killing time by jogging laps around the camp wearing nothing but cut-off fatigues.

"They are so darn sexy!" Deena remarked. Maggie, who was trying to read one of Billy's books, pretended not to notice. But her attention was just as riveted to the two men as they passed by the hooch. "Mmm," she mumbled and turned the page.

"Oh, come on, Maggie. Those two are so hot they sizzle, and you know it. Just because you're married doesn't mean that you can't look. Hmm, which one do you think is better looking?"

"I wouldn't know," Maggie remarked.

Deena sighed heavily. "I don't understand why you can't admit the obvious. Do you really think that I don't see you sneaking peeks at them as they go by? 'Fess up."

Maggie rolled onto her side. "Okay, I admit it. They aren't bad. But that's as far as it goes."

"Aren't bad? I wouldn't mind taking a roll in the hay with either of them! Personally though, I do think Fox is sexier. He's got that exotic cinnamon skin and silky long hair. And what about those bedroom eyes of his?" Deena sighed. "Oh, yeah, I'll bet he's really good in that room."

Maggie flushed. "Why don't you ask his wife?"

"You're such a spoil sport," Deena replied and continued to watch the two men.

It just so happened, that the two doctors were having an important conversation of their own about the nurses in hooch number four. Sex, however, was not on their agenda.

"Have you ever worked with Deena, Ray?"

"Uh huh."

"Uh, what d'ya think of her? As a nurse, I mean?"

Ray wiped the sweat off of his face with the back of his hand. He shook his head and rolled his eyes. "She's very nice and cheerful. And great with the patients, but…"

"Doesn't know one end of a scalpel from the other?" Billy finished.

"Right. Now I know why Maggie gave her the nickname Dodo." Ray paused and spit in the dust. "Is there anything we can do about it?"

"Aside from trying to send her back to Saigon, I really don't know. I guess I could limit her duties to pre-op and post-op until she gets reassigned."

"Uh, I don't know about pre-op, Billy. She's not too swift there, either. The other day she was trying to shove a chest tube into a poor guy's bladder instead of a Foley cath. And she blows more veins than gunpowder."

"Shit, that's just great. What about post-op only then? Or is there something I should know about that, too?"

"No, she's pretty good there, but that's about it. She's strictly bedside nursing. You know, she empties a mean bedpan."

"How about the other two girls? Have you worked with either of them?"

"Yeah, they seem to know their way around an OR pretty well. Not used to the way we do things up here, but they're learning. And Reynolds, of course, is excellent."

"Okay. So, it's safe to say that Cramer is the only problem?"

"I think it would be safe."

"Thank God. I suppose I should speak to Reynolds about her since she seems to be kind of the spokesperson for the nurses."

As they continued to jog, Billy looked up and saw the nurses' hooch approaching. "I guess I should get this over with. I think she's in her hooch right now."

"No time like the present," Ray laughed.

"Go ahead, laugh. You don't have to face 'Mighty Mouse' and her flame spewing tongue."

"Flame spewing tongue? Aren't you being a little harsh?"

"Harsh? She's worse than Kate in the *Taming of the Shrew*. She's constantly asking me questions like some high-powered attorney."

Ray looked at Billy quizzically. "Huh? That's weird, she never says a word to me. Must be you. Maybe she's in such awe of you that she doesn't know what to say in your presence."

"Up yours, Krause," Billy said, as he veered toward the nurses' hooch.

Deena answered his knock. "You ready for that shower, Doctor?" she asked sweetly.

"Is Reynolds inside?" Billy asked, ignoring her question.

Deena looked crestfallen, "yes."

"Send her to my office, please," he said, then departed.

"Sure," she said, closing the door. "Maggie, Major Fox wants you in his office on the double," Deena stated.

"What!" Maggie exclaimed. She jumped from her cot, tripped and almost fell as she headed to the door.

Deena laughed. "A little anxious, aren't you? Geez, don't kill yourself to get there, Mags. Especially since you wouldn't know if he's hot or not," she mimicked.

Maggie gave her a dirty look and slammed out of the hooch. She crossed the compound and knocked on the door of Billy's office.

"Come in," he called.

As Maggie entered, Billy was pulling on a t-shirt. "You wanted to see me?" she asked.

"Yes, I need to talk to you."

"Oh?"

"Here, have a seat." He offered Maggie his chair, then sat down on the edge of his desk. He wiped at the sweat on his face with a towel, then began, "It's about Cramer. Have you ever worked with her?"

"Of course. She's very nice."

"I know she's nice," he said impatiently. "We all like Cramer."

"Then what's the problem?"

"To put it bluntly, she's a lousy scrub nurse."

Maggie refused to meet Billy's eye. "What do you mean?"

"She knows nothing about surgery. You ask for a clamp; she gives you a retractor. You ask for something specific, she looks at the Mayo tray like it will tell her some secret, then she just grabs anything. Half the time, I end up getting my own instruments which is defeating the purpose of her being here.

"When a patient starts to hemorrhage and you ask for suction, she gets flustered and doesn't know what to do. I asked her to take the guard off the suction nozzle and she looked like a deer caught in the headlights. I had to finish the job that a mortar started on a guy's hand a couple of weeks ago. While doing the amputation, she threw up. Not only did she make a mess, but Joey had to come in and take over and I needed him elsewhere. If I didn't know better, I would think she failed nursing school. Or barely made it through. Or just doesn't like being a nurse. I'm not sure."

"She's probably just nervous. You guys can be pretty intimidating in the OR."

"Intimidating? Me and Ray? Come on. We may be a little arrogant perhaps, but on the whole we're decent guys. In fact, I think I have been extremely tolerant. There are things I could have said to her that would have had her running out of the OR in tears, but I didn't."

"Is she really that bad?"

"Yes."

"What are you going to do about it?"

"*You* are going to limit her responsibilities to post-op. I don't know how she made it in Saigon."

Maggie was unusually silent for several moments. Then she sighed and looked down at the floor. "Deena never finished nursing school," Maggie stated.

"What!"

"I'm the only one who knows."

"You mean you've been covering for her all this time?"

"I felt I had to."

Billy made an exasperated sound of disbelief. He got up and paced the floor for a few moments, then turned to Maggie, his arms crossed against his chest.

"I'm really surprised and disappointed in you Reynolds. I thought you were a professional. I respected you, even treated you as an equal," he said, shaking his head.

"Look," Maggie said, her hands outstretched in supplication. "She's a good kid. Her brother is over here somewhere. He's MIA. Neither she nor her family have heard from him in over twelve months. She had a little over a year to go before she could graduate. She lied to the army about her credentials so that she could come to Vietnam and look for some trace of him."

"How the hell did she get away with it?"

"I don't know, but she did. That's the real reason why we're here," Maggie said. "We thought if we were at a field hospital, she might be able to find out about her brother. Also, we thought it would be easier to fake her ability to do her job. In Saigon, she'd have been caught sooner rather than later, and God knows what would have happened then. As it is, it happened anyway," she bowed her head. "What happens to her now is up to you, Major."

Billy rubbed his eyes. "Great! Throw this shit in *my* lap! Damn it! If she was going to stay here for the rest of her tour, there wouldn't be a problem. We'd stick her in post-op and leave it at that. But did you two ever stop to think about what would happen when you left here? What if you aren't there to bail her out? What will happen to her then?" He shook his head. "What a mess!"

"I know. I'm sorry."

"Go get her."

"What are you going to do?"

"I don't know yet. Just get her in here now," he growled.

"Yes, sir," Maggie stood and left.

Billy's thoughts were in turmoil. What in the hell *was* he going to do? The proper procedure would be to expose her and hand her over to the colonel. Let *him* deal with the problem. She would probably be thrown out of the army in disgrace or worse and would never find out about her brother.

"You wanted to see me, sir?" Deena asked nervously.

"Sit down." When Maggie made to leave, he said, "Where do you think you're going? You're in this too, Reynolds," he glared. "You're both in a lot of hot water."

"What's wrong?" Deena asked, glancing at Maggie.

"What's wrong is you lied. Lied to the army, lied to all of us and Maggie allowed you to do it."

Deena looked at the floor. "What are you going to do?"

"I haven't thought that far yet. I know what my brain is telling me to do, but I just don't have the heart to do it."

"Isn't there any alternative?" Maggie asked.

"The only one I can think of is probably next to impossible."

"What's that?"

"We'd have to complete her education. Obviously, there are things Deena missed. We'd have to teach her the basic fundamentals of surgery. When she leaves here, she'll have to be good enough to pass for a bad scrub nurse. But not as bad as she is now."

"Who would teach me?" Deena asked, with wide eyes.

"Maggie," he paused for a few seconds. "And me...I guess."

"Do you think we can?" Maggie questioned.

"I don't know. But since you allowed Deena to get into this mess by continuing her charade, you are going to have to help get her out of it. Unfortunately, you both now have my ass involved as well."

"I'm sorry, sir."

"You know, Reynolds. I'm getting awfully sick of hearing you say that."

"Sorry, sir."

Billy gave Maggie a dirty look, then continued, "In the meantime," he said, addressing Deena, "I don't want you anywhere near an OR, triage or pre-op ward. You're confined to post-op and clean up until I tell you otherwise. You hear me?"

"Yes, sir," Deena said, her eyes downcast. After a moment, she looked up. "You don't have to do this, you know."

"I know. And it might not work. If it doesn't, our asses will all be in a sling, especially mine. So, pay attention and learn for God's sake."

"Yes, sir." She paused, "Major Fox?"

"Now what?"

"Thank you very much. You don't know what this means to me."

"Yeah, okay, now beat it, both of you. We'll talk later. I need to think things over."

The next day, Billy called Deena to his office. "This is what we're going to do. Between Maggie and myself, we're going to fill in the blanks of your education. Thank God we're slow right now." He handed her several hardbound books. "Here are some textbooks for you to read. They're mine. I want them back the way I gave them to you. Learn the information in them, it's very important," he instructed.

"Starting today, I'll work with you on the basic fundamentals of surgery, the equipment and instruments that we use, when they are used and why. Maggie will concentrate on triage—what to look for in a casualty and how to discriminate between an immediate OR case to one that can wait. She'll also help you out in pre-op: how to prep patients, start lines of IVs, collect vital signs, blood types, catheterize—all the things you should already know. Hopefully at least some of this will be review. Unless you're with Maggie or myself, I don't want you alone in any of those areas. Clear?"

"Yes, sir."

"Good, now sit down. I'm going to start by reviewing some basic surgical instruments and their functions." As he showed her different pieces of equipment, he lit one cigarette after another. In a short amount of time, the air in the room was thick with smoke.

Deena felt her eyes begin to water and started to cough. Billy didn't notice and continued speaking. He patiently explained scalpels and sutures and all the different types and sizes of retractors, forceps and clamps. He had just demonstrated how to make a sponge stick when he stated, "You're not listening to me." Standing in front of her, his hands on his hips, he remarked, "You haven't been for the past few minutes. Do you want to know this or don't you? I'm not doing this for my health."

"No, you aren't," she said, waving her hand in front of her face. "And if you keep doing it, I'm gonna suffocate," she said, coughing.

"What?"

"Your smoking, I can't stand it. You…never…stop," Deena said. "Just when I think, thank God, he's finished, you light up another one." She glanced pointedly at the overflowing kidney bowl he was using as an ashtray and said, "The way *you* smoke, you should be using a bed pan."

Billy stared at her as if she'd lost her mind. "My smoking? I'm talking about sponge sticks and you're ragging on about how many friggin' cigarettes I've smoked? Have you heard anything I've said at all?"

"No, you lost me after the fourth Marlboro. I haven't even tried to pay attention. I just want to get out of here. You have one hell of a problem, Doctor."

Billy glared at her. "Look Cramer, I'm doing my best to help you. I don't want to have to expose you. Yet all you care about is my smoking? Is it bothering you that much?"

"Hell, a court-martial would be a lot more healthful. Do you have to smoke?"

"I can't smoke in the hospital which is where I am for most of the day. Now, I can't smoke in my own office because it bothers you. You know, you're a real pain in the ass."

"You ought to quit."

"Why?"

"It's bad for you."

"I don't care."

"I do."

"I care more about whether or not you learn this stuff."

"I can't think in all this smoke."

"Well, what're we going to do?" Billy sat on the edge of the desk; his arms folded against his chest.

"I don't know," Deena said, miserably.

Just then, a chopper landed on the strip and things came to life in the camp. "We'll talk about this tomorrow. I've got to get to the hospital. Take all those instruments and run them through the autoclave," he said over his shoulder on his way out.

When Billy entered his office the next day, he had a pack of cigarettes in his hand. He threw them down on the desk in front of Deena. "See this pack of cigarettes?" he asked. "This is how you're going to become a nurse."

"I don't understand."

"You will," Billy said, tearing off the outer wrapping of cellophane. "There are twenty cigarettes in a pack. When I'm done lecturing you today, I'm going to give you a twenty-question quiz. For each correct answer, you get a cigarette. For every incorrect answer, I get to keep and smoke the cigarette. So, the more you know, the less I smoke. Got it?"

Deena nodded her head, dazed.

"I just bought three cartons of Marlboros. There are ten packs in a carton. You have thirty days to learn everything, and I have thirty days to quit. Fair?"

"Why are you doing this?"

"Oh for God's sake! Do you want me to quit or not?"

"Yes."

"Do you want to become a better nurse or not?"

"Yes."

"Then shut the hell up, listen and learn," he said scowling.

"Yes, sir!" she said, saluting. "And what do I do with the cigarettes I take from you?"

"I don't know. Start to smoke, sell them. What the hell do I care. Whatever you do, keep 'em away from me."

It became a game. Every day, Billy did his best to trick and stump Deena. And Deena likewise did her best to keep one step ahead of him. By the end of the first week, Deena had won three quarters of the cigarettes they were vying for. She studied the textbooks in her free time and Maggie grilled her continuously. Each day, she knew more and more, and at quiz time, was soon taking the whole pack.

Billy, on the other hand, was rationing the few cigarettes he won. He became irritable and foul mouthed and everyone with the exception of Maggie and Deena steered clear of him.

Two weeks later, he was seated on a bench reading a letter, his leg nervously jumping, when Maggie sat down next to him. Her silence caused him to look up. Staring straight ahead of her, her face was white and pinched.

"What the hell's the matter with you?"

"It's Wednesday."

"I know. That fuckin' bitch took every one of my goddamned cigarettes today. Why did I ever promise I'd help her?"

"It's Wednesday," she said again.

"So, it's Wednesday," he raised a shoulder.

"I didn't get any mail. Something's happened."

"Shit, Maggie. You know how things are around here. You can't think something's wrong just because you didn't get any mail."

"He's never missed a Wednesday."

"Maybe he's busy."

"No, something is wrong."

"Oh, for cryin' out loud, give the guy a break. I'm sure there's a good reason why you didn't get a letter today."

"Something's wrong," she said again. Even though it was hot and steamy, Maggie's teeth were chattering.

Billy felt her forehead. "You coming down with something?"

Maggie's teeth sounded like castanets. "Something has happened. I can feel it."

Billy was at a loss. "If something has happened, which I doubt, you'll hear right away. In the meantime, I'm sure you'll get a letter from your husband tomorrow."

"No," she said, shaking her head. "I'll not get another letter from Mike." She stood and went to her hooch. Billy frowned. He hoped she was wrong.

Two days later, Maggie was in the hospital during mail call. The clerk went from hooch to hooch passing out mail and packages. He by-passed the nurses' hooch and returned to the colonel's office.

Colonel Barnes and Billy were together when he knocked on the door. "Sir, I hate to interrupt, but I think you'd better look at this."

"What is it, corporal?

Higgins placed an envelope on the colonel's desk. It was an official document they had seen before and meant one thing—death.

"Who's that for, Higgins?"

"Lieutenant Reynolds, sir."

Billy stared at the envelope, but saw instead Maggie's face, heard her voice, 'I'll not get another letter.'

Barnes sighed. "These things are never easy. We don't often have a situation like this. Both Reynolds and her husband are over here at the same time," he said. "Well, I guess I'd better get this over with." Barnes stood, picking up the envelope.

It would be so easy to let him handle it, Billy thought. Instead, he took a deep breath. "Uh…Colonel? May I take care of this?"

Barnes handed over the letter. "Thanks, Major. It would probably be better coming from you."

Billy walked to the hospital, his brain numb. What was he going to say? He found her in the scrub room prepping mayo trays, her face pinched and pale. She looked up at him, silent for once. He tried to smile but couldn't. Maggie saw the pain in his face and knew. When he put his arms out, she went to him, and he held her tightly.

Finally, she pushed away, her eyes dry. "Is it a letter? Where is it? Read it to me," she commanded.

He pulled the letter out of his back pocket, opened it, and scanned the words quickly. He tried to hand it to her. "Wouldn't you rather read it yourself?" he asked quietly.

"No," she whispered, shoving her hands behind her back. "I don't want to touch it! Please!"

"Dear Lieutenant Reynolds," he began, "we regret to inform you that your husband, Captain Michael Reynolds, was shot down over the Bay of Tonkin… and…and…killed."

Maggie started making little mewling noises in her throat. "Nooooo." It was a moan of anguish. Her teeth were chattering, and she was shivering. Billy went to her, hugging her close. Rubbing her arms, he tried to warm her.

"Maggie?"

Her eyes met his. "I knew. I could feel it. Oh, nooooo."

Holding onto him as though she were drowning, she stared into the troubled, olive-green eyes—eyes so different from Mike's. Where were those laughing, dancing, Irish eyes now? The thought overwhelmed her, and she felt herself falling. The world around her spun out of control and went dark.

The next thing she knew, she was in the post-op ward lying on a bunk. Deena sat at her side holding a cool cloth to her forehead. Trisha stood nearby. Both girls silent, worried.

Maggie couldn't stand to see the pity in their eyes. Her throat closed up on her, fighting back tears. She turned her head away and concentrated on the rivets in the walls of the building. After a while, she must have dozed off. When she awoke, Billy was sitting beside her, and the girls were gone.

"Are you taking turns watching me?"

"We're concerned," he replied. "You had a terrible shock." He checked her pulse. "I had to be sure you were all right. Would you rather I left you alone?"

"No." After a moment, she said, "I feel stupid lying here, though. I'm not sick."

"What do you want to do?"

"Where is everyone?"

"We got a few casualties. Everyone is next door."

"It can't be that bad."

"Why do you say that?"

"Because you're here with me. If things were really bad, you'd be in the OR."

He smiled. "Well, most of them were ambulatory. I let the other guys handle what came in. But I really should go and check on things. Want to come?" He held out his hand and she took it in hers.

"Keep me busy and don't go too far away, promise?"

"I promise," he said, drawing her to her feet.

The only thing that kept Maggie from falling apart was Deena and her training. She stubbornly refused to go home for the funeral. For what? To see his coffin shrouded in the flag, to hear taps and witness a twenty-one gun salute? The thought of it all panicked her. She couldn't do it. Besides, it wouldn't mean a thing. Mike was gone. It was better to be busy, and she was needed here. Home would just be endless days, emptiness, and either pity from her family or disapproval and guilt from Mike's.

Never straying far from Billy's side in the hospital, she always found herself across from him in the OR. His eyes would smile encouragement and she felt comforted.

In the meantime, Deena learned quickly and was going to be a good nurse. She had been working in triage and pre-op either with Maggie or one of the other nurses and Billy felt she was almost ready to solo.

One day, Deena was alone in the scrub room quickly prepping trays and cleaning instruments when Billy banged open the swinging door with his hip. "Where's Reynolds?" he asked harried, already gowned and gloved.

"In triage. We got mass casualties. There are so many wounded that everyone's running around like idiots. I was in there helping, but Maggie sent me in here to keep ahead of things."

Billy assessed Deena quickly. "Get scrubbed and get into OR 1. I need you."

"But Doctor…"

"No buts, Cramer, get scrubbed. Now. Move it." As Deena scrubbed, her stomach churned with nervousness. Don't screw up, she thought. She rushed into the OR to find a black boy of about nineteen lying on a gurney. His hand was reduced to a bloody stump and the torn muscles and ligaments of his forearm were exposed.

Deena felt bile rise in her throat and gulped down a brief moment of panic when Billy reached for a saw. She glanced heavenward, offering up a silent prayer as he smoothed off the jagged ends of bone.

It was a long, tedious, and intricate procedure. Deena listened attentively and did what Billy asked. He was patient and helped her when she was unsure. The instruments no longer looked like a confusing bunch of crazy scissors and shoehorns on sticks. They now had names and she could distinguish between each and every one.

At first, she only did as instructed, but her eyes kept returning in morbid curiosity to the horrid wound. After a while, she became more confident. Her horror gave way to interest and fascination at what Billy was doing to stop the bleeding and knit the torn flesh back together. She thought about all that she had read, and what Maggie and Billy had been teaching her. She couldn't let them down.

Once, Billy looked up. The exposed parts of his face were bathed in sweat, his glasses perched precariously on the end of his nose. "Okay, Dodo?"

She nodded and hurriedly blotted his forehead and pushed up his glasses.

"Thanks. I'm almost finished here. I just hope this kid wasn't right-handed."

When they walked out of the OR, Billy pulled off his mask and snapped off his gloves. His face was serious, and Deena was frightened. She thought she had done everything right; but now, she wasn't sure.

"Do you know what you've just done?"

"Oh, my God, what did I do? I thought I did everything right. I thought I gave you everything you asked for. And I didn't pass out or puke. What's the matter?"

Just then, Maggie walked in from triage. "Deena, I hear you were in the OR. How'd it go?"

"She's done the impossible, Maggie," Billy said and gave a war whoop that startled them all. "She was wonderful!" he laughed.

Maggie felt herself smiling for the first time in many weeks. "You did it, Dodo!" she exclaimed.

"You should have been there. She was great," Billy continued. "We should celebrate later. But now, back to work. Let's make sure it wasn't beginner's luck."

"You mean I have to do that again?" Deena asked in mock anguish.

"Absolutely," Billy responded. "No excuses for you anymore, Cramer."

Later, they all gathered in the 'O' Club. A bottle of champagne was opened, and paper cups were handed around and raised. "To Deena!"

Billy refused a cup, but stood next to Maggie, one hand resting lightly on her shoulder. In his other hand, he held a small white package.

With tears glistening in her eyes, Deena said, "I don't know what to say except thank you. You all stuck by me. I could never have done this without everyone's support, especially the hours of instruction from Dr. Fox. And of course, Maggie, who put aside her pain to tutor and guide me." Deena hugged the two of them. "Thanks," she whispered.

"Here Cramer, catch," Billy said, as he tossed the small package he was holding to Deena. "This is for you. Thank you also."

She peeled away the paper then laughed, holding up an unopened pack of Marlboro cigarettes.

"I was saving those for a rainy day. Then I realized I wasn't even craving them anymore. Thanks, Deena, Maggie. Everyone who had to put up with me. Sorry if I was a little testy."

"Testy!" Ray commented. "That's not even close! You were downright impossible. You were meaner than a two headed snake. I think we all wanted to kill you on more than one occasion. But now, you're back to being your regular pain in the ass self! And for this, we're grateful."

"Thanks," Billy said dryly.

BILLY

It was a long day. Billy ate, did rounds, then decided to take a walk around the compound. Since he had given up smoking and wasn't much of a movie person, the evenings sometimes seemed to drag if they weren't busy with casualties. He was itching for a good run, but at dusk, it was too dangerous. He felt her presence before he saw her.

"Mind if I join you?" Maggie asked.

"Just taking a stroll through the neighborhood," he said, his hands deep in his pockets.

"It's quiet tonight."

"Yes, thank God."

"Tell me about Dong Ha."

"Why?" he asked, his voice guarded.

"That's where a lot of our casualties come from, right?"

"Uh huh."

"I'm interested in learning more about it, that's all."

Billy paused for a few moments. "Dong Ha is a supply station just a few miles south of the DMZ, which, as you know, is the area or line of demarcation between North and South Vietnam. It's where evacuated casualties from up north are brought."

"Do they have a hospital?"

"Sort of. It's a makeshift area partially underground in bunkers or in tents. The whole camp is very primitive. In fact, this is the lap of luxury in comparison."

"I suppose there are no women there, either?"

"You're right."

"Same reason?"

"Yes, in fact, it's even more dangerous there. The NVA have guns positioned above Dong Ha, and the camp gets hit heavily by artillery fire several times a week, if not once or twice a day."

"And you say there's a hospital? How does anything get done if they're getting shelled?"

"Mainly the wounded are just stabilized and sent on to places like our little company or further afield to real hospitals like the ones in Da Nang or Saigon or to hospital ships. Only rarely is major surgery done and most of the time only in life threatening circumstances."

"It sounds scary."

"It is."

"You sound like you know," Maggie pointed out, as they began another circuit.

Billy was silent for a long time. "God, I need a cigarette."

"I thought you didn't crave them anymore," Maggie smiled.

"I don't really. It's just that I need something to do with my hands."

"Ever think of taking up knitting?"

"I'm so nervous, I'd probably chain stitch myself to death or whatever you do with those big ass needles."

Maggie laughed softly. After a minute, she said, "You're avoiding my question."

"Did you ask me one?"

"I wanted to know if you had ever been in Dong Ha."

"Yes."

"Was it bad?"

Billy looked at her and nodded, "Yeah."

"Want to talk about it?"

"No."

Even in the twilight, Maggie could see the pain in his eyes.

"I lost my best friend there," he said.

"I'm sorry. By the way, I'm starting to feel like a cart horse. How many laps are we going to do?"

"Am I wearing you out?"

"Well, I have been on my feet all day."

"Come on," he said, walking over to a makeshift seat of wooden crates.

"Was your friend a doctor, too?"

"Yes," he answered shortly.

Maggie raised her eyebrows questioningly, and Billy let out an exasperated breath. "God, you're a pest. If you must know, we met in med school—both army; poor hoi polloi thrown into the DC upper crust. We spent more time together than we did at home—classes, anatomy lab, library. Then running the streets when time allowed in an effort to unwind. When John got married, I stood for him. You know, the whole nine yards.

"We did basic training at the same time and got our invitations to Asia the same day. A week or so before we left, his wife found out she was pregnant."

"Oh," Maggie was silent for a few moments, digesting all that he told her. "Did you both get sent to Dong Ha right away?" she then asked.

"No, I was sent to a BAS above Da Nang. John went to Chu Lai. After almost three months of treating dysentery, malaria and snake bites, doing short-arm inspections and setting broken fingers acquired in fist fights, I got sent up to Dong Ha. John was already there. It was a hellish place, but at least we were together and were able to make the best of it. Until…" Billy became quiet, lost in thought.

They sat companionably in the dark until Maggie broke the silence. "What happened then? You didn't finish your story."

Billy leaned forward on the crate, his elbows resting on his knees, hands clasped together. "It was crazy. First, we were shelled. Then, we ended up in a tent, removing some kid's spleen before he bled to death. Joey was with us as well."

"Our Joey?"

"Uh huh, that's where I first met him. I don't know what we'd have done without him." Billy's voice became soft. He was far away, reliving that fateful day.

Maggie was mesmerized as he spoke. She visualized the shelling, heard the whine of the bullets as they tore through the tent. She felt the sting in Billy's arm and John's indecision. When she looked at Billy, his head was in his hands.

"He should never have died," he said. "If I hadn't made him go, he would still be alive. I sent him to his death."

"You don't know that. You could have been killed instead."

"It would have been better that way. John had so much to live for. I don't." He paused. "His baby is due soon."

Maggie stared down at her hands, and her throat tightened. She felt tears prickle in her eyes and fought to hold them back.

Billy noticed her strained silence. "Are you okay?" he asked.

"Mike wanted babies," she stated. "But no, I had to have a career instead. Now, I wish I would have been a better wife and had his children. That all powerful career doesn't mean squat now." Turning away, she rubbed at her eyes.

Billy put his arm around her. "Don't do this to yourself. You had every right to have a career. Don't blame yourself because you never had a child. What good would having a baby do you now? You'd just be a widow trying to take care of a kid or kids on your own."

"At least I would have had something tangible left of Mike like your friend's wife has of her husband. What do I have? A few medals, some photographs, a couple mementos?"

"Either way, you shouldn't crucify yourself because he's gone. Having a career didn't shoot him from the sky, did it?"

"No."

"Then you can't take the blame."

"And you? You didn't kill your friend, either."

Billy stared at Maggie. "Somehow the two situations seem different."

"They aren't."

Billy squeezed Maggie's shoulder, then removed his arm. "You may be right, but I still can't live with myself."

"Neither can I," she said, as the tears again fought to take over. "Damn it," she said, wiping at her eyes. "I can't be doing this."

"What? Crying?"

"It doesn't change anything. He's still gone."

"You're right. It doesn't change things. But crying is a release. It may make you feel better in the long run."

"I doubt it. Besides, once I start, I won't be able to stop. I have to be strong."

Billy turned to Maggie and gently placed her hand in his. He looked into her eyes. "Listen to me. Crying when you're in pain is not a sign of weakness. Holding back tears, however, can actually make you sick inside. Trust me. I know." He looked away from her and rubbed her fingers as he stared into the growing darkness. "You know, Maggie, maybe you *should* take a leave. Go home for a couple of weeks. I'm sure the army would let you. You need to distance yourself from this place and be able to grieve properly."

"No, thank you. I'll have plenty of time for that when my tour is over," she said and, pulling a tissue out of her pocket, blew her nose. "I'll have a whole lifetime to mourn then," she mumbled through the tissue.

"Don't say that," he said, again looking at her. "You're a young woman. There's no reason why, after a time, you can't live again, even love again."

Maggie stared into his eyes for a long moment, then removed her hand from his. "No, Doctor. How can I love, if I'm not even certain what it means?" She stood abruptly and walked quickly off into the darkness.

The casualties kept coming, American and Vietnamese alike—soldiers, civilians, men, women and children. For well over twenty-four hours, the doctors, nurses and corpsmen of Phu Bai worked straight through.

Billy finally had to make several shifts so that his staff could get some much-needed rest. People were beginning to make mistakes. Casualties or no casualties, time was needed for rest and nourishment. Maggie fought him tooth and nail. If he wasn't taking a break, neither was she.

"Maggie," he reasoned, "you're tired. You haven't eaten or sat down for any amount of time, that's not good. You are going to pass out if you don't rest and get something into your stomach."

"What about you?" she asked, "I don't see *you* stopping."

"I will, trust me. As soon as everyone else has had a chance to take a break."

"I'll take a break, when you take a break."

"You'll go now, when I tell you to," he said, pointing a stern finger at her. "There's a method to my madness. I want you fresh for while I'm gone. Why do you always have to give me such a hard time?"

She saw the weariness in his bloodshot eyes. His back was stooped, and he seemed ready to drop. He looked—like Maggie felt. "I'm sorry," she said. "I'll go now. Can I get you anything?"

"Coffee, black, thanks."

She squeezed his shoulder and headed toward the mess. Billy followed her outside, searching for the chopper pilot of the last drop. He found him seated on a field chair smoking a cigarette. Lucky was stitching a gash in his upper arm.

"Is this shit ever gonna end?" Billy asked him.

"I don't know. Hell, I can hardly think to fly. It seems there's always another load waiting for me when I get back. We're flying everywhere, trying to spread this shit out. Up and down the coast to evacs, ships, hospitals, here… Crazy bastards, they don't care who the fuck they're blowing to bits."

As they were speaking, another chopper landed. Corpsmen no longer ran to unload, but walked tiredly out and half carrying, half dragging, got the wounded into triage.

Billy went to see what was arriving.

"Hey, Doc, how's it goin'?" On a litter, smiling his lopsided grin, was Joey.

Billy hurried to his side. "I thought I told you to keep your head down."

"Aw, I'm fine," Joey said. "It's just a little nick."

There was blood staining Joey's collar. Bending down, Billy carefully turned Joey's head a little to each side. What he saw made his stomach contract. It was a through and through, beginning at the base of Joey's skull and exiting just below the ear on the other side. "Little nick?" he asked.

"Yeah, no problem! Take the other guys first. They're a lot worse off than me. I'm just a little…cold," he said, shivering in the steamy heat.

"Hang on a sec, I'll get you a blanket."

When Billy returned, Joey was struggling to sit up. "Come on, buddy," Billy said, gently nudging him back down and tucking the scratchy, wool blanket around him. "Just relax. I know you want to help, but take it easy, okay."

"Should be helping you. Should…up…elp." With bewilderment in his eyes, Joey began mumbling nonsense.

Billy motioned to a corpsman to take him to x-ray, then to bring him into the OR as quickly as possible. He was in the scrub room when Maggie returned with his coffee. The fierce look on his face frightened her.

"What is it?"

"It's Joey. They just brought him in with a through and through to the head. He's already exhibiting signs that the bullet passed through part of his brain. He was talking to me as if nothing happened when I first examined him. Now…" he shrugged. "And there's not a damned thing I can do. I wish we had a neurosurgeon here."

They went to the OR together. The neg was already hanging in wait for Billy. "Jesus Christ!" he said softly. It was as he feared. Maybe in a hospital in the states, seen immediately by a neurosurgeon, with equipment like CAT scanners and accurate brain pressure monitors, Joey might have had a chance. But that was too many maybes. Unfortunately, all Billy could do was make Joey comfortable—and watch him die.

"What can we do?" Maggie asked, her eyes large, worried.

"Nothing."

"Nothing?"

"No, look," he pointed to the x-ray. "See the path of the bullet? It's right above the brainstem. Once the injury begins to swell, if it hasn't already, it's going to crush all the blood vessels in his brain and shut off the blood supply."

"Can't you do anything?"

"I'm going to start him on drugs to combat the swelling, but it's really too late. God knows how long it's been since he was wounded. The drugs probably won't help at all." He looked at the x-ray again and shook his head. "Joey told me he just had a little nick, and to take care of his buddies first. Poor son of a bitch."

As they were speaking, two corpsmen brought Joey into the OR. His eyes were open, but he wasn't aware of his surroundings. Billy gave him an injection and turned to Maggie. "Go get some rest. I'll call you if I need you."

"I want to stay."

"There's nothing you can do. Will you please listen to me for a change?" he said tiredly.

"You'll call me?"

"Sure, now get out of here."

During the long night, Billy kept returning to Joey. His breathing was shallow, and Billy could tell that the part of Joey's brain that told him to breathe was now affected. He inserted a trache tube and put him on a prehistoric respirator that did very little to help. Billy would treat a casualty, then go back to Joey. But no matter what he did, it wasn't enough. The drugs he gave him to keep the injured site from swelling weren't working. It was a battle Billy knew he had lost. Joey was already beyond help. Even if they would have immediately transferred him to one of the ships or to Da Nang, it still wouldn't have saved him. If it wasn't for the respirator, Joey would have been dead.

He should have called Maggie, but there just wasn't time to get her. There were still wounded to be seen, wounded that were going to live if they were taken care of immediately. Besides, she needed the rest. Her presence wouldn't keep Joey alive. Around 03:00 hours, Billy checked Joey's pupils. Even though he expected to see it, he was sick. The one pupil was fully dilated, the other, barely visible. Billy could hardly see it, even with the aid of his penlight.

"What do you think?" Billy asked Ray, who had just come in to relieve him.

"I think you were hoping for a miracle, Billy. This kid's gone," Ray said, "been gone probably for a while now. The brainstem's been crushed. You did all you could. In a hospital in the states, this kid would have been pronounced hours ago."

Billy shook his head, defeated. "He was such a good kid, Ray."

"I know. They all are," Ray said, placing a hand on Billy's shoulder.

"I hate this fucking place," Billy said wearily and turned the respirator switch off.

Two hours later, Billy finally stumbled to his hooch and threw himself on his bunk. He had only been asleep for about an hour when there was a pounding on the hooch door. He fought with the mosquito netting and sleepily got up and admitted Maggie.

"What is it?" Billy muttered.

Maggie stood before him; all five foot two inches of her were quivering with fury. "Joey's dead and you never called me! You let him die," she sobbed. "You think you're God, turning off that respirator. You should have sent him somewhere. But, no, you think you know everything."

"I couldn't do any more. I tried. I told you that yesterday. You knew he was going to die." He tried to put his arms around her.

She shook him loose. "You didn't try hard enough. Look at you, sleeping. Was checking on him too much? Was he keeping you from your bunk? You're cold and heartless. You pulled the plug on him so that you could go to bed!" she cried. "I hate you, you son of a bitch!"

Billy again tried to hold her, to comfort her. She was going to snap if she kept this up.

Again, she pushed his hands away and began to pound on his chest. "I hate you! I hate you!" she screamed.

Billy looked down at her. She didn't know what she was saying, yet it hurt. All the tears she'd kept bottled up when Mike died came flooding out. Over and over she hit and cursed him. He had to do something—she was starting to hyperventilate. But he couldn't hit her.

Instead, he grabbed her by the shoulders, pulling her roughly against him and pinning her flailing arms to her sides. He bent and kissed her, hard. She fought him and when he released her, she swung at him, striking his face with the flat of her hand.

"You bastard! How dare you! You're just like all the rest!" Turning, she ran from the hooch, slamming the door behind her.

Billy absently rubbed his cheek. The imprint of her small hand was red against his skin. He probably should have hit her, but he couldn't. It was all too much for her. Mike, Joey, this place. Billy rubbed the back of his neck. He felt like running from there as well.

He couldn't sleep now. Instead, he followed Maggie from the hooch and headed to the hospital. He hoped he could find her and help calm her down as well as checking on things.

On his way to the hospital though, Colonel Barnes stopped him. "Major, may I have a word?"

"Sure, Colonel."

"Come into my office."

Billy entered the room and Barnes offered him some coffee. "Thanks," said Billy, taking a mug.

"How is everything going?" Barnes asked.

"Okay, I guess. I've got all the personnel working in shifts to handle this mess. Is there any end in sight?"

"I've been in contact with the CO in Dong Ha by radio. Right now, things still look bad. In fact, that's the reason I called you in here. You got orders this morning, Fox. You're being reassigned."

"Oh?"

"Yes, they need a surgeon sent to Dong Ha ASAP. Only two GPs, and a few corpsmen are there right now, and a gas passer is en route as we speak. They're doing the best they can. But there are so many wounded, all the docs can do is sort injuries and ship them out. The wounded are laying around perhaps needlessly dying while they wait to be brought down here or sent elsewhere for treatment." Barnes paused for a moment, scrutinizing Billy's papers in front of him. "I see you've been there before."

"Yes, sir," Billy said, feeling ill.

"I hate to see you go, Major. You did a great job here and really cleaned this place up. Don't worry, I'll make sure it stays this way."

"Thank you, sir. Do you know when I'm to leave?"

"Now. As soon as the next fixed-wing or chopper comes along bringing more wounded, you're to go back with them. I'm sorry about the rush. Normally, we have more notice, but...they really need you."

"Well, if you'll excuse me. I'd better get packed and ready."

"Oh, one other thing, don't forget, you're due another week of R & R. If you want, I can schedule it for you."

"Whatever you say, sir."

"Do you have anywhere in mind? The medical corps usually has a lousy selection. Right now, they probably only have 'in country' R & Rs to Saigon up for grabs. However, the 106th had a few trips to Australia and Bangkok available last I checked. Of course, not just anyone can pull one of those locales, but I'll see what I can do."

"Where do you suggest?"

"I liked Bangkok myself. The women are really free and easy there. If you're in need of an oil change, I'd suggest going there."

"I just want to go somewhere quiet where I can rest."

"No tours or whores, huh? I think I know the perfect place. You leave the rest to me. I'll send you the paperwork. They probably won't let you go until things settle down anyway."

"Thank you, sir." Billy handed Barnes the empty coffee mug and turned to go.

"And Major…be careful."

"Yes, sir."

Billy found Ray in the hospital.

"What's wrong?" he said, seeing Billy's face.

"I've been reassigned."

"Where to?"

"Dong Ha."

"When?"

"Now."

"Christ, that's where all this shit is coming from."

"They need help up there. They probably should have moved me days ago. Ray, could you do me a favor." He quickly explained what had transpired with Maggie earlier. "I wasn't able to talk to her. When you see her, please tell her I'm sorry. Tell her…" he cleared his throat. "Tell her I said goodbye…please. And tell her that she and the other girls can help themselves to my finished paperbacks. I can't take all of them with me."

He shook Ray's hand. "I just wish there would have been more time. I hate leaving like this."

"I know. It stinks. But don't worry, I'll tell her. Take care of yourself."

"You too," Billy said.

He hurried back to his hooch and tossed clothes and books randomly into his duffel, his mind a million miles away. When he heard the rotors of an approaching chopper, he took a last look around, slung his duffel over his shoulder, and ran out to the Huey.

When Billy arrived in Dong Ha, the supply station was mass chaos. Wounded lay everywhere. Corpsmen slowly moved among them starting IV's and taking vitals. Two men, that Billy supposed were the GPs, were trying to sort the injuries. Billy walked up to the closest man and introduced himself.

"Thank God! The bastards finally sent us help. The gas passer got here about an hour ago. He's over in the second bunker getting his crap together. Right now, there are several casualties that'll never make the transport. Can you guys start with them?"

"Sure, have someone bring them in to us. Is the hospital still set up in the first bunker?"

"Uh huh, we'll get them to you. Sorry we aren't very organized, but this shit hit us without warning and hasn't let up."

Billy made his way to the hospital bunker and was shocked. Supplies lay haphazardly; the surgical equipment forgotten underneath. He quickly rear-ranged the disorder and made room for the first casualty. The gas passer entered with a corpsman and, without even the merest of formalities, the three men began working. They operated on five boys without stopping. Afterward, they helped clean and debride wounds and treat the less critically wounded. Things appeared to be slowing down.

Later that night, the confusion that greeted him was under control for the moment. The remaining wounded were either waiting for transport or were spending the night for observation before being moved or sent back to the field.

The mess was packed when Billy and the anesthesiologist finally went to get something to eat. Taking his tray, he sat down next to the man he assumed was one of the doctors.

"Sorry," the man said. "We never had a chance for formalities." He stuck out his right hand. "Brian Matthews, and this," he said, cocking his head in the direction of another man, "is Jerry Talbot."

"Billy Fox and Gordan Parker."

"You guys were real lifesavers today," Talbot remarked. "Thank God they finally sent someone."

"Our surgeon and gas passer were rotated back to the states last week and neither one has been replaced," Matthews explained. "I guess they figured things were tapering off since Nixon started recalling troops."

"I don't think anyone told the Vietnamese though," Talbot commented sarcastically, taking a mouthful of food and washing it down with some pink Kool-Aid.

"By the way," Matthews interjected, "our hooch is across from the hospital. You both can bunk with us."

"Thanks," Billy said, as he tried to cut into his meat. Having no luck, he pushed it aside and ate some beans instead.

"I sure as hell hope this stops soon. I had a great streak going when the shit hit the fan," Jerry said.

"A streak?" Billy questioned.

"Yeah, poker, we play as much as we can. You play?"

"Not really," Billy said.

"That's too bad, it's something to do in this hole. Although, where *you* came from, I hear you had some white women. How'd you get so lucky? You must've had a field day. Did you take numbers or what?" Jerry asked.

"They were nurses not whores," Billy replied.

"You mean they aren't one and the same?" he sniggered.

"No, they weren't," Billy said, then stood and picked up his tray. "I'd better go and check on my patients."

"Oh, they'll be okay," said Brian. "The corpsmen can take care of them."

"The corpsmen need a break, too. I'll go."

When Billy got to the bunker that housed the post-operative patients, a young private was sitting at the entrance. "Have you eaten?" Billy asked.

"No, sir."

"Then go now. I'll stay here while you're gone."

"Thanks. I haven't stopped since midnight last night. I won't be long."

"Take your time."

Billy checked each patient, then getting his gear, took it to the hooch. Returning to the hospital, he continued making better order of the mess. He didn't want to be as ill prepared when the next wave of wounded arrived.

Mac would have had a fit. With such a small amount of room, order was a necessity, not a luxury. From the way things looked, Billy was sure no one had given a damn about anything for the past couple of weeks.

After several days, the onslaught of casualties was finally over, and order restored. The poker game was back in business and Billy didn't see his hooch mates for hours at a time.

During Billy's second week at Dong Ha, he received a letter and papers from Colonel Barnes informing him that his week of R & R would start on Saturday. The colonel had taken the liberty of making reservations for Billy's flight and stay in Australia. All Billy had to do was pick up and pay for his tickets at the airport.

After taking a short flight to Bangkok, he would then transfer to Quantas and fly to Brisbane. There, he would be met and taken to the Byron's Beach Inn. Located in Byron's Bay, the inn was surrounded by ocean and rocks. No tours, no whores. If he wanted those, he was on his own. Saturday, that was only two days away. When he returned, he would have less than two months left 'in country.' Only two months, he thought. He couldn't wait to get the hell out of Vietnam.

MAGGIE

Maggie couldn't find Billy. He wasn't in the hospital, and he wasn't in the mess for dinner. He must be furious, and she didn't blame him. He had been so wonderful to her, and as thanks, she had treated him so badly. Swallowing her pride, she timidly knocked on the warped wooden frame of his hooch.

Lucky's voice bade her to enter. "Change your mind about having a little fun with me?" Lucky asked, while lying on his bunk reading a magazine.

"I'm looking for Doctor Fox. Have you seen him?"

"Haven't you heard? Our fearless leader has departed for greener pastures."

"What are you talking about?" Maggie asked.

"He's gone. Reassigned. And good riddance to red trash, I say."

She glanced at Billy's bunk and nightstand. The photographs on the chest were gone as well as his duffel. He can't be gone, she thought, and backed out of the hooch oblivious to remarks Lucky was making.

Maggie searched the compound in the twilight. She saw someone sitting on Billy's favorite bench and ran in that direction. At the last minute, she pulled up, realizing that it was Ray not Billy seated there.

Ray turned when he heard her. "Maggie, there you are. I've been looking all over for you. I need to talk to you."

"Where's Doctor Fox? Doctor Galbreath said he's gone," she gasped. "He can't be gone. I mean, he didn't say goodbye."

"Sit down, Maggie. After you ran from him this morning, Billy went after you. But was waylaid by Colonel Barnes. You know how we've been bombarded with casualties from Dong Ha these last few days?"

"Yes," Maggie answered.

Ray then went on to fill Maggie in about the surgeon shortage and Billy's reassignment.

"Will he come back?"

"Doubt it. He's almost a short-timer. They'll either keep him in Dong Ha or move him elsewhere. In any case, he took everything with him. He left a box of books for you girls with orders not to fight over them."

"But he didn't say goodbye," Maggie lamented.

"He couldn't. Barnes wanted him on the first available flight, hardly giving him time to pack. He felt terrible about what happened and not being able to say goodbye."

"I feel so bad about this morning. I really lost it."

"Yes, and your accusations were way off the mark. Billy was with Joey most of the night, monitoring his brain pressure, giving him drugs, trying to fight the swelling. And when he wasn't doing that, he was operating on several casualties. He was too busy to send for you. Besides, he also knew how tired you were and wanted you to rest."

Shock registered in Maggie's eyes. "All night?"

"Yes, he never got to bed until about five this morning."

"He must hate me," she whispered. "I said such horrible things to him."

"No Maggie, he doesn't hate you. He was very worried about you and was upset because he didn't get the chance to talk to you."

Maggie stared into the darkness. She could hear herself calling him cold and heartless—could feel the hurt she had inflicted. He wasn't like that, and she knew it. She just needed to take her pain out on someone, and he had been there. Now he was gone, and she'd never see him again—never be able to apologize. Billy had been her friend, and she had turned on him.

She didn't realize she was crying until Ray put his arm around her. "Maggie?" Leaning into him, and feeling him tighten his hold on her, she couldn't stop the tears. It was as if Mike had died all over again. But this time, her tears were for Billy as well. She knew how he felt about Dong Ha. How he'd be remembering the last time he was there and reliving the pain. Loss, that's what Vietnam was all about, she thought with sorrow.

"What are we going to do without him?" Maggie asked.

"I don't know. They'll send someone eventually. Hopefully it will be someone like Billy," Ray stated. "It's funny," he continued after a few moments. "He was the last thing I expected when he first got here. And I resented him like you wouldn't believe."

"Why?"

"Well, first of all, I expected to be put in charge myself. I'd been here for over two months and had been doing surgery in the states for a couple of years. I figured I was a shoe in. I couldn't believe that they'd send this young pup to do a man's job."

"Young pup?"

"Yeah, the other guys don't know this, so please keep it to yourself. But I resented Billy because he was just a rookie." At Maggie's puzzled look, he added, "You know, still a resident."

"You're kidding."

"Can you believe it? I was so angry when I found out that my boss wasn't even a full-fledged attending. I couldn't understand why I was bypassed and this kid, who was still wet behind the ears, and an Indian to boot, was put in charge of us old timers. But after I worked with him for a week, I understood why it was he and not I that had the oak leaves on his shoulders. Guess the army knew what they were doing."

"I just can't believe it. He never said anything to me."

"He wouldn't. He was so afraid guys like Galbreath would find out, then he would have no credibility or respect from them at all. He had so little to begin with. It was bad enough he was an Indian. A lot of the guys really fed him some shit over that. You could imagine what they would have done if they had found out he was still a resident."

"How did you find out?"

"He needed my help on something, and we were bunk mates. I guess he had to trust someone. If he only knew how I originally felt about him, he probably would never have asked."

"But I thought you two were friends."

"Sure, we were. He was a great guy. I'm gonna miss him. He was one of the best surgeons I ever worked with, and was decent, too. In fact, on more than one occasion, he actually helped *me* out. Really saved my ass. That was kind of embarrassing, but he just laughed and said that one good turn deserved another. That's how he was."

Maggie closed her eyes. She saw Billy's face before her and now understood why he always seemed so youthful. Gee, he was probably about her age. It made her feel even worse about the things she had said to him.

After a few moments, Ray stood. "Come on. Let's go get those books for you."

Galbreath was gone when they went inside. Next to Ray's bunk on the floor sat a small cardboard carton. Krause bent and picked it up. "Here, I'll carry this for you. It's heavy."

She pushed the door open for Ray and took a last look at Billy's empty bunk. She visualized him standing there earlier, his eyes bleary and confused at her accusations. She wished she could relive the morning. But it was too late.

Without Billy, Phu Bai was different. Maggie did her job but no longer socialized with her friends or the other doctors. She kept to herself and made a habit of walking the perimeters of the camp every evening. She was a solitary figure in the dusk. Her friends tried to cheer her, but to no avail. Maggie slowly alienated herself from everyone and spent the rest of her free time reading Billy's books.

Deena brought the matter up with Colonel Barnes since Billy had not yet been replaced as head of medical personnel.

"I was just about to come for you girls," Barnes said. "You and Maggie are being reassigned to Da Nang at the end of the week, and the other two girls will be returning to Saigon."

"About Maggie, Colonel," Deena interjected, "we're really worried about her."

"I'm going to arrange a week of R & R for her. We'll see what happens after that. If she's still in bad shape when she returns, talk to one of the staff psychiatrists at your new billet. It's a shame we don't have one here anymore."

"Yes, sir and thank you," Deena saluted.

"You girls did a fine job. We were a bit tense when we heard you were coming here. This isn't a situation women should have to deal with." He put up a hand as Deena started to sputter. "It's not that we don't think you can handle roughing it or being close to the fighting. We're just trying to be gentlemen. We hate to expose you to things even *we* would rather not see. Call it chivalry if you will. Some of us still believe in it. Anyway, it was a pleasure having you here. You're a credit to your profession."

"Thank you again, sir. I'll tell Maggie about her R & R and our new assignments."

As the plane circled Bangkok on its descent, Maggie saw the many canals that linked the city and the spires of several Buddhist monasteries. On her return trip, Maggie would have a night's stay here. At that time, she could get a better look at the city.

At first, she had been excited, but then remembered she would be seeing it alone. Mike had often written about getting their R & Rs together and meeting somewhere. That had been a lovely dream. Now, nothing seemed to matter anymore. She couldn't help but wonder why she was going to Australia.

She transferred planes without a hitch, then was on her way again. There was a jeep waiting for her and a trio of women tourists at the Brisbane airport.

"G'day," a strapping youth said to them, "you the sheilas to go to the Byron's Beach Inn? The other four guests were already picked up."

"Well," Maggie said uncertainly, "I'm going to the inn, but my name's Maggie."

The fellow threw back his head and let out a hoot of laughter. "Sheila, that's our term for a woman. Come on, get in." She caused another round of laughter when she went to get in on the right side of the jeep. "Strewth! Wanna drive, eh love?"

"What?" Maggie asked in confusion until her eyes focused on the steering wheel in front of her, and she flushed. "Oh dear."

"No worries, lady. Happens all the time."

The inn lay on the outskirts of a small, quaint, seaside town still relatively untouched by commercialism. It was a rustic, one story clapboard facing the ocean with tiny bungalows scattered on either side. The quiet was punctuated by the incoming rollers and sea birds wheeling overhead. Except for a few people walking along the beach, the grounds were deserted. Two or three older couples were seated on the veranda enjoying the early evening, as Maggie went in to register.

The main floor of the building held a dining room and library as well as a recreation area. French doors opened to the rear, exposing a brick paved patio surrounding a swimming pool on one side of the building and tennis courts on the other.

After taking the short walk to bungalow three, Maggie was pleasantly surprised. The cottage was an airy bedsitter and bathroom with a tiny porch that faced the ocean. Although there was no kitchen facility per se, the room was equipped with an electric kettle, percolator, and mugs. A large basket containing a selection of teas, coffee, some fresh fruit, one or two muffins, and a tin of cookies was placed invitingly on a coffee table.

Since the dining room was being kept open due to their late arrival, Maggie hurriedly selected one of Billy's books and went to dinner. It was wonderful to be able to order food from a menu. There were linens on the tables and the delicious meal was served on delicate china plates.

She glanced casually around at the scattered occupants. There were few. Business this time of year, the receptionist told her, was relatively slow—especially during the week. The weekends were a little busier until around November through February when Australia enjoyed their summer months, and the B & B was packed with people.

As she looked around, Maggie was startled to see at another table a person with a long, dark braid of hair who reminded Maggie of Billy. This was getting ridiculous, Maggie thought. She seemed to be imagining him everywhere—in the airport, on the plane and now, here.

In fact, as she was leaving the dining room, she glimpsed yet another person seated in a corner, who from far away resembled Billy. This person's dark hair was pulled into a loose ponytail. Engrossed in a book, there was something about the way they pushed up their glasses that made Maggie turn and take another look.

Maggie felt as though she was losing her mind. She went through the lobby and approached the registration desk.

The young woman looked up and smiled. "May I help you?"

"I was wondering if you could answer a question for me?" Maggie asked. "Could you tell me if you have a Dr. Fox registered here and if so what room he's in?"

"I'm sorry, ma'am. I'm not supposed to give out that kind of information."

"But it's very important," Maggie pleaded. "Could you please just tell me if there *is* such a person registered?"

"I don't see how that would hurt," the girl replied. Scanning the guest book, she asked, "What was the last name again?"

"Fox."

"William R. Fox?"

"Yes, that's it."

"He registered about a half an hour before you did."

Maggie felt dizzy. "Are you sure you can't tell me what room he's in?"

"No, I'm sorry." Staring at Maggie's crestfallen face, she then asked, "Are you in a room or a bungalow?"

"I'm in bungalow three."

The woman perused the pages of her book again. "I'd say your friend is a year older than you." She winked at Maggie, then continued, "I hope you enjoy your stay."

"Thank you very, very much."

She returned to her room, stunned. Billy, here! It seemed impossible. She racked her brain for ways to run into him. The girl at the registration desk inferred that he was in the next bungalow. Why not go next door and knock.

After some deliberation, she got up and went out. With her heart thumping wildly in her chest, she knocked at bungalow four. There was no answer, so she retreated to her room to decide what to do next.

She ventured out again about an hour later. This time, the door opened, and Billy stood before her wearing only a pair of khaki scrub bottoms. He looked as though he had just gotten out of the shower. His hair hung wet and loose, and a towel was draped around his neck. Astonishment flashed across his face.

"Maggie! What in the heck are you doing here?"

"I'm on R & R. Colonel Barnes arranged it for me."

"No kidding? Guess who got me my room?"

"Colonel Barnes," she answered smiling. "I thought I saw you at dinner this evening but, after already accosting several women with dark braids, I was afraid to try again."

Billy smiled. "Still putting those size fives where they don't belong, aren't you?"

"Of course."

"Well, don't stand there. Come on in, it's getting cool out," he said, as goose flesh appeared on his chest and arms.

She went in, closing the door behind her. Now that she was here, she didn't know what to say or how to begin. In Vietnam, he was as comfortable and familiar as an old friend. Conversation between them was always relaxed even though at times a little heated. But now, as a civilian, he was like a stranger and Maggie felt at a loss.

"I didn't think I'd ever see you again. And yet, here you are."

"Amazing, isn't it?" he said, gathering some clothes from a chair. "Sit down."

"Uh…I really shouldn't stay, Doctor."

"Maggie, please," Billy interjected. "We're not in a hospital, can't you call me Billy?"

"Oh…I'll try. Uh, I just thought if you were here, I wanted to come and apologize."

"Apologize? You, apologize? *Now* what did you do?" he grinned. The smile instantly transformed him from stranger to friend, and Maggie felt more at ease in his presence.

"You know. I was such a jerk. I felt awful about what happened that last morning and all the terrible things I said. Then you were gone without a good-bye." She felt tears welling in her eyes. Don't you dare cry, she commanded herself.

"Come here," he said, opening his arms. Maggie hesitated, then went to him. He hugged her tightly. "I felt pretty awful myself," Billy said. "I hated to leave that way. But they wanted me ASAP. I had no choice." He tilted her face up so that she was looking at him. "I'm sorry, too. I wish I could have at least said goodbye."

Maggie's vision swam. Laying her head against his smooth, bare chest, she tried to force back the tears that started to spill unbidden from her eyes. "I promised myself I wouldn't cry or act like a fool. Yet here I am doing both," she said.

"You're not acting like a fool." He rubbed her back and laid his head on top of hers. "You're acting like a person who's in pain. Like someone who has lost a great deal." He backed away and rested his hands on her shoulders. "I told you before, it's no sin to cry."

"I know," she whispered.

"You can only fight it so long. Look what happened in Phu Bai. Do you want to snap?"

"No," Maggie said glumly.

"Then give yourself a break."

"It's just that there's this huge emptiness inside that eats away at me constantly, like a hunger."

"Yes," he nodded. "And no matter what, it's always there. I know. I feel the same way." He gazed at her a long time—his eyes dark, unreadable, and hypnotizing in the lamplight.

Maggie returned the gaze, her tears still wet on her face. She could feel the heat of his body and knew before it happened that he was going to kiss her. When his lips finally touched hers, it was like a shock of electricity. Maggie's heart was pounding so hard that she thought it would burst from her ribs. Unlike the kiss in his hooch, this was very gentle, like a whisper.

She closed her eyes and gave in to the feelings that she had been running from since the moment she met him—feelings that were building within her as they became friends—feelings that when she thought about Mike, filled her with a tremendous amount of guilt.

Afterward, he broke away from her, his face serious, a question in his eyes.

"What is it?" she asked.

Suddenly, he grinned. "I'm waiting to see if you're gonna take a swing at me."

She smiled with a trace of sorrow and shook her head. "No, I won't hit you." Maggie was torn. She wanted him to hold her and love her; to comfort her and take away the pain and emptiness of death. First Mike, then Joey and all the rest of the young men they couldn't save. The needless waste of it all.

"Maggie?"

Her thoughts returned to the present. "I'm sorry. I was a million miles away, wasn't I?"

"At least," he smiled.

"I'd better go," she said, backing away. "It's getting late."

Billy nodded and didn't try to stop her from leaving. "Good night, Maggie," he said, then stood on his porch and watched until she got to her door.

"Good night…Billy," she called, then disappeared inside.

Maggie rose early the next morning after a night haunted by terrifying dreams. She opened her door and saw Billy on his porch, a steaming mug in his hands and waved.

"I have hot coffee if you're interested," he called.

"Be right over." Grabbing an empty mug and a sweater, she joined him. "Beautiful morning, isn't it?" she commented, as he filled her mug and handed her a blueberry muffin.

"The sunrise was really nice. It looked as though the ocean exploded."

"You've been out since then?"

"Couldn't sleep. I kept expecting to hear a Huey."

"I know the feeling. I think I slept with one eye open most of the night and when I finally did sleep, I had the worst dreams," she said, biting into the muffin. "Mmm, this is good."

"The fruit is good, too. I haven't had any fresh fruit since I was in Hawaii. The only problem is there's so much of it in my room, that I can't eat it fast enough. I envision either being attacked by a horde of fruit flies or getting the worst case of diarrhea imaginable."

Maggie laughed. "That would make quite a story for your hooch mates."

"Hell, this new group of guys I'm bunking with only care about two things—women and cards. And not necessarily in that order, either." He peeled an orange and looked at it thoughtfully. "I guess I'll have to throw caution to the winds," he said, eating a section. "What're you going to do this morning?"

"I don't know. Do you have any plans?"

"I was going to hike to the lighthouse everyone's talking about."

"Sounds like work."

"I need something physical to do. It's too early to swim and I don't feel like running. My eyes are tired from reading, and I don't want to go into town. The lighthouse was my last option."

"If you promise not to walk too fast, I'll go with you if you don't mind the company."

He smiled at her. "I promise I won't make you feel like a cart horse, all right?"

"Okay."

Situated high on a cliff, the lighthouse was accessible only by climbing a long, rocky path. Maggie was about to enter the building when she realized Billy wasn't behind her. Instead, he leaned against the base of the lighthouse and gazed out at the ocean.

"Aren't you coming?" Maggie asked, going back to him.

"I don't think so."

"But we came all this way. Why not?"

"I'm not real fond of heights," he replied.

"You, afraid of heights?"

"I didn't say I was afraid of them—just not fond of them."

"I'll hold your hand, if it will help. Please. I don't want to go alone." She held out her hand to him. After a moment's hesitation, he sighed, pushed away from the wall and took her hand.

Inside, the circular stairway seemed endless. No matter how many steps they climbed, there were always more.

When they finally reached the top, a narrow walkway circled the inside of the lighthouse. Billy exclaimed, "Geez, that was almost as bad as the freakin' Washington Monument!"

In the center of the building, the gigantic prism slowly rotated, sending its message far and wide. Billy stood in the stairway, refusing to go out to the glass wall.

"Chicken?" Maggie teased, holding out her hand again. Billy took a deep breath and joined her. "That wasn't so bad, was it?" Maggie asked.

"It's not the coming out, it's the going back in that's a problem."

"Fear of heights is not an inborn fear, you know."

"I know." Billy stared out at the ocean and the surrounding rocks; his face grim. "When I was a kid, my old man killed himself by diving off a cliff in front of me. When I went to the edge and looked down, I could see his body smashed on the rocks below. It kind of put me off heights."

Maggie's stomach tightened queasily. She visualized Billy as a child—saw the horror he had witnessed. "I'm so sorry. I think I would be better off keeping my mouth shut."

Billy smiled at her. "I think I've seen enough water to last me the rest of the day. How 'bout we race back down?" he said, backing slowly to the stairs with Maggie at his side. They ran the whole way, laughing and dizzy at the bottom. Once outside, they leisurely walked back to the inn.

"Feel like a cart horse?" Billy asked.

"No, more like I was back at Basic Training. Let's eat. I'm starving."

"I've been enjoying your books," Maggie said, as they walked along the beach after dinner. "Thanks for leaving them for us. Barbara sure has interesting taste in reading material."

"You can say that again," he said, kicking at a loose stone. "One month, she sends mysteries, the next, true crime or espionage. I'm getting so used to reading books where someone gets axed in the first chapter, that I'm beginning to expect it in all the books I read," he laughed.

"They aren't all thrillers, though."

"I know. In fact, the one book I can't find, isn't a mystery either," he said. "I'm afraid in the hurry to pack and leave Phu Bai, I must've lost it."

"Is it something you can replace?"

Billy put his hands into his back pockets and shrugged. "I guess I could go out and buy another one, but it wouldn't be the same. I've made notes in this one."

"Where did it come from?"

"It was a graduation gift from one of the padres at the mission school I went to, who was one of my favorite people." He paused, picked up the stone and skipped it on the waves. "Besides the book, I also lost my medicine bag."

"Medicine bag?"

"A small deerskin pouch on a leather thong."

"What was in it?"

He was silent, staring out at the water. "Memories," he murmured finally. "Reminders of who, and what, I am."

"What do you mean?" Maggie asked.

"It's kind of hard to explain. Medicine bags hold all sorts of things that are important to an individual. Things a person believes make them stronger in mind, body, and spirit. For instance, my bag contained a bear claw that to me signified courage because my grandfather and I faced and killed this bear before it was able to kill us. To remind me of home, I had some horsehair, a piece of turquoise and some dirt and sand from the ground where my grandparents live." He glanced at her sheepishly and smiled, "My last cigarette butt."

Maggie smiled back. "Now, that's one story I know."

"Let's see. What else? Oh yeah, pollen."

"As in plant pollen?"

"Yes, pollen is a very powerful medicine to my people."

"What's it used for?"

"Ceremonial purposes for one thing. Or to anoint the sick and dying for another. Hell, there are so many uses for it besides that. But now, it's all gone."

A breeze had picked up and the night had turned cool as they wandered back to the bungalows in a companionable silence. Finally, Maggie asked, "What was the name of the book?"

"It was *Meditations* by Marcus Aurelius. It's a philosophy book kind of on par with Plato's *Republic* or Descartes' *Discourse on Method.*"

"I remember reading those two in an intro to Philosophy course."

"That's where I read them as well."

"They sure aren't light reading material."

"No, they aren't exactly an Agatha Christie."

"From what I remember, they were work to get through. Did you like them?"

"They were okay. But Aurelius was my favorite. Reading him wasn't really work."

"What made him so special?"

"A lot of things, I guess. His writings and teachings apply to any situation in any given time, not just in the days before Christ and the first century. His wisdom reminded me of an old Apache medicine man I once met. Being in his presence made me feel as if I was closer to the creator—to something outside my understanding. He was truly a holy man. It just goes to show that there are some people who see and think beyond that of the normal human being no matter what race, education, religion or age of time."

"It's a shame more people don't think like that."

"I think most people see either black or white, never the shades of gray in the middle."

"I think that's what bothers me most about the medical profession."

"What's that?"

"The arrogance and close mindedness of the practitioners."

Billy looked at her and shrugged. "I don't think everyone is like that. You really shouldn't make sweeping generalities. Your constant assumptions are what always seem to get you into trouble, don't they?" he said, softening his reproach with a smile.

"You're right, as usual."

"Always," he grinned, ruffling her hair. "I'm a doctor, remember?"

"Oh you," Maggie said, giving his shoulder a shove. "You're terrible."

"I'll see you tomorrow," he said, when they approached her door. "I hope you won't be too sore from the hike."

"Good night," she replied and entered her room. Her eyes strayed to the night table. Lying next to the lamp was the book *Meditations*, the deerskin pouch hung from the closed pages like a flag. She stared at the book thoughtfully, picked it up, and went next door. "May I come in?" she asked.

"Sure," Billy said, his eyes questioning.

"I think I have something of yours," Maggie said, handing him the book. "I found this in the box you left in Phu Bai. Is this what you were talking about this evening?"

He took the book, handling it almost reverently. "Yes, Maggie," he said. "This is it. I can't thank you enough. I'm glad I mentioned it."

"When you left, Phu Bai was different. I hated it. It was as if I had lost my best and only friend. I felt alone and made it all worse by keeping to myself. I became possessive of your books, because they had been yours. It was all I had left of you. But then, I found this book and it gave me comfort. First, because I thought you had intentionally left it for me. And second, because it was as if you weren't so far away. It was a part of you that was still with me."

Her eyes became unnaturally bright, and she cleared her throat before she continued, "I've been reading some of it every day. It's almost like reading a journal. Like you said, the material in it pertains to any time," she commented. "Everything that happened in Phu Bai, the casualties, Mike, Joey, your friend's death, and then you leaving so suddenly, all seemed to be there within its pages."

A tear overflowed her eye and ran down her cheek. "There's one line I especially keep going back to. Not just to the line itself but to the notes that you made beside it."

Billy laid the book down on the dresser and moved closer to Maggie. "What was the line?" he asked softly.

"You may break your heart, but men will still go on as before." Her voice trembled and broke as she spoke the words. She glanced at him and noticed his eyes were filling with unshed tears. He stared at the ceiling, fighting his own inner demons, and nodded his head, swallowing hard. His arms encircled her, pulling her close against him. She could feel his tears falling on her hair—felt her own on her cheeks.

After a moment, Billy tipped her face up to his, allowing her to see the tears that he knew couldn't be hidden. He looked into her eyes, then kissed her forehead. Maggie's eyes closed as his lips caressed her face, moving from her hairline to her nose, to her cheeks, then finally her lips. She forgot to breathe as his mouth gently touched hers. The kiss deepened sending shock waves throughout Maggie's body as she responded.

After a moment though, Billy ended the kiss. Moving slightly away from her, he stroked her cheek with the back of his hand. His eyes locked on hers, an unspoken question surfacing from their olive depths. They stared at each other for many heartbeats before Maggie moved back against him in silent assent—giving in to the forces that neither one of them could control any longer. Their tears mingled as their lips met hungrily in a quest to salve the wound. And for a brief time, as their bodies merged, they held at bay the horrors of Vietnam and its many victims.

BILLY

They lay enfolded in each other's arms—Maggie's head against Billy's chest. He stroked her hair, smelling its sweetness.

"What's that noise?" she asked sleepily.

"Hmm? What noise?"

"A sort of grinding, clicking noise. It seems to be coming from you."

"That better?" he asked, as he shifted his position and laid slightly on his side, facing her.

Maggie listened for a minute. "I don't hear it anymore. What was it?"

"My ribs. A couple were broken when I was a kid and didn't heal quite right. When I lay a certain way sometimes the cartilage kind of crunches."

Maggie palpated his side. "I feel them. They feel kind of bent."

Billy jerked. "Hey, that tickles!"

"How'd it happen? Did you fall or get into a fight?"

"No," he said, and kissed her, keeping her mouth busy for a few moments.

"Mmm," Maggie sighed, slowly opening her eyes. "That's sure an interesting way of avoiding a question."

"Isn't it just? I could keep avoiding it for the rest of the night if you'd like."

"I bet you could. But you have my interest piqued. Come on. Please."

"Your interest is always piqued."

"I know. But don't you understand, you interest me. Besides, you just made love to me. I want to know more about you." She smiled shyly and placed her hand gently back on his side. "Please. Tell me."

"Look, sometimes there are things that are best left alone, best left unsaid. The more you know about me and the more I know about you, the more history we have together. By the end of the week, going our separate ways will be even more unbearable. Is that what you want?"

"I know it will hurt, but at least I won't feel as though we were just two ships passing in the night. Or a one-week fling."

"As far as I'm concerned, we are neither of those."

"I know, but…"

"Besides, it's not a nice bedtime story."

"Oh, don't be so dramatic. How bad can broken ribs be. If you're afraid I'll not want to be with you because you punched some guy out when you were ten, think again."

"I told you; I wasn't in a fight."

"So how did it happen? They just don't break by themselves."

Billy sighed. "If you must know, my mother kicked me."

"My God, on purpose?"

"Yes, Maggie, on purpose."

"But why?"

"Why? Because she didn't want me? Because I was a burden? Because her life changed when I was born?" he mused, rolling onto his back and staring at the ceiling. His arm tightened around her, pulling her against his side. "I don't know. That's just how my life was. If she wasn't ignoring me, she was making me pay for being alive in some way or another."

"How old were you?"

"I don't know. I guess around six? Maybe seven?"

"That makes me ill. I just can't imagine a mother inflicting pain on her own child. A child that she carried inside of her."

Billy absently stroked her arm. "Not every woman is mother material, sweetheart. Unfortunately, from the moment I was conceived, my mother hated me. And from the time I was born, she reminded me of that fact daily."

"By kicking you?"

"Kicking, punching…using me as a human ashtray, whatever turned her on at the time. Most days, I was lucky. She ignored me and left me to fend for myself. I think she thought if she didn't see me, I didn't exist," he said, his fingers continuing to gently stroke the smooth skin of her neck and shoulders.

"This particular day, she'd had a tough time of it the night before with my old man and took it out on me. After the first kick, I felt something give. Then she kind of lost it and wouldn't quit. After about a half a dozen times, she stopped and threw two buckets at me, ordering me to get her water so that she could wash her hair."

"Just like that?"

"Just like that."

"But why did you need the buckets?"

"The rain barrel was empty, and the nearest well was about a mile away."

"You mean you didn't have running water?" she said, shifting to look at him.

"God, Maggie, this was a reservation. We were lucky to have a well nearby. You don't know what poor is until you've been on a Rez."

"It must have been awful."

"It was all I knew."

"You were so little. How did you manage to get the water?"

"It wasn't easy. I couldn't fill them very full. Then staggering under their weight, I half carried, half dragged them home."

"After all that, was there anything left in them by the time you got home?"

"Good question, and no, I think, by then, they were pretty empty. My mother came outside, looked at the buckets, called me a useless brat, then dumped what was left of the contents over my head. 'I should have known you wouldn't do it right,' she said, then went back into the rusty trailer we lived in and locked the door."

"What did you do then?" Maggie asked, her voice tremulous.

"Crawled under the trailer and laid in this shallow hole I had dug. I was cold and wet, and my side was on fire. I think I must've passed out or fallen asleep, because after a while my father came and pulled me out and made me come inside."

"Did you tell him what your mother had done?"

"No."

"Why not? Couldn't he have helped you?"

"Help?" Billy laughed without humor. "I don't think so. You see, every day, my father sat around with the rest of the unemployed men in the piss hole of a Rez that we lived on. He spent what little money we had buying whiskey and eating peyote like it was candy. When he came home, he was either drunk or high or both. He'd take one look at me, realize that it was because of me that his life was shit, and hit me or worse. Then he'd go inside and work over my mother."

"No child should have to live like that. How could you do it?"

Billy didn't answer. Instead, he ran his fingers through Maggie's hair gently tugging on the silky strands. His eyes were closed, and his mouth was set in a grim line. The sight of him and what he had gone through was too much for her, and she began to cry softly.

"Don't," Billy said. Turning to her, he wiped at her tears with his fingers and cradled her in his arms. "You asked, remember? It happened a long time ago."

"But how did you ever become a doctor? How did you get out of that situation?"

Billy took a deep breath as though resigned to his fate. "I couldn't take the abuse anymore, Maggie. One day, when I was about eight, I stole my father's hunting knife, hiding it in my pants. When he came at me that night, I handed him the blade and told him that he might as well kill me. If not, I would do it myself, right then and there."

"Oh my God!"

"The crazy fucker was so damned proud of me. I was his son, a true Apache. A warrior! The next day, he grabbed me and threw me into his truck. We drove a good part of the day, going hundreds of miles. He finally pulled up in my grandparents' yard, pushed me out of the truck and left. That's how I ended up here. From one hell to another, huh?"

She clung to him; her face wet with tears. "Not many people would be able to overcome that. You must be a very strong and determined person to have come so far."

Billy was silent for a long time, as if bracing himself for an ordeal before finally saying, "I don't know, Maggie. I'm still my father's son…just ask my wife," he commented quietly. "It took a long time, but I eventually came to understand him. To understand his frustration at the way his life turned out. It made me realize how desperate a person can become. It happened to me, too."

"What do you mean?" she asked, after his pause dragged on into long minutes.

Billy looked at Maggie for a moment, then taking another deep breath, said, "Jessie came along, and my dreams went down the toilet. In my own frustration, I also started drinking, using drugs and finally, in the end, slapping her around. I found out that she had lied about so many things just so I'd marry her. And I realized my life was wasted because of it."

Taking his arms from around her, he lay again on his back, putting distance between them. Crossing his arms behind his head, he said, "I remember sitting in an alley in a pile of garbage, thinking that that was where I belonged—in garbage. I kept rubbing my thumb over the side of my knife blade trying to decide whether I had the guts to kill myself. I sat there a long thinking about my old man and how he had ended his life. I visualized the same thing happening to me."

Billy stared at the ceiling reliving his past sins and wondered how could Maggie ever understand?

"What changed your mind?" Maggie prompted.

"I thought about my grandparents and all our dreams, all the hard work and how far I'd come. After a while, I decided it took more guts to live than to die. But at that point, I still wasn't sure that I had the guts."

The room was quiet except for the sound of the surf that rode in on the breeze coming through the cottage window. For Billy, Maggie's silence lasted an eternity. Finally, he looked over at her, his face full of sadness. Tears trickled down her cheeks and into her hair. "Some story, huh? See, Maggie. Some things are better not known."

"Would you have kept all this from me if I hadn't pushed."

"Probably, why would you need or want to know all this shit? It's not like our relationship is going anywhere. After the end of the week, we'll never see one another again. Why tell you this, then have you hate me, ruining everything?"

"To me, intimacy isn't just about making love. It's about truly knowing someone. Knowing all the bad as well as the good. Even if it *is* only for a week. Evasion of the truth is a kind of lie, you know."

Billy got out of bed, pulled on his jeans, and went to the window. The light from the full moon illuminated the beach and incoming waves like lights on a stage. "So now you can add liar to my list of sins. Look, did you really need to know what kind of person I truly am?"

"What do you mean?"

"I'm nothing but a savage—an abusive husband, a drunk, a drug user."

"Those are your terms, not mine."

"Come on, Maggie. It's the truth."

"Okay, you slapped your wife. I don't condone that. But I have seen you pushed to your limit, and I've never once seen you resort to violence. When was the last time that you hit her and why?"

Billy turned from the window and stared at her for a few moments. "About six years ago, I guess. She showed up at the Wilson's and made all our lives miserable. She was being crude in front of Marian and the girls, then verbally went after me."

"And you punched her?"

"No, I slapped her across the face. I would never have punched her," he murmured.

"Did the Wilsons know about it?"

"Yes."

"And they continued to let you live with them?"

"Crazy, huh?"

"No, not crazy. You see, if you were so terrible, I highly doubt they would have let you continue to live with them, or be around their two little girls."

"You're making it sound like it was a frivolous thing. Put yourself in Jessie's shoes. Getting hit is getting hit. No matter what or whether you asked for it. I couldn't control my temper."

"I think you can now. No matter how much I pushed you at times, even tonight—especially tonight, you have always kept your emotions in check."

"Well, being sober helps."

"I guess that's why you've always refused alcohol and never hung out at the 'O' club."

"Yes."

"Are you an alcoholic?"

"I don't know. I just know that when things got bad, I would drink to forget. I abused it just like the drugs. Get drunk or high and forget. Just like my dad."

"When was the last time you were high?"

"My senior year at ASU."

"And when was the last time you were drunk?"

"It's been a while," he muttered. "I guess it was the summer between my first and second years at Georgetown."

"Why'd you get drunk?"

"I had just found out that Jessie was selling her ass to make money and had taken off for Vegas with some guy."

"I probably would have gotten drunk, too. Hell, my dad stopped at the bar every night after work and had a few. Still does. Yet I wouldn't consider him an alcoholic. Have you had any alcohol after that?"

"I had a sip of champagne at John's wedding."

"Did you get drunk?"

"No."

"An alcoholic wouldn't have stopped at a sip."

"I know. But I still don't trust myself with the stuff."

"That's being smart and playing it safe. If you know you have a weakness, staying away from it is practical."

"Look Maggie, you can rationalize all you want. But that doesn't change who I am and the fact that you probably won't want to be around me anymore. Telling you all of this has ruined everything. How can you like or respect me now that you know all this?"

Maggie got out of bed and pulled a blanket around her body. She went to him and looked out the window. "How did your being honest ruin things?"

"Because your feelings for me have changed."

"They have?"

"Sure."

"Let me tell you something. Not only have my feelings for you *not* changed for the worse, I now respect you even more. You owned up to something that you, yourself, are ashamed of."

"You're foolish. I don't deserve your respect."

"You're wrong. I know a good thing when I see it. Listen to me, Billy Fox. You tell me a story filled with words that if interpreted without thought, would mean one thing. But if interpreted another way, would mean something completely different. Sometimes you have to look beyond the words of the story to see the whole truth."

"And what do you see?"

"I see an honest man. A man who has been hurt more that anyone should ever be hurt. Someone who has overcome a vast amount of problems in order to help his fellow man. You're no savage."

"God, Maggie! You make me sound like a fucking saint."

"No, Billy, you're no saint. But then again, none of us are. You may break your heart, but men will still go on as before," she whispered. She kissed his shoulder and the fresh scar on his arm. Her lips grazed his skin like the wings of a butterfly.

Billy looked at Maggie in disbelief. Jessie had never given herself to him as this woman was doing. She had only taken—taken from him what she dictated he give. Maggie had lost so much, yet she was willing to give him what he had never had before. Not only unconditional love, but trust and respect.

"What are you thinking?" she asked.

Billy dragged himself back to Australia—to Maggie soft and warm beside him. He stared at her in wonder. "I was just thinking how lucky I am to have you here with me." He took her hand in his and kissed each finger. "*Gracias, mi amiga*," he whispered, then facing her, pulled her tightly against him and joined her lips with his own.

The next afternoon, they sat companionably, side by side at the pool's edge, their feet dangling in the water.

"You're rather quiet," Billy commented.

Maggie looked uncomfortable and shrugged.

"Have the second thoughts finally hit?" he questioned. Although it was spoken lightly, his insides were churning in fear that she'd changed her mind about being with him.

After a considerable amount of time, she said, "Yes and no."

"That doesn't sound very good."

"I noticed something in your belongings that rather upset me."

"In my belongings? What could that possibly be?"

"It's just that after all we went through together in Phu Bai, then after last night…" she broke off.

"What could there possibly be in with my things that would upset you more than all that I told you last night?"

"Well, didn't you say that you *weren't* looking for someone to sleep with?"

"That's right, I wasn't."

Maggie kicked at the water with her feet. "Well, if that were truly the case, why were there not one but two large boxes of contraceptives in your duffle bag? I mean, I could understand one or two condoms, just in case, but two dozen?"

Billy laughed nervously, slightly relieved but still not out of the woods. "For someone who wasn't even interested in sex, it does seem like I was expecting great things, doesn't it? Let's see, two dozen, divided by six. Wow! That's an average of four times a day. God! At my age, I'd be lucky with four times a month."

"You're making fun of me, aren't you?"

"No, Maggie, I'm making fun of myself. Do you really want to know why I have two dozen condoms with me?"

"Yes."

"Remember how I told you my new hooch mates had two things on their minds and one of them was women? Well, both of them put a dozen in my bag before I left with notes attached saying to raise hell and a lot of 'other things' while I was away. It was a big joke on their part. In fact, as you noticed, they were the *only* condoms I had with me. I hadn't even given them a thought until last night. And at that point, uh, they did come in handy, didn't they?" he asked, lightly bumping her shoulder with his own.

She nudged him back. "I guess." She was silent for a moment. "I just didn't want to be a number in an endless string of women. I was already feeling guilty, then I thought maybe you were handing me some line. The real truth being that you *were* some sort of stud who was expecting to participate in an orgy while you were here."

"You really thought that?"

"I don't know. I didn't know what to think. That's why I had to ask."

"I'm sorry, Maggie," he said soberly. "Let me say for the record, I did not lie to you about myself or the way I feel. When you asked me about my past, I was up front with you. I have never lied to you. I may have intended to hold back some things, but after you asked, I told you everything that you asked of me and more."

"Thank you. I always feel that I have been up front with you as well."

"Is that what you call being brutally honest?" he laughed.

Maggie smiled. "Am I really that bad?"

"No, sweetheart, you're not that bad. In fact, it's one of the things I love about you. From the moment you burst into my office that first day, you had me hooked. I think Joey and Ray both realized it before I did."

"So, you're not a stud?"

"Stud? I'll have you know that I have gone several years, not just months mind you, *years* without having sex. Don't you think that if I really wanted it, I'd have kept my horny ass in Bangkok. There, I could have had a different whore every hour and made good use of all that latex. No, I requested peace and quiet. That's how I ended up here."

"You're right."

He took her hand in his. "I know it hasn't been very long since Mike's death and I don't think that what happened is what either if us had in mind or planned. Did we?"

"No," she shook her head, tears beginning to form in her eyes.

"Besides, after all the time you've known me, do you *really* think I'm that kind of guy?"

Maggie glanced at him sideways, and her mouth turned up at the corner. "Yes," she said, stifling a giggle.

"Oh really? Well, it's just too bad you didn't bring Cramer with you. I think I could have satisfied both of you. What do you think? All three of us in the shower together?" he laughed. "With or without soap! In fact, we could have thrown the other two girls in just to make things interesting. As the only rooster in the henhouse, I think I could have kept you all happy. Hell, if we threw Lucky into the mix, we could have really gotten perverted!"

"Oh you!" Maggie laughed. "You're such a jerk!" She leaned over and pushed him into the swimming pool. Sputtering, Billy surfaced and gently holding her around the waist, pulled her in with him.

The only thing to mar their week was an incident that happened at dinner the night before they were to leave. Since the weekend was approaching, the inn was filling up. The dining room was much more crowded than it had been all week. Instead of their usual table in the corner, Billy and Maggie were given a table that was much more prominent.

They were holding hands and talking quietly as they waited for their meals to be served, when an older couple was seated next to them. It wasn't until a few minutes later that the older couples' conversation penetrated their discussion of alternative healing. Billy and Maggie froze as they listened to the comments being made about themselves.

"Are you sure that's a man?" the woman asked. "It's wearing earrings."

"Damn sure," the man replied. "I got a good look at his face. It's definitely a he."

"I can't believe the brazenness of it. This wouldn't be happening if he were one of ours."

"I know. I miss the days when all abos and darkies weren't allowed, period. Now, anything goes."

"…and in plain view, how shocking," the woman added.

"Who knows with these young people today, especially Yanks."

"Are they really Yanks?"

"Of course. Wouldn't get away with it, if they weren't. Always making a point and shoving it in our faces. Bet he's one of those wild abos from the States. Thinks he can come here and do as he pleases," the man stated, his voice getting louder as he pushed his point home.

"Are you sure she's not one of ours?"

"No, heard them talking earlier. They're both Yanks, that's for certain. Wonder what they're doing all the way over here? Bet he's dodgin' the draft.

Too gutless to fight. Or maybe they're what they call conscientious objectors. You know, hippies. Free love, sit-ins and all that rot. Wonder where the money's coming from? It's not exactly cheap to fly here. Her parents are probably wealthy and are footin' the bill. Wonder if they know she's with a boong?"

"Do you think the waitress would change our seats? Looking at them makes me sick to my stomach. I don't think I'll be able to enjoy my meal," the woman stated just as loudly.

"I'll ask the next time she's by."

Moments later, as the young waitress came to bring the couple their menus, the gentleman asked in raised tones, "Miss, me and the misses would like seats somewhere else. Can't abide sitting next to a boong. Don't know what the management is thinking letting people like him stay here as a guest: using the same facilities, swimming in the pool, eating in the same room just like he was one of us. If it was up to *me*, he wouldn't even be allowed on the property. How totally repulsive! He should be out back eating pig slop."

The young girl flushed, taking a quick glance at Billy and Maggie. After a moment's hesitation, she said, "Of course, sir," and proceeded to take the couple to different seats.

As the man passed their table, he practically shouted at Billy, "If you were any kind of man, you'd stick to your own kind instead of soiling a nice young white girl. And you," he said, pointing a finger at Maggie, "you should be ashamed of yourself!"

Maggie's face was bright red, her hand over her mouth. She looked as though she was going to explode, cry or be sick. Billy stared into space; his jaw clenched in anger.

The young waitress, who had been serving Billy and Maggie all week, came hurrying back a few minutes later, their dinners on her tray.

"What beastly people!" she said under her breath. "I'm so sorry. I would have liked to move them out of the dining room completely."

"Don't worry about it," Billy said, quietly. "You have no control over what people say."

Maggie's face was still mottled. "I…don't think I'm very hungry anymore."

Billy looked at the waitress with her heavy burden, "I know, neither am I. But you may be later," he said.

"I just want to get out of here."

"I could pack up your dinners for you to take back to your room if you'd like," the waitress said.

"That would be great," Billy smiled weakly. "Thanks."

When she returned carrying several bags, she waved off Billy's attempt to pay the check. "No charge, and again, I'm so very sorry. Those two are rude to everyone."

"Thank you," Billy said, taking the bags and leading Maggie out of the room. Patrons turned to stare as they departed. One or two seemed in total agreement with the older couple, but most of the patrons seemed embarrassed for them.

The minute they exited the dining room, Maggie said furiously, "Oh my God! I can't believe what those people were saying—about you, about us."

Billy put his arm around her, "Please Maggie, not here," he said, and gently steered her toward his bungalow. When they were inside, Billy walked away from Maggie.

Leaning against the dresser, he sighed and said quietly. "Except for the stuff about Vietnam and comparing me to an animal, he's right, you know."

"What? What are you saying?"

"He's right. I have no business being with you. I'm sorry, Maggie. This should never have happened. I was so selfish. It's just that I keep forgetting what I am, and that I don't belong with a white woman…any woman for that matter. God, he would really have crucified me if he had known I was married on top of everything else."

"Don't say that."

"It's true. I keep forgetting that the rest of the world isn't color blind. I thought that here, away from the prejudices of the American public, it would be safe to be with you. But I was wrong. Bigotry's everywhere."

"So, were we to hide in the shadows and pray that no one saw us together?"

"Not even that. I let this go too far. We should have gone our separate ways and pretended that we didn't know one another."

"That's ridiculous!"

"Yes, it is. But the world isn't ready for couples like us."

"That's too damned bad. Perhaps it's up to us to change things."

"No."

"No? What do you mean, no?"

"I mean, I would never do that to you. For one thing, what would your father think of me. He'd probably shoot me off your porch and you know it."

"Only if you were a Protestant," Maggie replied, her hands clenched in fists at her sides. "I hope that my Da would at least give you a chance before he reached for a rifle, even if you *were* a Protestant."

Billy stared at her for a second, then gave her a small smile. "Look, my people probably wouldn't accept you, either. My grandparents didn't like my mother for many reasons but one of them was because she was Navajo. Even if your father *didn't* shoot me off his porch, he wouldn't be happy at your choice. You would always be considered white trash just like I'll always be a savage or a red nigger."

"I don't care. I love you. It doesn't matter that you're an American Indian. So what? My people came from Ireland. Come to think of it, they're almost as far down on the bigotry chain as American Indians. And how about this…that son of a bitch is probably a relative of an inmate of a penal colony but now thinks he's Mr. High and Mighty."

"God, this is silly to even be having this conversation. I'm married to someone else. I shouldn't have involved you in my life, Indian or not. Because of me, someone ripped you apart and there was nothing I could do about it short of getting into a fist fight. Then I truly would have been accused of being a savage."

Maggie blew out a loud breath. "Look all this talk is ridiculous and it has to stop. You're making a mountain out of a mole hill. For God's sake, after tomorrow, I'll never see you again. And none of this will even matter. Do we really care that some jerk and his wife think we're trash? Let them. I don't care."

"You sure looked like you cared in the restaurant."

"I was in shock. I had never been attacked like that before. Without deserving it, of course. I would have liked to have told them both what a wonderful doctor you are and how you have saved lives. Face it, we both have, damn it!" she smiled. "Do we really want to spend our last night here arguing about something that will never come to be? Are we going to let two bigots ruin what could be a beautiful night? If we do, they win." Maggie held out her hand to Billy. "Do you want them to win?"

"You know me, jock that I am. I hate to lose," Billy smiled grimly, taking her offered hand.

Maggie pulled him close and kissed him fiercely. "I would much rather make love to you," she said. "You know, when the lights are off, we're both the same color."

Billy smiled and slowly began to unbutton Maggie's blouse. "Yes, but it's still daylight."

"So, close your eyes."

"Hell no, I want to look at you," he murmured, kissing her shoulder as her blouse slid to the floor.

Later, they picked at their cold food as they packed. "I just can't imagine life without you. How can I go back to the way things were?" Maggie asked, as she sat on the bed and nibbled on a piece of lettuce.

"You can't. But you'll still have Cramer."

"She isn't you."

Billy put his hand on her shoulder. "You know Maggie, you can't depend on other people to survive. You have to be strong and be your own person. Strength and happiness come from within. You can't get that from someone else."

"But why do I feel strong when I'm with you?"

He smiled and touched her face gently. "It's only temporary. You can't use me as a crutch."

"Is that what I'm doing?" she asked.

"Maybe, maybe in that respect, we're both using one another. But sooner or later, we have to stand on our own two feet—alone."

"What will you do when your tour is over?"

Billy went back to his packing, hesitating.

"Perhaps finish your residency?" Maggie questioned. Billy looked up, startled. "Ray told me," she explained.

"God, can't trust anyone to keep their mouths shut."

"If it matters, he didn't tell anyone else, and I didn't say anything to anyone. We're the only ones who know."

"Gee, that's a relief."

"It's nothing to be ashamed of."

"No, but every time I think of it, I wonder how I'm going to be able to go back to being a lackey after all this?"

Maggie shook her head. "I think that will be almost impossible. I don't know how you'll manage without breaking under the strain."

"Thank God it's only for a few months."

"Will you go back to Walter Reed?"

"That's up to the army."

"And after that, then what?"

He sat down beside her. "I used to know what I wanted to do with my life. Now everything has changed. All those dreams seem so trivial." He picked up her hand, kissing the knuckles.

"I meant to ask you if your friend's wife had her baby."

"Mmm, she had a boy. I got a letter from Marian Wilson telling me all about it."

"Have you talked to her?"

He shook his head. "I've wanted to, but I don't know what to say. I wrote her a letter, but...hell, I don't know. I guess when I get back, one of the first things I'll do is go and see her and the Simmonds family. It won't be easy."

"That's how I feel about seeing Mike's family and another reason I didn't want to go home. I can't bear to face them. They always thought I was such a lousy wife." Her lips began to quiver, and a tear trickled down her cheek.

Billy put his arm around her. "Hey, come on, don't do that. You're gonna have yourself down in the dumps again."

"I was all right until I thought about going back."

"Look on the bright side, we still have one night together in Bangkok."

"Yes, then I have to go back to Da Nang. Ooh! I hate it there. Our head honcho is a real creep named Cameron Taylor. You don't know him, do you?"

"I don't think so. I don't remember anyone by that name."

"If you'd met him, you'd remember. Not only is he a lousy doctor, he's arrogant and his inflated ego needs to be burst."

"Well, Mighty Mouse, you're the perfect person to burst any guy's bubble. If you try hard enough, that is."

Maggie slapped him on the shoulder. "Mighty Mouse?"

"You know what your problem is? You're just so used to working with the best that you can't stand mediocrity," he laughed.

"The best, huh? Cameron *never* gets crap on his pants or under his nails. Of course, he usually doesn't do anything to get dirty, period."

"Sounds like quite a guy."

"He is. You'd hate him."

In the morning, Billy went to settle their bills. He entered the lobby in his uniform and went directly to the desk, walking past the obnoxious gentleman from the dining room, who was reading the newspaper.

Janey, the owner of the Inn, greeted him warmly. "Good morning, Doctor," she said rather loudly. "Are you and Mrs. Fox ready to go?"

Billy gave her a weird look but went with it. "About as ready as we'll ever be. Maggie is having a hard time this morning. She just can't stop crying. She's trying to fix her face right now."

"I would be crying, too. Not knowing when she'll see you again or where you both will be sent. How much longer do you have in that hell hole?"

"I have about two months and Maggie is a couple of weeks behind me."

"Will the Army keep you together once you return home?"

"I don't know, but I'm not expecting any miracles."

"Biwwie!" Ellie, Janey's three-year-old daughter, and Billy's pool and reading buddy for the past week, came tottering toward him. "Don't go!"

"Got to Short Stuff. But I have something for you."

"A book?"

Billy smiled and hunkered down next to her. "How'd you know?" he smiled, handing her a wrapped package. "You know how my last name is Running Fox?"

Ellie nodded.

"Well, I found you a book that will remind you of me. There's something else to go with it. But you can open it later, okay?"

"Gonna miss you!"

"Gonna miss you too, kiddo!" Billy said, clearing his throat as the little girl jumped into his arms and clung to him like a monkey.

At that moment, Maggie, also in her uniform, entered the lobby after first opening the door for the bigot's wife. The wife's eyes were as big as saucers as she took in the uniforms and stumbled to a seat next to her husband, who was still hiding behind his newspaper.

Janey came from behind the desk and gave Maggie a long hug. "Please be safe. If you have the time when you get back home, please let me know that you both got back safely. It was an honor having you here. I must apologize again for the scene that couple created last night. When your waitress told me what happened, I was mortified. Please don't let it leave a bad taste in your mouth. I'm of a mind not to accept any reservations from them in the future."

Maggie smiled wanly. "I have your address. I'll try to keep in touch."

"Yes, please." She then turned to Billy as he handed her Ellie. "We are going to miss you both. Thank you for being so good to Ellie and the rest of the staff. And, if you hadn't taken a look at my pool filter and made a few repairs, I'd be looking at a huge plumbing bill right now."

Billy smiled. "It was nothing. I'm glad I could help." At that, Maggie began to cry again. He encircled Maggie with his arm, slowly steering her toward the door. "Come on, sweetheart, we have a plane to catch. Thank you again, Janey. We won't forget you."

And without a look at the seated couple, Billy walked Maggie out the door to the waiting jeep.

On their flight back to Bangkok, Maggie was upset to find that their seats were in different sections of the plane. Swallowing some bitter tears, she forcefully shoved her carry-on bag into the tightly packed overhead compartment. She kept reminding herself that at least they would have the night together even if they were apart during the flight.

As she sat down with a heavy sigh, a young Thai gentleman came up to her and asked, "Are you Maggie Reynolds?"

"Yes, I am," she answered.

"The gentleman in the back asked if I would switch seats with you. Apparently, he knows you," he said, gesturing to the rear of the plane where Billy stood in the aisle.

"Oh! Thank you so much!" she gushed, hugging the very surprised gentleman. "You're wonderful." She pulled at her now jammed bag in the luggage rack, almost falling as the bag suddenly gave way, then practically ran to Billy.

"It was too long a flight to be separated," Billy smiled. "I was getting worried though. I wasn't sure he was going to budge. I think he liked his window seat. I was getting desperate enough to offer him money."

"I'm glad your brain was working. I never even thought of asking someone to change seats with us. I was too busy feeling sorry for myself."

"Well, now you can relax," he said, "at least for a few hours anyway. That is, of course, if you don't mind being seen with me."

"You really are a jerk," Maggie smiled, snuggling against him.

Late the next day, when they landed in Da Nang, they saw Deena waiting with a young man and a jeep near the small terminal building. Maggie turned to Billy. "Please don't say anything," she begged.

"I don't kiss and tell," Billy replied, as they slowly made their way to the exit of the plane. "But anyone with an ounce of sense in their heads, would take one look at us and know what we've been doing," he whispered into her ear.

Deena ran to greet them as they hit the tarmac. Her look of incredulity made both Billy and Maggie smile.

"Well, well, well. What do you know? Did you come all the way to Da Nang to see me, Major Fox? I'm still a tad bit ticked at you for not saying goodbye."

"Sorry about that, Cramer, it wasn't intentional," Billy said, hugging her. "And please, do me and everyone else a favor. When you get back to the states, finish school for God's sake. What you had here was just a crash course. You hear me?"

"Yes, sir, I promise," she saluted. Deena then looked from Maggie to Billy and with a straight face asked, "Good shower?"

"Have to leave you guessing on that one," Billy grinned. "Now if you don't mind, I'd like to say goodbye to Maggie. It'll only take a minute."

As Deena retreated to the jeep, Billy turned to Maggie and tipped her face up to his. "I know we've said all there is to say. But I just want to thank you again. You'll never know what this past week has meant to me," he said.

Maggie nodded, not trusting her voice.

He pulled her into his arms, kissing her for the last time. "I tucked a piece of paper into your bag with the Wilson's address and phone number on it. If you ever need me, call that number. If I'm not with them, they'll know where I am."

"Thank you. Please Billy, be careful. I don't know what I'd do if something happened to you."

"You'd go on, just as before," he said gently and stroked her cheek. "*Te amo, mi amiga. Vaya con Dios*. Go with God."

"I love you, too." She paused, then added, "You know, Deena is gonna grill the heck out of me on the way back, and it's all your fault."

"You could always tell her it *was* a good shower. Or that we tried to put a dent into two dozen condoms in less than a week," he laughed, tweaking her nose. "Now *that* would give her something to talk about." He took his bags and, with a wave, went into the airport to see about getting transport to Dong Ha.

It wasn't long before he was sent back to Tam Quan. With troops being evacuated or moved either back to the states or into Laos or Cambodia, the artillery unit in Tam Quan was being relocated. Billy was brought in to take care of all the medical supplies and equipment still at the BAS. His final month 'in-country' would be spent taking inventories, packing and sending boxes. It was easy work and a rest from the grind of long hours of surgery.

The only downside was that the CO of artillery treated Billy like dirt. He was constantly checking to make sure Billy was doing his job and not stealing any supplies or drugs.

Due to the Vietnamese climate and the torrential rains they had been having, the virus Billy heard about in Saigon was spreading rapidly. It was a nasty problem that began as bronchitis and, in some cases, turned into pneumonia or worse.

Unfortunately, the special drugs being used to treat the virus needed to be requisitioned from Saigon. In Tam Quan, the only drugs Billy had at his disposal were regular antibiotics and standard medications. The CO refused to let him order anything more since the BAS was being dismantled. Consequently, Billy dispensed what little drugs he had left and was forced to evacuate the worst cases to Da Nang or Saigon for treatment.

"I don't know what else to do," Billy confessed to the company chaplain—his only bunkmate and fellow officer.

"Is there anything I can do?" the chaplain asked.

"Pray," Billy stated.

"It seems as though that's all I can do these days. Although, it won't hurt. Why is he being such a hardhead?"

"I don't know," Billy replied. "But at this point, I almost don't care. I'll just keep sending the tough cases out. In two weeks, I'll be gone, and it won't matter." Billy rubbed his neck and coughed. "God, I feel like shit myself. It would be just my luck to get this crap, too."

"Looks like me and the big guy upstairs are going to be busy for a while. In the meantime, why don't you get some rest?" the chaplain commented. "You don't look all that great to me. Of course, I'm not a doctor, but…"

"Maybe later, you heard the colonel, 'Get this shit counted and packed. And don't go stealing any of it either!'" Billy mimicked. He started to laugh but coughed instead.

Two nights later, Billy lay on his bunk, tossing and turning. Even without a thermometer, Billy could tell that he was running a high fever. His body was bathed in sweat as he shivered with chills. In the morning, he was so sick that he couldn't drag himself from his bunk.

The chaplain squatted by his side. "You need to get to Da Nang, buddy. You sound like an air hose that's bent in half. I'm going to tell the CO."

"Don't bother," Billy wheezed. "He won't believe you…and he won't care."

As if hearing his name, the CO stormed into the tent a moment later. "What are you doing in bed, you lazy damned Indian? Get your ass out of that bunk this minute," he said, kicking at the metal legs of Billy's cot.

"Colonel," the chaplain complained. "Dr. Fox is very ill. He needs to be sent to a hospital. He can't do any work like this."

"Are you telling me what to do, Father?"

"No sir, I'm just saying that Dr. Fox needs medical attention."

"Why don't you go back to your beads and leave the running of this camp to me? *Dr.* Fox can treat himself." Turning his attention back to Billy he said, "Now get up. I'm going into Da Nang, and I want you to finish your work and oversee the men left in camp. I expect those sandbags to be removed and loaded onto those two deuce and a halfs as well as those last cartons. I want everything packed, sealed, loaded and ready to go when I get back, or your head will roll. Understand?" With a final kick to Billy's bunk, the CO stalked out.

"I can't believe that man," the chaplain muttered. "He has no heart or brains."

"Don't worry about it, Father. I'll get my stuff done, eventually," Billy said, as he slowly crawled from his bunk. He wheezed, then coughed as he pulled on his clothes and boots then staggered outside into the ever-present mud and rain. He headed toward the mess tent and the waiting pile of cartons.

Since most of the men had already been sent to new locations, only a skeleton crew remained which included Billy, the chaplain and about a dozen and a half GIs. While Billy took care of his part of the camp, the CO expected the rest of the men to repair and collect the sandbags protecting the bunkers.

With the chaplain's help, Billy prepared the last carton of supplies in slow motion. Each breath he took was a stabbing pain. He was dizzy, and his vision was blurred. He was about to return to his bunk to lie down, when through the rain, he saw a woman come into the camp. She was an old crone, walking slowly, bent over as if in pain.

Billy sighed to himself and slogged through the mud toward her. He wondered what was wrong with her and hoped she didn't need any drugs. As she approached the bunker with the men, however, she reached into her jacket and pulled out a tin can.

Billy's mouth went dry. He'd seen homemade Vietnamese grenades before. Using two cans, they filled one with shrapnel that included rusty nails, bits of metal, or glass. Gun powder was added. Then, the cans were carefully stacked one inside the other. They were dangerous and very erratic in the way they behaved. Everyone knew never to play 'Kick the Can' in Vietnam. It was a good way to lose a few toes, a foot, a leg, or worse.

The woman smiled and rolled the can toward the men. Christ! Billy thought. She'll kill them all if that thing should blow in the bunker. He didn't realize he was running until he was upon the can. Without thinking, he kicked the can back at the woman and away from the bunker, hoping it was a dud.

As his foot connected with the can, it exploded with a blinding light. Billy felt excruciating pain as sharp metal pieces ripped through his leg. The force of the first explosion then a second, knocked him backwards into the bunker.

When the smoke cleared, the silence was complete. The men in the bunker were stunned and shaken. Billy opened his eyes and found himself upside down, draped over a sandbag. He was disoriented, and the pain in his leg was so intense that he had to clench his teeth to keep from screaming.

He tried to raise his head to look at what damage had been done, but it was too much of an effort. Instead, he reached down and gingerly felt his thigh. He couldn't tell how badly he was hurt except that when he pulled his hand away, it was covered in blood.

By then, the men in the bunker had surrounded him. They looked to one another for guidance. There were no corpsmen to take charge of the situation, and the injured person was their doctor. The chaplain came running and bent over Billy. He seemed to be saying something, but Billy couldn't hear him because of the ringing in his ears.

He groaned in pain and knew he couldn't hold on much longer. "Please," he gasped, grabbing at the chaplain's arm. "Don't let…them…take off…my…leg!" Then everything went black.

PART FIVE

"Love nothing
but that which comes to you
woven in the pattern of your destiny.
For what could more aptly fit your needs?"

~

"You may break your heart,
but men will go on as before."

Marcus Aurelius

MAGGIE

October, 1970

"Will this rain ever end?" Maggie complained to Deena as she looked out the window at the gray, dreary day. "I feel like jumping out of my skin."

"It's got everyone bitchy," Deena agreed, as she turned the page of a magazine. "Heck, this was our day off and here we sit in this little two by four of a room reading last year's magazines. By the way, what had Cameron Taylor in such a foul mood? I've never seen him so pissed."

Maggie continued to stare out the window. Her silence was out of character.

"What is it, Mags? See something interesting out there?" Deena questioned.

"No, I was just thinking about Taylor. His foul mood was my fault, I'm afraid."

"Now what? Did you tell him off again?"

"Not exactly."

"Well…?"

"He wanted me to sleep with him," Maggie finally replied.

"What!"

"He was about as romantic as a freight train. 'Hey, Reynolds,' he said. 'I haven't done you yet. Let's screw.' Like it was entertainment! You know, something to do to pass the time."

"What a pig! What did you say?"

"I told him 'No thanks.' Then I suggested that he do the deed by himself."

"You didn't?"

"I couldn't help it; I was so mad. Then he asked, 'Do you think you're too good for me?' And I said, 'No Doctor, I don't *think* it, I *know* it.'"

"Oh shit! No wonder he was in a snit. You shouldn't have been smart with him, Maggie. It's only going to cause you more problems."

"Was I supposed to go to bed with him? Keep him happy? That's ridiculous! Even Lucky, as bad as he was, didn't expect that," Maggie retorted. "Taylor is a real s.o.b. and I can't stand him. He's arrogant, sexist and, most importantly, as a surgeon, he's downright scary."

"I know," Deena said. "He doesn't give a rat's ass about the wounded. All he cares about is getting out of here at four-thirty every day so that he can hit the bars and the whores."

"Do you know what he told me his favorite piece of equipment was?" Maggie asked, turning from the window.

"Let me guess? A hacksaw," Deena replied.

"You got it. I never saw anyone get so much pleasure out of cutting something off. He's always saying it's easier to just amputate and get it over with than to try to repair the damage. It takes too much time and effort. Heck, even the GPs hate him. He hacks things off, then disappears, leaving the GPs holding the bag. Have you noticed how they all steer clear of him? I mean, we have some very good doctors here. I have no idea how he got to be in charge."

"I heard someone say that his father is high up in the army."

"So, that's where his clout comes from." Maggie sighed and turned back to the window. "What's sad is that, in most cases, he's needlessly removing limbs because he's lazy. I guess he figures if he calls in a vascular or orthopedic specialist for help, he looks bad. Billy would be sick if he saw Taylor in action."

"Now there was a class act," Deena commented. "I sure miss him. Heck, even Lucky was a better doctor than Taylor."

"I know, aside from the sex crap, Lucky actually was a decent doctor. He wouldn't treat the men coming in with the virus like Taylor," Maggie said.

"You mean how he makes them go from one test to another, then prescribes all the wrong meds and dosages."

"Yes, and when I commented to him about that, you know what he said? 'Nobody tells me what to do, especially not a goddamned nurse.'"

Deena shivered. "I can't wait to get out of here."

"Me too, Dodo!"

Late the next afternoon, Maggie was catching up on her charting when someone radioed in a casualty. Some guy at a BAS had kicked a homemade grenade and shredded his leg. On top of that, he was very sick with the virus. The ETA of the chopper bringing him in was five minutes.

Maggie listened in silence. What a jerk! Didn't these guys know that everything in this god-forsaken country was booby trapped? To some of these kids, playing 'Kick the Can' was like playing Russian Roulette. She had no sympathy for them when they got injured. From the sound of the injury, Taylor would probably get to use his handy dandy hacksaw.

The chopper arrived and the injured man was brought into the hospital. Accompanying him was a tall, thin man with the insignia of chaplain on his shoulder.

"Excuse me, miss," he said, approaching Maggie. "I need to talk to someone who's going to be taking care of this man."

"What is it, Father?"

"Please promise you'll do everything you can to save his leg."

"Save his leg?" Maggie snorted. "You know, Father, these kids crack me up. I see them play their games and flirt with disaster, then when it strikes, they want to be saved." She turned away from him and continued down the hall toward the gurney where the injured man lay.

"What are you talking about?" the man asked in confusion, as he caught up with her.

"He was playing Kick the Can, wasn't he?"

"What? No!" the chaplain said, shaking his head. "That's not what happened at all. Our doctor saved some GIs' lives by kicking a homemade grenade away from a bunker."

"Oh my God!" Maggie replied.

"Yes, and what good would a one-legged surgeon be? The poor man's also very sick with this rotten virus and has yet to get a drug for it."

"What do you mean?"

"Our drug supply was depleted, but the CO refused requisitions for any more drugs because our BAS was being dismantled."

Maggie felt sick. She could hear Billy's voice ringing in her ears. 'It's your constant assumptions that are always getting you into trouble.' He was so right, she thought. "Well, let's see how bad it is. I'm just a nurse. I can't promise anything, you know. Besides, it might not be possible to save the leg."

"I understand. I also apologize for his condition. It was raining so hard when he was injured, that we just couldn't cover him fast enough," the chaplain explained. "We threw that tarp over him, but he was already soaked. His leg's wrapped in our shirts since there were no bandages available either."

Maggie immediately went toward the legs of the man and pulled the tarp up to look at the injury. Without a glance at the man's face, she donned gloves and taking a pair of scissors, cut away the blood-soaked shirts wrapped around the leg, exposing the torn flesh. She calmly studied the site like Billy always did. 'Don't judge an injury right away, Maggie,' he once said. 'First look at the bone structure. Is it all there? What about the muscle tissue? The skin is the final and least important factor. A graft is a hell of a sight better than a prosthetic.'

She carefully examined the limb, feeling for broken bones. None appeared to be shattered or fractured and the leg was intact. The majority of the damage was to the skin and muscle tissue. Maggie flinched when she saw how badly they had been torn but thought the leg could possibly be repaired if enough time and effort were taken. Maybe a skin graft or two would be needed later on, but Maggie felt the leg had a chance.

She was about to begin prepping him when he began to thrash around, his breath coming out in ragged gasps. Maggie grabbed for his hand as it slid off the gurney. When she touched him, something made her stop and stare at his hand. It was rather small. On the slender ring finger was a worn, plain, silver wedding band. Looking further, she saw the still fresh scar on his upper arm.

Maggie's throat closed up on her as she frantically clawed at the tarp completely uncovering his body. She steeled herself to look at his face, terrified at what she was going to see. Although the rain had washed away some of the blood, there were powder burns on his face and bits of torn flesh in his hair. But it wasn't until she saw the dark, bloody braid snaking over his shoulder, that a sob caught in her throat.

"Are you all right, Lieutenant?" the chaplain questioned, his face full of concern.

Maggie felt lightheaded and put her head down to keep from passing out. You can't help him by falling apart, she said to herself. Let's move it.

"I'm okay," she replied, pulling herself together. She raced to the phone and summoned the vascular specialist. Next, she started an IV line, then sent him to x-ray with a corpsman.

"What's going on, Reynolds?" Taylor questioned. "What's all the hurry for?"

"I'm seeing to a casualty that needs immediate attention."

"Yeah, I heard the radio com. Stupid idiot blew his leg to pieces. I'll go get ready for him in the OR." He rubbed his hands together in anticipation. "I haven't done an amputation all day."

"You aren't going to, either. I called Dr. Hamilton down."

Taylor grabbed her roughly by the arm and pulled her to the side of the corridor. "Who the fuck died and left you boss, Reynolds?" he growled under his breath. "Am I not the head of medical personnel here? I say what goes, not you.

If I say the leg comes off, the leg comes off. You had no right to call Hamilton down. I don't need him."

As he spoke, a doctor walked up to them. "I heard my name. Did you say I'm not needed?"

"No!" Maggie said, jumping in front of Taylor. "We definitely need you. We have a man with a leg that needs to be repaired and may need some arterial graft work done. Right now, he's in x-ray. He'll be back shortly."

"You'll be sorry you did this, Reynolds," Taylor muttered into her ear. "I won't have you making a fool out of me. In fact, isn't your shift over?"

"No, I'm scrubbing for this one."

"Oh no, you're not!" he said. "You're off duty as of now. Cramer is here. Get out!"

Maggie saw the hopelessness of arguing. Thank God Deena was her replacement. She ran into her friend on her way out.

"Deena, it's Billy! They just brought him in. His leg is badly hurt. Don't let Taylor amputate, whatever you do. Also, make sure he starts him on the drug we've been using for the virus. I should have ordered a chest x-ray too. He sounds horrible, I wouldn't be surprised if he had fluid in his lungs," Maggie said quickly.

"Billy is here? What happened?" Deena questioned.

"I'll tell you later. In the meantime, keep your eye on Taylor. Don't let him go for his hacksaw. Please!"

"Sure Maggie, I'll do my best and let you know what's going on as soon as I can."

With bleary eyes, Maggie checked the clock. It was three a.m. and well over eight hours since she had left the hospital. There had been no word from Deena. Maggie knew she should try to get some sleep, or she'd be useless in the morning; but, when she laid down and closed her eyes, all she could see were the tears in Billy's leg.

She finally heard from Deena an hour before she was to go in to work. "Sorry I didn't call sooner. You must have been frantic. I couldn't get to a phone and when I did, Taylor had me running in another direction. It was as if he knew I was trying to call you."

"He was there all night?"

"He was in the OR with Hamilton and Billy. I was a nervous wreck the whole time. I have never seen that kind of surgery before. I wish you'd been here. I was terrified I'd do something wrong. Hamilton worked on him until early this morning."

"How is he?"

Deena hesitated.

"Tell me, Deena."

"Well, he's alive and has two legs, but he hasn't regained consciousness, his breathing is terrible, and Taylor won't order a chest x-ray."

"I knew it. Did he start him on any drugs?"

"Not yet."

"What's he waiting for?"

"I don't know, but he wants to ship him out."

"What! He can't do that."

"He sure as hell is going to try. Hamilton seemed pleased with his work, but he doesn't want Billy moved. Then the two of them got into it. Unfortunately, Taylor outranks him. Man, this crap never happened in Phu Bai. I almost wish he *would* get shipped out."

"He'd have a better chance if he had a better doctor. He needs drugs. Oh God, Deena, if Taylor lets him die, I swear I'll strangle him with my own hands. I have to do something!"

"Maggie, that's not all. You really scalded his ass yesterday. He's sending you to Saigon, ASAP."

"He can't do that!"

"Yes, he can. Remember those connections we talked about? You shouldn't have angered him."

"That bastard!"

"I'm sorry, Maggie. Uh oh, he's coming my way. I've got to get off the phone. I'll see you when you get here."

"Thanks, Do."

The minute Maggie got to the hospital; Taylor summoned her to his office. "Don't even start your shift. Go and pack. You're leaving for Saigon on the four o'clock fixed wing."

Maggie glared at him. "Do you always send away the women who don't do as you wish? Get in bed with me or else. Is that it?"

"You know, Reynolds, you should've been nice to me. Maybe now, I could have helped you. I found out from Cramer why you were so hell bent on saving that redskin. I hear you two were lovers. No wonder you wanted to save his leg. Don't want to screw a cripple, do you?" He leaned across the desk at Maggie. "You threw away the opportunity to do it with a real man in favor of a fool who kicked his leg to hell and back."

"If I had the choice, I'd take a quadriplegic over you any day. You're nothing but a self-centered, egotistical prick who doesn't know the first thing about medicine."

"Is that so? Well, I *do* know one thing. You can probably kiss your lover's red ass goodbye. He's not doing so well. And if I have anything to say about it, he'll be shipped out tomorrow. He'll never make it back to the states alive. He'll probably be awarded a medal for all his heroics." He gave a little laugh. "Posthumously, that is. Have fun in Saigon," he said, as Maggie slammed out of his office.

Deena sat on the bed as Maggie packed. "Tomorrow they're flying out a group of wounded. I overheard Taylor say that Billy will be with them."

"He'll die! I know it!" Maggie sat down next to Deena, wiping her eyes with a crumpled tissue. "He was so good to me. I don't know what I would have done without him."

Deena nodded. "What about me? I could have been court-martialed if he had turned me in. And what about all the time he spent teaching me. What are we going to do?"

"There's nothing we can do! Taylor has seen to that," Maggie growled. "I wonder if things would have turned out the same way if I had slept with him?"

"Get those thoughts out of your head. He's still a lousy doctor. He'd never have been able to save Billy's leg. Hamilton had to graft an artery from Billy's good leg to the injured one."

"Taylor can't even do simple things, let alone something as intricate as an arterial graft."

"I know. So, forget it. Look, I'll let you know what happens. At least I'll be here. It's the only reason I'm glad I'm staying. Just think, as of now, you have less than two months to go in this hell hole. And you won't have to deal with Taylor anymore."

"That's one consolation," Maggie sighed.

Deena deliberately went in to work early that afternoon, despite the fact that she had barely had eight hours break in between. She wanted to know what was going on and what Billy's status was, so that she could let Maggie know, if possible, before she left for Saigon.

Maggie had just finished packing when Deena called from the hospital.

"Billy is definitely leaving tomorrow. But guess what? My drop date has been moved up. I'll be flying home on the same plane and tending the wounded back to the states."

"Thank God. Please Deena, take good care of him. I'll call you tonight and let you know where you can reach me. Please let me know how he is when you get back."

"Sure thing, Maggie, I'll let you know."

MARIAN

Marian was used to the phone ringing in the middle of the night. She reached for the receiver automatically. "Hello?" she mumbled.

"Is this Marian Wilson?" a female voice asked, while static crackled in Marian's ear.

"Yes?" Marian was now fully awake. This wasn't a call for Rusty. He was already at the hospital and wasn't due home for hours.

"My name is Maggie Reynolds. You don't know me, but I'm a friend of Billy Fox. I'm calling from Saigon."

"What is it? What has happened?" Marian questioned, panicking.

"Billy was wounded and is being flown home. He should be in Washington by the end of the week and will probably be taken to Walter Reed. At least that's what I heard. I thought you'd want to know."

"Is he all right?"

"I hope so, I didn't get to see him before he left."

"What happened?"

"His leg was injured when he saved some men from being killed by a grenade."

"Oh my God!"

"I'm really sorry, but I have to go now. I just wanted to let you know he was on his way home. Please tell him I called."

"Thank you. You said your name was Maggie?"

"Yes, Maggie Reynolds."

"I'll tell him. Thank you again for calling."

Marian hung up in a daze. Billy had been injured. Her mind went immediately to John, and she felt ill. She got out of bed and went down to the kitchen. While making a cup of tea, she glanced at the calendar hanging on the wall. It was Wednesday. Maggie had said the end of the week. It was a long time to wait and worry. Maybe Rusty could call the hospital and see if they would alert him when Billy arrived. She wished she knew how badly he was hurt. Why couldn't Maggie have told her more?

When Rusty called Walter Reed later that day, he spoke to an attending physician named Patrick McDonald. The name as well as the booming voice seemed very familiar, Rusty thought.

"This is Frank Wilson from Georgetown University Hospital. I'm calling to inquire about a casualty that may be coming to you."

"Wilson? Rusty Wilson?"

"Yes, your name sounds familiar. Do I know you?"

"We were in Korea together. Most people called me Mac."

"Mac! It's been a long time. How are you?"

"I'm doing well, Rusty. In fact, I was just talking about you recently. I was in Vietnam for a year and ran into someone who knew you pretty well."

"Who was that?"

"Kid by the name of Billy Fox. He was one of the doctors in my unit."

"No kidding?"

"Great kid, good doc, too. How is he? He should be coming home soon."

"That's the reason I'm phoning. We got a call saying he'd been injured and is being flown home. Supposedly, they're taking him to Reed. Do you know anything about this?"

"Until a few weeks ago, we received wounded on a daily basis. But things have slowed down a bit. At any rate, we're due for another group within the next couple of days. Perhaps he'll be with them. If you give me your number, I'll let you know when he arrives."

"I'd really appreciate that. We're very worried. We don't know the extent of his injuries except that he hurt his leg."

"A leg injury? That doesn't sound like something they'd fly you out for. Usually, the ones we get by plane are pretty serious, Rusty. I don't want to worry you, but lesser injuries are usually shipped, then flown. If they're flying him directly here, something must be very wrong."

"I was afraid of that. But I didn't want to say anything to my wife. Please Mac, let me know when he gets there."

"Sure, Rusty."

"Thanks."

McDonald was on duty when the ambulances arrived. Of the original ten men on board the flight, the surviving six were being brought into the emergency unit. Billy was listed as pneumonia/leg injury.

Pneumonia, so that was the other problem. Mac called to one of the nurses, gave her the Wilson's phone number and the information they needed, then went out to meet the casualties.

A distraught young woman in crumpled fatigues accompanied them. She grabbed his arm. "Please, sir. I think one of my patients is going into respiratory arrest."

The patient was Billy. His face was grayish blue, and he was wheezing.

"How long's he been like this?"

"He's been having trouble all along, but today he was really laboring. I didn't know what to do. There wasn't any equipment available on the plane for intubating patients. I felt so helpless."

Mac had Billy hurriedly wheeled into the ER and quickly hooked him up to a ventilator. As the oxygen flowed in, Billy's color improved slightly.

"He should have been on special drugs right away. But the doctor in Da Nang didn't do anything for him."

Patrick was tired of incompetence. "What's your name?" he demanded gruffly.

"Deena Cramer, sir. Please. Can you help Major Fox?"

"I hope I can. I'm not like *some* medical personnel. Tell me about his injury."

"His leg was badly torn up by a homemade grenade. He was operated on, and the leg was partially repaired when an artery was grafted from his good leg to the bad one. The smaller tears were able to be sutured. However, the vascular specialist who did the surgery said Dr. Fox might need some follow up skin grafts to completely repair the leg since some of the wounds were so large that he couldn't approximate the edges. But they didn't have to be done immediately."

"When did all this occur?"

"Last Sunday, sir."

"And when were antibiotics first administered?"

"On Tuesday before he was shipped out."

"Not until Tuesday?"

"Yes, sir, and even then, it was with a fight."

"Did Major Fox ever regain consciousness?"

"No, not really, sir. On the plane, he kept spiking a fever and was delirious most of the time. I tried my best to keep his fever down. But nothing I did helped."

As they were speaking, Marian, Rusty and Jennifer Wilson hurried down the hall. Patrick saw Rusty through the windows of the doors and went to meet him.

"Billy was just brought in. Besides a major leg injury, he appears to have contracted pneumonia and is having trouble breathing. I've already got him on a ventilator and now I'm going in to evaluate him and see what else needs to be done. I'm going to order some chest x-rays as well. It may take a while, but I'll let you know as soon as possible what I find." Mac went back into the ER and left the Wilsons and Deena in the hall.

"Are you Dr. Fox's family?" Deena asked.

"Yes," said Rusty.

"We were in Phu Bai together. He was my commanding medical officer."

"Why don't we get out of the way?" Rusty said and ushered the women into a waiting area. "Let's sit down and this young woman can tell us all that she knows."

When Patrick finally returned, Marian jumped to her feet and asked, "How is he?"

Mac cleared his throat. "It's kind of soon to say."

"When can we see him?" Marian wanted to know.

"He's being moved to the ICU. Once he's settled, you can see him for a few minutes."

"How long will he be in intensive care?" Marian persisted.

"Take it easy, Marian. Let's listen to what Mac has to say," Rusty said.

"I'm sorry, but I want to know how he is. Is that too much to ask? If he has pneumonia and a leg injury, how bad can that possibly be? I want to see him and talk to him."

"I don't think you understand the severity of the situation, Mrs. Wilson. In fact, you all need to prepare yourselves for the worst," Patrick said.

"What? What do you mean, the worst?"

"Marian, please," Rusty interjected.

"I want to see him! Now!" she commanded.

Mac studied Marian. She was like a cat protecting her young. For such a petite woman, she was all claws and spitting fury.

He sighed and shook his head. "Come on."

The whoosh of the ventilator broke the silence in the room. Amid lines of IVs, and ventilator hoses, Billy was ashen against the white of the sheets. A monitor flashed his vital statistics constantly.

"He's in a coma," Patrick said. "He went into respiratory arrest twice since he's been here. His lungs are full of fluid and his body is shutting down on him. He should have been on special drugs and antibiotics as soon as he developed this. He's also anemic and I want to do a transfusion as soon as possible. Except for the work done on his leg, it appears as though he was mishandled by the doctor who saw him in Da Nang."

As Patrick outlined his plan of attack for treatment, Jenny stared at Billy. He looked like a corpse. The jagged red line of his heartbeat on the monitor was the only indication that he was alive. Her thoughts turned to John, and she felt dizzy and couldn't breathe. Deena, who was standing next to her, noticed and gently took her arm, walking her from the room. Sitting her down on a bench, she pushed Jenny's head between her knees.

"He's going to die!" Jenny cried hysterically. "He's already dead, isn't he? That machine is the only thing keeping him alive."

"No, Jenny," Deena said. "He's not going to die. Not if Dr. McDonald can help it. He's just very, very sick."

"Don't lie to me! I saw him. He's not breathing by himself. He's dead!"

"I'm not lying. But, right now, Billy's lungs can't work by themselves. Since he needs oxygen to live, that machine is helping him breathe until his lungs are better."

"Then why won't he wake up?"

"He can't right now. His body is working hard to fight a virus. It can only do so much."

"But Billy is so strong. Why can't he fight this?"

"If Billy wasn't so strong, he would probably be dead. We don't know how sick Billy was before he got hurt."

"I don't want him to die," Jenny whispered, shivering.

Deena took her hands. "I know, honey. None of us do."

Shortly thereafter, Deena had to leave. Washington was just a short stopping off point on her way to Fort Dix. She promised to keep in touch, then departed.

As each day passed, Mac became more frustrated. He couldn't accept Billy's lack of response to his ministrations. MacDonald had already gone beyond all regular treatments. He took an aggressive approach using the highest dosages of drugs available. But no matter what he did, Billy's condition remained the same.

Marian refused to leave Billy's side. Day after day, she sat in an old, cracked, vinyl chair next to his bed. Rusty tried to persuade her to come home at least at night, but she wouldn't budge.

Jennifer, in the meantime, refused to return to the hospital. It was Barbara who spent the long evenings sitting with her mother, keeping silent vigil. When Marian needed a break during the day, however, it was another woman who sat by his side.

Mary Agnes had become a constant visitor ever since she had been alerted to Billy's whereabouts and his condition. She gave Marian support and provided much needed time for Marian to either get something to eat or take a quick nap or stretch her cramped muscles from the time spent in the chair.

On this particular day, Mary Agnes brought pictures with her. "I just had these pictures of the baby developed and thought I'd bring them along since you haven't seen him yet. He looks just like John, don't you think?" she asked Billy's still form. "I can't believe how fast he's growing. You'd better hurry up and get well. Father Delaney is waiting for you. He says we can wait to have him baptized, but he's going to need his godfather."

Patrick McDonald appeared in the doorway. He hated to intrude, but he needed to check Billy's chart. As he entered the room, Mary Agnes flushed guiltily.

"Good morning," Mac said. "Haven't I seen you here before?"

"I was here yesterday, giving Marian a break. Do you think it's stupid for me to talk to him?"

"No," Mac shook his head. "Many believe that people in comas can still hear. Who knows? Anything is better than nothing."

"Is he going to get well?"

"I try not to think about the alternative."

"For someone who has only been his doctor for a short amount of time, you seem to be very close to Billy and his family."

"Billy and I were in Vietnam together."

"Really? Where were you?"

"Dong Ha."

Mary Agnes flinched when she heard the name. "Perhaps," she said quietly, "you also knew his friend."

"You mean John?"

"Yes."

"I knew him well. He and Billy were two of the best young surgeons I've ever seen. I still can't get over his death. I thought Billy was going to snap about the whole thing."

Mary Agnes got up from her chair and walked to the window, rubbing her arms as if she were cold. She looked out at the sprawling front lawn. The well-manicured grass ended at a wrought iron fence. A plain, ordinary neighborhood carried on its normal, everyday existence on the other side.

With her back to McDonald, her honey-colored hair hung like a curtain. "I miss him so much," she said. "You know, he was due to come home this week."

"Who? Billy?"

"No," she said, turning around, her eyes bright with unshed tears, "my John."

"John was your husband? Oh my dear, I'm so very sorry." Patrick went to her side and took her hands. They were cold and seemed so fragile in his large, warm ones.

"I still can't believe he's gone. It's so unreal to me."

Mac saw the baby pictures lying on the bed. "I remember John said you were expecting. He drove me crazy, asking questions about babies and deliveries; telling me what you were experiencing. He had no one else to talk to before Billy came. Poor guy had nothing in common with the other doctors. He was in a totally different realm—a rookie and a father-to-be. All he wanted was to be with you. It was a godsend when Billy showed up. John wasn't so alone anymore. Of course, if you ask Billy, his being there was the worst thing…"

Mac saw the tears slowly rolling down Mary Agnes' face and couldn't continue. He was silent for many moments then asked, "Is that the baby? May I see those?"

"Of course," Mary Agnes said, brushing at her tears with the back of her hand. She scooped up the pictures and handed them to McDonald. "He's almost three months old now," she said, trying hard to swallow her tears and to compose herself.

As Mac studied the photos, he smiled, "Looks just like his old man. Got that crooked grin and a twinkle in his eye. Bet he's quite a handful," he said, handing back the photos.

"He is. Thank goodness he's finally sleeping through the night. Now there's just one of us who can't sleep." She returned the pictures to her purse and made motions to leave.

Mac glanced at his watch. "If you have a few minutes, I'd like to buy you a cup of coffee. I know the cafeteria food is lousy, but the coffee isn't bad," he said, smiling.

"I could go for some coffee. That would be very nice. I don't have to be at my mother's to pick up the baby for another hour. Thank you." She bent down and kissed Billy's forehead. "Get better," she whispered. "Don't leave me, too."

MAGGIE

The reception desk at Walter Reed was busy with activity when Maggie walked into the hospital. "I'd like to see a patient please," she requested, after waiting several minutes for the harried receptionist.

"Name? Rank?" the woman asked.

"Major William Fox," Maggie replied.

The woman checked her roster. "Major Fox is in a restricted unit of the ICU. Only immediate family is allowed."

Maggie was a little shocked that Billy wasn't in a regular room by now but tried not to show it. She paused for a moment, then continued. "Yes, I know. I just returned from Vietnam and came straight here. How do I get to the ICU?"

"Oh, in that case, take that bank of elevators on the left to the second floor, then follow the signs. You'll have to check in at the reception desk up there."

"Thanks." Maggie walked quickly to the elevators before the woman could say anything more. At the doors to the ICU, Maggie was directed to the family waiting area. Huddled in a corner of the otherwise empty room, were two women and a tall, slender man with greying red hair. They resembled the family in Billy's picture. There was something about the trio, however, that made Maggie's stomach flip over. They looked as though they were grieving.

The trio looked up expectantly when Maggie entered, then looked away. With her heart in her throat, Maggie walked over to the little group. "Are you the Wilson family?" she asked.

"Yes," the man answered, a little startled.

"I'm Maggie Reynolds," she said, putting out her hand. The man took her hand, but looked at her as though he wasn't quite sure why she was talking to him. In fact, all three looked rather perplexed for a moment. Then recognition dawned in the face of the older woman, who Maggie assumed was Marian.

She stood, extending her hand. "You're Billy's friend from Vietnam, aren't you?"

"Yes," Maggie answered.

"Rusty, this is the woman who called to let us know that Billy was hurt."

"Oh, I see. Thank you so much for letting us know."

"How is he?" Maggie asked.

The Wilsons looked at one another, and the young woman sniffed and blinked back tears. At that moment, a large man dressed in scrubs and a lab coat came into the room. All eyes turned toward him. "We got him breathing again, but God only knows for how long this time. I had to drain his lungs for the umpteenth time," the doctor stated. "He's filling up with fluid so fast, I can't keep up with it."

"He's basically drowning, isn't he?" Marian asked her husband.

"I'm afraid so," Rusty said, putting his arms around her and holding her tightly.

"Can't you *do* something, Mac?" Marian asked the doctor.

"I've tried, Marian. Right now, I'm all out of ideas. We're losing him."

"Has anyone called his grandmother?" Maggie asked to the room at large. All eyes now turned to Maggie, as if seeing her for the first time. Mac looked at her questioningly, then at Rusty for an introduction.

"Mac, this is a friend of Billy's from Vietnam," Rusty explained.

"Maggie, this is Dr. Patrick McDonald. He was also in Vietnam with Billy."

"Dr. Fox and I were in Phu Bai together."

"Phu Bai? I didn't know there were any women there."

"Myself and three other nurses were on a special assignment there."

"Oh, well, what's this about Billy's grandmother?"

"She's a healer. Has anyone thought to call her?"

"They don't have a phone," Rusty replied. "We wanted to call to let them know of his condition, but there's no way to get in touch with them except through the mail, which takes too long. Why do you ask?"

"I remember how Billy and I used to discuss different methods of healing and how he said that sometimes for one reason or another, traditional medicines failed. In certain instances, he would look beyond regular healing techniques in order to help someone. Has anyone given that a thought?"

Marian looked at Mac, then at Rusty. "No, Maggie, I don't think anyone here has. Have you?" she asked Mac.

"Look, I'm no medicine man, Marian. I'm a doctor. I don't go waving rattles and dancing around in a circle when my patients are dying."

"I didn't say you should do that, but I remember similar discussions we used to have at home about the same thing. Why didn't we think of that Rusty?"

"Think of what?"

"Alternative methods of healing."

"What do you have in mind?"

Marian frowned. "I don't know. But I seem to recall when I was little and had pneumonia, my mother made me a mustard plaster."

"Billy mentioned those," Maggie stated. "He always said he couldn't understand traditional medicine's treatment of a fever. He said that a fever was the body's natural way of killing bacteria or whatever it was that was making a person ill. He said there was nothing like a good sweat to cure whatever ailed a person, and that a mustard plaster generated heat needed for a specific area. Of course, being too hot was also a problem."

"Mustard plaster?" Mac snorted. "Old folk remedies and wives tales."

"Maybe," Maggie answered. "But I remember we once had a kid brought in with some sort of fever and Billy made him warmer instead of trying to cool him off."

"Did it work?" Mac asked.

"Yes," Maggie replied, "the fever broke, and we sent him back to the field a few days later. Unfortunately, there was no similar remedy for stepping on a land mine. When Billy pronounced him, he said he should have given him drugs and sent him home instead of curing him."

With her words, the room became silent, all eyes looking at Mac. "What? You want me to make Billy a mustard plaster? I've given him every drug in this pharmacy and then some. None of them have worked," Mac said, his face flushed in anger. "And now this *nurse* comes in here and says make him sweat. What kind of a fool do you take me for?"

"I know I'm just a nurse, Doctor, but…"

"Yes, and like children, you should be seen and not heard."

"Now wait a minute, Mac," Rusty said. "Nurses are entitled to their opinions. I always listen to what people have to say, no matter *who* they are or *what* their profession."

"But Rusty, this is ridiculous! If the drugs haven't worked, why would this?"

Rusty looked at Maggie. "Any ideas there?"

"Billy once told me about a man that his grandmother had healed. He was sick for a while before she actually saw him. By that time, his body was so weak that he failed to respond to any herbal remedy that she gave him. She then decided to flood his body with vitamins and minerals to strengthen him before she continued to help him. He eventually got strong enough so that his body began to help heal itself. When his grandmother then added her herbal treatments, he recovered completely."

Rusty nodded his head. "I remember that story. But how can that apply here?"

"Don't you see? Billy's been sick so long that his body's too weak to fight."

"What are you suggesting?"

"Take him off the drugs. They aren't working."

"You mean, let him fight this out on his own? But you just said he was too weak," Rusty commented.

Mac snorted again and threw up his hands.

"Look, he's in a coma. Because of that, he's only physically being given the nutrients he needs to *survive*. He needs to artificially get more nutrients into his body beyond the normal dosages. Give him higher doses of vitamins and minerals in his slurry to help strengthen his body not just keep it alive. That way it can begin to heal itself or at least help to make the drugs more effective. I mean, at this point, it doesn't seem like they're doing any good anyway."

Mac stared at Maggie as though she had lost her mind. "I can't believe that I'm listening to this garbage. I've got a young friend and colleague swirling the drain, and you want to halt his regular treatment and do some sort of unorthodox, quack remedy instead?"

"I wouldn't necessarily call it quack and it can't hurt to try," Marian commented.

Mac stared at her incredulous. "I can't believe what I'm hearing! You think it's okay?"

"For a very short period of time, maybe," Rusty added. "Nothing else has worked so far."

"What if his fever returns?"

"Let him sweat," Rusty said. "In fact, we make him warmer."

"But, Rusty, we can't do that."

"We can for a short amount of time, as long as he doesn't get too hot. Face it Mac, the longer he's in a coma and on the respirator, the more complications we may encounter down the road if he survives."

"Are you willing to take responsibility for this…treatment? I don't want a lawsuit on my hands when, not if, he dies."

"Mac, he's been in a coma for almost a week and is just wasting away. The drugs aren't working. You keep shoving needles into his lungs and draining them. At this point, it can't hurt. Can it?"

Mac shook his head, looking at them as if they had lost their minds. "So now, you want me to treat him like a…friggin' guinea pig?" he spat out. When no one answered, he said, "I'll have to think long and hard about this. We'll talk again later. Right now, I have other patients that I need to see. Patients that *may* live." Giving Maggie a disgusted look, he strode from the room.

All eyes were again trained on Maggie. She hesitated, then asked rather meekly. "May I see him?"

"Of course," Marian replied, and taking Maggie by the arm, walked her into the ICU. At first, Maggie thought they were in the wrong room. She focused her eyes on Billy's swollen, unfamiliar face. Not only was it distorted by the ventilator hose in his throat and the tube taped into his nostril, but it was also bloated out of proportion with edema. She watched his chest rise and fall mechanically and wanted to cry.

Brushing a stray strand of hair from Billy's forehead with her fingertips, she caressed his cheek. Then picking up Billy's lifeless hand, she pressed his fingers to her lips. "Has he been like this since he arrived?"

Marian nodded her head sadly. "I'm afraid so."

Maggie looked at the monitor by the bed, noting the flashing lights and numbers that Marian always tried to ignore. "I thought he would be on the road to recovery by now. When I was sent home early, I came straight here. I was so happy that I was being sent to Walter Reed to make up that last month of active duty. I was hoping that I could see him before I had to report for duty tomorrow morning. I had no idea he would be in this condition." Maggie paused. "By the way, did you say Billy's doctor is Patrick McDonald?"

"Yes, why?"

"Oh great, he's the doctor that I'm to report to. I don't think I made a very good impression on my new boss. In fact, I think I've just gotten myself off on the wrong foot."

"Don't worry about Patrick. He's just very concerned about Billy. We all are. People aren't always at their best when someone they care for is very ill or in trouble."

"I know. But I should have kept my mouth shut. It's just that Billy's last doctor almost killed him, and I didn't want to see him being pushed aside again."

"There's one thing I am certain of, Maggie. Patrick McDonald is *not* going to push Billy aside. He may not like what you proposed, but if he thinks it may help, you can be sure, he'll try it."

"I just hope it's not too late," Maggie said, her eyes once again on Billy. The sight of his face made her bite her lip. She closed her eyes tightly to keep from crying. Marian Wilson didn't need to have her weeping at Billy's bedside. She had enough problems.

Then taking a deep breath, Maggie gave herself a mental shake and turned her attention back to Marian. "It's funny," she commented, "I feel as though I've known you and your family a long time. Billy spoke about you constantly, and we shared letters from home. It gave us something normal to talk about."

"It must have been very hard for you being over there," Marian said. "There are times when I can't stand to hear the name of that horrid place."

"I know what you mean. I try to pretend I wasn't there, but unfortunately, I can't. Vietnam stole a huge part of me that I'll never get back. I just hope it doesn't take any more."

Two days later, after much consultation and debate, with the exception of an IV of saline and the respirator, Mac took Billy off all drugs for the weekend. Instead, he was given extreme doses of vitamins and minerals and nutrients in his feeding tube slurry.

When Maggie finished her shift on Friday, she spent the remainder of her time off in the ICU with Marian, heaping blankets on Billy. Maggie told Marian about how she met Billy, their time together in Vietnam, Mike, and his death. By the end of the weekend, the two women felt as if they had known one another for a long time. They had become closer than some people who have been together for a lifetime.

As Maggie was leaving to go back on duty, Marian said optimistically, "Despite the fact that he had no drugs, he didn't get any worse."

Maggie shook her head. "But he got no better, either."

"You know it won't happen overnight."

"I know. I guess I was expecting a miracle. I thought we'd do this, and he'd snap out of the coma."

"You, of all people, know that things don't work that way."

"I know, but we're fighting against time, Marian," Maggie fretted. "How much longer can he stay in a coma, on the respirator and feeding tube? Every day he remains unconscious is another day closer to slipping away. I just can't bear the thought. Now I know how Deena felt when she lied to the army about her brother. Desperate people do desperate things."

"Did she ever find out what happened to him?"

"Her parents got a letter a week before she went home. He had been injured and captured. Then, he was taken to a prison camp where he was kept for over a year until he passed away. If he hadn't died, they'd never have known. It's so sad. There are still many who don't know and live each day wondering. At least I know for sure that Mike is gone, no matter how painful."

Marian went to Maggie, and the two women clung to each other. "Thank you for being here Maggie, and for all you have done." She gave Maggie a piercing look and said, "You must care for him very much."

Maggie lowered her eyes. "Yes," she said so softly that Marian could hardly hear her. "But I also feel so guilty."

"Why?"

"It seems as though I'm being unfaithful. God, Marian, despite all our problems, I loved Mike and miss him terribly. Yet, he hasn't been gone six months, and here I am worrying and caring about Billy. I'm so confused."

"Love is a funny thing, Maggie. You shouldn't feel guilty because of it. It surfaces when you least expect it and also disappears at odd times, too. Just because you feel something for Billy doesn't mean you're a horrible or unfaithful person or that you didn't love Mike or miss him. It simply means you care about someone. The human being has a huge capacity to love. It's just unfortunate many people either go through life without someone to love or afraid to love."

"I know," Maggie said. "These past few months have been awful. I don't know what I'd have done without Billy. He understood. Now I have no one."

"Yes, you do," Marian smiled. "You have me," she said, hugging Maggie again.

"Thank you, Marian, for everything, especially for listening."

BILLY

It was like being in a thick fog. Everything was out of focus and distorted. He heard disjointed voices that murmured nonsense. Gray shapes moved and flowed around him. But he was too far away to see what they were, and the voices still made no sense. The only thing that remained constant was the pain.

On top of the pain, something heavy pressed down on his chest. The feeling wouldn't go away. Even though the voices and shapes came and went, the heaviness remained. When it finally lifted, the shapes slowly began to take form.

At first, his eyes seemed glued shut. When he finally forced them open, it was quiet and the light dim. He was propped in a bed with metal rails and someone's head rested down near his hand. Curious, he stretched out his stiff, swollen fingers and touched the dark hair. It was silky soft. He lightly stroked the hair, liking how it felt against his fingers. He wondered why the head was on his bed, but it was too much of an effort to think.

The head lifted and a face stared at him. She looked familiar. After a moment, he realized it was Marian. What is she doing here? How did she get to Vietnam, and why is she sitting by my bed, he wondered?

Quietly, she began talking to him, though there was an undertone of excitement about her. But he was so tired, that he closed his eyes, and everything faded away. The next time he awoke, Marian was still beside him. He didn't know how long he had been asleep. It could have been days or minutes. He tried to speak to her, but his throat wouldn't work.

"Don't try to talk," she said, holding his hand.

But he needed to know where he was and why Marian was with him. His leg felt as if it was on fire, and he wanted to ask about that as well. But something was in his throat, hindering his speech. He became agitated and put his hand up to his face, trying to remove whatever was blocking his mouth.

"No, Billy," Marian said, pulling his hand away. "Rest." She patted his hand. "I'm here and I won't leave. Everything is going to be fine."

That seemed to satisfy him, and he closed his eyes and slept. Time had no meaning. It was like a very weird, hazy dream where people came and went. He could only watch and listen—a frustrated, silent observer.

During this dream, Mac appeared and said, "I'm taking you off completely today. You're breathing just fine now." He reached toward Billy and began doing something to his face. Billy felt as though he was suffocating and clawed at Mac. Marian hurried to his side and stilled his hands, talking to him quietly.

"Thanks, Marian. Doctors always make the worst patients," Mac smiled. "So, how are you feeling?" he asked, turning back to Billy.

Billy's throat was raw. He tried to say, 'confused,' but nothing came out but a hoarse whisper.

"You've been on the respirator almost two weeks, I'm afraid. But don't worry, you'll be as good as new in no time. I'll be back later to check on you. He's all yours, Marian," Mac said, then left.

"It's good to see your pretty eyes again," Marian smiled. "We've missed you."

Billy focused on his surroundings and croaked, "Where?"

Marian glanced around the room. "I guess when you were here before, you didn't spend much time in the rooms. You're back at Walter Reed."

"Reed?"

"They flew you here from Da Nang. Do you remember getting hurt?"

Billy closed his eyes. At first, all he remembered was the constant rain and packing boxes. He vaguely remembered the CO of the camp and being sick with a fever. He then focused on the fire in his leg and thought hard. Finally, an old woman swam into his memory followed by some sort of blast and… blood—his blood.

"My…God! My…leg!" He grabbed at the covers, pulling the blanket and sheet away.

"Hey, I don't think you want to flash me, kiddo," Marian smiled, gently tugging the covers back over Billy's legs.

"But…my…leg!" He panicked and grabbed at the covers again, weakly trying to push Marian's hands away. "Have…to…see! Grenade! Blood! My…hand…covered!"

"Calm down, Billy," Marian said firmly. "Yes, your leg was badly hurt, but it's still there. Right now, it's all bandaged up. You may need a little help walking for a while, but Dr. Mac assured us it will be fine and dandy real soon. And so will you. I promise."

Each day, Billy got stronger. He was able to speak more and more until he was stringing small sentences together. His voice was still very hoarse, but every day saw an improvement. Lines of IVs and drugs still ran into his arms; but, one by one, they were being disconnected. The confusion was finally going away, and Billy was up to date on what was happening and why.

One thing bothered him. Jennifer would not come to visit. "Why won't… she come?" he asked Barbara.

"She's having a hard time dealing with the fact that you were so sick. She was here the day you arrived, and you didn't look too hot. All she could think of was John, and she was sure we were going to lose you as well."

"But…I'm better. Do I look…bad?"

Barbara stepped away from the bed and cocked her head to the left and right. "Hmm, let's just say you won't be winning any beauty contests in the near future," she laughed.

"Thanks."

"Don't worry, she'll be here soon. I've been refusing to tell her how you are and I won't bring you her letters. I told her she had to deliver them herself."

The next evening, the door to Billy's room opened a crack and a freckled face peered in. Billy squinted at the door and cleared his throat. "Come in. I'm… decent." The rest of Jennifer followed her freckles into the room.

"Hello, Papa Fox," she said, her hands and back pressed tightly against the door.

"There's…my girl," he reached his hand out toward her, but when she refused to budge, he asked, "gonna stand…there? Not…contagious."

Slowly she walked to the bed and studied him. His face was still swollen and a bit gray. He had deep, dark circles under his eyes, a small plastic hose stuck in both nostrils, and one IV attached to his arm. But he was alive and awake. That was all that mattered.

"Do I…pass?" he asked, reaching for her hand.

She clasped his fingers and bit her lip. "I guess," she whispered.

"Missed you…Jenny Wren."

Jennifer looked down at her shoes and mumbled. "I missed you, too. But I just couldn't!"

"I know," Billy said, squeezing her fingers. The muscles of her face contorted, and Billy could tell what an effort it was for her to keep from crying.

Finally with a coughing sob, she collapsed onto the bed and threw her arms around him. "Oh Billy!" she cried into his neck. "I was so scared. I thought you were dead like John, and I couldn't bear it! I'm sorry. I know I should have been here sooner. Everyone else was. Barbara said that you'd think I didn't love you. But I do, I really do! Please don't be mad at me."

"S'okay…baby," Billy said, patting her back. "I understand."

"You're not mad at me?"

"Not mad."

Hearing the commotion inside, Marian opened the door slightly and peeked into the room. "Is everything okay in here?" she asked.

"Fine," Billy said, his arms still around Jennifer. "Come in. Have lots…to talk about."

Half an hour later, Jennifer and Marian were preparing to leave, when the door opened again. Maggie, still dressed in her uniform, came into the room. "I didn't know there was a party going on in here. Is that kind of behavior allowed in this hospital?"

"Only for today," Jennifer smiled.

"I'm glad to see you finally got your butt in here," Maggie said. "Someone I know was worried that when he finally got around to taking a shower, he wouldn't have any soap or shampoo."

Jennifer giggled. "I promised I would bring him some stuff tomorrow. That way, he can stop smelling like a dirty, sweaty, wet dog."

"Wet dog?" Billy grinned. "Get out!"

"All right! I'm leaving."

"Be back tomorrow?" Billy asked.

"I promise."

"Soap?"

"With soap." Jennifer hugged him one last time, then the two Wilson women departed, leaving Maggie alone with Billy.

"Hello, Major Fox," Maggie said, taking Billy's hand. "How are you today?"

"Okay now."

"Good, I'm glad she finally made her move. I was getting worried."

"Me too. But…so tired."

"You'd think with all the sleep you had, you'd be wide awake and rarin' to go."

Billy started to laugh but coughed instead.

"Just like a man," Maggie continued. "They think if a little of something is good, a lot is better."

"Couldn't get enough…of you," Billy commented hoarsely, squeezing her fingers.

Maggie blushed and refrained from comment.

Billy continued, "How was…your day? Busy?"

"It wasn't Phu Bai, but it wasn't the Shady Rest Nursing Home, either."

"Still scared of your…new boss?"

"More in awe than scared. He's a very good doctor. He kind of reminds me of another boss I had," she said, smiling. "With Dr. Mac I just happened to get off on the wrong foot."

"Sounds familiar," Billy grinned. "Size fives…got you in trouble, again."

Maggie looked down at her feet, then put her hands on her hips. "Well, these size fives came in handy when someone I know was in the drain."

Billy put his hands up in mock defense and cleared his throat. "Not complaining. Mac said you knew…your shit. From him…that's praise."

"Hmm, that's good to know," Maggie said. "If he likes me, maybe he'll keep me around a while, so that I can watch over you."

"I hope," Billy said, yawning. "Can't stay awake. Morphine taking…me down."

"I just came by to tuck you in, anyway," Maggie said and kissed his forehead.

"Maggie?"

"Yes?"

"Do I really smell…bad?"

"Only when the wind blows," she laughed. "Good night, Major. See you in the morning."

"Night."

The next morning, Mary Agnes arrived. "Welcome back," she smiled. "You had us all very worried."

Billy picked at the blanket. "How are you?"

"Surviving," she said. "Some days are worse than others. The baby keeps me busy."

"Bet he's…getting big."

"He's growing like a weed. In fact, I just happen to have a few pictures with me. Would you like to see your godchild?" She reached into her purse and drew out some photos.

"Miss my glasses," he mumbled, squinting at the snapshots. "Marian is gonna…try to find an old pair…at home." He studied the photos for several minutes then handed them back, struggling to keep his composure.

"He looks just like John, doesn't he?" Mary Agnes asked.

Billy nodded, turning his head away. He put his hand up over his eyes and tried to force away the tears. Mary Agnes laid her hand on his arm and a moment later, he clasped her fingers.

"So sorry, Mare. I relive that day…in my dreams. Will haunt me till I die."

"Tell me about it."

He wiped at his eyes. "Can't."

"Please, Billy. I need to know. Dr. Mac wanted to tell me, but I'd rather hear it from you."

"You'll hate me," he whispered.

"No, Billy. I won't hate you."

He began slowly, stumbling over his words, trying to explain what the camp and each day were like. It all came rushing back—the shelling, the ruptured spleen, insisting John take cover, and finally the last horrifying blast.

"You see…it was my fault."

"No, it wasn't," Mary Agnes said sadly. "You have to stop thinking that. You were being a good friend. Had he not been hit; he would have been safe in a bunker."

Billy shook his head. "Miss him."

"So do I. Some days I don't know how I make it. But the baby keeps me sane. It's as if God gave John back to me in a different form. It helps when I think of it that way."

"Can't wait to see him. But…I feel terrible. I don't have a gift…for him yet."

"Getting well will be the best present he could possibly have. Now hurry up and get out of here, so that we can get this poor heathen baptized."

"Heathen? Must take after…me," Billy smiled.

"Yes, he does," Mary Agnes smiled back, squeezing his hand.

Mac stopped in daily to check on Billy's progress. He would save Billy for the end of his shift, then stay and visit.

Billy told him how things were in Phu Bai, and the condition the hospital was in when he got there. "It was a mess. We worked like dogs to clean things up."

"Joey," Mac smiled. "What a kid! I wonder what he's doing now. He was thinking of med school or something in the medical field, when he finally got out of the army, wasn't he?"

Billy turned his head away, avoiding Mac's eyes.

"What happened?" Mac asked instinctively.

"He was hit from the side, a through and through at the base of the skull. Kid never had a chance," Billy said bitterly. "All I could do was watch him die."

"Son of a bitch," Mac said, getting up from his chair and walking to the window. He stood there a long time. Finally, he reached into his back pocket and pulled out a handkerchief. He wiped at his eyes and blew his nose, then went back to his chair, refusing to look at Billy. The two men then spoke of other things and never mentioned Joey again.

With each passing day, Maggie got more complacent. She enjoyed this new life she was living. She got to see Billy daily and the Wilson family was great. They insisted that she stay with them over the holidays and on the weekends that she wasn't working. Marian provided much needed friendship and treated Maggie like a younger sister.

The time she spent with the girls was enjoyable as well. Rusty, when he was at home, had a quiet sense of humor that reminded Maggie of Billy. He was easy to talk to and never made Maggie feel inferior.

At Walter Reed, Patrick MacDonald was a good boss and doctor. Maggie's fear and awe of him evaporated, and she began to enjoy working with such a talented and intelligent man. But all that was to end.

During the second week of January, Mac received papers announcing Maggie's transfer to an Army hospital in Maryland. "Compared to this place," Mac said, as he gave her the news, "Fort George Meade is going to be boring to say the least. I can't for the life of me figure out why they are sending you there. I wish there was something that I could do to change this," Mac said in a state of agitation. "We really need you here. You're an asset to this hospital."

"Thank you, Doctor," Maggie said, trying to hide her disappointment. "I really liked being here. I hate to go."

"And I know one patient in particular who's really going to miss you, especially in the upcoming weeks."

"What do you mean?"

"The burn specialist I requested is going to be starting skin grafts on Billy's leg next week. From past experience, I know that's not going to be pleasant. It would have been nice if you were here to help take his mind off the pain."

"Does he know?"

"No. I was going to tell him today. I may as well hit him with all the bad stuff in one shot."

"I guess," Maggie replied.

"Well, try to buck up. At least you're only going a short distance. It could be worse; you could be going to California instead."

"You're right."

When she stopped to see Billy later that day, he had already been given the news. "We knew this wouldn't last," he said lightly, taking her hand. "It's a wonder they had you here at all. Deena is already at her third location."

"Will you be all right?"

"Me? I'll be fine," he said, clearing his throat. "What's a skin graft or two for a tough Apache like me? I just want to get this crap over with. Get back to real life," he smiled. "Although, I'm kind of getting used to this."

"Being a patient?" Maggie asked.

"Sure. No work, three squares a day, pretty nurses to cheer me up. It doesn't get much better than this," he said.

"At least I'm leaving you a little better off than the last time I said goodbye."

"Did you say goodbye?" he grinned. "I must have missed it. Not too sure you said hello, either."

"Come to think of it, I guess I didn't."

"I think that makes us even," Billy smiled.

"Well, behave yourself."

"How can I misbehave when I'm lying flat on my back in bed?"

Maggie grinned. "I can think of a *few* ways."

"I don't know Reynolds, you keep talking that way, I might set off this heart monitor."

She kissed him lightly on the lips. "I don't want to hear any bad reports, you hear."

"Yes, ma'am."

"As you can see," McDonald explained a couple of weeks later, "the majority of the damage was done to the calf and the surrounding tissues and ligaments of the knee. Thanks to those heavy boots you were wearing, you managed to keep your toes. Had it not been the wet season, and you had lighter weight footwear on, you may have lost some toes or your foot. Fortunately, your hamstrings didn't get hit too hard. And except for that one big gash in the front of your quad, most of the shrapnel tears in those areas were small enough to be sutured."

Billy looked on in horror as Mac unwrapped his leg, describing in detail all the procedures that had been done so far. A highly regarded burn specialist had been brought in to perform several skin grafts on the larger gashes and both he and Mac were very pleased.

Pleased, Billy thought. It wasn't *their* fucking leg that looked like it had been through a meat grinder.

"There's no reason in hell why you can't go back to doing surgery. With physical therapy and exercise, you'll hardly know there was anything wrong."

Billy stared at Mac. Was he kidding? He couldn't believe what he was seeing and hearing. He looked with disgust at the still angry, red flesh of his right leg. The leg that had once propelled him over hundreds of hurdles and ran endless miles, was now withered—a mass of grafts and healing wounds. The left leg didn't look much better, except there were no grafts, only healing sites, where an artery and slivers of skin had been taken and a few small shrapnel tears had been sutured. Both legs were severely shrunken from atrophy, and he highly doubted that they would ever hold his weight again. What was the matter with these guys? Couldn't they see there was no chance in hell he'd ever be able to do surgery again—let alone walk?

"And see," McDonald continued, "the incision where the artery was taken is also healing nicely. You're lucky you had a specialist in Da Nang."

"Yes, I was very lucky," Billy grimaced, looking at the red line that snaked down the inner side of his left leg.

Mac must have missed the sarcasm for he continued to plan Billy's recovery. "I know you won't be able to do surgery right away, since you won't be able to stand for long periods of time. But I'm going to see what I can do about those last months of surgical residency. I know you'll have to put in the time. But right now, since surgery is out, we'll see if we can make some of what you did in Asia count," Mac said, rewrapping the thick pressure bandages around Billy's leg from ankle to thigh.

Good, Billy thought, closing his eyes. Cover that thing up.

"I'll let you know what the Brass say about the residency."

"Fine," Billy said without enthusiasm. "Whatever you say." In his head, he thought, you stupid fucking bastard, there's no way I'll ever finish any kind of residency. You're dreaming.

"I'm going to send a PT up here today to start you on some exercises you can do in bed. Then starting tomorrow, I want you out of bed a little bit each day. The PT can help with that as well. You have got to start moving and get those legs strong again. I'll have them bring you up a walker. That will give you more stability than crutches at first." He pulled the sheet back over Billy's legs and patted his shoulder. "You really are doing great. I'll see you tomorrow."

"Sure, Mac."

Billy stared out the window. For two weeks, he had done nothing but lay in this bed. Each subsequent surgery was more painful than the first. The specialist had taken a tool that looked like a combination razor/vegetable peeler to his good thigh and, even once or twice to his back, peeled up layer upon layer of skin. After an open wound was debrided and flooded with antiseptics, the doctor then sutured the harvested skin over the wound, wrapped it in bandages, crossed his fingers, and hoped for the best.

Billy thought he could handle pain, but this had been intense. It was too painful to make conversation or even be civil. He had given Jenny a tongue lashing just for bumping his bed by accident. After that, he had requested no visitors—none, period.

Rusty stopped by occasionally to talk to Patrick McDonald and would stick his head in the door. But most days, Billy spent the time either sleeping in a drug induced haze or laying on his side, gazing blankly out the window in an effort to ignore the never-ending pain.

As promised, Mac brought Billy a walker and helped him to stand. Billy had been in bed too long and was so wasted away that even with the aid of Mac and a Physical Therapist, he could only manage a few seconds on his feet.

Dizzy and nauseous with pain, Billy sank back onto the bed, his blood pounding in his ears. By the end of the week though, with the PT's help and encouragement, he slowly struggled from the bed to the chair across the room, his teeth clenched in pain. When he finally collapsed into it, weak and exhausted, he was bathed in sweat.

A few days later, Mac called the Wilsons, telling them he felt they should resume their visits. "Ignore him when he tells you to leave," Mac warned. "He's very depressed. I'm trying to pretend everything's fine, but it's getting harder and harder to do."

"How is he?" Marian asked.

"He hardly talks to me anymore. He drags himself to a chair in the ward and sits there all day. He talks to no one, picks at his meals, and hasn't touched any of the books you sent. If he does talk to the nurses, it's to chew them out for something. He's not exactly making points on the floor."

"We'll come," she said, and from then on, again became a constant fixture at Walter Reed. At first, she tried to talk to Billy. But after getting no response, she sat quietly beside him, occasionally reading magazines or books or at least pretending. She left the material by his bed at night hoping to interest him in something. By morning, however, she found Billy the same, the books and magazines untouched. It was discouraging.

MAGGIE

Maggie called several times a week to check on Billy. "He's the same," Marian would say. "He sits in that darn chair and stares out the window. Mac is frustrated, but there's nothing he can do to get Billy up and moving. I'm failing as well."

"If I can get a pass for this weekend, maybe I can get through to him," Maggie said.

A few days later, Marian met her in the hall. "Any improvement?" Maggie asked.

Marian shook her head sadly. "None, in fact, a nurse left him in a wheelchair after she brought him from therapy the other day, and he just stayed there. He hasn't used the walker since. If no one forces him to move, he doesn't. He refused to talk to the psychologist on staff and when Mac tried to give him an antidepressant, Billy threw it across the room."

When they got to the ward, Marian asked, "Would you like me to wait out here?"

"If you wouldn't mind, Marian. Thanks." Wolf whistles and cat calls followed Maggie as she entered. Patients called out to her from all over the room, asking her to stop and visit. Although she smiled and waved at them, her eyes sought out a particular patient sitting at the end of the room. He was propped up in a wheelchair facing the window, his eyes dull and unfocused.

Maggie was shocked. His once glossy hair was unkempt and dirty. The edema was gone, leaving Billy's pallid skin pulled taut over his cheekbones, his hands skeletal in his lap.

"Don't they feed you in this place?" she asked, pulling up a chair.

A flicker of recognition passed in front of his eyes, then his face closed up, and he went back to the window, dismissing her.

"Gonna sit there forever?" she asked him.

He grunted in reply.

Maggie glanced around the room looking at the other patients. "Hmph, some of these guys don't even *have* legs. But I don't see anyone else moping in this room. They're going on with their lives as best they can."

For a moment, Billy stared at her. "Are they really? Why don't you talk to *them,* then? Go and find out how they really feel."

"You know what I mean. You're very lucky and you know it."

As if to himself he muttered, "Yeah. I'm so fuckin' lucky."

"You should be ashamed of yourself."

"And you should go back to Maryland."

"Leaving you here to waste away? Is that what you want?"

He shrugged. "I want to be left alone."

"Why? Will you get off your butt any quicker?"

He gave a humorless laugh. "Off my ass? Don't you get it? I'll never get off my ass."

"You won't if you don't try. What happened to that tough Apache? I thought you had guts. What would Marcus Aurelius say?"

"Fuck Marcus Aurelius," Billy growled.

"I can't. He's dead."

"So am I."

"No," Maggie said, gritting her teeth. "You aren't dead, but you may as well be." She leaned her hands on his chair and got into his face. "You listen to me, Billy Fox. There is nothing you can't do. You can get up out of that chair and walk out of this hospital. You can perform surgery again. You could even *fuck* Marcus Aurelius if he was alive. All you have to do is get up. Are you going to feel sorry for yourself forever?"

"What if I do? What business is it of yours?"

"You're hurting your family. It hurts to see their pain."

"So leave," he snarled.

"And let you rot?"

"What's the use?"

"You're right," she glared. "What's the use? Once a cripple, always a cripple. Well, I have an idea. How about I bring you some whiskey to drown yourself in? Or better yet, why don't I take you back to the Rez and park your chair at the edge of that same cliff where your old man took a flying leap? That way you can follow in his footsteps completely. Is that what you want?"

He refused to look at her; his jaw clenched, his face a stony mask.

"Look at me," she hissed, slamming her hands down on the arm rests of the chair. "Everyone who cares about you is trying so hard to get you moving. Goddamn it, I'll move you. I'll even watch while you jump. You just tell me when. I'll take you," she said, jumping up and storming from the room.

Out in the hall, she began to sob, her hand pressed tightly against her mouth.

"My God! What happened?" Marian asked, steering her down the hall away from the ward.

"Oh Marian," she cried. "It was awful. I said some horrible things. I was just so damned angry. I couldn't stand to see him like that."

"None of us can, dear," Marian sighed. "He was depressed after John died, but not like this. I think it's everything. John, his injury, what he saw over there. It's just too much. Maybe you said something to shake him up."

"I shook him up all right. And now, I can't even stay and repair the damage."

"What do you mean? I thought you were staying for the weekend?"

"I can't," she shook her head. "I couldn't get a pass. I came up in an ambulance with a transfer patient and in a few minutes, I have to turn around and go right back."

"Oh no, that's terrible! We were looking forward to visiting with you."

"I was too. On top of that, the army threw me another curve. They're sending me to Fort Stewart in Savannah next month. They're allowing me a short leave to go and see my dad before that occurs," she sighed. "I hate this! Why couldn't they let me stay in Maryland? Damn it!"

"Will we see you again before you go?"

"I'd like to stop back before I have to report. Just to say goodbye and to see him one last time. If he'll see me, that is."

Marian hugged her. "Be careful, Maggie. Thank you for coming. I hope things have improved when you come back."

"If he gets worse, let me know."

When she returned to Walter Reed later that month, she went straight up to the ward, her stomach a mass of knots. The wolf whistles were the same, although the patients looked different. Maggie scanned the room for Billy, but he wasn't there.

She stopped a nurse in the hall. "Can you tell me where I can find Billy Fox?"

"*Major* Fox, you mean?" the nurse corrected and looked at her watch. "It's not my day to watch him," she muttered. "He could be anywhere right now. Check ward three," she pointed.

"Thanks," Maggie said, heading in that direction. It was a large room with about twenty beds. At one end, a wheelchair was parked in front of a double-sized window. The occupant had a long, greasy ponytail. Oh God, Maggie thought, her tirade hadn't done any good and she felt let down. She couldn't decide whether she should even bother speaking to him. As it was, he didn't know she was in the room. *No, I can't abandon him. He means too much to me. He wouldn't desert me*, she thought.

She squared her shoulders and walked purposely toward the wheelchair. With less than ten feet to go, she felt a hand heavy on her shoulder. A voice whispered, slightly out of breath, "Don't, Maggie. He has no legs. I just got him out of bed for the first time yesterday."

The voice was familiar, so was the hand. Turning, she locked eyes with Billy.

He smiled and shook his head. "Those size fives were about to do some major damage. Hell, I haven't moved that fast in weeks," he said, still slightly out of breath.

"Oh my God! Thanks for stopping me."

She inspected him from head to toe. He was wearing Walter Reed scrubs and a white lab coat. Although he was still extremely thin, his hair was clean, and his eyes were no longer lifeless. The right leg of his drawstring pants had been cut away to make room for the bandages. He held a chart in one hand and a crutch was propped under the arm of the other. A stethoscope dangled from around his neck.

"What are you doing?" she asked.

"Rounds. This is my ward. Why don't you go and talk to Roger while I finish here?" He motioned to the man in the wheelchair. "He could use a pretty little nurse to cheer him up."

Afterward, they went into a lounge. At this time of day, the room was empty, the television playing for no one.

"How long have you been back to work?" Maggie questioned.

"Just this week, Mac thought I should ease back into things by checking on a few patients. The doc who originally had this ward had never seen active duty. The guys kind of resented him and gave him a hard time."

"What about you? Do they give you a hard time?"

"Me? Hell no, I'm one of them. I resent the bastard, too. But even if they did have a problem, I doubt they'd bother me since I'm armed," he said, raising his crutch.

"Oh, I see," she laughed. "What else are you doing to stay out of trouble?"

"I have PT and pulmonary therapy three times a week."

"Pulmonary therapy?"

"My lungs are pretty messed up," he shrugged. "Thank God I quit smoking when I did."

"When did you get up?"

Billy touched Maggie's cheek, running his finger slowly down the side of her face and under her chin. "A couple of weeks ago after some little girl gave me a mental kick in the ass and read me the riot act."

"I was pretty nasty, wasn't I?"

"It wasn't what you said that bothered me as much as the fact that Marian actually yelled at me for making you cry. I felt guilty for pushing you to do something so hurtful."

Maggie took his hands. "I didn't know what else to say, and I knew I had to get you out of that chair, or you'd be there for the rest of your life."

"I'm just glad I caught you before you ripped into private Walters. I saw the look on your face; you were girded for battle, baby."

"I was, wasn't I," she smiled. "Will you be able to finish your residency now?"

"Right now, there's no way I can do any surgery. But since I did so much of it in Vietnam, Mac's going to try and make that count for something. That way I can finish out those last months doing general practice stuff."

"What about your inactive duty?"

"Mac's going to push for me to stay here. He wants to keep his eyes on me."

"I hope he can do that."

"So do I. Although what I'm doing now isn't exactly what I had in mind when I became a doctor. It's hard to go from what I was doing in Phu Bai to checking charts and removing sutures."

"I think I'd be bored out of my mind."

"I am," he said, smiling.

Maggie flushed under the intensity of his gaze. "I guess you heard that I'm going to be a Southern Belle."

"Yes, Marian was lamenting that fact again just the other day. She misses you."

"I miss her, too. She's a lovely woman, and I think we could have been good friends. I'm glad that I got the chance to meet the whole family. You're lucky. They're really great."

"I know. I've never met such genuine people. I don't know what I would have done without them…or you."

Maggie looked down at the floor, her hands still in his. Finally, she looked up and said, "I guess I'd better hit the road."

"You're leaving? You just got here."

"I know. But I'm taking the ambulance back to Meade."

"You mean you won't be able to see the family before you head down south?"

"I can't. I was lucky I had enough time to see you."

"They're going to be so disappointed."

"I'm sorry. It couldn't be helped. I'm disappointed, too."

"When do you leave for Georgia?"

"Tomorrow morning."

"Wow, that's cutting things pretty close."

"I know. But at least I got the chance to see you to make sure you were back on your feet. I don't think you'll be needing any more pep talks."

"I don't know," he said, bringing her hand to his lips and kissing her knuckles. "We can all use a pep talk now and then." He leaned on the crutch, shifting his weight.

"I guess. Well, uh…good luck with everything."

"And with you." He looked at her hand. "We keep doing this."

"What?"

"Saying goodbye."

"Personally, I prefer the hellos," Maggie said softly. "As violent as they can be."

Billy kissed the palm of her hand, then curled her fingers inward before releasing her.

Forcing a smile, Maggie looked at the clock on the wall, then backed away. "I really need to be going. I can't afford to miss my ride."

"Can I walk you down?"

"I'd rather you didn't. This is too hard as it is," she said, her voice wavering.

"I know. Well, then, *Adios*."

Maggie nodded. "Yes," she whispered, "*Adios*." Then turning, walked from the room.

CAL

Night after night, Cal hunched over the bar. He couldn't remember how many whiskeys he drank, but it was never enough. When Cal first came back from Vietnam, he was assigned to Fort Bliss for a year of inactive duty. Being at an Army base was difficult. It was too close to being in Vietnam. Many of his patients were transferred from Asia and the injuries and conversations were the same.

Cal tried to tune out the talk and all the things he had been running from since he had returned to the United States. He kept to himself and stayed aloof from his colleagues. He found instead a few decent whores that didn't need to make small talk in order to entertain him. They gave him relief from at least one basic urge.

He spent most of his waking free time in a dark corner of the officer's club. Alcohol was cheap and plentiful, and Cal did his best to drown out the horrific images, sounds and smells that surfaced when he wasn't careful.

The Le family haunted his sleep. He'd lay on his bunk at night afraid to close his eyes to scenes that kept replaying in his head—to scenes that would not let him forget.

At Bliss, Cal could always tell where a person had been stationed. The ones who saw little action, always talked the most. He once gave an exam to a colonel whose chest was so decorated with ribbons and medals that he looked like a colorful Christmas tree. The colonel talked of how hard it had been in 'Nam'; his stories bordered on myth.

"Where were you?" Cal asked.

"I was in Saigon," the colonel answered importantly.

"Oh really?" Cal's anger was almost visible beneath his forced smile. "I was in Saigon for a while until I was transferred to Pleiku in the southern end of the Central Highlands. I'm sure you're familiar with that area." He leaned back against the counter in the exam room, his arms folded across his chest, and studied the colonel.

The man had the decency to look uncomfortable under Cal's scrutiny. "I see," the colonel said, picking up his cap. "Well, I'd best be on my way, good talking to you." And with that, he was gone.

One weekend, Cal took a three day leave to Denver. He jumped from bar to bar and was in the process of heading back to his hotel when he inadvertently walked into a nasty antiwar demonstration. Spying his field jacket, the demonstrators taunted Cal. As he continued down the street, he tried to ignore the remarks being thrown at his retreating back.

A reporter jumped in front of him, shoving a microphone into his face. "Tell us. Were you in Vietnam?" Cal pushed the microphone away and continued to walk. Sticking to his side, the reporter asked, "Did you kill any women and children?" Cal glared at him, this time, pushing the microphone away roughly.

"Do you feel the United States belongs in Vietnam?" the reporter persisted.

By now, the demonstrators were following him as well and the taunting increased. People started chanting, "Baby Killer! Baby Killer! Murderer!"

Cal grabbed the reporter's microphone and addressed the mob. "Were any of *you* in Vietnam? Did any one of *you* kill anyone? You all talk of peace and harmony and have your sit-ins and love-ins. You all make me sick. You hide behind your signs and crucify those of us who did as their country asked or were forced to do through the draft. I'm a doctor. I went to Vietnam voluntarily because there were men, women and children who needed my help. I didn't ask if it was right or wrong. I tended the wounded, American as well as Vietnamese, just as I would tend to you if you needed me."

Cal raised his voice and began to shout at the crowd. "How many of *you* ran to Canada or claimed to be conscientious objectors? Some of you just protest for the sake of protest. You have no idea what is *really* happening in Vietnam except through the biased eyes of people like *him*," he pointed a finger at the reporter.

"So many of the media and Hollywood sit on their asses and scream indignation at the killin' and the carnage. They stir everyone up. How many women and children were killed in other wars? Do you really think no civilians were killed during World War I and II? What about Korea? Those men killed as well. How many of us came home treated as the 'pariah of society'—to demonstrations, derision and ridicule! Thanks to jackasses like all of you!" he yelled.

The reporter and the crowd backed away. "You should be locked up," the reporter said.

"And you can all go to hell. As for me, I was already there!" He tossed the microphone into the street and pushed his way through the crowd.

He got lost several times on his return to the hotel. When he finally made it back, the bar in the lounge was still open. He went in, ordered himself a double and downed it quickly. He ordered several more and didn't stop drinking, until he couldn't see straight. He staggered up to his room and fell onto the bed. The room was spinning, and Cal could hear the crowd in his head screaming, "Baby Killer! Baby Killer! Murderer!"

In his mind, he saw the Le children scattered at his feet in the dust. He smelled the pungent odor of their blood and fecal matter and heard the buzzing of insects as they gorged on the ripped flesh. Cal could taste the vomit as he lurched to the bathroom. He sat on the floor, his head resting on the toilet and sobbed. Oh God, he thought. Help me!

After his stint at Ft. Bliss, Cal returned to Flagstaff. He moved back in with his parents but had a hard time rejoining civilian life. His parents persisted in trying to cajole him into starting a practice. But for Cal, just the thought was too much of an effort. The only things that seemed to motivate Cal anymore was a bottle of whiskey and the bare flesh of a woman.

Much to his parent's dismay, Cal would disappear for days at a time, finding solace in one woman after another. But after a while, even that couldn't satisfy his aching soul. It wasn't until a friend of Cal's father steered him to Phoenix that things slowly began to change.

Dennis O'Shea had gone to school with Cal's father as an undergrad and the two remained in touch. Dennis had served in Korea and also Vietnam during the early part of the war. A general surgeon, he was the chief of staff and also a fledgling administrator at St. Mark's Hospital in Phoenix.

The small satellite hospital was in need of some major upgrades and expansions to keep up with the demands of the growing city. Dennis and the board felt that the place to start would be to enlarge the small emergency department, and also add a specialized trauma unit. They wanted to put St. Mark's on the map and offer what no hospital in the area had ever offered before—a center capable of servicing trauma patients from all over Arizona, perhaps beyond.

It was a monumental task, and one Dennis couldn't do alone. He was in the market for young talented surgeons and doctors who were used to battle practices. Thanks to his experiences in both Korea and Vietnam, O'Shea knew there were procedures that would be beneficial if brought from the field of battle to a hospital setting. By incorporating these procedures, he could revolutionize the way emergencies were treated.

At a chance meeting, O'Shea outlined his plan of attack to Cal's father. "Perhaps Cal would like to come on board. He could even have his own practice if he wanted. There's a medical arts building adjacent to St. Mark's. If Cal wants an office, it's there for the taking," O'Shea stated.

"I've been sending out feelers to a few other buddies who were with me in Korea and Vietnam. I need several good general surgeons as well as cardiologists, orthopedic surgeons, OB/GYNs, burn specialists, and pediatricians. We'll need to be able to handle any kind of emergency, not just your everyday mishap, heart attack or automobile accident but emergencies on a grand scale."

"How's it going so far? Do you have anyone?" Mr. Lewis asked.

"Yes, a friend of mine from Vietnam is a pediatrician. He's young and very enthusiastic about the idea. I also have a lead on a very good orthopedic specialist. If Cal would join us, that would be a start in the cardiology department."

Mr. Lewis sighed. "I don't know, Denny. Cal has been different since Vietnam. Things happened over there that he won't talk about. He's been fighting a severe depression and can't set his mind to anything. I suggested seeing a psychiatrist, but he flatly refused."

"Let's face it, we're all different since the war. Maybe being among others who had similar experiences will help him to overcome the depression as well as keep him busy."

"I'll send him to see you. He needs to get out of this funk. Your proposal could be just the thing he needs."

The meeting with Dennis had gone well. Although it wasn't exactly what Cal had originally planned, the idea of a trauma unit was intriguing. It was also somewhat exciting to be in at the beginning. Dennis was a great guy, and his ideas were interesting and on the cutting edge of medicine.

Working at a hospital seemed less like work to Cal than starting up his own practice. Besides, if he wanted to open an office in the future, Dennis assured him that there were places available nearby.

Three months after their initial meeting, Cal moved to Phoenix and started his new job. He found that being busy had its benefits. Most days, he came home exhausted. Being dead on his feet helped him to sleep a little better.

After only one week on staff, Cal felt that he was fitting in just fine. The other doctors that Dennis had lined up were all easy going. Fortunately for Cal, although most of the staff doctors were veterans, no one seemed very interested in recounting war stories or talking about their time in Vietnam.

The trauma center was starting to take shape; and, with the suggestions and recommendations from the gathering staff, Dennis was able to form a unit to serve the purposes of the center. There was only one doctor still to come from the original group. He came highly recommended by not one but two of Dennis' old mates from Korea. To Cal, this last guy sounded rather intimidating. He had very impressive credentials. If he came on board, he'd be second in command to Dennis. Cal just hoped that he wouldn't be a jerk or a stick in the mud. But only time would tell.

BILLY

"I think it would be a great experience," Mac said to Billy as they sat in Mac's office. "I've known Dennis for over twenty years, so has Rusty. He's a terrific guy and has a lot on the ball. This trauma center of his sounds like something that's right up your alley. I know one thing, you sure as hell won't be bored."

"But will my leg hold up to something so strenuous?"

"Sure, especially now that you're wearing the brace. If you're going to be on your feet for long periods, the brace will stabilize and strengthen the leg. Haven't you already been doing surgery here?"

"Yes, but not for twelve to fourteen hours at a clip."

"I've explained your situation to Dennis. He knows where you stand, so to speak. Don't worry. He's willing to let you ease into things gradually. He's not going to expect twelve-to-fifteen-hour shifts from you the first week. If I didn't have confidence in you, I wouldn't have suggested the idea."

"But…what about the army?"

"Look," Mac said, "you've done your time—active and inactive, which was a major hurdle. And you're now on the inactive reserve list. You're not only a full-fledged licensed attending, but you're also Board certified, and you have your FACS in Critical Care Surgery as well. Except for a few weeks a year, the Army has ceased to own you. And that was your choice."

"I know, but…"

"Come on kid, this is what you want, isn't it? It's trauma *and* surgery. It's everything you know and love. It's what you have been working toward since you became a doctor. Right?"

Billy sighed. "Yes, you're right, I guess."

"See? Who's got you covered?"

"You know Mac, you keep doing this to me."

"What?"

"Getting me into situations I would never have gotten into on my own. I'm not sure whether you're handing me a blessing or a curse."

"Well, you won't know until you try it, will you?" Mac smiled. "Besides, haven't you been saying how you need to locate your wayward wife? If she's somewhere in the old neighborhood, you'll have better luck finding her if you're in the vicinity as well. Phoenix is just a spit away from Tempe. How much closer can you get?"

"But I thought you were going to stay here forever?" Jennifer wailed. "What do you mean you're going home? I thought this *was* your home?"

"Geez guys, we knew this day would come. This is a great opportunity. I can't pass it up."

"But," said Marian, her eyes unnaturally bright, "I thought Rusty offered you a partnership. Are you going to turn that down?"

Billy's shoulders sagged as he glanced at Rusty. "Please don't think I'm being ungrateful. The offer of the partnership was overwhelming, and believe me, I was very tempted to take it. But it wouldn't have worked."

"Why not?" Barbara asked.

"I hate to keep reminding you all that I'm not a wealthy white boy from the neighborhood. Rusty, how many patients have refused treatment from me because of my race? Only yesterday, Mrs. Bryant wouldn't let me remove her sutures and do a post-op exam because she didn't want 'one of those red-skinned people touching her.' She went on at great length, very loudly, I might add, about not understanding why you would want to have someone like me in your office."

"Not everyone's like her," Rusty said quietly from his place by the window.

"I know. But face it, in Phoenix, I wouldn't be as conspicuous. Besides, I also need to address the problem of Jessie. As much as we all like to pretend she doesn't exist, I have to find her and either make a go of being married or get a divorce. I've been avoiding that issue for far too long," he said, shaking his head, as he paced back and forth in front of the piano.

From her seat on the sofa, Marian said, "Will you please sit down, you're making me a nervous wreck."

Billy smiled weakly and sat down next to her. He took her hand and looked at her with imploring eyes. "All that other stuff aside, in Phoenix, I'll be able to do something for my people which was the major reason I became a doctor. Staying here would be a cop out. I can't do it in good conscience. Please understand."

"We do," Marian said, squeezing his fingers. "But we'll hate to lose you."

"I hate to go," he smiled.

"We'll never see you again!" Jenny cried.

"If you believe that, you don't know me very well. How could I just walk out of your lives after all we've been through together? We're a family. I'm not leaving here forever. I'll come and visit. And you'll know where I am. I'll be near your Uncle Joe. I'll even leave some clothes here if you want. God knows, I don't know what I'm going to do with all the stuff I've accumulated."

"But it won't be the same. You'll be different!"

Billy thought for a minute before continuing. "Things can never stay the same, Jenny Wren. If they did, life would be boring. Look, even if I took the partnership, I wouldn't live here anymore."

"Why not?"

"Because I am a grown man, who has a job. I would want my own place."

"That's silly."

He shook his head. "No, it's not. If I was truly your brother, that's what would happen—would probably *have* happened even before this. Things change. Aren't you considering colleges? What if you wanted to go somewhere out of the neighborhood like say…Kentucky. You wouldn't be here either, right? What if Barbara had chosen Temple?"

Jenny sighed. "I get it. I just don't want things to change."

"But they will, they have to. Do you realize that with the exception of the time I spent in Vietnam, I've been here eleven years. Eleven years! This was only to be for a year, remember?"

"Time flies when you're having fun," Jenny pouted.

The Volkswagen Fastback was ready to go. Billy couldn't believe all that he had packed into the little car and still had room leftover for himself. The car had been an excellent acquisition. When he had gotten back on his feet, there had been no way that he could manage the Harley. The motorcycle had been too heavy to handle with a weak leg. It was also old and getting to be unreliable. Still, selling it had hurt. But it was leaving the Wilson family that tore him apart.

There had been many tears and promises to call and write. However, Billy knew that it would be a long time before he saw his *Anglo* family again. When he waved goodbye, he felt as alone as when he first arrived in Georgetown.

He had not known then what to expect and now, he was going back into unknown waters.

Before completing the journey to Phoenix, Billy spent some time with his grandparents. They were doing well and were thrilled to see him. Aside from getting older, they hadn't changed and were still as active as they had always been.

However, there were missing loved ones. Dog Too was gone as well as Sombrita. Billy found their deaths extremely painful. Since Vietnam, it had gotten very hard for him to control his emotions.

In the barn, he paused before Sombrita's empty stall; her old, worn halter hung forlornly on a nail in the wall. Conchita nickered, and he went to her. With his head against her neck, he held on to her warmth, a lump in his throat. Memories of Vietnam, John's death, and his own close call haunted him.

He released the chain on her stall, went in, and gathered Conchita's now gray mane into his hands. He used the strength of his arms to clumsily pull himself onto her back. For the first time since he was hurt, he felt free. He rode outside and into the hills.

A week later, Billy sat across from Dennis O'Shea and regarded the man with interest. In his early fifties, Dennis was slightly built with thick black hair that was graying at the temples. His azure blue eyes were surrounded by laugh lines and lashes that a woman would have envied.

After an interview that lasted close to two hours, Dennis concluded, "You're going to be just what we need. I've been told you thrive on hard work, are level-headed, know your way around an OR, and are no stranger to all types of emergencies."

"Geez Dennis, don't believe everything you hear. I think you'd better reserve your judgment until you've given me a fair trial."

"I trust both Rusty and Mac implicitly. If they say you're good, you're good."

"I just hope my leg is up for the long hours," Billy said.

"Don't worry," O'Shea replied. "You'll ease into them gradually. Haven't you been putting in long hours at Walter Reed?"

"Yes," Billy said, giving O'Shea a long, sober look. "But there's also the fact that I'm still pretty green. You know, Dennis, it's only been a little over two years since I finished my residency. And I only recently finished all the requirements for my fellowship."

"Patrick has already given me a very thorough verbal resume of all your qualifications and Rusty concurred. I know you were green when you were promoted. You had the responsibility of running a field hospital foisted on you. From what I hear, you did a great job. Better than those who had years of experience."

Billy opened his mouth to speak, but Dennis interrupted, "I know, I know, that's not quite the same as what we'll be doing here, but you're already used to major, pardon the pun, responsibilities. On top of that, you speak fluent Spanish. That's a huge plus since a number of our patients are Hispanic. I also don't think Rusty would have offered you a partnership if he didn't think you were capable."

"God, you know everything!" Billy exclaimed. "But is all that enough?"

"I need a second in command that I can depend on. We'll give you a couple months trial to get your feet wet and settle in. If, after that, you still feel overwhelmed or it isn't working out for you physically, we'll go to plan B."

"Which is?" Billy asked.

"I don't know, but I'll think of something," Dennis chuckled. "Come on, let me give you a tour of the hospital."

As they walked through the hospital complex, O'Shea explained his plans for the construction and arrangement of the center. When they approached the ER, the doors swung open from the other side and a man emerged.

"Oh Cal, would you come over here? There's someone I want you to meet."

Billy and Cal stared at one another for a moment, then grins broke out on their faces. "I'll be a son of a bitch," Cal exclaimed, slapping Billy hard on the back. "If it isn't the Fox. Great to see you, buddy."

Billy winced and rubbed at his shoulder. "Some things never change. How the hell are you?"

"Just swell," Cal smiled. "Are *you* the wunderkind we've been hearin' so much about?"

"Wunderkind? I don't know about that," Billy answered.

"You gonna join us?"

"I was. But now that you showed up, I'm not so sure," Billy replied.

"I see you two have already met," Dennis commented, dryly.

"Billy and I were roommates for four years at ASU as undergrads," Cal stated.

"Well, well. Small world, isn't it?" O'Shea said. Then, as if an idea struck him, he said, "Hey Cal, are you free right now?"

"I just clocked out. Why?"

"Maybe you could finish showing Billy around."

"Sure, Dennis."

"I was also going to tell him about the 'Squirrel Cage.' I know they have some vacant apartments over there. Some are even furnished."

"When we're done here, I'll take him over there and show him my place."

"Great, I would really appreciate it. I have another meeting in half an hour and I didn't want to give Billy the short shrift."

"Not a problem. Come on, Fox," Cal said. "You're gonna love this place. The other guys are cool, too. You won't be makin' a mistake."

"I'll see you tomorrow morning. How does ten sound?" Dennis said to Billy.

"Great, Dennis. Thanks."

As Billy and Cal continued down the hall into the ER, Billy asked, "The 'Squirrel Cage?'"

"That's what we call the apartment building across from the hospital. Many of the residents work at St. Mark's and we're all pretty nuts. The only problem is that the walls are so thin, you can hear the guy next door fart."

"I see. Well, I guess I'll fit in since I'm pretty nuts myself," Billy stated.

After seeing all there was to see at the hospital, the two men went across the street. Cal had a sunny apartment on the third floor of the newly renovated building. Located directly across the street from the hospital, it was convenient, clean, and affordable.

He and Billy sat at the kitchen table shooting the breeze, discussing the trauma center and the twists life takes. Through it all, Cal poured glass after glass of whiskey for himself. Billy watched as Cal's personality ran the gamut. He went from being his usual happy-go-lucky self to being overly loud and boisterous to belligerent.

"Hey Hound, how many of those are you gonna chug? I just got here today. I don't feel like mopping up vomit already."

"I'll drink as much as I want, if you don't mind."

Billy shrugged. "Suit yourself."

Cal's eyes narrowed. "What are you sayin,' Fox? That I'm drunk?"

"You're getting there. I just don't want you to get sick, too."

"Mind your own fuckin' business. I'll get drunk and sick if I want," Cal snarled.

Billy shrugged again.

"You know, you really piss me off," Cal said, getting into Billy's face.

"I'm just concerned."

"Bullshit!"

"Think what you want, then," Billy said.

"I think you're a pain in the ass."

"Maybe I am. But you look like you're on a mission."

"A mission? A mission for what?"

"To forget."

"What d'ya mean?"

"The way you're hitting that bottle, you remind me of myself when I was at ASU."

"Tell me something," Cal growled. "You must have been in Vietnam since Dennis is hiring you."

"Yes," Billy replied.

"Where were you? Saigon? Da Nang? One of the ships? You had to be in a fairly large hospital to have gotten enough experience for Dennis."

"I was in none of those places."

"So where were you?"

"What difference does it make?"

"I want to know."

"If you really want to know, I was in Tam Quan, Dong Ha and Phu Bai."

"Field units or evacs?"

"Field units and aid station."

"Ever kill anyone?"

"Not intentionally," Billy smiled slightly. "But who knows, it's possible I made a mess of somebody's insides in a hurry to save their ass."

Cal didn't return the smile. "That's not what I meant. Did you ever *kill* anyone?" Cal sounded desperate and a little crazy. As he shakily poured himself yet another whiskey, the amber liquid slopped over the edge of the glass onto the table.

Billy pushed the glass away. "Come on, Cal, that's enough. How about some coffee?" He stood and went to the counter.

Cal jumped to his feet as well. "Fuckin' bastard! Still tellin' me what to do," he yelled, shoving Billy hard in the chest. "You always thought you were so smart." The shove caught Billy off balance and sent him toppling backward to the floor in an ungainly heap.

When Billy failed to get to his feet, Cal sneered into his face. "What a pussy! Come on, stand up," he commanded, shaking his clenched fist in the air. "I'm not too lazy to hit you anymore. In fact, I could probably beat the shit out of you now."

He gave Billy's leg a vicious kick that lifted Billy's pant leg up, exposing the metal and plastic of the brace. "Get up! What the fuck's wrong with you?"

"Cal, don't," Billy groaned and grabbed his leg. Please, for God's sake, don't kick me again."

Something in Billy's voice made Cal stop and take notice. He looked at his friend curled on the floor. There was a flash of silver and white coming from Billy's leg. He knelt down and roughly pulled at Billy's pant leg, exposing more of the brace as well as the shiny, bright red, scar tissue.

"Jesus!" Cal exclaimed, jerking away. "What the hell happened to you?"

The two men stared at each other as Billy awkwardly sat up and pulled his trouser leg down. "I came between a homemade VC grenade thrown by an old woman and a small group of GIs in a bunker. In kicking it back at her, I probably killed her and at the same time blew my leg to shit. Had to learn how to walk all over again." He tried to say it matter-of-factly, but his voice shook. "I don't think I'll be winning any more races," he said, leaning back against the cabinets, his arms wrapped around his knees.

"Oh Christ!" Cal put his head into his hands. After several moments, he raised his tear-streaked face. "I killed five civilians. Two old people and three little kids. Most days, I want to kill myself as well," he sobbed. "They were VC and it was dark. They had fixed bayonets! Christ! What was I supposed to do? They would have killed us!"

Billy closed his eyes and reached out, resting his hand on Cal's shoulder, the lump once again in his throat.

"I've never cried in my life, Billy. But now, all of a sudden, I can't stop. I keep drinkin', hopin' it'll all go away."

"It doesn't though, does it?" Billy questioned. When Cal shook his head, Billy continued. "Some nights, I wake up in a cold sweat. I see the explosion, feel the pain. In some dreams, a masked doctor is cutting off my leg. When

I look closely, the doctor doing the amputation is me. Other nights, I dream about John."

"John? Your buddy in DC?"

"Yes, he was killed over there."

"Killed? What happened?"

"We were in Dong Ha. He got hit by in-coming while running to a bunker."

"Oh my God," Cal said, wiping his nose with the back of his hand. He stood and hauled Billy to his feet, then reached for the glass on the table.

Billy got there first. "Don't, Cal. It doesn't do any good. It'll only make you feel like shit later."

"Haven't you ever caved?"

"I've come damn close. But since that one summer in Tempe, I haven't tied one on again."

"You aren't turnin' into one of those tea totalin' fanatics, are ya?"

Billy smiled and shook his head. "No, I just see you going the same route I went, and I don't want that to happen to you."

"How else can I forget?"

"I don't think you can. I think you have to live with it, just like any other thing that comes along, good or bad."

"How?"

"I honestly don't know. But I do know one thing, neither alcohol nor drugs will make it go away. They only make things worse. Trust me. Now, how about that coffee?"

Billy took the position. The job sounded interesting and in a good location. Another plus was the availability of a furnished corner apartment at the 'Squirrel Cage'. Located down the hall from Cal, it was a corner apartment, full of windows and sparsely but tastefully appointed. Billy added some colorful Indian blankets and pottery, built and filled some shelves with books, and it became home for the small amount of time he spent there.

He also began working for the Phoenix Health Department two days a month, caring for indigent Indians and Hispanics in the area. Then, eventually opened a small office for his own practice in the Medical Arts building.

The majority of his time, however, was spent at the hospital in the rapidly emerging trauma center. Plans were being drawn for a new wing that would eventually house this center, becoming an entity that would overlap and go beyond the workings of the regular emergency department.

At the moment though, the trauma unit and ER were one and the same. Billy and Dennis reorganized the ER's structure and formed teams that consisted of doctors in all different areas of expertise.

Everything was going well. With the exception of missing the Wilson family, Billy's life fell into a regular pattern. Now, there was only one more problem to address. For that, he looked up an old running mate from his ASU cross country days.

Dylan Begay was a Navajo who had set up a law practice in Phoenix. Billy hired him to try to locate Jessie. It was a tremendous undertaking, and one Billy couldn't tackle on his own. With Dylan on the job, Billy could now give his thoughts completely to his new and interesting position without the addition of guilt to slow him down.

MAGGIE

"Dennis, this isn't going to work. We only have a total of twelve nurses on the trauma unit staff and one or two of them are worthless," Billy said, as he sat in O'Shea's office.

"Worthless? What do you mean? They're all qualified RNs. What's the problem?"

"Let me rephrase that. On the whole, they're decent nurses. In a regular med/surg ward, they're fine. But, since you want this new unit to be run like a field hospital or evac, they don't have enough experience to deal with the major traumas you're envisioning. For that, we'll need some nurses who have also seen active duty."

"Oh, I see what you mean. I'm sorry. I never gave that much thought. I guess I was too busy sorting out the doctor situation and figured that the nurses we already had on staff would work."

"Well, they won't. Look Dennis, if you want this idea to fly, we need to have the very best, most experienced nursing staff as well. How about some guys? I worked with a lot of very good male nurses in Vietnam and even in DC. I'd hate to go back to Walter Reed to get that."

"Hang on, don't get your jock in a bind. Now that I'm aware of the problem, I'll get you some nurses. Maybe I can put an advertisement in the Vet's newsletter as well as some trade publications."

"Good," Billy nodded, his face mock serious. "You'd better get off your lazy ass and do *something* around here. I can't do *everything* you know."

After a moment, the two men began to chuckle. Dennis finally sobered and said, "Not a bad impersonation of a hospital administrator, Fox. Maybe someday, you'll be as feared as I am. Although, I hear you already do a pretty good job in the intimidation department."

"Me? Intimidating?"

"Yes, I hear you tell people off right and left in the OR."

"Since when did telling it like it is become intimidation?"

"Is that what you call telling someone they have 'shit for brains'?"

"If you're talking about Connie, I don't call that intimidation, I call it telling the truth."

"Oh, hell, I thought you insulted her or something."

"Man, she is one employee I hope that we can replace, and soon. She scares the hell out of me. The way she passed a loaded knife handle the other day, I thought I was going to be the next patient."

"Well, maybe if you hadn't turned her down for a roll in the hay, she wouldn't be out for blood. It seems to me that you're very picky."

Billy snorted. "Can we please keep my sex life or lack thereof out of this conversation? All you need to know is that we need some good, qualified nurses. And you'd better get them for me before I mutiny."

"Yes, sir," Dennis said, saluting. "I'll see what I can do."

Maggie couldn't stop sweating. Phoenix in July was hotter than she had ever imagined. In the taxi, she blotted her forehead with a tissue as she checked the papers in her hands. She was to interview with a doctor named Dennis O'Shea, who was one of the administrators at the hospital. She had already spoken to him by phone, and he seemed a likable guy. His idea of a trauma center utilizing field hospital practices sounded intriguing.

Recently, Maggie had been considering moving back to New York City, until she had read an advertisement in a nursing trade journal. The ad had been for a trauma center nurse in Phoenix. The center itself, as well as the location, appealed to her. It shouldn't be boring and would be in a completely different setting. It might be just the move she needed.

After all the things she had seen and done in Vietnam, the small hospital in Watkins Glen was like eating baby food after a steak. She was overqualified and underpaid. The only thing that kept her sane was the fact that she was only several miles from her father and brothers.

But even that didn't help. Maggie was haunted by Vietnam. She had recurring dreams of Mike's death and the many horrors she had witnessed. Those experiences set her apart from everyone, including her own family. This made her lonely—lonelier than she had ever been in her life.

Although she had her dad and brothers, they were guys and weren't exactly girlfriend material. Her mom was gone, and Mike's family ignored her. She had no close friends and the only girls she talked to were right out of nurse's training. She felt ancient and had nothing in common with these fresh-faced young women. Maggie hoped this position in Phoenix would get her involved with people to whom she could relate. If not, she would go crazy.

When she arrived at the hospital, Maggie went to the admission's desk and asked for Dr. O'Shea. Several minutes later, a gentleman in his early fifties came toward her. He reminded her of an older, slighter version of Mike. His curly black hair was graying at the temples and his eyes were a deep blue with a bit of devil shining in them.

"Maggie Reynolds? I'm Dennis O'Shea. I hope you had a good trip."

"Yes, it was fine. No loss of luggage and the cab ride wasn't a treacherous endeavor."

Dennis chuckled. "Well, we're definitely not New York City. So, what do you think of Phoenix?"

"Hot," Maggie laughed, fanning herself. "Is it always this blistering?"

"Well, it is July," Dennis smiled. "We get a bit of a respite in the winter months. The temperature may drop into the low sixties or seventies."

"Wow! I guess that's something to look forward to. I don't know what I was expecting. Everyone said it was hot, but that it was a dry heat."

"I know. I'm originally from Boston, and I've heard that remark more times than I can count. But dry heat is still heat, isn't it?" Dennis commented, as they walked down the hall.

Dennis stopped at a door that looked like it led to a broom closet, and ushered Maggie into a very small office. Unlike many administrator's offices, this one felt right. It was shabby but appealing, the chairs old but comfortable. There were books and papers scattered all over, but Dennis seemed to know where everything was located.

O'Shea described the trauma center in greater detail and explained what the staff was trying to accomplish. "The surgeon heading the department is dissatisfied with the caliber of our nursing personnel. He recently informed me that I had better ship in some qualified nurses soon or he was shipping out."

"Are all the medical personnel veterans?"

"Most of the doctors are and so are a few of the techs, but the nursing staff is lacking. That's where I made a large tactical error. I'm hoping you'll help us out. The only problem I can foresee is that you're overqualified and won't agree to the measly salary we're offering. Since this is a new venture, and we don't yet have the financial support from the community, we can't offer you what a larger, metropolitan hospital would offer."

"At this point, Doctor, salary is the least of my concerns."

"And what would be your first priority?"

"I want a job I can look forward to every day. I'm a widow, I have no pets and no close friends. I'm available to start at a moment's notice, but I want a job that will keep me occupied. I thrive on responsibility, and I love what I do. If I can have that, I'll be the best darn nurse you ever had."

"What's the catch?"

"There's really no catch, but as you can see on my resume, I have worked in many different types of hospitals. I realize that not every doctor, nurse, and hospital employee is going to care for patients to the extent that I will. However, I have been in situations that have been intolerable due to the lack of concern and slap dash manner of the medical personnel. I have seen things that would curl, or in your case, straighten your hair," Maggie said, smiling. "If, after I'm here and I feel that there are areas that need improvement, I *will* voice my concerns. I'm not, as a rule, a complainer or a whiner, and I won't be constantly running to you to do that, don't get me wrong. I'm no tattletale. I just want to be proud of my place of employment."

"My head surgeon has the exact same goals. In fact, that's why you're here. When I first arrived at this hospital, there was a lot of room for improvement. We had a small facility and a smaller staff. I have been gradually replacing employees that I felt weren't up to the task. Now that we are enlarging the Emergency Department, we are currently bringing in more educated and experienced personnel. But again, the salaries being offered have, in some instances, been a sticking point."

"Although money is my least concern, I *will* need a salary that will allow me to pay rent and buy food. I'm not a total fool."

"I think that you'll be able to do that, and even put a few pennies away," Dennis said.

"That sounds reasonable. When would I start?"

"The surgeon in charge is requesting a probationary period for all new employees. He wants to work with each nurse individually both in the ER and OR for perhaps one or two days. It will be up to him to decide if the candidate is to be kept on or not. He wants to train each hire personally and refuses to put in all the time and effort to do so for someone he feels won't stick around or is not qualified for the position. All candidates will be paid for their time and will be, if necessary, as in your situation, given a stipend toward lodging and food expenses."

"I see."

"Still interested?"

"Actually, yes, I think that's a great idea. Because while he's assessing me, I can be assessing him. If I don't like what I see, I'll also be better able to make a decision as to whether I want to stay."

"Great! Now, how about a tour of the hospital?"

"I thought you'd never ask."

The hospital was small compared to New York City standards but larger than the small-town hospital where Maggie currently was employed. The layout was simple. The testing labs, ER, and ORs were located in wings on street level. The pharmacy and cafeteria were a level down and more offices and patient rooms were on the upper three floors.

They entered a waiting area that was partially full. A large television sat on a table, occupying one wall and an Admission's desk occupied the center of the room. Chairs lined the walls, and magazines and styrofoam coffee cups littered the small tables in between.

Dennis acknowledged the two women working at the desk and headed toward the double doors on the far end of the room. He pressed a button on the wall and the doors to the ER opened. Stepping out of the way of traffic, Dennis explained, "this is our emergency department. Eventually we'll be breaking ground for the new center that will be located in an adjacent wing. Right now, I'm working on updating some of our antiquated equipment. I'm trying to get the newest, most comprehensive replacements available.

"I've also been researching the feasibility of having a helipad placed on the roof of the building. There are a few hospitals that are now using helicopters to transport critical trauma patients, just as was done in Korea and Vietnam. It's a fascinating idea. I don't know whether it will catch on or not, but it sounds like it has potential. I'm not sure it's something that we'll be able to afford, have the building height for, or actually need; but I'm still considering the possibility. Hopefully, I'll also be able to get us the financial backing we need to make any and all of those purchases."

"What happens if you don't get the money?"

Dennis grimaced. "I don't like to think of that, but we still have the ER as it stands now and, with the money we *do* have at our disposal, I'll still be able to make some important and much needed improvements."

Dennis looked at his watch. "I'll have you wait here for a moment. I'm going to see if someone is available to meet you."

As Dennis walked over to the charge desk located in the center of the ER, Maggie looked around her. The ER was busy. There were at least eight to ten exam rooms surrounding the charge area on three sides. At this moment, they all seemed to be occupied.

Dennis returned moments later. "It appears as though someone used a serrated knife on their fingers instead of a loaf of frozen bread. He's in the process of putting them back together again. I guess I'll take you into the testing areas instead."

Passing through the ER to the furthest side of the room, they went through another set of double doors. As they did so, a man approached from the other direction. "Don't look now, Maggie. Here comes trouble with a capital T," Dennis commented. "I'd like to introduce you to one of our trauma team cardiologists. I hear he breaks hearts left and right, so you'd better be on your guard."

"Oh my God!" Maggie exclaimed. "Cal Lewis!"

"I can't believe my eyes," Cal said, grabbing Maggie and pulling her into a hug. "Maggie Sullivan! What in the hell are you doin' here?"

"Well, I see you two have already met," Dennis stated. "Maggie is an applicant for one of the nursing positions."

"Wow! That's great! I knew Maggie back when I was a lowly med student at Cornell. She was a nurse at New York Hospital."

"Small world isn't it," Dennis said, shaking his head.

"And getting smaller every day," Maggie commented.

Dennis looked again at his watch. "Cal, are you busy right now?"

"No, I'm done for the day."

"Would you mind showing Maggie around a little more? We were on our way to the labs. Unfortunately, I have another interview scheduled in five minutes."

"I'd love to. It will also give us some time to catch up."

"Great! Well then, Maggie, I'll leave you in Cal's capable hands. It was a pleasure meeting you. Let's have you come back tomorrow morning at, shall we say, eight?"

"That would be fine, Doctor. It was a pleasure meeting you as well. I'll see you in the morning."

As Dennis walked away, Cal questioned, "Where are you staying?"

"At the Hacienda Motor Inn near the airport."

"Not my first choice, but it's not too bad for a couple of nights, I suppose. Do you know how long you'll be stayin'?"

"I'm assuming three or four days."

"There's so much I want to show you. I know, I'll start by giving you a tour then takin' you to dinner. You're gonna love it here. It's not a bad place to live." Cal opened the door for her, and they exited the building.

"What about the labs?" Maggie questioned, as Cal walked down the sidewalk.

"Oh them," he shrugged. "They're boring. You can see them any time. I want to show you the good stuff instead. Come on," he said, taking her hand. "I live across the street in this very cool apartment building. We all lovingly call it the 'Squirrel Cage'. But don't let the name fool you. The units were all just recently refurbished, and an adjacent, brand new parking garage was added. I'm sure you'll be able to move right in. There are still a few vacant apartments left. In fact, there are a couple available on my floor."

Cal opened the door that led to the parking garage. In the darkened landing, he pulled her tightly against his chest and kissed her on the lips, catching her off guard.

He grinned, "God! I still can't believe you're here. It's like a miracle, you just showing up like this. Today, I'm the luckiest man in the world."

As the evening unfolded, Maggie did her best to keep attentive. But, with the time difference, and all that she had done that day, she was exhausted and couldn't wait to get back to her hotel room to get some sleep. Tomorrow was going to be another long day, and she wanted to be rested.

But Cal had other plans and didn't seem to notice or care that she was dragging. When she mentioned being tired, he waved it off. "You'll get your second wind, don't worry," was his only comment.

Cal hadn't changed. He was as handsome as ever and, with the exception of putting on some weight, could have passed for a husky version of Robert Redford. His personality hadn't changed, either. It didn't take Maggie long to remember why she hadn't gone any further in their relationship.

He was still self-absorbed, droning on about all his interests and accomplishments. He never once asked Maggie about what was going on in her life, or even gave her a chance to get the conversation back to St. Mark's, and the questions she wanted to ask.

Cal drove her around in his fancy, low-slung sports car, showing her all the sights he felt were important. Then afterward, he took her to an exclusive restaurant for dinner. Maggie knew that with a little bit of encouragement, he would have spent the night instead of just dropping her off at her motel. Maggie hoped that if she took this job, Cal wouldn't make things awkward.

"How were the first two applicants?" Billy asked, as he settled himself into the chair across the desk from Dennis.

"Not bad," Dennis replied, sifting through some papers. "Actually, the first was outstanding. She's a Vietnam vet and has more experience than half of the doctors here. The second doesn't have nearly as much experience but has worked the past several years at a Veteran's hospital."

"How will they be at working with others?"

"The first, I'm not sure. But the second is definitely a team player. That may make up for her lack of experience. Here are their resumes," he said, handing Billy some papers. "Take a look. I wanted to get them to you sooner, but you and I never seem to be available at the same time anymore."

Billy glanced at the resumes in his hand. The first belonged to a girl named Joni. She had graduated with a BS in Nursing only four years ago and was still pretty new to the field. As Dennis said, she didn't have any active-duty experience. She had, however, been working in med/surg at a VA hospital in Tucson for the past three years. She was battle green, but from the contents of her letter and her resume, she did appear to be worth a look.

Billy then turned to the next resume. His breath caught as he saw the name at the top. "This woman, she's the first one you interviewed today? The one with all the experience?"

"Yes, on paper she really seems to know her stuff."

"But…"

"Are you okay?"

"Okay? Uh…I guess."

  A.E. KAYSER

"I told her that you would meet with her tomorrow morning at eight. Is that all right?"

"Eight? Yeah, that's okay."

"The other girl will meet you late the following afternoon. In the meantime, I'm seeing a young fellow and another woman tomorrow. Then another guy and two more women the day after that. I'll let you know what I think as I see them."

"Sure, that's fine."

Dennis looked at Billy. He was still staring at the resume in his hands. His face looked rather pale in the fluorescent lights. "Are you sure you're all right?"

"Huh?"

"Are you all right?"

"Oh, um it's just that I…"

At that moment the phone rang, startling both men. Dennis answered. "Now?" he sighed. "Okay, I'll be right there. Thanks." He hung up the phone and rose. "It figures, I'm on call and they call me. Sorry to cut this short. Let me know what you think of Maggie."

"But Dennis…"

"Sorry Billy, gotta go. Don't forget, eight tomorrow morning. You can use my office if you want. I'll meet up with you later to see how things went." And with that, Dennis left Billy alone with his thoughts.

Maggie took a cab back to the hospital the next morning, despite Cal's wishes to pick her up.

"The doctor will be with you shortly," the receptionist stated, as she walked Maggie to Dennis' office. "He's running a little late this morning. He'll be with you as soon as he finishes his rounds. He told me to get you some coffee while you waited."

"Oh, no thanks. I think I've had my quota of caffeine for the day."

"Is there anything I can get you?"

"No, I'm fine. Thank you."

"Okay. If you change your mind about the coffee, come back out to the desk and I'll get you some."

"Thanks."

Maggie turned her back to the doorway and walked over to the window. She looked at the street scene before her. Definitely *not* New York City, she thought. Did she really want to go back to all that craziness?

She thought about her interview with Dennis, replaying it in her mind. She hoped she hadn't spoken out of turn and thrown her chances for the job. Except for the fact that Cal could pose some awkwardness, the job seemed to be just what she needed, and Dennis seemed like a great person to work for.

This new doctor, however, could make or break the situation. He could be a real jerk and she had worked with plenty of them in the past. In fact, waiting for him made her more apprehensive than her initial meeting with Dennis. She was so engrossed in her thoughts, that she never heard the approach of footsteps.

"I hear you put your size fives into your big mouth again, didn't you?" a man said, as he placed his hand firmly on her shoulder.

Maggie let out a strangled yelp and jumped. The voice sent shock waves through her body, and she twisted around in surprise. Billy stood behind her, a grin on his face. "Hello, Maggie."

"Oh my God! You almost gave me a heart attack!" she said, laying a hand on her chest. She swatted at him with her other hand. "Don't you *ever* do that to me again!"

Billy gently pulled her into a hug, "*Mea culpa* my darling Mighty Mouse. Please forgive me."

Maggie pushed back slightly. "Mighty Mouse, huh? Forgive you, huh? Just like that? You scared the crap out of me!"

"Really? Hmm, maybe I shouldn't be hugging you then," Billy smirked and backed away.

"Oh, you know what I meant," she said.

"Well, it's good to see that our track record for violent hellos still stands."

"Violent? You can say that again. Did you know I was here all this time?"

"I just found out last night. Here," Billy said, motioning her toward a chair, "have a seat. Did Gloria get you some coffee?"

"She asked, but I didn't want any. Good thing too, after being scared like that—caffeine is the last thing I need. So besides scaring me, what are you doing here in Dr. O'Shea's office?"

"I'm here to interview some crazy nurse that Dennis seems to think is the answer to our prayers," he said, taking a seat behind the desk. "I must say, I was rather shocked when Dennis handed me your resume yesterday."

"*You* are the head of the Trauma Center?"

"Not exactly, Dennis is the boss. I'm just technically in charge of surgery. Chief of Surgery/Trauma Center sounds very important but what it really means, I think, is that I get to do Dennis' dirty work."

"And that includes hiring more nurses?"

"Well, he's been pre-screening the applicants. If he feels that they're worth a look, then I take a look."

"And he felt I was worth a look?"

"Yes, and I'd better watch out. I think he feels you could do even *my* job. He was that impressed."

"Are the nurses here that bad?"

"No, but there are one or two that just don't have the experience we need. And in their cases, I'm getting tired of doing surgery alone. Deena, on her worst day, was better than one or two of these chicks."

"How long have you been here?"

"About six months."

Maggie gave him the once over. His long, white lab coat was unbuttoned revealing gray trousers and a white oxford cloth shirt with a buttoned-down collar. A navy and burgundy striped tie completed the outfit.

"You look terrific," Maggie stated. "One hundred percent better than the last time I saw you."

"Thanks, you're looking pretty good yourself."

"How do you feel?"

"Not bad."

"How's the leg?"

"It's holding up."

"Your walking is up for debate since I haven't really seen you do it yet."

"The walking isn't too bad. I've been wearing a brace for support when I'm working. And, if I had the time to work out, the strength would probably improve too. But…" he shrugged.

"What have you been doing since I last saw you?"

"I finally finished my residency under Mac at Reed. Then during my two years of inactive duty, I got my board certification and fellowship credentials."

"How did you end up here?"

"Mac was the one responsible for that. In fact, both he and Rusty know Dennis pretty well. One thing led to another and now I've come full circle, and I'm back where I started."

"I'll bet the Wilsons weren't too happy about that."

"You're right. In fact, Rusty offered me a partnership, but I had to turn it down."

"Why?"

"Come on, Maggie. I really don't belong in DC. I fit in better out here. It's not quite as prejudiced. Although there are still some patients that treat me like an orderly or janitor and refuse to be treated by me."

"Dummies, they don't know what they're turning down."

"Well…"

"So, um, is your wife out here as well?"

"I'm not sure. I have an attorney looking for her. So far, there's been no trace of her either dead or alive."

"You mean you haven't seen her since you came back from Vietnam?"

"No."

"That must be frustrating."

Billy shrugged. "I guess. But there's nothing else I can do. Anyway, enough about me. What have you been doing?"

"I finished out my time in Savannah, then went home to Watkins Glen. I've been there ever since, rotting away in a tiny suburban hospital. I was about ready to go back to New York City when this position caught my attention."

Billy picked up her left hand and looked at it. "And are there any men in your life?"

Maggie looked Billy in the eye. "My father and younger brother live about a mile from me. My other two brothers are within calling distance."

"That's not what I meant."

"I know what you meant. I thought I gave you a straight answer nonetheless."

Billy then questioned, "No dogs or cats?"

"No animals, friends or neighbors—only ghosts."

"Oh those, hell we all have them—some more than others. Do you keep in touch with Deena?"

"We write occasionally. She got her LPN in record time and is now attending a university in her area to get her bachelor's degree."

"Good, I'm glad she's finally official. Maybe when she gets her BS, she might consider coming out here, too."

"You never know. I do know for a fact that she feels as out of place where she's working as I do."

"Out of place?"

"You know, old and out of the loop. We don't fit in with the young or the old. We saw too much and participated in something the younger people don't believe in and the older ones don't understand. And we're alienated because of it."

"Well, you'll fit right in out here. We're all out of the loop. In fact, we're working on creating our own loop with this new trauma center."

"It sounds very interesting. Dennis told me all about your plans and showed me a little bit of the ER."

"What do you think so far?"

"I didn't see enough to make a complete evaluation. The ER as well as the entire hospital is bigger than where I am right now. But that's all I can tell you."

"Fair enough, how about we get you a better perspective? If you're up to it, I'd like to have you spend some time there with me today," he said, standing and heading toward the door.

"Sounds good," Maggie replied.

As they walked, Billy explained, "Right now, we have ten beds, which is kind of on par with other small city hospitals. But up until a few years ago, that's all we needed. Phoenix has been growing rapidly. People are realizing that they actually *like* a dry heat and living in the desert. Now, besides an ever-expanding city population, we are also seeing a growth in tourism as well. Dennis wants and needs to enlarge this area to keep up with all the growth. But until then, we still have ten."

The ER seemed different with Billy by her side. Maggie saw things that she had missed in her first cursory glance. At one end of the room was a huge white board.

Billy pointed to it. "Everything that's important is on that board. It lists the names of the attending doctors, residents, interns, nurses, students and techs who are working the shift. Which team members are on call and so on."

He walked over to the board. "The most important information on here, however, is about the patients. As you can see, all ten rooms are listed. Next to the room number is the patient's name, condition and status. For example, look at room one. It lists the patient: Jones. Condition: broken finger. Status:

patient/x-ray. For the patient in room two under status it lists: awaiting results/ upper GI. That patient will probably be here a while," he commented.

"If a patient goes from being an ER patient and is admitted, it will say admit with a room number, so that their family can find them. If a patient is taken to the OR, that is noted as well. This way, we don't look like idiots. At the bottom of the board are the patients who were here and treated, then DC'd."

"I think that's a great system," Maggie stated. "I wish they would have used something like that in New York City. So many times, we lost track of patients, or they fell through the cracks because we didn't have as detailed a system. But of course, we also had over double the exam rooms."

"All the more reason to cover your butt."

"You're right, as always," she said, and they both laughed.

They spent the day in the ER. Since Billy wasn't on as an attending, they stayed out of the way but oversaw all that went on in the busy area. Billy introduced Maggie to staff members as they were available. For the most part, they seemed friendly.

He also took her into the wings that housed the ORs and the testing areas. Maggie was impressed with the orderliness and cleanliness of the whole hospital. But then again, she remembered how Phu Bai had been run and was not surprised. She thought, this would be a great place to work.

CAL

Billy and Maggie were preparing to exit the ER, when Billy stated, "Tomorrow, be prepared to be on the team. You'll work with me on the daylight shift as if you were on staff. This will give you a better idea about how things are run. Also, I'll have a better idea about whether you have forgotten anything."

"Forgotten anything! Ha!" Maggie said. "What about you? Do you still remember how to handle an emergency?" As they were bantering, the double doors opened, and several staff members were coming back from the OR.

Dressed in scrubs, cap, and booties, Cal was leading the group. "Maggie," he said, pulling her tightly against him and surprising her with a rather long, lingering kiss on the lips. "How did it go today? Fox wasn't too hard on you, was he?" Without releasing Maggie, he turned to Billy and said, "So, what do you think of my lady love from New York City? Not bad, huh?"

Billy stared at Cal and at Maggie who was trying to extricate herself from Cal's grip. "What are you talking about?"

"You know, Maggie Sullivan. The woman I was seein' when I went to Cornell."

Billy looked from Maggie to Cal, and the truth hit him like a freight train. "You?" he said, addressing Maggie. "You're Maggie Sullivan?"

"I was. Back when I worked in New York City. Why?"

"I can't believe I didn't put two and two together," Billy muttered, shaking his head. "Boy, how dumb. All this time and I never knew."

"Never knew? Never knew what?" Maggie questioned.

"Maggie, this is Billy Fox, the guy I was always talkin' to you about. You know, my undergrad roommate. The guy I ran with at ASU. The Indian with the horses? Remember?"

Maggie was dumbfounded. "You?" she said, looking at Billy, her eyes wide.

"Me," Billy said. They stared at one another until Cal broke the silence.

"Is there something wrong?" Cal asked.

"No, it's just that I know Maggie as well.

"What?"

"Yes, we were together for several months in Phu Bai. She was one of my nurses."

"You're kiddin,' right?" It was now Cal's turn to look confused.

"No, I wouldn't kid about something like that. She was an excellent nurse. It's been great to see her again."

"Really? Hmph." Cal was silent a moment then continued. "What're you guys doin' now?"

"I'm taking Maggie over to the Squirrel Cage. As you know, there are a couple of apartments available on our floor. She might be interested in one of the unfurnished ones if she decides to take the position. If she stays, she'll be able to see what's available at a moment's notice. Then, I'm taking her to dinner before driving her back to her motel."

"Cool. Count me in. I'll join you as soon as I get cleaned up. You can buy my dinner as well. I'm sure it's on an account. Dear God, we wouldn't want you spending your own money. Since there is no such thing," Cal said, his face split into a devilish grin.

For Maggie, the rest of the afternoon and the evening that followed were not pleasant. At the Squirrel Cage, she and Billy looked at the two apartments available on the third floor. One was next door to Billy; the other was down the hall near Cal.

As Maggie walked through each apartment, Billy stood back quietly and let her look at both without making any comment. However, once Cal joined them, he began to loudly push for Maggie to take the apartment near his. He criticized the apartment next to Billy, pointing out imaginary faults.

Maggie's patience finally ran out after listening to his tirade for almost ten minutes. "Stop it, Cal. I like this apartment. It's bigger and has two bedrooms without costing more. I love all these windows. It gives a nice view of the area, without all the traffic and the noise that are on your side of the building. Besides, the other apartment is right across the hall from the elevator."

Cal couldn't understand her reasoning. "What's wrong with that? You'll be closer to an exit. Down here, you're away from everything."

"I like the quiet. I don't want to hear that elevator dinging all night."

"But, you'd be near to me."

"It's not like I won't be on the same floor."

Cal made an exasperated noise. He expected her to take the apartment next to him no matter what, then sulked when she refused to change her mind, *if* she decided to stay.

Dinner caused another heated debate. Cal wanted to go to a fancy restaurant located near Scottsdale which was about ten miles away.

"I was going to take her somewhere within walking distance of the hospital and the apartment building," Billy said.

"You mean to one of the local 'dives'? Don't be such a cheapskate," Cal retorted.

"Money isn't the issue. I want to take her wherever she wants to go. Maggie mentioned her interest in a neighborhood place. Somewhere she would eat if she were living here. I'm only doing what she asked."

Maggie quickly interjected, "Yes, Cal. I want to see what's available *if* I should relocate here. I also told Billy that I'd like something that I can't necessarily get back home."

"You mean like dysentery?"

"Don't be silly. I want something Mexican if possible."

"Fine, if that's what you want—cheap, local fare tonight, diarrhea tomorrow. Fox knows all the best places for that," he sneered, crossing his arms against his chest, his face a sour mask.

"You don't have to go," Billy said, grimly.

"Of course I do. Who will look after Maggie if I don't? Your indiscriminate Indian gut can take any kind of crap. Maggie is a delicate lady. She'll need someone to order for her."

"I'm a big girl, Cal," Maggie argued. "I can order for myself."

Cal shook his head. "You're a City Slicker. Until you get your feet wet, I'll take care of you."

"And what if Maggie wants to take care of herself? Since she has been doing that for how many years?" Billy asked rather heatedly.

"Not an option," Cal grinned, putting his arm across Maggie's shoulders and squeezing.

Maggie looked from one man to the other. They were like night and day. Cal blatantly and rather loudly ridiculed Billy and his opinions while Billy said less and less, his jaw clenched in suppressed anger.

By the time they had finally decided on a restaurant and walked there, the day had gone from bad to worse. Just like the previous evening, Cal not only ordered for Maggie, but also monopolized the conversation, never letting either Billy or Maggie say a word.

Afterward, Cal insisted on taking Maggie back to her motel.

"Fine. Take her," Billy said in resignation. "Maggie, I'll pick you up tomorrow morning around five a.m."

"Also not necessary, Fox. I'll get her and take her to breakfast before she has to be at the hospital." When Maggie began to sputter, Cal held up his hand. "I insist!" he said. Then, taking her hand, he pulled her toward his car and helped her inside.

Billy stood with his hands on his hips and watched them. After a moment, he turned and slowly walked toward the elevators. As Cal gunned the engine, Maggie watched Billy enter the elevator and wanted to cry.

Cal was whistling as he entered the doctor's locker room early the next morning. "I feel ten feet tall today."

Billy eyed him as he tied the drawstrings to his scrubs. "What the hell happened to you? You get lucky last night?"

"Seeing Maggie again, after all these years, I just can't believe it. It's the first time since I've been back home that I actually found myself smiling and forgetting about all the shit that went down in 'Nam. I feel like a new man," he said, pounding himself on the chest like Tarzan. "I have a reason to live again."

"Do you think she'll stay? Or did you scare her away?" Billy asked.

"You're such a kidder," Cal said, punching Billy's shoulder with a little more force than necessary. "If I have anything to do with it, she'll be stayin'. You can't imagine how happy I am."

"I can see that," Billy said, rubbing absently at his shoulder.

"Maggie told me about her husband gettin' killed in Vietnam. What a waste," Cal said, shaking his head disgustedly. "But hey, my gain, right?"

"Umm," Billy mumbled.

"Funny, isn't it?" Cal continued.

"What?"

"You knowin' her all that time, and never knowin' she was my Maggie."

"Yeah Lewis. *Your* Maggie! That's funny all right."

"Now that her husband's gone, we can pick up where we left off. What d'ya think?"

"Stranger things *have* happened. You did finally become a doctor, didn't you?"

Cal heard the sarcasm and looked up with a puzzled expression. "Geez Fox, what crawled up your ass and died?"

Billy shook his head. "Don't mind me. I'm just tired and my shift has only begun," he said, tying his shoes and heading for the door. "You did bring Maggie with you, didn't you? She's supposed to be working with me today."

"Of course. She's all breakfasted up and ready to roll. Now don't work her too hard today and don't you dare keep her over. I plan on taking her to dinner tonight, and I don't want her worn out."

"Sure," Billy said. "God knows, you wouldn't want her tired. Not that it would matter. Talk to you later."

"See ya," Cal said, and went back to whistling.

Maggie decided to stay. Despite Cal's urging, she still took the apartment next to Billy as originally planned. Although displeased with her choice, Cal was ecstatic that she was relocating to Phoenix.

It had taken a month, but Maggie was now moved in and settled. During that time, Cal refused to let Billy be alone with her unless they were working. He knew they were just friends but didn't like her being alone with any man—even his best friend. He had his future at stake.

Consequently, during their down time, it seemed that the three of them were always together. They would eat in the cafeteria and, when they weren't on duty, would hit the local eateries. Between he and Billy, they were trying to make Maggie feel at home.

Cal didn't realize how this appeared to an onlooker until he overheard comments made by one of the nurses. "There goes the 'Odd Squad,'" she commented snidely and snickered, as the three of them were leaving the cafeteria together. The name, unfortunately stuck. What could Cal say? There they were—a white woman, a white man, and a token. It just didn't look good.

A couple of days later, he took Billy aside when they were changing clothes. "Fox, we need to talk about the situation with Maggie."

"A situation? What are you talking about?"

"People are calling us the 'Odd Squad.' And spreading rumors about how we are all sleeping together."

"Who's saying this shit?"

"One of the nurses that you're trying to ditch as well as a couple of her friends."

"Sour grapes on their part. Maggie's a good nurse and they're jealous."

"Yeah, well if you weren't always around, maybe they wouldn't be making the ménage à trois comments."

"We work together. What am I supposed to do, ignore her? We're friends, remember?"

"Then stop being friends. You're her boss, nothing more. Besides, you're cramping my style. How can I woo her if you're always around?"

"Is *that* what you're trying to do? I thought you were just trying to run her life?"

"Run her life?"

"Yeah, you're constantly telling her when and where to eat, what to do in her spare time, and I guess now, who to be friends with. God, the poor woman can't even sneeze without you telling her how, when, and where."

"Bullshit! I'm looking after her. Which is more than I can say for you."

"I will say this again. We are *friends*. Unless I see her doing something that may be dangerous or harmful, I'm not going to interfere. She's a big girl and has survived by herself for thirty some years. I refuse to treat her like some empty-headed little girl."

"And that's what you think I'm doing?"

"Yes."

"All right. I'll back off…as long as you do."

"Me? Back off?"

"Yeah, start being a boss and stay out of our relationship. I'm working here. I want her. I always have. She could be the sanity I need in my life. Your so-called friendship can't be as important as my life."

"Fine. I'll back off. But remember, Maggie doesn't like being told what to do."

"I'll keep it in mind."

MAGGIE

"All right, Doctor. What is the problem? Don't I meet your high standards, either?" Maggie asked, slamming her hands down on Billy's desk and glaring at him.

"What are you talking about?" Billy asked, refusing to look up from his work.

"You won't work with me anymore. I haven't worked with you since those first couple of weeks. You have me continually working with Dr. Nelson. I want to know *why*."

Billy rubbed the back of his neck. "Look, Maggie, when Dennis and I created these teams, we had to put people together who would complement one another."

"I complement Dr. Nelson?"

"Yes, as a matter of fact, you do. You have more experience than he does, and when he runs into trouble, you're there to help him. I have to spread my people around so that the veterans are mixed in with the greenhorns. If I scheduled you on my team and put Joni with Nelson, well…"

"You'd have the blind leading the blind."

"Exactly," he said. "Is there anything else?"

"Will we ever work together again?"

He focused his gaze on the papers laying before him. After a moment, he looked up and said, "All things considered, I highly doubt it. Now, can I please get back to my work," Billy said curtly. "Or is there something else you need to discuss?"

"No, that's all. I'm sorry to have bothered you," she said quietly. As she walked from his office, Maggie ground her teeth wanting to shake him and shout, "What the hell happened to you? Where did the Billy Fox that I knew and fell in love with go?" It wasn't as if Maggie had asked him if he thought they could still be lovers, for goodness sake. She knew that part of their relationship was over. But they had been friends first, hadn't they? What was wrong with assuming that their friendship could continue?

When she had first moved in, they had done some things together. Of course, Cal was there as well, constantly hovering. But Billy provided a buffer between them. Now she was always having to fight off Cal and his attentions.

Not only was he being very physical when her guard was down, and sneaking kisses and hugs, he was always telling her what to do. It was getting on her nerves. She didn't know how to tactfully tell him to stop, and without Billy for support, things were becoming awkward. If only she and Billy could have worked together at least during some of that time, she would have felt better. But now, Billy had turned into a stranger. She was beginning to rue her decision to move to Phoenix.

One night about a month later, however, Maggie got her wish. There had been a multi-vehicle pile-up with at least four cars involved and as many as six to eight people injured. Maggie was on call and raced back to the hospital. The arrival of the first injuries was estimated at twenty minutes. Several people were trapped in their automobiles and at least three units of paramedics and fire companies were on the scene.

Through an odd shift of personnel, Maggie ended up across the OR table from Billy. Time fell away, and it was as if they were back in Vietnam. They worked so well together that their movements and thoughts appeared to be choreographed.

By the time the last of the injured were taken care of, it was morning. "What a night," Maggie said, pulling off her scrub cap and fluffing out her hair. "I didn't think we'd ever see the end of that mess. I can't wait to get home and put my feet up. Thank God I'm off today."

Billy poured himself a large mug of coffee. "I wish I could say the same. I'm going to have one hell of a day, and I don't even have time for a nap or a shower."

"But I thought you were off on Fridays?"

"Not exactly, every other Friday, I do pro bono work for the health department. I see sick Indian and Hispanic women, infants, children, and elderly patients. The other Fridays, I have office hours. Today is one of my office days. I'll probably be working until 5:00 tonight seeing them all, catching up on paperwork afterward, then I'll be back on at eleven."

"You'll be dead on your feet! How will you manage?"

He shrugged. "I've done it before. I'll probably sleep all day tomorrow. Although sometimes I wonder why I ever got an apartment. I should have just moved into the call room. But see, we did get a chance to work together."

"It was like old times," she said, smiling shyly. "I wish we could do that more often. It was almost…fun."

"Hmm," he replied. And reaching out, brushed a stray strand of her hair from out of her eye and tucked it behind her ear. "I don't know if putting people back together is fun. But I know what you mean." He smiled back at her, and Maggie felt herself blush.

He then seemed to shake himself. The smile disappeared, replaced by the dark, brooding eyes and grim countenance she was getting accustomed to seeing. He turned away from her and topped off his coffee, refusing to look at her again.

"Well, I've got to be going. See you later," he said, quickly leaving the room.

"Bye," she said to his retreating back, as her smile slipped from her face.

BILLY

"We're not going to be able to make it for Thanksgiving," Marian said on the phone.

"I understand," Billy replied, trying hard not to sound disappointed. "Maybe next year, you'll all be able to come out to visit then. What's more important is that Grandma Jean gets back on her feet."

"Ever since she fell and cracked her pelvis last month, we've been trying to persuade her to move in with us permanently," Marian said. "But Grandma refuses to admit she's too unsteady on her feet to be living alone. And she's so independent that she's miserable when she can't do even little things for herself. You know what she's like."

"Don't I?" Billy smiled to himself. "She's always been such a fireball."

"Yes, and you'd hate to see her so down. She's arguing that we should still visit you, but we just can't. I'm sorry. We were all looking forward to seeing you. Maggie too," Marian added. "Please give her our love."

"Uh…sure, I'll tell her."

"It must be wonderful to be together again."

"I guess. I don't really get to see her all that often. Different shifts, you know."

"Oh, don't give me that," Marian chided. "You're the boss. You could be working with her every day if you wanted. Plus, I hear she moved into the apartment next to yours. You can always see her when you're at home."

"I'm sorry, Marian, I have to go. I'll call you guys on Thanksgiving so that I can talk to everyone."

Marian heard the finality in his voice and sighed to herself. "That's fine. We'll talk to you then."

"Give Grandma Jean a kiss for me and tell her to behave."

"I'll do that."

Billy hung up the phone and put the kettle on for tea. He had been so looking forward to the Wilson family's visit that it was all he had thought about lately. It helped him to push thoughts of Maggie from his mind.

He allowed himself to think of her for a moment and the thought brought pain. What in the hell had he been thinking? Why had he let Dennis hire her? Had he really thought that the two of them could go back to being friends? Even without Cal and the relationship that he was trying to rekindle, Billy had left her wide open for ridicule for being friends with one of those 'red-skins'; a married one at that.

He had just run into the two of them in the hall a short while ago. Cal had put his arm proprietarily around Maggie's shoulder as they talked. Billy, meanwhile, had tried to keep from grinding his teeth in anger and frustration. Anytime he saw the two of them together, Cal did his best to prove she was still *his* Maggie. He was always taking her places in his expensive sports car—places Billy could never afford.

Billy thought about his Volkswagen—practical and plain. An Indian car, Cal had commented and laughed. It was well worn and, because of Billy's many trips to the nearby reservation to make house calls, in need of four new tires because of all the ruts.

"Does this thing really run, or did you buy it for show?" Cal had sneered. "Perhaps if you didn't give all your money and extra time to poor Indians and Hispanics, Dr. Bleeding Heart, you might be able to buy yourself a real car. At least buy some new tires, for God's sake. Or are you waitin' for them all to go flat first?"

Cal would also brag about the latest restaurant where he had taken Maggie, then casually ask Billy if he had ever been there. As usual, Billy had never even heard of the place. One day Cal said, "Look what I got. Front row seats to see the Phoenix Symphony. I plan on surprisin' Maggie tonight. They're doin' something by Harold Berly someone."

"You mean Hector Berlioz?" Billy had retorted. "I'd at least know his name before you surprise her, or she'll laugh in your face."

"Hmph, how would *you* know his name? What would someone like *you* know about the symphony?" Cal remarked.

"I've been to the freaking John F. Kennedy Center, seen concerts, plays, operas and ballets and I know a hell of a lot more than *you,* you philistine asshole," Billy had muttered under his breath as he walked away.

It was becoming increasingly difficult for Billy to be civil to Cal, and he tried to avoid him. Maggie, on the other hand, was getting harder to ignore. Billy had to be constantly on his guard around her. There were days when he would almost let his feelings show. Those days were the worst.

His mind then turned to Jessie. Billy wished that Dylan would have better luck. When he had talked to the attorney a week ago, the information Billy had received was not encouraging. Dylan had started his search by visiting the apartment building where Jessie and Anita had once lived. He found instead an empty lot. The building had been razed to make way for a new apartment complex. Tracing Anita had also been a dead end. There was no one in the neighborhood who knew her or remembered her. It appeared as though she and Jessie had vanished.

Dylan had also hired private investigators in Reno and Las Vegas in the hopes that she would turn up in one of the casinos or in the surrounding areas. In the meantime, he would continue to canvass the local neighborhoods, keeping Billy updated. The minute he found Jessie, or any information that could lead to her whereabouts, he would let Billy know.

But it was so difficult to sit back and wait. If Dylan found Jessie, then what? Would he try to salvage the marriage? It hadn't worked so far, why would it work now?

Since the Wilsons weren't coming to Phoenix, Billy volunteered to work on Thanksgiving. It gave him an excuse and a place to be for the day.

"You know, it's not your turn," Dennis had said. "Why don't you take the day off? You deserve a break. Since you've been here, you really haven't had a day off. And you always work the holidays."

"There's no reason to stay home. Let someone with a family have the day off."

"If that's the way you feel, I'm sure there will be plenty of doctors clamoring to have the time."

Holidays at St. Mark's were either quiet as the morgue or so busy no one had time to breathe. This Thanksgiving, Maggie's team and the rest of the personnel in the ER/Trauma Center were on their toes from early morning until late evening. It started with simple minor cooking accidents—burns and cuts. Those were followed by several automobile accidents, a fire, a drug overdose, two cardiac arrests and lots of miscellaneous miseries that had the waiting room and ambulance bays full.

Billy and Maggie worked on separate injuries for most of the afternoon until a freeway accident paired them up. The injuries of this particular accident were extremely gruesome, and the condition of the patients were reminiscent of casualties they had seen in Vietnam. When Billy saw the mangled flesh of a man's arm, his mind went back to Phu Bai. For a moment, he felt sick and wanted to run from the sight.

He happened to glance up at Maggie as he examined the man. Her look of nausea seemed to mirror his own feelings. He gave himself a stern mental shake, straightened and squeezed Maggie's shoulder.

"Let's go to work," he said quietly, his face and manner once again calm and matter of fact. When Maggie gave a tiny nod and a weak smile, his confidence returned, pushing away all thoughts of panic.

They both worked overtime, staying until the load was manageable for the next team. Billy then hurriedly changed and left the building, wanting to get home before Maggie.

He threw together a salad and ate while reading a new mystery purchased the day before. But the words on the page had no meaning for him. He was too preoccupied with thoughts of Maggie and kept straining to hear her footsteps in the hall. When he did hear her, he thought she hesitated at his door, but it could have been his imagination.

He washed his plate, then took a shower. Pulling on a pair of scrub bottoms and an old t-shirt, he went back to his book. But he couldn't concentrate. He was still wired from work, and the nearness of Maggie had his emotions in an uproar.

He went into the kitchen and put on a kettle of water. As he waited for the water to boil, he again tried to focus on his novel. When the kettle whistled, he made a pot of chamomile tea and, pouring a mug, was heading back to the couch when there was a tapping at his door.

MAGGIE

The plane was alone in the cloudless sky. Mike was in the cockpit, a smile on his face. He was happy doing what he loved. For a few moments, everything was fine. Then suddenly, there was a loud noise, and a trail of smoke came from the plane. The jet spun out of control, and Mike tried frantically to eject. He began to scream as flames shot into his face. In slow motion, the plane began to fall dizzily, then exploded with tremendous force, showering balls of fire through the sky.

Maggie's screams joined Mike's, and she jolted awake, trembling and sweating. She was crying and moaning, her legs twisted in her nightgown. She quickly turned on the bedside lamp. Despite the fact that she was awake, the vision of the explosion wouldn't go away. Maggie shuddered and rubbed her arms. She could feel the panic beginning to surge within her and knew that it would overwhelm her at any moment.

Without thinking, she grabbed her robe and key, then ran next door to Billy's apartment. Tapping lightly, she stood shivering, her bare feet icy on the tile floor. When his door opened, Maggie literally fell into Billy's arms, crying and whimpering, her hair matted to her head with sweat.

"What is it?" he asked. "What's the matter?"

"Hhhorrible nightmare," she said, her teeth chattering uncontrollably. Billy tightened his arms around her and pushed the door shut with his foot. He stroked her hair and murmured to her as she gradually calmed down and stopped shaking.

"I'm so sorry," she whispered. "I hated to bother you, but I didn't know what else to do. It was so real and so awful. I tried hard to fight the panic, but I couldn't."

"It's all right. You're not bothering me. I was reading and just made a pot of tea."

"I think it was that accident that came in today. All that mangled flesh. It brought it all back," Maggie gulped out and began to cry again.

"I know," he said, rubbing her back, as if she were a child. "It was pretty bad, wasn't it?"

Maggie nodded, her head against his chest, her tears soaking into his t-shirt. "Yes, and the dream was even worse. I could hear Mike's screams, feel the heat of his plane on fire, the spinning of it out of control. Will it ever stop?"

"I don't know, Maggie. I have dreams like that, too. I hope they'll fade with time. I remember right after my father killed himself, I used to have the worst dreams. Now, I hardly have those anymore. They've been replaced by visions of John and GIs with missing body parts and…my own blood. Right now, I think I'd gladly take back the nightmares of my old man."

Her small hands had a tight grip on his shirt, as if by holding onto him, he could take away the pain and the hurt, and most of all, the vision that wouldn't let her rest.

"It's not like I've never been around death. I mean, we're surrounded by it on a day-to-day basis and, for the most part, I try to make myself immune to it. But the one thing that I never witnessed is now what haunts me most."

"I guess it could be worse," he said.

"What do you mean?"

"It could be real. We could still be there, and the visions wouldn't be a dream," he said.

Maggie's tears slowed then finally stopped. With her head against his chest, in the safety of his arms, the warmth and smell of his body gave her comfort. The steady beating of his heart lulled her almost to sleep.

He continued to rub her back, the motion becoming more a caress than a pat. Billy was very aware of her in his arms and *what* she was wearing. He remembered buying her that silk robe in Bangkok on their last night together. Having her slight body pressed against him, in that robe, stirred feelings he had tried to push away for so long. He breathed in the scent of her hair, rubbing his cheek against its softness. Without thinking, he kissed her forehead.

Maggie sniffed and looked up at him, her red-rimmed eyes looking more like emeralds than ever. Their eyes met and held as they once did in a moment lost in time. They both seemed to stop breathing and, once their lips touched, there was a fierceness to their kisses that was almost violent.

Billy's fingers twined themselves in Maggie's curls, pulling her mouth closer to his. With his other hand, he undid the cinched belt of her robe. His hand slipped inside, feeling the beat of her heart against his fingertips. His hands continued to re-explore a territory known so long ago, so gently taken, and now, so desperate to repossess. He bent his head and pressed kisses down the smooth column of her neck.

The piercing ring of the phone jolted them both. Billy stumbled away from Maggie, breathing heavily. The insistent ringing was like a slap. Like one roused from a deep sleep, Billy made his way to the kitchen in order to answer.

"Hey, what time did you get out of work?" Cal questioned abruptly.

Billy cleared his throat, "Around nine thirty. Why?"

"I've been trying to get a hold of Maggie. She isn't answering her phone. Did she leave when you did or did she work longer?"

"I left before she did," Billy said. "But, if you're looking for her, she's here."

"What? What's she doing there?"

"She had a nightmare, and the fallout was worse than the dream. She came over for some tea and sympathy."

"You expect me to believe that?"

"Of course," Billy said, looking over at Maggie, who was in the process of tying her robe shut.

The line went dead. Billy stared at the receiver for a moment, then replaced it on the wall. "I have a feeling he's on his way over here," he stated quietly, his back toward Maggie.

He barely had time to get another cup of tea poured, when there was a pounding at his door. He grabbed his mug and shoved the other cup into Maggie's outstretched hand, then went to let Cal in.

"What the hell's going on in here?" Cal demanded, entering the room.

"I told you. We're having some tea. Would you like some?" Billy asked.

Cal shoved Billy in the chest, causing him to spill his tea. "Go to hell. Do you really expect me to believe that? I thought I told you to back off and stay away from Maggie. I want to know what you were really doing behind my back!"

Maggie's eyes snapped in fury. "How dare you! Billy told you why I was here. I had a nightmare, and it caused me to panic. He kindly offered to make me some chamomile tea. If you don't believe him, then you must not believe me, either."

Cal's eyes narrowed as he took in the innocent picture before him. Billy looked at the puddle of tea on the carpet, his half empty mug still in his hand. Maggie, who had been sitting on the sofa, her robe tightly belted, had been sipping from the steaming mug in her hands.

"I didn't think I had to check with you every time I left my apartment," Maggie said, standing.

"You don't. But Maggie, it's not right you runnin' around in your night-gown, especially not in front of *him*."

"Why not? Billy *is* a doctor. He's seen plenty of people in their underwear. Besides, I'm wearing a robe for God's sake. I'm not indecent or exposed. I'm also wearing it in front of you, aren't I?"

"That's different."

"What's the difference?"

"The difference is, he's a *married* man—a married *Indian* man," Cal said, glaring at Billy. "And he's *not* the one who's datin' you."

"You know Cal, sometimes you take too much for granted."

"What's that supposed to mean?"

"It means that I may go out with you on occasion. But that doesn't mean we're dating or that you own me. Remember that," she said, walking into the kitchen and placing her mug into the sink. "Thank you, Billy. The tea was just what I needed."

"Will you be all right now?" Billy asked quietly.

"Yes, thank you again. I don't know what I would have done had you not been home."

"You could have called me," Cal said.

"Yes, but I didn't. And now, if you don't mind, I'm very tired and would like to go back to bed. Good night," she said, and stalked from the apartment.

Cal gave Billy a departing glare and followed Maggie from the apartment and into the hall, slamming the door behind him.

"I'm sorry, Maggie," Cal said, taking her arm. "I know you weren't doing anything with him. Why would you? But I don't understand why you can't talk to me."

"You just don't get it, do you? Billy and I have a history. In Vietnam, when the shit was flying and people were bleeding and dying, it was the two of us. We spent hours talking. We sorted out all the bad stuff and tried to make it manageable. We were there for each other either to lend an ear or a shoulder to cry on. When Mike died, Billy helped to keep me from falling apart. That's the way it was. Why wouldn't I go to him when something like this happened? He understands. He's my friend."

"Friend," Cal snorted. "Women don't have men for friends. It isn't normal."

"Then I guess I'm not normal," she spat at him. By then, they were in front of Maggie's door.

"I'm sorry Maggie, that came out wrong. I guess I'm just a little jealous right now. Is it wrong to want you to myself?"

"Sometimes it takes a better person to share."

Cal scratched his head. "I never did like to share. Besides, Billy isn't the best person to be friends with."

"Why not?"

"Oh hell," he said, running his fingers through his hair. "Someone has to tell you. It may as well be me. But can I at least come in to talk to you. This kind of conversation shouldn't be done in a hallway."

"Fine. But please, can you do this quickly? I'm very tired. It was a long day and I have to be back to work by eleven tomorrow morning," she said, as she unlocked and opened her door. Cal followed her into the kitchen where she tossed her key onto the counter. "Well?"

Cal took a deep breath. "People are talkin'," he paused and looked down at his hands.

"About what?" Maggie prompted.

"About you and Fox."

Maggie raised her eyebrows.

"At first, they thought the three of us had something going on. Now, they're calling you a red lover and are saying that you're chasing him. That the two of you are having some sort of heathen affair, and that you're a whore."

"What!"

"You heard me."

"That's not true!"

"Are you sure?"

"What? That we're having an affair?"

"It sure looks that way."

"Oh, come on, I told you before, we're friends."

"Single women do not have married men for friends, especially not an Indian, whose wife is missing in action."

"Why not?"

"It's just not done."

"I am *not* having an affair with Billy. If evil-minded people want to talk, I can't stop them. But I am *not* going to stop being his friend just because some jerks at the hospital think I should, including you. If you all don't like it, that's too damned bad."

"So, you're going to keep being his *friend?*"

"Yes."

"And you don't care what people think?"

"No, I don't."

"Well, I can only stick up for you for so long."

"Is that some sort of threat?"

"No, for now, it's just a friendly warning."

"Well, thanks for the warning, *friend.* And if that's all you needed to tell me, I'm going back to bed. God knows, people may see you leaving *my* apartment and might start even *more* rumors."

Pushing Cal into the hall, she shut the door with finality and threw the bolt. With her back to the door, she softly began to cry, but this time, it was for a different reason.

JESSIE

Chet had said they were going to the opera. Jessie hoped to God that he paid her this evening. How much could that cocaine have cost? She had been working it off for the past three weeks. If she mentioned being paid, Chet would give her a sly look and make a snorting sound.

"You're still on the time clock, honey," he'd say. "Did you forget about that little package I gave you already?"

Tonight hopefully, she'd make some money. The rent was almost due, and she was a month behind. The apartment cost a fortune, but it was a good place to take customers. It was nice, without being too nice, and no one asked questions. She was quiet and discreet and had learned how to do business—at least most of the time. With a client like Chet, one had to be careful.

Chet was one of the wealthiest, most influential men in the city of Phoenix. With his unlimited funds, he financed new or failing businesses. He was the savior of many endeavors, hers included.

Good photocopy, he and his beautiful socialite wife were always gracing the social and business pages of the newspapers. They were the 'in' couple of Phoenix. By all outward appearances, they were the most loving and devoted of couples. But Jessie knew differently.

After many years of being in the sex business, Jessie had learned other skills involved with her trade. She knew how to 'stroke' a client in more ways than one. She listened as clients vented their frustration, anger, and depression once their bodily needs were assuaged.

It was a profession that wore one down, and Jessie was at the end of her rope. After all these years, she was tired of being a hooker, tired of being mistreated, tired of life. So many times, she wanted to just end it all.

She inspected herself in the mirror. Instead of a thirty-six-year-old in her prime, Jessie's sagging face and sunken eyes gave her the appearance of someone much older; someone who had been used and abused; someone who had seen it all and done it all. She laughed wryly to herself. Well, she had, hadn't she?

Jessie went to her closet and wondered what one wore to the opera. All of her clothing bore the stigma of hooker—slinky, slit, bare. All her options said, 'For sale.' After several minutes of rummaging, she found a pretty floral dress jammed in the very back of the closet.

For a moment, she stared at the dress wondering why it was there. Then, she remembered. She had worn it for Nick. "You look real classy, babe," he had said with a smile.

The memories washed over her in an unexpected flood, and she sat down heavily on the bed, her breath coming out in jerky gasps. Reaching for her bear, she feverishly stroked its fur in an effort to push away the feelings the memories brought. Eventually, her stroking slowed as her breathing quieted. Again, she was calm and matter of fact.

She pushed away the bear and all thoughts of Nick, then dressed carefully. For once, she wanted to look like a lady, not a cheap whore. She wore only enough makeup to hide the flaws, but not look like she was on the prowl. Before she left the room, she got out what was left of her stash of cocaine. Instant courage, she thought. Enough to boost the morale of several large men.

When she met Chet in the lobby of her building though, she could see he was not pleased with what he saw. "What did you do to yourself? You look like some wholesome schoolgirl. What kind of dress is this?" he asked, flipping at her ruffles with his hand.

"What's wrong with it? It's pretty. It's something a lady would wear."

"You're no lady," he snorted. "You're a whore. Whores aren't supposed to be pretty or ladies. Whores are supposed to look like whores. You're supposed to look like you want to be screwed."

"You said we were going to the opera. I wanted to make sure that I didn't embarrass you by being dressed wrong."

"I never said the opera. What I said was that we were going to hear a young woman scream sweetly. Now go back upstairs and get dressed for what you do best. I have something special planned, and I want you in the right clothing. Something easy access."

"Fine," Jessie said and sighed. All that trouble for nothing. If she had dressed normally, he'd probably have said to change into something decent. Men were such small-minded pigs. If they didn't have dicks, they'd be useless.

Chet's limo was waiting when Jessie returned. But when she got inside, there were four other men in the back with her client.

"What's going on?" Jessie asked.

"I said we were going to hear a young woman's screams. Aren't we fellas?" The men, who were dressed in business suits, snickered. "I'm entertaining some friends tonight, Jessie, and *you* are the entertainment. Good thing this limo has nice dark windows."

The rest of the evening passed in a blur as Jessie was passed from one man to another, often servicing more than one man at a time. After several hours, Jessie was exhausted, mentally as well as physically. She felt as though the proverbial 'red-hot poker' had been shoved repeatedly into her anatomy.

After his friends were dropped off at various locations, only she and Chet remained in the car. "You know, Chet, five on one is rather expensive."

"What do you mean? You're still working off that cocaine I gave you."

"You've got to be kidding! I know how much a kilo is worth. You got three times that in services since then, not to mention what you got tonight."

"My word against yours."

"What? Didn't Mrs. Chet pay your allowance this week?"

The crack of his hand hitting her face rang out in the car. "How dare you!"

"No, how dare *you*. You owe me and I want it."

"Too bad."

"Wouldn't the papers think it interesting that you spend so much time with a hooker?" Jessie asked, as she rubbed her cheek. "What about Mrs. Chet?" Jessie questioned.

Again, Chet's hand slapped her face. The slap was so hard that it knocked her back against the door of the limo.

"Go ahead, Jessie. Say something to the papers. Make a fool of yourself. Who will people believe? A well-respected businessman like me or a *whore* like you? You are nothing but scum."

"Funny you don't mind putting your dick into scum like me."

"No, I don't," he said, then straddling her, he forced himself into her repeatedly. When she fought him, he slapped her again and again.

"I'd say you were pretty scummy, too," Jessie said, as blood oozed from her cut lip. "At least *I* don't pretend to be a somebody. If it wasn't for your wife, you'd be nothing," she said.

Chet continued to thrust himself into her, then ejaculated into her face. "You," he grunted, "are nothing but a cunt." Getting off of her, he opened the car door and, as the limo continued down the street, pushed Jessie from the vehicle. The sidewalk rose up and met Jessie's face and body with brutal force. Her head hit the cement, then all went black.

BILLY

I t had been a long day and Billy's leg was throbbing. He had lost weight, and the brace was now digging into his thigh, causing a sore spot. However, the patients had been never ending, and there had been no chance to sit down for any amount of time. The enormity of what he was doing scared him. He hoped he hadn't bitten off more than he could chew with starting his own practice, as well as what he did for the health department.

Billy's office nurse, Ellen, had been as harried and haggard as he. They had worked side by side all day treating the constant flow of women and children that had come like waves. She had finally, at Billy's insistence, gone home.

Billy was lucky. Ellen had been a wonderful find; and, after only a few months, he couldn't function without her. She was a Navajo in her late fifties and the model of efficiency. She had worked for the health department for several years, doing inoculations, educating expectant mothers and teaching baby, infant and childcare. She also worked for the constant flux of doctors who revolved through the system. When he actually let himself think of Maggie, he imagined her turning into an Ellen when she got older.

After being on his feet all day, his walk had turned into a pronounced limp as he headed to his office. His desk was littered with insurance forms and health department papers that needed to be filled out. Plus, he also had the day's charting to finish. It would take several hours to sort it all and complete the work. On top of that, he was also on call.

Early that morning when he had done his rounds, everyone at the hospital had been talking excitedly about the Christmas party that was to be held later in the evening. Billy had wanted no parts of that. He just wanted to be alone.

He sighed and prepared to remove his brace while he worked. Taking it off would be a relief even for a short amount of time. He knew that with vigilant exercise and therapy he could strengthen the leg enough to ditch the brace, but he just didn't have the time or the inclination. Besides, the less he looked at the leg the better.

He had just undone his trousers and was about to let them fall to the floor, when he heard a knock on the outer door and the creak of hinges. Damn it, he thought, Ellen in her state of exhaustion must have forgotten to lock the door.

"Hello," he heard Maggie call, "anybody home?"

"In here," Billy called. He barely had time to re-zip his pants, before Maggie stuck her head in the doorway.

"Hi," she said cautiously. "Are you busy?"

"Yes, why?" he answered grumpily, as he sat down behind his desk and checked surreptitiously to make sure his fly was zipped completely.

"I just wondered if you had a minute."

"I guess. What for?"

"Well, I wanted to talk."

"Oh? About what?"

Maggie looked down at her shoes and said softly, "About last night."

"Oh," Billy said, refusing to make contact with Maggie's eyes.

"Um, for most of the time I've been here in Phoenix, I've been getting mixed signals from you. At first, you were like the Billy I knew in Vietnam. Then, all of a sudden, things changed. I felt that you, for some reason or other, were either mad at me or didn't like me anymore." She cleared her throat, "as a friend, I mean. Then there was last night, and now I don't know what to think…or feel."

"I see."

"Well?"

For many minutes, Billy stared sightlessly at the pile of papers that lay there. He opened his mouth to speak, then closed it again. Finally, he looked up and met Maggie's piercing gaze. He said, nodding, "Guess I lost it, didn't I?"

"Lost what?"

"Control—failure to hold in my feelings, failure to remind myself of who and what I am."

"Which is?"

"Let's see, how did Cal phrase it? A married man—a married *Indian* man. A man who shouldn't be with *his* woman, as a friend or otherwise. Because being *my* friend is a bad thing. I hear they're already spreading rumors about us at the hospital."

"Is *that* what this is all about?"

"What?"

"You treating me as though I don't exist, or that I'm someone you don't care to know?"

Billy remained silent.

"Tell me something. When we were on R & R, then later in DC, you said you loved me. Did you really mean it or were you just saying it because you had slept with me and felt you were expected to say it?"

"What do you think?" he spit out.

"I don't know, that's why I'm asking."

"Whether I meant it or not, it doesn't matter. Australia was a fantasy. It wasn't real. You know that. It didn't exist."

"It sure felt real to me. What do you mean, it didn't exist?"

"This is the real world, Maggie. What happened in Australia, can't happen here. Have you forgotten the conversation we had about the hazards of being in my company?"

"And have *you* forgotten what I said in reply? I don't care. Being your friend is much more important to me than any damage my stupid reputation may suffer because of it." She paused then said simply, "I miss you. You totally ignoring me hurts. So, did you mean it? Do you really love me or were you just using me?"

"Of course, I love you, goddamn it! I was *not* using you! How can you say such a thing?"

"I had to know," she said quietly.

"It doesn't change things. I can't be your friend anymore."

"Why not?"

Billy rubbed his forehead. "There are lots of reasons why, but the most important thing is that I honestly don't think I can go back to being your friend without the rest of it."

"You mean being lovers?"

"Yes, can you?"

Maggie paused a long moment, staring into space. "I don't know, I thought I could until last night. Now, I'm not so sure."

"You saw what happened. You had a bad dream and came to me. We talked. I held you. The more I held you, the more I wanted to hold you, and to love you, and it goes on and on."

"I see. And what did Cal mean when he said something about you backing off?"

"Cal wants me out of the way. Look, he doesn't know what happened between us, but he's suspicious because he doesn't understand or like the fact that we're friends. He wants me to leave you alone so that your precious reputation remains intact, that way he can move in for the kill."

"The kill?"

"You know he wants you. He expects the two of you to continue the wonderful relationship you had in New York City and make it official in all ways possible."

"That will never happen. When I left New York, our relationship was going nowhere, because that's just where I wanted it—nowhere."

"Does he know that?"

"As you know, Cal only sees what he wants to see and only hears what he wants to hear. At this point, I agree to go places with him, just because it's easier."

"You're leading him on."

"I am not! I just don't want to start a fight or hurt his feelings."

"That's what I call leading him on."

"Well, maybe it's because he's the only one around here that's nice to me," Maggie said, raising her voice. "*You* won't talk to me and the non-veteran nurses act like I'm some sort of freak. Dennis is nice, so is Joni, but I never see either one of them. I wish I had never come here."

"I'm sorry."

"Why did you let Dennis hire me in the first place?"

"We needed a good nurse," Billy said quietly. "You're the best."

"But what about your precious feelings?"

"I thought I could control them, and maybe I could have before Cal started making an issue of things. I didn't realize that he could make life so difficult and complicated."

"So why don't we tell him."

"Tell him? Tell him what? That we actually *did* have an affair? That we *care* about each other. Maybe even *love* each other. Are you crazy? I have enough scars on my body without asking for more."

"Maybe, but wouldn't having it out in the open be better?"

"No, it would not. Do you know, back when you two were dating in New York, Cal used to ask me repeatedly to help him get you into his bed. Like I was training some goddamned horse. What do you think he'd do if he found out that I had actually *slept* with you? My God, he'd kill me with his bare hands."

"He asked you for help?"

"Yeah, but please forget that I said that. I'm in enough trouble as it is."

"So, what are we going to do?"

"If you're a smart girl, you'll stay as far away from me as possible."

Maggie stared down at her twined fingers. "I see. And if I don't?"

"You'll give me no other choice than to leave this hospital."

"You'd do that to stay away from me?"

"If I have to."

"Because of Cal and my…reputation?"

"I would like to say yes, that as a gentleman, I'm protecting your reputation. But actually, if I told the truth, I'd be doing it for my own sanity," Billy said softly. "Because having you near me causes such severe pain that I would rather ignore you than look at you. That seeing you with another man, even if it's a friend, is slowly killing me."

They stared at each other for a very long moment. The silence was broken as the outer door banged open. Cal rounded the corner and stomped into the office.

"I knew I'd find you here," Cal said to Maggie, his face flushed with anger.

"I was trying to talk Billy into coming to the party."

"Why?"

"Because it's a Christmas party. You know, peace on earth, goodwill toward men?"

Cal snorted. "Peace, huh? I don't understand why they are having this party so early in the season, anyway? It was just Thanksgiving."

"Because it's less hectic right now. And more people are available."

"And you thought that beggin' Billy to come to this party was what? Goodwill toward men?"

"Something like that. I hated to see him alone when everyone else was having fun."

"If he doesn't want to come, he doesn't want to come. Don't force him. I know what can happen when you do. He'll end up drunk as a skunk and pukin' his guts out," Cal remarked snidely.

"God, who peed in your Wheaties this morning, Lewis?" Billy questioned.

"You know, Fox, I'm getting tired of always finding my girlfriend in your company."

"What are you saying?" Billy asked, standing.

Cal leaned over the desk and poked a finger into Billy's chest. "I told you to back off, you didn't listen. It was up to you to end this so-called farce of a friendship. But I see that you broke your promise."

"You know, Lewis, you're making my ass tired. I did *not* break my promise. I was here minding my own *fucking* business and trying to do some work when Maggie found *me*. And furthermore, if you want to talk about parties, let's talk about parties. I may have been drunk and vomiting, but you were the one that was screwing every girl you could find and in plain sight of everyone. Does your *girlfriend* know about all *that*?"

Maggie looked from one man to the other. The room was so full of built-up testosterone and tension, she knew that she had to somehow diffuse the situation before there was a violent explosion.

"All right, that's enough. Come on Cal, let's go. You're right. He doesn't want to come. I made a mistake trying to be nice. I refuse to beg someone to have a good time. Besides, I'm hungry. If he wants to go around looking like a sewing needle, that's his own business. Me, I'd rather eat. I know you would, too."

"I'm warning you Fox, stay the fuck away from her. I don't want to see her here again."

Maggie grabbed Cal's sleeve and began to tug at it. "Come on, let's go," she repeated.

"Well, you'd better tell your *girlfriend*. I can't help what happens if she initiates it."

"Cal, please," Maggie begged.

"She won't be bothering you again. I'll see to that," Cal replied, slamming his hand down on Billy's desk. "All right, Maggie. Let's go."

Billy watched them leave. He was shaking so hard inside that he had to sit down. He took several deep, cleansing breaths and was about to go and lock the door, when the phone rang.

"Dr. Fox," Billy answered. "Hi, Dennis, no, I'm not going to the party. I know I'm on call, what have you got? I can be there in about fifteen minutes. Sure, see you then." Hanging up the receiver, Billy sighed. Well, there goes the evening, he thought. It looked like it was going to be one of those nights.

Billy's first patient was a young man who was found in an alleyway. The unidentified man had slit both of his wrists in an attempted suicide. He was alive but bleeding heavily and only semi-conscious when they brought him in.

"Horizontal," Billy said, working on the wrist of the man. "Someone should have told him that if he wanted to do it right, he should have done it vertically and all the way up. That would have clinched it."

Joni handed him a suture and replied, "Unfortunately, someone probably will, and we'll see him again. He may not be as lucky next time."

"You can always tell when December rolls around," the anesthesiologist commented. "There are always a bunch of John and Jane Does that try to off themselves around this time of year. This is my third Doe this week. I think that's more than the other gas passers."

"I didn't know you guys were having a contest," Billy said.

"Unofficially, in fact, I hear we have a Jane Doe next in line. If that's the case, I'll be up to four this week."

"Let me guess, an OD?" Billy volunteered.

"Actually no," the passer said. "Officer Ramirez brought her in. Surprise, surprise! Although, this one doesn't seem to be self-inflicted, unless she purposely threw herself out of a moving vehicle."

"God!"

"Yeah, they were just taking her down to x-ray when I came in, probable concussion. She's been in and out of consciousness. Very disoriented. Lots of contusions, gashes and so on. You know, your forte. You'll be using all your skills to do some fancy cobbling on her face, to be sure. As to the rest, we may need someone from Ortho called in depending on what they say in radiology. And Ramirez will need to talk to you about both of these patients for his reports."

"Sounds lovely. Poor Tony always seems to be on duty when the shit flies," Billy replied.

"It does seem that way, doesn't it. He was just minding his own business, doing his beat when he saw something that looked like a pile of rags lying in the gutter. When he got closer, he realized it was a person and called the Paramedics. Tony thinks she's a hooker," the anesthesiologist said.

"How could he tell?" Joni asked.

"By the way she was dressed for one thing. Plus, she smelled heavily of *Eau de semen*. It was all over her. The poor bitch probably asked for her money and got to kiss the street instead."

Billy shook his head. "Well, we'll soon get a look at her. Mr. Doe is about ready to face the world again or try for two. We'll need to keep him tonight.

Perhaps he should have a little talk with Jeff Stark before he's released. It doesn't hurt to have a psychiatrist do an eval."

As the anesthesiologist had predicted, Jane Doe was their next patient. Billy went to examine her face, which was covered with blood and dirt.

"Doctor? Are you all right?" Joni asked, as Billy stumbled and grabbed the gurney to keep from falling.

"Uh yeah," he replied. "Lost my footing for a moment. I'm fine." He looked again at the face of Jane Doe and knew that Dylan could call off the search for his wife.

MAGGIE

Billy had disappeared. Although Maggie didn't work on his team, she always caught glimpses of him at the hospital—either coming on or off a shift, heading to his office, even eating in the cafeteria. But since the night of the Christmas party, she hadn't seen him.

In fact, A shift was just coming on as she was leaving, but instead of Billy getting notes from Nelson, it was Dennis. She hung around for a few minutes as the two men went over the roster of patients being seen at the moment in the ER.

When Nelson departed, Maggie cornered Dennis. "Hi Dr. O'Shea, I didn't expect to see you here. Where's Dr. Fox?" she asked.

"Hello Maggie. Dr. Fox has been a bit under the weather the last couple of days. I've been working his shift for him."

"I wondered since I hadn't seen him. I hope he's all right?"

"I'm sure he'll be back up and running by tomorrow. But until then, the patients will have to take their chances with me."

"I'm sure they'll be fine," Maggie smiled. "Sorry to bother you. It's just that I was concerned."

"Nice to know someone cares. Now, I must see to the patient in six," he said, and quickly walked away.

Under the weather? Maggie thought. In all the time she had known Billy, he had never been too sick to work. As she made her way home, she did a mental inventory of her pantry and fridge. The minute she got home, she'd put on a big pot of chicken soup—the panacea for every illness.

Thank God her mother had been a firm believer in pressure cookers. By mid-morning, Maggie had a steaming pot of soup ready to deliver to her neighbor. When she rang the bell, it took forever for Billy to answer.

"Did I waken you?" Maggie questioned, as she entered his apartment.

"Not exactly," he said, with a look of bewilderment on his face.

"I brought you some chicken soup," Maggie explained, putting the pot down on the stove. "Dr. O'Shea told me that you were under the weather. I thought you could use some liquid penicillin."

"Uh…thanks," he said. His eyes refused to meet hers. When she did catch a glimpse of them, they were bloodshot and enhanced by deep, dark circles underneath. There was a heavy smell of cigarette smoke in the air which made her look at Billy more closely. If she didn't know better, she would have thought he was either hung over or hiding something—perhaps both.

In fact, the strange way he was acting had her wondering just what was wrong with him. Her imagination took over, and she started thinking the worst. Had he gone on a bender? She surreptitiously checked out the trash can in the kitchen and the counter tops. There was no sign of any liquor bottles, empty or otherwise. However, a pack of Marlboros and a lighter were lying on the kitchen table. Oh dear God, she thought, it looks as if he's smoking again. What if this was all her fault?

She walked over to him and put her hand on his forehead. It was cool to the touch. "No sign of fever," she said. "Was it a twenty-four-hour thing?"

"Uh…not exactly," he said again, backing away from her.

"What's going on out there?" a woman called, as she slowly shuffled out of Billy's bedroom, wrapped in what looked to be Billy's bathrobe.

Maggie froze. The woman's long dark hair framed a face that was puffy and bruised. She had a large gauze bandage on her forehead and two black eyes. But despite these things, the woman was beautiful. Maggie looked again at Billy, then at the woman in front of her.

"Oh my God!" she blurted out, "I didn't realize you were *with* someone. Why didn't you say something? I'll…uh just get out of here. I'm sorry."

The woman looked from Billy to Maggie and sneered, "And just who the hell are you?"

"Jess, this is my neighbor, Maggie Reynolds. She's a nurse at the hospital. Maggie, this is Jessie, my…wife."

"Well, well, how convenient," Jessie spat. "Work *and* play. Boy Fox, you had me going the other day. I really fell for your poor wounded warrior story. No wonder you turned down my offer of a pity fuck, you've been having little Miss Nightingale on the side. Does *she* screw you for pity, too? Do all those scars turn her on, or does she get excited doing it with a wild, red man? Some say that white women can't go back to their own kind once they had a taste of…"

"Knock it off, Jessie," Billy said tiredly.

"The truth still hurts, doesn't it Fox?"

"I said, knock it off. Please."

"Do you hit her too?" Jessie gestured to Maggie. "I hear there are women out there that like to be slapped around."

"Jessie, please," Billy begged, his voice rising in desperation. "Maggie and I are just friends. We were at the same field hospital in Vietnam."

"It's…nice to meet you," Maggie said, wanting to fall through the floor and disappear.

"That's what you think!" Jessie smirked at Maggie, then turned to Billy. "So, if you two are only *friends,* what brings her to your apartment bringing…" she sniffed, "smells like soup?"

"It *is* soup," Maggie quickly said. "I was told Billy wasn't feeling well."

"Not feeling well? Is that what you call babysitting me, Fox?"

"It's no one's business what I do on my time off."

"Except your nosy neighbor. She seems to have made it her business. Did you miss a quickie in the broom closet or something?"

"There is *nothing* going on between us. Please stop."

"I'd better go. I'm sorry to have bothered you," Maggie said, backing toward the door.

"Don't let the door hit you in the ass, *neighbor,*" Jessie said, then gingerly sat down at the kitchen table and reached for the pack of cigarettes. She shook one out and lit it, her eyes dark and defiant. Exhaling two streams of smoke through her nostrils, she looked like an evil dragon.

"Thank you for the soup, Maggie. It was very kind of you," Billy said, as he opened the door for her. "And probably just what she needs, actually," he muttered under his breath.

"You're welcome," Maggie said to Billy, then fled.

"Nothing like being a bitch to the first person you meet," Billy said, shutting the door.

"Who is she, really?"

"I told you," Billy said, as he got out bowls and spoons.

"No, you gave me her name, rank, and serial number."

Billy ladled some soup and placed it before Jessie. "Maggie was in my unit in Vietnam. We became friends. End of story."

"No husband?" she asked, as she began to eat.

"He was killed in Vietnam."

"Aw, that's too bad."

"That's all you have to say?" Billy said, serving himself a bowl.

"Yeah, life's tough," Jessie shrugged. "What do you want me to say? Some mushy lie?"

"A mushy lie is a lot kinder than being a bitch."

"Look professor, I don't need a lecture. I am what I am. Like it or lump it."

Billy shook his head, as he sat down opposite her and began to eat. "You must be feeling better. You're back to being your old acerbic self. I guess I can look forward to some real stimulating conversations in the future."

"I'm very good at stimulating. Remember? In fact, I bet I could even stimulate a poor cripple like you."

"Thanks. I'll keep that in mind," he said, continuing to eat. "The soup is good, isn't it?"

"Yeah, I guess," Jessie answered grudgingly.

From then on, Maggie saw very little of her next-door neighbors. When she did see Billy at work he was distracted and not inclined to talk. One evening however, she met up with Cal and Billy as they were on their way home. They were discussing an article in the latest medical journal Billy had gotten.

"Would you mind lending it to me to read?" Cal was asking.

"I guess, as long as I get it back."

"Yes, mother, I promise," Cal said agreeably. Since Jessie was back in the picture, he was in a much better frame of mind. He turned to Maggie, "What's for dinner?"

"I have a tuna fish salad sandwich waiting for me at home," Maggie replied tartly.

"Tuna fish," Cal said, wrinkling his nose. "That's not dinner, I need something more substantial than that."

"Who said you were invited?" Maggie stated.

Billy looked at the two of them and shook his head, a small smile on his lips.

"Go ahead, make fun," Cal said to Billy, "but what's *your* little woman cookin' up for the two of *you*?"

This time, Billy actually let out a small laugh. "You *must* be joking, Lewis. Jessie doesn't know what a stove does, let alone how to turn one on."

"We could all go out," Maggie suggested, as they walked into the Squirrel Cage. "You know, all four of us."

"I don't think that's a good idea," Billy answered.

"Why not?"

"It's just not, okay?"

"If you're sure," Maggie said, approaching her apartment door.

"Hang on," Cal said. "I may as well pick up that journal while I'm thinking about it."

"Sure," Billy said, opening the door of his apartment. As he entered though, a puzzled look came over his face. He sniffed at the air. The puzzled look was replaced by one of such anger that Maggie was actually frightened.

"Jessie!" he yelled, then turned to Cal, who was also sniffing the air. "I'll get you that article later. This isn't a good time," he said, and basically pushed Cal and Maggie from the apartment. They heard him shout Jessie's name again, then all was silent as they entered Maggie's apartment.

After a few moments however, the silence was broken by the sounds of furious screaming and shouting from Jessie. "No! Don't you dare! You bastard! No! Don't!"

Pressing her head against the wall, Maggie heard Billy mumbling and grunting, then sounds of scuffling ensued. "Give it to me, Jessie!"

"No, you bastard! Stop!"

"Give it to me right now."

"You can't force me!" Jessie yelled.

Then Maggie heard the ringing crack of a slap and more scuffling. Jessie cried out, then the fight seemed to move into the other room, and the voices progressively diminished until Maggie heard nothing at all.

"Oh my God!" Maggie said. "What's going on in there?"

"It's none of your business."

"He could be hurting her."

"Leave it alone."

"You mean you're going to just let him go after her like that?"

"It's none of my business what happens next door, either."

"How can you say that? What happened? What made Billy so angry?"

"*That* is also none of my business."

"But you know why he was mad?"

"Let's just say I have a good idea."

"And you're not going to tell me?"

"It's…"

"No, don't you dare say it."

"Come on, Maggie," Cal said, as he came up behind her and put his hands on her shoulders. "Don't get involved. As much as Billy's my friend, his life's his own." Cal turned Maggie to face him and tipped her chin up to look at him. "I don't know how many times I have to tell you. Billy is not who you, in particular, want to hang around with. Indians are different from us. I know when we were in college, he smacked Jessie around. I don't think he wanted to, but hell, he couldn't control her. Indian men treat their women differently than us whites."

"That's not true! There are plenty of white men who beat their women, some of them, just for the hell of it. And I also know that Indian men aren't all abusive or drunkards. That's racist and wrong. And I can't believe you would say such a thing, especially about your friend!"

Cal put up his hands. "Okay, you may be right. But the relationship between Billy and Jessie isn't something you can fix."

"Why did he get so mad? What did he smell?"

Cal sighed. "You won't let it go, will you?"

"I just want to understand."

"I think Billy smelled grass in the apartment."

"Grass?"

Cal grimaced, "Marijuana."

"Oh? That would make him so violently angry?"

"Shit, Maggie. Think about it. He's an Indian. That's one strike against him already. He's trying to become a respected doctor in a world where color is a huge deal. He comes home and there's not only the aroma of an illegal drug in his apartment, but maybe some physical remains of it as well. You realize that would be the end of Dr. William Fox? Even if he could prove that the drug wasn't his, it's in his home. He could still be arrested for possession. With Indians, the fuzz act first, think later. If I were him, I would have beat the shit out of her myself."

"What! How could you?"

"Very easily, I'd never let some woman, especially a whore, destroy me. And I've been tellin' Billy that for years. But does that fool listen? No. Hell, he still thinks he's gonna save her. Ha, there's no savin' that bitch. Now come on, let's get out of here and get something to eat. I'm starvin,' and I don't think tuna fish is going to cut it right now."

The next day, when Maggie walked into the cafeteria, she spied Billy getting himself a cup of coffee and went after him. She wasn't quite sure what she was going to say, but she had to confront him about what she had heard the day before. She was almost upon him when he turned around suddenly and almost ran into her. One look at him, and anything that she might have said was stifled. His eye was puffy, and he had scratches on his cheeks.

"My God! What the hell happened to you?" she asked, instead.

He looked at her strangely, as though he knew what she had been thinking. Finally, he said, "Had a run in with a feral cat. It didn't like me flushing its catnip down the toilet." Without waiting for a reply, he stalked off toward the ER, and she didn't see him for the remainder of the day.

BILLY

"What do you mean, a black-tie affair?" Billy said to Dennis.

"You know, formal," Dennis responded.

"But why are we invited to this Christmas party in the first place?"

"Look Billy, this is a very important invitation. The Birminghams are obscenely wealthy. Our job is to go to this thing and schmooze. If we make a good impression, Mrs. B. may make a very generous donation to the new wing of the hospital."

"But why do I have to go? You're King Schmooze around here, not me!"

"Mrs. B. specifically requested your presence. She's very active with the Phoenix Health Department, and some of the big wigs have been singing your praises. Now, she wants to meet you."

"But Dennis, I'm not good at this kind of thing! Please don't make me go!"

"Oh, for God's sake, don't go getting your 'nads in a twist. I'll be there with you, so will Cal. Our mission at this party is very simple. We all need to impress Mrs. B. with what we're trying to accomplish, petition her for funds, and perhaps get her to join the Board of Directors."

"That's simple?"

"Yes. With your looks, you could have her eating out of your hand before an hour is up. I hear she's also active with the Veteran's Association. She has kids in the local schools writing to GIs in Asia as well as sending them care packages. Limp a little, tell her some battle stories and the money's ours."

"Just like that?"

"If you show her some of your scars, I'd bet we'd get even more."

"You're crazy!"

"Yes, I am. But without money, the Trauma Center is just a dream. I need the support of the Birminghams, and people like them, to make it a reality. If you like your job, getting the Birmingham's backing will help you to keep it."

"This is blackmail."

"Yes, it is. But without you, I don't have a snowball's chance in hell. I told you, you're the reason we got this invitation. Now let's make good use of it."

"But I don't own a monkey suit."

"You think I do? Rent one like the rest of us peons. Oh, and don't forget, it's a couples affair as well. You'll have to bring your wife. Make sure she's dressed in evening attire."

"What? I can't bring Jessie."

"Why not? She's a very beautiful woman."

"Until she opens her mouth."

"Don't worry, Reynolds is going with Lewis. She can keep an eye on Jessie."

"Oh, that'll be great. Jessie will have her ripped to shreds before we get to the front door."

"I find that hard to believe. Maggie won't let Jessie get to her. She's very calm and no nonsense. She'll keep Jessie in line. Trust me."

"Trust you? You are friggin' *loco*. This thing has fiasco written all over it."

"I know. Just pretend we're Marines going into combat. We'll all go down together."

Billy stared at Dennis for a few seconds, a sour look on his face. Finally, he shook his head. "All right, I'll go. I'll come dressed like some white fool and even bring Jessie, but we turn into pumpkins when an hour has passed. That's it."

"Sure, as long as *you* understand what needs to be done and can work fast. After that, I don't care what the hell you do."

"We're going where?" Jessie asked.

"To a Christmas party at some wealthy Anglo's house. You'll have to get some kind of dress. Maybe Maggie can help you. She's going to this party, too."

"Oh, I can see it now. The two of us shopping together like girlfriends."

"Whatever happens, please try to be nice."

"I hate this."

"Look, I don't want to go, either. But I have to. It's for the hospital."

"Why can't O'Shea and Lewis go by themselves?"

"Because the lady of the house specifically asked for me."

"God, Fox, sounds to me like you're nothing but a whore yourself."

"Thanks. In that case, maybe you can give me a few pointers."

"Sure, smile a lot, act like she's the only woman in the world, and what she's saying is fascinating, and you're halfway there."

"And the other half?"

"Have a ten-inch cock and make her toes curl for a few hours."

Billy gave Jessie a disgusted look and exhaled. "Okay. I'll smile a lot. The rest, as you well know, would probably be impossible."

"The ten inches, for sure. But even with *your* equipment you could probably make her toes curl quite a bit. I know. Mine did."

"Such flattery."

"And what is my part in this little drama?"

"You get to be nice to the man of the house while I'm being nice to his wife."

"How nice?"

"I don't think that you're expected to make *his* toes curl, if that's what you're getting at. In fact, I think Dennis would appreciate you acting like a lady, if you can manage it."

"With my bag of tricks, I could probably have gotten your money in ten minutes flat."

"Just like you got paid the last time?"

Jessie stared at Billy for a long second, then bowed her head and turned away. "Yeah Fox, you're right. I can't even do that, can I?"

Billy sighed. He went to her and laid his hand on her shoulder. "I'm sorry. That was a shitty thing to say."

Jessie rubbed at her eyes with the sleeve of her shirt. "True though."

"That guy was crud. These people aren't like that. Don't worry."

"People are people. Once their clothes are off, they're all the same."

"Tell me about it," Billy said. "One appendix looks just like another. The rich ones don't have diamonds embedded in them."

Jessie turned back to Billy. "See, I told you we were alike, didn't I?"

"Yes, you did."

"This is going to be one hell of a party. Two token Indians all dressed up as the entertainment. I can hardly wait."

"Well, don't you all look nice," Dennis said, surveying the two couples as he entered Billy's apartment with Joni, Billy's team nurse, on his arm. "You all clean up very well. Even you, Fox."

Billy, who drew the line at a bow tie, was wearing a turquoise bolo at his neck with his rented tuxedo. "Yeah, well, we'd better get this show on the road, before I chicken out or fall off the wagon. A whiskey would go really good right now."

"Sure, let's go," Dennis said. "Shall we all go together?"

"I'll drive Jessie and I," Billy answered.

"You're going in the VW?" Dennis questioned.

"What's wrong with that?"

"It's not exactly a good impression car."

"What do you mean? I just spent a small fortune buying four new tires and yesterday I washed and waxed the damned thing. Did you expect me to rent a Rolls as well as the tux?"

"It may have been a good idea."

"You know, Dennis. You're starting to piss me off. Besides, aren't we supposed to need money? Why would I want to go there looking like a rich person?"

"Because money begets more money."

"Just be happy I'm going to this thing. I hate parties and I don't do well at them."

"Jessie and I can vouch for that," Cal added with a smirk.

"You may be surprised," Dennis commented. "You might actually have a good time."

Billy grunted. "I highly doubt it. At this point, I think I'd rather be back in Vietnam."

"It's only for an hour."

"You can bet on that. That's why I'm taking the VW."

"The choice is yours," Dennis shrugged. "What about you, Cal? Are you and Maggie coming with us, or shall we meet you all there?"

"We'll meet you. I like having my own wheels as well," Cal responded. "Although I do hope my Corvette meets with your approval as transportation."

"Don't be smart. We'll see you there," Dennis said, as he and Joni departed.

"That would be all we need, arriving with the boss," Cal said. "It's bad enough, we can't go to have fun."

"Let's just get this over with," Billy said.

The Birmingham's lived in a new development of multi-million-dollar homes about ten minutes out of the city. Their home was not only brand new but sprawled the entire length of the block. The façade was of stone and stucco. Giant terra cotta planters full of blooming flowers and palm trees lined the circular driveway. Jessie gasped. "Holy shit! We're going in there?"

"I suppose so," Billy answered, putting the car in park as a uniformed man opened his door. "Just leave the keys," the man said. "I'll park it for you." When Billy hesitated, he continued, "Don't worry, *sir*, I think I can handle a Volkswagen. When you are ready to leave, just let one of us know and we'll get your *vehicle* for you."

Billy got out and went to Jessie's door. He opened it and extended his arm. Dressed in a long, black beaded gown with matching shawl, Jessie was shaking. "I don't think I can do this. What if I screw things up?"

"Don't worry. Everything will be all right."

They entered the double doors along with Maggie and Cal. Maggie turned to Jessie and gave her a reassuring smile. "You look lovely, Jessie. Don't worry. You'll be fine."

When Jessie answered by snorting loudly, Billy elbowed her in the side and said into her ear, "Be nice."

A large open foyer spilled down two steps into a formal living room the size of a gymnasium. Floor to ceiling windows provided a magnificent, panoramic backdrop of the mountains of Phoenix, which, at this time of day, were bathed in the purple golden light of the setting sun. A massive fieldstone fireplace occupied another wall. Waiters circulated among the guests with glasses of champagne and hot and cold hors d'oeuvres.

A tall, elegantly dressed woman in a blood-red, strapless evening gown approached the foursome. Her blond hair was pulled up into a French twist, highlighting her bare shoulders. "You *must* be Doctor Fox," the woman said, giving Billy her hand. "I'm *so* glad that you could make it. I'm Kathryn Birmingham."

"I'm very pleased to meet you," Billy said, looking at her hand with trepidation. Out of the corner of his eye, he saw Cal bring his own hand to his mouth with a grin and a wink at Billy. Swallowing hard, Billy brought the proffered hand to his lips and grazed her knuckles. "Thank you for inviting us."

Ignoring the other three, Kathryn slipped her hand into the crook of Billy's arm. She turned to a hovering waiter and said sharply, "Simon, neither Doctor Fox nor I have a drink." The man named Simon flushed, then handed them both glasses of champagne from his tray before slinking away.

"Here's to a healthy new relationship," Kathryn said, looking at Billy from over the rim of her glass. Billy glanced back at Jessie who smiled and leered at him. He raised his glass to Kathryn and smiled, then took a tiny sip, wishing it was bourbon.

She steered Billy into the sea of guests, and commented, "There are so many things I want to talk to you about and so many people I want you to meet."

Billy turned back to his friends with a look of terror. Maggie and Jessie smiled and waved. Cal, meanwhile, took a woman on each arm and entered the room. They made their way through the throng, drinking champagne and nibbling on elegant canapés. Toward the center of the room, a rather large, florid man stood in the midst of some people. He appeared to be telling a joke for those gathered around him were laughing.

"If I'm not mistaken," Cal remarked, "that's the man of the house. We met once before at the country club. Chet is nice enough, but a lousy golfer and a lousier loser. But then again, what man really likes to lose?"

Jessie looked at who Cal was referring to and her stomach lurched. "I…I'm going to be sick," she gasped.

Maggie turned to her and said, "Jessie, what's wrong?"

"Gonna be sick," Jessie moaned. "Get me out of here."

"Sure," Maggie said, and taking her quickly by the arm, the two women headed back to the foyer, leaving Cal a little confused.

Maggie stopped a waiter. "Where may we find the rest room, please?"

"Down this hall toward the kitchen."

"Thank you," Maggie said, and propelled Jessie in that direction. Jessie, in the meantime, had her head down and her hand over her face. "Hang in there, Jessie. We're almost there."

Fortunately, the powder room was empty when Maggie pushed open the door. Jessie slid down to the floor and pulled her knees up to her chest. "Lock the door," Jessie commanded.

"What's wrong?" Maggie asked, concern filling her face.

"I can't go back out there," Jessie whispered.

"Why not?"

"Go find Fox. I need him."

"Sure, Jessie. Will you be okay by yourself?"

Jessie was shivering. "I'll lock the door."

"I'll be back as soon as possible."

"Only Fox, you hear. No one else."

"Sure, Jessie, I'll get him."

Maggie finally found Billy in a remote corner; Kathryn pressed closely to his side. "Doctor Fox?" Maggie said.

Both Billy and Kathryn looked up—Billy in relief, Kathryn in annoyance. "And who might this be?" Kathryn asked.

"Kathryn, this is Margaret Reynolds. She's one of our nurses in the Emergency Department and a Vietnam Vet as well. She's here with Doctor Lewis, another vet, whom I don't think you have had the pleasure of meeting yet. He's a cardiologist at the center. Maggie, where's Dr. Lewis?"

"I'm not sure, but Jessie needs you. She's ill."

"Ill?"

"Yes."

"Where is she?"

"She's in the powder room by the kitchen."

"Maggie why don't you take Kathryn and introduce her to Drs. Lewis and O'Shea. In the meantime, I'll go and check on Jessie."

"Yes, Doctor, I know that they are both *very* anxious to meet you, Mrs. Birmingham."

With a look of disappointment on her face, Kathryn said, "Now don't you disappear on me Doctor Fox. I'll find you, if you're not back in a flash."

"Of course," Billy replied and hurried off to the kitchen. He found the powder room and knocked on the door. "Jessie?"

"Fox?"

"Yes," as he said this, the bolt slid back, and the door opened slightly. Billy slipped inside and found Jessie huddled on the floor. With her arms wrapped tightly around her body, she rocked back and forth. Her hair was a snarled mess. And, tears had run through her make up, distorting her face. "Help me!" Jessie moaned.

Billy locked the door, then awkwardly hunkered down beside her. "What is it? Maggie said you were ill."

"It's him. The guy who threw me out of the limo."

"He's a guest here?"

"No, worse. He lives here."

"Oh my God!"

"I've got to get out of here!" Jessie cried, grabbing onto the lapels of his jacket.

Billy put his arms around Jessie and held her. "Don't worry, Jess. I'll get you out."

"How? He'll see me."

"I'll think of something."

There was a light tap on the door. "Jessie? Billy? It's me, Maggie. Is everything okay?"

Billy looked at Jessie who, after a long moment, nodded. He struggled to his feet and unlocked the door for Maggie. "No, everything's not okay," Billy said, returning to Jessie's side.

"What's wrong?" Maggie asked.

"To make a long story short, it's very important that I get Jessie out of this house quickly and without anyone, especially Mr. Birmingham, seeing her."

"How long have we been here?"

Billy checked his watch, "Almost forty-five minutes."

"Did you do what Dennis wanted?"

"Sort of."

"Can you finish what you started in a few minutes?"

"I can try. What do you have in mind?"

"I'll stay here with Jessie while you go and say goodbye to Kathryn. Make the excuse that your wife is ill. Maybe you could arrange to meet her for lunch. That way you can get her off your back, yet still be in her good graces. After that, have the valet get your car. See if there's a back entrance, so that we can get Jessie out without anyone seeing her. Then you two take off, and I go and cozy up to the master of the house."

"Do you think it'll work?" Billy asked.

"I hope so," Maggie said.

"It's all we can do, I guess."

"Don't leave me," Jessie begged Billy.

"It'll only be for a few minutes. I'll be back. Don't worry. We'll get you out of here. It's a good thing I didn't know sooner. Had we been introduced, I may have broken his nose, or worse."

"Just as well, you forgot your cape at home," Jessie smiled weakly.

Billy shook his head, then stood slowly and turned to Maggie, "Thanks for your help. I really appreciate it. I'll be back as quickly as I can."

When he left, Jessie glared at Maggie. "Why're you doing this?"

"It's what friends do."

"You're not my friend."

"Maybe not. But Billy's my friend, and I'll help him if I can."

"Friend my ass, lover's more like it."

Maggie looked at Jessie, startled. "Lover? Where would you get that idea?"

"I'm not blind, you know. I see the way he looks at you. And you, you look at him like he's lunch. Why don't you stick to that blond asshole you're supposedly dating?"

"That's ridiculous, I am not having an affair with your husband."

"Maybe not now, but you did. Didn't you?"

Maggie looked off into space for a moment before replying, "I would prefer to say that we had something very special while we were in Vietnam. But it's over."

"Over?"

"Of course. Billy never led me on. He told me up front he was married and, whether you believe it or not, is very committed to you. It was over before it even started."

"If you think it's over, think again."

"It's over," Maggie said stubbornly. "It has to be."

Jessie stared at Maggie with hate and something akin to craziness in her eyes. "Damn right! He's mine and don't you forget it," Jessie snarled and began to rock back and forth again. "It's me that gets him hot. It's me that he wants— me, you hear?"

Maggie swallowed nervously and backed away, "Of course, Jessie. He's all yours."

Jessie continued rocking, a mantra of 'It's me he wants' coming from her lips, her eyes glazing over. Then just as quickly as it began, Jessie stopped rocking and sneered at Maggie. "Of course, I guess we're even."

"What are you talking about?"

"Your boyfriend."

"I don't understand."

"How dumb are you? I screwed him. Screwed 'em both."

"At the same time?"

"Christ! What kind of slut do you take me for. Though blondie would have liked that. He liked strange things. Used to give me drugs for it, till his daddy found out. Then he gave me the ass like he was too good for me. But he always comes back. He always knows he can get what he wants from me."

"You mean you're still…uh…sleeping with Cal?"

"Off and on."

"But he's Billy's friend."

"So? What do I care? It's business. As long as he pays me, I'll even bark like a dog. 'Course he couldn't even satisfy a dog in heat. Two, three strokes and he's finished. Now Fox can really last. But you already know that, don't you, bitch?"

Jessie had begun to rock again, when there was a tapping on the door. "The coast is clear," Billy said, when Maggie opened the door a crack. "We'll go out through the kitchen. The car is already there."

"What about Kathryn?" Maggie asked.

"I have a lunch date with the vampire on Wednesday at the hospital. Hopefully there will be hundreds of people there for protection. I guess I'll even throw in a tour as well. She seems very interested in both joining the board and of donating some money to the cause."

"That should make Dennis ecstatic."

"I just hope it isn't my butt that's the price. Now let's get out of here before someone else needs a place to pee or hide."

"Okay. I'll go run interference while you and Jessie disappear."

"Thank you, Maggie, for all your help this evening."

"That's what friends are for," she said, looking nervously at Jessie.

"Thank you, Maggie," Jessie said sweetly, and rising, took Billy tightly by the arm. "Okay," she said, shaking back her long, now sweaty hair. "I'm ready to go."

Maggie stared after them, her brow furrowed. She shivered and shook herself slightly. She snagged a glass of champagne from a passing waiter and downed the Dom Perignon a tad bit faster than the expensive wine deserved. Catching another waiter, she swapped out her empty glass with a full one. This time, she sipped genteelly, savoring her drink. Then finding a waiter with food, selected several small bites to go with it. After one more glass swap, she straightened her shoulders, sighed, then went to find Cal.

The interior of the small car was dark and cozy, reminding Jessie of a womb. She curled as close to Billy as the bucket seats and gear shift would allow. He put his arm around her and stroked her hair. "I'm so sorry, Jessie. Thank God, we got you out of there before any damage was done."

"You'd never have gotten any money if he'd seen me."

"The hell with the hospital, I'm talking about damage to you. He's already hurt you. Unfortunately, there's no way I can return the favor."

"Money always wins, Fox. Why do you think I couldn't get what he owed me? Who'd people believe, me or him?"

"I know. Boy, his wife's a real scary bitch, too. She acted like she owned me when she introduced me to some of her friends."

"The perfect couple."

"Just like us," Billy smiled.

Jessie was still shaking when they entered the apartment. "Relax, Jess." Billy said as he removed his jacket and tie and undid the top buttons on his shirt. "Don't think about it anymore. It's over and done with. Thank goodness."

"I wish," Jessie sighed. She sat down on the sofa and kicked off her shoes, grabbing up her bear that was lying on the cushion. "God, why couldn't that bastard have killed me when he pushed me out of his car? That would have been the best thing to happen."

"Don't say that."

"It's true."

Billy sat down beside Jessie and took off his shoes. "I'm glad I found you."

"Why? I'm nothing but a problem."

"That's not true."

"Yes, it is," she said. "I'm nothing—a whore, a nobody. No one loves me. Even you. You don't love me. You never did. But I know who you *do* love. You love Maggie."

"Please leave her out of this."

"I can't. I know you love her. I can feel it, and I have eyes. I can see it. You want her."

"No, I don't."

"Bullshit."

Billy sighed and went to stand. "Think what you want."

"Wait," Jessie said, clutching his sleeve. "Don't go away. Hold me…please."

Billy put his arms around her. "Did I tell you how beautiful you looked tonight?"

"I'm not sure. You could always tell me again."

"You looked beautiful tonight."

"I didn't spend much time at the party."

"No, but for the small amount of time that we were there, you looked terrific in that pretty dress."

Jessie tried to smile as she gazed up at him, but her eyes were full of grief as sobs shook her body. Billy couldn't bear to see her naked pain. He could not imagine any of Jessie's 'clients' ever saying anything like that to her. He stroked her cheek, wiping at her tears. What was he going to do with this poor broken woman, Billy thought, as he gently rocked her back and forth like a small child—her bear a furry lump between them?

Several hours later, Billy awoke from disturbing dreams. He could smell Jessie's cigarette before he saw its glow in the dark. Getting up, he went into the living room. She sat on the sofa, the bear in her arms covering her nakedness.

"Are you okay?" he asked, looking down at her.

Jessie shrugged in the dark.

"What's the matter?"

Jessie shrugged again and took a hit on her cigarette. She exhaled and sighed. "God, I wish this was a joint."

"Jessie, you know you can't have that."

"Why not?" she said, viciously stabbing the cigarette out in the ashtray on the coffee table.

"We've been over this all before. How many times do I have to explain it to you?"

"I don't care. I need something. If you loved me, you'd help me. Why can't you write me a prescription for painkillers? Or let me smoke some pot."

"I can't. I could lose my license. I could lose everything."

"So."

"So? And then what? We'd both be back out on the street, or in jail."

"Nick would have done it for me. He gave me everything, no matter what."

"Nick?" Billy asked, as he puzzled over who she was talking about.

"Yeah, Nick, now *he* loved me. Didn't he?" Jessie asked, addressing her bear. "He was the only one who ever did. He never worried about his precious reputation. He gave me drugs. All that I wanted. I could be with him now. If only…"

Billy thought back to the guy that Jessie had been working for in Vegas. That had to be who she was talking about, he thought. The guy she thought died while trying to get her away from her pimp. Billy sat down next to Jessie and laid his hand on her arm.

"I'm sorry. I really am. I wish I could give you what you want, but you know that's impossible."

Jessie shook him off fiercely, screaming, "Don't touch me! I hate you!" she cried, bursting into tears.

"Jessie, please calm down," Billy said, as he tried to hold her.

"I gotta get out of here." She got up and ran toward the door. But in the dark, she tripped on the leg of the coffee table and fell heavily. Billy went to her, again trying to calm her, but she balled her hands into fists and struck him repeatedly.

"NO! Don't touch me! You bastard! Leave me alone!" Her crying became hysterical, and she started to gasp for air.

Billy hurried into the kitchen and got a brown paper bag from the cupboard. Hunkering down on the floor next to her, he forced her to breathe into the bag.

"Come on, Jessie. Breathe. It's okay. Come on now, calm down. It'll be all right."

Although her breathing slowed, her crying continued. Taking the bag away from her face, Billy held Jessie as she rocked back and forth.

"I hate you," she continued to say through her tears. Billy picked her up and carried her back into the bedroom. He got her bear, and wrapping the two of them into his arms, held her tightly until she'd cried herself to sleep for the second time that night.

Billy laid awake long afterward. He worried that Jessie was close to the breaking point. He'd have to get her help. The kind of injury that Jessie had was something he couldn't fix by himself.

JESSIE

The next day, Billy had a long talk with Dennis. "She needs help. But I don't know how to fix a broken mind. She's crying one minute, laughing hysterically the next. I'm afraid to leave her alone for long periods of time."

"I know you're not going to want to hear this. But maybe the kindest, smartest thing to do is put her in a place."

"You mean commit her?"

"That sounds harsh. Don't think of it as committing her, think of it as placing her in a hospital that knows how to care for her kind of illness."

"It's still committing her."

"But at least you'll know she'll be safe and well cared for."

"What about Jeff Stark? He's on staff. It wouldn't be such a permanent move, at least not yet."

"I know that Stark is good, but he's only here part-time for counseling."

"Do you think he'd see Jessie?"

"I don't see why not. Ask him. See what he has to say. Maybe he could at least do an evaluation and let you know what he thinks. In the end, he may still tell you to commit her."

"If that's the case, then I'll start looking around."

"I know from reputation that New Hope is a good place. Stark is on the staff there as well."

Billy shivered. He'd heard of New Hope. They usually sent patients there in straightjackets, screaming incoherently. It was not what he would want for Jessie. Hell, she wasn't crazy, she was just…well…unstable.

"I guess I'll talk to Stark first. Maybe between the two of us, we can get her the help she needs without sending her away."

"I'd at least have a back-up plan," Dennis suggested.

"I will."

Billy met with Jeff Stark the next afternoon. Stark agreed to see Jessie for an evaluation. Then, perhaps see her for a few visits, until he was sure of the best possible course of treatment.

When Billy got home, he found Jessie curled on the sofa. As he rummaged in the refrigerator for something to make for their dinner, he casually commented, "I want you to start seeing a doctor at the hospital," Billy said.

"Why? I'm not sick. You already patched me up. What do I need to see another doctor for?"

"I think you need some help."

"Help? For what? I don't have clap or syph. Are you afraid you're gonna get that shit from me? Is that why you won't fuck me now, or when you did, you've always done me all covered up like some prissy grandma?"

Billy took a deep breath and let it out slowly. "I'm not worried about that."

"Then what is it? Why else would I have to see some doc?"

"I'd like you to see one of the staff…psychiatrists."

"A shrinky-dink?" Jessie spit out, her eyes narrowing. "No way!"

"I think it would be a good idea."

"Why? You think I'm nuts?"

"No, Jessie, I do *not* think you're nuts. I just think that you might be depressed and need someone to talk to."

"What's he gonna tell me? That I'm screwed up?" she said, sitting up on the sofa. "No shit. I don't need a shrinky-dink to tell me that. Besides, being depressed is something only rich people can afford to be. Like that Birmingham bitch. It's okay for *her* to be depressed," Jessie said, putting her hand dramatically against her forehead.

"That's not true, Jessie," Billy replied, sitting down next to her. "Everyone is entitled to feeling down or being depressed."

"But only the rich can afford to be treated for it."

"You're wrong, especially now. I work at a hospital, for God's sake. I can get you the help you need."

"Too late, Fox, I'm tellin' ya, no shrink is gonna change me."

"Maybe not right away, but someone may be able to help at least a little bit. You don't want to spend the rest of your life like this, do you?"

"The rest of my life? God, the way you say it, it sounds like a prison sentence."

"That's why you need help," Billy said, exasperated. "You can't continue to feel this way."

"Look asshole, get it through your thick, fuckin' head. I don't want to be here. Why can't you just leave me alone?"

"There are medications out there that might be able to help you."

"Like heroin?"

"No, not that."

"And what will they do for me? Make me high?"

"They'll make you feel…better."

"So, they'll make me high?"

"No, but they'll help."

"Help, schmelp. I want the good shit or nothing."

"Come on, Jess."

"Where're we going? You know, you kill me. You fix me up, pay what I owed on my rent, bring all my stuff here, then treat me like a fucking prisoner."

"I am *not* treating you like a prisoner. But the way you're acting scares me. I'm afraid to leave you alone."

Jessie made a rude noise and waved at the air with her hand.

"I just don't want to see you end up like my father."

"Why not? It worked for him."

"Maybe he'd still be here if someone had helped him."

"Like you? Get lost. He wanted to end it. Get over it."

"Jessie, you're here with me now. I'm doing my best to take care of you, just like I promised. When you were cut and bleeding, I patched you up. What's wrong with trying to patch up your mind when it's hurt?"

"Who do you think you are? God?"

"No, but I refuse to give up on you."

Jessie sighed and laid back down on the sofa, curling back into a ball. "Fuck off."

Billy stared at her back for a long moment, his eyes blurring. In his mind, he saw his father—arms outstretched, embracing the wind, as he propelled himself off the cliff. Then he heard Rusty's voice in his head repeating, 'It's not your fault.' He blinked and shook himself. Then rising, Billy walked slowly back to the kitchen.

In the morning, Jessie refused to get out of bed. Billy tried to coax her to eat something, but she ignored him. He sat down on the edge of the bed next to her. "I'm leaving for work. Are you going to be okay?"

Jessie remained silent.

"If you need me, you know where I am," he said.

There was still no response as he picked up his briefcase and jacket and left the apartment. On his way to the hospital, he ran into Maggie, who was returning from work.

"Hi, Billy, how's it going?" she asked.

Billy shook his head.

"What is it?"

"It's Jessie. I'm so damned worried about her. She sounds like a suicide waiting to happen."

"Are you sure?"

"Yes, I'm sure."

"Would you like me to look in on her and maybe talk to her for a little bit?"

"I don't think she'll talk to you. But, if you'd look in on her during the afternoon, I wouldn't worry as much. That way I could concentrate on what I'm supposed to be doing."

"Sure, I can do that."

"Thanks. I would appreciate it."

Later that day, Billy was paged at work. There was a phone call for him from Maggie. "Billy? It's Jessie. I went over to check on her, but the door is locked and the key you gave me isn't working. The door seems to be stuck. Can you come over here? I'm really worried. She isn't answering me."

Billy turned to one of the residents, "Can you please cover for me? I'll be back as soon as possible. Send an ambulance to my apartment." Then without waiting for a reply, he hurried out.

Maggie was outside the apartment when he arrived. "I still haven't heard anything from inside," she said.

Billy put his key into the lock and turned it, but the door still refused to open. "God! She must have barred the door with something." He threw his shoulder into the door and shoved. The door moved a fraction.

"What's going on?" Cal questioned, hurrying down the hall. "Denny said there was trouble over here."

"Help me," Billy stated, as he again threw his shoulder into the door. With Cal's help, they got the door open enough for Billy to shimmy through. "Jessie?" he yelled, going through the apartment.

He found her in the bathroom, naked and lying in the tub. She had a broken mirror from her powder compact in her hand and blood was running over her fingers. Her left wrist was open and bleeding profusely as she tried to make a cut on the other side. She looked at him in a bit of a daze, as he quickly grabbed the mirror from her hand.

Wrapping her in a towel, he picked her up and carried her from the room as the paramedics hurried down the hall to the apartment.

"No, don't!" Jessie cried. "Leave me alone!"

"Hush, Jess," Billy said, as he laid her on the gurney. He grabbed a kitchen towel and, tearing it in two, picked up Jessie's wrist. Jessie squirmed and tried to resist him as he used one half to pad the wound. The other half of the towel he tied tightly around her wrist in a tight knot. "Let's get her next door," he directed.

Jessie continued to struggle as the paramedics fought to strap her to the gurney. With her good hand, she punched Billy in the face as he tried to calm her down. She writhed on the gurney, screaming obscenities and crying tears of frustration as they wheeled her down the hall to the elevator.

"Do I have to hire a babysitter for you?" Billy asked Jessie later, as he escorted her back to the apartment.

"Fuck you," she said.

He pretended that he didn't hear her and continued, "You have an appointment with Doctor Stark tomorrow morning at nine. I rearranged my schedule so that I can go with you."

"Fuck you," she said again, as she entered the apartment and plopped down on the sofa.

"Is there anything I can get you?"

"Pain pills."

"All I can give you is acetaminophen."

"What the hell is that? I want some coke."

"No."

"How about some grass?"

"You know I can't get you that."

"Then go to fucking hell! What good are you?"

"Not much good, I guess. If I was, maybe you wouldn't feel the need to kill yourself."

"Oh, for God's sake! Here we go again."

"I just feel bad, Jessie. I want to help you, but you won't let me."

"If you hadn't had your *friend* checking up on me like some sort of undercover dick, I could have been dead and gone by now. Happy at last. My very best Christmas present to myself. But no, thanks to you, I'm not only still here, but in pain. Thanks, a whole hell of a lot."

"I'm sorry." Billy sat down next to Jessie. For a long time, the two of them sat side by side, not touching, not speaking, not looking at each other. Two strangers tied by vows that had no meaning, yet bound by an unspoken moral obligation.

"How's Jessie?" Maggie asked Billy the next day, when they met in passing at the hospital.

Billy shrugged.

"How did things go with Doctor Stark?"

"They didn't. She refused to talk to him."

"Why?"

"Because she wants to die and that's that. Stark says he can't help her. After I left the room, he said they sat for fifty minutes in silence, then Jessie looked at her watch and said, 'Time's up, Starky. See you later,' then flounced out. Now I have both Stark and Dennis recommending that I have her committed. God! I hate to do that. It would break her completely."

Maggie sighed. "I'm sorry. I wish there was something I could do."

"Damn it," Billy growled in frustration. "Why can't Stark help her? Is it too much to ask of someone? Shit, when someone comes into the ER, I don't give up right away because it's too much work. No, I go above and beyond to do something to help."

"But this is mental illness. It doesn't work that way and you know it."

Billy ran his hands over his head and groaned. "Yeah, I know. But I still don't like the thought of sending her away. It's a cop out."

"It is not! It's giving her the help she needs."

"It's too late. Jessie needed help when she was six, not now. I don't see anyone being able to help her. Her mind's made up. I just live in fear of when and how," he said, his shoulders sagging. After a moment, he continued, "And now, as much as I hate the thought, I'm going to go out to New Hope and see if they have a room for her. Hope, what a shitty name for a place like that."

Maggie placed her hand on his arm and remained silent. Finally, she looked into his eyes. "I'm truly sorry. There's nothing else I can say. I just wish things were different for the both of you."

Billy stared at Maggie's hand for a long moment before moving away. "Thanks. It's good to know that someone else out there besides me cares about her."

The days slowly dragged for Jessie. She met with her doctor as requested. It was senseless, but Jessie did it because she knew that it was what Billy wanted. She thought about her feelings for her husband, turning them over and over in her mind. They made no sense. He worked, came home, took care of her and the apartment, shopped, cooked, and slept. He was something that she still couldn't understand.

No matter what she said or did, he was kind to her. There was a part of her that actually looked forward to his home coming each day. She would listen for his step in the hall, and her heart would beat loudly in her ears when she heard his key in the lock. He would smile at her, and she would pretend not to care. But that smile meant a lot.

On the other hand, Jessie hated Billy. Hated him with all her being. He was between her and what she wanted—death. All she wanted was a nice quiet ending, a smile playing on her lips as she lived her last high in peace. It was this thought that she dwelled on, no sentimentality for her. No way, it would only make things difficult.

There was a guy that Jessie knew. He could get her what she wanted, but she had to come up with some major cash. She thought about hooking for the money while Billy was at work but was afraid to risk it. Unfortunately, whatever she did, she was going to have to move fast. She had overheard Billy talking to her doctor the other day. She supposedly was next on the waiting list for a hospital that sounded worse than a prison. She was running out of time.

The miracle came the day after Christmas. Jessie was taking a walk through the apartment building when the mailman arrived. She went over to the bank of mailboxes.

"Oh no! I forgot my key," she said in dismay.

"What number?" the mailman asked, smiling.

"Three fourteen."

"Here you go," the man said, handing Jessie a stack of mail.

"Thank you so much," Jessie gushed. "You're wonderful."

She took the mail up to the apartment and riffled through the junk mail, bills, and envelopes. One envelope among them stood out. She had hit the jackpot. It was Billy's paycheck. She ripped open the envelope and found not only his regular pay, but his Christmas bonus as well.

She sat at the kitchen table a long time, plotting. She knew what she wanted to do and knew what she had to do to get what she wanted. It would take cunning, skill, and several phone calls. The heroin was available, but did she have the money? She stared at the figure on the paycheck. It wasn't a fortune, but it was more than she needed to make a purchase. The drug would be hers. All that she wanted—no, needed.

But to get the check cashed, she needed numbers. And Billy was the one with the numbers. She tore the apartment apart, looking for his bank statements and his checkbook. She finally found them, hidden in an empty cereal box in the back of the pantry. She forged his name, signed hers, then added the account numbers. She dressed carefully—a little something for the guys, yet businesslike enough for the women. She aimed for the young male teller and flashed a lot of cleavage and a plausible story.

The money was in her hands before she could say 'Captain Jack.' A mega dose of heroin changed hands for the paycheck. It was just what the doctor ordered. Jessie then rushed back to the apartment, knowing that she had little time.

Billy was with a patient when his office nurse interrupted an exam.

"It's the bank," Ellen said. "They say it's very important."

After a very brief phone call with the bank manager, Billy left the office and raced to the apartment. The door was again barred but Billy, in his panic, was able to open it enough to get through. She was on the couch, the mangy teddy bear clenched in her arms. The evidence of what she had done on the floor.

"Jessie!" Billy cried, as he ran to her side.

She opened her eyes drowsily and said, "Damn, not fast enough."

As Billy stood to go to the phone, Jessie grabbed his arm. "No," she pleaded. "Let me go!"

"How much did you do?" Billy asked, as he eyed the needle and empty vials next to him.

"Enough, please. Won't take…long. Just…hold me."

As Jessie spoke, Maggie peered into the doorway, her eyes wide in fright. Unseen by Jessie, she saw Billy's face and ran back to her apartment to make a phone call.

Jessie held tightly to Billy's arms. Then, trying hard to focus on his face, she said clearly, "Tell me you love me."

Billy touched her cheek. "I love you, Jessie."

"Thanks," she whispered, then smiling, closed her eyes.

After making her phone call, Maggie quickly returned. Billy, in the meantime, had gotten Jessie onto the floor and was in the process of giving CPR.

"I called for an ambulance. Do you need help?" Maggie asked, hurrying to his side. Billy nodded toward Jessie's head as he counted chest compressions.

Maggie knelt at Jessie's head and began mouth to mouth resuscitation. By the time the police and ambulance arrived, Jessie was blue. Maggie moved out of the way of the paramedics and huddled in the doorway of her apartment. She knew from experience that in Jessie's case, their efforts would probably not bring her back, but they had to try.

BILLY

Billy stood like a statue in the quiet room, not the bringer of bad news this time, but the recipient. He stared at Jessie's face in death. It was calm and peaceful.

"I'm sorry, Billy," Dennis said, patting him on the shoulder. "She must have taken enough to kill an elephant. There was no way we could bring her back."

"I know," Billy replied. "I just wish there was something I could have done."

"You did all you could. Just remember, the most important thing is that you were there for her. That's all she wanted. Are you going to be okay?"

Billy sighed. "Yeah, I'll be fine. At least now, I won't be constantly worrying that she's going to do something crazy."

"Sometimes anticipating the tragedy is far worse than the actual event, isn't it?" Dennis asked.

"I guess."

"Is there anything I can do?"

"Not really, I know people are going to talk. They already are. Hell, there has been enough shit going on in my life since I got here to give the gossips a field day. I just wish we could have kept this kind of quiet. I don't need the staff sending me shit or asking a bunch of personal questions, that right now, I'm not quite prepared to handle."

"I can do my best. But you're right about how rumors run rampant around here. You know Billy, with all that's happened these past couple of weeks, why don't you take a couple of days off? Once you get everything straightened out, get out of here. Go see Rusty or go home to the reservation. Go anywhere—anywhere but here."

Billy looked at Dennis for a long moment then said, "I'll let you know what I decide." Then looking down, he ran his finger lightly over the healing gash on Jessie's forehead. It seemed like years since he had stitched it up instead of several weeks. Had it healed completely, there would have been little scarring. He shook his head, then taking one last look, he pulled the sheet up over Jessie's face and left the room.

Tony Ramirez was waiting for him in the hall, looking rather uncomfortable. "Hey, Doc. I'm really sorry about your wife."

"Thanks, Tony."

"I hate to do this now, but…"

Billy looked at the young police officer, who had found Jessie weeks ago. He looked like he wanted to be somewhere else.

Billy sighed, "What do you need from me?"

"Well, Doc. I tried to make things as painless for you as possible. I already spoke to Maggie and Dr. Stark. Then I got a statement from your office nurse and called the bank for verification. We put Jessie's movements in a timeline, but unfortunately, between the bank and your apartment, we lost her trail. So unfortunately, whoever sold her the smack is still at large. Now, if you could just confirm your own actions, that'll be great."

"Sure, I did my rounds at the hospital around five-thirty this morning, then got to the office by about seven, since it's my regular office day. I was there all morning and early afternoon—I'm not sure what time the bank called, maybe Ellen knows. I just know that it was after two, because she and I sat down for a minute to eat before seeing the afternoon patients. Neither one of us left the office until the bank called. I went to the apartment immediately after that, leaving poor Ellen with a real mess," he said, shaking his head.

"When I got to the apartment, I had trouble entering because Jessie had jammed a kitchen chair against the door. It took several minutes to push my way in. By the time I got to her, she was pretty far gone. Maggie heard the commotion and appeared at the door. She was the one to call the paramedics, then she helped me give CPR until they arrived." Billy paused to give Ramirez time to catch up with what he had told him.

"Then what happened?" Ramirez asked, writing quickly.

"Things were pretty much out of my hands by then. I followed her over here and Dennis was already with her. I guess she was DOA, but they still tried to resuscitate her," Billy said, looking down at his hands. He shrugged, "I can't think of anything else to tell you. Except that she was a bit unstable, and we were waiting for a bed at New Hope Hospital. In the meantime, I had people checking on her while I was at work, plus she was seeing Jeff Stark. That's about it."

"Thanks Doc, that's great. Everything corroborates with what I already have. You'll need to come down to the station to sign the printed statement. We'll call you when it's ready. I'll have them try to hurry things along. It's a pretty open and shut case, no queries as far as I can see. I just need to touch base with Dr. O'Shea, and that will be that."

"Thanks, Tony. Anything else?"

Tony glanced at his notebook. He coughed a little uncomfortably. "Let's see, Dr. O'Shea said he sent blood samples to Toxicology to confirm cause of death. Once those results are in, and the coroner gets it all together, then her body can be released to you." He looked at Billy, apologetically. "I'm sorry. Have to give the usual speech. I don't know why I'm telling you all this, you know the drill. This is just a formality."

"It has to be done," Billy smiled ruefully.

Tony shook his head, "It's just weird being on the other end of the situation, you know. I feel strange having to say this stuff to you, of all people."

"It definitely is weird hearing it, but you're just doing your job. Thank you for being so efficient."

"Uh…you may want to call the department later today to find out when the statement will be ready to sign. They may also be able to tell you when you can have her…picked up. Again Doc, I'm so sorry."

"Thanks, Tony."

The condition of the apartment shocked Billy when he returned home. It looked as though a tornado had gone through the small living area. Furniture had been moved, wrappings from the paramedics' equipment lay on the floor. Evidence of what had recently transpired was everywhere. Absently, he bent and picked up the wrappings on the floor and threw them away.

Billy saw Jessie's bear lying forgotten under the coffee table. He picked up the bear and walked through the apartment. Her jacket and cigarettes lay on the kitchen table; her toiletries were on the counter in the bathroom; her nightclothes lay on the unmade bed—all the detritus of human existence—all worthless.

Billy was exhausted mentally and physically. He went into the kitchen like a robot and called Ellen at the office. His wonderful nurse was still there. He explained to her what had happened. He asked her to make sure that the Health Department was not taking any patients the next Friday because of the holiday, and to reschedule all his regular patients into the second week of January for the same reason. He then disconnected and called the police department. He had just put on a kettle of water for tea when the doorbell rang.

"Hi," Maggie said quietly, when he opened the door. "May I come in?"

Billy backed away from the door and retreated into the living room, where they stood facing each other.

"I wasn't sure that you'd want anyone stopping by, but I just had to come and tell you how very sorry I am about Jessie."

"Thanks," Billy said. "I appreciate all the help you gave me this afternoon."

"You're welcome. I just wish I could have done more."

"There really was nothing more any of us could do," Billy said.

"You look like you could use a hug."

Billy shrugged.

Taking a deep breath, Maggie bridged the gap between them and put her arms around Billy. For a moment, he froze—not moving, barely breathing. Finally, he placed his arms around her and pulled her close.

"I don't know what to say," Maggie whispered into his shoulder. "I just feel so bad." For several minutes they stood together, until a pounding at the door broke them apart.

When Billy answered, Cal stood on the threshold. "Is Maggie here?" he asked brusquely, looking into the apartment. "Never mind," he said, as he saw her standing there. "Of course, she is. Why would I think she was any where else? You know, Fox, I am so sick and tired of always finding my girlfriend in your apartment," Cal said angrily, as he entered the room.

"I came over here to give Billy my condolences," Maggie said, rather heatedly.

"Oh yeah, I heard at the hospital that you're finally free of your weight," Cal remarked flippantly.

"How can you say such a thing?" Maggie said. "A woman's dead, and you're treating it so callously."

"And your point is?"

"Look, Cal, despite all our problems, she was still my wife," Billy said, his eyes dark and full of anger. "I don't intend to go running out into the street shouting for joy."

"God, you're such a hypocrite. You act like you loved her," Cal sneered.

"I might not have loved her, but I still didn't want her to kill herself."

"Yeah, yeah, whatever you say," he flapped his hand at the air. "Come on, Maggie. I have reservations for dinner this evening at six," he said, looking at his watch, "and it's half past five already. You'd better move that cute little ass of yours if we're going to be on time."

Maggie glared at Cal. "Is dinner all you care about? Where is your sense of decency?"

"What? Am I the only honest person around here? Why are you making such a fuss? In my opinion, Jessie was the biggest problem Billy ever had. He should be glad she's gone. If it was me, I would be thrilled."

"You disgust me," Maggie retorted.

Cal threw his hands up in the air. "If being honest is disgusting, well that's too damn bad."

"What if I said, 'go without me?'"

Cal shrugged. "What are you going to do? Use the excuse that you have to stay here and hold Fox's hand? He's a grown up. He doesn't need you. And just because Jessie is now out of the picture for good, doesn't mean that you can go running back to your *friend*."

"All right," Billy spit out. "I've had about all the shit I'm going to take. Listen Lewis, you and I need to get a few things clear here," he said, trying to remain calm. "I am *sick* of you accusing me of doing things with Maggie. I'm also *sick* of you telling me that we can't be friends, and I am especially *sick* of the patronizing attitude you have toward her. You don't own her."

"What are you going to do about it?" Cal asked, clenching his hands.

Billy noted the fists and threw his hands up into the air. "For God's sake Cal, I'm not about to get into a fist fight with you."

"I'd beat the shit out of you, you know."

"Probably, but can't we talk about this like grown men, not kids. We were friends—good friends, and now…"

"Well, it's your own damn fault. You won't leave my girlfriend alone."

"For one thing, I am *not* chasing your girlfriend. For another, is she really your girlfriend? I remember when you first met Maggie. You said that you didn't know what to do with her. That she wasn't your type at all. Had she slept with you the first week you two met, you would have moved on to someone else without looking back. The only reason you want her now is because she's a conquest. She's the fish that got away. And if you were honest with yourself, she's not what you want. She's just convenient. You two have nothing in common, except the fact that you work in the same hospital. Your thoughts and philosophies about life are totally opposite."

"So? Opposites attract."

"She doesn't look very attracted," Billy said, as Maggie glared at them both.

"What do you mean, we're dating!"

"Meeting at a restaurant for dinner or sitting with her in the cafeteria isn't what I call dating," Billy commented. "Neither is sponging off of her for dinner in her apartment."

"Sponging? How would *you* define dating then?"

"Do you have a physical relationship?" Billy asked.

Cal looked uncomfortable. "Sure."

"Really? You hug and kiss and make love?"

"Ugh, I have heard enough of this!" Maggie ground out.

"No Maggie, you haven't heard anything yet. I'm just getting warmed up. You're the one who wanted to be honest, so let's be honest. It's time Cal understands that I am *not* gonna back off. That I am *not* going to walk away. That if we want to be *friends*, that's our decision not his. It's about time you told him the truth and quit leading him on."

"What are you talking about?" Cal asked, getting into Billy's face, his hands still clenched.

"Billy don't…" Maggie began.

"Don't what?" Billy interrupted, "tell him the truth? Who once said to me that avoiding the truth was a kind of lie? Are you going to keep lying to him? Why do you think she has never let you get to first base?" Billy asked Cal.

"You're in the way. If you'd left her alone, I would be on my way to home plate by now."

"Just like you scored with her in New York?"

"I was getting there when her mother got sick, and she went home."

"Do you really think that a woman as strong willed as Maggie would have dragged her feet about sleeping with you if she really wanted to sleep with you?"

"How would *you* know?"

"Because I know Maggie," Billy said, looking at her. "She can be brutally honest. She says and does what she feels is right. She acts first and thinks about it later. She has apologized to me more times than I can count for blurting out what was on her mind. She is the kind of woman who, if she loves you, loves with her whole being, no matter what the cost."

"Excuse me, but am I allowed to say anything here?" Maggie asked, her face a mottled, angry red.

"Feel free to jump in at any time," Billy said, holding out his hand.

"Cal, this relationship isn't working. It didn't work when we were in New York, and it won't happen now."

"But I need you. I want you."

"Do you? I don't think so. On one hand you're chasing me, yet you're still having all your little trysts in the doctor's lounge."

"Did *he* tell you that?"

"No, *he* didn't have to tell me anything. I *do* work at the hospital. I *do* hear things. I'm tired of you treating me like a piece of property."

"Well, if you'd give me some once in a while…I'm not like Fox, you know. I need more than a hand job in the shower to satisfy my needs."

"No Cal, even if you were *getting* it from me, you'd still be sniffing around. Maybe I *should* have slept with you in New York like Billy said. Then after a few nights, you would have dumped me. He's right. I'm not enough for you. And that isn't Billy's fault. You can't keep blaming him for the fact that I'll never be yours."

"So," Cal said, hotly addressing Billy, "what's all this to you?"

"I'm just saying that I shouldn't have to end a friendship with Maggie simply because your relationship with her is going nowhere."

"But what about the race thing? Aren't you forgetting that you could ruin her reputation?"

"Again, Maggie is a strong-willed person. If her reputation meant something to her, she wouldn't be my friend."

"She doesn't know what's good for her."

"Here you go again. Will you please let Maggie make her own decisions. She made it through thirty-four years of her life without you telling her what to do."

"You know, I'm still of the mind to deck you—just because."

"If it would make you feel better, go ahead, hit me."

"You fucking bastard!" he growled and reaching back, punched Billy as hard as he could, snapping his chin. "You both can go straight to hell!" he shouted, then walked out, slamming the door behind him.

Billy and Maggie stared at one another for a long moment, then Billy let out a long, drawn-out breath. "Well, that went well," he said, rubbing his chin and opening and closing his mouth.

"I'm so sorry, Billy. This is all my fault. I should have nipped things in the bud right away. But he was like a steamroller. It was hard to argue with him. Had you not done what you just did, I would probably be on my way to dinner with him at this very moment."

"You don't have to apologize. First of all, I know how hard it is to say no to Cal. It's sometimes almost impossible. Secondly, this isn't the first time he's slugged me. It probably looked worse than it was. Cal's been this way for as long as I've known him. He's a spoiled, lazy, rich boy. Cal is only truly happy when he's getting his way, and that includes having as much sex as he can get. And he doesn't care who he uses and hurts to get it. I know for a fact that he screwed Jessie before and even after we were married."

"Do you think he will make things more awkward for us?"

"That, I don't know. But just in case, I'd stay out of his way for a few days."

"What about you? Will you be all right?"

"I'll be fine."

"Is there anything I can do at all?"

"No, I'm okay. Cal's right, I'm a grown-up, remember?"

"Are you sure you don't want some company? Or someone to talk to?"

Billy smiled wanly, going to the freezer for some ice. "I'm sure. Thanks again for the offer. Now, you had better get out of here before the rumor mill has me seeking comfort in your arms before poor Jessie's even cold."

Maggie looked at him for a long moment, then walked from the apartment, not quite slamming the door, but not exactly closing it quietly.

It took all the strength Billy could muster to sleep in the apartment that night. He lay awake most of the night, his mind reliving the events of the day. When he finally fell asleep, his dreams were haunted by Jessie, Maggie, and Cal.

The next morning, he went to the police department, signed their paperwork, then spoke with the coroner. Dennis had already sent the required test results, and everything was in order. He then went and made arrangements for Jessie's burial. It wasn't an easy task no matter what the circumstances. He had always been the one whose name was on the death certificate, now here he was requesting one.

There was to be no viewing, no funeral. He had never known Jessie's father's name and didn't even know if he was still alive. There was no one to contact—no one that needed to be informed. He gave the old, ratty, teddy bear to the undertaker. It was all she really had and all she had ever cared about. It should stay with her. He went and made arrangements at the local cemetery, then went back home.

He didn't have to go to work until late the next morning, but he felt he should go and check in with Dennis. He looked down at his jeans, shirt and boots and figured why bother changing.

He found Dennis cloistered in his office surrounded by paperwork. "I told my secretary that I didn't want to be bothered, but hell, I need a break from this mess. Thanks for saving me," Dennis said.

"You're welcome."

"Are you okay? You look like shit. Is that a bruise on your jaw?"

"The bruise is nothing. But it was a rough morning."

"You get everything taken care of?"

"Yeah, thanks for getting those test results back so quickly. I spoke with the coroner a little while ago and everything was under control."

"Well, let me take your mind off things. I got some good news for you," Dennis said with a large smile. "All your hard work paid off. We got the Birminghams to make a huge donation—so huge that the new center is going to be called the Birmingham wing. And since Mrs. B. now has a vested interest in the hospital, she has joined the board. How about them apples?"

"That's great! But this isn't going to cost me anything more, is it?"

"I don't know. You really impressed her. She mentioned that she hoped she'd see you at the monthly board meetings."

"Absolutely not! Dennis, this has gone far enough! I'll work double and triple shifts, holidays, any time you want, but I refuse to be a whore for this hospital," he said.

His thoughts quickly strayed to the night of the party and how people like the Birminghams could destroy someone like Jessie without a second thought; yet would give thousands of dollars to a hospital because a wing would be named after them. Giving himself a mental shake, he concluded, "I never signed on for that."

Dennis sighed. "I know. I'm sorry. How was I supposed to know she had a thing for you? I just wanted her money. Don't worry, I'll figure out some way to get her off your back. Hopefully without her taking her money away as well."

"You'd better."

"Alright, enough about them. Back to you. Are you going to be okay?"

"Sure, why?"

"I just want to know if you need some well-earned time off?"

"I'll be fine. Eight o'clock tomorrow morning is the burial. I'll have an hour or so before I have to be back on at eleven. I should be okay."

"Are you sure?"

"I guess," he said, standing. "I'd better let you get back to work. I'll see you later."

"Okay, kid."

Billy spent the night tossing and turning. Thoughts of Jessie and Maggie mingled in his mind, creating dreams that had him sweating and twisting in the sheets. When his alarm went off at six the next morning, Billy was exhausted. Breakfast had no appeal, so he passed on eating. What followed was a blur. Without all the formalities of a regular funeral, the burial was short. In fact, Billy was back at his apartment before nine.

He was tired and tried to nap; unfortunately falling into a doze about a half hour before he was to go in to work. He was groggy and out of sorts as he dressed.

There were already several patients occupying beds in the ER when he arrived. He checked the board to see what was going on. Holding a cup of coffee, he settled on a stool next to Nelson to hear a report.

"Nothing earth shattering," Nelson stated. "Several cases of a rogue virus— lots of vomiting. A kid with a broken finger—he's in radiology. One brought in by ambulance, an older woman—nasty fall. Hit her head pretty hard. She's also in radiology, that's about it. The paperwork is all done. The nursing shift already switched over and I'm out of here, if you don't need me."

"I think I can take it from here."

"By the way, I heard about your wife. I'm really sorry. Is there anything I can do?"

"No, but thanks."

"Later then," Nelson said, then stood, stretched and departed.

When the patients came back from radiology, Billy checked the x-rays, set the broken finger, and admitted the elderly woman who showed signs of a concussion.

An hour later, a possible drug overdose was radioed in. An ambulance was en route bringing with it a young hispanic female. She was unconscious, her pulse weak.

Billy and his team were waiting when she was quickly wheeled in. Billy got a jolt when he looked at the patient. Her long dark hair curtained a pretty, smooth skinned face—a face reminiscent of Jessie's.

Unfortunately, while Billy was assessing the patient, she went into cardiac arrest. He immediately began CPR. His team performed cardiopulmonary resuscitation for at least fifteen minutes with no response. The patient was pronounced dead less than an hour after she had arrived in the ER.

Joni saw Billy slump before the rest of the team. Her gasp brought people hurrying to his side. Shaking his head, he appeared to be dazed.

"Get Dr. O'Shea," Joni instructed.

When Dennis arrived, Billy was on his feet and waving off Joni's ministrations. "I'm fine," he stated. "I just got a little lightheaded, that's all."

"Are you sure that's all?" Dennis asked.

"Yeah."

"Go to my office and wait for me," Dennis said.

"What? But I'm fine."

"Go."

Dennis entered his office a short while later. "So, what really happened?" Dennis asked.

"I told you. I got a little lightheaded. I had been giving CPR for over fifteen minutes. You know what that's like."

"Yes, we all do. And you've done it for longer periods of time without feeling anything."

"So?"

"Joni said you also staggered a bit when the patient was first brought in. Then, when you came to, you had the shakes."

Billy's head was down, and he mumbled something.

"What was that?"

"Look, Dennis," Billy said, picking his head up, "the chick looked like Jessie that's all. It hit me funny. I lost my balance when she first came in and I saw her face. After that, it just seemed as though I was repeating everything that happened with Jess. The stress of the CPR, added to the fact that I haven't slept for several days or eaten since lunch time yesterday must have put me over the edge."

"Oh," Dennis sighed, pacing the room.

"What is it?" Billy asked.

"I said this the other day and I mean it. I definitely think you need some time away."

"I'll be fine."

"Sure you will, but you're not all right now, are you?"

Billy shrugged his shoulders. "Nobody feels one hundred percent all the time. I'm sure even *you* have an off day now and then."

"Yes, but I didn't just go through what you went through."

"I said I'll be fine."

"Look Billy, I not only have to worry about you, but I also have the hospital and patients to consider. I can't have the head of my staff passing out or making mistakes. It's not fair to you. It's also a poor reflection on me and the hospital. I don't need a lawsuit on my hands."

"I didn't make any mistakes," Billy said, standing.

"No, but you could have."

"You don't trust me."

"That's not what I'm saying."

"Then what *are* you saying?"

"I told you; I think you need to take a few days off."

"You're letting me go because my wife OD'd," Billy said, raising his voice. That's it, isn't it? I'm an embarrassment."

Dennis sighed and shook his head. "Calm down. I am not firing you. And if you were thinking with a cool head, you'd know that. You are *not* an embarrassment. You are going through a trauma of your own right now. That is why I want you to take a couple of days and get your head together. You need to get into different surroundings and not look into the face of death every other minute. That's all." He looked at his watch. "Look, I gotta get back downstairs. Go home and relax. Take a nap or something. I'll bring a pizza over tonight when I'm off, and we'll talk."

Billy went back to the Squirrel Cage and entered the apartment. Jessie's things were everywhere, and the place smelled of stale cigarette smoke. Billy opened all the windows, then went to the basement and found some abandoned cardboard cartons. He returned to the apartment; and, going from one room to the next, packed away all of Jessie's belongings. As he did so, he began cleaning the entire apartment.

Starting in the bathroom, he scoured and sanitized the little room, gathering up all the towels. Working into the bedroom, he gathered sheets and began to empty drawers, moving furniture as he went. He took the linens and headed back to the basement laundry room, then returned upstairs.

It was at the back of Jessie's underwear drawer. A small white box that contained the wedding ring he had given to her so many years ago. It looked brand new. She had never worn it but had kept it all this time. He looked at his own hand and slowly worked the ring off his finger. He added the ring to hers and put the box back in the drawer. He slowly shook himself then went back to work.

It was exhausting but served a dual purpose. It was something to do to take his mind off of reality and was also a ritual cleansing. There had been a violent death in those confined quarters. Billy needed to rid the area of any negative energy, or he wouldn't be able to continue to live in that space.

He had worked his way through the apartment and was finishing the living area, when he saw a small piece of notepaper filled with Jessie's scribble under the sofa. Picking it up, Billy looked at it with a sense of dread, then sat down and began to read.

Fox, don't be mad and for God's sake don't feel guilty.
This had nothing to do with you.
I've been wanting to do this ever since I was a kid.
If it hadn't been for you, I'd have done this a long time ago.
Sorry I fucked up your life. That's what I did best.
Now you can start over.

Billy reread the note, then sat lost in thought. Finally, he took the note and added it to the box with the rings then went into the kitchen. He found some small pieces of dried sage and sweetgrass and crumbled them into a clay pot. He lit the material and let it burn for several minutes. With the fire out, but smoking, he cleansed himself with the smoke then also cleansed a large feather. Starting at the door, he went from room to room, circling each several times as he wafted the smoke with the feather. A pungent, bittersweet aroma soon permeated the small living areas.

As Billy smudged, he began to feel more at peace with his surroundings. He let the remaining herbs finish smoldering, as he took the filled cartons and stacked them in the hallway. He then made a few phone calls to make arrangements for the cartons. The woman from the Department of Indian Affairs said they would be happy to have the clothing and other miscellaneous items. She would send someone to pick everything up as soon as possible.

Later that evening, Dennis showed up, as promised, bearing a pizza and a six pack of beer. Billy let him in and the two sat down at the table.

"How's it going?" Dennis asked, pulling a slice of pizza out of the box and placing it on a plate that Billy had handed him.

"Not too bad."

"How are you feeling? Still lightheaded?"

"No, I'm feeling better. I packed Jessie's things away and smudged the apartment."

"Ah, that's what that smell is. For a minute, I thought I had walked into a Catholic church during a Benediction service." Dennis picked up a beer, opened it, and took a long swallow.

"It isn't going to bother you, is it?" Billy questioned.

"No, it's not a bad smell once you get used to it. Don't worry, it takes a lot to put me off my feed. Even when some med school friends and I worked at the morgue, we were still able to eat. We'd just slide out an empty tray for a table."

"Nice," Billy commented, dryly.

"Sure, all the comforts of home."

The two men sat at the table and ate some pizza. Dennis was working on his third beer when he said thoughtfully, "You know, I probably could have used something like that smudging several years ago when my wife left me," he said, sitting back into his seat, his beer nestled into his hands. "I had just finished my tour of duty in Korea and had gone home to…hell, where were we living at the time? San Antonio, I think. Anyway, I had just gotten settled in and she tells me she's going back to Boston, taking the kids and the dog with her. She was tired of being an army wife and the love was long gone."

"I'm sorry, Dennis. I didn't know."

"No one does. Anyway, that was a long while ago. She's remarried now to an old school friend—a banker. He's not going anywhere, that's for sure. He adopted the kids, and they don't even write anymore. The dog…well he never was one for correspondence. Anyway, why I'm telling you these miserable details of my life is because after that, I was pretty much a mess. Couldn't eat, couldn't think. I was depressed as hell. All I wanted to do was sleep. I was working at the army base hospital and one of the guys brought in wasn't feeling right. I was so depressed that I really wasn't paying very close attention. I ran some cursory tests but missed a pulmonary embolism. While I was sitting on my ass feeling sorry for myself, it burst, and the guy hemorrhaged before I could put away my hankie." Dennis stared at the can in his hands, then took a long swallow of beer.

"My CO came close to tossing me out on my ear," he said, continuing. "Instead, he gave me a month's leave of absence, put me on some meds and told me to get my shit together. And that, my friend, is what I'm going to tell you."

"What? You're letting me go! You can't do that! I didn't do anything wrong."

"Calm down. I'm *not* firing you. I'm giving you a *week's* vacation. You need it. You already work too hard. With the exception of being in a coma and recuperating from your injuries, you have never had any real time off after you got home from Vietnam. Now, you're out here and you work every holiday and most weekends. You work for the health department and have started your own practice. What in the hell are you trying to do?"

Billy stared at the table and didn't answer.

"Working your ass off isn't going to make you forget or feel better. You need some time to mentally heal as well. So now, I'm making you take the time. I don't need a doctor with battle fatigue, burn out, and depression."

"You don't trust me."

"Listen, Billy. You know that as a trauma team specialist, you face death with over fifty percent of your patients."

"I know."

"Are you going to react each time someone codes like you did today?"

"Of course not! I'm going to react the way I always do."

"How can you be sure? Look," Dennis said patiently, "I don't want you in the same situation I was in. You need to distance yourself from here, from Jessie, and from the old grim reaper that lives in the bowels of that damn hospital, that's all. I want you back so that I can give you even more responsibilities."

"And what if I don't take it?"

"Come on, kid. It's just for a week, two at the most. You need it. If you don't, I may be forced to let you go, and that's something I don't want to do."

"You're not giving me much choice."

"Sure I am."

"Yeah, take it or leave it. And when am I supposed to start this leave?"

"As soon as possible."

"Who's going to cover for me?"

"I have a friend out in California who's been straddling the fence on this project for over a year now. Perhaps if he knew that it would just be for a week or two, he'd help us out. Who knows, maybe he'd like it and decide to stay."

"And take over my job?"

"No! For God's sake! Billy, how many times do I have to tell you, I'm not getting rid of you! But you yourself have said on many occasions that we could always use another good pair of hands."

"Fine. I'll go. But what if I decide not to come back?"

"That will be a decision that only you can make. Look, we'll talk about this later. In the meantime, I'll put in a call to the coast and see what's shaking out there."

"Does that mean that as of now, I'm off the clock?"

"Yes." Dennis then pulled a prescription pad and pen out of his inner jacket pocket. "I'm also going to give you a script for a med that helped me."

"No, thank you," Billy said quickly. "I'm not depressed or anxious. If I start taking one of those drugs, I may as well follow Jessie into hell. Next thing you know, you'll want me to start seeing Jeff Stark."

"That may not be a bad idea."

"No, thank you," he said again, rather heatedly.

"Look Billy, I don't want to argue. I value you as a colleague and friend. I just want to help you get through a bad time. I'm not firing you. I'm not embarrassed by you. All I'm saying is that we all go through things that leave us a little off center. Sometimes we need to step aside for a moment and refocus before we do anything else. You have the luxury of being in a position where we care tremendously about those we work with. Take this opportunity to have some R & R. You deserve it. Please!"

Billy looked at Dennis' sincere face. He knew that what he was saying was true. "I'm sorry, Dennis. I understand what you're saying. It's just that, I find it hard to admit that I need anything, especially if it appears to be a weakness. If you think I need the time, I'll take it. I won't argue anymore."

PART SIX

*"Never let the future disturb you.
You will meet it, if you have to,
with the same weapons of reason
which today arm you against the present."*

~

*"Everything is but what your opinion makes it;
and that opinion lies with yourself."*

Marcus Aurelius

BILLY

December, 1974

The lights of Washington, DC were a white smudge against the dark night sky as the plane circled for a landing. Billy prepared to disembark as the plane slowed to a stop. With the exception of Grandma Jean, the whole family was waiting for him. As he made his way down the ramp, the girls threw themselves into his arms.

At eleven thirty at night, the airport was rather quiet. As hugs and kisses were passed around, Billy said, "It's great to see you all. I'm just sorry it's so late in the evening."

"Don't worry about that. Do you have a lot of luggage?" Rusty asked.

"Just this," Billy said, holding up his carry-on bag.

"Good, let's hit the road," Rusty said, "we can talk on the way home. Actually, it's a good thing you picked this flight, there shouldn't be much traffic at this hour."

Marian linked her arm in Billy's as they walked. She looked into his face for a long moment. Billy looked back at her questioningly and gave her a small smile. "What?"

"Nothing," Marian shook her head.

Barbara grinned. "That'll be the day when it's nothing. I know the look. We all do."

"Where's the Tank?" Billy asked, as they approached a brand-new Volvo station wagon in the parking lot.

"The Tank finally bit the dust," Jenny said. "Daddy said it didn't like the way I drove, but don't believe him. It was old."

"Hell, it was old when I first moved in. I'd say it was pretty ancient by now."

"Hey," Rusty exclaimed, laughing. "Whose side are you on?"

"Only speaking the truth," Billy said, grinning.

As Rusty pulled onto the highway, Barbara said, "Okay mother, go ahead. We're just dying to hear what 'nothing' you have to say to Billy."

Marian sighed. "I hate to ruin this wonderful reunion, but I have a strange feeling that this isn't just a spur of the moment, holiday jaunt. Is it?" she asked, looking back at Billy.

For a moment, Billy was silent, then said, "No. You're right. How could you tell?"

"Oh please," Jenny said, "she's going to tell you it was written on your forehead. Like when we were little and told a fib. She always knew that, too."

"No, I'm not," Marian smiled. "It's just that Billy's a little too thin, and his smiles are a little too forced, that's all." She looked again at Billy. "Am I right?"

"You're always right, Marian."

"Well? What has happened to send you back to the bosom of your family? You're going to have to tell us eventually. No time like the present," Marian said.

Billy sat in the dark of the back seat; a sister snuggled on either side of him. For a moment, all was quiet.

"It was actually Dennis who sent me here. He felt that I needed a little time off."

"Time off?"

"Yes, I…uh…I buried Jessie yesterday."

"Oh my God! What happened?" Marian asked, her hand up to her mouth, as she looked back at Billy.

"She overdosed the day after Christmas."

"Was she with you?"

"Yes, she was brought into the ER the day after Thanksgiving. One of her customers threw her from his car. I had her move in with me after she was released from the hospital."

"Oh my goodness!"

It didn't take long for Billy to recount the events of the past month. As he spoke, there was complete silence in the car.

When he finished speaking, Marian said. "That poor girl! I'm so sorry, Billy."

"Why didn't you tell us what was going on when we called at Christmas?" Barbara asked.

"I didn't want to ruin your holiday and have you worrying. You couldn't have done anything, anyway."

"No, but you may have felt better talking about it," Jenny chimed in.

"I know. But Jessie was in the same room, and I couldn't very well discuss her with her sitting across from me, could I?"

"No, you're right," Marian commented. "I just wish we could have been with you or done something."

"There wasn't anything even *I* could do," Billy said sadly.

"Now don't you dare be feeling guilty. Do you hear me?" Marian said. "Jessie wouldn't have wanted that."

"I know, she told me that repeatedly."

"She must have known you pretty well," Marian stated.

"I think sometimes she knew me better than I know myself."

"I'm glad Dennis talked you into coming here," Rusty added. "He's right. You needed to get away. Even if it's only for a few days."

"At first, I wasn't sure. It felt to me like I was running away."

"You've got to get over that," Rusty said.

Billy sighed. "I know."

"Have you gone back to the apartment?" Marian asked.

"Yes, I cleaned out all of her things and smudged the whole place. The atmosphere is a lot better now. And I think I'm feeling a little better as well."

"We already planned our yearly New Year's Eve get-together. It will just be the Simmonds and Kuchta families, Mary Agnes and Jack. Patrick MacDonald and a few other doctors from the hospital are stopping by. But I'll cancel if you're not feeling up to it."

"It's okay. The more noise and confusion the better."

"I never realized we had so many things," Marian said, looking at the large collection of crystal and figurines that sat on the dining room table. "Since Grandma moved in, we've been sorting through all our knick knacks to decide what we want to keep and what we want to give away. The auxiliary is having a tag sale this spring, and I'm going to bring them our discards. Before I do, is there anything here you want?" she asked Billy, who was sipping a mug of tea and getting out silverware from the sideboard.

"No thanks, Marian. I don't have room for any of this fussy stuff."

As Marian continued to remove and clean the contents of her mahogany breakfront, she took out a beautiful cut crystal vase. "Ahh, I know someone who would love this. Maggie admired it when she stayed here."

"Maggie stayed here?" Billy asked, surprised. "When?"

"While she was stationed at Walter Reed. She spent the holidays and a couple of weekends with us. In fact, she stayed in your room. Didn't she tell you?"

"No, she never mentioned it."

"Maybe you ought to talk to her a little more instead of avoiding her."

"I am *not* avoiding her."

"What do *you* call it then?"

"I don't want to talk about her. There's nothing to say."

"Really? Nothing to say? You know, Billy, I was always under the impression that the two of you cared for each other. Perhaps, even loved each other."

"Whatever gave you that idea?"

"Maggie mentioned it."

"She did? What did she say?"

"She told me about the friendship you two forged in Vietnam. And how you met again in Australia while on R & R."

"Australia? She told you about Australia?"

"Yes."

"She told you…everything?" he asked quietly, looking down at his hands.

"Yes, everything."

"God! I suppose she gave you all the gory details. Nothing like talking about me behind my back."

"It wasn't like that at all. Look, it's not like we were idly gossiping about you. She had already lost her husband and now there was a very good possibility that she would lose you as well. She was, to put it mildly, distraught."

"Oh," he said.

Marian took a deep breath. "Um…since we are already talking about taboo subjects…and it's just the two of us in here at the moment, can I ask you a personal question?"

Billy sighed. "You're going to anyway, right?"

"Well, it's about the bruise on your face that you've been trying to hide. Were you punched?"

"You have eyes like a freaking hawk!"

"Don't be crude," she admonished. "Of course, I do. I'm a mom."

"Don't I know it."

"Well?"

"It's a very long, stupid story, but it ties in to all that you've been grilling me about."

"Can you give me a Reader's Digest Condensed version?"

Billy looked at her a long moment, then sat down at the table. "I can try," he said. "Let's see, I was in Phoenix about six months when we decided that we needed some nurses who had more experience, in keeping with the docs on staff. When Maggie responded to the ad, it was the best and the worst thing to happen. I should have told Dennis right away that there could be complications and not to hire her. That I could have a problem. But I figured it had been several years, and maybe we could go back to the way things were in Vietnam. I mean, in Phu Bai, we were good friends. But there was also a whole gang of us, so it wasn't as if we were off by ourselves. Then, I found out that Maggie was the girl Cal had dated when he was a med student in New York. When he found out that Mike was no longer in the picture, he did everything he could to ensure that their relationship continue where it left off. By then, it was kind of too late to do anything."

"And Maggie liked Cal?"

"I don't know. At the time, I wasn't sure what Maggie was feeling. But I did know how Cal felt."

"I can't believe she would fall for that lunkhead. He has no substance."

"Lunkhead," Billy snorted. "I don't know about that, but he has sure been a thorn in my side. He basically told me that I couldn't be Maggie's friend and to stay away from her. Since the first day that she was in Phoenix, he has monopolized her, told her what to do, where to eat, what to eat, you name it. If I'd been Maggie, I'd have told the bastar…him…off right away. But, in her defense, I also know that it's very hard to say no to Cal. When the three of us kind of hung out together, it wasn't bad. But Cal took offense—especially after a nurse I had turned down for a quickie started calling us the 'Odd Squad'. Cal accused me of ruining Maggie's reputation. Leave her alone, I'm working here, he said."

"Working? Wooing someone shouldn't be a…a job. How did Maggie feel about all this?" Marian questioned. "She couldn't have liked what was going on."

"I don't know. She went with him places, so I didn't know what to think. In the meantime, I did what he asked. I basically left her alone and hated it.

Maggie didn't seem too thrilled either but…what was I supposed to do? Then came Thanksgiving. God, I missed you guys!"

"I felt bad about not coming to visit, but you knew we couldn't leave Grandma here alone," Marian said.

"I know. But I was still down because you couldn't be with me. Just to keep busy, I filled in for a doc who wanted the day off. Maggie's team was also on staff and, when we worked an MVA together, it was kind of like old times. It was also bloody and gruesome and very similar to injuries that we saw in Vietnam."

"How do you all do it? Seeing things like that. I couldn't."

Billy shrugged. "You have to get around that. I knew that in order to save this person's life, I needed to focus on the task at hand. Anyway, we both stayed over. I left before she did, which was around 9:30. I got something to eat, showered, and was reading. I had just made some tea around 11:00 when there was a knock at my door. It was Maggie. She has this recurring nightmare of Mike being blown out of the sky. That night, it was worse than others, and the panic set in quickly. She was a real mess—crying, shaking, the whole bit."

"I remember her telling me about those dreams. She said they were very vivid."

"Yes, they are. Too vivid, poor thing. At first, I just tried to calm her down. She was close to hysterical. I held her and did my best to comfort her. But it was so difficult, and the longer she was in my arms, the worse it got."

"Difficult?"

"Well, first of all, I was shocked to see that she was wearing the silk robe that I had bought her in Bangkok," he said, sipping at his tea, and refusing to make eye contact with Marian.

Marian cleared her throat and raised her eyebrows.

Billy shook his head. "She had seen this beautiful robe in an outdoor market and commented on it. Being well trained by you and the girls, my ears pricked up and I got a good look at it. It was very pretty. When we got into the hotel, I noticed a similar one in the shop in the lobby. While she took a bath, I ran downstairs and purchased it. It was of better quality and the print wasn't just painted on, but actually part of the material. It could be cleaned and returned if it didn't fit. Fortunately, it fit, and she loved it and…I got to see her in it," he said, his face flushing a little.

After a few moments, he continued. "Anyway, she's in my arms, she's crying, she's in this robe, and I did what every dumb man in the same situation would have done…I kissed her. Which unfortunately was like letting loose Hoover Dam—not just for me, but for both of us," he said quietly.

"Then Cal called, interrogating me on what time I had come home and when Maggie had left work. I told him that she was with me and got the phone slammed in my ear. I had just enough time to pour Maggie some tea, when he burst into the apartment throwing accusations everywhere. It was unpleasant at best," he said, shaking his head.

"The next day, Maggie showed up in my office and kind of called me on it. But we never had the chance to really talk because Cal showed up again. He and I came close to getting into it then, but Maggie dragged him away. Two hours later, Jessie was brought into the ER."

Billy took another sip of tea and stared into his mug. "While Jessie was with me, things kind of settled down. At least Cal was happy and non-combative. Jessie, however, took one look at Maggie and said, 'Uh huh,' like it was written on my forehead."

Marian smiled. "I wouldn't say it was written on your forehead, but when the two of you are in the same room, an astute person can tell," she stated.

"Then the day after Christmas, well, you know what happened. Maggie had been the one to call the EMS, then helped me give CPR until the paramedics arrived. She stopped by afterward to give her condolences. Then Cal showed up, yet again. And I let him have it. I kind of yelled at Maggie too, for leading Cal on. At the end of the discussion, he said he wanted to hit me, and I said go ahead. Now, I have a lovely multi-colored bruise that everyone has not only noticed but keeps asking me about. And that, was basically the last six months in a nutshell."

Marian opened then closed her mouth several times, but no words came out.

"You look like a bass on a hook," Billy commented.

"I can't believe you actually told me."

"Why not? You asked. Didn't you want me to?"

"Of course! But you mean to say that every time we called, and you said things were great, this is what was really going on?"

"If I had told you the truth, what could you have done?"

"I know—nothing," Marian agreed. "But I can't believe he actually punched you!"

"It could have been worse. My whole face could be black and blue, or he could have broken one of my teeth. Since I knew it was coming, I moved with the punch. Besides, he's such a wuss there really wasn't much behind it. Now, had *I* hit *him,* he'd still be on the floor, and my hand would have been broken," Billy said, looking at his knuckles.

"I'm glad that you controlled yourself. It's amazing how much you have grown up in the last couple of years. I'm proud of you."

"Thanks, Mom. It's all your doing," he grinned.

"So after he punched you, what happened with Maggie?"

"Uh…I said that she should leave because I didn't want people saying that she threw herself into my arms the minute my wife died."

"How did she take that?"

"I think I came close to getting a similar bruise on the other side of my face. But all that she did was slam the door on her way out."

"And now you're here."

"Yes, ma'am."

Marian shook her head. "All this in less than a year. Wow! You work fast."

"Life's short," he grinned.

"You know, I used to be so jealous of the little heart to heart talks that you and Rusty would have. I always seemed to miss out on all the good stuff."

"Hang on, I seem to recall plenty of little talks that you and I had, especially the heated ones. And now, you're privy to this sordid mess. Although, I didn't know that you and Rusty were competing."

"We aren't," Marian laughed. "I'm just always being a mom. And that means wanting to know all the details, sordid or otherwise. Now, I think I finally understand everything."

"I suppose you think you're going to fix things. Don't you?"

"How can I possibly do that?"

Billy smiled, "I don't know, but somehow…"

At that moment, the phone rang. Marian went into the kitchen and picked up the receiver. "Hello? Hi!" she said, looking to see whether Billy had followed her in. "Long time no talk. It's wonderful to hear from you. Hang on a minute, please. Billy, why don't you go out to the sunroom with Grandma and the girls. I think they are trying to figure out how many chairs we will need to bring up from the basement? I'll be out in a few minutes."

"Sure," Billy said, taking his tea and wandering off to join the planning committee.

MAGGIE

I t was late in the afternoon when Maggie clocked out for a couple of well-deserved days off. At that time, she noticed that it was Dennis and another gentleman taking notes, instead of Billy.

She approached Joni, who had just come on shift. "Hi, have you seen Billy?" Maggie asked.

"I guess you haven't heard. It all happened suddenly. Billy was a little shaky at work the other day and Dennis encouraged him to take a week off. The doctor that he's talking to right now just flew in from California. He's going to be filling in until Billy gets back. Dennis is also trying to talk him into sticking around permanently."

"I see. Do you know if Billy went anywhere?"

"I think he was going to DC. Dennis said he has some family there."

"Thanks for the info."

"Sure, by the way, I hear you have the holiday completely off. Lucky duck. I guess working several holidays and weekends in a row, has its upside."

"Yes, I was kicking around the idea of going home to visit my dad. But I'd have to be back by the 2nd. That's cutting things pretty short. Even if I could get a flight."

"I have off the 2nd. Would you like me to work for you? I owe you at *least* a day, if not more."

"Wow! That would be great. Are you sure you wouldn't mind?"

"No, Dennis is working too, so I'll get to be with him. I'll let him know I'm covering for you. I'm sure he won't have a problem with that."

"Well, that's wonderful, thanks. Guess I better go and see if I can get that flight."

"Good luck and have a happy New Year!"

"Thanks, you too."

When Maggie got back to her apartment, she immediately made a phone call. "Hi! How are you? Fine. Sure, I'll wait." After a short pause, she said, "I think you just answered my question. I was calling to see if by chance you had a house guest. You wouldn't happen to have room for one more, would you? Just for tomorrow and the first? I have to be back to work on the third. Great! Let me see if I can get a flight. I'll call you right back. Thanks."

Maggie was in luck. There was a flight leaving Phoenix Sky Harbor at 11:57 p.m. She was able to book a reservation and a return flight for the second.

She then made another call, letting Marian know all the particulars. "I'll call from Dulles to let you know I got in, then I'll grab a taxi. I should be at your place by around 8:30 tomorrow morning, depending on the traffic. Are you sure this won't be an inconvenience? No, please don't say anything to him. Thank you so much. Can't wait to see you all."

She threw some clothes into an overnight bag, ate some dinner, then cleaned up the apartment in order to kill some time. Around ten p.m., she went down to the lobby to meet her taxi.

The flight was uneventful, although the time difference threw her a bit. After making her call from Dulles, Maggie was able to get a taxi right away. The traffic wasn't too insane, and she arrived at the Wilson's close to 9 a.m.

The Wilson home was all decked out in its holiday finery. All the windows were decorated with fresh, red-ribboned wreaths and electric candles. Matching garland wound around both columns, flanking the front doors on which hung colorful Williamsburg wreaths.

Maggie looked up at the house and bit her lip nervously. What am I doing, she thought? This whole thing could backfire terribly. But she knew that she needed to talk to Billy without any interruptions. If this was the only way she could do it, then that's what she was going to have to do.

She slowly walked up the sidewalk to the front door, her stomach a mass of knots. Taking a deep breath, she rang the bell.

BILLY

Billy awoke early on New Year's Eve to the ringing of the phone. Thank God that's not for me, he thought. As he threw on a pair of jeans and a sweatshirt that he had left in his dresser, he had the feeling that he was on a different planet. It was as if the family had absorbed him into their midst again, and life had never changed—that the last year had been a dream, and he had never left.

He walked barefooted into the kitchen as a flurry of activity was going on. Preparations for the party that evening were evident on every counter.

"Good morning, I'm glad to see you're awake. Hope you slept well," Marian said, as Billy entered the kitchen.

"Like a rock," Billy smiled. "The phone never rang, and no one died. It doesn't get any better than that."

"There's fresh coffee on the stove. What can I make you for breakfast? Eggs and bacon? Toast? Cereal?"

"How about just the coffee right now?"

"Only if you promise that you'll make yourself breakfast in a little bit. Please. You need to eat, and it may be a while before lunch. Dinner, as you know, will be after eight tonight."

"Where's Rusty?"

"He's at the hospital, then will be going in to the office for a while to make up for taking off tomorrow. Grandma is also at the hospital, doing her volunteer work. A friend of hers will bring her home later this afternoon," she explained. "The girls and I have to run out for a little while and get some last-minute things. Nothing is off limits in the fridge, so help yourself. If the doorbell rings, please answer it. I'm expecting a delivery."

"Sure," Billy replied, heading to the coffee pot. "And please don't forget the brioche for tomorrow morning," he said, as they headed out the door. "Or it will have to be pancakes."

He shook out the Post and looked at the headlines as he drank some coffee. After reading the comics, he opened the refrigerator and took out a carton of eggs and some butter and cheese, thinking an omelet sounded like a good idea. He was just getting out the bread, when he heard the doorbell ring.

Wonder what kind of delivery is coming, he thought as he walked down the long hall to the front door. He opened the door expecting to see a delivery person, but instead, saw Maggie standing there. Astonishment flooded his face, and he felt as if he had been kicked—hard. "Delivery my ass," he muttered, under his breath.

"Hi," Maggie said, quietly, her face stained red in embarrassment.

"Hi," Billy said, standing in the doorway, awkwardly.

"Uhh…may I come in?" Maggie's voice cracked in nervousness.

Billy backed into the entryway, opening the door wide as Maggie entered, carrying a small overnight bag.

They stared at each other for a long second, then Billy said, "Here, put down your bag and let me take your jacket. I assume you're going to be here for a while." He hung up her jacket in the closet then asked, "Are you hungry? I was just about to have breakfast."

"I'm starving. Breakfast sounds great."

Billy walked ahead of her into the kitchen and pulled out a chair. He poured another mug of coffee and set it in front of her along with cream and sugar, silverware and a napkin.

"Thanks."

Billy went back to preparing his omelet. He cracked in another egg and added some cream to the mixture as well as cheese and some seasonings. He put two slices of bread in the toaster and poured the egg mixture into a skillet. In several minutes, he had two plates of food ready and handed Maggie a plate.

"God! There must be something really wrong," he said. "You've been in this house almost a half an hour and have hardly said a word."

"I'm sorry."

Billy smiled. "Well, that's a step in the right direction. Things are usually all right when you start apologizing," he said. "You haven't asked about the Wilsons or anything else for that matter. Which leads me to believe, even though I shouldn't, that I've been set up? Am I right?"

Maggie took a bite of her omelet. "Wow! This is good," she said, wiping her mouth with her napkin. "I don't know if we actually set you up. I just knew that I had to talk to you, and I wanted to do it without any interruptions or distractions."

"Is eating a distraction or can you talk and chew?"

"I don't know. This is so delicious, I may have to eat first, because it could become a distraction."

"So eat," Billy said, shaking his head. "I take it you just flew in?"

Maggie chewed and nodded.

"And the Wilsons knew you were coming?"

Maggie nodded again.

"Does everyone in Phoenix know that you're here?" Billy asked, forking in some eggs.

"They think I'm in New York visiting my dad, which was my original plan. But when I heard that you were in DC, I changed my mind and came here instead."

Maggie finished the contents of her plate in record time. "Yum, that was delicious. Thank you. God! You can cook, too."

Billy stood and cleared off the table. He washed the dishes then left them to air dry. He brought the coffee pot to the table and poured them both another mug.

"Okay, your food is gone. If you are going to talk, do it now. If you wait too long, Marian and the girls will be home. Or do you guys have some pre-arranged signal?"

Maggie's face broke into a small grin. "No signals, but you know, I rehearsed this whole speech on the plane. I thought I had it memorized verbatim, but now that I'm here, it's gone." She moved her napkin around on the table pushing at some imaginary crumbs. "How are you feeling? I hear you had a little episode on Saturday that prompted your coming here."

"You flew all the way from Phoenix to ask me that?"

"It's just a lead in, but I really want to know. I also wondered how your jaw was."

"Besides the fact that everyone and his brother can tell that I was punched, I'm okay. Although…I woke up this morning feeling as though this past year never happened. That it was all a dream."

"A bad dream?"

"Not all of it. It definitely had its moments."

"What were they?"

Billy stared at her for a brief second. "Seeing you again was definitely one of the better moments."

"And what about the bad ones?"

"Uh, well…it's the old double-edged sword. Seeing you again would definitely have been one of the bad moments, as well."

"Bad?"

"I should have told Dennis up front that hiring you wouldn't be a good idea. That it was a conflict of interest. I just didn't know how much so until you had already moved in and started working with us. And by then, it was too late."

Billy stared into his mug, looking for inspiration. Finally, he continued, "As I explained to you on several occasions, your proximity to me and the complications that Cal threw into the mix had me ready to run back to Walter Reed. Then Jessie showed up, and I had a small tornado brewing inside of me."

Maggie took a sip of coffee. "Since our talk after Thanksgiving, I now understand what was going on and why you were acting the way you were. But… did you ever stop to think how *I* must have felt during the past six months?"

"Sure I did. You were miserable," Billy said simply.

"Yes, I was. And you knew that?"

"Of course."

"And you did nothing about it?"

"I couldn't."

"Why?"

"Look, aside from having it out with Cal last week, this is really the first time we have actually been allowed to have a dialogue with one another since you moved to Phoenix. The times we worked together were few and far between. They also were not exactly a good place to discuss anything that wasn't related to a body that was swirling the drain."

"You're right," Maggie said quietly.

"Unfortunately, I'm not sure that talking is going to solve anything. I could lay my heart on my sleeve, and tell you how much I love you, and how unhappy I am because I'm not with you. But would that do any good?"

"Well, for one thing, I would know how you felt."

"I guess. But in all this mess, I still don't really know how *you* feel. I know you're miserable, but are you miserable for the same reasons that I'm miserable?"

"I'm miserable because for months you refused to acknowledge my existence, even as just a friend. I'm miserable because I thought we could still be friends and, until Thanksgiving, I was under that delusion. And now, I know that I was only kidding myself. I'm also miserable because I feel that I am the only one of us to openly admit my feelings."

Billy shook his head and drank some coffee. "I don't know. I thought I made my feelings quite plain on Thanksgiving and the day after as well. But, as you also recall, until the day after Christmas, I had no right to acknowledge anything of the sort."

"I know."

"And right now, I can't just jump up and down with joy and immediately start acting upon my feelings."

"I understand that, too. But at least if I knew we were of the same mind, it wouldn't be so bad."

"Aren't you forgetting about the race issue?"

"I thought you told Cal that it was my choice if I wanted to ruin my reputation."

"And, if I remember correctly, that was a discussion about friendship, nothing more."

"But didn't you also say to me that friendship was no longer enough?"

Billy squirmed in his seat and looked down at the table uncomfortably.

"I don't want to argue with you," Maggie said. "But I refuse to go through the rest of my life wanting something that *you* say I can't have. Why does only *your* opinion count? You sound almost as egotistical as Cal," Maggie said, a little heatedly. "Ever since I left Australia, I made a conscious effort to really look at couples. And I noticed that not all couples were of the same race or different genders for that matter. I saw whites with blacks; blacks with Hispanics; whites with Asians; men with men; and women with women. And you know what I thought? Good for you! You're all being honest. You aren't letting anything stand in the way of your happiness."

She looked down at the table for a moment then continued, "If you loved me as much as you say you do, think of *my* feelings for a change. Think about how much *I* want to be with you. I distinctly recall you telling Cal that I was a big girl and could make my own decisions. Why don't you practice what you preach?"

She looked up and met his eyes. Her green eyes were bright with unshed tears, but she held it together.

"I'm sorry, Maggie," he said, and reaching out, put his hand over hers. He clasped her fingers gently and said, "You're right. I'm being as bad as Cal, if not worse. My good intentions of protecting you have led me straight to hell. I want you to know that I have heard everything you said. I just need some time. Can we talk about this more later?"

Before Maggie had a chance to reply, the station wagon pulled into the drive.

"Whew! Saved by the bell!" Billy said, sheepishly. Maggie sighed and shook her head, smiling slightly.

Marian and the girls had jumped out of the vehicle and were peeking into the kitchen window.

"I guess we'd better let 'em in before they break down the door. I'm sure they're dying to see you," Billy said, as he let the women in.

A lot of kissing and hugging ensued and Billy wandered outside to let the girls have their reunion. He thought about what Maggie had said and knew in his heart that she was right. Why was he being so stubborn? Was there really a chance for them? After maybe a bit of time.

MAGGIE

Marian and the girls burst in the kitchen door and enfolded Maggie into a huge hug, as Billy walked past them, and out the door to start unloading the car.

"It's wonderful to see you," Marian said. "I'm so happy that you were able to come. We've all missed you!"

"I've missed you all, too," Maggie said. "It seems like forever since I was here."

"Have you been here long?" Barbara asked.

Maggie looked at her watch, "Almost two hours."

"When did you eat last?" Marian wanted to know.

"Um…just a little while ago. Billy made breakfast."

"He did? That's good."

"Yes, actually, it was. He made a cheese omelet and toast. It was wonderful."

"He makes a mean omelet. Just wait till tomorrow!" Jenny crowed.

"What's tomorrow?" Maggie questioned.

"It's been a family tradition that since Mommy always has this party, Billy has been making breakfast for the past ten plus years, except for when he was in Vietnam. His specialty is French toast made with brioche, pure maple syrup, sausage and bacon on the side."

"*If* you were able to get me the bread." Billy said, as he began to rummage through the bags he had put on the counter.

"We got you two loaves, day old just like you wanted. Will that be enough?" Barbara asked.

"At the time I asked, I didn't know that we were going to have extra company. But unless Maggie can throw down an entire loaf of bread, I think we'll be all right."

"Be nice," Barbara said, giving Billy an elbow to the ribs.

"God! When did Bubba turn into Momma Marian?"

"Will you quit calling me that. I'm no longer ten."

"Bubba?" Maggie asked. "How did a sweet girl like you get the nickname of Bubba?"

"One part Jenny not being able to say Barbara, one part Billy and John being jerks."

"We were not being jerks! We thought it was cute! Jenny was Jenny Wren. You had to have a nickname, too."

"But Jenny Wren is cute!"

"So is Bubba!"

"No, it's not! You and John were horrible! You made me sound like a big, ugly wrestler, or something equally as uncomplimentary and unattractive, instead of a delicate little girl."

"That's why it was so cute. Because you were the total opposite. I remember when I was nine, I probably weighed well under 60 pounds soaking wet. But an old family friend, who was very large, used to call me Chubs. *Me!* Look, if we hadn't loved you so much, we would've never teased you." He paused, then continued, "Wait until I tell your date tonight," he said, laughing.

"You wouldn't dare!" she stomped her foot. "Mom! Can I hit him, just once? Please!" she said, swatting at him.

Billy spun away from the swat. "It's bad luck to hit a cripple, you know."

"Children, will you please behave. I'm so sorry, Maggie," Marian said smiling and shaking her head. "I thought I reared them well, but every once in a while, they act like a bunch of heathens."

"Pfft! Guess who's going to get blamed for that," Billy asked dryly.

"Billy, why don't you take Maggie up to your room, so that she can get settled?" Marian commented.

"Really! You *want* me to take her up to my room! Are we sharing?"

Marian sighed. "No, I want you to remove your things and take them to the spare room, get her clean sheets and towels, and be the perfect host."

"Rats, I thought perhaps you were suggesting I show her my etchings or possibly have a nooner," Billy grinned.

Marian sighed again and shook her head.

"I know, I know, don't be crude! Come on Reynolds, you heard the boss." He walked back into the hallway and picked up Maggie's overnight bag. "God, what do you have in here? Bricks?" he asked, as he headed toward the stairs. "I hear you have been to our humble abode before."

"Yes, while I was at Walter Reed."

"A little daunting, isn't it?"

"A bit."

"I was traumatized when I first arrived here."

"I can imagine."

"One look at the 'Fiddler on the Roof' staircase and I almost shit myself."

"Fiddler on the Roof?"

"You know, 'One stairway going up, one going down and one leading nowhere just for show!'"

"How do you all decide which side to use?"

"Me? I usually go up the side closest to my room. The girls and I would race on them when no one else was around. Marian always wanted to know why the girls were always so tired after I babysat them. I figured if I exhausted them, they would go to bed early. It was the only way I could get some peace and quiet to study."

"Cruel."

"Maybe, but they had fun, and we all got some exercise."

"I love your sleigh bed," she said, as they walked into the adjoining bathroom.

"I never even knew what a sleigh bed was, and here I was sleeping on one," he said as he got out a clean set of towels and laid them on the counter.

"You don't think I had one of these in New York, do you? I was on a twin bed, but at least I had my own room. My three brothers had bunk beds and a twin in a room they all shared. Had I been a boy, we would've all been in the same room with two sets of bunk beds."

"Hell, before I was eight, I was sleeping on the floor of a rusted-out trailer."

He went back into his room and prepared to strip the bed. Maggie put a hand on his arm. "No. Please. You don't have to do that."

"You heard the General."

"Yes, but…I…I really don't mind sleeping on your sheets," she said, slightly red in the face.

Billy looked at her quizzically, then sighed. "Fine. If I get into trouble because I didn't change the bed, you can tell Marian why *you* wanted to sleep on *my* dirty sheets," he said, giving her a devilish grin.

Maggie reddened again. "I don't understand why I can't sleep in the guest room. You're all going to too much trouble."

"*You* are special company. I'm family. Don't worry about it. Just don't forget you're sharing the bathroom with Grandma Jean. You may want to keep your bathroom door closed. You don't want her to accidentally wander into your room during the night."

"Has she ever done that?"

"Not yet, but then again, I always keep my doors closed and locked. And not because of Grandma, but because of the little turds bursting in on me at odd times of the day and night," he smiled.

Billy grabbed up some clothes from his chair then went to his closet. He selected something to wear for later, then started back to the guest room.

Maggie walked beside him. "Do you think your Apache family would accept me?"

Billy was quiet for a minute, "I really don't know. I'm sure my grandparents would be happy, because I was happy. But I also know how they felt about my mother. Of course, she was not you," he said, as he deposited his things on the other bed. "You up for a walk?" he asked, as they headed back downstairs.

"You aren't going to make me feel like a cart horse, are you?"

Billy gave her a very long look. "I highly doubt that I could walk like that now. How about just a stroll? Then you can come back and take a shower and a nap or something, so that you won't be dead on your feet later."

"That sounds like a great idea."

Back downstairs, Billy popped his head into the kitchen. "Are you girls okay in here? You need me to do anything?"

"I think everything is good here. You did all of the stuff I needed to be done yesterday."

"Well, if you don't need anything, I think I'll take Maggie for a walk around the neighborhood. Show her some *real* houses," he laughed.

"Sure, have fun. But don't wear her out," Marian warned. "I'm going to put something out for lunch in about an hour, since our company is coming around eight. After lunch, she'll probably want to rest."

"I know. I figured as much. We'll be back in a little bit."

As they wandered down Q Street, Billy asked, "And what about *your* family? I mean you asked about my grandparents, but what about your dad? Your brothers? You could be setting yourself up for a hard time."

Maggie thought a few moments. "I honestly don't know how they will feel, and I don't care," she said, her jaw out-thrust. "I said I love you; I mean it. Whatever happens, happens. I'm miserable without you. I'd rather be ridiculed with you, than be without you, and be only a shadow of myself. Wouldn't you?"

"Don't you think we should at least get an idea of how they might feel?"

"Why? They aren't the ones who matter. We are."

"If that's the way you feel. I just don't want you to lose your family because of me."

"The Wilsons seem to like me."

"Yes. They love you."

"Then, that's all that matters to me."

"But Maggie," he said quietly.

"Yes?"

"There's one other thing."

"What's that?"

He took both her hands in his and forced her to look at him. "I still have a lot of…issues. I'm not like I was."

"Neither am I. The only difference is that my scars are all on the inside, where yours are both on the inside *and* the outside. Billy, we went to hell and back and survived."

"But…my legs. They aren't very nice to look at anymore."

"I know. I saw them when they were raw. You needn't tell me what I already know. Do you really think that some scars will turn me off?"

Billy looked uncomfortable and didn't answer.

"If you think that I'm the kind of person that makes superficial shit important, then I guess you don't know me as well as I thought you did," she said, looking as though she was about to cry.

"No, I don't think that," he said, squeezing her fingers gently. "I also wanted to remind you that, that guy who sat in a wheelchair for weeks at Walter Reed, the one you yelled at, might still exist inside of me and, every once in a while, may rear his ugly head."

"I understand. As long as *you* remember that my demons usually come at night, and I may wake you up with my screams."

"Two damaged people trying to maintain some sense of normalcy in their lives."

"We make a great couple."

"I guess," he said grudgingly. "But remember too, in light of my present situation, we'll have to try the friends first approach. Maybe after a couple of months, we could try dating. Then go from there? I refuse to do it wrong this time and put the cart before the horse."

"I understand. That's all I needed to know at the moment."

Billy brought her hands to his lips and kissed them lightly. Then, dropping one, he turned and began walking back to the Wilson's house, Maggie's hand firmly in his.

BILLY

"Hey, stranger!" Mary Agnes exclaimed, when Billy answered the door that evening. "What a wonderful surprise!" She and Billy hugged, then Mary Agnes turned and said to the little boy at her side, "Look who's here sweetie. It's Uncle Billy!"

The little boy's eyes were huge as they took in his mother and this strange man embracing. Billy glanced at Jack and his breath caught. It was like looking at a miniature version of John. He collected himself, then awkwardly hunkered down and shook the little boy's hand.

"My goodness, I can't believe how big you have grown in a year. I'll bet you don't even remember me, do you?"

"You're the man who sends me all the neat books."

"And the money," Mary Agnes added.

"I like the books," Jack said. "I brought some with me. Could you read to me?"

"Jack, honey, not now. We're at a party," Mary Agnes said. "Maybe Uncle Billy will stop by and spend some time with us while he's here."

"I'm only here till the weekend, Mare. But I'll try to stop by later this week."

Jack looked crestfallen until Billy said, "Although I don't see why after we eat, and I greet a few other people we can't sneak off and read a bit."

The smile transformed Jack's face and he put his hand into Billy's. "Please!"

The bell rang again, and Billy turned to open the door. He was happy to see Patrick MacDonald.

"Mac, come in."

Mac's face creased into a grin. "Hey! No one told me the prodigal son was going to be here."

"Surprise."

"Uncle Pat!" Jack cried and ran into the older man's arms.

"How's my little guy?" Patrick said, picking up the boy.

"Good, my Uncle Billy's here. He said he'd read to me!"

"Hello, Patrick," Mary Agnes smiled and lightly kissed him on the cheek. "I'm glad you could make it."

"Me too," he said, as he put Jack down. "It was well worth the effort. I get to see not one, not two, but three of my favorite people. This is my lucky day."

Billy raised his eyebrows at Mac and said, "Maybe even four. I guess this is a day of surprises for all of us."

At that moment, Marian came into the hallway and said, "Ah, Patrick! Good, you and Mary Agnes are here. Rusty should be home any minute. The girls and I are just getting the buffet set up in the dining room. You know where the bar is. Please go and help yourself."

Mary Agnes and Jack followed Marian back to the kitchen.

"Come on, Billy," Mac said, "let's go get a drink, then we can talk."

After Mac poured himself a whiskey and Billy got a soda, the two men got comfortable in the library.

"What brings you back to Georgetown on such short notice?"

"Dennis felt I needed to get away for a few days."

"Is he working you that hard?"

Billy smiled. "Like a dog."

"Didn't take long for you to get your feet wet then, I take it."

"Not really."

"How are things going with the building of the trauma center?"

"They're coming along."

"How's the leg holding up?" Mac asked.

"It's holding," Billy replied.

"You know, if you'd exercise that leg more, you'd be just as strong as you were before," Mac stated, shaking an index finger at Billy.

"Yes, mother, I know. I just don't have the time."

"Time," Mac scoffed. "How much time does it take for a quick walk around the block?"

"Come on, Mac. I didn't come home for a lecture."

"So why are you really here?"

"Is it that obvious that I'm here for a reason?"

"It's just unexpected, that's all."

"Jessie OD'd the day after Christmas," Billy said simply.

"Christ! I didn't even know you had found her. I usually hear from Mary Agnes everything that's going on out in Phoenix."

"I see the good old Georgetown grapevine is still in action."

"You'd better believe it."

"The Wilsons didn't know that I had found Jessie. I never had the chance to tell them and, when I did, it was too late."

"What happened?"

Billy quickly recounted the events of the past few weeks.

"Geez kid, I'm sorry. I mean, I know you guys weren't Romeo and Juliet, but I know it must still have hurt, especially the suddenness of it all."

"Thanks. I'm glad you understand. It's funny, but I didn't think her death would affect me as much as it did. I mean, those last couple of weeks were hell. But yet there were times when we almost seemed like a couple—not necessarily a normal one but…I don't know, it was weird."

"I'll bet it was." Mac looked at him sharply. "Are you okay?"

"I guess," he shrugged, took a sip of soda, then said casually, "So, what's up with you and Mary Agnes?"

Mac cleared his throat nervously. "Do you mind?"

"Mind? Mind what?"

"You know. I visit her. First it was a leaky toilet, then it was a stopped-up sink. I'd do some odd jobs for her, and she'd feed me dinner. After a while, I started going over just to visit and play with Jack. She's a very special girl, Billy. And Jack's a great little kid. He needs a man in his life."

"I'm glad they have you, Mac. Why should I mind?"

"I don't know. I wasn't sure how you'd feel about me wanting to see Mary Agnes since John was your friend."

"And you weren't? Look, John's gone, and Mare needs someone. Even if it *is* just to fix the toilet," Billy said, smiling. "And you're right. Jackie needs a man around."

"I think I'm in love with her."

"I could tell when I saw the two of you together tonight. It shows."

"But don't you think I'm too old for her?"

"You're not that much older, are you?"

"A little over twenty years."

"If she were fifteen, I'd worry, but not now. She's a grown woman. I don't think you should let age get in the way of how you feel about her. If you both don't mind the difference, you shouldn't let it or anyone's opinions matter."

"I know. Hell, I don't know why I'm worried. I'm not even sure how Mary Agnes feels about me. I know she likes having me around, but I'm not quite sure where it goes from there. I'm giving her a lot of room. I don't want to push."

"Well, good luck. I seriously think that you two need to talk about this, and soon. It's been over four years since John died. Don't waste any more time. You guys make a very nice couple."

"Speaking of which, I hear Maggie Reynolds is out there working with you."

Billy sighed. "The Georgetown grapevine again?"

"Of course. We have nothing better to do than gossip about other people's lives. It keeps us from thinking too hard about our own. So, is she?"

"Yes, she is. In fact, she's here right now."

"What? Here? As in here? Georgetown?"

"She showed up this morning after taking the red eye from Phoenix."

"I'm speechless."

"Yeah, I was too when she rang the bell. I guess it was another spur of the moment thing. But I also think I was set up."

"Why? I mean I know it's none of my business, but I thought you two had a thing for each other."

"We did. But well…it's been awkward. My old roommate, who is also at St. Mark's, knew Maggie when he was in med school, and seemed to think they were still an item. Just the other day, the day Jessie died to be exact, he and I kind of had a rather heated discussion about that."

"Ahh, that explains the bruising around the jaw."

"Jesus, everyone is such a freaking doctor!"

"Bruising aside, I always thought you and Maggie were well suited for each other."

"Wrong color, remember?"

"I don't know about the color thing. I think it's a lot like the issue of age, isn't it? A wise man I know once said, if both people don't mind, one shouldn't let the opinions of others get in the way of their happiness."

Billy looked uncomfortable. "With all that's happened with Jessie, it's not like I'm really available right now."

"I'm sure that if Maggie feels as strongly for you as I think she does, she'd wait a little bit."

"I know. You're right," he paused, then changed the subject, "So, how are things here?"

"Not busy like it was when you were on staff. In fact, I spend most of my time in my office now instead of doing actual doctoring. I leave that to the residents, interns and students. I don't know whether I like it or not. I miss being a doctor. I'm not sure I'm really cut out for this administrative crap. I've been thinking seriously of retiring."

"You? Retire? You're too young to retire. What would you do with yourself?"

"Not that kind of retire. I mean, retire from the Army. I've been considering starting my own practice or going in with someone or a group. Hell, maybe I could even take up plumbing as a second career."

"I've been telling him that he and I should go into practice together," Rusty said, as he walked into the room, with a drink in his hand.

"Now there's a good idea," Billy agreed. "A match made in heaven. Something to think about in the coming new year." And before the conversation could again focus on him, Billy said to Rusty, "Have you seen our little surprise?"

"You mean, Maggie?"

"Yes. I guess you were in on this as well." Billy stood. "Come on, let's go find her. I'm sure she will want to reconnect with her old boss, and I'm sure she'll want to say hello to you, too," he said, looking at Rusty, who had the decency to turn a bit red.

The party was in full swing by 10 p.m. There was a pool tournament going on and two foursomes were squared off in heated Scrabble contests. Billy was playing against Barbara, her date, and Maggie. It was the first time he had gotten to meet the two young men who were seeing Barbara and Jennifer.

Barbara's date was also doing his student teaching at the moment and seemed very nice. The two had met at a teacher conference over the summer and had been dating ever since. He was a very good Scrabble player and, at the moment, he and Billy were putting one another to the test.

Jennifer's date, a good-looking young man with pleasant manners, was in her sophomore class at Georgetown. He and Jennifer were both pre-med and seemed to have a lot in common, especially their fiery personalities. In fact, they were presently squabbling over a compound word at the next table, and Billy tried to hide a smile. It had always been he and Jennifer who were usually the ones playing cutthroat Scrabble.

It was strange to see the girls with dates, and he wasn't quite sure how he felt about it. He was feeling maybe a little bit overprotective. After speaking to Rusty about it later, he found out that Rusty felt the same way. Neither man knew how to react to their little girls being with dates.

After winning his part of the tournament, Billy went in search of Jack, who was in the living room with both sets of his grandparents, Grandma Jean, and Marian. He was quietly playing with the train set under the Christmas tree.

"Come on Jackie, let's go someplace where I can read to you."

The little boy's face lit up. "Oh yes, please!"

Billy took Jack by the hand, and they walked through the library and out into the sunroom. Jack crawled into Billy's lap with his small pile of books. It reminded Billy of another day, many years before, when a little girl had also taken his hand and had him read to her. How far he had come in those past years.

As the time neared midnight, everyone stopped what they were doing and gathered into the library around the television set. Jenny tuned the channel to Dick Clark's Rockin' Eve, which had made its debut only the year before.

"What? No Guy Lombardo?" Mac asked.

"It's the young people's world now," Rusty replied, then sighed. "I think we're about to get phased out. The minute we hit fifty it was all over."

"Guess we'll just have to learn to Frug," Mac laughed. "Got to beat them at their own game. I refuse to lay down and die."

"Me too!" Rusty laughed.

"Are we going to Frug?" Grandma Jean asked, as she walked into the room with her cane. "I'm not sure my hip is up for it, but I don't want to lay down and die, either," she chuckled. "How about the Hokey Pokey or the Bunny Hop instead? I think those are more my speed. Of course, with this cane, I'm well equipped to Shuffle off to Buffalo."

"Rusty, have I ever told you that I adore your mother," Mac laughed, wrapping his arm around Jean and giving her a kiss on the cheek.

Mary Agnes went in search of Jack and Billy and found them both asleep in the sunroom. She gently shook them awake. "Come on you two, it's almost time. Don't you want to see the ball drop?"

Billy put Jack down, stood up, and stretched the kinks out of his back. "It's midnight already?" he yawned.

"Yes," Mary Agnes replied.

Maggie, in the meantime, was helping Marian fill and distribute glasses of champagne. As Billy emerged from the sunroom, she handed him a third of a flute of champagne.

"It's a short one. Is that okay or do you want something else?" she questioned.

"I think I can handle a mouthful," he smiled, then took a small sip as 1975 was toasted in.

When the ball began its descent and the countdown began, Billy found himself standing next to Marian. As cheers of Happy New Year rang out, Billy turned and gave Marian a hug and a kiss on the cheek. "Thanks for having me here. I love you," he said into her ear. "And…thanks for setting me up."

"And…?" Marian asked, raising her eyebrows—giving him her mom look.

"You always get your way, right?" he smiled.

"Right now, my *way* is for *you* to be happy," she smiled back.

Billy then went around the room hugging and shaking hands and wishing everyone a happy 1975. When there was no one left to wish well, he turned and looked for Maggie. She was standing near the door of the sunroom watching him with trepidation on her face. Billy caught her gaze and slowly walked toward her; his eyes dark—his face serious. When he got to her, he continued to look deeply into her eyes as if searching for her soul.

Finally, pulling her into an embrace, he slowly bent and kissed her gently on the lips. Maggie's arms reached up around his neck and pulled him closer. The kiss went from gentle to searing in a matter of seconds. After a long breathless moment, Billy broke the kiss. He glanced around and was surprised to see that the room was empty except for the two of them.

"Boy we're good. We cleared the room," he said, seriously.

Maggie remained silent; her eyes still fixed on his.

"Happy New Year, Maggie," he said quietly.

"You promise?" she asked, shyly.

"I promise," he said smiling and crushing her to him, kissed her again.

ABOUT THE AUTHOR

A.E. Kayser is a writer from Pittsburgh, PA who started her journey at Duquesne University, receiving a BA in Journalism and a BA in English. Kayser graduated in the early 80's, during a time when there was a glut of young writers vying for any and all writing jobs.

photo credit E.E. McNeil

She took a side road into Marketing and Communications, then realized that she hated everything about sales. From there, she got into Aquatics and has been there ever since. She loves the smell of chlorine in the morning.

Other roads taken were in dentistry, culinary arts, physical therapy and personal care and more education that if added together would have earned her at least one doctorate.

She has been working on the saga of Billy Running Fox for over 20 years.

WA